Monsters at Midnight
Copyright © 2023 Nick Clausen

Edited by Diana Cox
Bonus stories proofread by Joe Manza

The author asserts his moral rights to this work.
Please respect the hard work of the author.
If you don't, monsters will come and eat you at night.

CONTENTS

- Introduction
- **They Come at Night**
- **Blind Date**
- **Chills & Creeps vol. 1**
- **The Girl Who Wasn't There**
- **Chills & Creeps vol. 2**
- **Dreamland**
- **Human Flesh**
- **Bonus Stories**

INTRODUCTION

Thanks for picking up this collection!

I wanted to tell you a bit about what to expect, but ... that turned out harder than I thought. This is such a ragbag of different stories. Some are short, some are long. Some are dark, some are weird. There are elements from Gothic fiction, sci-fi, and even fairy tales.

What they all have in common is that they aim to **scare, spook, and creep you out**.

There are a total of 29 stories. They were written over the span of a decade, from 2007 to 2017. I was in my twenties and basically just a kid.

As I polished them for this collection, I was surprised at just how simple and straightforward my writing was back then. And yet the stories kept pulling me in, making me forget I was supposed to be editing. I hope you'll have the same experience. And I hope you'll find that, while these stories were written by a not-yet-fully mature author, they all have a lot of heart.

As you can imagine, coming up with a title for this collection wasn't exactly easy either. I eventually settled on *Monsters at Midnight*. 'Monsters' because there are almost any kind of monster in here you can imagine—vampires, werewolves, ghosts, witches, wendigos, psychotic murderers, killer fish, even a churel—and 'midnight' because, well, that's a great time to read the stories. That, and it sounded cool.

You might have already come across one or more of the stories in this collection. Some were available in the Kindle Store a few years ago. I took them down, not because they weren't good enough, but because of how different they were. I was trying to establish a brand, so throwing spaghetti at the wall, as was my strategy to begin with, didn't really seem helpful. Having a scattering of odds and ends was a bit confusing to new readers.

But instead of just having all these fun stories lying around on my hard drive, I figured I'd bunch them all together and give them a second life, presented in a new, collective wrapping that—hopefully—makes it easier to know what you're getting into.

If you're a longtime reader of mine and have already read all of these stories, then thank you first and foremost for supporting me by picking up this box set anyway. And as a special treat, I threw in eight brand new short stories that have never been for sale anywhere! You'll find them in the last section, called "Bonus Stories."

Anyway, I won't spoil much more about the journey you're about to undertake. I trust that since you chose this collection, you're the adventurous type—just like me—and you probably don't mind going in blind. So, I'll get out of your way and let you dive into the first story.

Very fittingly, *They Come at Night* was the very first book I ever got published, so it's kinda special to me. I still think it's a cool story, and I really hope you like it.

THEY COME AT NIGHT
The locals keep a secret

PROLOGUE

To whomever finds this!

I write this so the world may know what happened.

For a year I have mourned the loss of my beloved wife, Elvina. She was taken from me in the most gruesome way, and I never thought I would see her again. For a year people have been telling me I am crazy, that Elvina had just left me, without a trace or a note.

Even though I was there to witness her death, I began to doubt if I really was crazy. Perhaps it had all just been a terrible nightmare? The trap that I'd made, in case the foul creatures would return, now seemed ridiculous.

But then, last night, Elvina suddenly stood there, tapping on my window. It took me a long time to realize I wasn't dreaming, and even longer to convince myself that she wasn't a ghost. It really was her, my beloved darling, in flesh and blood, exactly as I remembered her.

I opened the window to let her into the bedroom. My heart almost burst with joy and relief; after so many nights of sorrow and longing, I was finally able to hold my Elvina once more.

I was happy. And because of that, I was weak. I let her trick me into removing the one thing that kept them out.

As we lay down to sleep, I was the happiest man in the world. As I awoke again a short time later, my fortune had turned abruptly. The beasts were upon me! They had entered the house, and, by God Almighty—Elvina was one of them!

I hurled myself through the window, cutting myself badly. The creatures followed. I was bleeding. It was an uneven fight. I was struck. Torn. Bitten.

I managed to throw one of them into the trap. That saved me—it made them hesitate and gave me time to escape beyond their reach. I could now await the break of dawn, when they were forced once again to return to whence they had come—Elvina and the rest of the damned souls.

They made me one of them. I am now a monster. I can see it; I can feel it. Come nightfall I will be compelled to follow them to my new home.

But I won't be alive by then. I don't know what fate awaits me, but I'm certain that death is a much better way.

May God forgive me.

ONE

"Ouch! I stepped on something sharp ..."

Sienna stopped and looked under her bare foot. A tiny red spot appeared on the heel.

"Shoot, I'm bleeding. I'll get sand in it."

"I'm sure you'll survive," Richard said, throwing the frisbee across the beach.

Spike barked happily and went sprinting after the pink disc, sending the sand flying around him.

Max and I were walking behind the others. The sun was baking down on me and my three friends (four, if you count Spike). Not a breeze stirred, and behind us the sea was stretched out, greenish blue and completely calm and inviting.

Sienna tried to walk without stepping on the wounded area of her foot. "Could you please help me, Jayden?" she asked, hopping to me on one leg.

I quickly looked down to avoid staring at her suntanned breasts bouncing alluringly under her bikini.

"Sure, you poor thing," I laughed nervously and gently put an arm around her slim waist.

I thanked heaven that I had been in the chill water just a minute ago. If not, a specific part of my body would undoubtably have celebrated the physical contact with Sienna in a highly inappropriate manner.

"Oh, it stings," she complained. "I hope we have a Band-Aid in the house. Do we, Richard?"

Richard pushed his glasses up his nose. "I already told you, I don't know the place any better than you guys. My parents have only been here once, and they didn't bring me."

"Speaking of," Sienna said, "it was really nice of them to let us stay in the cottage for the whole weekend!"

I snorted.

Sienna looked at me. "Did I say something funny?"

"Well," Richard began, shrugging his skinny shoulders. He looked particularly pale in his tight black swim shorts and his curly hair clinging to his head like a wet cloth. "The thing is, I never really got around to asking them."

"What? You didn't just take the key, did you?"

"I kind of did," Richard smiled, not the least bit embarrassed. "They'll be in Paris for the week, so they'll never even know we were here."

"But ... how about the electricity? Was the house just, like, on?"

"I turned on the relay when we got here," Richard explained. "And I'll turn it off Sunday night when we leave."

"The perfect crime," I added.

"Jesus," Sienna laughed. "I sure wouldn't want my parents to catch me doing something like that."

"Richard's folks are pretty cool," I said. "Hey, Richard, you remember when we filled the exhaust pipe of your dad's Mercedes with snow? We just did it as a joke, but it messed up the engine really bad. It had to go to the shop and everything. He hardly even got mad when he found out we did it."

"He's pretty laid back about things like that," Richard said. "He just ... hey, what's up with Max?"

Sienna and I turned to look back at Max, who had stopped and was staring down at something in the sand. He was the only one of us still wearing his T-shirt. Max was heavy, almost fat, and didn't really share many similarities with his adorable younger sister. He was also a year older than the rest of us. Max and I had been friends for many years. I really liked the guy, though he could sometimes be moody. He had his good and bad sides to him, just like all of us.

"What's up, Max?" I called. "Found something cool?"

"Yeah, come check it out!"

We went back. Sienna still had her arm around me, and I could smell perfume and salt water from her skin—although I tried not to notice it too much, as I could already feel a warningly stir in my swim trunks.

"What's that?" Sienna asked when she saw what Max had found.

"It looks like ..." Richard began.

"I think it's a skeleton," Max finished. "I just can't figure out from what animal."

The trace of a twisted spine and two parallel rows of ribs were protruding from the sand. The tiny white bones were pointing upwards.

"Yuk!" Sienna sneered. "Please don't tell me that's what I stepped on."

"It's pretty big," I said. "I've never seen a skeleton that size before."

Spike came running back with the frisbee. The retriever dropped the toy and started sniffing eagerly.

"It smells rotten," Richard murmured. "Like old fish."

"Nonsense, a skeleton doesn't smell," Max corrected him.

"Spike looks like he begs to differ," I said.

The dog was investigating the bones with the enthusiasm of a forensic scientist. Then, suddenly, he pulled away and started growling.

"What's the matter, buddy?" I said, letting go of Sienna and crouched down. I had only very rarely seen Spike bristle before, but he was really upset and didn't even look at me.

"He doesn't like the nasty fish skeleton," Sienna said, crossing her arms. "I don't blame him."

"If that's a fish it has to be at least a dolphin," Richard interjected.

Max sighed. "A dolphin is a mammal, you goof. Just like whales, turtles and giraffes."

Richard looked at Max with mild insult. Though he didn't say anything, I knew what he was thinking. Max and Richard were very different. For the most part, they got on well enough with each other, but it was no secret that I was kind of the link holding them together.

"I don't care what it is," Sienna said. "Can't we just go back to the house and get some lunch? It's got to be almost one o'clock, and I'm really starving."

"You have an impressive appetite," I said teasingly, as I once again put my arm around her, and we ventured on up towards the tough green reeds that grew in the dunes. Richard's parents' cottage had appeared between two of the soft hills.

"Hey, just because you're a girl doesn't mean you don't eat three meals a day, you know," Sienna defended herself. "Besides, I'm still in the growing age."

"The growing age?" Richard repeated with a grin. "Seventeen? I think you're kind of done growing at our age."

"Yeah, the only growing you do now is outwards," I added.

Sienna counterargued with an elbow to my ribs. "What's that supposed to mean? Are you saying I'm getting fat?"

"No, no," I laughed. "I just mean ... well ..."

"What do you mean, really?" Sienna gave me an arch smile, which made my heart race faster. "Can't talk your way out of that one, can you?"

It was at that moment I noticed the figure disappearing between the reeds about a hundred yards away. "Did you see that person over there?"

"Right, just change the subject."

"No, I'm serious, someone just ran behind the dune right there." I pointed.

"I think I saw him," Richard said. "A guy in a red T-shirt, right?"

"Yeah!"

"At least there's one other living soul out here," Max said, coming up beside us. He had picked up the frisbee, and Spike was jumping and yelping to get him to throw it. Like the rest of us, the dog had already forgotten the unidentified skeleton.

"Yeah, it's actually kind of weird that we had the beach all to ourselves," Richard remarked. "This area is one of the most popular vacation spots."

"I think it's just great," Sienna smiled. "More room for us!"

We approached the cottage and the station wagon, which was parked in the driveway. Max had talked his parents into letting us borrow it for the trip.

The cottage was made of wooden beams and had a tarred roof. On the side facing the sea was a garden door leading out onto a terrace. On the other side was the driveway and the front door. We had come in the morning and had hardly unpacked before heading down to the water.

"What's up with that thing above the door?" Sienna asked, looking at Richard.

He pushed his glasses up. "It looks like an anchor. I guess it's adornment."

"I'll just get my phone, I left it in the car," I said, slipping around the house as the others went inside through the terrace door.

When I turned the corner, I was met by a strange sight. The boy in the red T-shirt had dragged the garbage stand in front of the door and was now standing on top of it. He had a small hammer in one hand and was apparently trying to drive a nail into the woodwork.

"Uhm, hi there," I called. "What are you doing?"

The boy gave a startle. He looked at me with surprise, then jumped down onto the grass. At the same time the front door opened and bumped into the garbage stand. Richard poked his head out. "Hey! What do you think you're doing?"

The boy did not intend to answer, he just bolted out the driveway and disappeared behind a row of trees.

Richard squeezed himself out the door and came to me. "Why didn't you stop him? What the heck was he even doing? Ravage? Does he think it's Halloween?"

"I didn't even think to stop him," I confessed. "I think he tried to put a nail above the door. Look, he dropped this."

"What's that? Another anchor ..."

We studied the black piece of iron that was shaped like an old-fashioned ship anchor. It was the size of a palm.

"It looks a lot like the one above the terrace door," I observed. "But why in the world would he want to hang it up here?"

Sienna and Max had joined us.

"I saw him from the window," Sienna said. "He wasn't that old, was he? Like ten, maybe."

"If he comes back for his anchor, we can ask him what he was up to," I said.

"I really hope he comes back," Richard sneered. "I don't like people who think they can just mess with other people's property like that."

"Perhaps the anchor means good luck," Sienna guessed.

"No, you're thinking of a horseshoe," Max corrected her.

"You don't know what I'm thinking of, Max."

"Sure, it's really quite simple, since there aren't really that many options. Boys, makeup or clothes."

"So what?" Sienna retorted. "At least my best friends aren't my books."

"Well, if you ever learn to read, you can borrow one of them. I can probably find an early reader with lots of pictures in it."

Sienna was about to answer, when I cut her off.

"We didn't come here to listen to your family squabbles. Let's go eat. You can finish arguing later."

TWO

I had a good feeling: it was going to be a wonderful couple of days in Richard's parents' cottage.

That night we grilled sausages, steaks and mini pizzas on the terrace. The barbeque and the patio furniture we had found in the garage.

Later we were all gathered in the living room in front of the television, watching one of Max's favorite horror movies. Outside, the sun had set and the sky was overcast by black clouds. A rather harsh wind blew in from the sea.

"It doesn't take too long to figure out that the gardener is the killer," Max said, cramming a fistful of popcorn into his mouth.

Richard was slumped over in the armchair, completely absorbed by the movie. Max had thrown himself onto the larger coach, so Sienna and I had to share the small one—not that I minded. Spike was lying underneath the coffee table, occasionally looking up at the screen whenever someone was screaming while being dismembered alive.

"Easy for you, you've seen it before," Sienna remarked, reaching for her Coke.

"And with good reason," Max said cheerfully. "It's five-star entertainment!"

"Sssh," Richard hushed. "I think that maniac with the hacksaw is hiding somewhere between those bushes …"

"Of course he is," I laughed. "Wouldn't be a splatter if he wasn't. It's so predictable."

"The plot is not important," Max argued. "It's all about the effects. Notice how realistic it looks when she gets her thumb cut off in a moment …"

"Don't spoil it!" Sienna protested.

"Oh, sorry," Max said, opening another beer. "Jayden, you want one? They're ice cold."

"No, thank you. I really only drink when I want to get wasted."

"Me too," Sienna said. "Especially beer. I don't know how anyone can drink it just for the taste of it."

Max gave a loud sigh. "You guys are a couple of girls. Real men know how to appreciate a cold beer. Right, Richie?"

Richard tore himself away and looked at Max. "Huh?"

"You want a beer?"

"Nah, I'll wait for tomorrow."

"Suit yourselves," Max grumbled. "I for one intend to … hey, it's about to go down!"

Max chuckled with delight as The Mad Gardener, armed with a wide range of rusty garden tools, snuck up on a group of oblivious teenagers whose only crime was to visit the closed garden center after dark.

I was so into the movie that I didn't even feel Sienna lying down until she placed her legs on my lap. She smiled at me innocently. "Is it okay if I put them there?"

"Sure," I said.

"Thank you. I really need to stretch. My legs are kind of sore after the swim today."

"I thought you were used to exercise," Max said. "You're down at the gym all the time."

The only forms of exercise Max ever embarked on were when his parents made him mow the lawn or when he got the chance to throw snowballs at smaller kids.

"I guess it's some other muscles you use for swimming," Sienna said. "Do you mind massaging my calves a little, Jayden?"

I gulped discretely. "Sure ... I can do that."

My clammy hands started fumbling Sienna's slim, firm legs through her pants.

"Ow! Did you see his ankle in that nasty fall?" Max whooped, sending bits of popcorn flying from his mouth. "It looked so real!"

Richard sneered with disgust. "Yuk, that was nauseating. He doesn't stand a chance now, that's for sure. Pass me the candy, please."

"I wouldn't be too sure," Max smiled secretively.

"Max!" Sienna exclaimed as she pushed the bowl of candy across the table to Richard. "Stop spoiling."

"Sorry."

"Mmm, that's good right there, Jayden." She closed her eyes for a moment.

Butterflies started fluttering in my stomach. Was Sienna coming on to me? I'd had a crush on her for almost two years now, but I'd never had the courage to do anything about it. As far as I knew, almost all the boys at school were crazy about Sienna, Richard included.

I snuck a quick peek at her. She was watching the movie. Her dark hair was gathered in a ponytail. She drank from her Coke. I had to force myself to look away as she licked her lips.

We had reached a point in the story line where the two only surviving characters—heavily amputated though still alive—had fought their way to the exit, which now lay open before them at the end of a long corridor with a lot of obvious hiding places. And, of course, the man with the hacksaw was nowhere to be seen.

None of us said anything—we awaited the inevitable shock. It didn't come from the television, though.

Suddenly, someone hammered at the terrace door.

Sienna gave a shriek, and Spike jumped to his feet, banging his head against the coffee table before running to the door, barking angrily. Max choked on a sip of beer and started coughing.

"Spike!" I called and got up.

"Fuck, I think I shat myself!" Richard exclaimed. "Who the hell could that be?"

"It's not your parents, is it?"

"I doubt that."

"Well, it's probably not the fucking mailman, either," Max coughed, wiping beer off his chin. "Goddammit, I almost went belly up ... but hey, choking on beer wouldn't be the worst way to go, I guess."

The dog jumped at the door and barked aggressively.

"Spike, cut that out!" I commanded and pulled him away. The upper half of the door was glass, but I couldn't see anything out there besides darkness. The dog quit barking but instead started whining with concern and slinking around my legs.

"Who is it?" Sienna asked.

"If it's Jehovah's Witnesses just tell them we're busy slaughtering goats in honor of the devil," Max advised.

"I can't see anyone," I said.

Richard came over. "You think we ought to open it?"

"It's your parents' house, so it's your call," I reminded him heroically.

Max had paused the movie, and the house was suddenly a little too silent. We could hear the wind tugging at the roof.

Richard pushed his glasses up and put his face to the glass. "No one's out there. The terrace is empty."

Sienna had also gotten up from the couch. "Perhaps someone was just trying to scare us?"

"Yeah, it could be that boy again," I said, stroking Spike, who was finally settling down.

"Maybe," Richard murmured. "But I'm going to lock the doors now, just to be safe."

There was no more knocking that night.

We watched the rest of the movie, but the good mood was kind of gone.

At eleven we agreed to go to bed. Max and Sienna got the master bedroom with the double bed, and Richard and I were given a children's room each.

When I said good night to Sienna, she sent me one of her special smiles, the ones that make your head tinkle just a bit.

I turned off the light and crawled under the covers. Spike jumped up and lay to rest by my feet. I smiled at him, knowing he was determined to defend my life—and keep my toes warm.

The house had gone quiet besides the storm outside.

I drifted off to sleep thinking about Sienna.

I didn't think to check my watch, so I never knew what time it was, but I awoke sometime during the night because Spike was giving off a soft whimper.

"Buddy?" I muttered, rubbing my eyes. "Where are you?"

I saw the dog by the door—which I had left ajar. Spike was staring out towards the living room.

At that moment I became aware of the scratching noises. It reminded me of something gently clawing at a wooden surface, like nails on a table. I was only halfway awake and too tired to investigate, so I told Spike to come back to bed, turned towards the wall and immediately drifted back into sleep.

THREE

A couple of hours later I awoke by bright sunlight hitting my face. I opened my eyes and realized I was sweating profusely underneath the blanket. Spike was on the floor next to me, snoring.

I trudged out into the kitchen only wearing my briefs. Richard—who's always been an annoying early bird—was sitting by the table, all dressed and reading something on his phone.

"Morning, Sunshine," he said without looking up. "We have yogurt and cornflakes if you're hungry."

"Thanks, I'll just grab a banana," I mumbled. We'd shared the cost for the food, which according to the calculations should last all weekend.

"Did you notice the barometer?" Richard asked.

"What the hell is a barometer?"

"It's a thing that predicts the weather."

"Huh," I said, peeling my banana.

"It says Rain," he continued, pointing to the disc on the wall. "So, I guess it's going to rain ... if you believe the thing."

I took a bite of the banana and walked over to the barometer to study it closer. It was pretty much just a clock face but without the numbers. Instead, the hand could point to one of five possible scenarios: Rain, Storm, Change, Quiet or Sunny. Right now, it was pointing to Rain.

"I had a really weird dream last night," Richard said, as I sat down next to him. "Something about the four of us being stranded on a desert island in the middle of the ocean. We wanted to get out of there, so we found a helicopter."

"How convenient," I remarked.

"I know. Max was like: 'Don't worry, I know how to fly this thing.' But I guess it was out of gas or something, because he couldn't get the rotors going ... I don't remember the rest."

"I dreamt about Sienna," I said, chewing thoughtfully.

"Again?"

"What's that supposed to mean?"

"You dream about her a lot. You're in love, man."

"Shut up."

"You shut up. Freckles."

"Four eyes."

We started laughing. We'd had those nicknames since we were very young.

"I can tell, you know," Richard kept on, smiling. "But I can't blame you. She's very cute."

"Who's cute?"

Both Richard and I gave a startle as Sienna came waltzing into the kitchen. Her hair was a bit fuzzy and she was only wearing shorts and a tank top.

"We were just talking about Jayden's sister," Richard said casually, saving my ass—I was still too groggy to come up with a quick excuse myself.

"Really? I didn't even know you had a sister, Jayden," Sienna said, sitting down across from me.

"I didn't either," I smiled stupidly, gobbling down the last of the banana.

Sienna looked very confused. Luckily, at that moment, Spike entered the kitchen, providing a much-needed distraction.

"Morning, buddy."

The dog wagged its tail and licked my hand.

"Max is the only one still sleeping," Richard observed.

"Don't count on seeing him anytime soon," Sienna said, resting her head in her hand. "It would take an atomic blast to wake him up."

I got up to discard the banana peel when I remembered the noise I'd heard during the night. I asked Richard and Sienna if they'd noticed anything.

"Nope, I was sleeping," said Richard.

"I didn't hear anything either," Sienna said. "The bedroom is pretty far from the living room, plus Max was snoring like a boar."

I went to the terrace door and opened it wide. The sunlight came streaming in, blinding me for a moment. I stretched and yawned as Spike slipped past me and started looking for the exact right place to take a leak.

I stepped barefoot out onto the wooden deck. The landscape was a soft, wavy belt of beige-colored sand with green blotches of reed scattered about. The cottage was less than two hundred yards from the water, which could be glimpsed between the dunes, looking particularly velvety and copper green this morning.

As I turned to go back inside, something crunched underneath my foot. I looked down and saw a piece of seaweed that had been completely dried out in the sun.

Then I noticed the rest of the terrace. It was all plastered with more dried seaweed and a couple of seashells. Large, white stains were visible on the decking. I crouched down and traced my fingertips across it. The smell left no doubt in my mind: it was traces of salt.

"What are you looking at?"

I turned to see Sienna squinting at me from the doorway.

"What the hell?" Richard said, making his way past her. "What happened out here?"

"It looks like someone poured out a bucked of seawater," Sienna observed. "Look, there's even a dead starfish!"

"I don't think anyone did it," I said standing back up. "I think the sea came up here during the night. Don't you remember the time we learned about the tide in science class?"

"No," Richard said.

"I do!" exclaimed Sienna. "Ebb and flow and all that stuff. The water actually comes really far inland during nighttime some places."

A slight breeze made the terrace door close with a soft creak. We turned around and uttered a collective gasp.

"Shit!" Richard said.

"Did the water do that, too?" Sienna asked.

THREE

The outside of the door was covered in thin cutmarks. It looked like someone had gone crazy with a sharp tool. The wood hung in shreds.

"That looks more to me like something a dog could have done!" Richard said, darting a malicious stare at Spike, who was happily running around sniffing the seaweed.

"What are you talking about?" I said, shaking my head. "Spike couldn't have done that, not even with his teeth. Look how thin and deep the scratches are. It's clearly been cut into the door with something a lot sharper ..."

Sienna put a hand to her mouth. "Don't say that, Jayden. Do you think it was that guy who knocked last night ...?"

"Well, maybe. I'm not saying he used a knife or anything, I'm just saying it's way sharper than a dog's claws. Besides, Spike has been with me all night."

Before Richard could answer, Max came trudging out. He looked like a grumpy bear who had been awakened prematurely from its hibernation. "Morning," he grumbled. "What's the cause for the general assembly?"

"Look at the door," Richard said grimly. "What am I going to tell my parents?"

"How the fuck did that happen?" asked Max.

"We were just asking that same question," I said. "It looks like the tide has been all the way up here, flooding the terrace during the night."

Max looked around. "Huh. Well, fuck me. I didn't think it came so far inland. Lucky it didn't seep under the door, or we would have ..." He stopped talking as he apparently noticed something.

I followed his gaze and saw the footprints in the soft, sandy ground next to the terrace. There were many, at least a dozen.

"Apparently, someone had a garden party out here while we were sleeping," Max observed drily.

We went around the cottage but didn't find any more footprints or any other damages done to the building.

"They've only left footprints where the ground was wet," I concluded. "And the water only just reached the terrace, not all the way around the house."

"Those prints must have something to do with the knocking we heard," Richard said. "Who the hell was running around out here in the middle of the night?"

"Huh," Max said. He was closely studying the vandalized door and the footprints. I think we all awaited his suggestion for an explanation. He was the oldest but also the most intelligent. He finally shook his head. "It looks really weird. Obviously, they didn't try to enter the house, since no windows or doors have been broken. And the car is still here, so they probably weren't trying to steal anything, either."

I noticed Sienna crossing her arms with a shudder despite of the warmth. I reached over and squeezed her shoulder.

"So, what's the explanation?" Richard demanded.

"Your guess is as good as mine," Max shrugged.

"Perhaps they were just trying to mess with us?" I offered.

"Probably," Max said.

I didn't feel convinced, and judging from the expressions on the others' faces, they didn't either.

FOUR

"It's not exactly like this place is overcrowded," Richard said.

We were standing on top of a dune a fair distance from the cottage. The other cottages were spread out along the coastline as far as the eye could reach, but neither cars, bicycles nor people were seen anywhere.

"Perhaps people are still at work," I suggested.

After examining the terrace door and agreeing on the fact that there wasn't really anything we could do about it, Max went back to bed. He didn't feel fully rested—it was only ten o'clock, after all.

Sienna pulled one of the loungers out onto the terrace and changed into a bikini. When she started rubbing her body with sun lotion, it got too much for me, so I asked Richard to join me for a walk.

"It looks like it's going to be a really hot day," I prophesied, pulling out my T-shirt's already damp collar.

"How many of the houses do you think are used as year-round homes?" Richard asked.

I shrugged. "Most of them look like vacation homes to me, but I guess some people live here all ye—"

"Hey, look!"

I followed Richard's pointing finger. The boy in the red T-shirt was standing about fifty yards away. He slipped behind a bush when he realized we were looking at him.

"That's that kid from yesterday."

"Come on, let's find out if he knows anything about what happened!"

Richard set off running, and I followed him. Soon, we reached the bush.

"You go that way," Richard instructed. "I'll take the other."

We snuck in opposite directions around the bush. We met on the other side.

"What the hell ...?"

"There he is!"

The boy was running like a madman.

"Damnit, he must have seen us coming. Get him!"

We took up the pursuit, sprinting across the plain, jumping over patches of heather and reed, and slowly gaining on the kid.

"He's ... headed for ... that house!" I panted.

"We'll ... get him!" Richard said, upping the speed even more. "Hey, wait up, kid! ... We just ... want to ... talk!"

The boy darted a fleeting glance over his shoulder without slowing down—it made him miss a step, and he went tumbling to the ground.

We reached him before he could get to his feet, grabbing his arms and standing for a moment heaving for air, like a couple of racehorses.

"You better ... explain yourself," Richard sneered. "Why did you ... cut up ... our terrace door?"

"Easy, Richard," I panted. "Let's not ... scare the kid ..." I looked at our captive. "What's ... your name?"

"Chris," he answered, staring from us to the house.

"Do you know anything about who visited our cottage during the night?"

The boy looked even more scared. He shook his head firmly.

"So, you don't know who ruined the door either?" Richard demanded.

"N... no."

"Tell us what you were doing yesterday when I saw you on the garbage stand."

"I was ... I was just trying to help you guys!"

"Help us how?"

"There's no anchor above your front door ..."

Richard and I exchanged a puzzled look.

"I'm aware there's no anchor above our front door," Richard said. "Why the fuck would that be any of your concern?"

"I already told you—I wanted to help you!"

I was beginning to think the boy might be taking the piss out of us. If that was the case, Richard would very soon lose his patience.

"Help us with what?" I asked.

"With protection," the boy said, lowering his voice. He was talking to Richard now. "Your parents don't know any of us locals, so they don't know about the anchors."

Richard frowned. "What are you talking about? Stop speaking in riddles."

"Ouch, you're hurting my arm!"

"Richard," I said. "Ease up, man. We don't know if he did anything yet ..."

Richard reluctantly let go of Chris's arm. I did the same.

"All right. Now, explain to us how you thought you were going to help us ... or protect us."

Chris rubbed his arm, looking very uneasy. "My mom says I'm not supposed to tell anyone about it. Everyone around here knows, but ... no one ever speaks of it." He took a deep breath and lowered his voice even more. "You need to make sure your doors are protected. Some people died because they failed to do so. For instance, the old couple living in your house before your parents bought it. I heard my mom talking about it with the neighbor. She would definitely not be pleased if she knew I was telling you about this. I'm not supposed to breathe a word to anybody." The boy stopped speaking and looked at us with big eyes.

"Jayden, look! Above the door ..."

Richard pointed. I looked at the house and noticed the anchor above the front door.

"Everyone around here has them," Chris whispered. "It's protection."

"Protection against what?" I asked, trying not to sound anxious.

Chris pulled back a little. Then, he got himself together and looked straight at me. "Against them. Promise me you'll put up the anchor before dark. Promise!"

Richard and I looked at each other. I didn't know what to say, and neither apparently did my friend.

Suddenly, Chris spun around and ran to the house.

"Weird kid," Richard mumbled.

I nodded, but said nothing.

Sienna had fallen asleep when we returned to the cottage. She was still lying on the lounger, glistening in the sun. Spike had found himself a place in the shade, wagging his tail lazily when he saw me.

Sienna heard us coming and opened her eyes. "Oh, hi," she said, stretching. "How long were you guys gone?"

"Almost an hour," I said. "Did you get a good nap?"

"Mmmm."

"Is Max up yet?" Richard asked.

"I haven't seen him."

"You guys feel up for a swim?" I suggested. "I could really use a cool-down."

"I'm in," Sienna said, getting up. As she waltzed past me, I got a whiff of her perfume and sun lotion. "Are you coming or what?"

"Sure thing. Spike, you want to come?"

The dog got up and followed us as we started walking down to the beach. We hadn't gone very far, when we heard an audible CLONK! from underneath Richard's sandal.

"What the hell ...?"

He crouched down and examined the ground. When he pushed the heather aside, the corner of a big, rusty metal plate became visible.

"What's that thing doing there?" Sienna asked.

"I have no idea, but it's really big," Richard said. "At least one square yard. And it's right on top of this little rise." He knocked on the plate with his fist.

"Judging from the sound, there's air underneath," I observed. "Maybe it was put here to cover a sewer pipe or something. Who knows? Let's go, I'm sweating like a pig."

"Last man is a chicken!" Sienna said and started running.

Richard and I ran after with Spike barking in amusement right behind us.

FIVE

At around ten that evening the rain started trickling down the windows. An hour later, darkness had descended and it was raining steadily. The barometer turned out to be right—of course, at that point we were all way too drunk to care about the weather.

Max—who'd finally gotten up at around noon—had asked me to help him carry his precious loudspeakers and amplifier from the car and set it up in the living room. The stereo was now blasting out music, and Sienna had insisted on lighting candles all around the room. It created a dim, but I must admit also pretty cozy, atmosphere.

Richard and Sienna were performing something that could hardly be described as a dance on the living room floor. Normally, Richard was too shy for this kind of display, but he had been going at the beers pretty heavily.

Sienna was laughing with amusement while trying to keep up with him. She was also fairly drunk, yet enchanting as ever.

Max and I were sitting on the couch, each with a beer, discussing the Second World War—one of Max's favorite subjects.

"Did you know," he said loudly, trying to outshout the music, "that Nagasaki wasn't the original target for the bombing of Japan? Another town called Kokura was supposed to be blown up, but it was cloudy that fatefot ... uh, fatful... uh, that day. So, it was changed to Nagasaki instead."

"That's crazy," I said, taking a sip of my beer. "Imagine being saved by some clouds!"

"It just goes to show that tiny things can have a huge impact on the larger scale of life," Max philosophized, raising his beer. "Let's drink to that, buddy!"

I laughed and touched bottles with Max. At that moment the song ended, and there was a blessed interlude in the music.

"I'm going to grab some grub!" Richard announced and staggered towards the kitchen.

Sienna laughed. "I had no idea you were such a great dancer, Richie!"

"It's all in the hips!" he said, shaking his skinny butt before leaving the room.

The next number began in comparably gentle tones. Sienna came over and grabbed my wrist. "Come on, Jayden! I love this song, I have to dance to it!"

"I can't dance," I protested, as I was dragged to my feet. The alcohol was starting to make me light-headed.

"It's easy," Sienna promised, pressing herself against me. "It's a quiet song. Just follow my lead."

I had never seen her eyes this close, and I couldn't look away. She was smiling warmly and biting her lip. I could smell her sweet beer-breath—my own was probably a lot worse. I chucked down the last of my drink and put the bottle on the windowsill.

Sienna slipped her arms around my neck and rested her head against my shoulder. I put my trembling hands around her waist, and we started dancing slowly.

"Are there any more cold ones?" Richard champed, returning to the living room with a slice of leftover pizza.

"Coming right up," Max said and handed him a bottle.

I enjoyed the alluring scent of Sienna and felt her soft body against mine.

She squeezed my neck. "See, I knew you could dance."

"I feel like a bag of potatoes."

She laughed in my ear.

"Spike!" Richard called. "Where's the"—burp—"dog? I can't eat anymore of this."

The dog came trudging.

"Here, boy! Catch!"

Richard threw the half-eaten slice in a way-too-high arc over Spike, who didn't stand a chance of catching it. The slice landed on a shelf, knocking two candles to the floor.

"Oh, fuck me!" Richard howled, running over there.

"Watch out, Sienna," I said, as she almost stepped in the hot wax that had spilled out over the wooden floor.

"Don't just stand there, help me clean this up!" Richard pleaded, blowing at the mess, even though the candles had gone out already. "Shit, I hope it doesn't leave a stain ..."

Max turned the music down, while I got a dish cloth from the kitchen and handed it to Richard, who grabbed it and started scrubbing to get the wax off.

"Just my luck," he grumbled. "If this doesn't come off ... hey, what the hell? It feels like this board is loose." He knocked on the floorboard, producing a hollow noise. "Check this out, Jayden! I think there's a cavity of some kind."

"Well, try and lift the board, then."

Richard fumbled helplessly.

I sighed. "Move aside, Four-eyes, you're drunk as a skunk."

Richard shuffled to the side. I crouched down and started pushing and prodding the board, which was about two feet long. Finally, I got it up.

"It's a secret room," Richard exclaimed over my shoulder. "Do you think they made it on purpose?"

"It kind of looks like it," I said. "And there's something down here." I stuck my hand down the hole and pulled up a small metal cylinder.

"Awesome!" Richard said, crouching down next to me. "What is it? Can you open it?"

Max came over. "What did you find?"

Richard lost his balance, tipped backwards and bumped into Max, who almost fell over. Richard grabbed my arm, making me drop the cylinder. Max spilled most of his beer, soaking both Richard and me.

"Now, look!" Max complained. "Good beer going to waste!"

"Sorry, dude," Richard said, precariously getting to his feet. "Let me buy you the next one."

Max flung his arm around Richard's shoulders. "Never mind, buddy. Let's get you something to drink. You need it. That wax isn't going anywhere."

On the way to the couch one of them must have kicked the cylinder, making it roll under the couch, because that was where I found it later on.

Right now, Sienna was smiling at me, and I forgot all about cylinders, secret rooms and hot wax. I quickly put the floorboard back and got up.

"Thank you for the dance," she said softly.

"The pleasure was all mine," I assured her and made a clumsy bow.

She laughed. "You're silly. Oh, I really need to pee." She hurriedly left the room.

I slumped down next to Richard and Max, who had just opened a couple of beers. The way they chatted made me smile. Alcohol has a way of making people friends. My own head was really spinning now.

After a couple of minutes, I got up and went to the bathroom door. I needed to take a piss, and just as I was about to knock, Sienna opened the door.

I gave her my best smile, and she took my arm.

"Jayden, there's something I want to tell you."

The words made my world turn a couple of times.

"Sure, what is it?"

"Not now. Can we talk tomorrow, when we're sober? It's a pretty big thing for me, you see." She smiled secretively. God damnit, I loved that smile.

"Of course, Sienna. I ..."

A movement caught my eye from the nearest window. It seemed to me that a person had just passed by outside. Even though I was fairly drunk, I felt my stomach tighten.

"Jayden? What are you looking at?"

Before I had time to answer, Richard shrieked from the living room. Spike started barking. Sienna and I ran into the room.

Max was still sitting on the couch, looking up at Richard, who had jumped to his feet and pointed to the terrace door. "Someone just walked past right outside!"

"Shut up," Max scoffed.

"I'm telling you, it's true! It was a tall figure. Like, a man, maybe."

"Who would go out in this weather? It's raining like a cow pissing on a flat rock."

"I don't care, I saw someone. The dog saw it too!"

"He's only barking because you started yelling. I bet it was just your own reflection you saw."

Richard glared at Max. "I know what I saw, damnit!"

"Fine, I'll check it out."

"No, wait!"

But Max had already gotten up and went to the window. He pulled it open and stuck his head out. "You see? There's nothing out here, except darkness and ... oh shit!"

"What is it?" Richard said.

"Come and see for yourself."

We all three went to the window and looked out. Sienna gasped.

The whole area was completely flooded. The water had crawled up through the dunes and had reached the cottage. The terrace was hidden under water, and small waves were beating rhythmically against the woodwork.

"Christ," Max muttered. "If we had a fishing rod, we could catch flounders from in here."

"I guess we were right about the tide," I said. "It did flood the terrace last night."

"Yeah," Sienna said. "I can't believe anyone would build their houses around here."

None of us had any good answers. Max spat out into the water and closed the window. He turned to say something, when a loud screeching noise came from the window right behind him.

I thought I saw an arm disappearing out of sight. Four clearly discernable scratches had been drawn across the glass.

Sienna screamed and backed away.

"What the hell was that?" Max yelled and turned around.

"Someone scratched the glass!" I said. "There really is someone out there!"

"Is it that stupid kid again?" Max said, trying to sound tough—but he was backing away from the window like the rest of us.

"I didn't have time to see who it was."

"Christ, what am I going to tell my parents?" Richard cried. "The whole damn house is being destroyed."

Max went out to the hall. "No more of this shit. I'll fucking show them ..."

"No, Max, please don't go out," Sienna pleaded, running after him. "What if it's some kind of ... psycho?"

Max stopped. "It's just some idiot having fun scaring the crap out of us," he said, scowling at the small window in the front door.

"Can't we just call the police then?"

"No!" Richard shouted. "If we do, my parents will know we are here."

"So what?" Sienna said. "You said they probably wouldn't get mad."

Richard flung out his arms. "That was before the terrace door had been all fucked up!"

While my friends were arguing, I was thinking of Chris. My intoxicated brain was trying its best to think rationally. Richard and I hadn't put up the anchor. On the way home, we had agreed that the kid was probably just a nut job. We had even laughed.

But right now, I didn't think the things Chris had told us sounded the smallest bit funny. Quite the opposite, in fact.

I went out and locked the front door. "There. At least they can't get in."

"What do you mean, 'they'?" Max asked.

We hadn't told Max or Sienna about what Chris had said. I decided that now was not the time, so I just shrugged. "We don't know if there is more than one out there."

Richard went to the couch and slumped down heavily. "Well, I'm fucked ... as soon as my parents find out about this, they'll ground me forever."

The rest of us joined him.

"There isn't really anything we can do," Max murmured, spinning an empty beer bottle with his finger.

"I wish I wasn't drunk," Sienna said, sounding like she was about to cry.

I put my arm around her, and she leaned against me.

I looked over at the four scratches on the wet window and couldn't help but shiver.

SIX

I don't know what woke me up, but I suddenly opened my eyes and stared up into the darkness. My mouth felt like sand. I sat halfway up, and the movement released an avalanche of pain in my skull.

I groaned and licked my dry lips. My phone was in my pants somewhere on the floor, so I had no way of telling the time. I could tell from the silence it had stopped raining outside, but it was still dark.

Carefully I swung my feet to the floor and sat up. Spike woke and looked up at me.

"You're lucky dogs don't get drunk," I mumbled.

I got up and shuffled to the kitchen, feeling like someone who had just underwent major surgery. The display on the microwave said 04:11. Another hour before sunrise.

I poured myself a big glass of cold water and drank it greedily. I didn't feel nauseous, but that would probably come soon enough.

After the episode with the window, we had sat and talked for a while. We were all pretty shaken up, but we were also drunk, so we kind of forgot about the creepy incident, and when Richard started yawning, we said good night and went to bed.

As I was standing in the kitchen, trying to collect myself, I looked out the window. Far out in the twilight I could glimpse the tops of the dunes and the black water behind them. The tide seemed to have retracted and returned to the ocean.

Suddenly, I saw a group of figures amongst the reeds. I blinked. It had to be my imagination, but—it really looked like someone was standing out there. Four or five people, maybe even more. Without moving. Just standing there.

I went to open the terrace door. A cool, salty sea breeze met my naked upper body and made me shiver. Even though the rain had stopped, the sky was still overcast by heavy, black clouds.

From here I had a better view of the dunes—but now I couldn't see the figures anywhere. I looked for a couple of minutes, but they were gone. Or rather, they had of course never been there.

I stepped down into the moist grass. Now that the water had pulled back, the sandy ground was already starting to dry itself up. As soon as the sun rose, it would be a matter of minutes before the last traces of water had evaporated.

I pulled down my briefs and started peeing with a deep sigh of relief. It took me almost two minutes to empty my bladder.

When I was done, I was beginning to freeze, so I wanted to go back inside—but then I saw the footprints. There were a lot this time. All the way along the cottage on both sides.

I looked around. I was alone.

I crouched down to get a closer look at the prints. They were made by big, bare feet. The unknown guests had trudged back and forth right on the outside of the cottage.

I went to the other side, the one facing away from the sea, where the driveway and the front door was located. On this side the ground was completely dry and had no prints.

My heart was beating a bit too fast. The nausea had come after all. I continued around the cottage. When I reached the window that Max had opened, I quickly examined the scratches.

I moved on, soon the ground became soggy again, and the footprints reappeared. It was clear to me that the footprints only went as far as the water had gone.

Who in the world was sneaking around out here at night? Were the locals pranking us? Had they walked around out here, barefooted, and cut up the door and scratched the window? That didn't seem like a plausible explanation.

A violent shiver went up my spine. It was at that moment I finally admitted to myself that something was really wrong.

A sudden wind made the heather rattle around me. I darted a glance out into the landscape. Still alone.

I hurried back inside and locked the door. Spike came to greet me. I went to the kitchen to get a couple of aspirins. A nasty headache was starting to throb in my temples.

As I flushed down the pills with another glass of water, I went to the living room. The barometer was pointing to Change. The room was a mess. Empty bottles, clothes, pizza boxes and other stuff were thrown about.

I noticed something. Across the hall ran a trail of muddy shoeprints. They came from the front door and led to Max's shoes, which were soaked and caked with mud.

Had Max been outside during the night? What had he been doing there? If he had heard something and gone to investigate, why hadn't he woken up the rest of us?

Spike's impatient whining pulled me out of the gloomy thoughts. The dog was looking at me pleadingly, then sniffed underneath the couch. It could only mean one thing.

"Did you lose your frisbee?" I asked, crouching down. But when I reached under the couch, my fingers found something round and cold. I pulled out the object and stared at the cylinder. I had completely forgotten about it.

I sat down by the dining table and fumbled a while with the cylinder before I got it open. A rolled-up piece of paper dropped out. I unfolded it and started reading. It was some kind of odd suicide note. I read it three times over. With each reading my hands grew a little bit sweatier.

SEVEN

Someone gently shook me.
Then, Sienna's lovely voice: "Jayden? ... Jaayden?" She laughed quietly. "What a weird place to sleep ... Jayden?"
I opened my eyes and sat up straight. I had been sleeping slumped over the dining table.
"Good morning," Sienna smiled, running a hand through my messy hair. She had apparently just showered, because her hair was wet and she smelled of shampoo. "Why on earth are you sitting here?"
I rubbed my eyes and tried to get my brain going. I felt like I had just awoken from a coma. The sun was streaming through a halfway clouded sky and lighting up the living room.
"I ... uhm ... I went to pee, and ... I sat down for a moment. I must've fallen asleep."
I remembered the letter and looked around for the cylinder. It had rolled to the floor, so I picked it up.
"Looks like you did," Sienna said and walked to the kitchen. "How's the head?"
I tentatively shook said body part. No avalanche this time. "Okay, I guess. What time is it?"
Sienna returned with a glass of water and sat down across from me. "Half past eleven. Richard isn't up yet. That's a new one."
"Well, he got pretty drunk last night," I mumbled.
A lot of thoughts were going through my head. The footprints outside. Max's shoes, all wet. The figures in the dunes.
"What have you got there?" Sienna nodded towards the cylinder.
"It's the thing we found underneath the floorboard."
"Oh! Did you get it open?"
"Yeah, it was just empty," I lied.
"Too bad. It would've been cool if it had a treasure map inside." She smiled and looked around. "Christ, we made a mess in here. Just the thought of cleaning all this ... hey, who made those?" She pointed to the muddy footprints out in the hall.
"Max did," I said, getting up with difficulty; my legs were kind of numb from the awkward sleeping position. I glanced at the barometer, noticing it was now predicting Storm. "I guess he must've been outside sometime during the night. Did you hear him leaving your room?"
"No, I slept like a baby," Sienna said. "But he used to sleepwalk a lot when he was little. We could ask him if he remembers anything when he wakes up."
"That could be hours," I murmured.
Sienna gave me a curious look. "Is it important?"
I shook my head and looked out the window.

"Jayden? What's wrong?"

"I just ... have a feeling that something weird goes on at night."

I didn't really want to tell her about the things Chris had said, nor about the strange letter. I saw no reason to make her nervous.

"I don't like what happened either," she said. "It creeps me out just thinking about someone being outside while we slept. But we're going home tonight; we won't spend another night here."

"I know. And I'm glad."

We were silent for a little while.

"You want to go for a bike ride?" Sienna asked.

"Sure," I said. Honestly, I was happy to get out of the house. And maybe Max and Richard would be up when we got back.

The skies were heavily overcast with grey clouds as we some minutes later walked along the gravel road, which wound its way through the duney landscape. The bikes that Richard and I had used yesterday when we picked up pizza in the city were both flat when we found them in the garage, so Sienna and I decided to walk instead.

"We probably drove through some broken glass without noticing," I said. "And then the tires lost the air during the night."

"Well, I don't mind walking, do you?"

"It's fine," I said, looking up at a couple of seagulls soaring overhead.

My worries had eased off a little since I got out into the fresh air. Same went for the hangover, which by now had been reduced to a mild dizziness.

"By the way," Sienna said. "The thing I wanted to talk to you about ..."

My pulse immediately spiked. I had completely forgotten. "Yeah?"

Sienna looked at me and smiled. "Okay, I'm just going to come right out and say it. I've got a boyfriend."

I'm not sure if I managed to keep a straight face—luckily, Sienna looked down at her feet, so she probably didn't notice my look of utter surprise—but the disappointment must have been painted on my face in that dreadful moment.

"I ... that's really ... congratulations ... I guess."

Sienna laughed. "Thank you, Jayden. I'm just so happy. He's so sweet. We've been keeping it a secret so far."

"I see," I said, swallowing something bitter. "Who ... is he? If you don't mind me asking?"

For a brief, gruesome moment I thought she might say Richard. In my head I quickly ran through the fastest ways of committing suicide.

But Sienna said, "It's Tommy. You know, from Max's class?"

"Tommy?" I exclaimed. "But he's ... I mean ... I really didn't expect that."

Sienna sniggered. "I almost can't believe it myself. I can't wait to go back home and see him again."

I didn't know what to say. I just glared down into the gravel as we trudged on.

"I don't know if I dare to tell Max," Sienna said. "I'm not sure how he will react to me dating one of his friends."

I gleefully envisioned Max chasing down Tommy and killing him with an axe. It probably wouldn't go down like that—I wouldn't be that lucky.

"I was hoping you could give me some advice, Jayden. You know Max better than me when it comes to those things."

"I don't know, Sienna," I said, kicking a small rock. "Why not just tell him straight up? What's the worst he can do?"

Sienna mulled over my suggestion. "Maybe you're right ..."

"He can't tell you guys what to do," I continued. "If he gets pissed off, let him be pissed off. You know Max—it'll pass."

Sienna looked at me. "You know what? I think you're absolutely right."

"Just call me Dr. Phil," I grunted.

"I'm going to tell him as soon as we get home. Maybe Tommy can even be there when I do—we could tell him together!"

"Sure, why not?" I mumbled.

"Thank you so much, Jayden," she said, squeezing my hand. "I knew you would have the answer." And then, as if to really rub it in, she said the worst, most cruel sentence in the world: "You're such a good friend!"

EIGHT

"Hold on for a second, I forgot to lock the door!" Richard jumped out of the car and ran back to the house.

The rain was pouring down in buckets and the wind was blowing violently. We were all stuffed in the car, soaking wet, our luggage crammed in the trunk.

When Sienna and I got home earlier, Richard was up. He looked like he had been run over by a truck with a trailer and twin wheels. An hour later Max, too, had joined us. I had shown him the footprints, but he didn't remember leaving the room, so we concluded that he must have been sleepwalking.

We used most of the afternoon cleaning up and packing. It was now eight o'clock and I was starving. The plan was to hit a McDonald's on the way home, since we were pretty much out of food.

Richard came back and threw himself into the car next to me. "All right, we're good to go!"

Max was in the driver's seat looking at his phone. "That's weird. The signal has gone. It's probably the storm."

"Who gives a damn?" Sienna sighed, leaning back her head. "We're going home."

"Home to the civilized world," Richard added, drying his glasses in his shirt. "Aw, it smells like wet dog in here!"

Spike was sitting between my feet, looking innocent.

I gazed out the window. The rain was streaming down the glass, distorting the view. Far out on the horizon above the sea, the first lightning flashed on the already dark skies. The barometer would once again turn out to be right: it was going to be a dreadful storm.

"Can't wait to sleep in my own bed again," Sienna said, running a hand through her damp hair.

"Me too," Richard said. "I mean, my bed, of course. Not yours, Sienna."

Sienna laughed.

"Son of a bitch," Max muttered. He turned the key a couple of times, but the engine just went TICK!

"Something wrong, Max?" I said, leaning forward.

"It's completely dead."

"What?" Sienna asked. "Is it out of gas?"

"Yes, it's out of gas," Max snapped at her, unfastening his seat belt. "It's a diesel engine, you dummy. And the tank is more than half full." He pushed a button, opened his door and stepped out into the rain.

I could see him lifting up the hood. I went to join him. "Do you see the problem?" I asked, walking to the front of the car.

Max was just standing there, staring down. When I saw, my heart sank.

EIGHT

The engine was completely filled up with seaweed. It was everywhere. Stuffed into every nook and cranny.

"Who the hell did this?" Max asked.

I had no answer. Sienna and Richard came out of the car.

"Holy shit," Richard said. "How the fuck did this happen?"

We all just stood there for a moment, exchanging uncertain looks, saying nothing, getting drenched by the rain.

"Well, we sure as shit aren't going anywhere in this car for the foreseeable future," Max said, slamming down the hood. "And I really don't feel like standing out here trying to fix it while it's pissing down. Let's go back inside."

"Won't your parents start to worry if you're not home in time?" Richard asked, looking at Sienna and Max.

All four of us were sitting in the living room. Spike was the only one who seemed unfazed by the situation—he was just looking up at us with his usual curious expression, waiting to see what would happen next.

"We just told them we would be home before midnight," Sienna said. "So, I guess we still have plenty of time. But if we can't get the car working, we'll have to call them at some point."

"Do you have any service?" Max said, throwing his phone on the table. "Mine is gone."

"Mine too," Richard said.

Sienna checked her phone and sighed. "Mine too. How about you, Jayden?"

I looked up when my name was mentioned. "Hmm?"

"You have any service on your phone?"

I found my phone and got the same answer.

"Goddamn storm," Richard growled. "We need to borrow a landline from one of the neighbors."

None of us were particularly eager to go back outside.

"You sure you can fix the car, Max?" Sienna asked.

"I don't know. First we need to get all of that seaweed out."

"Who on earth would do such a thing?" Sienna asked, throwing out her arms. "Do you guys think it's the same person who messed up the door and the window?"

"The odds are pretty good," Richard said.

"I'll go out as soon as the rain tapers off a bit," Max said, throwing himself on the couch. "Until then, why don't we see what's on?"

"I'll just dry my hair," Sienna said, leaving the room.

Richard went to join Max. I kept sitting by the table, staring at my hands.

"Oh, come on," Max said. "The TV is dead, too!" He was searching for a channel, but all he found was static.

"How can that be?" Richard asked.

I got up and wandered about. I stopped and leaned my forehead against the wall.

"Maybe the wind knocked down the antenna. Or the TV company shut down the signal."

I realized I was standing right beside the barometer. The hand was moving rapidly from side to side.

"There's another possibility," I said, turning.

Max and Richard looked at me.

"Someone cut the outside cables."

My words hung in the air for a moment.

"Why would anyone do that?" Richard asked.

"I'm going over to talk to Chris," I said. "I'll borrow their phone and call my dad, so he can come and get us. You guys stay here and lock the door when I leave."

"You're scaring me, man," Richard said.

"You've been oddly quiet all day," Max added. "What's up? What did that kid tell you, anyway?"

"Richard, you tell him," I said, going for the door. "Spike, you stay here." I gave my friends one last look. "And don't open the door to anyone else, okay? No matter what."

NINE

It took me ten minutes or so to run to Chris's house. It was pretty much dark by now. The storm whipped the raindrops into my face, making it hard to see. At one point I almost lost my sense of direction. Lightning was flashing all around me, and the thunder grew louder with each clap.

Finally, I saw the lights from the windows. I thought about knocking on the door, but then I remembered what Chris had said about his mom. I was afraid that she would just slam the door in my face if I asked her to talk to Chris.

So instead I snuck around to the back, checking the windows along the way. Through the window I saw a man with a moustache was sitting in the living room watching TV. In the kitchen I saw a woman doing the dishes.

The next window showed me a kid's room. Chris was lying on his bed, playing on his computer. I tapped the glass gently. At first, Chris didn't hear me, so I tapped a little harder. He turned his head and looked directly at me, his eyes widening.

I waved and signaled for him to come and open the window.

He didn't move—he just shook his head.

I waved at him again.

He got up, but instead of coming to the window, he went to a drawer and took something out. He came over and opened the window ajar. "What do you want?" he asked, giving me a suspicious look through the wet glass.

"I just want to talk," I said, pulling my collar up. I was soaked to the bone. "Would you please open it all the way?"

"You're not coming in," Chris said. He leaned forward and looked down at my feet. "And I won't talk to you before you touch this …"

The thing he had been hiding behind his back was, of course, an anchor. He stuck it out the window.

"Sure, no problem." I took the anchor, turning it over. "Satisfied?"

He nodded and looked a little bit less uneasy. "Give it back, please."

I handed him back the anchor, and he opened the window all the way.

"Was that some sort of test?" I asked.

"Yes," Chris said. "And you passed. I had to be sure you hadn't become one of them."

"Who is 'them'?" I asked. "You have to tell me what you know, Chris. I think we might be in danger."

"If you put up the anchor like I told you, and you stayed inside at night, you should be safe, and there's no need to—"

"We didn't put up the anchor!" I interrupted. "And at least one of us has been outside last night."

Chris's eyes gleamed with fear.

"Tell me what the hell is going on around here!" I demanded.

"All right, all right," Chris said. "But keep your voice down. My mom—"

"Yeah, I get it. Your mom will kill you if she sees you talking to me. I'm sorry, but I'm tired of you guys and your secretiveness. Now, spill it!"

Chris bit his lip for a moment. Then, he started talking. "I don't know when it started. Maybe it has always been like this. But you and your friends chose the worst time to come here. It only happens once a year, and never more than three nights in a row."

"What happens?" I whispered.

"The tide, of course. It floods the whole area. But I guess you noticed by now. Everyone around here knows about it. You can see it on the barometers, they warn us about it, so most of the people leave home while it's happening. We used to go to my grandparents', but my granddad is very ill, so my parents decided to stay home this time. We have put up plenty of anchors, so no harm can come to us."

"Who is trying to harm you?" I asked. "Who are they?"

Chris was about to answer, when lightning flashed, illuminating everything for a split second. The thunderclap followed immediately.

"How far has the water come at your house?" he asked.

"Well ... the first night it just reached the terrace. But last night it went halfway around the house."

"You have been very lucky," Chris said. "The front door is facing away from the sea, right?"

"Yes, why?"

"That's the only reason you guys are still alive. That's the only thing that has kept them from entering the house. You see, they can only go as far as the tide allows them. They can't leave the water. That's why I looked at your feet before I asked you to touch the anchor—I was checking to see if you were standing in water."

My legs suddenly felt like jelly, and I grabbed the window frame so as to not fall down.

"They are lost souls," Chris continued quietly. "They have been cursed to live in the ocean. I once heard my dad refer to them as 'sea demons.' Three nights a year they get the chance to come up here and find new souls. Once you've been scratched or bitten, there's no way back. In a matter of hours, you'll become like them." He raised his hand, holding up the anchor. "The only protection is this. An anchor works on them like a cross on a vampire. Sea demons can't survive touching an anchor, and they can't pass through a door with an anchor above it. I know from experience. They knocked on our door one night some years ago. It was storming like crazy, like it is right now. It's always storming on the third night. That's when the tide reaches its highest."

I became aware that I was shaking all over, and it wasn't because I was soaking wet. "I don't get it: why would anyone want to live here?"

Chris shrugged. "We know how to protect our homes, and we make sure it's done properly. Plus, everyone sleeps with an anchor under their pillow."

"But what happens ...?" I swallowed and thought of Max. "What happens if someone comes in contact with these creatures?"

"Within a day, the person will turn into a sea demon. Then he must go to the ocean and stay there for the rest of his life with his new kind."

"Can you tell if a person has been ... infected?"

When Chris shook his head, my throat closed up. "That's the worst thing about them," he whispered. "They can still take their human form. For a while, at least. You see now why I couldn't trust you before you took the anchor?"

I tried to answer, but no words came.

"I mentioned the couple who lived in the house before, you remember?" Chris went on. "Well, the wife disappeared suddenly. The man was talking to everyone about some strange creatures from the sea who had taken her. Of course, we all knew he was telling the truth, but since we don't talk about it, no one would admit to him that he was right. Exactly one year later he too went missing. Rumor has it that he'd gone out into the sea and drowned himself."

Something made me turn around, and in that instant, a new flash of lightning tore through the darkness and revealed the grey sea behind the dunes. I saw to my horror that the waves were closer now than before.

"Holy hell," I whispered. "The tide is already coming."

"Yes. It will probably have flooded the whole area within half an hour. You'd better hurry back and put up the anchor, before it's too late. Here, keep this one, too. I have plenty more."

I stared at the anchor. Then, I grabbed it and looked at Chris. "Thank you."

I turned and ran as fast as I could.

TEN

I was getting closer to the cottage, but I wasn't the only one. The water had passed the dunes and came rolling a little closer with every wave.

On my way back, confused and frightened thoughts ran through my head. The flat tires on the bikes. The seaweed in the car engine. It was suddenly clear to me that someone didn't want us to leave.

And what was more: someone couldn't have gotten to the bikes in the shed or to the car engine without the keys. The key to the shed was hanging on a nail in the hall, and the car key was probably in Max's bag. Besides, the water hadn't reached the shed nor the car any of the previous two nights. Which meant that it had to be one of us who had punctured the bikes and sabotaged the car.

If Max had been outside last night, had he been scratched and infected? Had he turned into one of the creatures, but was hiding it from the rest of us? I hadn't seen any wounds on him, but he had been fully clothed at all times, so a tiny scratch could easily be hiding somewhere on his body.

Finally, I got the cottage in sight. I stopped for a second, trying to catch my breath—when, suddenly, I realized I was standing on something hard. It was the metal plate that Richard, Sienna and I had found the other day.

What's underneath that plate?

I threw a glance out at the sea, which was quickly approaching. I couldn't see anything but the waves. So, I crouched down and removed the heather, uncovering the rest of the plate. It was a couple of square feet. I squeezed my fingers under the edge and pulled upwards. It was really heavy, but I managed to lift it up and drag it aside.

The hole was deep enough for a grown man to stand in it—if it hadn't been for the spikes, of course. A dozen or so huge rusty iron spikes with pointy ends were standing upright at the bottom, welded onto a large iron anchor. A bunch of scattered bones from something that might very well be a human were visible down in the darkness.

I realized I was staring down into the trap which the former resident of the cottage had described in his final letter. I carefully walked around the hole, my heart pounding.

The sky was lit up in yet another flaming flash. I spun around and saw a group of dark figures out in the water. It was the same figures I had seen that morning—although at the time I had told myself it was just my imagination. This time, however, I couldn't fool myself—they were really there, and they were coming closer.

I ran to the cottage and pounded on the door.

"Who is it?" Richard called.

"It's me! Open the door!"

He opened. I tumbled in, slamming the door shut. My ears were ringing and I was dripping wet. Spike came to greet me, tail wagging.

"Finally," Richard said. "We were starting to worry that you—"

I pushed him aside and walked into the living room. Max was sitting at the table with a game of solitaire in front of him. He looked up with surprise. "Hey, man. You look like a drowned horse. Did you find a phone?"

"No," I said. "But it doesn't matter, because we won't have time to wait for help to come anyway."

I was approaching Max while clutching the anchor behind my back. I felt like a maniac in a cheesy movie, but I had no choice.

"What do you mean?" Richard said from behind me.

"And what's that you're hiding?" Max said, getting up.

I leaped forward, reached out the anchor and pressed it into Max's chest.

He screamed and almost fell over. Then, he stopped and stared down at my hand, which was still pressing against his chest. He looked at me, eyebrows raised. "What the fuck are you doing, dude?"

I licked my lips and removed the anchor. "I ... I just ..."

"Jayden, what the hell, man?" Richard said. "What's gotten into you?"

"Thank you for that," Max said. "Now I have no more clean underwear. I thought you were going to fucking stab me, you maniac!"

"I had to be sure," I muttered, running a hand through my wet hair.

"Where have you been, Jayden?" Richard asked.

"At Chris's house. He told me everything. You guys remember the cylinder we found underneath the floorboard?" I spilled out the whole story. The letter, what Chris had told me, and the approaching sea.

"And you actually believe that?" Max said, grinning. "I know you're scared, Jayden, but that kid sold you a bunch of bullshit."

"I don't care if you believe me," I said. "I saw them, okay? They are coming for us right now. We need to get the anchor up before the water reaches the house. It's a matter of minutes. Richard, where did you put the anchor? The one Chris dropped that day he was here?"

"I ... uhm ... I don't remember."

"Never mind, we'll use this one. Find a nail and a hammer." At that moment, it finally hit me. "Where's Sienna?"

Max and Richard exchanged a look, as though they both excepted the other to know.

"She went out to dry her hair before you left," Richard said. "We haven't seen her since."

I frowned and went to open the door to the hallway.

"Jayden, what are you –"

"Just shut up for a moment."

I checked the bedroom. It was empty. I placed my ear against the bathroom door. No sounds came from inside, but the keyhole told me that the lights were on.

"Sienna?"

No answer.

With bated breath I turned the knob. The door wasn't locked. Slowly, I pushed it open. It hit something soft on the way: Sienna's clothes were lying in a pile on the floor.

When I saw her in the tub, my first instinct was to turn away out of sheer embarrassment. Sienna was completely naked—her suntanned skin stood in sharp contrast to the white tub. Her eyes were closed, so I assumed she was sleeping—but then I noticed that her face was under the surface.

I felt a bolt of fear. She had fallen asleep and slipped down below the water. Maybe it wasn't too late to save her.

"Sienna!" I yelled, jumping forward, leaning over the tub, and just as I was about to reach down and grab her—she opened her eyes and stared right up at me.

I recoiled.

Her beautiful brown eyes were gone—in their place were two shining yellow irises. Sienna's mouth contorted into an unnaturally wide smile.

I backed away, bumping up against the wall.

Sienna sat up, making the water slosh about. I noticed her skin had taken on a yellowish hue.

"Hi, Jayden," she said in a voice that was thin and hoarse, almost snakelike. "I was just taking a nap—hope you don't mind."

I think I was fumbling for the door—I'm not sure, the adrenalin was pumping through my veins, and I couldn't take my eyes off Sienna.

"You see, it's kind of hard for me to be without the water for so long at a time," she whispered, still smiling. "Honestly, I don't know how I could ever stand it."

Her hands grabbed hold of the edge of the tub. The skin was yellow, the nails were dark and pointy, and the fingers were webbed.

"You ... you ... I don't ... understand," I heard my voice say.

Sienna didn't say anything, but her smile grew even wider, revealing a row of pointy, fishlike teeth.

In a flash it all came to me. The skeleton Sienna had stepped on—it had been from one of them, that's how she got infected.

"The seaweed in the car," I croaked. "That was you ... and you were outside last night, not Max ... you just used his shoes."

"Jayden," she hissed softly.

"This ... this is not happening ..."

There came a scream from the living room, and Spike started barking.

Sienna gave a spitting hiss and jumped up from the tub. I stumbled out into the hallway, pulling the door shut behind me and ran into the living room.

Richard was standing frozen, staring at what was happening out in the hall by the wide-open front door. Spike was jumping around, frothing and barking, but without enough courage to come close to the creatures who had grabbed Max and were shredding him to pieces. The salty seawater was pouring in through the doorway.

The sight of the creatures made me hesitate for a fateful moment. They were naked and their skin was scaly and glistening in yellow-green tones. On both sides of their necks was a row of open slits that could only be gills. Their faces were the most shocking: no noses, only huge fishlike mouths with way-too-many teeth and those shining yellow eyes.

Behind me, I distantly noticed the bathroom door being opened, as Sienna came stomping out. I heard her breath right behind me and felt it on my neck—I'll never forget it. The sound was sticky, as though her throat was filled with goo, but the smell was even worse: her breath reeked of rotten fish.

She was just about to sink her teeth into my shoulder when my eyes caught the anchor lying on the floor in front of Richard. I threw myself forward.

TEN

"Help! Get them off! Let me go!" Max screamed and fought frantically against the two sea demons who were attacking him while hissing eagerly. He had lost his glasses and had been torn badly on his face and arms. His T-shirt was nothing more than a bloody rag at this point, and one of them suddenly bit down hard on his forearm. Max shrieked and tried to pull loose, but the other one grabbed him from behind.

I picked up the anchor, held it out in front of me and approached Max.

"Back off!" I roared, trying to outshout Max's desperate screams and the hissing of the creatures.

To my amazement they actually recoiled towards the doorway, but they dragged Max along. My poor, bloody friend threw himself down and tried to crawl away, but the sea demons grabbed his legs and pulled him back.

"Nooo! Let me go!" Max howled and kicked at them. He was halfway out the door when he managed to grab the frame. "Help me, Jayden! Help me!"

"I'm trying! Let go of him, you bastards!"

"Jayden, behind you!"

Richard shouted just in time to warn me. The creature who had been Sienna just minutes ago, but now bore almost no resemblance to that beautiful girl I knew, was inches away from grabbing my neck and shredding the skin with her sharp nails. I spun around and thrust the anchor into her face.

She pulled back with a fierce hiss, holding up her arms to protect herself from the invisible force of the anchor.

"Take this and keep her away!" I yelled, handing Richard the anchor.

Max was now holding on to the doorstep with just one hand, and his screams had turned into dying sobs. Three new creatures walked right past him and entered the house.

I grabbed a chair and threw it at them. It knocked them back just enough for me to jump forward and slam the door shut, just as Max's fingers let go. I turned the lock.

Immediately, the window in the door shattered, as one of the creatures punched its arm through the glass and grabbed at me.

I jumped back and turned towards Richard and the creature who had been Sienna. They were stepping around each other like two wrestlers about to fight. The anchor in Richard's hand prevented Sienna from attacking him.

Spike was barking and lunging at Sienna's legs, trying to bite her. The dog seemed to be of no interest to the creature, whose eyes were fixed on Richard.

"Give me that," I said, yanking the anchor from Richard. "Fuck off!" I roared, stepping towards Sienna, forcing her to back away. "Follow me, Richard!"

We walked past the creature at a safe distant, while I made sure to hold out the anchor. Sienna hissed and sneered at us, but couldn't come closer.

"Come on, Spike!" I called, and the dog ran with us into the living room.

Sienna followed closely behind, watching our every move. I kept her at bay while Richard opened the terrace door. The water came rushing in, soaking our shoes. We stepped out onto the flooded terrace. There was nothing but water in every direction. Lightning was flashing overhead, the thunder was roaring.

The sea demon stopped in the doorway and looked up. It couldn't pass due to the anchor. I realized faintly I hadn't seen Sienna ever using the terrace door.

"Come on, Richard," I said, turning. "We have to—"

I fell silent when I saw them. They were all around us, standing in a half-circle. Their yellow eyes gleamed in the darkness, their hissing voices came sneaking through the stormy air.

"Keep as close to me as you can," I told Richard over my shoulder. "If we start fighting them, it's over. This anchor is our only way out, you got it?"

"Y... yes."

"We need to get out of the water. They won't be able to follow us."

One of the creatures stepped forward.

Spike lunged at it. It retreated.

"You're damn right!" I shouted. "That means stay the fuck away from us!"

The creature glared at me, showing its sharp teeth in a hateful sneer.

We started moving slowly. We walked along the house, the creatures following us and gathering ever so slightly closer.

"You stay back!" I demanded, holding out the anchor. "Come on, Richard. As soon as we reach the other side of the—"

Richard hadn't seen the edge of the terrace because of the water, so he stepped right out and fell down with a splash. He spluttered and fought to get back up.

The sea demons were frighteningly fast. One of them instantly lunged forward and bent down to grab Richard. I swung my fist—the one clutching the anchor—and hit the creature right in the back of the neck. The creature fell over, Richard managed somehow to kick it off of him, and then he was standing again.

It had only taken a couple of seconds, but that was all the other creatures needed to make their move. I sensed something closing in from behind and spun around, swinging my arm blindly and connecting with my elbow right to the chin of one of them—there was an audible SMACK! and the creature went sprawling.

Now they really went for it. Richard was grabbed by his ankle, making him almost fall over once more. He used his other foot to kick the creature while pushing another one away.

I had my own trouble: a pair of cold, sticky arms were swung around me from behind. I flung my head back, hitting the attacker square in the face. It was just enough to make it loosen its grip and allow me to wrestle free, but two new creatures came at me at once.

I dodged to the side, grabbed Richard around the waist and pulled him away just as a sea demon was about to bite down on his shoulder.

"Come on!" I shouted, pulling Richard along.

They had completely closed the ring around us—there was only one way open for escape, and that was straight out towards the sea. We fought our way through the knee-high waves with the creatures right at our heels.

I saw a small island straight ahead, like a single safe heaven.

"Over here," I panted.

We tumbled up on the island, getting out of the water, but the nearest sea demon followed us.

A hand grabbed my collar, forcing me to stop. The creature jumped on my back before I could do anything, and we fell to the ground, rolling around, its slimy, cold body was on top of me, and the hideous face was right in front of mine.

It hissed with triumph, causing a droplet of ice-cold drool to dripple down onto my cheek. As it opened its mouth to bite off my nose, I was sure I was done for.

That was when Spike sank his teeth into the throat of the sea demon and tore at it with the fury of a tiger. Dark-green blood came gushing out, drenching my face, and I heard the hoarse shriek from the creature, as Spike dragged it off of me.

I fought my way back up as the sea demon was battling Spike, trying to get the dog to let go, but Spike was in no mood for an argument, and was holding on with all his might. I helped him by kicking the creature hard in the chest, making it roll back down into the water.

"Jayden, watch out! Another one's coming!"

I ran for my life, sensing the creature right behind me. And suddenly, I saw the hole right in front of me. I threw myself through the air and landed on the other side. I looked back just in time to see the sea demon disappear down the hole.

There was a splash followed by shrill shrieks of pain. I crawled to the edge and looked down. The creature was lying at the bottom in a twisted position, the rusty spikes had penetrated it several places, and the blood was flowing out, mixing with the muddy rainwater. The creature writhed about desperately, trying to get free. Being so close to the big anchor was obviously too much for it, and the screams soon died out. Within only ten seconds or so, it was dead.

I got to my feet, and Richard and I were just standing there. We looked at each other, and then we looked at the creatures, who had gathered around us. But surprisingly, they didn't seem interested in us anymore—they were staring down into the hole. Spike growled warningly at them, but they didn't even notice the dog.

"Come on, Richard," I muttered. "Let's get out of here."

We stepped down from the island and back into the water, making our way through the waves. When I looked back, I saw the sea demons standing on that lone island, completely still, as though in mourning. I suddenly understood what that guy had meant in his suicide letter.

That saved me—it made them hesitate ...

I don't know if it was sympathy for their fallen peer or just plain morbid fascination that made the creatures unresponsive—and honestly, I don't really care. All I know is that it enabled Richard and me to reach safety.

As soon as we got out of the water, we collapsed panting next to each other in the wet heather. My body was shivering with exhaustion and fear and relief. The thunder was becoming distant, and the rain had almost stopped.

We just lay there for several minutes, until Spike started growling. I lifted my head and almost screamed.

The sea demons were only a few yards away. They had come in complete silence, and they were merely standing there, at the edge of the water, staring at us with hate and vengeance glowing from their yellow eyes. They didn't make a move, they didn't make a sound, they just stared at us until, a few minutes later, the water started retracting back towards the sea, and they were compelled to follow.

EPILOGUE

When I think back on last summer, it all seems like a bad dream. But dreams don't take away your friends, no matter how bad they are.

I haven't seen or heard from Max or Sienna since that night. Losing them might have been easier to cope with if Richard hadn't gone too.

Later that horrible night, as we were on our way home in the backseat of a police car, he lifted up his soaking wet shirt to reveal three long, thin and bloody scratches on his stomach. He'd gotten them during the fight with the sea demons. I still remember the look on his face as he stared at me. I'm pretty sure he knew what it meant.

The next day he disappeared. His parents—who had taken the first plane home from Paris after the police had informed them about what had happened—were devastated. They sold the cottage not long after.

Richard still hasn't returned. But I know where he is.

I've been thinking about the skeleton from the sea demon, the one that Sienna stepped on. I wonder if it had died of old age—if they even can die that way—or if it might have been the remains of the man who lived in the cottage before. His body could have washed back ashore after he drowned himself.

Not that it really matters either way. All I know is that Sienna got infected from that skeleton, and I only realized it all too late.

The whole thing happened exactly one year ago to the day. Outside the sun is setting. The sky is clear, and only a mild breeze is stirring. But I know somewhere a storm is gathering right now.

I'm sitting here, thinking about Richard, Max and Sienna, my three friends. I think of Chris and all the other frightened people. I'm glad I'm more than three hours' drive away.

Safe and secure on the mainland.

Far from the sea and the rising tide.

BLIND DATE
Never go home with a stranger

The simmering sensation in Lily's stomach intensifies as the evening wears on. Perhaps the wine has something to do with it—she has almost drunk half a bottle—but she's pretty sure it's also because of him.

She didn't know him at all before they met at the restaurant—she only knew he was twenty-one, his first name was Jake, and according to Georgia's description, he was really good looking. Lily doesn't completely agree on the last part; he is handsome, but not super-hot, and a little too skinny for her taste.

On the other hand, he has a really winning smile which makes his face light up, and he's extremely pleasant to talk to. There is a nice chemistry between them, and she's guessing he feels the same, because he orders another bottle of wine when the first one is empty.

"I'm not sure I should drink anymore," she says, smiling and touching her temple. "I think I'm getting a little drunk."

"It's not for you," he says, grabbing the bottle from the waiter and pretending to drink directly from the bottle in big, loud gulps.

Lily can't help but laugh at the silly gesture, as she gazes around a little nervously. It's a really fancy place, way too expensive for anything Lily would ever visit on her own; all the other guests are wearing suits or beautiful dresses, even the waiter strikes her as an old-fashioned British butler, butterfly tie and all. He forces a strained smile at her date's practical joke and reaches a pale hand out for the bottle. "Would you like me to serve the wine, sir?"

"Thank you, we'll manage, Lurch," Jake says, filling Lily's glass. "We'll ring the bell if we need you."

Lily sniggers once more, feeling like a silly school girl, as she tries to hide it and the waiter marches off. "That wasn't very nice," she whispers across the table.

"He knows I'm only joking," Jake says, serving himself another full glass. "He's a friend of my parents; they come here all the time."

"What was it your father does?"

"He owns a movie company."

"Which one?"

"It's called BT Productions."

"I haven't heard about it."

"Well, I didn't take you for the type who watches a lot of porn."

Lily almost chokes on a sip of wine. "Do they make ... porn?"

Jake nods earnestly. "That's where the big money is."

"You're kidding, right?"

"Oh no. BT is an acronym for Big Tits."

Lily looks around to see if any of the neighboring tables have heard them, as she feels her cheeks starting to burn.

Jake goes on, swirling the wine nonchalantly around the glass. "It's fine with me, of course, I just kind of wish they wouldn't shoot so many scenes at home, you know. The whole house is littered with dildoes, and ..." He breaks off as he apparently notices something on her face. "Wait, are you blushing?"

"No, I'm not."

"I think you are."

"It's just the wine."

"Red cheeks look good on you."

Lily takes her napkin and dabs her upper lip, discretely trying to cover her face. "So you were just jerking me around?"

"Yeah, they just produce regular, boring movies."

"Are you like that to everyone?"

"Like what?"

"A jerk."

He shrugs. "Only to the ones I'm trying to impress."

She raises one eyebrow, forcing herself not to return his smile this time.

He reaches a hand across the table. "All right, I'm sorry. Can you forgive me?"

She looks at his hand for a moment, then takes it. Her hand is a little damp, but his is dry and soft. He holds on for a couple of seconds, giving the back of her hand a quick, gentle stroke with his thumb before letting go. The touch makes the simmering in her stomach grow stronger.

What are you doing? spurts a voice in her head, sounding like a strict old lady. *You're falling in love with this guy. You don't even know him.*

"I need to pee," Lily says—partly because she really does need to pee, but mostly as an excuse to escape the situation which has suddenly gotten a little too intense.

She adjusts the skirt—it has an annoying habit of creeping up, but it's still her favorite, since it makes her ass look nice—and walks towards the bathroom, concentrating hard on not wobbling. Luckily, she decided against the heels right before leaving for the bus.

The air in the bathroom is a little cooler, and it feels nice against her hot face. She's also glad to get away from the many buzzing voices; the only sound out here is low, pan flute music floating from hidden speakers.

Lily locks herself in a stall, pulls up the skirt and sits down with a sigh. She pees with her eyes closed and feels the effect of the wine pulsating in her body.

Am I seriously planning on going home with him if he asks? A total stranger?

Except he's not—Georgia knows him. She was the one who put her up to the blind date. She said he was really nice, and so far, Lily has no reason to disagree. In fact, he's pretty interesting. Not many twenty-one-year-olds run a firm they created themselves. He told her about it during the dinner, an IT firm of some kind, making some security-thingy. She didn't really understand it, and she honestly didn't care, but it's apparently going well, since he's about to start shipping overseas.

Of course, his parents helped him with the funding, but he was very adamant about stressing the fact that he built everything himself ground-up, his only help being a partner who left the company recently.

Lily can't help but wonder if Jake sees her as just a silly teenager who has just only turned nineteen and is still living at home.

The thought of home makes her check her phone. There's a message from Dad.

Hi, hon. Mom said you were going on a date tonight. Exciting! But don't forget your date with Daddy tomorrow. Have fun. Love you.

Lily can't help but smile. After the divorce, Dad has tried his best to spend more time with her, to invest himself in her life, and Lily loves him for it. She can't really think of a good response, however, so she puts the phone back in her purse and finishes up. As she's washing her hands, she looks at herself in the mirror. It's hard to keep eye contact, because Mirror Lily keeps drifting out of focus.

You're already drunk as a skunk. There's that demanding voice again. *No more wine, no matter how charming he is. And if he asks you to go home with him, you'll say no. You don't go home with anyone on the first date, even if they are really sweet.*

"The *first* date?" Lily murmurs at the mirror. "So you're already expecting a second one?"

She smiles and leaves the bathroom before the voice in her head can come up with a snappy retort. As she reenters the restaurant, a lot of the tables are empty, and two more couples are leaving.

Jake is sitting with his phone out, but puts it away as soon as he sees her. "I was starting to worry you might have bailed on me. Jumped out of the window or something."

"I would never do that," she smiles and sits down.

"So, I'm not that bad after all?"

"Not at all." She leans a little closer.

Jake leans forward too, smiling.

Get a grip of yourself! You're flirting like crazy! At least play a little hard to get.

Lily leans back again and breaks the eye contact, but she can feel Jake keeps looking at her, and the simmering in her stomach returns.

"Looks like people are leaving," she says casually. "When does this place close up?"

"At ten."

"It's a quarter to ten now."

"Yeah." He grabs his glass and drains it. "Should we leave?"

"I think we'd better," Lily says, unsure whether it's an invitation.

"I'll go and pay the bill."

"I'll pay for myself."

Jake shakes his head. "Don't worry about it, it's on the firm."

While he's paying, she goes to the wardrobe and puts on her coat and scarf. Jake joins her, grabs his jacket and pushes open the glass door, making room for her to leave first.

"Thank you," she says, stepping out into the cold November evening. She gives a shiver and blows out a white cloud.

Jake gets in front of her and smiles. "Well," he says.

"Well," she answers, feeling a bunch of butterflies take flight in her stomach and thinking: This is it. Goodbye or go home together.

"I would love to invite you home with me for a cup of tea or something," he says, "but I don't take you for the type of girl who goes home with a guy on the first date."

Lily swings her body a little from side to side. "Normally, no. But if the guy is really nice, I could make an exception."

"Have I been really nice?" Jake asks, stepping a little closer.

Lily looks at his mouth, and before she even knows she's going to do it, she leans forward and kisses him.

"I'll take that as a yes," he says, as their lips part. He slips an arm around her waist. "Come on, let's grab a cab."

***

The voice in her head makes several objections during the ride, but Lily ignores them all. Jake holds her hand, and she rests her head against his shoulder.

Twice, Jake takes out his phone, checks it and puts it back in his pocket. It irritates her a little, but she assures herself it's just a habit a lot of people have—he's probably not even aware of it.

The third time, she can't help but say something. "Are you waiting for a call?"

"No," he mutters, smiling a little guiltily. "Sorry, it's just … I got a pretty weird message back at the restaurant."

"From whom?"

"From my former partner. I haven't heard from him since we split up."

"What did he want?"

Jake shakes his head. "Just something about him not being angry with me anymore."

"Why would he be angry with you?"

"The way we split up wasn't exactly very smooth. I suppose it was mostly my fault. To be honest, I kicked him out."

"Why did you do that?"

Jake sighs and runs a hand through his hair. "I guess I just realized I didn't really know him as well as I thought."

"Well, it's good he's not holding a grudge anymore."

"I guess so," Jake says, but sounding insincere for the first time. "It's just a little odd that he would suddenly write me on a Friday night. And the way we ended things … he was so pissed at me; you wouldn't believe it. Honestly, I never expected to hear anything from him again." He shakes his head and smiles. "Never mind. This evening isn't about him."

"What's it about then?"

Jake answers her with a kiss, longer this time. He's a really good kisser; she can taste the wine on his tongue, and she almost doesn't want it to end, but at that moment the cab pulls over.

She looks out at an enormous building. "Is this your place?" she asks amazed.

"It's my parents' place," he says, paying the driver. "They're in Monaco for a couple of weeks, so I stay in the house."

They get out, and Lily peers through the metal gate at the huge yard and the dark stone mansion behind it.

As the cab leaves, Jake takes out his phone, smiling. "Let me give you a demonstration of my product."

The phone plays a short melody, and the gate starts rolling aside.

"Impressive," Lily says, shivering in the cold.

They walk across the courtyard and reach the front door, where Jake uses his phone once more, making the lock snap open. The lights in the entrance hall turn on automatically as they enter.

"So you need your phone to get in?" Lily asks, pulling off her coat.

"Yeah, or one of my parents' phones. Here, let me get that." He takes her coat and hangs it in a closet. "Come on, I'll show you how it works."

He leads her through a big hall and into a living room bigger than a normal-sized house. The furniture is very modern looking, and everything is spotless. There is an open fireplace, a home cinema and a huge aquarium with large, colorful fish swimming lazily about. The lights, once again, turn on by themselves.

Jake activates a screen in the wall above the fireplace, and low, cozy music starts playing from hidden speakers. He throws himself on the couch, patting the seat next to him. Lily sits down.

"Look at this," he says, showing her the phone. "This is a map of the house. It shows that all the windows and doors are locked right now. If anything is opened, it will alert me. And you see this room here, which is blue? That's the living room. It's blue because we are in here."

Lily looks at him, wonderingly. "How does it know?"

"Because every room has sound and movement sensors," he says, pointing up into the corner, and Lily sees a small metal ball. "There are still a few bugs I need to work out. Like, the sensors are a little bit too sensitive. They react to things like a curtain moving in a breeze."

"So if we keep absolutely still and don't make a sound, the system won't register us?"

"Well, yeah, but you always move a little, even in your sleep."

"But someone could be in the house right now?" Lily goes on, teasing him. She looks around and whispers: "Someone standing completely still ..."

Jake grins. "In theory, yes. But would a burglar stand completely still? Besides, he couldn't have gotten in without a verified phone." He leans closer and says: "Rest assured, it's only you and me."

Lily smiles. "I hope so."

Jake kisses her briefly, then jumps to his feet and opens a drinks cabinet. "You want something? What's your favorite drink? I think we can manage almost anything."

She knows she shouldn't drink anymore, but she finds herself saying: "I love Cosmopolitans."

"That's the one with lime, right?"

"Yeah, and cranberry juice."

Jake opens another cupboard, revealing a refrigerator filled with fresh citrus fruits, different berries, juices, milk, cream and everything else you would need to make any kind of drink.

Jake mixes a Cosmopolitan and pours it into a fancy glass which he hands her.

"Thank you," she says, tasting it.

"Approved?"

"Mmmm, yes, it's really good." She licks her lips and notices Jake watching her do it.

He smiles. "Good. Now it's your turn. Mix something for me—anything, surprise me! I'll just go and change into something more comfortable."

"How strong do you want it to be?"

"Depends on how drunk you want me to be." He winks at her, grins and leaves the room.

Lily just sits there for a moment, smiling to herself and listening to the music. The voice in her head seizes the opportunity to assert itself again.

You aren't planning on spending the night here, are you? I mean, my God, you've only known him for four hours ...

Lily doesn't feel like listening anymore, so she drowns out the voice with a large swig of her drink, then gets up to mix something for Jake. She explores the many bottles and decides on a Manhattan.

When the drink is made, she puts it on the table and takes a walk around the impressive room while sipping her Cosmo.

Five minutes more pass by, and still no Jake.

He's taking his time.

Lily finishes her drink and sits back down again, finding her phone, and decides to write back her dad.

Of course I haven't forgotten about you, Daddy. But I might be a little hungover tomorrow. Call you once I wake up. Love you.

There is a noise from upstairs. It sounds like something heavy being dropped on the floor, or maybe a door slamming shut.

At least he's still alive up there. He really doesn't mind letting people wait.

Ten minutes more go by, and Lily starts to become restless and annoyed. She wonders if Jake might be playing a game. Perhaps he wants her to come looking for him. Perhaps it was something completely different he had in mind, when he said he was going to change into something more comfortable. She gets a picture of him lying butt-naked on a bed surrounded by rose petals.

Lily snickers and gets up. Game or not, she doesn't feel like waiting around all evening, so she goes out to the hall, where a wide, winding staircase leads to the first-floor landing. She listens for a moment, but can't hear anything from upstairs, so she slips up the steps.

The first floor is split by a long hallway with lots of rooms on each side. One of the doors is ajar, and a stream of light is floating out. Lily goes to take a peek and finds a large bathroom.

"Hello?" she whispers. "Jake?"

No answer—except for something dripping. It sounds like a leaky tap.

drip ... drip ... drip ...

Lily pushes the door open all the way, no sound from the hinges, only the dripping growing slightly louder, but still the same, slow rhythm.

drip ... drip ... drip ...

She steps inside, looking around. Everything is shining blindingly white. The tub is more like a small pool, and behind a tinted glass wall is a sauna. Her date, however, is nowhere to be seen, so Lily goes to turn off the tap.

But the tap isn't dripping. Instead, she finds something strange in the sink: a clear plastic bag, sealed up with a tight knot and containing a large hammer. The bag is red and sticky around the head of the hammer.

"Yuk," Lily mutters with a sneer.

Is that supposed to look like blood? What kind of a sick joke is this?

She looks up into the mirror, and finally she sees Jake. Or rather, Jake's arm. It's hanging over the edge of the tub. She didn't notice it before because she took it for a towel at first glance.

"What are you doing?" she asks, turning around, starting to get really upset. "If this is your idea of a practical joke, you really need to get your head checked."

Jake doesn't answer and doesn't move his arm.

Lily strides over to the tub, about to tell him off—but stops abruptly as she gets a proper look at him.

The picture is all wrong. Jake is lying there in a twisted position, head resting on one shoulder, eyes and mouth open. Across his left temple is a large, open gash, from where blood is oozing out. It runs down his cheek and drips from his jawline down into the tub

DRIP ... DRIP ... DRIP ...

where a pool of it, screaming red against the white tub, has made its way to the drain and is disappearing.

Lily can't move, can't scream, can't think. Her brain is struggling to process what her eyes are perceiving.

Is he acting? He must be—all that blood can't be real ...

But Jake's eyes are telling a different story. They are staring across the room, seeing nothing, dead, they are dead, Jake is dead, he is dead and

DRIP! ... DRIP! ... DRIP! ...

the blood is real. And now she can even smell it; a sharp, metallic odor hangs in the air. The blood is running from his head and dripping down into the tub with thunderous bangs, still louder and louder, and the noise

DRIP! ... DRIP! ... DRIP! ...

isn't just coming from the dripping blood, it's everywhere in the room, it's filling the whole house, it's coming from the hallway.

The hallway ... steps ... someone is coming ... hide ...

Amazingly, Lily's body obeys her flickering thoughts. She doesn't really have any say in the matter, her body just operates on a primitive survival mechanism, making her stagger to the door, slide in behind it and press her back up against the wall, seconds before a large person enters the room.

Lily isn't really there. She's pretty sure she holds her breath, but she has no idea for how long. Half a minute, maybe, or it could be half an hour. She feels convinced it's all just a dream, yet somehow, she knows it's not.

The door blocks her view, so the sounds are all she has to go on in guessing what's going on in the room.

Crackling of plastic; it sounds like a large piece being spread out. Steps across the floor. A muffled grunt. Small, shrill shrieks from skin rubbing against porcelain. She's guessing Jake is being lifted out of the tub. A couple of bumps as he's laid down on the floor. Then, more steps. More crackle of plastic. The shredding sound of tape being pulled from a roll.

"Goddamn mess," a deep voice mutters.

Then there's another grunt. The steps leave the room and fade away down the hallway.

Lily stays put a moment longer. She knows she needs to move, needs to get out, but her body feels like an ice sculpture only slowly thawing. Finally she regains enough control to get moving, and she staggers out from behind the door.

Jake is gone. All that's left is his blood all over the tub.

Lily steps closer to the doorway and listens intently before peeking out into the hallway. It's empty in both directions. She assumes the killer has carried Jake's body downstairs. Perhaps he even left the house. The thought fills her with something which feels like a faint hope.

Her hand goes to her pocket, but the phone is in her purse, and the purse is on the coffee table in the living room. She can't call for help, which means her only remaining option is to get out of the house. So, she tiptoes down the hallway towards the staircase. She can hear the music still playing downstairs, and she's just about to step out onto the landing when the sound of heavy footsteps suddenly comes from the stairs.

Lily spins around and runs down the hallway, passing the bathroom and wrenching the next door open, jumps inside and closes the door. She tries not to slam it, but it still gives off a noise, which in Lily's ears sounds like the firing of a gun. She turns, heart in her throat, to see a dim bedroom with a huge double bed and a flat-screen on the wall. There are only two hiding places: the bed or the closet.

Lily drops down on the floor and crawls under the bed. She turns so she can see the door, breathing rapidly through her mouth.

He didn't hear it ... he didn't hear it ...

She listens for footsteps, but can't hear anything but her own pulse.

Then, suddenly, the door is opened and Lily almost screams, cramping her throat shut to keep in the noise.

A stream of light falls in from the hallway, and two large, black boots steps in through the doorway. A click, and the lights come on in the room.

Lily stops breathing completely, her pulse pounding behind her eyes, making her vision blurry with fear.

The killer walks around the bed, his steps painfully slow, almost casual. Lily follows the boots with her eyes, but is too afraid to turn her head even an inch.

The killer seems to be gazing out the window for a moment or two, then he walks back around the bed, but instead of leaving the room, he goes to the closet and opens both doors. The hangers rattle as he pushes them aside. Seemingly finding nothing of interest, he shuts the doors again with a scuff.

Then, Lily hears him give off another sound, as he sniffs twice.

He can smell my perfume ...

The thought sends icy lightning down her spine. For a moment she's sure the killer knows she's hiding in here somewhere, and soon he will kneel down and check under the bed. She prepares for the shock of seeing his face and meeting his eyes as he will stare directly at her.

But that doesn't happen. To her astonishment, the killer leaves the room. He doesn't close the door, but leaves it ajar. She hears him walk down the hallway and open another door.

Lily starts breathing again, her lungs gulping for air.

Do I stay or do I run?

Being under the bed makes her feel like a mouse in a trap; if he comes back for a second look and finds her, she has no way of escaping. Whereas, if she leaves her hiding place, even if he does see her, she'll still at least have a chance of getting away.

So she crawls out from under the bed and gets to her feet, her legs feel shaky. She goes to the window and peers out. She can see the neighbor house from up here, and in one of the windows a lady is watering her plants. Lily waves frantically and jumps up and down.

Look up here! Come on, look up here!

For a moment it actually looks like the lady gazes up at her, but at that same moment comes a noise from the hallway, and Lily whirls around to stare at the door, ready to dive under the bed.

Nothing happens, however, and there are no more noises from the hallway. She sneaks over and carefully peeks out. No sight of the killer, but she can hear him somewhere nearby, rummaging through something.

All right, you can do it. Count to three and then make a run for it. Don't look back. Just run for the stairs. Ready? One ... two ...

The killer comes out from a room. Lily only gets a brief glimpse of him before she pulls her head back, but he's a lot bigger than she thought, tall and broad, and he's wearing a black ski mask.

Lily steps behind the door and listens. The killer walks by the door, and a moment later the water starts running in the bathroom. She can hear the sound of scrubbing on porcelain.

He's cleaning the tub. Now is my chance.

She steps out into the hallway. The door to the bathroom is wide open. She slowly starts walking towards it, feeling extremely exposed in the hallway without anywhere to hide; at any second he could step out and see her. Except she can still hear him scrubbing the tub.

She gets close enough to peer into the bathroom, and she sees him crouched in front of the tub, scrubbing away on the inside, while the tap is running. He pauses briefly to rinse off the sponge, and Lily sees the pink blood pouring from it. Jake's blood. The guy she was kissing twenty minutes ago. The thought hits her like a fist in the stomach.

Don't think about it now. Concentrate on getting out.

Lily forces herself to focus. She just needs to pass the bathroom door. It's three steps at the most, then she will be out of sight and have a free run to the stairs and the front door.

Lily steps forward, time slows down, and for two infinite seconds she is completely in plain view of the killer. He would only need to turn his head slightly, and he would see her.

But he doesn't.

And then Lily is past the bathroom.

She runs for the stairs, takes them two steps at a time, careful not to slip. It's difficult to make her shaking legs slow down, now that they know escape is right in front of her.

At the foot of the stairs she almost trips over a large bundle on the floor. Lily stops in surprise and looks at it for a second, before she realizes what it is.

It's Jake. He is wrapped in black plastic like a mummy.

Lily feels her throat tighten and her eyes tear up. She puts a hand to her mouth and steps around the bundle, making an effort to take her eyes off it, as she staggers to the entrance hall. She doesn't even think about finding her jacket, just goes directly for the handle and pulls it. The door is locked. She fumbles for the lock, but finds only a little, black box. There are no buttons or display or anything. Lily recalls how Jake unlocked the door with his phone. Perhaps the phone is also needed to get out.

She turns reluctantly, desperation rising in her chest, and looks towards the bundle. Is the phone still in Jake's pocket? Lily bites her lip. The mere thought of opening the plastic and reaching inside makes her stomach churn.

Perhaps she could just smash a window and jump out. But that would definitely make enough noise for the killer to hear, and she's not sure she will be able to get out of a smashed window without cutting herself if she only has a few seconds to do so.

Lily finds herself walking towards the bundle, as though her instincts are telling her the way to go. She bites down hard and kneels. Carefully, she grabs the plastic and tries to rip it. It's difficult because the killer has taped it up good, but finally her fingers find an opening and manage to squeeze inside, all the while she's keeping an eye on the upstairs landing and listening for any noises. She can still hear the faint sound of running water.

Her hand searches the inside of the plastic, finding cloth, going farther down, and—

Lily lets out a gasp as she feels Jake's hand, which already is cold to the touch. She puts her other hand to her mouth, but it's too late, the sound already escaped her, and she can only pray it wasn't loud enough for the killer to hear.

She hurries up, groping her way under the plastic, locating Jake's belt, a little farther down, feeling his jeans, and—there! His pocket! She squeezes her fingers into the pocket and feels a wild urge to scream with joy as she finds the phone.

At that moment she hears a bump from upstairs. The sound of the water has stopped.

Quickly she pulls out the phone, as the sound of footsteps approaches the landing. She jumps up and runs through the nearest opening, entering a large kitchen, which is instantly lit up by the automated lights. She runs around the table and ducks down behind it, clutching Jake's phone to her chest and her thrumming heart.

A few nerve-racking seconds pass by. She listens intently, realizing the music from the living room has stopped.

Then the killer enters the kitchen; the soles of his boots making the unmistakable, high-pitched squeaking noise from rubber against the tile floor. He stops, as far as Lily can tell, right on the other side of the table.

She holds her breath, as a movement catches her eye and makes her look up. In the reflection of the dark window she can make out most of the kitchen, including the large man on the other side of the table. He takes off a pair of leather gloves, then reaches up and pulls off the black ski mask too, revealing a pale, bald head.

If he looks into the window, he will see me staring back at him.

But he doesn't; he pulls out his phone, and several minutes pass in intense silence, as the killer apparently tries to do something with the phone, but not succeeding, he grows visibly annoyed. A few times he mutters: "Piece of shit ..." Then finally, he lets out a grunt and puts the phone to his ear, turning his back to the table.

Almost another minute passes in silence.

Then he suddenly says: "It's me. I have ... yeah, I know, but I ... listen ... shut your mouth and listen! I know I'm not supposed to call you, but I need your help. This stupid fucking system you made isn't working ... yeah, I'm inside ... it's already done ... yes, it's taken care of ... well, the problem is I think there might be someone else in the house."

Lily's body tightens in every muscle. It's all she can do to keep from jumping up and fleeing in blind panic.

"I'm not sure," the killer goes on. "It could just be a cat or something, but I'm pretty sure I heard a noise ... yeah, he came home like you said, but he could have had company ... of course I searched the house, what do you take me for? The problem is, there's a thousand hiding places in this fucking place ... listen, you said something about this system of yours being able to detect movement—that means I can see if someone is in the house, right? ... Fine, how do I make it show me then?"

Lily looks up into the window, seeing the killer starting to fumble with the phone.

"Hold on ... hold on, damnit ... I'll put it on speaker ... right, go ahead ..." He puts the phone on the table.

"*Did you find the app?*" a much lighter voice asks from the phone—it sounds like a young man.

"Yeah, I just opened it. What do I choose?"

"*Choose Overview.*"

The killer presses something on the phone. "Right, now it shows a map of the house."

"*Good. The room you're in right now is blue, right?*"

"Yeah."

"*Are there any other blue rooms?*"

"No."

"*Then we're fine; no one else is in the house.*"

"But couldn't the person just be standing perfectly still? Like you told me to do?"

The voice on the other end hesitates. "*Well, it would need to be someone who knows the system, a pal of his, maybe. Did you check the entrance hall?*"

"There are no hiding places in the entrance hall."

"*No, I mean if you checked for shoes, you idiot. If he brought home a friend, there might be an extra pair of shoes in the entrance hall.*"

"Oh, I see. Good thinking."

"*The rest is up to you. Think you can handle it?*"

The killer overhears the snark remark. "You can transfer the other half of the money now. Like I said, it's done."

"*You'll get paid once I hear about it in the news—that was the deal. And remember to trash the phone once you're done.*"

"Sure, I'll—"

"*It needs to be properly trashed. If they find even a piece of it, that will directly point to me.*"

"I know, damnit."

"*Right. Don't call again.*"

The killer disconnects and mutters to himself: "Goddamn punk ..." He checks the phone once more before stuffing it into his pocket. Then, he leaves the kitchen.

Lily listens. It sounds like the killer goes to the entrance hall. Lily's shoes are out there, but so are several of Jake's mom's—Lily noticed them when she came. The killer probably won't be able to tell the difference.

A minute goes by. Then she hears the killer pass the kitchen and walk upstairs again.

Lily breathes out slowly through her mouth. She doesn't dare to move a finger, she's afraid to even blink. Even the slightest movement might set off the sensors, and she has no way of knowing if the killer might check his phone again.

Maybe I should just stay here. Wait for him to finish up and leave. Maybe that's the safest course.

But the thought of her accidentally making a move and revealing herself to the killer is too claustrophobic. If he comes back into the kitchen, knowing she is here somewhere, she will have no way to escape.

She realizes she is still clutching Jake's phone and feels a pang of hope. She can call for help! But if she does, she will activate the sensors, and she will have to wait at least ten minutes before help arrives.

There is another way. A better way. She can use the phone to unlock the front door.

Without moving her head, she turns her eyes down to the phone. Moving her thumb as little as possible, she activates the screen—luckily, she noticed Jake's pin code as he showed her how the system works—and she navigates to the app called Perfect Lockdown.

As she opens it, the phone plays a brief tune, and Lily's heart jumps in her chest. But the killer can't possibly have heard it from all the way upstairs.

She scrolls through the menu items: Lock ... Unlock ... Overview ... Help

It's probably Unlock she needs, but she decides to hit Overview first, and the map of the house appears. The upstairs bathroom is blue, all the other rooms are black.

Good. He's still up there. And the sensors haven't picked up on me.

Lily returns to the menu and hits Unlock.

A message pops up: *Place device close to door or window.*

Now she knows how it works. She just needs to reach the front door. She checks the map once more, making sure the killer is still in the bathroom. He is. Lily bites her lip. Now is as good a chance as she'll ever get. She can make it to the front door in ten seconds. She's not going to waste any time putting on her shoes; she'll just open the door, sprint across the yard to the gate, open that too and run down the street.

You can do this. Even if he hears you, you'll have a head start. You can outrun him.

She tries her best to encourage herself, but she is trembling all over with fear, and she won't be able to calm down before she is out of danger. So she counts to three and does it.

Jumping to her feet, she runs around the kitchen table, almost slipping on the smooth tile, and just as she is about to leave the kitchen, she stops abruptly and stares at the table.

Suddenly, everything moves in slow motion.

The gloves and the ski mask are still on the table.

He ... forgot ... it ...

Even her thoughts are unnaturally slow. She manages to lift the phone and stare at it. It's still on the map. Now, two of the rooms are blue: the kitchen and the upstairs hallway. But the hallway changes in that instant to the hall right next to the kitchen, and Lily hears the heavy steps coming down the stairs.

Time jumps back into speed. Lily can't make it around the table, so she jumps to the side and presses her back up against the wall right next to the entrance.

A second later, the killer enters the kitchen. He goes directly for the table, muttering to himself: "There it is ..."

Lily stares at his back, as he stops and puts the gloves on. She is completely exposed. As soon as the killer turns around, he will see her. She moves sideways, sliding her back against the wall until the wall disappears and she can move backwards out into the hall, just as the killer puts the ski mask in his pocket. Lily jumps out of sight the moment he starts turning around, and she bolts for the only hiding place in the hall: the stairs.

Just as she ducks under the staircase, the killer comes back out from the kitchen. The steps of the staircase have space between them, which makes Lily able to peer out at the killer, who starts climbing the stairs, making it tremble slightly with every heavy stamp of his boots.

For a second, Lily is sure she made it. The killer will proceed upstairs and she will be able to make it out the front door.

But then he stops halfway up the stairs. He sniffs.

"There's that perfume again," he murmurs.

Then he turns around and walks back down again.

Lily is completely paralyzed with terror. She can't move a muscle, can only stand there, watching the killer through the steps. He stops at the foot of the stairs, darting a glance around, but not looking back at the stairs. Then he goes to the entrance hall.

Lily stretches her neck slightly to the side and sees him opening the closet and pulling out a coat.

Her coat.

He buries his face in the fabric, sniffing deeply, then examines the pockets, but apparently finding nothing of interest, he puts the coat back.

Then he returns to the hall and stops in the middle of the floor, looking around slowly. The look on his face makes Lily even more terrified; he is obviously suspicious, maybe even certain that someone else is in the house. For the first time, Lily gets a chance to see his face properly. He is around the same age as her dad, but way bigger and way more repulsive. Bags under his piggy eyes, reddish blotches on his skin and a gray, stubbly beard.

He mutters something incoherent and marches off to the living room. Lily hears him give off a curse in there, before he returns holding her purse.

Lily's heart stops beating, as the killer bites off his gloves and frantically starts going through her purse, making her lip gloss and a few coins spill out on the floor. He pulls out her phone, tries to activate it, but can't get past the screen lock. Instead he finds her driver's license and squints as he stares at the photograph.

Another curse as he goes to his pocket, producing his own phone. Suddenly, and completely unexpectedly, he looks up and roars: "I know you're here, Lily Amber Jackson!"

Lily jumps but manages to bite back a gasp.

The killer listens briefly for a reply, looking around in all directions. Then, when nothing happens, he turns his attention to the phone again. "Why the fuck can't I see her?" he growls. Looking up once more, he bellows: "I know where you live! How would you like me and a few friends to come pay you a visit someday, huh? Why don't you just come out, so we can settle this right now?"

Lily holds her breath.

The killer waits impatiently for half a minute, pacing back and forth, constantly checking the phone. Until, finally, he loses patience and mutters: "Right, missy. You're going the same way as your date. Let's start down here ..." He strides out to the kitchen, and Lily can hear him starting to rip open the cupboards and tip over chairs.

She's trapped. It's only a matter of minutes before he'll find her if she stays. In order to get out of the house, she has to get past the entrance to the kitchen, which means she will very likely be seen. If she's lucky, however, he will have his back turned.

She is just about to make a run for it, when a phone starts ringing out in the kitchen.

"Fuck!" the killer exclaims, then a second later he barks: "Hello? What do you want? I thought we weren't supposed to talk anymore ..."

Lily hesitates, listens.

Heavy footsteps, as the killer comes stomping in to the hall once more, phone to his ear. "Not yet," he growls. "But I'm positive someone's here. It's a bitch he brought home with him—I found her purse." A short pause as the killer listens. From between the steps of the staircase, Lily can see now his cheeks turn red with anger. "How the fuck was I supposed to know he had company? You were the one who was supposed to make sure he ... Listen, you little punk, who the hell do you think you're talking to? I'll rip your fucking—huh? ... No, she didn't call the cops ... Because I have her phone. And they would have been here already ... What's that?" The killer breathes heavily as he listens for a moment. Then he looks around. "I'm in the hall—why?" He listens again shortly, before he checks the phone screen. "No, none of the other rooms are blue. Don't you think I already checked? She must be standing perfectly still somewhere, and I'm going to find her and ... Huh?" The killer frowns. Then he mutters three words which make a chill run down Lily's spine: "The same room ...?"

Lily stares at the killer, as his small, piggy eyes search the hall.

"That can't be," he murmurs. "There are no hiding places here ... except for maybe ..." His gaze stops at the staircase. He glares directly into Lily's eyes. His mouth drops open. Then a nasty grin spreads across his face. "I'll be damned ... yeah, I'm looking right at her." He disconnects the call and slips the phone back into his pocket. "You sneaky little bitch—you almost played me for a fool."

Lily's heart is pounding hard in her throat as she steps out from under the stairs, her legs feeling wobbly. There is no furniture in the hall, nothing to hide behind, nothing between her and the man who wants to kill her. Only Jake's body is lying on the floor.

Less than twenty feet separates Lily from the killer, and he's blocking the way to the entrance hall, the kitchen and the living room. Lily is completely cornered. Her only way out is the staircase. Maybe she can jump up and climb—

But apparently the killer gets the same idea, because he moves a little closer to the stairs, preventing her from taking that way too.

His smile grows wider. "I like your perfume—reminds me of my ex."

Lily never thought it possible to be this scared. And yet her fear reaches even higher as she picks up on something in his voice, and the terrible realization comes to her: *He's going to rape me before he kills me.*

One last fleeting hope flies across her mind as she becomes aware of the phone in her hand. She dials 9-1-1—her finger trembling so much it's almost impossible, but she manages to make the call.

The killer charges at her.

Lily screams and tries to jump aside, but he grabs her arm and rips the phone from her hand. Without even bothering to check the screen, he throws it onto the floor, causing it to explode in several pieces.

Lily tries to pull free, but he is too strong. He snarls something at her, but she doesn't register it, her mind has gone into blind survival mode. She is screaming and struggling, punching and clawing at him, she even tries to bite him. Then he grabs her hair, and her head is flung aside as he slaps her hard enough for her ears to ring and her eyes to water. She feels dizzy, as though she is about to faint. She fights to stay awake, but her body isn't really responding anymore, and the next thing she knows she is on the floor on her back, with him towering above her. He says something—the words are lost in the ringing—but he's not smiling anymore. Then his giant hands close around her throat with crushing force.

Lily tries to scream, but no sound comes out. She blinks and almost can't open her eyes again.

I'm going to die ... This will be my last thought ...

Darkness closes in, all sounds grow distant, even the pain goes away, and Lily floats away, floats away into the dark, and she's not afraid anymore, she's not even worried, in fact she feels quite good, almost like she does just before slipping into a pleasant dream, and then ...

***

... she can breathe again. The world returns, everything comes floating back. Lily gasps and opens her eyes.

The killer has let go of her. He is still poised above her, but he has turned to the side as something else seems to have caught his attention. "What the hell?" he roars, and Lily can hear something odd in his voice—is it fear? "Let go off me!" Yes, it's definitely fear.

The weight of him lifts as he scrambles sideways, and Lily is able to sit up, still panting and rubbing her aching neck. What she sees doesn't make any sense at all.

The killer is pulling and tearing at his leg, trying to wrench it free from something which has caught it. And that something is Jake's hand protruding from the plastic.

Lily's brain is trying to understand. Her first thought is that Jake has somehow come back to life as a vampire or zombie. But slowly, the only logical explanation dawns on her.

He wasn't dead at all—he was just unconscious!

But how is that even possible? She saw his face. He wasn't breathing; he was definitely dead.

Except he wasn't, apparently. And even though part of her knows what's happening doesn't make sense, a bigger part of her feels like this isn't the right time to question it.

"Let go of me, damnit!" the man roars and pulls his leg back hard enough for the plastic bundle to slide across the floor, but the hand doesn't let go—its grip seems almost unnaturally strong, like a dead man's cramp.

Lily looks up and sees the front door out in the entrance hall. Then she sees the killer's phone, which has slipped out of his pocket and is lying on the floor. She scrambles to her feet and picks up the phone.

The killer doesn't even notice her as she staggers past him, he is too busy fighting to get Jake to let go. Lily reaches the front door and uses the phone to unlock it.

"Hey!" the killer roars from the hall, and she can hear him getting to his feet, apparently finally free. "Stop! Come back here, you bitch!"

Lily opens the door and stumbles out into the cool evening air, down the front steps and starts running across the gravel yard. The gate is getting close, jumping up and down in front of her eyes. Behind her the sound of the killer's running footsteps.

The phone almost slips out of her sweaty hand, but she manages to hold on to it, as she stops and runs it past the box on the gate. It unlocks with a snap and starts moving aside. As soon as she can squeeze through, she chooses Lock on the phone and holds it close to the box on this side. The gate immediately changes direction and closes itself, just as the killer comes crashing into it. He grabs the bars and shakes them violently, but the gate is too heavy for him to break it down.

Instead, he glares at Lily; his face scarlet and his eyes black. A string of spittle hangs from his lower lip. "I promise you I'll make you regret it if you don't come back in here."

Lily backs away from the gate, looking down at the phone as she is about to dial 9-1-1 once more—but then it starts ringing in her hand. It's from a number unknown.

The killer falls silent and just stares at her.

Lily answers the call without saying anything.

"*Did you find her?*" the squeaky voice of the young man asks. Lily can hear his bated breath. "*Hello? ... Speak to me, asshole! ... Is it fucking done?*"

Lily's fear suddenly turns into something else. "Fuck you," she snarls into the phone. "I know who you are, and you're going to prison, you psycho."

A gasp of surprise as she disconnects.

The killer is now trying to climb the gate, but he is too heavy, and the metal is slippery, so he slides right back down again.

Lily makes the call, as the killer succumbs to simply staring at her, like a prisoner behind bars, hatred burning from his eyes, and a friendly female voice sounds in Lily's ear: *"Nine one one, what's your emergency?"*

Lily tells her, and the lady tells her in turn to stay put, that help will be there shortly. And it's true, in a matter of minutes she hears the sound of sirens, and police cars show up, and then ...

***

... suddenly, strangely, she finds herself walking down the hallway of a hospital, realizing a few days have past by like the blink of an eye. She stops at the door marked with number 12, briefly looks down at herself, fixing her clothes, and then she knocks on the door.

"Come in," a familiar voice calls.

Lily opens the door and steps in the room.

Jake is sitting up in the bed. He has a bandage around his head and is eating a big lunch from a tray on his lap. "Oh, hi," he says, putting the tray on the table next to his bed. "I was just thinking about you."

Lily smiles and goes to the bed. "Sorry I didn't bring you any flowers."

"That's okay, I have plenty." He nods at the forest of bouquets on the table.

"How are you doing?"

"Fine, considering. They said I'll be able to make a full recovery."

"I'm so happy to hear that," Lily says, smiling. "I still can't believe you even survived. I mean, getting hit in the head with a hammer ..."

"Well, I might suffer a few minor things," he says gravely. "The doctor says my face might sometimes ..." He cuts himself off and screws up his face in a silly grimace for a second. "Look, it just happened!"

Lily can't help but to laugh. "At least you didn't lose your bad sense of humor."

"I can ask them to do another surgery and remove it if you don't like it."

"No, keep it. It does have a certain charm."

Jake smiles, and a moment's silence passes through the room.

"I spoke to the police," Lily says. "I told them all I knew. He'll get life, and that partner of yours is also going to prison."

A distant expression settles over Jake's face. "Good. I'm still shocked he actually hired someone to kill me, just so he could take over the firm."

Lily wants to ask Jake what he remembers, but they haven't spoken about it, so she's not sure how he feels about it. It turns out she doesn't need to ask, because Jake starts speaking on his own.

"I don't remember anything. I went to the bathroom to pee, and I think I heard a noise behind me, but then everything is just black ... Next thing I remember, I woke up inside the plastic without a clue as to where I was. Honestly, I thought I was dead."

"I thought so too," Lily whispers and suppresses a slight shiver by the thought of Jake's face as she found him in the tub.

"I tried to speak, but I couldn't," Jake went on. "I tried moving, but only my hand got free, and I just grabbed the first thing I found and held on to it with all my strength."

Lily looks into his eyes. She gets an almost dreamy feeling looking at him like this. It's kind of like déjà vu, like they already had this conversation a thousand times. Not that it bothers her, though. She could easily live through it a thousand times more. In fact, she feels like she could stay in this moment forever.

"You saved my life," she says softly.

Jake just shrugs. "I had to. Or I wouldn't get to see you again."

Lily looks around. "I guess this technically counts as our second date."

Jake raises his eyebrows. "You're right. The first one was such a success, right up until the point where I took a hammer to my head."

Lily snickers.

"You want to sit down?" Jake moves aside, making room for Lily, and she sits down on the bed. He takes her hand and smiles wryly. "So, I got you into bed after all."

Lily bites back her smile. "That surgery you were talking about—I think I changed my mind."

Jake laughs out loud, and Lily laughs too, before bending over him and kissing him.

Behind her the door to the room opens, Lily turns her head and her ...

***

dad enters, a bouquet of roses in his hand.

He swallows hard at the sight of his daughter lying there. It's still hard to look at her, but he can't help it. She looks so peaceful, like she's only sleeping and might wake up any moment.

He finds a spot for the flowers on the already crowded table, bends down and plants a kiss on her forehead. "Hi, hon, Daddy's back. I just needed to go home for a quick shower. Mom called—she will be here later."

It's the fourth day he spends at the hospital, and except for a few quick visits to the house, he hasn't left his daughter's side.

The television on the wall is still on, though the sound is muted. A news reporter is telling the story he already knows, and he grabs the remote and shuts it off, just as they show a picture of the guy.

Oswald Brand, previously convicted, several accounts of aggravated assaults and two attempted murders. Out on parole last month. This time, he won't get out ever again. But what good is that? The damage is done.

He can't help but blame himself. If he had only called her that night ...

He sighs deeply and slumps down on the chair next to the bed. It's no use thinking about it now. They can only thank God for the neighbor that saw Lily waving desperately from one of the upstairs windows and decided to call the police. When they arrived twenty minutes later, they heard commotion and forced their way into the house. In the hall they found the body of Lily's date wrapped in plastic, next to Oswald Brand, who was strangling Lily. She was already unconscious and had they come just half a minute later, he would now be visiting her in the morgue instead of the hospital, and there would be no hope of her ever coming back to life ...

He shakes his head, trying to get rid of that terrible thought. He doesn't want to sink into despair. Instead, he looks at her face. Her expression is serene, almost happy. Is that a slight smile in the corner of her mouth?

He gently takes her hand and holds it. He hopes with all his heart that she will wake up. And if she doesn't, then at least he hopes she has pleasant dreams.

***

 I originally intended to end this story with Lily getting away clean. But it just didn't feel like the proper ending. Then the idea of the coma dream came to me, and it was so damn beautiful and so damn awful at the same time that I just had to go with it.

CHILLS & CREEPS 1
Eight scary stories

The Well

"Did you know you can see stars during the day if you're standing at the bottom of an empty well?"

Oliver looks up from his lunch, forgetting to chew the piece of sandwich he just bit off. Mason is standing in front of him.

"Uhm ... no," Oliver mutters. "I didn't know that."

"Well, you can. I saw it in a YouTube video. Don't you think that's awesome?"

"I guess."

Oliver is very surprised—Mason is speaking to him! He hasn't done so for several weeks. Ever since the math exam, which Mason failed, even though he got all the answers right. But the teacher found out he had bought the answers from an eighth grader.

"Would you like to try?" Mason asks, leaning over the table and lowering his voice. "Felix knows about an old well somewhere. Me and him are going there after school today."

"I can't today," Oliver says. "I have to walk Alex home."

"He can walk himself, can't he? He knows the way."

Oliver hesitates. "I don't know. My mom will be furious ..."

"I'll pay off Alex not to tell," Mason says. "Your mom will never know."

Oliver can't help but smile. That's Mason for you—always getting what he wants, even if he has to cheat.

"Honestly," Mason goes on. "Aren't you curious? Stars—in the middle of the day."

Oliver nods. "All right, then."

"Awesome! See you, dude."

"Hey, Mason?"

Mason already turned to leave, but now he looks back. "What's up?"

"Are you ...? I mean, are you no longer ...?"

Mason laughs. "Nah, come on, man. I know you didn't tell on me."

Oliver feels great relief. "So we're cool again?"

"Cool as ice!" Mason blinks and walks away.

Alex accepts the bribe with no pause to think.

"You'll go straight home," Oliver demands. "And if Mom asks ..."

"Yeah, yeah, I get it. If Mom asks, we walked together."

"Exactly."

All four of them are in the schoolyard. Oliver, Mason, Alex and Felix. The bell just sounded the last time for the day, and the late summer weather is sultry.

Alex stuffs the bill in his pocket and looks up at the older boys, squinting against the sun. "Where y'all going?"

"None of your business," Oliver snaps.

"We're going to a strip club," Mason says.

"Can I come?" Alex asks immediately.

"Sorry, you're not old enough to look at boobies. Now, scram."

Alex reluctantly slinks away.

The three boys wait until he's well out of sight. They agreed no one can know where they're going. The well is in a garden somewhere in town, and even though the house is vacant, they will still be trespassing.

"Where is it?" Oliver asks.

"It's called Tenmile Road," Felix says.

"Show the way, sailor," Mason says.

The boys start walking with Felix leading the way through town. As they walk, Oliver can't help but glance at Mason now and then. He's glad they are on good terms again, but he's also a little puzzled at how abruptly it happened.

"Mason?" he asks.

"Huh?"

"Why did you change your mind?"

Mason looks at him. "You mean about you telling on me?"

"Yes."

The mood immediately gets a little tenser between them. Felix pretends like he's not listening.

Mason shrugs. "I don't think we need to talk anymore about it."

"But I thought you thought I was the one who—"

"Felix told me who ratted on me."

Oliver looks at Felix in surprise. "Who was it, then?"

Felix's eyes flicker. "Uhm ... Brad."

"Brad? That guy from eighth grade?"

"Yes."

"But I thought ..." Oliver looks at Mason. "Wasn't he the one who sold you the answers?"

"Yeah, and then he told on me," Mason growls. "That fucking asshole."

"I overheard him talking with his friends the other day," Felix says. "He was bragging about getting Mason to fail the exam."

Silence between the boys as they walk on.

Oliver thinks it over. So, Brad was the one who told on Mason. And he probably started the rumor to put the blame on Oliver, too. What a scumbag. Oliver hopes he gets what he deserves. But for now, he's just happy the truth is out. He and Mason have been best friends since first grade, and the falling out between them really hurt him.

"There's something you need to know," Mason says with a crooked smile, pulling Oliver out of his thoughts. "A small detail we forgot to mention."

"What's that?"

"The well is haunted."

Oliver raises his brow. "Haunted? You mean by a ghost?"

"No, by a camel, you idiot. Of course it's a ghost. A ghoooooost!" Mason dances around him, moving his arms.

Oliver laughs and pushes him away. "Get a grip, man. I don't believe in those kinds of things."

"Fine. Then you have no problem hearing the story?"

"Bring it on."

Mason looks at Felix.

Felix clears his throat. "Okay, well, I have it from my dad. I don't know if it's even true. Sometimes he makes up—"

"Just tell it, man," Mason interrupts.

"I'll warn you, it's pretty creepy."

"Oliver says he doesn't buy any of that stuff," Mason says, jabbing Oliver in the ribs with his elbow. "Right?"

Oliver laughs again. How he has missed hanging out with Mason.

"All right," Felix begins. "The story is about a woman who once lived in the house with her husband. They were from India or someplace like that, and they believe in all kinds of weird gods over there. They also believe in spirits and curses and stuff like that. Well, the woman got pregnant, but the man didn't want to have the child, so he moved back to India, and the woman was all alone. She was afraid of hospitals, so she gave birth at home. In the well."

"In the well?" Oliver repeats. "You can't do that."

"Sure, because back then the well was full of water. It's not uncommon for a woman to give birth in water. My aunt did so—not in a well, of course, but in her tub."

"That's weird," Oliver says. "Why wouldn't you just do it in a bed or something?"

"It's something about the water relieving the pain."

"But d—"

"Shut up and let him tell the story," Mason interrupts.

"Right, where was I? Oh, yeah, the birth. It didn't go well. Both the woman and the child died. Since she didn't have any friends or relatives, the woman's death went unnoticed, and her corpse just stayed in the well until it dissolved. When someone finally came by several years later, they found the house empty and the well dried up. At the bottom was the skeleton of the woman, her flesh had probably been eaten by rats and bugs."

Felix pauses and looks at Oliver, his eyes seeming to ask: "Well, are you creeped out?"

"That's a lovely story," Oliver says, playing cool.

"There's more," Mason interjects. "What was it called, that thing she turned into?"

"A churel," Felix says. "In the Eastern world there's a myth saying that whenever a woman dies during childbirth, she turns into a churel. It's an evil spirit that looks like a woman, but has a long, black tongue and its feet face the wrong way. It resides in the place the woman died and seeks vengeance on any males who come too close. Her thirst for revenge can never be satisfied; the more victims she can get, the better. She either kills them outright or turns them into very old, frail men."

Oliver feels a chill run down his spine, in spite of the warm weather.

"Now the churel lives in the well," Felix concludes. "A couple of witnesses have seen her."

"But don't worry," Mason says. "She only comes out at night; we'll be long gone by then." He studies Oliver's face. "You look a little pale, dude. You're not scared, are you?"

Oliver straightens up a little. "Nah."

Mason slaps him in the back. "That's the spirit!"

***

Tenmile Road leads out of the town, and the house is located just on the limit. It's not really that big, and from the outside it looks quite ordinary, except it's pretty decrepit; the roof has several holes, the windows are cracked and the grass and the hedge are growing wild.

Felix checks the mailbox. "There are two names here, but I can't read them. Vassa-something-or-other. The other one has been scratched out."

"Probably after the guy left," Mason says, looking up at the house. "It's definitely the right place. Can't you just feel the mean atmosphere?"

Oliver tries to feel what Mason is talking about—and he actually can. The air is somehow cooler, the wind a little quieter. He can't hear the sound of traffic, either, and—have the birds stopped singing? It's almost like—

Mason snaps his fingers right in front of Oliver's face, causing Oliver to jump with surprise.

Mason laughs. "You're completely gone, man. I'm just kidding. I can't feel a damn thing."

"No, I know," Oliver mutters. "Me neither." But he sends Felix a sideways glance, and it definitely looks like Felix is feeling something too.

Mason pushes open the rusty garden gate. "Are you guys coming or what?"

Oliver and Felix follow him through the gate. The boys trudge through the tall grass of the front yard, making their way around the house, stopping by the first window to look inside. They see an almost empty room, the only piece of furniture being a tipped-over stool.

"No one's home," Mason remarks.

They go to the backyard and find a terrace with a moldy parasol lying on the overgrown tiles and something that might once have been flower pots, but are now swallowed up by weeds. The yard is pretty big and everything has grown wild for several years.

Mason throws out his arms. "I don't see any well."

"I'm sure it's here somewhere," Felix says.

Oliver isn't really listening—he has noticed something through the terrace door. The living room is empty except for something standing right in the middle. It looks like a doll. He steps closer and puts his hands to the glass.

"Hey, Oliver?" Mason asks. "Found something?"

"I'm not sure," Oliver mutters. "Come take a look."

Mason and Felix join him by the glass.

The thing on the floor is not a doll—it's a figurine made of clay. It's almost two feet tall and is supposed to look like a pregnant woman, but something about it is wrong. Her arms and legs are too long and too thin, insect-like, and her feet are turned the wrong way. The mouth is open wide, revealing a long, black tongue slithering down her chin.

"That's the churel," Felix whispers. "Goddamnit, it's creepy as hell."

"Why is it here?" Oliver asks.

"No idea. Someone put it here, I guess."

"Well, now we know what awaits us if we don't get out of here before nightfall," Mason says, forcing a smile, but Oliver can tell even he is a bit shaken up. He turns towards the garden. "Let's find the damn thing."

The boys search the garden, being careful not to step anywhere without looking, in case the well is hidden under the grass. But they don't find anything. Oliver is relieved, but also a little disappointed. Just as they are about to give up, Felix exclaims: "Here! Here it is!"

He's standing at the farthest corner of the garden, next to an overgrown rosehip bush. Oliver and Mason go to him, and Oliver spots the well underneath the branches of the rosehip bush. It consists of a circle of brown weather-beaten bricks and a crumbling wooden plate on top.

"Good work," Mason says, slapping Felix on the shoulder. "I already looked down here, but I didn't see it. Come on, let's get these branches out of the way."

They carefully break off the branches and pull them aside, revealing the well.

Mason lifts up the plate, woodlice sifting off. "Jesus, it smells like rotten eggs!"

Oliver smells it too; a stench of mold and rot and mud comes pouring up from the deep. He holds his breath and leans forward in order to see down the well.

The sunlight only reaches a few meters down, so it's hard to judge how much farther the well continues. There is no trace of water.

Mason picks up a tennis ball-sized stone and drops it over the edge. The darkness swallows it up. Then, a second or two later, they hear a soft blob.

"It's dry as a bone," Felix remarks. "At least we don't risk drowning."

Mason activates his cell light, which dispels some of the darkness, but still can't reach the bottom.

"We'll never get all the way down," Oliver says. "Not without a huge ladder or something."

"How about a rope?" Mason smiles, swinging off his bag, opening it and pulling out a roll of rope. He unrolls it and ties one end to the stem of the rosehip bush. "All right, now pull it, all at once!"

Felix and Oliver grab hold of the rope, and together, all three boys pull with all their might. The bush bobs slightly, but there is no chance of it uprooting.

"It'll hold," Mason says. "Who'll go first?"

Oliver and Felix exchange a look, none of them volunteering.

"Chicken shits," Mason sighs. "Right, rock-paper-scissors, whoever loses goes in first."

They embark on a short tournament of rock-paper-scissors. Mason beats Felix, and Felix beats Oliver.

"It's you and me," Mason tells Oliver. "If you win, it's a stalemate, and we'll have to do it all over again. If I win, you go down first, and then Felix."

Oliver's heart is beating fast. What should he pick? Mason chose rock before, so he probably won't go for it again—or will he? Maybe it's his favorite. Oliver doesn't have any more time to think. They hold out their fists, and Mason counts to three.

Oliver has rock.

Mason has paper. He smiles. "Sorry, dude. You lose."

Oliver takes a deep breath. He really doesn't feel like going down the well first, but he won't appear like a scaredy-cat in front of the others, so he takes off his bag.

"Do you have anything in your pockets?" Mason asks.

"Only my cell."

"Better leave it up here."

"Why?"

"I don't know, so you don't drop it or anything. It would be hard to find down there."

"But I'll need the light."

"No, that will only blind you, so you can't see the stars. Your eyes need to adjust to the darkness."

Oliver nods. It makes sense. He takes out his cell and puts it in the bag, right after checking the time. It's three o'clock. What time does the sun set? He's not sure, but they still have plenty of time. He looks at his friends. "If I don't have the strength to climb back up, you'll pull me, right?"

"Sure," Mason says.

"And if anything happens ... you'll get help."

"Like if what happens?"

"I don't know. Anything."

"Sure, don't worry about it."

Oliver picks up the rope and throws it down the well. He takes a few deep breaths and climbs over the edge, clutching the rope. As he sits with his feet dangling over the abyss, he almost regrets it.

"You can do it, man," Mason whispers behind him.

That gives Oliver the courage. He lets himself slide down and hangs by the rope. The cold, clammy air immediately engulfs him as he starts climbing downwards. Oliver is pretty good at sports, and he has no real problem in holding his own weight as he works his way down the rope. He walks his feet down the inside of the well like a rock-climber.

The darkness draws in closer, the smell intensifies, the temperature drops, as Oliver descends farther and farther down.

He looks up. The opening is now a light-blue circle, the dark silhouettes of Felix and Mason peering down at him.

"You all right?" Felix asks, his voice ringing hollowly around Oliver.

"Sure, I'm fine," Oliver says, but he doesn't feel very fine. He looks down, but can still only see darkness beneath him.

How much longer do I have to climb down? What if the well just keeps going? That's silly, I heard the rock hit the bottom. But what if something is waiting for me down there?

He recalls the figurine in the house, and suddenly he can vividly imagine the churel standing at the bottom of the well, staring up at him in bated silence, the long black tongue slithering hungrily across the broken lips, as she waits patiently for him to come close enough so she can reach up her abnormally long arms and grab him by the ankles ...

Oliver is close to panic. He clutches the rope feverishly, closing his eyes hard, unable to take even one step farther down.

"Something wrong?" Mason asks.

Oliver is breathing rapidly through his nose, trying desperately to keep the panic down, telling himself over and over again that nothing is waiting below him except for the bottom of the well. He could really have used a flashlight right now. But after a few seconds he gets a little hold of himself, and he's able to call out: "No, still fine!"

He climbs down another yard. Two. Three.

*How deep **is** this goddamn thing?*

Then, finally, his foot finds solid ground. Carefully, he steps onto the bottom of the well. The ground is soft, but not soft enough for him to sink in. He very hesitantly lets go of the rope.

"Are you down?" Mason asks, the voice causing a series of echoes.

"Yes!"

"Well done! Do you see anything down there?"

Oliver looks around, his eyes are starting to make out the surroundings. The walls are glistening from moisture, and moss is growing in between the stones. The ground is mud and dried up rosehip leaves.

"No!" he answers. "There's nothing down here."

"Can you see the stars?"

Oliver looks up and sees the tiny outlines of Mason and Felix. "Move aside!"

They pull back. A couple of branches from the rosehip are visible, but other than that he has a clear view of the sky. It seems a lot darker than before, as if time has been fast-forwarded, and as he looks at the dark-blue circle, something amazing happens: a tiny star appears. And one more. And one more. Soon he counts a dozen.

"Yes!" he shouts. "Yes, I see them now!"

No answer from above.

"Hello? Guys?"

Still no answer.

They're probably playing a joke on me. Typical Mason to—

Oliver hears something rustling behind him, and he spins around, seeing something move on the wall and almost screams when he realizes what he's looking at.

It's the rope. It's quickly rising. Oliver stares at it dumbly for a second, then he jumps to grab it, but the end is already out of reach and still rising.

"All right, very funny!" he calls out. "Give it back now!"

But the rope continues upwards until it disappears out of sight. Then, Mason's head pops up. "Howdy!"

"It's not funny," Oliver says. "Give me back the rope. I want to get up now."

"You'll get it in a moment," Mason promises. "First I just need to hear you say something."

"What's that?"

"That you were the one who told on me."

Of course it's one of Mason's stupid jokes—but there's something in his voice Oliver doesn't care for. Something which tells him this might not be a joke.

"It wasn't me—you know that!"

"No, I don't know. All I know is I was made a fool in front of the whole damn school, and everyone is saying you did it."

Oliver throws out his arms, even though he knows Mason can't see him. "That's just rumors. Brad probably started them. Felix said—"

"Felix said what I told him to say." Mason looks to the side. "Felix? Come over here."

A moment later, Felix appears. "Uhm ... I really don't like this," he mutters.

"Shut up. Tell Oliver you lied about Brad."

"Oh. Yeah, that was a lie. You told me to say that." Felix looks at Mason and whispers: "Shouldn't we let him up now?"

Mason doesn't seem to hear him. "Did you get that, Oliver? You thought you would get away with telling on me, that I was blaming someone else. But I tricked your ass, and you went for it, hook, line and sinker. And you're not getting up from there until you confess."

"Come on, Mason," Felix pleads. "You said we were only going to tease him a little."

Mason shoves Felix out of sight and stares down at Oliver. Even though he's only a dark shadow against the blue sky, Oliver can feel his eyes. "How about it, Oliver? Do you confess?"

Oliver is really afraid now. Mason is acting totally strange, like something has possessed him. Even his voice sounds distorted from down here.

"It wasn't me, Mason," he says.

"What? I couldn't hear you."

"It wasn't me!"

Mason groans. "Come on, just fucking admit it, man. I know it was you! Everyone knows it was you! You stabbed me in the back."

"Why would I do that?"

"Because you didn't want me to get a better score than you."

"That's crazy! I don't give a fuck who gets the higher score!"

"Confess. Then we can go back to being friends again."

"I can't confess to something I didn't do!" Oliver is shouting at the top of his voice now, his own words resounding all around him. "And friends don't do this kind of shit to each other!"

Mason falls quiet. Oliver hopes he got through. Then, he hears Mason mumble: "Friends don't tell on each other either." Raising his voice, he goes on: "Do you know what my dad did to me when he got the call from school? Do you know?"

Oliver knows Mason's dad can get violent; the day after the exam Mason came to school with bruises on his neck.

"I'm sorry, Mason, I really am. But that wasn't my fault ..."

Suddenly, Mason disappears from sight.

Oliver hears Felix ask: "What are you doing?"

A moment later, the opening starts to grow smaller, as Mason pushes the plate back over the well.

Oliver panics. "No! Don't do that! *Stop!*" He jumps and screams, tries in vain to climb the wall. "*Mason! Don't! Please, don't!*"

The plate stops halfway, and Mason's silhouette appears once more. "You have something to say?"

"Seriously, Mason. You can't do this!"

"Yes, I can. Until you confess."

Oliver is close to tears. "All right, I confess. I confess!"

"Confess to what?"

"I was the one who told on you."

Mason hesitates for a moment, then shakes his head. "You don't mean that. You're just saying it to get up from there."

"No! It *was* me!"

"Listen, Oliver, here's what's going to happen. I'm going to write a message to your mom from your phone. I'm going to tell her you'll spend the night at my place. Felix and I will come back tomorrow morning. Spending the night down there will probably make you more honest."

"No, Mason! You can't do that! Mason! Felix! *Felix, help! Tell my parents!*"

"Catch!" Mason calls out and throws something down the well.

Oliver jumps aside, as the thing lands on the ground. It's the water bottle from his bag.

"See ya!" Mason says from above. "Say hi to the churel from us."

Then the plate is pushed into place, and the darkness becomes complete. Dirt sifts down and hits Oliver, but he doesn't even notice; he is too busy screaming.

***

After what feels like an eternity, Oliver can't scream anymore. His throat is raw.

The silence settles around him, deafening, the darkness thick and oppressive. The only thing he can make out is a thin stripe of daylight seeping in from one edge of the plate. Everything else is pitch black.

Oliver can hear himself breathing—it's not a nice sound. He tries to get his breath under control, but it's difficult. His heart is also racing.

He makes an attempt to climb the wall, but it's hopeless; the stones are moist and slippery, the cracks between them aren't deep enough for his fingers.

Instead, he sits down, resting his back against the wall. He shuts his eyes and breathes deeply. It helps a little. The thoughts even slow down a bit; he starts to see the situation more clearly. He forces his mind to go through it step by step.

Mason and Felix have left. No one else knows where he is. No one can hear him yell out. He has no phone. And he has no chance of getting out of here on his own. His mom believes he's spending the night at Mason's. Tomorrow is Saturday, so they don't have school, and no one will miss him until dinnertime at the earliest.

All this leaves him with no other choice than to wait. Perhaps Mason and Felix will return soon; perhaps they haven't even left for real; they might be waiting up in the garden, just wanting to give him a scare.

But somehow Oliver knows Mason was serious; that tone he heard in his voice. He has to prepare himself for spending the night down here.

In pitch blackness.

All alone.

All alone?

Maybe not. Maybe he'll have company.

No. He can't think about that. It doesn't help. And besides, it's just fiction. Ancient superstition, like the Norse gods. They learned about them in school lately. Back in the day, people in Scandinavia believed thunder was created by Thor driving his chariot across the sky.

Oliver tries to laugh at the notion, but the sound is all wrong, and he quickly stops again.

He reaches out his hand, feels his way across the soft ground, finds the bottle. Luckily, it's full. He drinks a little, soothing his sore throat. But he can't allow himself to drink too much; the water will have to last all night.

Oliver's suspicion turns out to be right: Mason and Felix don't come back, and he spends the rest of the day in the well. He doesn't have a watch, but the strip of light tells him that time is moving by, getting slowly weaker as day turns into evening.

Oliver waits.

Now and then he senses something crawling in the dark, but it's only bugs.

Oliver waits.

Eventually, evening turns to night, the strip of light dwindles and dies, leaving him in total darkness.

Mason and Felix still don't show up.

Oliver still waits.

Something awakes him up abruptly, making him sit up with a jolt. For a second, he is amazed he even fell asleep.

His first instinct is to look up, but he still can't see the strip of light, which means it's still nighttime.

How long was he gone? An hour, maybe two. It's hard to tell. What was that noise that woke him up? It sounded like a branch breaking.

He holds his breath and listens. Something is rattling around up there.

Probably only a squirrel or maybe a cat. Nothing to be scared about.

But then Oliver hears something that definitely doesn't come from a squirrel or a cat. It's a low, drawn-out hissing noise, like something exhaling heavily.

The small hairs on the back of Oliver's neck stand up.

The wind. Just the wind.

But he is not able to convince himself, because now he can also feel someone up there. It could be Mason, finally coming back to let him out. Oliver really hopes so.

A few nerve-racking moments pass by in complete silence, nothing but Oliver's own heartbeat is audible.

Then, the plate slowly starts to glide aside. Oliver sees the night sky appearing, a myriad of stars blinking down at him. When the opening is completely free, everything falls silent once more.

Oliver's heart is in his throat, making it difficult for him to speak. "He ... hello?" he croaks. "Mason? Is that you?"

Only the whispering echo answers.

Then, a head appears, and Oliver has to stifle a scream. It's definitely not Mason; he can't make out the face, but the neck is far too long and skinny, and the hair is long and tattered.

It's her!

No. It has got to be a trick. He needs to keep his cool. Mason has made some sort of doll, which looks like—

But then the noise comes again, the long, hissing breath, crawling down the well and wrapping itself around him with an icy breeze and a smell of decay.

"Who ... are ... you?" Oliver whispers, barely audible. He suddenly needs to pee.

The creature at the top of the well doesn't answer. Instead, two hands with long, boney fingers appear, grabbing the edge.

The next thing that happens erases the last bit of hope in Oliver that this might be an elaborate prank played on him by Mason.

The creature crawls out over the edge.

But it doesn't fall, like it should. Somehow, magically, it's able to stick to the inside of the well, like an overgrown bug. Slowly, it starts to climb down towards him, head first, the thin elbows and knees moving like the legs of a spider.

Oliver tries to scream, but only produces a meek whimper. His lungs are empty, his legs soft, almost not able to support him. Warm urine runs down his thighs, but Oliver doesn't notice; he just stares up at the churel coming closer.

She stops a few feet above him, and Oliver's legs give out. He slumps to the ground, still staring up the creature hanging right above him, black against the starry night sky. Luckily, it's too dark to make out her face, otherwise he probably would have lost his mind.

But the tongue is visible. It moves from side to side, slithering like a snake ready to strike. The churel opens her mouth and hisses at him once more, this time he gets the full blow of her breath, which smells like a thousand rotting corpses.

Oliver presses his back against the wall, wishing he could disappear into the cracks between the stones. He knows he only has a few seconds left. At any moment the churel will attack him.

But then she speaks. At least it sounds that way. The voice is hoarse and uneven, more like a snake hissing, and Oliver can only make out some of the words.

"... old ... or ... dead ..."

Oliver can only stare up at her. He thinks his lips are moving, but he's not sure.

The churel speaks again, a little louder this time: "Old ... or ... dead?"

Oliver blinks as he realizes she is posing a question. She is offering him a choice to decide his own destiny. Does he want to die? Or would he rather be turned into an old, weak man? What fate is worse?

"No," he whines. "Please don't hurt me ..."

The churel hisses angrily, then repeats the question: "Old ... or ... dead?"

"None of them," Oliver pleads. "I'm sorry ... for what happened to you ... but please don't ..."

The churel lets go of the wall and jumps down onto the ground. Oliver screams and tries to recoil, but there's nowhere to go. The creature towers above him, unnaturally tall, as she bends forward, grabbing his arm with a cold and immensely strong clawlike hand.

"*No!*" Oliver shrieks. "*Let go of me!*"

He tries to tear himself loose, but the churel is way too powerful. She pulls his arm closer, and he feels the tongue, cold and rough and slimy, as it wraps itself around his hand. Just before the churel bites off his hand, a single, clear thought shoots through Oliver's brain.

It's Felix's voice, saying: "*... the more victims she can get, the better ...*"

"Wait!" Oliver shouts. "I have something to offer you! Please listen!"

To his astonishment, the churel actually hesitates, her mouth still open a few inches from his hand.

Oliver puts forward his proposal.

Afterwards, she stares at him in silence for a while. He can sense her eyes as two black buttons underneath the ragged bangs. It is almost as though she's trying to make out if he's lying.

"I promise, I'll do it," he says hoarsely. "If you'll only let me live ..."

Another moment of silence. Then, the churel lets go of his arm. She steps back, turns around and starts climbing up the wall. In a matter of seconds, she has reached the top and disappears over the edge.

Oliver stares at his arm. The skin is moist from the tongue, but unharmed. He can't believe it. It worked! He's still alive!

Oliver looks up at the night sky, just as the rope comes flying. He reaches up and grabs it. Taking a few deep breaths, he notices how exhausted he feels; hunger and fear have drained him of energy.

He's not sure he can make the climb ...

***

It's almost ten o'clock when Mason and Felix finally return to the house on Tenmile Road. It's another lovely late-summer day, the sun is shining, and the birds are singing.

"I hope he hasn't been too scared," Felix mutters.

"That was kind of the idea," Mason remarks dryly.

They enter the garden and head for the rosehip bushes in the farthest corner. The plate is still on the well, exactly like they left it, the rope is lying in a neat, rolled-up bunch on the ground, and Oliver's bag is resting against the well.

"Let's see if he's up yet," Mason says, grabbing the plate and pulling it aside. "Ahoy down there! How are we feeling this lovely morning?"

No answer comes from Oliver. Mason squints, trying to see the bottom, but it's not possible.

"Peek-a-boo!" he calls merrily. "Are you playing dead or what?"

The only answer is his own echo, returning from the darkness below.

"Uhm ... Mason?" Felix says behind him.

"Shut up a moment ... Hey, Oliver!"

Still no answer.

"Mason, take a look at this ..."

Mason turns around, annoyed. "What is it?"

"Did you roll up the rope yesterday?"

"What? I don't remember. Why?"

Felix bites his lips. "It's just ... I think I remember we just threw it in a pile."

"You remember wrong, then." He turns to the well once more. "Hello? Why aren't you saying anything? Don't you want to get up from there?" Mason pauses for a moment, then mutters: "Something's wrong. Give me the rope."

Felix picks up the rope, just as someone comes crashing out from the bushes. Felix only just has time to see Oliver swinging a thick branch, hitting Mason squarely between the shoulder blades, knocking him forward, causing him to tip over the edge and disappear down into the well with a scream.

Felix is too shocked to react, but Oliver doesn't hesitate: he jumps at Felix, grabbing him by the arms and forcing him towards the well. Felix stumbles against the edge, almost falling backwards, but at the last second, he grabs a hold of Oliver's shirt.

"No, wait, Oliver! Wait!"

Oliver doesn't listen. His face is completely different, his eyes are dark and terrifyingly determined, and he just keeps pushing Felix backwards, trying to wrench his hands free from the shirt.

"It wasn't my idea!" Felix tries desperately. "I swear! It was all Mason. I had no idea what he was going to do. I'm sorry, Oliver! I really am. I tried to make him stop, I really did!"

Oliver hesitates for a moment, panting through gritted teeth and glaring at Felix.

Mason's pained voice reaches them from down the well: "Help me ... my leg ... it's broken ..."

Oliver doesn't seem to notice. "You started the rumor," he growls into Felix's face, his voice hoarse and rugged. "You made everyone believe I told on Mason."

Felix licks his lips. "I just ... I just wanted to be friends with Mason. He only wanted to spend time with you. Please, Oliver, please don't do it."

Oliver slowly shakes his head. "I'm sorry. But I promised her two." He grabs Felix's wrists and twists them hard, causing Felix to lose his grip. Then he lets go, and Felix disappears with a look of utter shock on his face.

Oliver turns his back to the well and puts his hands to his ears. He doesn't want to hear Felix scream on his way down. He doesn't want to hear him hit the bottom. Perhaps he hits Mason. Oliver doesn't want to hear any of it.

But he has to take away his hands from his ears for a brief moment, while he picks up the plate and puts it on top of the well. He hears their voices. They call for him. Plead with him.

Oliver feels nauseous as he grabs his bag and walks away.

**

Yikes, this one was pretty mean, wasn't it? I think it might be one of the darkest stories I've done. That churel-creature is a real myth figure from Indian folklore, by the way—you can Google it, if you have the nerve to see it illustrated. Even though she's really creepy, I think what makes this story so gruesome is actually more the interactions between the boys, don't you? The betrayal, the broken friendships, the things they are willing to do to survive.

If you liked the premise of *The Well*, you should check out Koji Suzuki's *Ring*, even if you've already seen the movie adaption. The book is excellent.

Snapper the Fish

Ring-a-ling!

A bell chimes as Mary opens the door. The smell of sawdust and fur greets her. She turns around and waves. "Come on, Dad!"

Dad is busy on his phone. He steps into the store and looks around. "That's funny. I never noticed a pet shop here."

"I can choose whichever one I want, right?"

"Sure, sweetie. You just look around. I need to make a quick call to John from work."

Mary runs to the section with rodents. They're peering out from behind glass walls, mice and rats and guinea pigs. They're cute, but they are not what she wants.

Mary goes on to the birds. They chirp and whistle. She pauses briefly in front of a yellow canary. It's pretty, but it's not what she wants, either.

In the back of the store she finds the fish tanks. There are fishes in all sizes, shapes and colors. But they're kind of boring, they just go around and around.

Mary is disappointed. Why don't they have any *exciting* pets?

Then, she notices the door. It's just slightly ajar, and on the other side it's dark except a looming glow.

Mary looks to the register. The owner is selling cat litter to a lady. Dad is jabbering on his phone.

Mary slides through the door.

The small room smells of coffee. On the table is a fish tank, and that's where the glow is coming from. The light is making strange shadows on the walls.

Mary steps closer. The fish tank looks empty. The bottom is covered with black sand, and in the middle is a grey rock with a hole the size of Mary's fist. She puts her nose to the chilly glass and squints her eyes. Is there something in the cave?

Suddenly, two orange discs appear. A couple of eyes are looking out at her.

Mary gasps and pulls away, but then she smiles. "Wow, you're scary. It's you I want!"

Steps behind her make her turn around.

The owner comes into the room. It's an old guy with white hair and wrinkly cheeks. He smiles. "You're not allowed back here, little lady. This is not part of the store."

"I want to buy that fish," Mary says and points.

The owner shakes his head. "It's not for sale."

"Why not?"

"Because it's a very special fish."

At that moment, Dad comes. "Here you are. Did you find anything, sweetie?"

"Yes, I want that fish."

Dad looks at the tank. "What fish? That tank is empty."

"No, it lives inside the rock."

The owner smiles at Dad. "Like I was just saying, the fish is unfortunately not for sale."

"Oh, well. You have to find another one, sweetie. There are lots of other pretty fishes ..."

"I don't want any of those. They are boring." Mary crosses her arms.

"You heard the man," Dad tries. "This one is not for sale."

Mary gets mad. "It's not fair. You promised I could choose whichever one I wanted." She starts to tear up. She's good at crying at will.

Dad sighs. "Listen, how much do you want for the fish?"

The owner shrugs. "It's not for sale."

"Of course it is. How about a thousand bucks?" Dad gets out his wallet.

"It's not about the money," the owner says. "It's about the price you pay to own this fish."

"And what price is that?"

The old man hesitates. "I can't really tell you. Please, let's go back out to the store. We'll forget about the whole—"

"I *want* this one, Dad!" Mary exclaims. Her chin is quivering.

"Two thousand," says Dad. "It's a bargain of your life."

The old man thinks it over. Then, he turns to Mary. His expression has changed, his eyes are strangely empty. "You know what? I think you're just the right owner for this fish, young lady." He looks at Dad and lifts a wrinkly finger. "Just don't say I didn't warn you."

Luckily, the tank isn't that big. Dad and the owner carry it to the car.

"How much did we agree on?" Dad finds the money. "Was it two thousand?"

"Keep it," the owner says and pulls out a bag. "Here you go. It's the food for the fish. That should be enough for a week or so."

Mary takes the bag. It's cool and heavy and soft.

"I made it myself," the owner says. "It's the only thing it'll eat. When it's gone, you'll have to make some more."

The bag has a sour smell. Mary sneers.

"It's very important that you remember to feed it," the owner continues. He looks demandingly at Mary. "The more you give it, the longer before it gets hungry again. Don't worry about overfeeding it; it can eat more than you, me and your dad put together."

Dad closes the trunk. "Is there anything else we need? How about a pump?"

"That's not necessary."

"I thought the water needed to be kept oxinated, or whatever ..."

The owner shakes his head. "Like I said, it's a very special fish. It only needs its food."

"Well, thank you."

The owner takes a deep breath and looks to the sky. He smiles and mumbles: "No, thank *you*."

***

"Mary?" Mom is shouting from downstairs. "It's the third time I'm calling. Dinner is ready!"

Mary is sitting at her desk, looking into the water behind the glass.

The fish is nowhere to be seen. In fact, it hasn't been out for even a second. It's probably timid.

A high-pitched scream sounds from downstairs. It's Lisa. She's only six months old. Mary can't stand her smaller sister. All she does is cry, pee and scream.

Mary gets up and goes downstairs. Mom, Dad and Lisa are sitting at the table.

"There you are," Mom says. She's feeding Lisa with a spoon. "I almost went to look for you."

Mary slumps to her seat. "Yuck! Shepherd's Pie again. Why do we always get potatoes?"

"Because Lisa loves potatoes," Mom says. "Here comes the airplane ..." Mom makes a sound that makes Lisa laugh and open her mouth.

Lisa. Always Lisa.

Mary takes a spoonful on her plate. She's not even hungry. She looks at Dad. "The fish hasn't been out of the cave yet."

Dad doesn't reply. He's busy reading something on his laptop while he eats.

"Dad? Are you listening?"

"Mm? What's that, sweetie?"

"The fish is still in its cave."

"Well, I guess it'll come out soon."

Lisa spits out a lump of mashed potatoes. Mom is ready with a new load, but the baby flails its fat arms and knocks the spoon out of Mom's hand. It flies across the table and plumps down onto Mary's lap.

"*Yuuuck!*" she screams and pushes the spoon to the floor. "That's so disgusting!"

Lisa starts wailing.

"Now look, you scared Lisa," Mom says and picks up the baby. "Why do you always have to scream like that, Mary?"

Since Lisa came along, it's like Mom only has one child. Like Mary just doesn't matter anymore. Mom only talks to her when she's correcting or scolding her.

"Please give me the spoon, Mary," Mom says.

"It's all greasy."

"Then rinse it off in the kitchen."

"I don't want to touch it."

Mom sighs and looks at Dad. "Frank? Are you going to say anything?"

"What? Eh, yes. Pick up the spoon and give it to your mom, Mary."

Mary looks angrily at him. She hates it when he takes Mom's side.

Lisa's hissy fit has already blown over. Now she's jabbering and clapping awkwardly with her small fat hands. Mary sends her an evil stare, tries to scare her with her eyes, tries to make her cry again. But Lisa just smiles stupidly back.

Mary bends down, picks up the nasty spoon and throws it on the table. Then, she gets up and marches out of the room.

Before Mary goes to bed, she decides to feed the fish. She still hasn't seen it, but maybe it'll come out when she drops food in the water.

She unties the bag and opens it. The sour smell become worse, to the point that it almost makes Mary nauseous. She holds her breath and sticks two fingers into the bag. They touch something moist and soggy. She gathers a small portion and looks at it with disgust. It reminds her of minced meat.

"Yuck, it stinks ..."

She drops the red and gooey lump into the water.

Instantly, there's a loud

SSSSHUISH!
as something bolts through the water.

Mary bends down and looks through the glass. The water has been stirred up. The food is gone, only small pieces are floating around. There is no sight of the fish.

"Damnit! I missed it."

Mary waits a couple of minutes. Tiny bubbles come out from the hole in the stone and float to the surface, but she doesn't get even a glimpse of the fish.

***

"Fish? Hello?"

Mary taps the glass. She just woke up.

The two orange discs appear in the darkness of the cave. The fish blinks at her.

"Heey!" Mary smiles. "Would you like some breakfast?"

She gets a lump of the disgusting food and lets it fall into the water. This time she's ready: her eyes are fixed on the cave. But the fish doesn't come out.

The red lump slowly dissolves. The eyes of the fish are staring out at her. Like it's waiting.

"Come on, fish ... come on out here ..." Mary whispers to it. "Let me see you ..."

The door opens behind her. Mary turns around abruptly.

Mom is standing in the doorway. "Good, you're up ..."

SSSSHUISH!

Mary turns her head. Too late. Most of the food is gone. The water is still moving a bit.

"Oh, come on! You made me look away, Mom!"

Mom comes into the room with a puzzled look on her face. "What are you doing?"

"I'm feeding the fish. But it only comes out when I'm not looking, and it moves really, really fast."

Mom shakes her head. "I still don't get why you chose a fish. Why not a cute little hamster or a furry rabbit?"

Mary glowers at the bubbles coming from the cave. "I don't want some stupid pet that everyone else has."

"Well, get dressed, you're late." Mom goes to the door. "I need to change Lisa's diaper, so you have to make your own breakfast. You know where the corn flakes are, just don't spill the milk."

***

Mary gives up on seeing the fish when she feeds it, because no matter how long she waits, it just stays in its cave—until she looks away.

She even tried turning off the light in the tank, but not even the darkness can lure the fish out of hiding.

The next morning, she throws in the last of the food, when she suddenly notices something. A small clear shell is floating on top of the water. It came from the bag, that she just emptied.

"What's that?" Mary mumbles and reaches down to catch the thing. She takes a closer look, gasps and quickly drops the thing back into the water. "Yuck, how nasty!"

The thing is a fingernail. She looks at the empty bag. What kind of disgusting stuff has she been feeding the fish?

"*It's the only thing it'll eat.*" That's what the pet store owner said.

Mary looks at the tank. "You really are a special fish. I think I'll call you Snapper. What do you think of that, Snapper?"

The fish just looks at her from its cave.

Mary smiles. "I'm glad you like it."

She turns away and goes to pack her school bag. Behind her, Snapper immediately shoots through the water and swallows his breakfast in one big bite.

"Its name is Snapper," Mary tells Lynn in the schoolyard. "I came up with the name just this morning."

"Snapper?" Lynn asks. "That's a weird name."

"It's because it always jumps out and *snaps* its food, like lightning!"

"Is it a piranha?"

"No. But the guy I bought it from said that it's very special. Do you want to come home with me and see it after school?"

"Sure. If my mom says I can."

Lynn gets permission to go home with Mary. They walk home from school and find the house locked. Mom has probably gone shopping. Mary retrieves the key from her bag and lets them in. They go straight up to Mary's room.

"That's it, right there," Mary says proudly and points to the fish tank.

"Gosh, it's really boring. There aren't even any plants or anything."

"It's not the tank I want to show you, it's Snapper!"

"I see. But where is it?"

"It's hiding in the cave in the stone."

Lynn steps closer. "Is it always hiding?"

"Oh, no. It's probably just shy because you are here."

Lynn darts her a skeptical look. "A fish can't tell a thing like that."

They just look into the water for a moment.

"Can't you lure it out somehow?" Lynn suggests. "Maybe with a little bit of food?"

"I already told you, it eats so fast that you won't see it happen. And besides, it got the last of its food this morning."

All of a sudden, the water starts stirring.

"Hey, don't push the table!"

"I didn't touch it," Lynn says.

"Then why is the water moving?"

"How should I know?"

The water is still shaking, as though someone were kicking the tank.

"Weird," Mary mumbles. She puts her hand on the glass, but quickly removes it again.

"What happened?" Lynn asks.

"It's hot ... try to feel it."

"No, I don't want to."

Mary is getting more and more confused. She has no idea what's going on.

"Look! It's steaming!" Lynn exclaims.

"Oh no! What if the fish can't tolerate water that hot? It'll die!"

Lynn holds her hand on top of the tank to feel the steam from the water.

At the same moment, a voice calls from downstairs: "Mary?"

Both girls turn their heads.

Instantly, there is a whizzing noise as Snapper shoots through the water. Mary hears a loud smack of strong jaws snapping shut. She turns just in time to see

Lynn pulling her hand away with a shriek. Something that looks like a thick snake disappears down into the water with a splash.

Then, Lynn starts screaming. "It bit me! It *bit* me!"

"*Mary?!*" Mom calls again and comes running up the stairs.

Mary is dumbfounded. Lynn is crying. Blood starts dripping from her finger. There is water all over the floor, and some of it has drenched Lynn's clothes.

Mom bursts into the room. "What's happening?"

"The fish bit me!" Lynn cries and shows the bloody finger.

"Come, let me see. There, there, honey, it's only a small cut."

Lynn sniffles. "It really hurts."

Mom looks from the tank to the girls. The water is calm now. "Did you say the fish bit you?"

"Yes. It came all the way out of the water. It was enormous … like a snake … and … and its mouth was full of teeth. It wanted to eat my whole hand!" Lynn sobs.

"Calm down," Mom says and hugs her. "The fish just looked a lot bigger because you got so surprised."

"No! It was huge! It's way too big to be in that small cave!"

"All right, then. We'd better find a Band-Aid for your finger. Come on, now. Mary, get this water cleaned up, and stay away from the fish tank from now on."

Mom takes Lynn downstairs.

Mary is left alone with her pounding heart. The orange eyes of the fish are glistening in the darkness of the cave.

***

Lynn wants to go home, so Mom calls her parents, and she is picked up a couple of minutes later.

"What happened up there?" Mom demands with her arms crossed.

"I didn't see it," Mary lies. "My back was turned. All of a sudden, she just started screaming."

"I guess she must have cut her finger on something," Mom mumbles. "Well, Grandma and Grandpa are coming to dinner tonight. Go clean up your room."

Mary shuffles upstairs again and starts tidying up her things.

After a short while she becomes aware of a strange noise. It's like a deep rumbling, and it comes from the tank. She turns around and sees the bubbles coming from the cave in the stone. They're a lot bigger this time. She steps closer.

"What's wrong, Snapper?"

The noise increases, it sounds almost threatening.

Mary is scared now, she backs away. "I think we'd better get you some food, Snapper. So you can be happy again."

Then, out of nowhere, she has an idea.

Mom has started making dinner. Mary sneaks down the stairs and past the kitchen without being noticed.

She goes down to the basement, turns on the light and tiptoes across the cold concrete floor to the fridge.

The pale glow illuminates her face as she opens the lid. She pulls out a frozen bag of minced meat and shuts the lid again.

She sneaks back upstairs, bringing the meat to the bathroom, where she runs hot water over the bag until it starts turning soft. She opens it and brings it back to her room.

"Well, Snapper, just look at this now. I got something for you."

The sound from the tank has ceased.

Mary breaks off a lump of the meat and drops it in the water. She steps back and turns around. "All right! Have at it."

She waits anxiously. No sounds from the tank.

When a minute has gone by, she can't take the excitement any longer, so she turns around to look.

The meat is still floating around on the surface, untouched. It has started dissolving.

Mary catches the orange irises of Snapper. They are staring out right at her, and they seem angry.

Once again, she recalls the old man's voice. "*It's the only thing it'll eat.*"

Mary goes to flush the rest of the raw meat down the toilet.

***

That evening, they're sitting around the dinner table in the living room. Grandma and Grandpa are here.

"How she has grown," Grandma chuckles and tickles Lisa's chin.

The baby drools with delight.

"What an absolute darling! Did you weigh her recently?"

"Yes, we did so yesterday," Mom says. "Fifteen pounds nine ounces."

"My goodness! What a fitting weight for such a wonderful little lady."

The conversation goes on like that. Mary tries not to listen.

"How is the new stroller?"

"How does she sleep at night?"

"She is so cute."

"She is so lovely."

Lisa, Lisa, Lisa.

"How about you, Mary?" Grandpa suddenly asks. "Aren't you happy about your new little sister?"

"No," Mary says. "In fact, I hate her."

"Don't you start," Mom warns her.

Grandma laughs. "Of course you don't hate your sister, Mary.

"Yes, I do. I wish she'd never been born."

"That's the last warning, young lady," Mom says. "Next thing out of your mouth and you can finish your dinner up in your room."

"I don't like it anyway," Mary says, pushing the plate away. She remembers that she's out of food for the fish. "Dad? I need more food for Snapper."

"Then we'll have to buy something tomorrow."

"But don't you remember? The man said the fish would only eat that special stuff he gave me."

"Well, was there a name on the bag?"

"No, because it was something he made himself."

"Did you get a fish?" Grandpa asks.

Mary lights up. "Yes. Its name is Snapper. Do you want to see it, Grandpa?"

Grandpa is about to answer, when Lisa lets out a loud burp and starts laughing.

"Oh, baby doll," Grandma laughs. "You're such a good girl!"

Mom and Dad smile. Grandpa waves at the baby. Lisa chuckles and hits the table with both hands. She's happy. She's once again the center of attention. Mary has yet again been forgotten.

"What an appetite."

"She is such a sweetheart."

Mary can't take it anymore. She feels a lump in her throat. She pushes out the chair and gets up. "I'm going to my room."

No one answers, because no one notices her leaving the table.

***

A noise wakes her up. She sits up in bed and rubs her eyes.

It's dark in the room, except for the fish tank, which is trembling slightly on the table. The water is sizzling and giving off steam. The fish is making its angry growl.

"You really are hungry, aren't you?" Mary whispers.

Snapper keeps on roaring. The light is on in the tank, because Mary is too scared to go close enough to shut it off. Tiny shreds of minced meat are still floating around the surface.

The eyes of the fish are glaring out from the cave, giving off their orange glow, shining with hunger.

Mary shudders. She pulls a little closer to the wall. "It's not my fault, Snapper. We'll get some more food from the weird old man tomorrow."

The tank seems to settle a bit.

"You'll get as much as you can eat," Mary promises. "I swear!"

As if Snapper understands her, the water stops boiling, the eyes disappear, and the room becomes silent.

***

Dad picks up Mary from school, and they drive by the pet shop, as they did last week.

Mary is looking out the window while rubbing her earring. She could only find one of them this morning. She hopes the other one isn't lost. They were a birthday present from Dad, and she really likes them.

"You got it, John." Dad is jabbering on his phone. "My words exactly. We can't just sit with our hands in our laps waiting for them to come to the table. There're so many other buyers in Europe, and we ... John, I'm sorry, I have to call you back." Dad slows down the car and brings it to a halt. "What the heck?"

"What's wrong, Dad?"

Mary realizes they are right next to the pet shop; she recognizes the building. But the nice sign with toucans, cats and turtles is gone. Instead, there's a note in the window. FOR SALE, it says.

"Wait here, sweetie." Dad gets out and runs to the shoe shop across the street. A minute later he comes back out, gets into the car and mumbles: "The pet shop closed down the day after we were here."

***

As soon as Mary gets off her shoes, she realizes that something has been gnawing at her foot all day. She shakes the shoe, and out falls a tiny rock. She is sore from where the stone has been rubbing her sole.

Up in her room she finds the fish tank calm. Mary sits down on the bed and pulls her sock off. A small blister has formed on the skin. She rubs it gently with a finger, and a small piece of skin comes off.

Mary gets up to go to the bathroom to throw the piece of skin into the toilet. But she stops in the doorway, hesitates. Instead, she goes to the tank and drops the piece of skin into the water.

Mary isn't really expecting anything to happen. But Snapper instantly leaps out like a torpedo, and it's gone again just as fast. The water sloshes around and only slowly settles down.

Mary's heart is pounding. She sits down on the bed. It was lightning fast, but this time she actually got a glimpse of the fish. It looked like an eel, black and grey and shiny, with gills on the side and sharp fins down its back. And a huge mouth.

Mary shivers.

A short series of bubbles leaves the cave.

"Mary! Could you come down here?"

Mary goes downstairs.

Mom is breastfeeding the baby, and she looks angry. "Guess what I found in Lisa's bed."

"How should I know?"

Mom holds up a tiny golden thing between her fingers.

"My earring!" Mary exclaims, reaching out to take it.

But Mom puts it in her pocket. "Oh, no, you're not getting it back. First of all, you promised to look out for your jewelry. They cost a fortune! And secondly: What were you thinking? Leaving a small thing like that just lying around? What would you have done if Lisa had swallowed it? She could have choked on it!"

"It wasn't my fault," Mary argues. "I didn't leave it anywhere, I looked out for it."

"Then how did it end up in Lisa's bed?"

"I ... I don't know." Mary is close to tears, and it's not fake tears. "She probably stole it!"

"That's just nonsense."

Lisa lets go of the breast and sends Mary a wide, milky smile.

"Stop looking at me!" Mary shouts. "It's all your fault! *Stupid brat!*"

The baby blinks with surprise.

"You don't yell at her like that," Mom hisses. "Go to your room!"

"Give me my earring!"

"You'll get it back once you apologize to your sister for shouting in her face."

"*Never!* I'll never apologize! I hate her! *I wish she was dead!*"

Mary runs out of the living room and up the stairs as the tears start flowing. She slams the door and throws herself on the bed. She sobs on the pillow for a while.

Then, she lifts her head and sniffles, looking at the fish tank. She suddenly gets an idea.

"Don't you worry, Snapper," she whispers and wipes her nose. Her face is expressionless. "Now I know how we'll get you something to eat ..."

***

After dinner, Mary is sitting on her bed playing her Xbox. It's dark outside. The fish tank has been calm since she gave Snapper the small piece of skin, but Mary knows that the fish is still hungry.

There's a knocking at the door. Mom comes in. "Hi, Mary. Aunt Tina just called. She locked herself out of the apartment again, so I have to go over there with the spare key."

"Sure, Mom."

"Could you look after Lisa while I'm gone? I already put her to bed. She's sleeping in her room, so you just need to listen, and if she wakes up, you just talk to her until I come back."

"Sure, Mom."

"I'll bring my cell. If anything happens, just call me."

"Sure, Mom."

Mom looks puzzled for a moment. Then, she smiles. "Thank you, Mary. That's a good girl. I'll be back in ten minutes."

Mom goes downstairs.

Mary listens. She hears the rattling of keys. Then, the slam of the front door. And finally, the car starting up.

Mary sneaks into Lisa's room. The baby is sleeping in the crib with her pacifier between her lips. Next to the crib is the carrycot.

Gently, Mary picks up her little sister. Lisa grunts in her sleep. As carefully as possible, Mary puts her into the cot. She manages to do it without Lisa waking up. Mary carries the cot into her own room. It's heavy, so she needs to take a couple of breaks.

Finally, she is standing in front of the fish tank. The glass is vibrating, the water is boiling. Snapper is excited.

"All right, all right, take it easy," Mary whispers and moves the chair next to the tank. By now the tank is shaking so violently, Mary is afraid it might tumble to the floor. The fish is growling from inside the cave, and the water is spilling out the sides.

Now comes the hard part. Mary steps onto the chair, bends down and picks up the cot. With a lot of effort, Mary gets it up on top of the tank.

The shaking stops immediately. The water sloshes and bubbles for a moment, then becomes completely calm.

Mary is about to step down, when the baby wakes up. She looks sleepily up at Mary, and for just a moment, Mary feels a pinch of doubt. Can she really go through with this? Mom and Dad will probably be heartbroken. But that will pass. Soon, they will have forgotten about Lisa, and then they will only have Mary again. Things will go back to how they were, back when Mom and Dad still loved her.

The thought makes Mary smile. She yanks the blanket off the baby. Lisa is wearing her yellow pajamas. Mary grabs the soft legs and pulls them out over the edge of the cot, so they dangle just above the water.

Lisa spits out her pacifier and starts to whimper, almost as if she knows what is about to happen.

Mary leaves the room and shuts the door.

She stays on the other side of the door, listening to the baby crying. Snapper will strike any moment now and stop the noise forever.

All off a sudden she hears a car outside the house. Mary's heart jumps. Mom is back already! If she comes in and finds the baby before Snapper eats it, everything will be ruined. Mary must buy some time. She must make sure Mom doesn't come inside the house yet. She runs down the stairs and opens the front door.

Mom's car is not in the driveway. Mary gives off a sigh of relief. It was just the neighbor coming home.

Mary shuts the door and hurries upstairs again. She stops in front of the door and holds her breath as she listens.

Complete silence from the room. Slowly, she opens the door.

The carrycot is still standing on top of the tank, but the baby's legs are gone.

A tickling sensation in Mary's stomach. "It worked," she whispers.

She goes to the tank. She isn't scared of Snapper anymore. Now the fish must finally be full and satisfied.

She gets up on the chair and looks down the water. "Well, how was the meal? Did you …?"

"Bluuh!"

The sound comes from the cot. Mary's eyes grow big. Lisa is still in the crib; she just tugged her legs in.

Mary doesn't get it. Why didn't Snapper eat her? The fish must be starving. Perhaps it's so starving that Lisa isn't big enough? Perhaps … Mary gasps. Perhaps Snapper is out for a bigger prey?

She hears the familiar
SSSSHUISH!
as the fish comes shooting up through the water with its mouth wide open.

***

Fifteen minutes later the front door opens.

Mom takes off her shoes and goes up the stairs. She goes to check on Lisa, but finds the crib empty.

"That's weird," the mumbles. Perhaps Lisa woke up, so Mary took her out to play with her. She goes to Mary's room. "Mary?"

No answer.

Mom is just about to close the door again, when she notices the carrycot. It's standing on top of the fish tank. She goes over and finds the baby smiling up at her.

"But, sweetheart. What did you do, Mary? Why on Earth is Lisa sitting on top of your fish tank?" She lifts the cot down. "Mary? … *Mary!*"

Still, no answer.

"And there's water all over the floor again," Mom mumbles. "She should never have gotten that stupid tank, when she obviously isn't big enough to … Wait, what's that?"

Mom sees something glimmering at the bottom of the tank.

"Oh, that does it. She threw her earring into the water. Mary! You come here right now and explain yourself, young lady!"

***

I grew up with three smaller siblings, so I know just how annoying they can be. How they steal the lamplight. How you, as the oldest, is always the one getting blamed for everything. Now and then I could have easily fed my siblings to a killer fish.

Headless

"Did I ever tell you guys that this place is haunted?"

Jack looks across the coffee table at Murray and asks, slightly startled: "Haunted?"

The old man nods eagerly. "Uh-huh."

"Cut it out, Grandpa," Kyle says, helping himself to another cookie, while sending Jack a reassuring smile. "Don't listen to him, he's always making up stuff like that."

"It's true," Murray insists. "We have a real ghost here."

"Have you ... seen it?" Jack asks.

"Not myself, no, but I've heard others talk about it. Do you guys want to hear the story?"

Jack nods and sits back in the couch.

Kyle pretends not to be interested, but Jack can see he's listening.

Murray glances out into the kitchen, then he leans forward and whispers: "Have you seen the old swamp? Behind the barn?"

"No," Kyle says abruptly and sends Jack a firm look. "We weren't allowed to go over there, Grandma told us so. She said it's dangerous."

"She's right," Murray says. "That swamp is like quicksand. Well, the story goes like this. Back in the day, this place was a big farm, with lots of fields and cattle and all. The whole thing was owned by a stinkingly rich farmer. There were rumors going around that the farmer was kind of crazy, you see. For instance, one day he caught one of his farmhands stealing, and he went ballistic. He grabbed his axe and ran after the hand. The poor guy fled into the stable and jumped on a horse. He rode out to the courtyard, but the farmer was still in pursuit and managed to cut off his escape by barring the only way out. The noise had drawn the attention of the rest of the people working on the farm, and they all came out to watch. The hand was trapped in the courtyard, riding around and around in circles, looking for a way out, while the mad farmer was running after him, swinging the axe. Finally, the hand was cornered, and the farmer came charging with the axe held high, ready to ..."

At that moment, Dorothy comes into the living room with a pot. "Tea is ready!"

"Uhm ... yes ... thank you, dear," Murray says. "Say, did you turn off the water heater?"

"It turns off by itself."

"Oh, right."

Dorothy sits down next to Murray and starts knitting. "Why, isn't this nice and cozy? So, what were you boys talking about?"

The boys look to Murray, but none of them answer. Jack really wants to hear the ending of the story, even though he's also somewhat anxious. Stories like that tend to give him nightmares. But he's thirteen now, and too old to believe in ghosts.

"Don't be polite and hold back on the cookies," Dorothy says. "I baked a bunch, so there's more where that came from."

Murray shovels the last cookies off the tray and shoves them all in his mouth. "I fink fat was fe laft onfe!" he exclaims, spewing crumbs all over the floor.

"Murray, you moron! I was talking to the boys. You know you shouldn't eat so many sweets. And could you at least take one at a time, like someone with decent manners?"

Murray smiles with his mouth full. "Forry, dear ..."

Dorothy sighs, gets up and brings the tray out to the kitchen.

"Now, where was I?" Murray finishes chewing. "Oh, yeah! The farmer caught up with the hand. He jumped up and chopped his head off with a single, brutal swing of the axe! The people watched in stunned horror. The farmer let out a crazy laugh. The horse panicked. It took off, still carrying the dead body on its back. It crashed through the barrier and ran out into the swamp, where it immediately got stuck. Even though it thrashed and wriggled, it just sank farther down into the mud. The people didn't have time to save it. Within a minute, the poor animal was gone, and so was the body of the hand." Murray lowers his voice. "The farmer made his people swear that they would never tell anyone outside the farm what they had just witnessed. Then, he threw the chopped-off head into the swamp as well, but ... for some strange reason, it just wouldn't sink. So, he had to fish it out again, and instead, he buried it somewhere here on the farm."

The living room is suddenly silent, except for the TV. Jack can feel his heart beating in his throat.

"That's creepy," Kyle whispers. "When did it happen? I mean, supposedly."

"A long time ago. The farmer and his people are all long dead. But the swamp is still there, and it's said that it's not to be disturbed. If anyone digs around in it or messes with it somehow, that same night, the hand will rise up on his horse and go looking for his head."

Jack glances at Kyle, and Kyle glances back.

"But that's not all," Murray whispers, leaning forward even farther. "Once the hand has been reunited with his head, he'll turn his anger onto the people of the farm. He thinks he can get his revenge over the farmer that way." Murray looks out the black windows. "Imagine. For all those years, the swamp has not been disturbed."

"So, you ... uhm ... you believe in the story?" Jack asks.

"Of course! The story is true, no doubt about that. The question is, if you believe in ghosts." Murray chuckles. "Dorothy and I don't. We bought the farm twenty years ago, and we haven't seen no headless guy or his dead horse." His smile fades a little as he mumbles, almost to himself: "But then again, we never disturbed the swamp."

Jack winces. He can still see and hear the splashes from the stones that he and Kyle spent all afternoon throwing out into the swamp.

Dorothy comes back, landing a fresh batch of cookies on the table. "These are with raisins. Say, you boys look a bit pale. I hope you haven't caught a cold. A whole day out in the fresh country air can hit you quite hard, you know."

***

Murray sticks his head into the chamber. "I hope you guys are comfortable in here." The beds are made for two. A skylight lets in the pale moonshine.

"Sure, thank you," Jack says.

"Dorothy and I will be sleeping in the room right next to you. If you need to pee, just use the bathroom down the hall."

Kyle throws his bag on one of the beds. "That's good to know. Jack is a night pee-er."

Jack shrugs embarrassed. "I almost always wake up in the night because I need to pee."

"As long as you don't sleepwalk," Murray says. "Kyle used to do that when he was little. Do you remember, Kyle?"

"It's a long time ago," Kyle mutters.

"One time, he came to our bedroom in the middle of the night," Murray says chuckling. "He was mad because the elves had taken his blanket."

Jack laughs. "Seriously? Is it true, Kyle?"

"I was only like five years old."

"Well, sleep tight, boys." Murray is about to leave, then, he hesitates. "By the way ... I hope I didn't scare you with that silly old story."

"Nah, we don't even believe in that kind of stuff," Kyle says and pulls off his shirt.

"That's good. I guess you're old enough to tell the difference between fact and fiction anyway. Actually, I just remembered ... I forgot to tell you the best part."

Jack isn't certain he wants to hear any more of the story.

"Rumor has it that the axe—the one the farmer used to kill the hand with—is still on the farm to this day. When we moved here, I checked the barn, and wouldn't you know, I actually did find a small axe. It's very old, but still sharp. I never used it, though. If it really is the same axe, I guess we'll never know."

The words hang for a moment in the room.

"It's a creepy story," Jack says.

"I thought you would like it," Murray smiles. "But not a word to your grandma, Kyle."

"Don't worry, Grandpa."

Murray winks at them. "Good night, boys." He closes the door behind him.

The boys change into their pajamas and crawl into bed.

"Your grandpa is nice," Jack says.

"He's kind of crazy, but he's all right," Kyle replies. He stretches and yawns. "I'm totally wasted."

"Me too."

For half a minute, none of them say anything.

"Kyle?"

"Hmm?"

"Do you believe in ... ghosts and stuff?"

"Nah, I don't believe in anything I can't see with my own eyes."

"But ... do you think it was a mistake to mess with the swamp?"

"We didn't mess with it. We just had a little fun."

Another long silence. Jack can hear the wind whistling over the roof. It kind of sounds like voices.

Kyle snickers.

"What?"

"Do you remember when I threw that big stone? The mud was splashing to all sides. It even got you right in the face."

"Well, how about that time when you slipped and fell on your ass?"

The boys laugh. Then, they both yawn and say good night.

Sometime during the night, Jack wakes up. He has to pee. Kyle is sleeping with his back turned, quietly snoring.

Jack gets up. The wooden floor is cold, but luckily, it doesn't creak. He slips out into the hallway and down to the bathroom, where he turns on the light, stands in front of the toilet, and—

A strange noise. It stops again immediately.

Jack holds his breath while he listens. Was it just his imagination?

He doesn't feel like peeing now, but if he goes back to bed, the urge will surely come back. So, he closes his eyes and concentrates.

And then the noise comes again, very quietly, like a whisper.

hiiiiiuuuuuhhh

Jack looks around, startled, but can't see anything. His eyes stop at the shower curtain. It's white with red flowers, and someone is standing right behind it. The curtain moves.

HIIIIIUUUUUHHH

Jack spins around on his heel, bolts out of the bathroom and back down the hallway, slams the door to the chamber behind him. The noise wakes up Kyle.

"What's going on? Jack? Is that you?"

Jack grabs Kyle at the shoulders. "It's the ghost," he whimpers. "It's come to get us. We have to wake up your grandpa!"

"What are you talking about? What ghost?"

"It's in the bathroom. I saw it with my own eyes!"

"You just had a bad dream, you nut," Kyle says. But he doesn't sound quite sure. "Hey, let go, you're hurting me."

"I was *not* dreaming. I went to pee, and there it was, right behind the shower curtain. I heard it, Kyle! I'm not messing around …"

Kyle looks from Jack to the door. "I still think you were dreaming. But let's go and check. If I see and hear the same as you, we'll wake up Grandpa, all right?"

"All right. You go first."

"You really are a cowardy custard."

"I already saw the ghost, I don't need to see it again."

Kyle goes to open the door. He peeks out into the hallway before waving Jack to follow him. The boys sneak down to the bathroom.

"It's right in there," Jack whispers.

"Come on, you also have to go in."

"Why? I thought you weren't scared?"

"I'm not. But if something happens, I might need backup."

Jack follows him hesitantly. When he sees the figure behind the curtain, he freezes up and can't take another step.

"Fuck me," Kyle whispers. "It really does look like someone is—"

HIIIIIUUUUUHHH

Kyle turns around and bumps into Jack. The boys trip over each other and tumble out into the hallway. Jack trips and struggles to get back up, as Kyle grabs him by the arm.

"Wait! I know what made the sound! It's not a ghost …"

Jack feels like running far away, but forces himself to stay. "It … it's not?"

"No, I just remembered," Kyle smiles. "Look …"

He steps back into the bathroom, and while Jack looks from the doorway, Kyle pulls the curtain aside. A bathrobe hangs on a hanger. And through a small window, which is slightly ajar, a chilly breeze comes in, making the howling noise and causing the curtain to move.

hiiiiiuuuuuhhh

Kyle turns around with a grin. "There's your ghost. We're such suckers!"

Jack's heart drops down back into place. "Jesus. I was sure it was the ghost."

"I told you, it's just an old wives' tale."

"You got scared too."

"Only until I remembered Grandpa's bathrobe."

"That still counts."

"How about you? You almost pissed yourself."

That reminds Jack, he still needs to go. "Could you please get out, so I can pee?"

"Are you going to be okay? Or do you want me to wait outside?"

"Shut up."

Kyle grins and shuts the door behind him.

Jack pees and washes his hands, then he goes back to the chamber. When he enters, Kyle is not in the bed. He's standing on a chair under the skylight.

"What are you doing?"

Kyle jumps. "Jesus, you scared me."

"What are you looking for?"

"Nothing. I just thought I heard something, that's all." Kyle steps down from the chair and crawls back into bed.

"Heard what?" Jack insists.

"Someone snorting."

"Snorting? You mean like a horse?" Jack smiles. "You're messing with me."

"No, I'm not. But it was probably just the wind, that ... Hey, do you hear that?"

Jack listens. He hears the sound, very faintly.

clop-clop ... clop-clop ... clop-clop

Jack stares at Kyle. "How did you do that?"

"Do what?"

"Make that sound?"

"It wasn't me! It came from the courtyard." Kyle looks to the window and whispers: "It really was a horse I heard, then."

Jack's legs start to shake. "Of ... of course, it's not a horse. It's just a branch knocking against something, or maybe ..."

CLOP-CLOP ... CLOP-CLOP ... CLOP-CLOP

This time, there's no denying it: The sound comes from outside, and it's hooves walking across cobblestone.

For several seconds, the boys just stare at each other.

"If this is some kind of trick, it's really not funny," Jack whispers.

"I want to see it," Kyle says and climbs on the chair to look out the skylight again. "I can't see anything ... it's too dark out there."

"It's probably nothing anyway."

"What do you mean 'nothing'? You heard it just as I did. There's a horse down in the courtyard. Maybe it escaped from one of the nearby farms."

Jack hadn't thought of that. But he still doesn't want to look into the case. In fact, he just wants to crawl back under the blanket and sleep until the morning.

Kyle, of course, has other ideas. "We have to go down and check."

"Check on what?"

"If the horse really does belong to one of the neighbors, we have to call them." Kyle has that special glint in his eyes, the one he always gets when he senses something exciting. He starts putting on socks. "Come on, hurry up!"

"Do I have to come?"

"You can also stay up here, all alone."

That prospect appeals even less to Jack, so he quickly gets dressed.

The boys sneak out into the hallway. A loud snoring is audible from the bedroom.

"Your grandpa is a really heavy sleeper," Jack whispers.

"That's not Grandpa, that's Grandma. Come on."

They slip downstairs and find the living room with undrawn curtains. They can see the garden with the apple trees, which looked so friendly in the sunlight, but now remind Jack of skeletons lurking in the dark.

"We can see the courtyard from the kitchen," Kyle whispers, leading the way.

They lean over the sink and look out. The courtyard is empty. Murray's tractor is parked by the barn. Dead leaves are dancing across the cobblestone, but other than that, nothing moves.

"There's no horse," Jack observes. "Can we please go back to bed now?"

Kyle is visibly disappointed. Then, he lets out a gasp. "Look! There's light in the barn ..."

He's right. Two of the small, dusty windows are lit up.

"Your grandpa just forgot to turn it off," Jack suggests.

"Nah-ah, there wasn't any light when I looked from the chamber just a minute ago." Kyle squints his eyes dramatically. "There is someone out there, Jack."

Jack's stomach tightens up. "Do you mean a burglar? We have to call the police then ..."

"What are they going to do? There's a thirty-minute drive from the city. He's long gone once they finally arrive."

"But—"

"Besides, it's probably just the neighbor, looking for his horse."

At that moment, Jack notices a shadow passing one of the barn windows. Someone really is out there.

"Come on, let's go out there," Kyle says.

"No! Are you crazy? What if it's ... *him*?"

Kyle places his hands at his sides. "Do you mean the ghost? Use your brain, you dummy. Why would a ghost turn on the lights? Don't you think they can see in the dark?"

"Well ... shouldn't we at least wake up your grandpa?"

"By the time we get him out of bed, it will probably too late. Come on!"

Kyle runs to the scullery. Jack has no other choice than to follow. They put on their shoes, unlock the door and slip out into the cool night air. The lights are still on in the barn, and the door is open ajar. They run across the cobblestone and stop in front of the door.

Kyle steps forward to stick his head in.

"Kyle, wait!"

"What?"

"Look!"

Jack points down. A trail of footprints leads into the barn. Because of the darkness, it almost looks like blood, but Jack can see that it's really mud. The trail runs along the barn and disappears around the corner.

"Holy shit," Kyle whispers. "It comes from the swamp. It really is him!"

Jack feels a strong urge to sprint into the house, slam the door and lock it, regardless of whether Kyle wants to join him or not.

But just at that moment they hear dragging steps from inside the barn.

The boys jump behind the door.

A second later it's pushed open. The heavy wooden door squeezes them up against the wall, and as it slowly swings back, Jack sees the most insane thing he has ever witnessed.

The man who has come out of the barn is now walking across the courtyard in an uncertain stride. Only, it's not a man. Not a *whole* man, anyway.

His head is missing.

Jack takes in a deep breath to scream his lungs out.

But Kyle slams a hand over his mouth. "Sssh! Do you want him to see us?"

"Mhe ghoft! Mhe ghoft!" Jack mumbles into Kyle's palm.

"I know it's the ghost," Kyle whispers into his ear and takes his hand away. "But there's no reason to scream about it."

The dead man has reached the house. Instead of going for the door, he disappears around the corner.

"Wh-where is he g-going?" Jack whimpers.

"To the garden, of course. Didn't you see the shovel?"

"The shovel?"

"Yes, he'd taken Grandpa's shovel. That must have been why he went to the barn. You really didn't notice it?"

"No, I didn't notice the shovel. I just noticed that *he didn't have a fucking head!*"

"Calm down," Kyle hushes. "Don't you remember the story? He wants to find his head. It must be buried somewhere in the garden."

"What do we do?"

"We follow him, of course." Kyle starts walking.

Jack jumps in front of him. "Are you out of your mind? What are you planning on doing? Stopping him?"

"Why would I do that? No, I just want to see him dig up his head." To Jack's amazement, Kyle isn't scared, only excited. "Don't you think it's freaking cool? It's like being in a horror movie!"

"People get killed in horror movies!"

"Not kids. Come on, just a quick look. We'll keep a safe distance."

"This is goddamned madness," Jack mumbles, but follows his friend anyway.

"We'll go the other way around the house," Kyle decides. "That way, we don't risk running into him."

They turn the corner. Jack looks back to check that the headless ghost hasn't snuck up on them. Because of that, he doesn't see Kyle stopping, and bumps into him.

"Why are you stopping?"

Kyle doesn't answer. He doesn't need to.

The horse is tethered to the clothesline pole. It's standing halfway in the shade of the house, so only the rear end is visible in the moonlight. The fur is grey, as far as Jack can tell, but it's really more brown because of the dried mud, which also dangles in big clumps from the tail.

"Christ, it stinks," Kyle says and holds his nose. "It's like an open sewer."

Jack breathes in through his nose and instantly regrets doing so, as he almost throws up. The horse really does stink of sludge. But it also smells of something else, something worse. It's rotten flesh.

The ghost horse apparently hears them, because it turns its head.

Jack stares into the eyes of the beast. They are glowing red as blood. The horse lets out a loud snort and white clouds shoot out from the muzzle.

"Jack? Are you coming?"

Jack detaches himself and runs after Kyle, as the dead horse follows them with its shining red eyes. Kyle sneaks up to the corner and peaks out into the garden.

"Do you see him?" Jack whispers.

"No. But listen ..."

Jack notices the sound of someone digging.

"It's coming from down there," Kyle points and starts walking across the garden.

Jack hurries to follow Kyle. They cross the lawn and pass the apple trees.

"Right there!" Kyle whispers. "In the rose bed. Do you see him?"

Jack sees the hand among the rose bushes, several of which are trampled to the ground. The boys sneak behind a bush, from where they can see the ghost.

"Holy shit, Grandma is going to kill him," Kyle whispers.

"He's already dead," Jack points out.

The ghost is digging diligently, although he has some difficulty in keeping his balance and operating the shovel at the same time. To be fair, Jack thinks, it's probably difficult to do *anything* without a head. And it doesn't make it easier that the roses keep grabbing his clothes, as if they try to stop him in his endeavors.

"I didn't think ghosts could touch stuff," Jack whispers.

"What do you mean?"

"Well, the shovel, for instance. He doesn't really look like a ghost, either. He looks like a regular person, made of flesh and blood. Except for the missing head, of course."

Kyle bites his lip. "You're right. Maybe he's more of a zombie."

"A zombie? But they eat humans ..."

"Maybe he's a mixture. Or maybe—"

"Sssh!" Jack hushes. "Can you hear someone talking?"

They listen. A voice is audible somewhere.

"I think ... I think someone's coming," Jack whispers and looks around.

It sounds like the voice is getting closer.

Then, the hand throws down the shovel, drops down on his knees and starts digging with his bare hands. The voice gets louder.

At last, Jack understands where the voice is coming from.

At that moment, the ghost pulls up his head and holds it up high, almost triumphantly, in the moonlight. The skin is dark with dirt and rot, the hair is straggly and stringy. The head has only one eye left, the other seems to have rotted away. The mouth is spewing a stream of nonsense.

"Hantala kampu gram taka mahala dansaki!"

The hand places the head under his arm and steps out of the rose bed. The boys huddle behind the bush, as the ghost walks right past them. The head speaks constantly, but doesn't make any sense. The stink that's left like a trail from the dead body makes Jack nauseous.

"Yuck," Kyle whispers. "It smells like that time we came home from vacation and the power had gone. The meat in the fridge was completely rotten ..."

The boys follow the hand as he goes to the other side of the house. It's easy to locate him because of the head's incessant jabbering. At the corner of the house the boys stop and take a look.

The hand is standing by the ghost horse. He has untied the rope, fastened the head onto the saddle, and now jumps up himself. The horse turns around and starts walking across the courtyard.

"Where is he going now?" Jack whispers.

"Probably back to the swamp," Kyle mumbles. "He has gotten what he came for."

But the hand doesn't ride to the other side of the barn. Instead, he stops by the open barn door, jumps off the horse and walks inside. The head is still sitting in the saddle talking.

"What is he doing in the barn?" Jack whispers. Something tells him that this is far from over.

"How should I know?" Kyle replies. "Look, there he is again. What's that in his hand?"

The head bursts into a hoarse laughter.

"Oh, no," Jack gasps, as goose bumps spring out all over his body. "You've got to be kidding me. It's ... it's the axe!"

"Fuck me," Kyle whispers. "This is not good, Jack."

"It's all our fault," Jack whimpers. "We shouldn't have thrown those damned stones into the swamp!"

The hand reaches up and takes the head. With the head under one arm and the axe in the other hand, the ghost starts striding towards the front door of the house.

"Fuck! He's going to kill your grandma and grandpa! We have to wake them up, Kyle!"

"Wait, I got a better idea. We lure him back to the swamp."

"How?"

"You distract him, and I'll steal the head."

"*What*? Are you crazy?"

"He's not very fast. Look, he hasn't even reached the door yet. We can easily outrun him." Without waiting for an answer, Kyle jumps out and waves both arms. "Hey! Hello! Over here!"

The hand has stepped onto the stairs and is just about to grab the knob, as the head sees Kyle and starts hissing angrily. "Kanta makkadakka pulpu!"

"That's right, we're right here, moron. Come and get us!"

The hand forgets about the door and instead approaches Kyle.

Kyle darts a look at Jack. "Now it's your turn."

"I didn't agree to this stupid plan ..."

"Just do it!"

"Do what?"

"Lure him towards the swamp. I'll sneak around him and grab the head."

Kyle grabs Jack by the arm and pulls him out in plain sight. Jack stumbles out into the middle of the yard, his legs shaking and threatening to give in with every step. The hand turns to follow him, the head is scolding him viciously.

"It ... it's working," Jack says, gaining a bit more courage. "Yeah, you ... you come here, you ... come this way ... that's right ... nice and easy."

Slowly, Jack pulls the hand in the direction of the swamp. Then, he notices Kyle coming from behind the ghost. The head is oblivious to Kyle, it just stares at Jack with its one good eye.

Kyle makes his move. He grabs the head and runs away.

The ghost jumps in surprise. The head starts screaming.

"I've got it!" Kyle yells. "Quick! To the swamp!"

The boys run around to the other side of the barn. The head screams and curses them. "*Mikka tulla kanda bralla!*"

They stop by the edge of the swamp.

"Throw it!" Jack yells. "Hurry up, before he gets here!"

"Christ, take a look at him," Kyle says and holds the head out for Jack to see.

Jack almost can't handle looking at the head. The lips are broken, the mouth has lost almost all of the teeth, the remaining ones are black. The single eye is rolling like crazy, and in the empty socket, maggots are squirming.

"Just throw it, Kyle," he pleads, struggling to keep Dorothy's cookies from coming back up.

Kyle pulls back to throw the head like a handball. "So long, asshole. Don't come ba..."

A loud *SNAP!*

Kyle screams and drops the head. "*Fuck! He bit my finger!*"

The head lands in the grass. It spits out something and laughs vindictively. "Har, har, har! Grala panu kokka!"

Kyle stares at his hurt hand. Jack just gapes.

The index finger is missing. Blood is spurting out.

Jack registers a movement from the side. He just has time to turn around. The headless ghost is standing in front of him. It shoves him hard to the ground. Jack hits his head and blacks out for a second. Somewhere nearby, Kyle is shouting.

"Help! ... What are you doing? ... Let me go! ... Jack! ... No, not the swamp! ... Jack, help me!"

But Jack is only halfway conscious. It takes him a minute or so before he's able to sit up and look around. The night is quiet now. He is alone by the side of the swamp.

"Kyle?" he croaks. "Where ... where are you?"

He gets no answer except for a couple of bubbles bursting out in the swamp. Then, he hears a loud snort and spins around.

The ghost horse comes trotting right by him. As it passes him, it darts him a glance with its gleaming red eyes, before walking straight out into the swamp. It sinks immediately. It's gone in less than a minute. The swamp lets out a burp. The eerie silence returns.

Jack gets up, staggers and rubs his temple. His head is pounding, he feels dizzy.

He tries to think straight, but it's difficult. What has happened? He's not sure.

He sees something in the grass, picks it up and puts it in his pocket. He starts to shiver. The night air is cold. He walks across the courtyard and enters the house, slips upstairs, undresses and goes to bed.

***

Jack opens his eyes. The sun is shining. It's morning.

First thing he remembers is the horrible dream. It was so lifelike that he actually took it to be real. But that's silly, of course. He was only dreaming.

He turns to the other bed. "Kyle? Are you up? I had the most insane dream ..."

Kyle's bed is empty.

He probably already got up, Jack figures, so he starts getting dressed.

He hears someone coming up the stairs. A moment later, Murray sticks his head in the room. His expression is bewildered as he scans the room.

"Morning," Jack says. "Is something wrong?"

"Where's Kyle?"

"Uhm ... I don't know. I just woke up."

"Did you guys go outside in the night?"

"Outside? No. Why?"

Murray enters the room and grabs Jack's shoulders. "Did you hear Kyle leave his bed during the night?"

"I ... I didn't hear anything. Has something happened?"

Murray sits down on Kyle's bed and runs his hands through his hair.

Dorothy shows up with a worried look. "Murray? Did you find him?"

Murray shakes his head. "He is nowhere in the house, and not in the garden, either. I'm afraid there might have been an accident."

"An accident?" Jack exclaims, as his hearts starts pounding. "Like what?"

"Someone has completely dug up the rose bed. The lawn has track marks from horseshoes. Someone has been in the barn rummaging through my tools, and there are mud prints all the way to the swamp."

Jack is dumbfounded. He feels like reality is slipping.

It can't be true. It was just a nightmare.

Dorothy covers her mouth. "Do you think Kyle might have been sleepwalking? That he might have walked out into the swamp?"

"Let's not assume anything now," Murray says and gets up. "We'll look everywhere once more. If we still don't find him, we'll call the police."

Dorothy and Murray leave the chamber.

Jack is still sitting on the bed. He can't move.

It was only a dream. Kyle will show up any minute. Perhaps they both sleepwalked. Yes, that makes sense. They made the marks in the lawn, they went to the barn and messed with the tools. They did everything themselves while asleep, and that's why—

Jack's hand goes to his pocket and finds something. He pulls out a tiny cold lump.

It's Kyle's index finger.

***

This story is based on a childhood experience I had. When I was Jack's and Kyle's age, I went on weekend holiday at my friend's grandparents' farm. The grandpa told us a story of a man who was once killed and now haunted the place. That night I dreamt of the ghost returning to seek vengeance. Luckily, *my* experience was only a dream.

All Birds Hate Me

"And how long will it be? Until you are well, I mean." Dad dips his hot dog in mustard and takes a big bite. "Did the doctor say anything about that?"

Eagle finishes chewing. "A couple of months. Perhaps longer."

"A couple of months? Are you supposed to take pills for a couple of months?"

"I have to."

"Hmmm. Did he say anything about side effects?"

"Dry throat and insomnia."

Dad doesn't look convinced. He flushes with a swig of Coke. Tonight's menu is hot dogs with fries. Dad's specialty. It's only eight o'clock, yet it's already dusky outside the window.

"I would rather have problems sleeping," Eagle says, "than having the problem of ... what happens if I don't take the pills." He shrugs. "I can't leave the house. I already lost two shirts. And look at this ..." He pulls up his sleeve. The most recent scratches are not healed yet.

"I get it," Dad mumbles. "How did you get those?"

"It was Falcon's canary. I came too close to the cage."

"That Falcon is a weird guy ..."

Raven comes into the kitchen. Eagle is glad he came. Dad was just about to start one of his speeches about all the faults of Falcon. Falcon is Mom's new boyfriend.

"What took you so long?" Dad exclaims. "I called twenty minutes ago. The hot dogs are almost cold now. I damn near thought you got stuck to the can."

"I had to do my hair," Raven says. He plumps down onto the chair. "*Someone* in this family has to look good, you know."

Dad snorts. "And that someone is you? I think you need glasses."

"Shut up."

"Watch your mouth." Dad smacks Raven in the back of his head.

Raven just laughs. Raven is sixteen. He goes to college. He is old enough to do what he wants. According to him, anyway.

"What were you guys talking about?" Raven snatches a hot dog from the pan. "Eagle's bird problem?"

"It's a disease," Eagle says. "A virus in my blood."

"Like hell it is. You're just weird, that's all."

"The doctor said it's a very rare condition. There have only been four recorded incidents in history. It's called ..." Eagle finds the note. "*Omnia Avesodio.*"

"That's Latin," Raven says. "And it means 'all birds hate me.'"

Dad laughs, almost choking on a fry.

"It's not funny," Eagle says. "It's actually very serious."

Dad clears his throat. "You're right. Stop teasing, Raven."

Raven dips in Eagle's ketchup. "I just don't get it. How could you have gotten that virus on the vacation? None of the rest of us got it. Not Mom, not Falcon, not me."

"Didn't I tell you?" Dad grumbles. "That vacation was a bad idea. Going to Greece, when the weather is perfectly fine here at home. I bet it was Falcon's idea …"

"The doctor said," Eagle hurries to interrupt, "that it probably was a mosquito. Like malaria. Except that I'm not contagious."

"Do you know what I think?" Raven asks. "I think it's more like AIDS. You know how the first human got AIDS?"

Eagle doesn't answer. He just glares at Raven.

"He got it by screwing a monkey …"

"Raven!" Dad yells.

"That was probably how you got it," Raven laughs. "You snuck out into the woods at night and …"

"That's enough!"

Dad reaches to grab Raven, but Raven is already on his feet and flees the kitchen, laughing.

Dad sits back down and glances at Eagle. "Don't listen to him. He's just messing with you."

"I know," Eagle says. "Besides, there aren't even any monkeys in Rhodes."

"There aren't? Well, what do you know." Dad ruffles Eagle's hair. "You're such a clever boy, Eagle. I bet you got that from me."

Eagle smiles.

Raven sticks his head in room. "I'm going out."

"Going out?" Dad asks. "You didn't say anything about going out."

"Well, I say it now. And by the way … don't forget to take your medicine, bird boy."

Eagle flips him off. Raven laughs and disappears.

"You're home before one o'clock!" yells Dad.

A moment later they hear the front door.

"Well," Dad says. "How is school? Are you still getting good grades?"

Eagle is just about to answer, when his phone rings. He looks to see who it is. Then, he quickly gets up. "I have to take it."

"We're eating …"

"Sorry, Dad." He hurries into the living room. Closes the door and answers the call. "Hi, Lark."

"Heeeey, Eagle. Where are you? Did you forget my birthday?"

"No, no. Congratulations. I would've called."

"Thanks. But I would rather you come over here. The party has already started."

He can hear the music in the background. People shouting and laughing.

Eagle turns toward the window. Dad's apartment is on the first floor. The sun has almost set. The town is inky in the twilight. Three black birds are sitting on the neighbor's roof.

"I'm sorry, Lark. I really want to. But … you know … my illness."

"I thought you got medicine? Doesn't it help at all?"

"Yeah, it works, but … my mom still doesn't want me to go out alone." Eagle regrets saying that. He sounds like a baby.

Lark sighs. *"All right. I was just looking forward to seeing you."*

Eagle closes his eyes. He knows Lark has a crush on him. Dove told him so. Eagle has been crazy about Lark since third grade. Now he finally has the chance. And then this stupid virus is going to ruin everything.

"I ..." he begins.

"*Hey!*" Lark exclaims. Some noise and fumbling.

Then a new voice shouts: "*Eagle? Hiiii. It's me, Dove. Lark just said that you'll get a kiss if you come over right now.*"

Dove sniggers. Lark protests in the background. Something like "give me my phone back."

Eagle smiles again. He doesn't have time to answer, before Lark comes back.

"*Sorry about that. Dove is pretty drunk.*"

"Yeah, I could tell."

The music fades a little. Lark has probably gone someplace quieter.

"*Eagle?*" Her voice is lower now.

"Yes?"

"*What Dove said, you know?*"

"Yes?"

"*It's true.*"

Then, she hangs up.

Eagle is standing there with his heart pounding. Just staring at the phone.

That settles it. He has *got* to get to Lark's party. Birds or no birds.

***

The evening is chilly as Eagle lets himself out into the yard. The door slams behind him.

Dad gave him permission to go—as long as he promised only to drink three beers, and to be home before midnight. Those conditions are more than acceptable to Eagle.

He hurries to the garage. Unlocks the door, drags out the bike and locks the door again. He's just about to jump in the saddle, when he notices a noise from the container. A white cat comes sneaking out from behind it.

"Hi, Ibis. Are you allowed outside this late?"

Ibis belongs to the old lady who lives downstairs from Dad. Almost every morning as Eagle goes off to school, he meets the cat here in the yard. He notices something in its mouth.

"What've you got there, Ibis?"

The cat drops the lump in front of his feet.

Eagle recoils. It's a dead sparrow. The eyes of the little bird are closed. The wings are spread out. There's blood around the beak.

"Yuck," Eagle whispers. "Did you kill it, Ibis?"

The cat swings its tail proudly. Then suddenly it raises its ears. With a hiss it runs out of the yard.

Wonder what got into it, Eagle thinks. *It was as though something scared it.*

Eagle turns towards the bike. He gasps. On the roof of the garage, just above the door, sit three large, black birds. Eagle doesn't know much about the different species, but he's pretty sure these are crows. They don't make any noise. Just sit there and stare. There is something accusatory in their black eyes.

Eagle glances down at the dead sparrow. "It ... it wasn't me. It was already dead." He realizes how silly he sounds. He's talking to birds.

But it's no wonder that he's nervous. Lately he has had plenty of reasons to become paranoid.

It started out small. Blackbirds would fly close by him, grazing his hair. Then small birds began landing in front him, pecking at his shoelaces. One day at recess a seagull came flying. It kept soaring around just above Eagle's head, shrieking and flapping its wings.

After that things just got more crazy.

Pigeons would come out of nowhere, diving at him like fighter pilots. A murder of crows started sitting outside his window day and night. As soon as he opened the door, they came flapping and tore at his clothes. Falcon's canary went nuts each time Eagle got close to the cage.

Finally, Mom took him to the doctor. It took a lot of tests to find the diagnosis, but finally, they got it. The explanation was pretty simple: The rare virus makes Eagle's skin send out a smell that humans can't detect, but makes birds go crazy with rage.

Now Eagle has been taking the pills for four days. There hasn't been a single accident since. All birds have been acting normal around him again. None of them have even glanced in his direction.

But he's still nervous. And the way those three crows are looking at him ...

I already took the pill for tonight, he reminds himself as he gets in the saddle. He glances up at the crows once more. *They won't hurt me. I'm protected.*

Eagle rolls out of the yard. He looks back. The crows don't take to the air. They just sit and stare after him.

Eagle feels better once they're out of sight. He rides along through town, the buildings passing by. There are lights in the windows, and the streets are almost empty. No one is out at this hour. Most people are probably sitting in front of the TV.

Eagle thinks about Lark. It makes his stomach flutter with butterflies. What's he going to say when he sees her? He tries to think of something clever.

He passes the park. It gives him an idea. He's going to pick some flowers for Lark. He turns into the gravel path, but he can't really see any flowers. Maybe it's too late in the season?

He's getting closer to the lake. A couple of swans live in the park. Eagle can make out the two white figures on the water. They're probably asleep.

A man is sitting on a bench. He's wearing a padded jacket and a beanie. A bottle in his hand. Eagle can hear him talking to himself.

Eagle spots a small cluster of blue flowers growing beneath a bush. He stops and jumps off the bike. But as he reaches for the flowers he realizes that it's in fact not flowers, just a blue plastic bag.

Disappointed, he gets up. *Rats. No flowers. I have to come up with something else, then. Maybe I can ...*

"Fssssh!"

Eagle turns around. The swans have come to the shore. Now, they're waddling towards him. Their necks are craned, and their heads are bobbing up and down. It looks rather silly, but Eagle isn't really amused by it; he's pretty sure it means the swans are angry. He must've gotten too close. One of them opens its mouth, hisses loudly and flaps its wings.

Eagle turns around and runs back to the bike.

But the swans are not intending to let him get away that easy, so they up their speed. Eagle steps hard in the pedals. The swans take up the pursuit. Luckily, Eagle is faster. He quickly increases the distance. He passes the bench where the bum is sitting and hits the brakes hard, making the gravel spray.

"Hello there," the guy drools, lifting the bottle. "To what do I owe the honor, young man?"

"I think you'd better watch out," Eagle says and points. "The swans are angry and they're coming this way."

The man blinks. "The swans? Yeah, those are some crazy birds all right. But they leave you alone as long as you don't ..."

"Fssssh!"

"Fssssh!"

The swans are coming. They're halfway running, halfway flying now.

The man gets to his feet. "Christ on the can! They're really looking for a fight. What did you do to them, kid?"

"Nothing!" Eagle says and gets back on the seat. "Get away from them!"

Eagle sets off. He looks back. The birds are coming fast. The bum doesn't have time to flee. He utters a yelp and jumps onto the bench. "Keep away, you beasts! I'm warning you ... these pants are brand new, I've only had them for four years!"

But the swans aren't interested in the bum—or his pants. They go right past the bench.

They're only out for me, Eagle thinks and feels a cold shiver down his back.

He steps hard in the pedals. A little too hard. His foot slips. He struggles to keep his balance, but tumbles to the ground.

Before he can get up, the swans are upon him. One of them jumps him from behind. The large wings beat repeatedly against the back of his head. He can feel the strong feet kicking his back. The other one squawks and snaps at his face.

"*Stop!*" Eagle shrieks. "*Get away from me!*"

He flails his arms. One of the swans catches his sleeve in its beak, the other one starts biting his leg. Eagle grabs one of the birds around the neck and pulls it to the side. It loses its balance for a moment. That gives him the chance. He gets to his feet. The other swan spreads its wings to cut him off, but Eagle jumps across the tipped-over bike. The bird steps on the bike and tumbles over with an angry shriek.

The bum has come rushing. He tries to help Eagle by flapping his jacket. "Shoo! Get lost, you stupid fowls!"

Eagle runs over behind the man. The swans don't even look at the bum. They just waddle around him to get to Eagle.

"Holy moly!" the bum exclaims. "They've really got a bad eye for you, kid. Better get the hell out of here!"

Eagle turns around. He doesn't give a damn about the bike anymore. He just storms along the gravel path. He can hear the birds hissing behind him. But he doesn't stop running until he's out of the park.

Eagle is sweating heavily when he finally bends over to catch his breath. He is sore in many places from where the swans pinched him. He has abrasions on his palms from the crash, and his pants got a pretty big tear.

"What the hell got into them?" he whispers.

Of course, he'd like to think that the swans attacked him because he came too close to their nest, and not because ...

The pills have stopped working.

On the other hand, it's pretty well known that swans are aggressive. It's not uncommon for them to even attack humans. But the question is: Why only *him*? Why not the bum?

Perhaps they've seen the bum before, so they know he's not a threat.

Yeah, that's probably it. It's got to be. Eagle feels a bit calmer. It makes sense. Of course the medicine is still working. And he took a pill just before he left home.

Still, he doesn't go back to get the bike. It can wait for tomorrow. If someone steals it, so be it. It was kind of old anyway.

Eagle walks through the streets. Lark lives twenty minutes away. He reaches the pedestrian street. The stores are empty behind dark windows. He catches his own reflection. He looks terrible. He stops to brush off the jacket and fix his hair. It helps a little bit, but he still looks like someone who just got—

"What are you looking at?"

Eagle looks around, startled. He's prepared to meet someone who has snuck up on him. But the street is completely empty.

"Hello?" he asks hesitantly. "Is someone here?"

No answer.

The voice sounded kind of like that of a child, except it was weirdly distorted.

Eagle shakes his head. It must've been his imagination. He's about to walk on, when the voice comes again.

"What time is it?"

This time Eagle is able to determine that the voice comes from inside the store. He looks in through the glass. A tiny orange eye is starring back.

Eagle lets out a gasp and steps back. Then, he realizes that the eye belongs to a parrot. It's sitting in a cage. The shop is a pet shop. Eagle smiles with relief.

The parrot opens its crooked beak and squawks: "I seeeee you."

Of course, it's just something the owner has taught the bird to say.

Eagle taps the glass. "You don't know what you're saying, do you? You're just a stupid bird."

The parrot shakes its feathers and exclaims something akin to laughter. The sound makes the hair in the back of Eagle's head stand up. The bird must've learned the noise by listening to people laugh.

Then, it says: "You're the stupid one."

Eagle frowns. "Do you ... do you understand what I'm saying?"

The parrot doesn't answer. Instead, it crackles: "Are you afraid? Are you afraid? Are you afraid of the swans?"

Eagle's lungs are all of a sudden unable to take in air. He stumbles backwards. "What ... what did you say?"

The parrot flaps its wings as though to take off. "We'll get you. Before the night is over. We'll get you." It throws back its head and breaks out into the fake laughter once more.

Eagle starts running down the street. Faster and faster, until he's sprinting. He only stops when he can't run anymore. He leans against a lamppost and heaves for breath.

It can't be real. He didn't just meet a parrot that made threatening remarks towards him. It's too far out. It simply can't be—

"Crrruuuuh!"

Eagle looks up. On top of the lamppost sits a pigeon. It looks down at him curiously.

Oh no ... not you too.

Eagle slowly walks on. He doesn't take his gaze of the pigeon. The bird's eyes follow him. It's like a stare contest: Who will look away first?

Something big and grey comes swooping through the air and whizzes close past Eagle's head. He screams and ducks down. Then, he cautiously looks up. It is a second pigeon. It flies up and lands on top of the next lamppost.

*No, it can't be happening ... They're starting again! But why? I don't get it ... I **did** take the pill, damnit!*

More cooing makes Eagle turn around. On the next lamppost sits another pigeon. And another one. And another one. All the way down the street they're stationed, like a row of fighter pilots ready to take to the air. One after another they jump off and spread their wings. Then they dive towards Eagle.

He flees in a random direction. The birds tear by just over his head while they peck at him with their beaks and grab at him with their claws. He protects himself as best he can with his arms, while he feels a wing smack his neck and hears the jacket tear in the back.

A pigeon strikes him in the ribs, another one grazes his thigh. Eagle almost takes a tumble. The birds don't care about their own well-being, they happily risk their necks and wings to get him, as they hurl themselves at him. Eagle strikes out blindly. He catches one hard with his elbow. It squawks in pain and goes to the ground.

"Ha!" Eagle shouts in triumph. "I got you!"

But in that moment a new kamikaze hits his shinbone hard and knocks him off balance. He falls and rolls around several times.

It's a painful fall, but there's no time to cry about it. The pigeons only intensify their coordinated attack. They hit him again and again. He feels a sharp pain on his jaw as he gets to his feet and tries to run, but his leg is really hurting.

Then, he sees two round lights ahead. A bus is coming this way. He's saved!

Eagle waves his arms frantically. The bus slows down and stops. He knocks away one more pigeon and jumps in through the open door.

"My goodness," the driver says. "Was that *pigeons* attacking you?"

"Yeah," Eagle pants. He tries to explain about his disease, but he realizes from the face of the driver that his explanation doesn't make much sense, so he gives up and just pays for a ticket.

The bus is almost empty. Eagle sits down all the way in the back. He looks out through the windows, but can't see the pigeons anywhere. They must've lost the scent of him.

Eagle tends to his wounds. He's got a big bump on his shin and a cut on his jaw that is bleeding a little. He will get a lot of bruises all over his body tomorrow.

What the heck is going on? It's like he forgot to take the pill. But he didn't, he's sure of it, he did it just before he left the apartment. So why is it suddenly not working?

Something pops up from his memory. A tiny detail. When he went to take the pill, the bottle wasn't in the windowsill like it usually is. Eagle always keeps it in the exact same place, so he's sure he won't lose it. But this time he found it on his desk. Someone had moved it.

Eagle narrows his eyes. "Raven," he whispers.

Eagle finds his phone and calls up his brother.

Loud music in the background, as a voice shouts: "*House of the Lord, God speaking!*"

"Did you touch my medicine?"

"*What?*"

"Did you touch my medicine?"

Raven laughs. He sounds drunk. "*So, you noticed, huh? Do you feel a difference? Have the birds started coming for you again?*"

Eagle is furious. "Yes! They damned near tore me to shreds. You dick! What did you do?"

Raven sniggers. "*I switched them for **mints**!*"

Eagle doesn't even know what to say. He's so mad he's practically frothing. "You psycho! You might get me killed, do you know that?"

"*Well, look on the bright side ... at least you die with fresh breath!*" Raven splutters with laughter.

Eagle growls and hangs up. He should've guessed it. It actually hit him as something weird when he found the pill bottle in the wrong place, but he was so preoccupied thinking about Lark that he dismissed it. And he didn't even notice the taste of the pill, he just flushed it down with a glass of water as usual.

A message ticks in. It's from Lark.

Hey! <3 Are you coming or what? :'(

Eagle feels like crying. Lark is waiting for him, but now he probably won't get his kiss, thanks to Raven, that asshole. He needs to go get his medicine. But he can't bring himself to tell Lark that he won't come.

He bites down hard. He wants that kiss, damnit, and he'll get it. Neither Raven nor the birds are going to stop him.

He has an idea. Lark lives only a couple of streets from Mom and Falcon's house, where Eagle has another pill bottle. If he goes there first, he'll be able to get to Lark's place ten minutes later. So, he writes her:

Sorry sweetie. Running a little late, but will be there ... Promise!

***

Five minutes later the bus stops.

The driver gets up. "Last stop, buddy. We don't go any farther."

Eagle gets off. He looks both ways. No birds in sight. He's in a part of town that he knows well, very close to Mom's house.

He runs down the sidewalk while he constantly glances up at the sky and listens for squawks or the flapping of wings. He crosses the street, turns, turns again, and finally, he sees Mom's house. Relieved, he runs to the driveway. The windows are black, the front door is locked.

That's right, Mom and Falcon are spending the weekend at a couple of friends' place.

In the garage he finds the spare key. He's just about to unlock the door when he hears whistling. He flinches and turns around. In the driveway a blackbird is sitting, staring at him.

Eagle turns the key, opens the door and rushes in. He slams the door and locks it. His heart is pounding.

All right, now I'm safe ... The pills! Quickly!

He kicks off the shoes and runs to the kitchen. The bottle is on the table. He opens it and shakes out a pill. Swallows it and drinks from the tab.

He lets out a burp and takes a deep breath while he closes his eyes for a moment. It'll probably be a couple of minutes before the effect kicks in. But now he only needs to wait.

Eagle hears a faint chirping. The sound comes from Falcon's office. He remembers the canary. He goes to the room.

The small yellow bird is flapping about in the cage. It should be asleep at this hour, but Eagle's presence makes it go crazy. It's chirping angrily and trying to get out through the bars.

Eagle has an idea. He can use the canary as an indicator for when the medicine in his system has started working. He sits down in the chair and folds his hands in his lap. Then, he waits.

The tiny bird is chirping and flapping, chirping and flapping, like it's never going to stop. But after five minutes it suddenly calms down.

Eagle looks up from his phone. The canary is just sitting there, in the bottom of the cage. The feathers are ruffled, and the bird seems exhausted.

Eagle smiles and get up. He goes to the cage and sticks his finger through the bars. The canary just looks up at him.

"Yes! It's working."

He hurries to the kitchen, leaves the house and locks the door. He looks around the driveway. The blackbird is gone, and there are no other birds in sight.

Eagle is normal again, thanks to the medicine. He goes to the sidewalk and heads off towards Lark's home.

**

"Heey, Eagle!" Lark smiles as she opens the door. "You finally got here!"

She hugs him. She smells of perfume and booze.

"Sorry I'm late," he says. "I had a small problem ..."

"Hey, what happened to your cheek?"

Eagle almost forgot about the bruise. "Oh, it was just a branch."

"Come on, come in!"

Lark grabs his hand and pulls him in. The living room is packed with guys and girls from the class, drinking and dancing to the music.

Lark puts her mouth to Eagle's ear. "You can say hi to everybody later. First, I have something to show you."

"Sure!"

She takes him to her room. Dove is sitting on the bed, talking on her phone. She looks up and smiles. "Hey, Eagle! I didn't think you would come."

"Please leave, sweetie," Lark says. "I need to show Eagle something."

"Ooh la la," Dove says, getting up while batting her eyelashes. "What are you going to show him?"

"Something secret," Lark says and shoves Dove out the door.

When the door is closed, Lark turns to Eagle. She's smiling, but she also seems nervous. Eagle figures he'd better take the first step. He steps closer, his heart in his throat.

She closes her eyes, purses her lips and leans forward. Eagle does the same.

BANG!

Something hits the window. Lark gives off a scream.

Eagle stares at the glass, which is stilling vibrating. There's a greasy mark right in the middle.

"What was that?" Lark asks.

"I ... I don't know," Eagle mumbles, although he has a nagging suspicion.

Out of the darkness comes a bird—a crow, as far as Eagle has time to see—heading directly towards the window. It hits the glass with a new, loud

BANG!
and falls to the ground.
No, no, no. This can't be happening!
Lark grabs him by the arm. "It was a bird, Eagle. Did you see it?"
"Yes, I ..."
Eagle is cut off when three crows comes flying and hit the glass almost simultaneously.
BANG! BANG! BANG!
The glass is shaking violently, and a small crack appears.
Eagle and Lark step back.
"What's going on?" she yells. "Why are they doing that? Has it something to do with your ... condition?"
Eagle doesn't get time to answer.
BANG! BANG!
Two more birds. White ones this time. And larger. It looks like seagulls. By now there has to be a pile of dead birds outside the window.
"This is crazy," Lark says. "I'm a little scared, Eagle. What can we do to make them stop?"
Eagle sticks his hand in his pocket and takes out the pill bottle. He reads the label, as if it will provide him with the answer. And it actually does. It says with clearly readable writing:
ONSET OF ACTION: 20 MINUTES
Eagle thinks back. The canary didn't settle down because the pills was starting to work, but because it was exhausted. How long has it been since he took the pill? Fifteen minutes? It has to be close to twenty. Perhaps he's lucky that the effect will soon—
BANG! BANG! BANG!
This time the window really cracks, leaving a big, starshaped hole with bloody feathers stuck to the edges. The cool night air seeps in.
Eagle grabs Lark and pulls her to the door.
At that moment, two more birds hit the window and shatter the glass in a hail of shards. The birds crash-land on the floor, shrieking and flapping their wings.
Lark screams. Eagle pulls her out of the room and slams the door.
Another bang somewhere in the house, followed by the sound of glass shattering. A girl screams.
"Oh, no!" Lark exclaims. "They're in the house!"
Eagle turns to her, talking fast. "Listen to me, Lark. It's only me they're after. I have to run. I don't know if I'll make it, but I—"
"Watch out, Eagle!"
Eagle spins around. A big crow comes flapping down the hallway. He bolts through the house, pushing people aside, reaches the front door, yanks it open and stumbles out on the lawn.
He senses a whooshing sound above, it almost sounds like gathering thunder. He stops and looks up and freezes on the spot.
Above him, in the black sky, is a cloud of birds. They're so plentiful that it's impossible to count them all. Crows, seagulls, blackbirds, pigeons, small birds, birds of prey, seabirds and loads of others that Eagle doesn't know the names of.
They have all come to end him once and for all.
Eagle runs blindly in a random direction.

The first birds dive and hit him. He manages to keep his balance despite the blows. But then they really come down on him, like a house collapsing.

Eagle falls and lands on the grass. The sheer weight of the birds crushes him into the ground. He is unable to get up, he can't even turn around. He can only huddle into a fetal position and cover his head with his arms.

He screams, but the sound is drowned out by the shrieks and cooing and chirping of the birds. Everything is feathers and beaks and claws. The birds peck and tear at him. His clothes are ripped. Then comes the pain. He is torn all over, his arms, his legs, his back.

Eagle is going to die. He is certain of it.

He has no idea how long it goes on. Maybe only twenty seconds. But it feels like an eternity.

All of a sudden, the pressure eases off. The birds continue to peck and scratch for a couple of seconds, but then they cease all together. Eagle can hear them taking to the air. Their shrieks grow distant.

And then it's all over. Eagle is not sure whether he is still alive. He cautiously lifts his head, opens his eyes and looks around.

The lawn is littered with lost feathers in all colors and sizes. A couple of birds are still hanging around, but they have completely lost interest in him. The rest have taken off and are now leaving the place in all directions.

"Eagle?" a voice says.

He sits up and turns around. Everyone from the party is standing in front of the house, staring at him.

Lark steps forward, looking terrified. "Are you ... are you all right?"

Eagle is hurting all over. He looks down and realizes that his clothes are almost gone. His skin is covered with bloody scratches. He touches his head. His face is relatively unharmed, but he can feel that tufts of hair are missing from his scalp.

And yet, he's alive. He made it.

"I think I'm all right," he mumbles.

"Call an ambulance," Lark says to the others. Then she comes closer and kneels down in front of him. "I was so scared, Eagle."

"Me too. Say, Lark?"

"Yes?"

"Do I still get that kiss?"

Lark bursts into laughter. "You are not normal."

Eagle smiles. "Yeah, I know, but at least—"

He's interrupted as Lark presses her lips against his.

***

Omnia Avesodio is not a real disease—I made it up. But what Eagle's brother says about the meaning of the name is actually almost true. I came up with the name using the Latin words *omnia*, *aves* and *odio*, which translate to *all*, *birds* and *hate*.

It's crazy how many people are afraid of birds. I don't mind them at all, but I've heard from a lot of readers who tell me this story is like a nightmare come to life for them. To me, it was just a cool idea. As you might have guessed, it was inspired by Daphne du Maurier's *The Birds*. That's one of the best and most atmospheric stories I've ever read. You should really check it out if you haven't already.

Oh, and by the way, did you notice all the characters in the story are named after birds? Even the cat.

Under the Skin

It's really pouring down. Peter is soaking wet. He runs down the street, trying to use his collar as a guard against the water, yet it seeps in anyway and trickles down his neck.

Lightning flashes across the sky, illuminating everything for a brief second. Then comes the thunder, deafeningly loud. A car rolls by, the water splashing from its tires.

The storm started just before class ended. Peter waited at the school for an hour, but the rain just kept coming, until finally, he decided to make a run for it.

He stops for a moment to catch his breath. Peter is rather heavyset, and he's not in good shape.

"Hi there!" a voice calls.

Peter turns around.

A wrinkly hand waves at him from a doorway. "You there! Yes, you! Come inside, you're getting all wet."

"Thank you, but I'm almost home," Peter says.

"Nonsense," the voice insists. "You'll catch a cold. Come on, now!"

Peter doesn't want to be rude, so he goes to the door. An old lady peeks out at him. She is so short that Peter for a moment thinks she might be on her knees. But as she opens the door all the way, he realizes that she simply is very hunched over and only about four feet tall.

She smiles broadly, making her whole face wrinkle. "Hurry up, son. Before we let out all the heat."

Peter steps into the hall, where the atmosphere is stuffy and dusty. The lady closes the door, making the storm quieter and more distant, yet Peter can still hear the next thunderclap rolling across town in that very instant.

"For a moment I took you for my grandchild," the lady says as she shuffles past Peter into the living room. "You look just like him. Now, get that wet jacket off, and I'll fetch you a towel."

Peter obediently pulls off the jacket. He catches his reflection in a mirror on the wall. He looks like a drowned mouse. His freckly skin is glistening with water, and his red hair sticks to his forehead. He notices a family photo on a shelf.

"Ah, yes, that's my grandchild," the lady says, returning with a towel. She points to a picture of a redheaded boy about Peter's age. "His name is Jonathan. He's such a good boy. Perhaps you know him?"

Peter takes the towel and starts drying his hair. "Well, I think I saw him before, but I'm not sure."

"You probably did. Come on in, the tea is ready."

"Thank you, but ..."

The lady is already gone. She keeps talking as she goes. "You know, I don't very often get visitors nowadays. Jonathan used to come here all the time, but not anymore. He probably got too big to visit his old grandmother. So, now I live here all alone ..."

Peter feels sorry for the lady. She probably just wants some company, and Peter knows what it's like to be lonely. Due to his weight and hair color, he's the lowest chicken in the pecking order at school. None of the others want to be his friend.

So, he steps out of his shoes and follows the lady into the living room. It looks a lot like Peter's own grandparents' home. A couch, a piano, an armchair, an antique dining table, a bureau, a fireplace, an ancient television and a cuckoo clock in the corner.

"Sit down," the lady demands. "I'll get the tea and cookies."

Peter takes a seat on the couch. It's made of leather in an odd color, kind of pinkish, almost like a pig, and with a subtle, spotted pattern. In the fireplace small flames are crackling, making the room nice and warm.

A moment later, the lady returns with a tray. She puts two cups on the table and a bowl of cookies.

"Here you go, son," she says, settling down next to him. "Well, now. Tell me a little about yourself."

Peter is about to bite into a cookie, but hesitates. "Eh ... about myself?"

"Yes. Your name, for instance."

"Oh. My name is Peter Matheson."

"And do you live in this town, Peter?"

"Yes. We live on Pine Hill Drive."

"Do you like going to school?"

Peter tries the cookie. It's a bit dry. "Well ... sometimes it's boring, I guess. I usually spend the recesses by myself. I read books and stuff. But I like art. That's my favorite subject, and ..."

Peter realizes that the old lady is no longer listening. She just stares straight ahead, eyes becoming moist behind the glasses.

"Is ... is something wrong?"

The lady sniffles and comes to. "I'm sorry, son. I just thought of Jonathan. You remind me so much of him, you see. He's such a good boy, but he never comes to visit anymore."

Peter doesn't quite know what to say, so he takes another cookie.

"Try the tea," the lady says with a smile. "It's better when it's still hot." She apparently forgot about her grandchild for a moment.

Peter sips at the tea. It's rather bitter, but he doesn't say anything.

"Jonathan has red hair, just like you," the lady goes on. She smiles and ruffles Peter's hair. "And freckles, too. I always had a liking for red hair and freckles, you know."

Peter can't help but smile. It's the first time anyone has ever complimented him about his hair color. And he does have a lot of freckles, not just on his face, but all over his body. He hates gym class, when he has to change with the other boys. They always laugh and point.

"Who did you get it from?" the lady asks. "Your mom?"

"My dad," Peter says.

"Do you have any siblings?"

"A little sister."

"Does she also have red hair and freckles?"

Peter shakes his head. "She has brown hair, like my mom, and no freckles."

"That's a shame. But I guess we can't all have red hair and freckles. It wouldn't be anything special then, would it?"

"I guess not."

"Do you like the tea?"

"Uhm ... sure," Peter lies. "But it's still a little too hot."

"It's best while it's hot."

Peter politely takes another sip. "So ... eh ... what do you do?"

"Well, I rarely get any visitors. But I keep myself occupied with different things. My hobby is upholstery."

"Upholstery? What's that?"

"It's putting fabric on furniture. I buy old chairs and couches at yard sales and then I reupholster them. I made this couch, and that armchair. What do you think?"

Peter glances at the couch. It's hideous, but he smiles and says: "It's really nice. I can't believe you did it yourself."

"There's nothing unbelievable about it, really. I worked as an upholsterer in my younger days, in a large factory." She shakes her head. "The only problem is, you really can't find any good leather these days. They just don't make it like they used to."

"Oh." Peter doesn't really know what to ask next.

Outside a new thunderclap is rumbling.

The lady gets up and trundles to the fireplace, where she starts to root around in the embers with a poker, before putting another log on the fire.

"I'd better get on my way," Peter says, getting up and putting the cup on the table.

The lady spins around. "Already? But ... you haven't even drunk your tea."

"I can't drink anymore."

"And you're not even dry. Come a little closer to the fire. Your clothes are still soaking wet." She grabs an ottoman and drags it in front of the fireplace.

"I ... well ... all right," Peter says. It can't hurt to spend a little more time with the old lady. Besides, it's still raining heavily outside. The water is pouring down the windows, making everything blurry.

"That's it," the lady says smiling, as he sits down on the ottoman. She strokes his cheek. "You make sure you get nice and warm now, son. You wouldn't want to catch a cold. Do you know what? I think you should take off your sweater. It'll never get dry as long as you are wearing it."

Before Peter has time to object, she has unzipped his sweater, and with brisk efficiency she strips it off him. Peter is left with just his T-shirt on. The lady puts the sweater on a hanger and puts it on a rack next to the fireplace.

"There," she says with a satisfied smile. "Now it'll get dry in no time. You can ..." The lady gasps. "Oh no! What's *that*?" She stares at Peter in horror.

"Uh ... what do you mean?"

"That!" She points at him.

Peter looks down at himself, unsure of what to look for, expecting maybe a spider crawling on him or something.

The lady gently touches the scar on his elbow.

"Oh, that," Peter smiles with relief. "I got it when I fell off my bike."

"It looks terrible!"

"It's okay," Peter says, a little taken aback by the lady's reaction. "I got used to looking at it, really. And when I wear a shirt, no one can see it."

The lady doesn't seem to be listening. Her expression is concerned, and she mumbles something to herself. "That really won't do. No, not at all." Then, she comes to and smiles. "Oh, well. It'll be fine anyway. Here, drink your tea." She takes the cup and hands it to him. "It's homemade with herbs. It'll do you good."

Peter sends her a strained smile.

"I'll just dust a little. It looks a mess in here."

To Peter the living room looks nice and clean, but the lady finds a dust broom and goes to work while she hums a tune.

Peter sits and listens to the storm while pretending to drink the tea, which has left a bad taste in his mouth. He looks down and notices that he has spilled some tea on the ottoman. He tries to wipe the stain away, but it doesn't come off. It's not a stain, but part of the pattern, he realizes. It really is a strange style, he has never seen that kind of leather before.

He lets his eyes wander. Above the fireplace hangs another photo of the lady's grandchild. He is smiling at the photographer. Peter furrows his brow. The boy does look familiar.

"How old is Jonathan?" he asks.

The lady is dusting the piano. She stops and comes to Peter. "Jonathan is eleven years old. Why? Do you know him?"

"Maybe," Peter says. "I think I've seen him somewhere, at least. I just can't figure out where. Does he go to school here in town?"

"No. He lives far away. That's why he never comes to visit anymore. Are you getting warm?" She feels his arm. "Yes, you're getting there. Tell me, isn't your skin terribly dry?"

Peter feels his skin. "A little, I guess."

"I always get such dry skin when I sit in front of the fire. You know what? I have a really good lotion. I'll just get it." She shuffles out of the living room.

Peter gazes after her. He's getting a weird feeling. The lady says so many strange things. He considers if he should leave. But he can't bring himself to just go without a word. Instead, he uses the opportunity to pour the rest of the tea into the potted plant next to the television.

He goes to study the picture of Jonathan. Where has he seen him before? Something about Jonathan's smile makes Peter nervous for some reason. The floorboards creak behind him.

The old lady has returned. She has brought a large, white bucket. "Here you go," she says, pulling off the lid, and digs out a handful of the thick, white lotion. She slaps it on Peter's arm. "There! Now just rub it in nicely, and your skin will become oh so soft."

"Uhm ... all right." Peter rubs the lotion on his arm, and then the other arm. The lotion has a weird smell to it.

The lady just stands there, smiling. Then, she exclaims: "You know what? I think you ought to do your legs too. And your stomach, while you're at it."

"No," Peter says, shaking his head. "I don't want to do that."

"Why not? Are you shy? I'll turn my back."

She hands him the bucket and turns around.

Peter hesitates. This has gone too far; the situation is simply too weird. "I have to go home now," he says, handing her back the bucket. "My mom just called me. She was worried about me."

"Really?" the lady asks with surprise. "I didn't hear your phone ringing."

"It did," Peter says, automatically going to his pocket, then remembering that the phone is in his bag, which he left in the hall. But of course, the lady doesn't know that, so he sticks to the story. "My mom told me to come home right away."

"Are you allowed to lie, son?"

"I'm ... not lying."

"Oh yes, you are." The lady pulls something from her own pocket. It's Peter's phone. "I found this in your bag. That means you haven't spoken to your mom."

Peter blushes. "Uhm ... well ... I ..."

The lady sniffles. "You don't want to be here. You're exactly like Jonathan. He never wants to visit me, either. I just live all alone here in this house and never get any visitors."

Peter feels ashamed. But at the same time, he doesn't like that the old lady has gone through his bag. "I'm sorry," he says. "I'm sorry I lied. But I do have to go home now. Can I have my phone?" He holds out his hand.

The lady takes a step backwards, looking at him assessingly. "You'll get if you use the lotion on the rest of your body."

Peter frowns. "Why is it so important that I rub myself with your lotion?"

"Because your skin is very sensitive. That's how it is when you have freckles. You get easily sunburned and the skin tends to turn dry. I should know, I was a redhead myself in my younger days."

"And so what if my skin becomes dry? Why does that matter to you?"

The lady doesn't seem to have an answer, so instead she starts sniffling again. "You are just like Jonathan. You don't listen to me, either. I'm just trying to help, but no one wants to listen ..."

"Fine," Peter says and pulls the T-shirt over his head. "Give me the lotion, then."

The old lady lights up in a big, wrinkly smile. "Oh, my." She looks down Peter's body hungrily. "You really have a lot of freckles."

"I know. Just give me the lotion."

She hands him back the bucket. Peter quickly rubs himself in the lotion. The lady smiles as she watches him do it.

After it's done, he puts the T-shirt back on. He feels embarrassed, confused and a little angry. "Now I'll have my phone, please."

"Of course, son." She hands it to him.

Peter puts it in his pocket. "I'll go home now."

"Already? But you haven't even—"

"I've finished my tea," Peter interrupts.

"Oh, you have? Did you like it?"

"It was all right."

The lady nods satisfied. "I'm glad. Jonathan didn't really care for my tea. He would sometimes pour it out when I wasn't looking."

Peter tries not to betray himself by showing surprise. He goes to take his sweater. It's almost dry, so he pulls it on and zips it. "Thank you for the tea and cookies," he says. "Goodbye."

"Would you like to see my workshop? Jonathan loved to see it."

"No, thank you. I'm going home."

The lady sighs and slumps down onto the couch. "Goodbye, then," she says sadly.

Peter exists the living room. In the hall, he puts on his shoes, jacket and bag, even though everything is wet and cold. When he tries to open the door, he finds it locked.

The lock is the old-fashioned kind, where you need a key both from the inside and the outside, and the key is not there.

Peter sighs. He takes off his shoes once more and goes back to the living room. The lady is still sitting on the couch, glaring into the fireplace.

"The front door is locked," Peter says. "Where's the key?"

"I miss my Jonathan so much," the lady says. It sounds as though she's talking to herself. "It has been such a long time since I last saw him."

Peter notices that she has taken down the photo of Jonathan and is holding it. She is caressing the picture.

"He was such a good boy," she mumbles. "Back when he still came to visit."

All of a sudden, Peter gets a flash of memory. Now he knows where he has seen Jonathan. "It was on television ..."

The lady turns her head. "What did you say?"

"I remember I saw Jonathan on the news. It was only a couple of weeks ago. They showed a picture of him, but I can't remember what it was about ..."

"I have no idea what you're talking about," the lady hisses. "My Jonathan has never been on the news. He was a good boy. He never got into trouble."

"It wasn't because of any crime he had done," Peter mumbles, churning his brain to remember. He feels a little dizzy. It's probably the heat. The temperature is stifling in here. "It was something about ... about ..." Suddenly, something else hits him, and he looks at the old lady. "Why do you keep saying he *was* a good boy?"

The lady mumbles something that Peter can't make out. She's talking to herself again.

Peter lets out a gasp as he finally remembers the story. "He had gone missing! That's why he was in the news. They said it was a suspected kidnapping."

The lady doesn't answer. Instead, she begins to chuckle.

Peter feels suddenly anxious. The lady isn't just weird, there's something really off about her. Something dangerous.

He doesn't give a damn about being polite anymore. "Unlock the front door. Right now. Or else I'll call the police."

"The police?" The lady chuckles even louder. "What would the police do, son? They couldn't find Jonathan. What makes you think they'll find you?"

"All right, I'm calling them now," Peter says, taking his phone and dialing 9-1-1.

"Stop being such a fool," the lady sneers. She gets up and shuffles right past him. "Come on, I'll unlock the door."

Peter is relieved. He follows her to the hall, but still he keeps the phone ready. His head is spinning a little. He's looking forward to getting out of the warm house, to breathe in fresh air.

The lady stops in front of the door and goes through her pockets. "Darn it, where did I put it?"

"You don't fool me," Peter says. "Find the key."

"Stop bossing me around, young man." She points at him with a thin finger. "Jonathan also spoke to me like that, and I won't tolerate that tone. It's not easy being old, you know. You forget stuff, and you lose things."

Peter sighs. "Don't you have a back door?"

"Sure, I do. We can go out through the basement. Come with me, son."

"I'm not your son. Stop calling me that."

The lady chuckles again, as if she's having her own, private joke. She shuffles through the house, and Peter follows her. They go down a staircase to a dark room. There's a heavy smell of leather in the air.

When the old lady turns on the light, Peter looks around and sees furniture everywhere. Chairs, ottomans, even a couch. Some of them are naked, some are halfway done. They all have the same, pig-colored leather. In the middle of the room is a large worktable filled with tools. Peter gets overwhelmed by exhaustion and feels like sitting down to rest his legs.

"This is my workshop," the lady says proudly. "I'm glad you wanted to see it."

"I *didn't* want to see it! Where is the door?"

"Just let me show you around for a second. Look at this. It's a chair I'm doing for my friend. And this couch is a request I got, all the way from Canada. Isn't it pretty? I have so many costumers, I can hardly keep up."

"That's nice," Peter says dreamily, even though he finds the furniture ugly. He glances at a chair, noticing a button in the middle of the seat. His head is buzzing. "Is there really a way out from down here? Or was it just something you said?"

"Do you know these tools?" The lady goes to the table. "This is a pair of leather scissors, I use it to cut the fabric into shape. It's very sharp. This is my pincer, for when I have to pull out a nail. And the awl ..." She takes something that looks like an oversized needle with a handle. "It's very multipurpose. For instance, it's good for poking holes in stuff." She points the tool at Peter and smiles.

Peter starts to sweat. It's even warmer in the basement. A faraway thunderclap makes the floor vibrate. The dizziness returns, he has to sit down on the chair, wiping the sweat from his brow. "I ... I really want to go home now ..."

"Did you know that leather actually is skin?" the lady asks, turning her back to Peter. "There are many different animals whose skin is suitable, but the best comes from humans."

Peter freezes. "Did you say ... *humans*?"

The lady doesn't answer. She touches something on the table.

Peter gets up. Stares down at the chair. Now he sees it. The button is really a belly button. And the funny spots on the ottoman are moles.

Finally, everything falls into place for Peter.

He turns and runs for the door. He reaches it, but he can't open it: There is no knob on this side.

He turns around.

The lady glares at him. She is holding a hammer. "It would have been a lot easier if you had just drunk the tea, son. We wouldn't have had to do it this way. But no, you just had to throw it away when I wasn't looking. Just like Jonathan. He was very impolite."

Peter looks around at the furniture. He almost can't grasp it. All that skin. "You ... you're insane!"

"Now, what did I tell you about that tone of voice?"

"You've killed people! You killed your own grandson!"

The lady shakes her head regretfully. "It didn't have to end like that. If he had just treated me kindly. After all, I'm just a lonely old lady. All I want is a visit once in a while—is that really too much to ask?"

Peter suddenly remembers. There have been several cases in the media lately, not just Jonathan. He recalls three, maybe four other kids that have disappeared. All with red hear and freckles.

And he's about to be next. He walked right into the trap.

Peter walks along the wall. His legs feel wobbly. Now he understands that it's because of the tea. Luckily, he only drank three sips—but was it too much? Will his legs be strong enough to get him out of here?

"I prefer to use children." The lady is talking as she walks after Peter. "Children have the nicest skin. It hasn't been ruined by unhealthy habits, like grown-ups with their cigarettes and their booze. Not to mention tattoos—have you seen the things people draw on themselves nowadays? Goodness gracious! It looks awful. How could you ever get a nice couch out of that?"

Peter bolts for the table and grabs the awl. He points it at the lady.

She just chuckles. "Come on, son. You're not going to hurt me. You couldn't bring yourself to that."

"Yes, I can. Keep away." Peter is backing up.

The lady follows him slowly, swinging the hammer from side to side like a pendulum. "I think I'll make a lazy boy out of you. It would suit you."

"Shut up!" Peter yells. "You're not getting my skin!"

Suddenly, he gets an idea, as he recalls what the lady said when she saw the scar on his arm: *"That really won't do."*

Peter turns the awl to his arm. "Stop right there, or I'll scratch my skin."

The lady stops. Her face turns expressionless. "Don't."

"I'll do it! If you come just one step closer ..."

The lady glares at him. Then, she smiles. "Come on now, son. You're not being serious ..." She comes closer.

Peter presses the sharp point of the awl against his arm and drags it swiftly upwards, leaving a long, red stripe. It doesn't bleed, but it stings.

The old lady's eyes get big and wide. "No! Cut that out! Are you out of your mind?"

"Stay where you are!" Peter shifts the awl to the left hand. "I'll do the other arm next."

The lady bares her grey teeth in a snarl. "You fool. You have no idea what you're doing. That precious skin ..."

"Open the door. Let me out of here."

The lady hesitates. At first, she looks mad. Then sad. And finally resigned. She sighs and goes to the door, while she finds something from her pocket. It's the handle, Peter sees. She puts it in the door and opens it.

"There," she says. "Run off, then."

"Step away from the door."

The lady shuffles aside.

Peter walks to the door, holding the awl ready, if the lady tries anything.

He's almost out, when he hears the voice. It's very faint, barely audible.

"Grandma? Is that you?"

Peter stops. "Where did that come from?"

The lady looks oblivious. "Where did what come from? My hearing isn't that good anymore."

"Stop lying. I know you heard it."

"Just get out of here. Wasn't that what you wanted?"

"Quiet," Peter demands and listens.

After a couple of seconds, the voice asks again: *"Grandma? Please let me out. I promise to be nice."*

Peter looks down. There's a hatch in the floor. He goes to it.

The lady follows him with her gaze. She looks very displeased now.

Peter kneels down and pulls up the hatch. Nothing but absolute darkness. Then, a pale face appears—a freckled face. Jonathan blinks and looks up at Peter. "Who are you?"

"My name is Peter."

"Where's my grandma?"

"She's right here."

The boy immediately looks scared. "Watch out! She's insane! She wants to—"

"How dare you talk about your sweet old grandma like that?" the lady shrieks. "You rude kids! I'll teach you some manners!" She charges at Peter.

Peter barely has time to get up. The lady swings the hammer. He ducks. The weapon passes his head within a few inches. The lady loses her balance, screams and falls down the open hatch, landing somewhere down in the darkness with a crash.

Peter can see her lying down there. Jonathan is standing next to her, staring at his grandma. His clothes are dirty. Peter tries to remember how long it has been since Jonathan went missing. Fourteen days, at least. That's a long time to live in pitch darkness.

The lady grunts and starts moving.

"Quickly!" Peter says, reaching down. Jonathan grabs his hand. He isn't very heavy, so Peter pulls him up with only little difficulty.

"Jonathan?" the lady mumbles and tries to get up. "Jonathan, help your old grandma."

"Fuck you, Grandma," Jonathan says and slams the hatch shut. He sighs deeply and hides his face in his hands. his shoulders start shaking as Jonathan cries.

Peter doesn't really know what to do. He squeezes Jonathan's shoulder.

Jonathan sniffles and looks at him. "Thank you so much. I didn't think I would get out of there." He wipes his nose with his sleeve. "Did she try to get you too?"

Peter nods. "I thought she wanted to ... you know ..." He drags his finger across his throat.

"You're right. She has already done it to others."

"But why didn't she kill you? Was it because you're her grandchild and she couldn't bring herself to do it?"

Jonathan scuffs. "No, it wasn't because of that." He pulls up his shirt. There are scratch marks across his belly. "Every time she tried, I would do this to myself with my nails. So, she had to wait for the scratches to heel up." He notices the red line on Peter's arm. "I see you got the same idea."

The boys smile at each other.

From under the hatch the lady has started making noise. She alternates between yelling, crying and laughing.

Jonathan shivers, as if he gets a chill. "She has always been fucked up. My parents wouldn't let me visit her. I kind of felt sorry for her, so I started to visit her. I just thought she was a little weird, you know. I had no idea, that she ..." He looks around at the furniture.

For a moment Peter feels like they aren't really alone in the basement. Outside, the thunder has finally ceased.

"Let's get out of here," Jonathan says.

Peter nods. "I'm with you. What about her?" He points to the hatch.

Jonathan glances back. "We'd better call the police, let them handle it. But if it's okay with you, I'd like to wait a little. I think she deserves some time down there."

Peter can't help but smile, although the situation is crazy. He shrugs. "It's your grandma, you decide."

Jonathan laughs and puts his arm around Peter's shoulders. They leave the basement and walk up the stairs, supporting each other. Jonathan is weak after his long stay in the basement, and Peter is still a little dizzy from the tea.

That evening, Jonathan once again makes the news. But this time, it's *good* news.

***

I once worked for a short period of time at a furniture upholsterer. I quite liked the job. Some of the tools were really chilling, especially the awl. It always made me think of a murder weapon, so it was pretty ideal inspiration for a scary story. I also liked the smell of the leather. I never asked where it came from, but it didn't have any freckles.

If you liked this story, check out *The Landlady* by Roald Dahl. It's really, really good, and it served as inspiration for *Under the Skin*.

Drip-drip-drip

bloop!

Nadia becomes aware of the sound of water dripping. She can smell chlorine and hear children laughing. She's at the public swimming pool. She's standing on the high springboard. She can see everything from up here. A father swimming with his kids, an old lady wearing a bathing cap.

Above Nadia is a big skylight, which lets in the sunshine and makes the water glitter invitingly.

"Come on!" a voice says. "What are you waiting for?"

Nadia turns her head.

Alice is standing behind her. "Are you a coward?"

Nadia smiles. "You're the coward." She jumps off yelling: "Bombs awaaay!" She hits the water with a splash, diving deep, almost deep enough to touch the bottom. She blows bubbles out her nose and watches them as they float upwards. She swims after them and breaks the surface with a big breath.

She wipes the water from her eyes and looks up at the springboard, but she can't see Alice. Instead, she notices the big, heavy clouds that are now blocking out the sun from the skylight. The atmosphere has become dim.

"Alice?"

Nadia's voice echoes between the walls. Suddenly, there is dead silence. She looks around and notices that she is alone in the pool. Where did all the other people go?

bloop!

There it is again, that dripping sound. What *is* that?

Apparently, the pool is closing for the day. That must be the reason everyone left. Nadia better leave too, so she starts swimming.

Then, she hears another sound. It's a whirring sound, like an engine of some kind. Nadia stops as she sees the plate of glass. It slides out from the edge of the pool and covers the water like a lid. It's got to be some sort of protection for the water, although Nadia fails to see why water needs protection.

She turns around and swims the other way. But another plate of glass is coming from this side. Nadia has no choice but to dive to avoid getting cut in half. A second later the two glass plates meet above her head with an audible *clang!*

It's only now that Nadia realizes the horrifying fact: She is trapped under water!

bloop!

Nadia bangs the glass, but it's way too hard to break, like solid stone. She tries to find the joint, but the plates have melted together.

Nadia panics. She swims back and forth, looking for a way out, but to no avail. She can't hold her breath any longer. She opens her mouth to scream, and the water pours down her throat as she

***

sits up in bed.

She's completely entangled in the blanket, like a fly in a spider's web. She fights her way out and looks around the room, panting.

It was just a dream.

Nadia sighs deeply and covers her face with her palms. Her hands are sweaty.

I thought I'd outgrown that old nightmare by now, she thinks. Nadia is thirteen. Ever since she was little, she has had the same nightmare about the glass plates covering the pool, trapping her below. It's her deepest fear, and the reason she never goes to public swimming pools. She has always been—

bloop!

Nadia stiffens. It was the sound from the dream. She listens intensely. But the sound doesn't come back.

Just my imagination.

Nadia gets up and gets dressed. She looks out the window. The backyard is big and green. She hasn't quite gotten used to the view. They have only been living here for two months. The rest of the family loves the garden. Mom tends to the roses, dad is building the porch, and Anton is playing soccer against himself. Nadia mostly keeps to her room. She still misses their old home in the city, where all of her friends—

bloop-glook!

Nadia spins around. This time she's certain: The sound is real, it came from the bathroom. Nadia leaves her room to go check. She finds the water in the toilet bubbling and gurgling. She breathes a sigh of relief. The toilet is clogged, that's all.

She goes to the stairs and yells: "Dad! The toilet is messed up again!"

No answer from downstairs. Now that she's aware of it, she notices that the house is unusually quiet.

Nadia remembers that she is home alone. It's the middle of the summer vacation, but Mom and Dad still have to go to work, and Anton is at kindergarten, so Nadia has the house all to herself. The new, wonderful house, that everyone loves, except Nadia.

She goes back to the bathroom. The toilet isn't bubbling quite as much now, and she really needs to pee, so she pulls down her pants and sits down.

For some reason Nadia doesn't like being alone in the new house. Maybe it's because of all the empty rooms, or the many quirks of the house. How the doors squeak, how the hall closet opens by itself, the strange sounds from the water pipes in the walls or the old boiler down in the basement.

"The charm of the house," Mom calls it. Nadia believes that the house is haunted. The thought makes her shiver.

She gets up and flushes. Water pours down the bowl, rises alarmingly high, and then starts bubbling again, even more so than before.

BLOOP-GLOOK-BLOOP-GLOOK!

"Dad'll fix it when he comes home," Nadia mumbles to herself, leaving the bathroom. She goes downstairs to the kitchen and pours herself a bowl of muesli. While she's eating, her phone rings.

She pulls it from her pocket and answers. "Hey, Alice."

"Morning, sweetie. Did I wake you?"

"No, I was already up."

"This early? You know it's the holiday, right?"

Nadia takes a spoonful of muesli. "Yeah, I know. It was only because this stupid house woke me up."

"How so?"

"Something's wrong with the toilet. I think it's clogged or whatever." Nadia feels a sudden urge to tell Alice about the nightmare. She's never told anyone, not even her mom. Instead, she asks: "What are you up to today?"

"I was thinking about going to the swimming pool."

Nadia stops chewing. "What did you say?"

"I said, I was thinking about going to the swimming pool."

ploink!

The sound makes Nadia turn. A drop is hanging from the tap. It lets go and falls into the sink with another

ploink!

Nadia stares at the tap. How long has it been dripping? It's almost as if it started when Alice mentioned the swimming pool. But that's silly.

"Hello? Nadia? You there?"

"Yeah, I'm here."

"You disappeared for a second."

"It was probably just the connection. The signal isn't that good out here."

Nadia glances toward the sink. The drops are falling regularly now.

ploink! ... ploink! ... ploink!

"So, what do you say? You want to come swimming?"

"I don't think it's a good idea."

"Oh, come on!"

Nadia goes to tighten the tap. It stops dripping. "My throat is kind of sore," she lies. "I think I might be coming down with something."

"Bummer."

"We'll do it some other day," Nadia promises.

"Okay, feel better," Alice says.

Nadia puts the phone back in her pocket and looks at her breakfast. She really isn't hungry anymore. Outside the window, the sky has become overcast. It looks like rain.

She cleans her dish and goes to the living room to feed the hamster. The tiny rodent looks out at her from the cage. Nadia gives it food and watches while it gorges itself.

The hamster is actually Anton's pet, but he doesn't really take care of it, ever since it bit his finger.

Anton has been rather unlucky lately. One night, Dad was firing up the barbeque, and Anton accidentally bumped into it, burning his elbow. Just the other day, he pinched his finger pretty bad in the refrigerator door.

Now that she is thinking about it, it's not just Anton. Dad tripped over a box and got an electric shock when he was trying to fix the light in the bedroom. Mom spilled burning hot tea on her leg and cut her finger while peeling potatoes.

Nadia furrows her brow. Could it all be coincidences? It doesn't seem like it. It seems more like ...

No, that's crazy. Just her imagination running wild.

But still. The accidents started after they came to this house. Perhaps there really is something wrong here, just like Nadia's gut keeps telling her. Could it be the house causing the accidents? Is it trying to hurt them?

She shakes her head. It doesn't make any sense. They love the damn house. All of them, except Nadia herself, and she is the only one who hasn't had any accidents. So, if the house is trying to harm them, wouldn't it be most mean to her?

Nadia smiles at her silly thoughts. She goes to brush her teeth, but as she passes the kitchen, she hears the sound of the tap going again, faster this time.

ploink-ploink-ploink-ploink-ploink-ploink!

Nadia sticks her head into the kitchen. The tap just keeps going, as though to spite her. She closes the door to the kitchen and goes upstairs. In the bathroom, the toilet, too, is still going.

While she's brushing her teeth, the toilet suddenly gives a burp, sending a cascade of water onto the floor and getting her leg all wet.

"Oh, come on! That did not just happen!"

The toilet keeps bubbling spitefully. Nadia pushes the button several times, making it flush over and over again. The water just rises, until finally it seeps over the edge and runs to the floor.

"Stupid crap," Nadia growls, watching the water run across the tiles towards the drain underneath the sink.

Nadia brings clean clothes from her room and goes to the downstairs bathroom, where she undresses and steps up into the tub for a quick shower, making sure to wash her leg where the dirty toilet water hit her.

When she's done, she steps out of the tub, noticing it being halfway full. She reaches down to find the drain, but realizes that the plug isn't in.

How is that possible? Is this drain clogged, too?

Nadia turns off the shower—or rather, she tries to do so, but when she turns the knob, the water just keeps pouring.

Nadia looks at the shower head and bursts into laughter. "My god, this is too much. The toilet, the kitchen tab, and now the shower. Has this whole house gone mad?"

She chuckles while drying off with a towel. She suddenly feels like leaving the house. Maybe go down to the mall. She could get an ice cream.

This stupid old house can go to hell for all I care. It's not my problem.

Nadia gets dressed and goes to the hall, when she notices a new sound from the kitchen. She opens the door.

The tap is no longer dripping; now it's spewing like a fireman's hose, hitting the sink and sending droplets all over the kitchen floor. The tab is shaking under the violent flow, as though it's going to explode.

And that is exactly what happens next.

With a loud, bang the tap goes flying, hitting the ceiling while a fountain shoots up and splashes out into the room, soaking everything. Nadia screams. The tap lands in front of her. It's all twisted and crumbled up, as if it had been chewed on by a large set of jaws.

For a couple of seconds Nadia is unable to move. She just stares at the fountain.

"I ... I have to call someone." She finds the phone while talking to herself. "Okay. What do you call a person who knows how to fix something like this? A plumber?" She finds a number for a local guy and makes the call.

First ring.

I hope they're not closed for the holiday ...

Second ring.

Come on, pick up ...

Third ring.

You've got to be kidding me!

Fourth ring—and then someone says: "*Tony's Plumbing, Tony speaking.*"

"Yes, hello, my name is Nadia. I have a really serious problem. I think you need to come, like right now!"

"*I see,*" the plumber says calmly. "*What's the deal?*"

"I know it sounds crazy, but ... everything in the house has gone insane. The toilet is clogged, the showerhead can't be turned off, and the kitchen tap just exploded ..."

"***Exploded?***"

"Yes! There's pouring water all over the place. Please, you have to come. I'm home alone and ... and my parents won't be home until later and ... and I have no idea what to do!"

"*Easy now, young lady. Calm down for a second. We'll fix it. Just tell me how it started.*"

"Uhm ..." Nadia is trying to think. "The toilet! It started with the upstairs toilet."

"*All right. And is the toilet still clogged?*"

"I ... I guess."

"*I need you to go check.*"

"Okay, just a minute." Nadia runs upstairs. She is just about to open the bathroom door, when she notices the puddle. Water is seeping out from under the door. "Oh, no ..."

"*What's that?*"

She tries to open the door, but it's stuck. She has to put her shoulder to it, pushing with all her weight. Finally, the door gives and a flood wave comes flushing out. It soaks her legs and almost pushes her off balance, as it runs across the hall and splashes down the stairs.

"*Jesus Christ,*" the plumber says in her ear. "*Is that **water** I hear?*"

Nadia is unable to answer and unable to move. She just stares into the bathroom. Before she opened the door, the water level must have been knee height, because the paper roll is soaked. Even though it's quickly sinking now that the dam has been breached, more water is welling up from the bowl.

"*Are you still there?*"

"Yes," Nadia croaks.

"*I'll be right there. Give me the address.*"

"The address?" Nadia racks her brain. "I don't ... I don't remember the address. We just moved here."

"*Well, can't you check the mailbox or something?*"

Nadia turns and runs down the stairs, which has now been turned into a long waterfall. The steps are slippery and Nadia's socks are wet.

"*You know what?*" the plumber says. "*Forget about the address for a moment. Something's obviously really wrong. You need to find the main valve and turn off the water completely. Is there a basement in the house? The valve is probably located—*"

Nadia doesn't hear the rest, because she slips and almost falls. She manages to grab the banister and stay on her feet, but she drops the phone. "*No!*"

It tumbles down the stairs. Nadia runs down and picks it up. It's completely wet. The screen is black and unresponsive.

"No, no, no!"

Nadia realizes that she is standing in water up to her ankles. The whole ground floor seems to be flooded.

Nadia starts to feel fear. This is no longer just an irritating problem. It's dangerous. There are electric appliances, wires and stuff. She could get electrocuted.

She's got to get out of the house. Right now.

She runs to the hall, grabs the front door and almost crashes into it, because it doesn't budge. Nadia checks the lock, but it's not turned, and the door should be able to open.

"What's the problem? Open up, damnit!"

She tugs violently. The door doesn't move an inch. It's like it has never been opened before.

Nadia steps back, breathing heavily.

"Jammed," she mumbles. "That's all. It's just jammed."

But suddenly she feels the malice of the house. It's like eyes watching her, laughing at her, enjoying her fear.

Get a grip. There's a logical explanation. It's not the house trying to ...

Her thoughts are interrupted by a deep rumbling. It's almost like thunder, except it's coming from below, not above. It makes the whole house tremble. Something tips over somewhere, a picture falls from the wall.

Then it stops.

"Was that ... an earthquake?" Nadia asks, turning around. Her gaze goes to the door underneath the staircase. It leads down to the basement.

Didn't the plumber say something about the basement? That she had to find a valve or something?

Nadia goes and opens the door. The darkness is thick like tar. Her fingers search for the switch.

Click!

The dusty staircase appears. But only the three top steps, because the rest is under water. Nadia stares in amazement at the things floating around. A cardboard box, a garden glove, a tennis ball. Underneath the water she can just make out the tumble dryer and Dad's workbench.

The heavy rumbling returns. The water rises with visible speed. It looks unnatural. As though some force is pushing the water from below.

The rumbling is not thunder and not an earthquake. It's water. A whole lot of water.

Nadia slams the door, runs to the living room and yanks hard on the terrace door. But that, too, is jammed and does not move an inch.

"Let me out!" she cries, only too aware that she's talking to the house. "Open this door! Open it!"

The terrace door doesn't yield no matter how violently she tugs the handle. She tries the windows: jammed as well, impossible to open.

Nadia's gaze is caught by the glass ball on the windowsill. It's a souvenir from a trip to Egypt. It's big as an apple and very heavy. Nadia picks it up and steps back. She used to play handball, so she's a good thrower. She takes the position as though she's about to execute a penalty throw. Her heart is thumping. How will she explain to her parents that the living room window is shattered? She hears the water rumble from the basement, and she decides that she really doesn't care how much trouble she'll get in for breaking the window. Right now, she just wants to *get out.*

She throws the glass ball.

It hits the window with a loud bang and falls into the water with a splash. The window vibrates, but the glass holds. Nadia can't believe it. She steps up to the window and takes a closer look. Not so much as a scratch is visible.

She picks up the glass ball once more. This time she makes a run-up and puts all her strength into the throw.

The glass ball hits the window and practically explodes. The pieces rain down into the water. Yet the window remains intact.

"No, it can't be. It can't be!" Nadia pounds the glass with her fists. "*Hey! Can anybody hear me? Hello!*"

Who would hear her? She's alone, several miles outside of town, far from the nearest neighbor, who is probably at work right now. Mom and Dad won't be home for at least four hours. The mailman is the only one who might come by, but he has most likely already been here. She's completely cut off from the world.

She turns and glances around the living room. Once again, she gets the feeling of the house looking right back at her. And suddenly she gets it: why it hasn't done anything to her yet. It has been saving its strength, waiting patiently, watching, planning. It wanted Nadia to get the worst of it, because she didn't care for the house, but it had to lure her in. And now that she's finally home alone, it has trapped her like a mouse in a glass cage that is slowly going to get filled up with …

No. She won't think the thought. There *has* to be a way out.

She gets an idea. She's only physically cut off: she still has the Internet! The laptop is in her room. She runs out to the stairs; the water is now knee-high and splashing around her legs.

Just as she reaches the hall, the basement door is flung open. It gives way for the water, which now comes roaring out in a crashing wave, hitting Nadia and slinging her against the wall. She screams and fights to stay on her feet, as the water quickly fills the room and she makes her way to the stairs. Water is also coming down from the top floor, making every step a struggle. She grabs the handle and pulls herself up. Finally, she reaches the top.

A hard-streaming river is running from the bathroom, across the hall and down the stairs. Nadia jumps over it and runs to her room. The laptop is on the table. She turns it on and waits impatiently for it to start up. Her clothes are soaked, her heart is racing.

When the computer is ready, she opens a chat window. Only one other person is online: Alice.

Nadia writes a message: *Help me! The house is going crazy! I'm trapped! Call the pol*

She stares at the word. Then, she changes it.

Call someone who can break into the house!

Twenty seconds pass before Alice replies. It feels more like twenty minutes.

Hey sweetie. What are you on about? Is it a joke?

"No!" Nadia screams.

No joke! I swear! Hurry up! I'm scared!

She hits Send, just as a message appears on the screen:

Connection lost. Problem with router. Please check the cables.

Nadia slumps back into the chair. She knows what has happened. The router is downstairs in Dad's office. The water must've drowned it. She has lost her last contact to the outside world.

Did Alice get the message? Maybe. Maybe not.

Will she get help from the outside? Maybe. Maybe not.

Out of nowhere, a thought jumps into Nadia's head: The guinea pig! It's still down in the living room.

"Oh, no!"

She runs out into the hallway. But she forgets about the stream, and her wet socks slip on the floor.

Nadia's head hits the floor with a thump.

***

She awakens slowly. Blinks and sees the ceiling. For a moment, she just lies there, collecting her thoughts, listening. There's absolute silence.

Nadia sits up, realizing she's at the top of the staircase. There's no water. The floor is completely dry. Same goes for her clothes.

She raises her hand and gently touches the back of her head. She finds a sore spot.

I was dreaming, she thinks, feeling great relief. *I must've been sleep walking. That was why I fell down. But everything was just a horrible nightmare.*

She carefully gets to her feet, feels dizzy for a moment, then goes to the bathroom door and opens it. No water. She steps over to the toilet. The water in the bowl is still like a forest lake.

Of course.

She goes downstairs. No trace of water. The house is still very silent. No flushing, no dripping, no rumbling from the basement. Just to be sure, she opens the door underneath the staircase and turns on the light. The basement looks normal. No water.

Of course.

She checks the kitchen. Nothing unusual. The tap is intact.

The living room. Dry as a bone. The guinea pig is sleeping peacefully in the cage. A warm sunshine even comes through the windows.

Nadia starts to feel convinced. She smiles. She has had a lot of nightmares, but never one as real as this one. And the first dream, the one with the swimming pool, that must've been a dream within a dream. Crazy!

Nadia feels like going outside. The weather is perfect for a bike ride. She will call Alice. Maybe she wants to join her for a trip to the park.

Nadia goes and puts her shoes on. Just before grabbing the doorknob, she hesitates.

What if it won't open?

The door opens without any resistance.

Of course.

Nadia laughs at her own nervousness as she steps out into the sunshine. The birds are singing in the garden. She whistles along while she walks to the shed. She finds her phone and calls Alice. She can't wait to tell her about the crazy nightmare.

A weird noise comes out of the phone. It's like a distant rumbling, almost like thunder. She looks at the screen. The call has been disconnected.

"That's odd," she mumbles, and for some reason she gets the shivers.

Suddenly, she just wants to get away from the house. She runs to the shed. Her shoes give off a funny sound with every step.

slop-slop-slop

Nadia looks down. Her shoes and pants are wet. In fact, she's drenched all the way up to her navel.

Nadia starts breathing faster. The birds are no longer singing. A dark cloud has covered the sun.

She spins around. The front door of the house is wide open. It looks like a mouth.

This isn't real, Nadia thinks. *I'm dreaming. But if this is a dream, then ... The rest must have been real! Oh, God ...*

Nadia gasps and

***

sits up.

She is back at the top of the staircase. The water has reached the top most steps. The whole ground floor is now flooded! And the water is still rising.

She screams and jumps to her feet. Feels a sharp pain from the back of her head, but ignores it. She runs down the hall, tries every window in every room. Her parents' bedroom, Anton's room, finally her own room. None of the windows can be opened.

She slams the door to her room. The water has already flooded the floorboards with a couple of inches. She can hear it rising on the other side of the door, pressing against it. A thin stream is trickling through the crack at the bottom. How long will the door be able to hold it? Probably only a couple of minutes.

Nadia walks back and forth as she starts to cry. The fear is pervading her entire body.

Have to keep looking. Must be some way out of here.

She looks around. The windows can neither be opened nor broken. There's no attic in the house, so she can't go any higher up.

There's no way out. Soon the water will likely break down the door and fill the room.

I'll finally get to experience what it's like to drown. It's my old nightmare coming to life. And it's the house that's doing it.

"*Fuck you!*" she screams and stamps the floor. "*Fuck you, I hate you!*"

Suddenly, silence. The roar of the water dies down. The same with the rumbling from the basement. The house falls completely quiet.

It heard me, Nadia thinks, astounded.

Then, it starts again. More loud and frantic than ever. The house makes a noise like a wild animal roaring. Everything trembles. The door flies open. A flood wave comes crashing into the room, tipping over the desk and the bookcase, swallowing everything.

Nadia jumps on the bed, but that too is flooded. In a matter of seconds, the room is halfway filled.

Nadia panics. She fights her way to the window, bangs the glass, scratches it with her nails, screams at the top of her lungs. "*Help me! Somebody! Heeeeelp! I'm drowning!*"

And then she sees it.

Water. Running down the glass. But on the *outside.*

Nadia blinks. It's not raining, so where does the water come from? The roof?

It suddenly falls into place. "The chimney! The boiler in the basement!"

If the water can get out that way, then maybe she can, too. It's her only chance. The water is neck high now. She turns and swims for the door. Around her, she notices the fishes from the tipped-over tank.

Nadia swims out into the hallway. As she reaches the staircase, the water is almost at the ceiling. In order to get downstairs, she has to dive. She breathes deeply a couple of times. Then, she goes for it.

Nadia swims down the stairs. It's a surreal feeling, to swim inside the house. There are a lot of things around her that she needs to avoid. Dish towels, shoes, papers, chairs. She uses the walls to navigate.

She reaches the hall, turns and swims underneath the staircase. The door to the basement is open, but it's pitch darkness down there. Nadia has no chance of finding the boiler in the dark. She tries the switch, but the lightbulb is dead, drowned.

Suddenly, a small furry ball floats in front of her. It's the guinea pig. Nadia lets out a scream, losing precious air. She can't worry about the guinea pig now, or she will end up the same way.

A flashlight, she thinks. *Dad has one in the closet. He used it when the power went out.*

The closet is hanging on the wall halfway down the basement stairs. She swims down there, opens it, finds the flashlight and turns it on. It works!

Nadia puts it in her mouth and swims on downwards. This way she can see, but her air is also starting to run out. The pressure from the water is a lot heavier down here. She can feel the weight of the entire house resting on top of her.

She swims to the boiler. It's in the corner, looking like a big, sleeping beast. Above it, the chimney runs upwards. There's a hatch, which is open. It's big enough for a human to get it. Perhaps it's meant for the sweeper.

Nadia hasn't got time to speculate. Her lungs are heaving for air. She sticks her head in the hatch and twists her body upwards. The tube is tight, and the water just makes it worse. She loses the flashlight. The darkness is strangling. She pushes on. Her arm is stuck. She manages to get it free. She fumbles, claws her way upwards, as she sees a faint light. She fights, fights, air, must have air!

And suddenly, her head is above water.

Nadia gasps and coughs and breathes. Feels the fresh air filling her lungs. The daylight makes her squint.

She looks around. She's at the very top of the big house. Water is pouring out around her, splashing down the roof.

She made it. She really made it! She cries with relief. She defeated her nightmare.

She pulls herself together. "All right, the worst part is over. But I still need to get down from here without breaking my neck."

Carefully, she climbs down the chimney. She can just reach the roof, but it's very slippery. As soon as she lets go of the chimney, she starts sliding.

Nadia screams and clambers for something to hold on to. But the roof is too steep. The gutter and the neck-breaking fall come rushing towards her.

Her hand catches the antenna. She stops with a yank and clings to the metal rod. That was a close call. The water gurgles beside her. Laughs at her.

Nadia just hangs on for a while. Gets her heart rate down, gets her strength back. At the gable of the house a large tree is leaning over the roof. If she could just get over there ...

It's doable, but she has to crawl a couple of meters to get there, and if she slips, it's going to be a free fall. She breathes deeply, sinks her nails into the tiles, and starts to make her way across the roof.

For a short second her foot slips and she's certain she's going to die, but she doesn't. She makes it. She reaches the branches of the tree and clings to them. With shaking arms and legs, she crawls from the roof and onto the tree. Then, she makes her way down. Slowly. Carefully.

And finally, she's standing on the lawn. She stumbles away from the house, but after a few steps, her body gives in and she falls to the ground, shaking, sobbing.

Nadia sniffles and looks up at the house. It's a crazy sight to behold. Behind every window the water is pressing. Furniture and stuff are floating weightlessly around. From the chimney, water is still spouting.

"I won," she whispers. "You didn't get me."

Nadia smiles. She stays seated on the grass. Doesn't have the strength to get up. She can't believe what she has just been through. It doesn't seem real. Maybe it isn't. Maybe it'll turn out to be another nightmare. She could wake up any minute now.

Yet, she has never felt more awake.

***

As a kid I would often play with the idea of what I would do if the house suddenly got filled with water and I couldn't get out. It was almost like a horror fantasy. The thought was both scary and fascinating. Of course, I knew it was silly. Stuff like that doesn't happen in real life.

But what if?

What *if* ...?

Lights Out

"This is the six o'clock news, good evening.

Top story today is of course the mysterious occurrence that shook the world. At 12:08 PM, the sun went out. The phenomenon lasted for nine minutes before the sun came back on and the daylight returned. It was not a solar eclipse, scientists agree, although no one has been able to come up with an explanation.

The occurrence has caused worldwide panic and chaos. Riots have struck several large cities, among them London, New York, Cairo and Beijing. Several hundred people have been reported dead or maimed so far.

We now go live to our reporter downtown, where the police are still fighting the unrest ..."

Mike is the one who comes up with the nickname. Mike is good at coming up with nicknames.

"Hey, Lights Out!" he shouts at Noah one day at recess.

Everyone in the schoolyard hears it and starts laughing. Noah feels embarrassed.

Since then, he has been known as Lights Out. But it's not his fault. He doesn't do it on purpose. Turn off the lights, that is. It just happens.

It began one night in winter.

Noah is on his way home from badminton. It's seven o'clock. The streetlights are on. Not many people in the street. People are home enjoying dinner. Noah strolls along the sidewalk, beanie pulled down, sports bag across his shoulder. He walks alternately in light and in darkness.

Poof!

Suddenly, the light disappears.

He looks up. The lamp above him has gone out.

That's weird, Noah thinks. *What are the odds it would happen exactly when I was below it?*

He walks on. Behind him, the lamp comes back on. Noah turns around and looks at it. Something must be wrong with the bulb.

He continues on his way. Just as he reaches the next lamppost—

Poof!

—it turns off, too.

Noah shakes his head. Perhaps something is wrong with the electricity on this street. But as he walks on, and the lamppost comes back on behind him, he starts getting nervous. What if the next lamppost turns off?

Noah cautiously walks on.

Poof!

Sure enough, the third lamppost turns off.

This time Noah decides to wait for the light to come back on. He stands there, arms crossed, patiently waiting. Two minutes. Five. Ten. The lamp doesn't turn on. Noah starts to freeze. Finally, he's sick of waiting, so he walks on.

The lamp turns on immediately. It really is like it was just waiting for him to go on. Exactly like the previous two.

Now, Noah speeds up. He doesn't like this. He walks fast along the sidewalk.

Poof!

The fourth lamppost goes out.

And turns back on behind him.

Poof!

There goes the fifth.

Turns back on behind him.

Noah is running now.

Poof!

The sixth.

Turns back on.

Poof!

Back on.

Poof!

Light.

Darkness.

Light.

Darkness.

Running as fast as he can. Sprinting.

Poof! Poof! Poof!

Finally, he reaches the house. His heart is pounding, he's sweating despite the cold weather. Now, it's over. Now, he's home.

He walks up to the house on shaky legs, and is just about to grab the handle, when he hears another

Poof!

and the lamp above the front door goes out. Noah is standing on the stairs in darkness. He hurries inside. No light in the hall. He finds the switch and flips it. Nothing happens. He flips it again. Still nothing.

Noah opens the door to the living room. Thankfully, the lights are on in here.

His mom is sitting at the piano playing. She looks up and smiles. "Hi, Noah. Did you have a nice time at practice?"

Noah doesn't answer. He hasn't taken off his shoes as he steps into the living room. At once, the light goes out. In return, the light in the hall turns on behind him.

"Oops," Mom says. "Must have been the lightbulb burning out."

"No," Noah hears himself saying. "It's me causing it."

Mom doesn't hear him. She calls for his dad. "Harry! The lightbulb is dead. Would you be a sweetheart and change it?"

"It's not the light bulb, Mom."

Mom looks at him. "What do you mean, Noah?"

"Watch."

He steps back out to the hall. The light comes back on in the living room, but turns off in the hall. Noah steps into the living room, and the opposite happens. No matter what room Noah is in, the light doesn't want to be there with him.

Mom gapes. Then, she laughs. "I don't believe it."

Dad enters the living room. "What's going on?"

"Look at this, Harry. Noah has a trick."

Noah shows dad his "trick."

"That's funny," Dad says. "It's got to be a faulty wire somewhere. Perhaps underneath the floorboards. Let me try, Noah."

Dad pushes him aside. It doesn't work when Dad tries to do it.

"It's not just the lights in here," Noah says, and tells them about the streetlamps.

Mom isn't laughing anymore. Dad scratches his hair.

"Try it with the lights in the kitchen, Noah."

Noah tries the kitchen. The bathroom. His own room.

The same thing happens everywhere. None of the lightbulbs want to give off light as long as Noah is in the room. None of the lightbulbs in the entire town, actually. Perhaps the entire world.

The doctor is baffled. Noah gets sent to specialists. They run a lot of tests. They find no answer.

Mom buys a gas lamp for Noah's room. If he has to get up to pee in the night, he has to turn on a candle.

Noah brings a note to school. The teacher explains his problem to the class. Mike, of course, laughs at him. The others look kind of uncertain. Like they don't really know what to make of him anymore.

Noah is terribly embarrassed. He hates his problem, or whatever it is. He wishes it would have never happened.

That is, until the day he finds out that he can actually control it.

It happens one evening when Noah is home alone.

He's sitting in his room, reading. It's a book about a superhero he found at the library. It's really exciting. He has only one chapter left, when the gas lamp suddenly burns out.

"Aw," Noah grunts.

Mom and Dad are at a concert, so Dad can't fill more gas on the lamp.

Noah gets up and brings the lamp with him to the garage. He doesn't even try to turn on the light—he has already gotten used to living in darkness. He knows Dad isn't fond of him touching the cylinder, but he has to finish the book. He fumbles with the valve, but can't get it to work.

"Guess I have to use a candle, then."

He goes to the living room, where Mom keeps the candles in the bottom drawer of the dresser. But the drawer is empty. Noah remembers that he used the last candle yesterday.

He sighs. Goes to his room again. Tries to read, but it's too dark. He looks out the window. The streetlights are on. He gets an idea. Maybe if he is careful to not get too close ...

He goes to put on his shoes and jacket. Brings the book to the sidewalk. Gets closer to the light. But just as the letters starts to become visible—

Poof!

Noah throws the book down on the pavement. "Give some goddamn light already! I'm sick of this!" He glares angrily up at the lamp. "Turn back on, you piece of crap! Turn on, I say!"

The lamp turns on.

Noah blinks in stunned amazement. He walks a little from one side to the other. Expects the lamp to turn off again. But it doesn't—it stays lit. He breaks into a smile. He looks to the next lamp. It could just be a coincidence. He has to test it.

Slowly, he walks to the lamp. It turns off as he comes close. Noah stops right beneath it. Points up at the lamp. "Turn on!" he commands.

And he is showered in light.

Noah claps his hands. It's fantastic! He can get the light back!

He turns towards the house. Dare he try it inside? Noah runs into the hall. The light, as usual, goes out.

"Turn on."

The lights come back on.

Noah laughs loudly. He runs to the living room. Turns on the light. Out into the kitchen. Turns it on. The bathroom. Turns on. His own room. Turns on, too.

Noah rejoices and throws himself onto the bed. Finally! It's finally over!

Or is it?

The lights still turn off whenever he enters a room. But now he can turn them back on. The thought gives him an idea.

He sits up and looks at the bulb in the ceiling.

"Turn off," he says.

Poof!

There is darkness.

"Turn on!"

There is light.

Noah is stunned. He tries it again and again.

On, off, on, off.

It works every time. It's magic!

***

The next day at school Noah demonstrates that the lights can be on, even though he's in the room.

The teacher smiles. "That's great, Noah. Perhaps, you are ... well again?"

"Sort of, I guess."

"What do you mean, 'sort of'?"

The whole class is staring at him. Noah feels uncomfortable. But he does it anyway. He looks up the lamps. "Off," he says.

The lights go out.

A whisper runs through the classroom.

"Back on," Noah says.

All the lights come back on.

"Wauw!" someone exclaims.

"Amazing," someone else says.

The teacher looks a bit frightened. He tries to smile. "That's ... that's a crazy trick, Noah."

"It's more like a superpower, really," Noah mumbles.

"Yeah, you could be the villain in a movie!" Mike shouts, jumping up. "Lights Out! That would be your name."

Noah glares at Mike. "I'm not the villain ..."

"Sure you are! You're trying to turn off all the lights in the entire world. That's your evil scheme! You want to lay the whole world in darkness."

"Shut up," Noah says.

Mike doesn't shut up. "But luckily, the hero Mega Mike comes to the rescue and saves the day as he stops you just in the nick of time …"

"That's enough, Mike!" the teacher demands. "Sit down and be quiet."

Mike laughs, but sits back down. Someone else is snickering, too. Noah's cheeks turn hot. Why is Mike always pestering him like that? Noah was actually proud of his ability. Now, he just feels stupid.

"All right," the teacher says. "Now that we have the lights back on, let's go on with the assignment from last time …"

Noah doesn't listen. He looks at Mike with a mean face. Mike just smiles stupidly back.

Noah gets an idea. He looks up and whispers: "Off," so low that no one hears him.

The light above Mike turns off.

Everyone looks at Mike. Even the teacher turns around.

"Looks like you're Lights Out now," Noah says.

Everybody laughs. This time, Mike is the embarrassed one.

***

It was a mistake to tease Mike.

At the last recess, Noah comes back into the classroom to find a note on his desk.

hi ligts out
u shood have never turned of the ligt above me
it made me vary angry
u will regret it
regards MEGA MIKE

At first Noah is frightened. But during the lesson something weird happens. His fear goes away. Instead he gets angry with Mike. *He* was the one who started it. And he always thinks he is the toughest. But Noah will show him. He writes a note:

Hello Mini Mike
You should probably learn to spell before trying to threaten someone.
And I'm not scared of you. You're too fat to catch me anyway.
Sincerely, Lights Out

Noah looks at the letter. Without even thinking about it, he signed it as Lights Out. He's actually beginning to like the name. It sounds cool. A bit dangerous. He crumbles up the note and throws it to Mike while the teacher isn't looking.

Mike catches the paper ball, grinning at Noah. He's probably expecting the letter to say "sorry" or "please don't hurt me" or "I promise never to do it again."

As Mike reads the letter, something happens to his face. It changes color. Finally, Mike looks at Noah with eyes full of lightning. He puts a finger to his throat and slowly drags it across. The message is unambiguous.

Noah looks up to the light. *On, off, on, off,* he thinks. The light blinks.

The others look at Mike and start snickering. Mike looks around, confused.

Just as the teacher turns around, Noah stops blinking the light. "What's so funny?" the teacher asks.

Mike stands up and points to Noah. "You're dead, Lights Out!"

"Mike!" the teacher shouts. "I won't have talk like that. Get out of here, and don't come back in!"

Mike grabs his bag and slowly exists the classroom without taking his eyes off of Noah. He slams the door behind him.

The teacher looks at Noah. "What was that all about, Noah?"

Noah looks innocent. "I have no idea."

Of course, the teacher believes him. Noah has never been in trouble before. So, the lesson goes on.

Noah feels excitement. His superpower is growing; this time, he turned the lights on and off using only his thoughts!

***

The lesson is over way too soon.

When the bell has chimed, Noah waits for everyone else to leave. Then, he sneaks out into the hall. Mike is nowhere in sight. The school seems empty. Everyone has gone home. Noah runs to the exit.

Mike is standing right on the other side of the glass door. He smiles at Noah.

Noah turns to run to the other exit. But down the hall comes Tommy. He is in the grade above Noah, and he is Mike's best friend.

"Hi, Noah," Tommy smiles. "I just need to talk to you really quick."

Noah doesn't buy it. He turns and sprints down the hall.

Tommy is in pursuit. Noah knows that he can't outrun Tommy. So, he turns and enters a classroom. It's empty, and there is no lock on the door. Tommy is right behind him. Noah zigzags between the desks, reaches the window and pulls it open.

"Where do you think you're going?"

Tommy grabs the back of his shirt.

"No, let go off me!"

But Tommy is too strong. He laughs and shouts: "Mike! I got him!"

Noah thinks fast. He looks up at the ceiling. The lights turn on.

Tommy turns to see who hit the switch. In that instant, Noah gives him a hard shove. Tommy tumbles into a desk. Noah climbs up and jumps out of the window. He lands hard on the pavement.

"Lights Out!" Mike shouts, as he comes running across the yard. "You're not getting off that easy!"

Noah runs to the cellar stairs, jumps down the steps and into the bicycle cellar. It's a long, cool room lit up by a row of neon tubes. There are almost no bikes here now.

"Tommy!" Mike shouts somewhere behind him. "He's in the cellar! Cover the other exit!"

Noah gets behind one of the pillars carrying the ceiling.

From one end he can hear Mike panting. From the other Tommy's steps are coming closer.

"Do you see him?" Mike asks. His voice echoes.

"Nah. But he hasn't passed me, so he's got to be still down here."

"He's hiding. That little coward."

The boys are blocking both exists. Noah is trapped between them, and they are coming closer.

"Keep close watch," Mike says. "He's fast." Then, he begins to sing. "Oh, Noooooa ... come out, come out, whereever you are!"

Noah gets a crazy idea. He covers his mouth with his palm, so his voice gets distorted, and says loudly: "I am not Noah. I am Lights Out!"

Simultaneously, he makes all the lights go out. The cellar is suddenly pitch black.

"What ... what the fuck?" Tommy exclaims. "What happened? Who did that?"

"It was just him," Mike says. "Don't get fooled."

Noah goes on in the fake voice: "I am the one who decides when there is ... light!" The lights come back on in a flash. "And when there is ... darkness!" The lights tuns off once more.

"Holy crap!" Tommy shouts. "How is he doing that? That's goddamn witchcraft or something ..."

"It's just a silly trick he learned," Mike says. But he also sounds a bit shaken up. "Listen carefully. He'll probably try and use the darkness to escape."

But Noah has other plans. He sneaks out into the middle of the hall. He positions himself with feet apart and bowed head. Like a superhero would be standing. Then, he turns on the light—but only the one right above his own head. He can hear Tommy gasp.

"Do you morons really think you can catch me?" Noah asks. "Then come on. I'm right here."

"Get him!" Mike shouts.

Noah can't see them in the darkness. But their running steps are coming rapidly closer from both sides. Noah waits until they come into the light. Then, he turns off the light and jumps aside.

A loud noise as Tommy and Mike collide.

"Ouch, damnit!" Tommy grunts. "You knocked the wind out of me ..."

"I got him!" Mike howls.

"That's me, you idiot! Let go!"

"Fuck! Where did he go?"

"How should I know? I can't see shit. Ooh, it fucking hurts ..."

"You think you are hurting? You almost broke my nose."

While they argue, Noah sneaks right past them and runs for the exit. As he reaches the stairs, he can't help himself. He turns on the light above him.

"Hey!" he calls. "Are you coming or what?"

"There he is!" Tommy shouts.

"Get him!" Mike shrieks.

Noah runs out, shuts the door and turns the lock. He runs up the stairs, across the schoolyard to the other end of the cellar. He slams this door too, and locks it. His heart is pounding wildly, but he is also smiling.

He runs all the way home.

***

When Noah comes to school the next day, the whole place is upside down. Many of the students are outside in the yard. Everyone is whispering and darting nervous glances. A group of teachers are talking to each other with very serious faces.

Noah asks Gaby what's going on.

"You didn't hear?" she says. "It's Mike. Him and Tommy from sixth grade was found in the bicycle cellar this morning. They have been down there all night."

Noah tries hard not to smile. "Oh. How did that happen?"

Gaby shrugs. "Someone must've locked them in. It's really crazy. The police have been looking for them all night. When the janitor found them this morning, they were completely hoarse from screaming for help. Mike had a juice box or something in his bag. That's the only thing they've had to drink for almost twenty hours."

Noah blinks. He didn't even consider that. "So ... where are they now?"

"At the hospital. Didn't you see the ambulance? It just left a couple of minutes ago."

"No, I ... didn't see it." Noah clears his throat. "Uhm ... did they say anything about ... who might have done it?"

"No, they wouldn't say. The teachers are probably discussing it right now. But I don't think they have any suspects."

Noah feels kind of relieved, but he's still worried. Things could have gone really badly. And why haven't Mike or Tommy told on him? Is it because they are afraid to do so? Afraid of him? Maybe. But he thinks it more likely the bullies just don't want to involve the teachers. They want Noah all to themselves.

Noah feels his throat tightening. This time, Mike will surely kill him.

Noah clenches his hands into fists. He can't let the fear take him over now. He has got to stay tough. He has a superpower. Mike can't bully him any longer.

He just needs to make a plan for what he'll do when Mike returns for his revenge.

***

The next day is Saturday, so Noah has the whole weekend to prepare. He starts practicing, training his superpower.

He sits in his room turning the lamp on and off faster and faster. By the end it's blinking so fast that it's almost imperceptible.

If he concentrates, he can turn on the ceiling light and turn off the desk light simultaneously.

That evening Noah is playing badminton. When he comes out to his bike, it's become dark. The football field next to the sports center is filled with people. The local team is playing against the neighboring team. The large spotlights are on.

Noah looks up at them. They are hands down the biggest lamps he has ever seen. He doesn't know if can turn them off. He squints his eyes.

Poof!

The spotlights turn off. All four of them. The football field goes dark. The players stop. The referee blows his whistle. The crowd boos.

Noah turns on the spotlights again and hurries towards his bike. No one notices him.

It's Sunday night. Noah is standing on the sidewalk outside the house.

How many lights can I turn off at once?

He can see seven streetlights in both directions. Fourteen total. He strives. All fourteen turn off. He lights them up again and smiles.

He can do even more. He can feel it.

So, he rides his bike to the hill outside town. From here he has a clear view over most of the houses. There are lights in almost all the windows. Plus the streetlights and the cars driving around. All in all, he's probably looking at more than a thousand lights.

"All right," Noah whispers. "I can do it. I'm Lights Out." He lifts his arms and shouts: "*Off!*"

The town immediately turns dark. Like someone just pulled a gigantic plug.

Noah feels goose bumps all over.

Then, he hears the sounds. A car honking. Someone shouting. Screaming brakes.

Noah quickly turns the town's lights back on.

He snickers to himself as he rides home.

***

Mom and Dad meet him as he enters the living room. Their faces are grave.

"Where were you?" Dad asks.

"Just out for a bike ride."

"The lights went out while you were gone," Mom says. "Do you know anything about that?"

Noah shrugs. "I wasn't home. How could I have done it?"

"It wasn't just our house," Dad says. "The whole town went dark."

Noah considers if it would be wise to confess. "It was probably a power failure," he says.

"That's what they say on TV," Mom says. "But they also said it was very peculiar, because it was only the lights that went out. Not the power. And it only lasted a couple of seconds."

Noah says nothing.

"Come with us, please, Noah," Dad says.

They go to sit down on the couch. Noah is getting kind of nervous. He has never seen his parents like this before.

"We know that you have … learned to manage your problem," Mom begins.

"It's not a problem, Mom. It's a superpower."

Mom smiles in a weird way. "All right. Anyway, you can decide if the lights should turn off or not, when you enter a room. You showed us."

"I can do even more," Noah says proudly. "I can turn it on and off, super quick, using only my mind. Look."

He doesn't even need to look up to make the ceiling lamp blink.

"That's nice," Dad says. "But please stop, Noah. It's not good for the bulb."

Noah stops.

Mom leans her head to the side. "Are you sure that you didn't cause the lights to go out all over town, Noah?"

"Perhaps it was me," Noah admits hesitantly. "But so what if it was? I turned it on again instantly."

"Not instantly enough," Dad says. "There were three traffic accidents. A man fell down the stairs. A lady cut her finger with a knife. They said so on TV. No one was seriously hurt, but that could easily have been the case."

"We're not angry with you," Mom says. "But you can't go around turning the lights off for other people. It's dangerous."

"All right," he mumbles. "I won't do it anymore."

"Of course, it's just until we find out what's wrong with you," Dad says. "Once the doctors find a cure, they can treat it, and everything will go back to—"

"I don't want them to treat it," Noah exclaims. "It's not something that needs to be cured. It's a superpower. I told you guys already."

Mom and Dad look at each other. Noah notices something in their eyes. It's fear. *Are they afraid of my superpower? Or are they afraid of me?*

Noah suddenly doesn't feel like talking anymore. He gets up and runs to his room.

Mom and Dad don't get it. Noah *needs* his superpower. Without it, Mike will kill him. He needs to turn off lights. He's Lights Out.

Noah spends the entire night brooding. How can he use his superpower to protect himself from Mike?

He thinks about the man who fell down the stairs. Maybe he can make Mike do the same? Of course, he doesn't want him to get hurt, just a few bruises maybe. That way, he will get too scared to come after Noah.

But that idea requires quite a bit of planning. For instance, they need to be in a room with a staircase but no windows or at least very dark curtains. If it's not completely dark, it won't work.

But how will he lure Mike into such a room? He will obviously get suspicious.

Noah lies awake pondering. No matter what idea he comes up with, the problem is always that it can't be during the day, because the sunlight will—

Noah sits up abruptly.

The sun! Of course.

He grabs his computer and reads about the sun on the Internet. It's a burning ball of gas, the biggest light source in the solar system. It's so big, that Earth is a grain of sand in comparison. It's so far away, that it takes the light eight minutes and twenty seconds to reach Earth. The sun provides not only light but also heat. Without it, the Earth would become cold. Plants and animals would die. The oceans would freeze over. Humanity would become extinct.

But what if it only gets turned off for a second? That probably wouldn't cause any problems.

Now he knows how to scare off Mike for good.

***

Next day Mike comes to school, but he doesn't look at Noah. He pretends like nothing has happened. But Noah knows he hasn't forgotten.

It's almost like the other students can sense the bad blood between Noah and Mike. There is a rumor running around that it was Noah who locked Mike in the cellar. Everyone darts nervous glances after him.

At recess, Noah finds Mike in the schoolyard and goes up to him. He taps him on the shoulder.

Mike turns around, making his eyes small. "What do you want?"

"I want to tell you where our final stand should take place."

"Our final stand?"

"Yes."

"And where might that be?"

"Behind the school. On the lawn by the hang glider. At twelve o'clock."

"I see. And what will happen then?"

Noah smiles. "You get to beat me up. If you can catch me, that is."

Mike sneers. "You'll just tell on me. You'll make sure the teachers are there, so I'll get in trouble."

"No. I promise the teachers won't be there. It will only be you and me. Lights Out against Mega Mike."

Mike mulls it over. "And you're not going to cheat? You won't use that sneaky trick of yours?"

Noah shrugs. "How could I? We will be outdoors at high noon."

That makes Mike smile with malice. "All right. I'll meet you for our final stand. But don't forget that you asked for it."

***

As soon as the bell rings for the twelve-o'clock recess, Noah runs to the playground. The rumor has spread. Already a crowd has formed by the hang glider.

Noah waits patiently in the sunshine.

Two minutes later, Mike shows up. He rubs his knuckles, as if he is warming them up. The boys stand opposite from each other on the grass.

"You all know me," Noah says loud enough for everyone to hear. "But my name is no longer Noah. From this day on, I shall be called Lights Out. I will fight my nemesis, Mega Mike." He looks around at the crowd. "Prepare yourselves, for in a moment, I will do something that has never been done before. I will turn off the biggest light in the whole world ... the sun!"

There is a gasp. Someone whispers. A small girl starts crying and runs away.

Noah stares at Mike. His enemy seems nervous, but keeps his cool. Noah points to the sky and shouts: "*Off!*"

Everyone holds their breath. No one moves. Even Mike glances nervously upwards.

But nothing happens. The sun shines on.

"*Off!*" Noah yells again. "I command you to turn off! I am Lights Out! You will obey me!"

The sun doesn't obey. Noah feels a pang of panic. *No, it can't be. Why doesn't it turn off?*

Someone laughs. The crowd starts cheering.

Noah sees Mike coming towards him. He smiles grimly. "It's my turn now, Lights Out."

Noah has no other choice but to flee. He runs around the hang glider. Mike is right behind him. The crowd is shouting excitedly. Noah manages to hold off Mike for some minutes. But Mike is determined to get his revenge, so he keeps up the chase. The boys are panting and sweating.

Suddenly, Noah slips in the grass.

Mike immediately seizes the opportunity and pushes him onto his back. He crouches down on top of Noah and strikes at his head. Noah moves his head, dodges the punches and tries to push Mike off of him. But Mike is too heavy, and he keeps throwing the punches.

"Take that, Lights Out! And that! And that!"

The punches are raining down over Noah. It's all he can do to not get hit, but some of the punches connect to his forehead, his chin, his nose. It hurts. He can taste blood.

"Did you have enough?" Mike pants angrily. "Do you surrender?"

"Never," Noah hisses. He can't believe the words are coming from his mouth. But he can't surrender. He is Lights Out.

Mike keeps pounding him.

And suddenly, it happens.

Noah's eyes are closed, so he doesn't see it happen. But Mike stops punching. Gasps and shrieks around them.

Noah opens his eyes, but he can't see anything. It's pitch darkness.

Mike gets to his feet. "What ... what happened?"

Noah sits up and looks around. Everything has become night. The other students are vague shadows. The sky is black. The sun is turned off.

Mike stares at him. "It was you ... you're a freak! You're a monster!" He runs away.

Noah realizes what has happened. *Damnit! I forgot about the eight minutes and twenty seconds delay.*

He gets up and wipes the blood from his nose. All around him, scared eyes are watching him. A boy steps forward. "Could you please turn the sun back on, Mr. Lights Out?"

"What? Oh, yes, sure." Noah points to the sky. "Turn back on! I command you!" Nothing happens. Noah looks to the boy and mumbles: "It'll just be eight minutes and twenty seconds."

Noah suddenly recalls the things he read about. Oceans freezing over. Animals and plants dying. Humanity becoming extinct.

He glances up at the black sky.

It'll only be darkness for nine minutes. Nine minutes without the sun can't cause any real damage. Can it?

***

I know this story isn't hardcore horror. It's more like something from *The Twilight Zone*. Or maybe a dark superhero story. But I really liked the premise, and I think it's certainly got an eerie atmosphere.

The inspiration for it came one night, as I was out walking. It was January and the sun had already set. Suddenly, the streetlight turned off right above me. I got a pretty good scare. Of course, I knew it was just a coincidence. But I couldn't help but ask myself: What if the next one also turns off as I'm right below it? It didn't do so. But the thought gave me the idea for *Lights Out*.

I hope you read the story with the lights on.

Whiskers

Alvin runs through the forest as fast as he can, panting and heaving, tripping over a heap, getting back up, pushing away branches. He has no idea where he is going, he just wants to get away. His dad will never see him again.

Alvin hates his dad. He has done so for a long time; perhaps forever; or perhaps since Mom left. Alvin was only four years old back then, and he barely remembers her anymore. All he really recalls are the fights, the screaming, and his dad telling her to leave if she didn't like it here—until one day, she left. Alvin hasn't seen or heard from her since.

Or maybe Alvin's hatred didn't really start until Dad dragged him out to live in the woods, away from all his friends, away from everything he knew.

Yet only now, as he runs through the forest, tears streaming from his eyes, does Alvin realize just how deeply he truly hates his dad.

Because Dad gave Rocky away.

Rocky is Alvin's best friend, his only friend, really. He is a German shepherd, three years old. Alvin has had him since he was just a puppy. He found him in the woods one rainy day, all soaked and whining. Alvin brought him home and dried him with a towel. The puppy had no collar and no name tag. The nearest neighbors lived miles away, and none of them knew anything about a lost puppy.

As he couldn't find the owner, and since no one seemed to be looking for him, Alvin decided to keep the puppy. Dad wasn't happy about it.

"I bet it has all kinds of bugs," he grunted. "Or maybe there's something wrong with its head. That's probably why the owner got rid of it."

The puppy bared its teeth and growled at him, as though it understood what he said.

"Can I keep him then?" Alvin said.

Dad pointed at him. "I don't want anything to do with it. You clean up after it if it shits on the floor. And it's your job feeding it and all."

Alvin nodded eagerly. "Sure."

And for three years he has taken care of Rocky. He didn't have any bugs, nothing was wrong with his head. In fact, he turned out to be a big, strong and healthy dog. And now ...

Alvin trips over a log and falls to his knees, pine needles stinging his palms. He stays down, heaving and sobbing. Wiping the tears away from his eyes, he sees a print in the soft ground. It's from a paw. It could be from Rocky—he loved to roam the forest and would often go for a walk on his own—if fact, it almost certainly was Rocky's print, because what else could have made a print that size? There were no wolves in this part of the land.

The thought that Rocky has walked past here makes Alvin cry even harder. He jumps to his feet and starts running again.

Dad never grew to like Rocky, and the dislike was obviously mutual.

Rocky would growl in a low tone whenever Dad entered the room. He jumped out of the way if Dad ever tried to touch him, and he protected Alvin whenever Dad got mad and wanted to punish him.

It happened for the first time only a few months after Rocky came to the house. One day as Alvin was fetching firewood from the shed, a log fell from the overfilled basket just as he carried it across the living room and made a large dent in the floorboards.

Dad heard it from the kitchen and came stomping in, a mug of coffee still in his hand. He glared at Alvin like he was a criminal, then looked down at the dent. "What the hell? You goddamn moron! Will you look at my floor!"

Rocky was lying on the couch, still only a large puppy, but already big and leggy—and he had just gotten his molars, which he now displayed in an ominous growl.

"It was an accident," Alvin sighed, putting down the basket. "It's too heavy for me, I told you I can't carry it."

"Oh, so now it's my fault?" Dad asked loudly, stepping closer. "Because I ask you to help out a little?"

"No, I'm just saying—"

"You're a man, aren't you? Or are you a little girl? Can't you even carry a little firewood without dropping it all over the house?"

"Stop calling me names!" Alvin demanded. "Or you can carry your own stupid firewood."

Dad's eyes grew dangerously narrow. "What did you say to me?"

"Nothing," Alvin scuffed, trying to walk past him to get out of the room, but Dad cut him off.

"You're not leaving," he said, putting down his mug and pointing down to the floor. "Give me that log."

"Why?"

"Just give it to me."

Alvin could see something in his dad's eyes. Something he didn't like at all. He glanced over at Rocky. The dog had laid back its ears, and the eyes were fixed on him, shining brightly, very alert, like they were saying: *Go on, Alvin. Do it. I'll make sure he doesn't try anything.*

So Alvin bent down, picked up the log and handed it to his dad.

Dad took it and turned it over, studied it intently. "You know my granddad built this house," he said conversationally.

"Yes, you've told—"

"Shut your mouth. He built it with his own bare hands, and he lived here for all his life. Chopped his own wood, lived off of pheasants and rabbits he would shoot in the forest. My father was born here, and he lived here too for his whole life. Now that he's gone, *I* live here, and when *I'm* gone ..." Dad pointed the log at Alvin. "*You'll* live here."

"Never," Alvin said, crossing his arms. "I'm moving as soon as I turn eighteen."

To his surprise, Dad smiled. "Oh, you are?"

"Yes, I am."

"Eighteen, you say? Well, that gives me four years to change your mind."

"I'm not changing my mind," Alvin said stubbornly, his heart pounding now. "I hate living out here."

"That may be the case, but as long as you live here, you will still treat this house with respect."

Without any warning, Dad raised the log to strike him. Alvin gave a yelp and held up his arms.

But the log never connected.

Rocky came bolting through the air, catching the log between his teeth mid-swing, and ripped it out of Dad's hand. Then he landed on the floor and dropped the piece of wood with a clunk, getting in front of Alvin, staring defiantly up at Dad, daring him to try another move.

Dad stepped backwards a few feet, looking exactly as dumbfounded as Alvin felt. "What ... what the hell got into that beast? He can't go charging at people like that ... You didn't raise him properly!"

"Yes, I did," Alvin heard himself say, his whole body tingling with a mixture of excitement, shock and relief.

Dad stared from Alvin to Rocky for a second or two, then he bellowed loudly enough to make spit fly from his mouth: "You get that filthy mutt under control, you hear me? Or I swear I'll get rid of him!" Turning on his heel, Dad then proceeded to march out of the living room, slamming the door behind him.

Alvin stared after him until he felt Rocky licking his hand. Alvin looked down and smiled, still shaking all over. "Thank you, buddy," he whispered.

Since that day, Dad never again tried to lay a finger on Alvin. Whenever he got in a bad temper, Rocky would be there, watching from the sideline, ready to intervene within a split-second, which caused his Dad to swear to Alvin several times how he would soon be getting rid of the dog. But he never made good on his threat.

Not until today.

When Alvin got home from school earlier, he wasn't greeted by the familiar, happy barking, and Rocky wasn't lying on the porch, waiting for him, as he usually was.

Alvin searched through the house, but found nothing except—curiously—Rocky's collar, thrown casually on Alvin's bed, and a handful of coins on his pillow. He ran out to the shed—already a quickly growing fear in the pit of his stomach—and found his dad busy chopping wood.

"Where's Rocky?" he asked immediately.

Dad only glanced at him, the lit cigarette bobbing slightly between his lips.

"Where is Rocky?" Alvin shouted.

"I gave it away."

The breath was sucked out of Alvin's mouth. Even though he had suspected it, he still can't believe what he had just heard. "You did ... *what*?"

"I gave it away," Dad said again. "Sold it, actually. To some guy upstate. He came for it while you were at school. I got two hundred bucks for him. It's on your bed, you can keep it. Spend them on whatever you like."

Everything in Alvin had turned to white-hot stone. "I don't want two hundred bucks," he heard himself say, his voice trembling with rage. "I want Rocky."

He doesn't really remember the following conversation, except for himself screaming and begging and threatening. Urging his dad to call the guy and get Rocky back.

But it was too late. The guy had left no name or number. And Rocky was already hundreds of miles away.

"It wasn't right in the head anyway, that damn mutt," Alvin recalls his dad saying, as he continued chopping. "You'll see, in a week you'll have forgotten about it."

Alvin comes into a clearing where he stops and heaves for breath. He puts down the bag for a short rest. In it are his most essential things. A couple of sandwiches, some clothes, the two hundred dollars and Rocky's collar.

He looks around, has no idea which direction to go. The forest seems to stretch out endlessly all around him. His only plan is to find Rocky. He will get back him back if it's the last thing he does.

He needs to find a way to get upstate, but first he needs to get out of the goddamn forest. His legs are shaking with exhaustion. How long has he been running? An hour, maybe. And yet he doesn't seem any closer to reaching the edge of the forest—it's like the place is bewitched and doesn't want to let him leave.

Alvin needs a rest, so he sits down on a heap, wiping the sweat from his forehead.

It's fall, and the air is chilly, the ground is covered with leaves in rusty colors, and most of the trees are naked.

A rifle shot echoes from somewhere far away. Alvin is quite used to the sound by now; it's hunting season, and the neighbors are hunting for deer in the forest.

Alvin looks up at the grey sky overhead and thinks about Rocky and where he might be right now.

"Don't worry, buddy," he whispers. "I'll see you again soon, I swear to you."

He can't cry anymore; there are no more tears. Instead, he feels completely drained. So he slumps down on his back and closes his eyes.

A noise calls him back. Alvin blinks and sits up straight.

It's dark around him, as the night has fallen on the forest, glittering dew covers everything, and the coldness has crept into his bones.

"Hello?" he croaks, clearing his throat. "Is anyone here?"

His voice is swallowed up by the silence of the forest. Not even the slightest wind is blowing, no leaves are stirring.

So what made the noise he just heard?

Alvin gets to his feet with difficulty, every muscle in his legs feels cold and hard. He bends down to pick up his bag, when he hears the noise once more and spins around.

A woman comes striding into the clearing. She looks tiny and frail, all dressed in grey, her hair hidden under a scarf and her face pale in the darkness.

"Who ... who are you?" Alvin asks.

"My name is Syphina," the woman creaks, her voice thin and rusty. "I'm a witch."

Alvin suddenly realizes he is dreaming, and immediately his fear subsides. He gives himself a painful pinch on the arm—but it doesn't wake him up.

The woman stops a few paces from him, tilting her head to the side. "Your name is Alvin. You've come because you seek something."

"Yeah," he mutters. "But how do you know?"

The woman looks up at the sky, which is hidden by clouds, only a faint greyish light coming down over the forest, but just enough for Alvin to make out the woman's features. She is very old, her skin creased like cracked concrete.

"I can help you," she says, looking once more at Alvin. "I can help you find what you seek. But we must hurry; it's almost midnight."

"What happens at midnight?" he asks.

"You'll see. Come on." She waves impatiently at him with a hooklike hand. "Come on now, boy! Get your bag."

Alvin obeys, picks up his bag and starts following the witch. She leads him out of the clearing in the direction she came from. Even though she must be at least a hundred years old, Alvin almost has to run to keep up with her. She darts in and out between the trees, disappearing for a moment, only to reappear in the next instance. Clearly she is very used to faring in the forest.

They suddenly reach another clearing—or is it the same one? Alvin thinks it just might be.

The witch takes her place in the middle and looks up. "Good," she mutters. "The clouds are behaving themselves. Good."

Alvin can make out a few cracks in the clouds, a pale moonlight protruding.

"Come on over here," she demands.

Alvin steps a little closer.

"Stand here," she says, grabbing his shoulders with her tiny, strong hands. "Right here. And you need to keep the money ready."

"The money?"

"Yes, a coin. How else are you going to make the wish? Tell me, have you no idea how a wishing well works, boy? Haven't you ever read a fairy tale?"

"Uhm ... yeah, I have. But I don't see any well ..."

"Just find a coin."

Alvin unzips his bag, rummaging around for his purse.

"The well is only visible in the light from the full moon," the witch explains, stepping behind him. "As soon as you see it, make your wish, and then throw in the coin. You might only have a few seconds, so be quick. Once the clouds block the moonlight again, your chance will be lost forever."

Alvin finds his purse and pulls out a dime. He gets to his feet and is just about to turn around to ask the witch if a dime will do or if he needs to use another coin, when she shrieks: "*No!*" and grabs him by the neck, turning his head forward again. "Don't look at me while the moonlight hits me!" She lowers her voice to a hoarse whisper. "Look. Here it comes ..."

Alvin looks straight ahead as the silvery moonlight shines down brightly on the clearing, causing the trees to throw sharp shadows. And right in front of him an old well materializes.

Prompted by a prod in his back from the witch, Alvin steps forward, puts his hands on the old, mossy bricks and looks down into the well. He can just make out the water, glinting black far below.

"Make your wish," the witch whispers from behind.

"I wish ... I wish Rocky will return to me. I wish he will protect me again." Alvin glances nervously sideways, not daring to look all the way over his shoulder. "There. I said it."

"Now, the coin," the witch urges.

Alvin holds out the dime and drops it. A tiny *plim!* sounds as it hits the water, causing ripples in the surface.

Then the moonlight starts to fade, and the darkness comes creeping back. The well disappears before Alvin's eyes, and the clearing is once again empty.

It's over. Whatever just happened, it's over.

Alvin turns around. "Thank you for—"

But the witch is gone. Alvin is alone.

***

He sits up and looks around, blinking.

He is still in the clearing, sitting on the ground, resting against the heap. It's dark all around him except for a pale stream of moonlight shining down from above, and he is shaking from the cold.

There are no signs of the witch or the well.

"It was all just a dream," he mutters, feeling both relieved and disappointed.

Or was it? a thought whispers in his mind.

Just to be sure, Alvin finds his purse and checks it. There is a dime missing. He counted the money before he left home.

Maybe it wasn't just a dream? ... Don't be stupid, of course it was. You just counted the money wrong.

Alvin becomes aware how quiet the forest suddenly is. And how dark. It's like the trees are holding their breath while watching him.

He gets up and puts on his bag. For some strange reason, Alvin doesn't feel like running away anymore. He still hates his dad, but something tells him he doesn't need to go looking for Rocky. He feels assured things will work out on their own accord. Rocky will come back to him. He just knows it.

Alvin starts walking home.

He knows it was just a dream, but he can't help but feel hopeful in spite of himself. What if his wish has been granted? What if Rocky really will come home?

Dad hasn't even noticed Alvin was gone most of the night. When he finally gets home, sunrise is only an hour away, and he simply sneaks in through the window and crawls into bed.

Every day as Alvin runs home from the school bus, he listens intently for the familiar barking, but he doesn't hear it, and the porch remains empty.

Alvin's hope fades a little.

After a week with no sign of Rocky, he finally realizes his dog isn't coming back. And without a name or an address, he will never be able to find him. The terrible truth sinks in: he will never see his buddy again.

Alvin submerges into deep sorrow. He can't eat, can't sleep, can't think. He doesn't go to school, just lies in bed all day, staring at nothing, clutching Rocky's collar.

At first, his dad gets angry. "If you think you're just going to lie around like that," he begins, until he sees Alvin's face. Then he falls quiet, leaves the room and closes the door gently behind him. After that, he doesn't say anything to Alvin.

Alvin thinks about Rocky constantly. All the funny little habits. Like how he would paw the door when he needed to go out for a pee. Or how he loved sniffing about in the forest. How he would sometimes howl when Alvin left for school, and how he barked from joy when he saw him again.

Days and nights go by. Alvin doesn't care. The world can go on without him.

Then, something happens which calls Alvin out of his sorrow.

***

One morning he feels something under his nose and goes to check it in the bathroom mirror. He finds four or five grey hairs pointing to each side.

Alvin feels a mild surprise. He has grown a moustache, and it has apparently happened over night, although it's already half an inch long. But the hairs don't really look like an ordinary beard, more like—

The door opens behind him, and Dad comes in. "Awakened from the dead, have we?"

Alvin turns around.

Dad's expression changes. "What the hell? You've grown a moustache, boy." He pats Alvin hard on the shoulder. "You're becoming a man. Move, will you? I gotta take a leak."

Alvin leaves the bathroom without a word. He suddenly feels an urge for fresh air, so he goes out to the porch. It has been raining all night, and everything is still moist with droplets. Alvin breathes deeply through his nose. It's like the forest smells more vibrant than usual; he can almost smell the ground, the moss, even the bark of the trees.

Alvin isn't quite sure why, but he feels better inside, almost reborn, and he is suddenly in the mood for a walk. He walks for an hour, trudging along the paths, just taking in all the perceptions of the forest, the birds singing, the breeze stirring, the trees smelling.

Alvin speeds up. He feels like moving faster. He starts running. Then sprinting. He races through the forest at enormous speed, jumping over heaps, dodging between the trees, slipping through shrubbery.

And suddenly, he is standing in front of the house again. He stops, panting with surprise. He has found his way home without even realizing it. He licks the sweat off his upper lip, his tongue touching the new hairs. They feel a little longer than he remembers. But of course, that can't be.

Or maybe it can.

The hairs turn out to be growing at an incredible speed. The next morning they are two inches long. They are light grey, almost transparent, and are now reaching across his cheeks. There are eight on the left, nine on the right. It looks silly, so Alvin cuts them off before going to school.

But as he wakes up the following morning, the hairs are back, almost full length once more.

And as Alvin stares at his own, groggy reflection in the bathroom mirror, he finally admits to himself what the hairs really are.

Whiskers.

* * *

Alvin notices other small changes in his body during the next couple of days.

His fingernails become narrower and thicker. His tongue becomes longer, as do his ears. The hair on his head turns thicker and bushier, and his voice sounds deeper.

It's not big changes, not enough for others to notice. Except for the whiskers, of course, as they are now five inches long and move whenever he talks.

But it's not only Alvin's appearance which changes. He also starts acting differently. He will scratch himself behind his ears more often, and when he has an itch somewhere, he will use his teeth to scratch it. Before going to bed, he turns around a couple of times, for no apparent reason. And most of his time he spends in the forest, running around, searching for interesting odors, chasing for mice and squirrels.

His senses are much more acute than he has ever felt. He can hear pine needles falling to the ground. He can smell a bird dropping several yards away. And he can hear far more rifle shots than usual.

One day, Alvin puts on Rocky's collar. He is not sure why, he just feels like it, and the feeling of the leather around his neck is oddly pleasing, so he starts wearing the collar all the time—but of course he hides it underneath his shirt collar, so no one notices.

Alvin's appetite has returned with a vengeance. One evening, as he and Dad are eating dinner, Alvin chows down the pork chops without using either his fork or his knife. When he is done, he licks his fingers clean, then the plate too, and then he stares hungrily at Dad's unfinished meal.

Dad puts down his fork. "All right, what is it with you?"

Alvin looks at him. "What do you mean?"

"You look ... different somehow. Did you cut your hair?"

Alvin shakes his head and stares at the pork chops on Dad's plate.

"Then was is it? Have you hit puberty?"

"How should I know? Are you going to finish that?"

Dad glances down at his plate, then mutters something and shoves it across the table to Alvin, who immediately throws himself at the pork chops.

He doesn't notice Dad staring at him.

He doesn't notice the eager growling coming from his own throat, either.

***

Later that same evening, as the sun has gone down, Alvin wants to go for a walk. He goes to the hall, but doesn't put on his jacket, as the cold outside doesn't seem to bother him anymore. Likewise he has stopped wearing both socks and shoes—they simply feel wrong on his feet, where his toenails have grown dark and pointy.

"Alvin!"

He spins around, staring at his dad, who has come out from the living room and is now staring back at him.

"What the hell are you doing?"

"What do you mean?" Alvin grunts annoyed.

"You're scratching at the damn door."

Alvin suddenly realizes that he was in fact scratching the door with his fingernails. "I ... I just want to go for a walk," he mutters, feeling oddly embarrassed.

"Then why don't you just open the goddamn door?"

Alvin stares at the knob, hesitating for a moment before closing his hand around it and turning it. He darts a fleeting glance at his dad, mumbling: "Sorry, I just ... forgot how to open it."

Dad steps up behind him, shoves the door shut and grabs Alvin's arm, pulling him into the living room.

"What are you doing? Let go of me!" He rips himself loose, backing away while showing his teeth. "Don't touch me."

Dad is breathing heavy and is apparently just about to say something, when he notices the collar around Alvin's neck, which is peeking out from under the shirt collar. "What the hell is that? Are you ... are you wearing the dog's collar?"

Alvin pushes the collar inside his shirt without saying anything.

"Look, we need to have a talk, Alvin," his dad says, sounding surprisingly reasonable—he even uses Alvin's name for a change. "I don't know what on earth has gotten into you, but it ends now, you got it? If this is some kind of attention stunt, you can cut it out."

"If *what* is a stunt?" Alvin says, throwing out his arms. "What are you even talking about?"

"About your sick behavior!" Dad roars, pointing at him. "You think I haven't noticed? I've seen you through the windows, running around on all fours, sniffing the trees. I know you're sleeping on the floor next your bed at night. And now this! Do you honestly want me to believe you don't remember how to open the goddamn front door? What is going on?"

Alvin doesn't really know what to say. A part of him understands what his dad is saying and sees why he is worried. Another part of him, however, doesn't feel like listening and can only think about getting out to the forest.

"Is it because of the mutt?" Dad asks, lowering his voice slightly. "Is that why you're acting out? I've told you, you're not getting him back. He lives upstate now."

Alvin is about to answer, when he picks up on something in Dad's voice. It's very subtle, but at the last few words, the tone rises ever so slightly. It can only mean one thing.

Alvin narrows his eyes. "You're lying."

Dad blinks. "What? What did you say? Are you accusing me of lying?"

"Where is Rocky? Where did you send my dog?"

"Upsta—"

"Stop lying!"

Alvin means to shout, but the words sound more like a thundering bark. He feels the hair on the back of his neck stand on end.

Dad steps back a few paces, before regaining control, the brief look of fear on his face turning into rage. "That does it; I'll teach you to shout at me!"

He lunges forward, grabs hold of Alvin's arm and flings him across the room. Alvin flies, lands, rolls around and ends up on all four. He stares up at Dad, baring his teeth in a menacing growl, every muscle in his body ready to pounce.

"I said cut that out!" Dad roars as he comes charging at him once more. "You know what? If you're going to act like a fucking dog, I'll treat you like one!"

He snatches the newspaper from the coffee table, rolls it up and starts whacking Alvin with it. Alvin jumps around to avoid getting hit, giving off loud barks and snapping at the newspaper with his mouth. Instead, he catches the sleeve of Dad's shirt, ripping the fabric with a *RITSCH!*

Dad freezes for a second, staring from his ripped sleeve to the piece of cloth between Alvin's teeth. Then he jumps forward and grabs Alvin by the neck, forcing his head down to the floor and drags him out to the hall, out of the house and across the lawn. Alvin fights to get free, but Dad is too strong. He picks up the chain which is tied to a tree and slaps it around Alvin's neck, slamming the lock.

Alvin immediately starts pulling to get it off, but to no use. He is trapped in Rocky's old chain.

Dad backs away a few paces, panting but looking triumphant. "You can spend the night out here. Maybe that'll get your head straight." He turns and goes inside.

Alvin breathes fast, pacing back and forth, exactly like Rocky used to do, whenever Alvin put him on the chain. Finally, he sits down, lifts his nose towards the dark sky, purses his lips and lets out a long, keening howl.

***

Alvin awakens early the next morning to the sound of a rifle shot.

He has spent the whole night curled up on the ground. Although he is cold, he is not freezing. He gets up, stretches his legs and listens.

More shots, the echoes ringing through the forest. Something about the sound makes Alvin very uncomfortable. He has always feared a stray bullet might hit Rocky as he was roaming the forest, and now ... now something finally clicks into place.

His mind stops. Everything stops.

That day. That day he came home and Rocky was gone. He heard a shot. As he walked home from the bus. A single shot. Very close by. A single shot.

"No," Alvin croaks. "No, that can't be."

But the more he thinks about it, the more it makes sense. Dad would never bother finding a buyer for Rocky. And why would some guy from upstate come all the way down here to buy a two-hundred-dollar dog?

No, what happened to Rocky is a lot simpler, a lot more obvious. Alvin can't believe he didn't see it before. The lie he heard in Dad's voice now seems ridiculously transparent.

Dad hated Rocky. And he finally had enough.

So he shot him.

Alvin has no trace of doubt in his mind. Rocky is dead. His dad shot him. But he needs to be absolutely sure. So he puts on an act when Dad comes out to unlock the chain.

"Well, are you ready to act like a person again?"

"Yes," Alvin says.

Dad eyes him for a moment. "Will you take off that stupid collar then?"

Alvin takes it off.

Dad nods, satisfied. He doesn't seem angry anymore; he even pats Alvin briefly and awkwardly on the head. "Good thinking, son. Are you coming in?"

"I'll just be a minute."

"All right. I'm frying bacon for breakfast."

"Sounds good."

Dad looks at him one last time, apparently trying to figure out if Alvin is being sincere. Alvin looks back at him, completely expressionless. Dad gives him a brief smile, then goes inside.

Alvin waits for the door to close behind him. Then he puts his nose to the ground and starts sniffing. He searches all around the house, until he finally picks up the scent from behind the woodshed. He finds a spot where the ground has been newly dug up.

His heart beats faster as he starts digging with his hands, slowly at first, then faster and faster, until the dirt is flying everywhere. His eyes are watering, his throat is throbbing. He knows what he'll find, but he can't stop.

And suddenly he finds it. Rocky's paw is pointing straight up at the sky.

Alvin takes it gently in both his hands. It's not warm like he remembers, but cold and stiff. Alvin starts crying, the tears spilling from his eyes, as he holds his dead dog's paw for a long while.

"Alvin?"

Dad's voice is calling.

"Alvin? Breakfast is ready! Are you coming or what?"

Alvin sniffs and wipes his eyes with the back of his hand, leaving dark traces of dirt on his cheeks.

"Yeah," he whispers. "I'm coming."

***

Half an hour later, the local police receive a peculiar call. A hoarse voice is mumbling something which sounds more like animal sounds than actual words.

The officer on call frowns and says: "I'm sorry, sir. Could you repeat that?"

The voice repeats the message, making it a little more comprehensible.

The eyes of the officer grow bigger. "I must have misunderstood you, sir. It sounded like you said you just bit someone to death."

The voice on the other end croaks out an address. Then the connection is lost.

The officer writes down the address, looks at it for a moment, considers if it could be a joke. He decides to send someone to check it out. Just to be sure.

The police arrive twenty minutes later. They discover the bloody corpse of a middle-aged man sprawled on the kitchen floor. On the stove a pan is sizzling, the bacon is all burnt.

In the backyard they find a woodshed. Behind it, a dead German shepherd is buried. There are imprints in the soft ground from naked hands and feet.

The whole forest is searched. All they find are bloody pieces of something which might once have been clothing, and more imprints. But these aren't from a human; they seem to belong to a large dog.

For many years to come, the police receive several calls from people living near the forest. They've seen a furry figure running around in there. Some think it's a stray wolf, others say it looks more like an overgrown German shepherd. No one ever knows for sure, though.

And on moonlit nights you can often hear a wailing howl echoing through the forest, a note of sorrow in the sound, almost like a dog missing its owner.

***

Even though *Whiskers* was a really hard story for me to write, it's also one of my personal favorites.

I've lost a dog myself when I was younger, and it broke my heart, so I really understood Alvin's heartache. I was really rooting for him, and I hated his dad with a passion. But when Alvin got his revenge in the end, I was surprised to find it didn't really help, I still only felt sad for him. Maybe that's the moral of the story, I don't know—I'll leave that part up you.

If you have a dog, go give him a hug and a treat. Love him while you can. And when you one day have to say goodbye, don't go looking for a witch or a magical well. It won't help bring back your friend. Instead, you might end up growing whiskers yourself.

THE GIRL WHO WASN'T THERE

Monsters are real. And they steal kids.

PART ONE
ANDY WISLER

DAY 1

It happens on a perfectly ordinary grey Tuesday afternoon in late March. They're on their way home from school. Andy is pushing his bike and Rebecca is walking next to him on the sidewalk, skipping along to some annoying song playing on her phone.

"We have to make a quick stop at the library," Andy says, stopping by the intersection next to the red brick building. "I need a new book."

"I don't want to," Rebecca says, shaking her head. "I'll just keep walking and you can catch up."

Andy steps in front of her, cutting her off. "No. Mom says we should always go together."

"You're the one who doesn't want to go together. I don't want to go into the stupid library."

"Why not?"

"I just don't feel like it. Books are so boooring!"

"It'll only be a minute. And could you please turn that off?"

Rebecca doesn't pause the song, instead she crosses her arms. She's wearing her thick, purple winter jacket, which makes her look even more stern. "You go ahead into the library," she says, smiling falsely. "But you can't make me go with you."

Andy frowns. "Are you going to wait out here then?"

"Perhaps," Rebecca says, glancing up at the sky.

"Perhaps?" Andy repeats. "What's that supposed to mean?"

"It means: Perhaps I'll wait, perhaps I won't."

Andy feels irritation arise. They've been down this road so many times before, and he knows exactly how it'll end. Whenever Rebecca is like this, there's no way of bending her will. Neither prayers nor threats can make her obey. Still, he points at her and says, putting on his sternest demeanor: "You'll wait here until I get back."

Rebecca doesn't reply; she just stands there, avoiding his eye, humming along to the music.

Andy stares at her menacingly for another moment, attempting to intimidate her into staying put. Then, he crosses the street and parks his bike by the bike rack. As he darts a glance back across his shoulder, he sees Rebecca on the other side of the street, one arm raised to wave sarcastically at him, the way old ladies wave in the movies.

Later, Andy will think back to this moment a thousand times. He'll come to wish he had waved back at Rebecca, even though he knew she only waved to annoy him. But an ironic wave of goodbye would still be a lot better than no goodbye at all.

Then again, if Andy had known what was to come, he would have simply never gone into the library. He would have walked right back to Rebecca, and they would have gone home together and nothing bad would have happened.

But Andy doesn't know the future.

And he's angry with Rebecca at that moment.

So, he scoffs and turns his back to her, then marches into the library.

As soon as the glass doors slide shut behind him, Andy's anger dissipates like fog in the sunny morning air. He's entered the world of books, and he can't be angry here.

Not many people are at the library this afternoon; in fact, he seems to be the only one. It's a small-town library with only a few librarians, and they're only here every other day.

Andy unwraps his scarf and inhales the scent of the books. Ever since he learned to read, Andy has loved books more than anything, and he feels the old excitement bubble up now at the mere thought of the countless universes lurking between the pages. In those universes he can get lost for hours on end. And there is no one bullying or annoying him, no one making demands or yelling at him.

Andy goes down row B and lets his gaze glide across the spines, searching for one that looks intriguing, when, suddenly, the tip of his shoe bumps into something.

He looks down to see a book on the floor. He picks it up. It's an older one with an anonymous, red leather binding. There is no text on the spine, nor on the front cover. Only a title engraved into the leather in scratched gold letters:

THE WENDIGO

Andy has never come across the book before, and he's never heard the title mentioned either; he has no idea what a wendigo is. There's something intriguing about the name, though; it sounds somehow ominous.

He leafs briefly through the pages and skims the text. The story seems promising, so he brings the book to the terminal and beeps it through.

A cold gust of wind leaps at him the moment he steps outside the library again, biting his cheeks and forehead. His gaze immediately seeks the other side of the street, where he last saw Rebecca, but he can't hear her music playing, and she's no longer to be seen.

Of course she's gone. That little brat.

Andy looks in both directions just in time to catch a glimpse of purple, as Rebecca turns down a side street a couple hundred yards away. Andy grabs his bike and takes up pursuit.

Apparently, Rebecca is intent on jerking him around, as she is walking the opposite way from home. Her plan, no doubt, is to give him a good scare by making him believe she's gone home, then, when Andy shows up to find the house empty, he will panic.

But I saw you, you sly devil, Andy thinks, a triumphant smile tugging at his lips. *You're not fooling me.*

Thanks to his bike, Andy is a lot faster than Rebecca, so it takes him only a moment to reach the street where she turned, and once again he's just in time to see her turn down a new side street.

Andy decides to play along.

Rebecca obviously thinks she has the upper hand, since she doesn't know Andy is onto her. So, he rides along at a comfortable speed, following along every time she makes another turn, making sure to stay far enough behind so as to not be seen in case Rebecca decides to look back. She doesn't look back, though, not even once—which proves to Andy just how confident she must be in the fact that she fooled him, and it makes him chuckle to himself.

Then, she suddenly turns into the driveway of a random house, goes to the front door, opens it and disappears inside.

What the heck?

Andy speeds up and reaches the house. He has no idea who lives in there, and the names on the mailbox don't make him any the wiser. He looks up at the house, but can't see anyone in the windows.

Andy just stands by his bike for a moment, brooding.

Could it be a trick? Did Rebecca spot him after all and is now trying to throw him off?

No, he doesn't think it likely she would walk into a strange home just to mess with him. She might be devious, but she's not stupid.

Which means, of course, that Rebecca must know the people who live in the house. Probably someone from Rebecca's class.

So, that was her plan all along. Go to one of her friends' house and let me rush home alone, totally worried about where she might be.

Andy bites off his glove and pulls out his phone. He types a quick text.

You can come out now. I saw you.

He keeps an eye on the front door, but it doesn't open for several minutes. And Rebecca doesn't text him back.

Soon, Andy begins to lose patience. He's also freezing. He puts his bike on the stand, goes up to the front door and knocks on it, loudly.

The door is opened, and a girl from Rebecca's class looks out at him with an expression of mild surprise. Andy can't recall her name—maybe Freya or Faye or something like that.

"Hi," the girl says, as she apparently recognizes Andy. "What do you want?"

"You can tell Rebecca to come out now," Andy says, sniffing. "I'm taking her home."

"Rebecca isn't here," the girl says, her tone innocent.

"Yeah, she is."

The girl shakes her head, causing her bangs to swing. "No, she really isn't."

"Well, I saw her go in."

"When?"

"Just a minute ago."

The girl—her expression still serene—shrugs. "I haven't seen Rebecca since class today. Honestly. It's just me and my mom home."

Andy is growing annoyed with the girl and the way she's covering for Rebecca. Rebecca probably instructed her to play oblivious, and the girl is doing a pretty good job pretending.

He stretches his neck and sees Rebecca's jacket on the rack. "I can see her jacket," he says, pointing. "The purple one."

The girl looks back briefly, then says: "That's *my* jacket."

Andy opens his mouth to answer, but is suddenly struck silent, as something falls into place. He never really saw the girl in the purple jacket up close, did he? No. And come to think of it, he couldn't hear any music playing, either. And the way she walked without glancing back ...

Andy realizes the girl is still looking at him with patient bemusement.

"I, uhm ... I'm sorry," he mutters, backing away. "I think ... eh ... there's been a misunderstanding ..."

He turns around and hurries back out to the sidewalk, finds his phone and calls up Rebecca.

She doesn't answer. After the fourth ring it goes to voice mail.

Right, don't panic now, he tells himself, putting the phone back into his pocket. *She's obviously just gone home, and she knows the way. We've walked it together a million times. Nothing happened to her, she's just—*

Andy is so distraught he goes to cross the street without looking. A yellow van comes out of nowhere, its horn blaring angrily, and Andy leaps back onto the sidewalk, almost tripping over his bike, as the van rushes past. It slows down, and for a moment Andy is sure the driver will jump out and yell at him. But the van only slowed down in order to make a turn at a crossing. It holds and waits for a break in the passing traffic, only one of the brake lights glowing red.

Andy is just about to jump on his bike, when he hears something.

It's a knocking.

He looks towards the van. It could have been the engine. But it could also have been someone knocking from the inside of the van.

Then the brake light goes out, the van revs up, rolls out into the crossing, turns and disappears out of sight.

Andy rides home as fast as he can, panting and sweating under his clothes despite the cold spring air, a nagging sense of dread growing steadily larger in the pit of his stomach all the way.

If Mom finds out Rebecca has walked home by herself, she'll blow a fuse—and Andy will be the one blamed. Mom has instructed him several times that since he's the older one, Rebecca is *his* responsibility whenever there are no grown-ups around.

*Never mind the fact that she can be a pain in the butt and fight me every step of the way just because she's in a foul mood! But oh, no, it's still only **my** fault if something happens to her!*

But there's still hope he can avoid a scolding: if he's lucky, Mom won't be home from work yet, which means she'll never know Rebecca and Andy split up.

Of course, Rebecca might tell on him as soon as Mom gets home—it would be just like her, ratting him out to get him into trouble—but Andy can always deny it, which at least would give him a fifty-fifty chance that Mom will believe his side of the story.

Andy reaches the house, drops his bike in the driveway—which is empty, meaning Mom isn't home yet—and runs to the front door. It's locked. Andy stares at it for a moment, confused. Then he scrambles for the key in his bag and lets himself in.

The first thing he notices in the hall is that the purple jacket is not on the rack. Still, he calls out: "Becca! You here?" then holds his breath and listens. Only silence from the house. Dad always works late, and Cindy is probably out with her college friends.

Andy pulls out the phone and calls up Rebecca once more.

Four rings. Then voice mail.

"Pick it up," Andy hisses and tries again immediately. He knows it won't do any good, but he does it anyway.

This time, there's only a single ring before it goes to voice mail. Which means the call has been declined. Or that the phone was shut off. But why would Rebecca do any of those things? Just to mess with him? It's not completely unlikely, of course—her being somewhere nearby, sniggering at his call—but Andy doesn't think so. Rebecca has never taken a prank this far before.

His heart by now is pounding away in his chest, and the anxious feeling in his stomach has grown into full-fledged fear. He checks the time. It's been more than half an hour since they split up by the library. Would Rebecca really still be mad at him? And if so, where could she be?

Maybe she's still just wandering around town. Or maybe she's lost and can't find her way home. But then why would she turn off her phone? Maybe it ran out of battery.

Andy decides him standing here dialoguing with himself won't do any good. Mom could be home any minute, and when she finds out Andy has come home without Rebecca, she won't just blow a fuse—Andy is afraid her head might simply explode.

So, he goes out to look for Rebecca, locking the front door behind him, as he knows Rebecca has her own key.

Andy rides around town for almost an hour. He checks all the places Rebecca might be: the school, the mall, the park, the playground, even the library. She's nowhere to be found.

Finally, he goes back home. He's really scared now. His last hope is that while he was out looking, Rebecca has come home on her own. That this has all been a mean joke on her part. That she has just been wandering around the streets, biding her time until she was certain Andy was freaking out. He tries to imagine the situation play out. The front door will be unlocked, and he will barge in, call out her name, and she will come striding out casually from the living room to greet him, put her hands to her sides and ask: "What took you so long?"

"What took *me* so long?" Andy will burst out. "How about you? Where have *you* been? I've looked all over town for you!"

And Rebecca will smile her most devilish smile and say: "I took another road." Or: "I met Anna from class, and we talked for a while." Or simply: "That's not any of your business."

Andy has a well-developed imagination, and the conversation is so vivid in his mind, he actually has himself convinced that's how it will play out—he's even smiling to himself as he parks his bike in the driveway the second time. He leaps up the steps and grabs the knob.

His smile withers.

The door is locked.

And when he lets himself in using his key, he finds Rebecca's jacket still not on the rack.

Then suddenly, standing in the empty, silent house, Andy hears something knocking. The sound is coming from his own heart. But it's also coming from the yellow van. It's growing louder and louder inside of him, until it feels like his ribcage is going to break open. That single, red brake light is glaring at him in his mind's eye, burning him with its evil, monstrous stare. His thoughts begin arguing.

She's gone.
No, she can't be.
Someone took her.
No, that's not true.
She's not coming home.
*She **is** coming home!*
Stop being a baby.
Shut up!
Stop pretending.
Shut up!

Andy breathes out heavily and realizes he's seconds away from crying, which makes him even more scared. He clears his throat and swallows hard.

Andy knows there's only one thing left to do now, and he dreads it more than anything. It will wipe out the last hope. It will break the illusion that Rebecca still might show up on her own in a minute or two. It will make it real.

At the age of thirteen, this is the hardest thing Andy has ever had to do—and that includes the time he crashed on his bike and dislocated his shoulder and had to have the doctor pop it back in. The pain, which was already intense, grew to unfathomable dimensions for a few seconds, and the shock of it almost caused him to faint, scaring him out of ever trusting any doctor ever again telling him that "it'll only hurt a bit." But just like then, he has no choice now. The difference is, this time he knows what's coming. Which makes it even worse.

He takes out his phone and makes the call.

Dad answers right away: *"Hey, Andy, what's up?"*

"Dad," Andy says. His mouth is dry. His voice is trembling. "I think ... I think Rebecca is missing."

DAY 50

Andy completely forgets about the book tucked in the back of his schoolbag, until finally one evening, he pulls out his atlas to do his geography homework, and the book incidentally pops out and falls to the floor.

He looks down at it and is instantly reminded of Rebecca. Not that he ever forgot about her, of course, but brief intervals have begun showing up, maybe half a minute or so passing without him thinking of her. Now, at the sight of the book he took out of the library that fateful day, it all comes rushing back for the millionth time, and Andy chokes up.

The first days after Rebecca disappeared were full of questions and police officers and solemn looks and more questions.

"What was the last thing Rebecca said to you?"

"Did you see which way she went?"

"Did you guys fight before you separated?"

"How long were you inside the library?"

"Did you hear her talking with anyone?"

"Did she mention anything about where she might go?"

"Did anyone threaten you or Rebecca earlier that day?"

And so on.

Andy answered to the best of his ability. He also told the police about the yellow van.

"Did you see the van parked outside the library, Andy?" the officer with the deep voice asked him.

"No, but ..."

"Did you see Rebecca through the rear window when the van went past you?"

"There was no rear window. But the knocking ..."

"You said you thought the sound came from the van's engine?"

"That was what I thought at first, yeah, but ... then I got the idea, you know, what if it was Rebecca knocking?"

The officer gave him a long look, then he nodded, and did not ask about the yellow van again.

Andy's not stupid; he can see there's no evidence to support his theory. No one else reported seeing the yellow van near the library that day. Andy didn't see who was driving it. The van could have had absolutely nothing to do with Rebecca's disappearance.

Yet Andy just can't forget about the knocking, or the red brake light staring at him like an evil eye. For every day passing without the police finding Rebecca, Andy has grown more and more certain that the knocking was Rebecca pounding on the inside of the van. If he had only thought to take down the license number, then the police could at least have found the van and checked it out.

He has tried telling both Mom and Dad about it, but neither of them really seem to listen anymore. They've both gone into a strange state Andy has never seen them in before. It's like they aren't themselves anymore.

Mom's eyes are always glazed, and some days she doesn't get out of bed. Other days she walks around the house and tries to do normal things, like vacuuming or doing the laundry. But she keeps stopping, staring out into nothing. As though she forgets for several minutes what she's doing.

Dad mostly keeps to himself and very rarely speaks. Andy sees him cry now and then, when he thinks he's alone. In the beginning, he went for long drives in his car, returning hours later without a word to anyone about where he had been.

One day, when Andy saw Dad take the car keys, he mustered up the courage and asked where he was going.

Dad just looked at him with an empty gaze and said: "Where do you think I'm going, Andy? I'm going out to look for my daughter, of course."

There was no anger in the voice, yet Andy felt the words land on him like bee stings.

No one has ever said it outright, not Mom or Dad, not Cindy or Aunt Clair who had visited a few times, not the police officer with the deep voice or the shrink Andy went to see for a couple of weeks, not the teachers at school or any of his classmates, not even the neighbors or anyone else in town. Yet they all know it. Andy can feel it right under the surface. They all agree on that simple, horrible truth.

If Andy hadn't gone into the library that day ...

If he had only kept his promise to not let Rebecca out of sight ...

But Andy *did* go into the library.

He *did* leave Rebecca out of sight.

And he's been trying desperately not to think about that day ever since.

But now, as he is standing in his room, staring at the book he took out only a few minutes after he saw Rebecca for the last time, the feelings of dread and guilt and regret come rushing back, and Andy tears up, his bottom lip begins bobbing.

He hasn't picked up a book since Rebecca disappeared, hasn't read a single page; he just hasn't felt like it, although he used to read at least a book a week, usually two or three. But the mere thought of going near the library now makes him almost physically ill.

Andy chokes back the sobs, wipes his eyes and picks up the book. With a sigh, he sits down on his bed and studies the secretive, dark-red cover. It must have gone way past its due date, and he probably owes a library fine on it now.

He opens the book and finds the author name on the title page: Algernon Blackwood. Andy has never heard of that author before, but the book looks to be at least a hundred years old, so the guy is probably long dead.

He absentmindedly leafs through the first few pages, reads a couple of paragraphs, and then he disappears.

The language is fluent and colorful, the descriptions so vivid that Andy has no problem getting immersed in the plot.

The evening grows dimmer outside the window, the church bells chime somewhere in the distance, marking the hours passing by, and Andy turns the pages.

The story plays out way up in Canada more than a century ago. It follows a group of men on a moose hunt, venturing deep into the huge Canadian forests, reaching territory where no man has ever set foot. In there, they encounter something strange.

A demonic creature dwells in the forest, luring in people who have gone astray by imitating voices. Wendigo, the monster is called. If it catches you, it'll break down your psyche and suck the life force from within you, until you're nothing but an empty shell. But first, it'll light your feet on fire and poke out your eyes.

Why?

Because eyes and feet are the only two things that can save a person lost in the woods.

Andy feels the fear come creeping like ants on his skin, his heart pounding away in his chest. At one point, he has to close the book and look around, making sure he's still safe in his room and not trapped in an endless forest. A part of him wants to put away the book and never pick it up again. It's late, and he has to get up tomorrow morning to go to school. But another part of him wants to keep reading, *demands* it. That part needs to know how the story ends.

It's just a story. Wendigos aren't real. Get a grip, you big wuss.

Andy takes a deep breath, peels open the book once more and dives back in.

Andy has already read quite a few horror stories in his life. He has even taken on some of the heavier monsters, like Dracula, or Cthulhu, or Pennywise the Clown. But the wendigo scares him in a way none of the others ever managed to do. There is something absolutely terrifying about that invisible thing lurking in the woods, just waiting patiently for someone to come close enough ...

The plot flows along easily enough to begin with, the mood getting slowly darker despite nothing really happening. Until about a third of the way in, that is; then something happens which almost makes Andy scream out loud.

The men have set up camp for the night, when suddenly, one of them is dragged to his feet and flung out of the tent, like some invisible force pulling him away. And as he disappears into the darkness of the woods, his voice can be heard by the other men:

»Oh! oh! My feet of fire! My burning feet of fire! Oh! oh! This height and fiery speed!«

Andy reads the line again and again, and every time he does so, his palms grow sweatier. He understands what has happened to the poor guy, and yet he doesn't. Something—the wendigo—has taken him. And the part about his feet burning—is it meant to be taken literally, that they simply burst into flames, or did the man lose his mind on the spot, like a house of cards collapsing? What exactly does the invisible demon do to him? The text simply isn't clear enough and leaves it up to the reader's imagination—which somehow only makes it worse.

Andy reads on with bated breath. More than once he tries again closing the book. The problem is, his fingers don't obey him anymore; they just eagerly keep turning pages.

When he finally reaches the conclusion of the story, he feels dizzy. He looks to the clock on his nightstand. It's past 2:00 AM. His parents have long since gone to bed. Andy doesn't recall ever having been awake at this hour, not even on New Year's Eve.

He's about to put the book away, when he notices something. On the very last page, a piece of paper is pinned. It's a library receipt, one of those automatically printed out by the terminal when you borrow a book. Someone apparently used it as a bookmark. The text is faded but still readable.

Lisa Labowski, the name on the receipt reads. The date is August 16, eighteen years ago.

Amazing to think the paper has been in the book for eighteen years without someone removing it. Perhaps the book simply hasn't been read by anyone for that long.

Andy reads the name again.

Lisa Labowski ... I think I heard that name before ...

He tries to remember, but he's too exhausted to think straight, so he closes the book and falls asleep the second his head hits the pillow.

In his dreams, Andy travels to the Canadian woods to hunt for moose. It's winter, and it's very cold and dark.

Suddenly, he sees Rebecca between the dead trees. She has her back to him. Andy feels his heart leap and he runs towards her. But it's difficult to move his legs right, so he only very slowly gets closer. Instead, he calls out for her.

"Becca! Becca, it's me! I'm coming!"

Rebecca turns her head sideways, as though she hears him. But something is wrong with her eyes. Is she crying? No, Andy realizes to his horror, it's not tears streaming down Rebecca's cheeks—it's blood.

Then, the wendigo steps out from behind the tree. The demon is even more terrifying than he imagined. It looks kind of like a human, but at the same time not at all. It's much taller and sickly skinny, the skin is ashy gray and paper-thin, clinging to the bones and revealing the dark veins underneath. The eyes are small and dark and deep-seated, the lips are cracked and bloody.

Andy can only look in horror as the creature goes to take Rebecca's hand and leads her away, his sister following along willingly, like a sleepwalker or a zombie, completely unaware of what's going on. Andy tries to scream to her, but no sound comes out of his mouth. Rebecca turns her head to look back one last time just before she disappears into the darkness with the wendigo, and Andy sees her lips mouthing the words: "Help me."

Andy sits up in bed with a choked cry. He stares around his room, his heart in his throat.

"The wendigo took Becca," he whispers hoarsely. "It was the wendigo ..."

DAY 51

The next morning, as Andy is awakened by the alarm, the images from the nightmare have mercifully faded to nothing but vague shadows at the back of his memory.

On his way to school, Andy rides past the town church as usual. The old, white building surrounded by the graveyard is located right up against the park, so Andy takes the shortcut through the park, when he suddenly sees three girls a hundred yards away, blocking the path. Andy recognizes them immediately. It's Sheila from Andy's class and two eighth graders, Kimmie and Stacey. They're posing for a group selfie. When they look at the result, they laugh out loud.

Oh, crap, Andy thinks to himself, realizing he won't be able to get past them unnoticed. *That's just my luck ...*

Ever since Rebecca disappeared, everyone in his class has acted differently whenever Andy is around. They fall silent. As though not sure what to say. Even the teachers become awkward.

Andy is used to being the quiet boy in class—the one who's always reading a book at recess and only seldom gets any attention or is spoken to. And that hasn't changed, but now he can sense everyone staring at him.

Only Sheila is acting like she used to. She's still bullying Andy like she has always done. In a strange way, Andy finds it somewhat comforting that at least this one thing hasn't changed.

But that doesn't mean he's in the mood for Sheila today. He sees the gate leading into the churchyard and makes a quick decision to cut across instead of going through the park.

Just as he gets off his bike and starts for the gate, he hears one of the girls exclaim: "Hey, isn't that Wisler from your class, Sheila?"

Andy turns his head to see the girls looking in his direction.

"Yeah, it is," Sheila says. "Hey, Andy! Why are you going into the churchyard?"

Andy doesn't answer, but opens the gate and pulls his bike through. He restrains himself from running, just walks briskly along the gravel path winding through the many graves.

"Andy! Hey, Andy! You got gravy in your ears, man?"

Sheila's voice is followed by shrill laughter. Andy is unsure what, but something makes him stop. It's obviously a mistake; he should just keep moving. But he turns to look back.

The girls are at the gate. Sheila is wearing a tight black top, way too cold for this time of year, which reveals her boney shoulders and flat chest. Kimmie is sucking noisily from a McDonald's cup.

Sheila glares at Andy with a stupid smile. "Come on over here, Andy. I need to talk with you real quick."

Andy feels the heat rise to his face. It's part embarrassment, part frustration with himself for stopping. Now that they're staring right at each other, he can't just turn and leave.

Of course you can. Why should you stay and listen to her bullcrap? She's only going to humiliate you. Go. Just go!

But he stays rooted.

"You can have the rest of Kimmie's milkshake if you come," Sheila says alluringly.

Kimmie almost chokes with laughter, spraying out pink milkshake on the gravel. She holds up the cup and dangles it in the air. "Come on, piggy! Come get a treat!" She tries to say something more, but is interrupted when Stacey breaks into hysterical laughter.

Sheila is the only one not laughing. She just holds Andy's gaze, her smile widening ever so slightly. "Seriously, Andy," she says in an almost friendly tone, stepping into the churchyard. "I just have one little question for you."

Andy turns and starts walking.

"Hey, Andy!" Sheila calls out, a clear note of insult in her voice now. "I'm talking to you! Don't just walk away—that's rude!"

Andy keeps walking. Now that he finally got moving, he walks fast enough for his backpack to jump up and down.

"Let him go, he probably got hungry!" Kimmie shouts, sending Stacey into another manic case of high-pitched laughter.

"Fat idiot," is the last, scornful words Andy hears from Sheila, before the girls' voices dissipate behind him.

Andy looks back to see them no longer at the gate. His pulse is beating fast, as though he was just running, and he waits a moment for his heart rate to slow down.

What the heck got into her? I know she's always picking on me, but she's definitely gotten worse lately. It's like she—

Andy's gaze falls on the tombstone by the grave right in front of him, and his thoughts immediately stop as he reads the engravement:

Lisa Labowski
Here lies our beloved daughter

Andy just stares at the name for several seconds. Then he reads the date at the bottom. July 17, eighteen years ago. At first, he doesn't really get it. Not consciously, anyway, but something inside him begins to feel very funny at the sight of the date, until suddenly, it dawns on him.

No ... that can't be. I must remember it wrong.

He needs to know for sure, so he takes off his backpack and finds the book, opens it and takes out the receipt. His fingers are shaking as he holds it up.

He stares at the date on the paper.

Then back at the tombstone.

Then back at the paper once more.

He didn't remember it wrong. Which means there has to be some other logical explanation for the impossible discrepancy in the dates. And there are plenty of possible answers, all clambering in his mind, like eager students wanting to be heard by the teacher.

It has to be a flaw in the library system, one thought suggests. *The machine simply printed the wrong date.*

It's not Lisa Labowski herself who borrowed the book, another one argues. *Someone just took it out in her name.*

It's not even the same Lisa Labowski, a third thought interjects. *There are two of them: the one who borrowed the book and the other one who's buried right here.*

All of the answers are reasonable. All of them make sense. All of them could be true.

And yet, none of them *feel* true to Andy. None of them can fight back the goose bumps making their way up his spine. And if none of the answers are true, then he's left with one simple fact.

Lisa Labowski borrowed the book from the library a month after she died.

Andy can't really shake the thought of Lisa Labowski. All day in school he has to strain to concentrate on anything else, since his thoughts keep going in circles about the dead girl.

Luckily, Sheila has apparently forgotten their little rendezvous by the church; she's busy talking with her friends and doesn't bother Andy. This gives him time to brood.

Did Lisa Labowski really borrow the book after her death? Despite Andy's vivid imagination, he doesn't really believe in ghosts or other fantasy creatures. Part of him wants to think they really do exist somewhere in the world, and that you can encounter them like people do in books and movies, but that's mostly the child in him. The rational, soon-to-be-a-grown-up part of him knows it's all just made up.

And yet he keeps thinking about Lisa Labowski as a ghost girl. So, he decides to investigate—if nothing else, at least to give himself peace of mind.

So as soon as school ends for the day, Andy heads straight for the bike shed, grabs his bike and rides through town.

For the first time since Rebecca disappears, Andy stops by the library. He looks up at the red building. It looks completely the same: friendly and inviting. He has been riding past it almost every day, but hasn't had the nerve to really look at it, much less go in. Even now the thought scares him a little.

But he needs an answer to the Lisa Labowski paradox, so he puts the bike in the rack and strides towards the glass doors. They greet him with their old, familiar hiss as they glide open.

Andy steps inside the entrance and stops to close his eyes for a moment, inhaling through his nose. The atmosphere is exactly as he remembers it, and it brings the same feeling of security and peacefulness it always has. Andy can't help but smile.

I've been so silly. Why was I afraid of going in here? It wasn't like the library caused Rebecca to disappear.

He proceeds to go inside and sees Regan—or Libraregan, as she calls herself on social media—by the desk, busy sorting out returned books. A couple of girls Rebecca's age are sitting by the computers and an elderly man is reading a newspaper in the armchair in the farthest corner.

Andy goes to the desk and says: "Hey, Regan."

Regan turns around with a look of surprise. "Andy? Heey!" she beams at him. "Great to see you! It's been so long—got to be a new record."

"I know." Andy smiles shyly.

He notices Regan is about to ask him something, but then seems to think better of it. Something unsaid passes between them, and her smile fades a bit. Of course Regan heard about Rebecca, but did she also hear how it happened? Does she know it was Andy's fault? If she does, then she doesn't say it. Instead, she asks: "How are you holding up?"

"Okay, I guess," Andy says with a shrug.

Regan is pretty young for a librarian—no more than twenty or twenty-one, if Andy had to guess. She's not much taller than Andy and wears glasses too. But unlike Andy, Regan is very thin. She has a tiny pigment spot on her right cheek bone where the skin is noticeably brighter than the rest of her face. It reminds Andy of a teardrop and gives Regan a look of eternal sadness—although she smiles most of the time. Yet Andy has always sensed a loneliness from her, very much akin to his own, and he's pretty sure she doesn't have a boyfriend; she's in love with books, just like Andy.

"So, what did you read this time?" she says, her smile returning, as she goes on sorting books.

Andy finds the book from his bag and shows it to her. "It's called *The Wendigo*. It's really cool."

"*The Wendigo*? Don't think I've heard about it ... who wrote it?" She takes the book from Andy and opens it. "Algernon Blackwood ... huh, what an old-school name."

"I know," Andy says. "I never read anything else by him—did you?"

"I think I'd remember a name like that, so no, I probably haven't." She hands him back the book. "Is it a horror story?"

"Yeah, and it's freaking scary. Definitely too scary for you, Regan."

Regan puts her hands to her sides. "I'll have you know I've read several horror books in my time, thank you very much. In fact, I recently finished *Pet Sematary* ... and now I have to sleep with the lights on for the rest of my life."

Andy sniggers. Then he remembers why he came. "I need to ask you something, Regan."

"Sure."

Suddenly, Andy doesn't know how to put the question. Somehow, "Are dead people allowed to borrow books?" doesn't really seem like the right way to go about it.

"It's just because ... uhm ... I found this note ... here, let me show you." He leafs through the book till he gets to the last page. The receipt isn't there. Then he remembers he put it in his pocket. Or was it the bag? "Eh ... give me a second," he mutters and begins rummaging for the note.

"Do you mind me helping the gentleman behind you, Andy?" Regan asks, and Andy looks back to see the old newspaper guy standing in line with an impatient look on his face.

"Yeah, sure," Andy says, scurrying aside. He keeps digging for the library receipt, but he can't find it anywhere. "Damnit," he murmurs, scratching the back of his head. How can he put the question to Regan if he doesn't at least have the note proving Lisa Labowski was dead at the time the book was lent out?

He glances towards the desk, where Regan is still talking with the old man. Andy looks down at *The Wendigo*, flipping through the pages absentmindedly, just to double-check if he by chance put the receipt in somewhere else, when a certain paragraph catches his eye. It's the one where the man is pulled from the tent. Andy immediately feels his skin begin to prickle, and he can't help but read the passage one more time.

What happens next is the most curious and inexplicable thing Andy has ever experienced.

The line is changed.

Of course that's not possible.

Words printed in a book can't change; they're ink on paper.

But the line has changed nonetheless.

And it's no subtle change, either. Had the wording been only slightly different, Andy could have explained it by him simply not remembering the line correctly. But the words he reads now are nothing at all like the ones he read last night.

The line, as Andy recalls it, went:

»Oh! Oh! My feet of fire! My burning feet of fire! Oh! oh! This height and fiery speed!«

But now it's only one word:

»hello«

Andy is dumbfounded. He reads the word twice over, then a third time, spelling it out, scrutinizing every letter.

He's not reading it wrong. And there's nothing wrong with his eyes, either. The new word is really there. It shouldn't be, but it is.

I must be at another place in the story ...

He reads the paragraphs leading up to the line, but he's not in another place. The man is awakened in his tent, and just as he shoots out through the opening and disappears into the night, he screams out in distress, that disturbing line which ...

Which now is completely wrong.

"Andy?"

He jerks and spins around, almost dropping the book.

Regan—who is no longer talking to the old guy—is looking at him with an uncertain smile. "Are you okay? I heard you muttering to yourself."

"There's ... there's something wrong," he croaks. "With the book."

She looks at *The Wendigo* in his hand. "The one you just read? What's wrong with it? I thought you said you liked it?"

"Yes, well, it's ... I'm just ..."

Regan eyes him patiently.

For a crazy moment, Andy considers the possibility that she is the one playing a trick on him. She was holding the book in her hands a moment ago—could she have switched it for another one?

Of course she couldn't. This is the same book.

"There's an error in the text," Andy says. "Look."

He shows Regan the page and lets his finger run down the text until it reaches the line. They both read it.

Andy gapes.

Regan frowns. "Well, it does sound a bit odd, I'll give you that. Burning feet of fire, what's that mean? I don't think it's an error, per se, but I agree it's a weird way to phrase it."

Andy attempts to moisten his lips with a dried-up tongue. "Yeah, very weird," he manages.

"That book really did a number on you, didn't it?" Regan asks, squeezing his shoulder. "You look like you saw a ghost!"

Andy murmurs something about him being very tired due to the fact that he was up all night reading. Regan laughs heartedly and says she knows exactly what he means; she usually refers to the phenomenon as a "book hangover." Then she goes back to sorting books.

Andy is just standing there for a minute, discretely holding the book at arm's length, as though it is something poisonous. He goes to row B to put it back on the shelf, when he suddenly gets the urge to look one more time.

Why would you do that? a voice in his mind immediately objects. *What could you possibly have to gain? If the text is normal, there was no need to check in the first place. If it's changed again, then there must be something wrong with your head. Do you really want to know if you're going crazy?*

The voice makes a good point, but Andy looks anyway. His curiosity gets the better of him. He opens the book once more and finds the page.

The line is changed again. But to something new this time.

»afraid?«

Andy slams the book shut, shoves it in a random place on the shelf and leaves the library in a hurry, not even bothering to answer Regan, who says his name from somewhere. As soon as Andy is outside, he grabs the bike, jumps on it and rides home as fast as he can.

DAY 54

Andy naturally concludes the library must be haunted, and he swears to never go near it again, ever. Instead, he begins to spend his free time at home in his room.

Ever since Rebecca disappeared, Andy has avoided being in the rest of the house as much as possible, only leaving his room to eat or go to the bathroom. He just can't take The Silence—that's how he thinks of the word, with a capital S.

Before Rebecca, his parents would no doubt have noticed how Andy isolated himself.

Mom would have asked him if he was feeling okay, would have checked his forehead with her cool palm.

Dad would have come into his room, sat down on the bed next to him and asked him if everything was okay.

But those kinds of things are in the past now, and his parents are simply drifting through the days, hardly noticing anything. Andy will sometimes imagine them going on like this, growing more and more distant, talking less and less, until they completely lose the ability to speak or recognize anyone around them. Or maybe they will even begin to grow transparent, simply fade away like ghosts, until one day, there will be nothing left but the occasional creak of a floorboard from Dad's office or the faint smell of Mom's perfume. No one would be able to explain exactly what had happened, only Andy would know that The Silence had finally swallowed up both his parents.

Still, there is one other thing besides food and bathroom visits which can make Andy venture out of him room, and that's Tweety. When Rebecca went missing, Andy took it upon himself to feed and look after her parakeet. Whenever he enters Rebecca's room, he's greeted by a squawking voice: "Hello, ugly!"

"Hello, Tweety."

Tweety reminds him in many ways of Rebecca, and Andy suspects that parakeets adopt the personality of their owners just like dogs will. As Andy steps inside and closes the door behind him, the bird gives a whistle and flies up on its perch. He hesitates for a moment, like he always does, looking around the room. Everything is neat and tidy. The bed is made, the floor is clean, not a trace of dust or laundry. It's almost like Rebecca moved out and the room is now waiting for a new occupant.

Andy dislikes the thought, and besides, it's not true; Rebecca will come home, of course she will. No one else will move into this room.

"Most children who run away from home get found within twenty-four hours," Andy recalls one of the officers telling his parents. "In rare cases, it takes up to a week."

The word, which the officer discretely avoided, and which no one has said aloud yet—at least not when Andy was listening—is of course, "kidnapped." Although Andy hasn't heard the word uttered, he can sense it lurking in the air all around him, immersed within The Silence. And behind it, buried even deeper, lies another word—a much, much worse one.

For some reason, Andy is reminded of the nightmare he had recently about Rebecca being taken by the wendigo, and his stomach tightens. What if it wasn't merely a dream, but some sort a warning? He once saw a documentary about twins who were able to sense each other's pain and distress even over great distances. Perhaps he and Rebecca have a similar connection?

"Hey, you!" Tweety calls out, pulling Andy from his train of thoughts. "Whaddaya looking at?"

Andy goes to the cage and pours seed into the bowl.

"Bon Appetit! Bon Appetit!" the bird squawks and begins eating.

Andy stands for a moment and studies it, the shiny green feathers and the gleaming orange eyes. "What do you think, Tweety? Will Rebecca come home?"

"Becca!" the bird answers and stops eating for a moment, as though it genuinely remembers.

Andy feels his heart speed up. It's silly, he knows that; of course the bird doesn't know who the word refers to, it simply repeats what it's heard.

"Becca!" it says again.

"Is that a yes? Do you think she will come home?"

The bird eyes him intently for a moment, then it says: "Hello, ugly!" and resumes eating.

Andy bites his lip, his gaze growing distant. "Up to a week," he mutters, not even aware he's speaking aloud. "Seven days."

It's almost two months since Rebecca disappeared.

DAY 57

Of course Andy can't avoid the library for the rest of his life; he needs something new to read. And after only a couple of days, The Silence is getting on his nerves.

Besides, it isn't really the library that scares him, it's the book. Or rather, the strange, changing line.

The notion which he has been trying to ignore is that the line wasn't just a random thing, but a meaningful message addressed to him. Not any reader, but him, Andy Wisler.

Andy has been going over the scene in his head several times. It really was exactly as though the book was talking to him.

No, not the book. The message came from someone else.

The name trying to force its way into Andy's mind is of course Lisa Labowski. But that wasn't only not possible, it was also insane.

Andy often reads books where the main character encounters something inexplicable, and usually the reader is given a rational explanation later on in the story, but sometimes ... sometimes it turns out there aren't any.

That's just stories. I'm not a character in a book. This is the real, boring world. And there is no such thing as books with changing lines.

So, Andy makes up his mind to be brave and go back to the library. He decides to wait until Friday at five o'clock. At that time the library will probably be empty.

He lets himself in with his password and begins by walking casually around the rows, making sure he's alone. Then he takes his time checking out Regan's newest display of popular books. Nothing really catches his attention, though, so he goes on to the rows.

He keeps glancing nervously over at row B, but as the minutes pass by and nothing happens, the calming atmosphere of the many books makes him feel at ease. He even begins to smile to himself.

God, I've been so stupid. I got scared by a brief moment of imagination. That's all it was. I'll bet I can go to the book right now and read the line and it'll be exactly as it has always been.

And he decides to do it. Just to put this silly thing to rest once and for all. He goes to row B and finds *The Wendigo*. He takes it out, leafs through the pages and finds the scene with the tent.

The line goes:

»Oh! oh! My feet of fire! My burning feet of fire! Oh! oh! This height and fiery speed!«

Andy lets out a long breath he wasn't even aware he was holding, and his shoulders drop down an inch. Apparently, he wasn't quite as confident as he acted, but he's still glad he looked, because now it's confirmed.

"It was just my imagination," he mutters. "Nothing more than that."

He puts back *The Wendigo* and finds another book which looks promising: *Solaris* by Stanislaw Lem. He sits down in the armchair by the far corner, kicks off his shoes and makes himself comfortable.

Andy reads the first chapter. He sits quietly and turns the pages, completely undisturbed and utterly absorbed by the story.

Solaris is about a young astronaut visiting a space station on a foreign planet called Solaris. But as soon as he arrives on the station, it becomes clear that something is wrong. What remains of his colleagues still on the station are frightened and scattered and acting extremely weird. When the main character talks to one of them, the dialogue quickly turns odd as the colleague warns the protagonist of great undefinable dangers aboard the station.

»Who could I see?« I flared up. »A ghost?«

»You think I'm mad, of course. No, no, I'm not mad. I can't say anything more for the moment. Perhaps ... who knows? ... Nothing will happen. But don't forget I warned you.«

»Don't be so mysterious. What's all this about?«

»Keep a hold on yourself. Be prepared to meet ... anything. It sounds impossible I know, but try. It's the only advice I can give you. I can't think of anything better.«

»But what could I possibly meet?« I shouted.

»lisa«

Seeing him sitting there, looking sideways at me, his sunburnt face drooping with fatigue, I found it difficult to contain myself. I wanted to grab him by the shoulders and ...

Andy is so caught up in the story that he reads on another few lines before it finally dawns on him. He stares at the last line of dialogue. The way it's written; no capital letters. No punctuation. And the name ...

Everything inside of him stiffens up, as though his body temperature has dropped way below zero. He stares at the name, feeling his skin turn to ice all over.

It's her again! his mind screams at him from someplace far away. *She's in this book, too! Get out of here! Run!*

He manages to get up on shaky legs while squeezing the book hard enough to crinkle the pages, afraid that it might jump on him if he lets go. Then, he drops it all at once, while simultaneously spinning on his heel and bolting for the exit. His elbow graces one of the shelves and knocks down a couple of books, but Andy pays no mind, he just runs as though his life depends on it, only slowing down as he approaches the glass doors.

"Come on, open!" he cries out, as the automated doors take their sweet time gliding aside. They're no more than a few inches apart when Andy leaps forward to squeeze through—but then, completely unexpectedly, the doors close again, almost pinning Andy's nose. He stumbles backwards, taken aback, staring at the doors. "What? No, no, open! Open up!"

He flails his arms, stepping back and forth, trying desperately to activate the doors again.

They finally react, gliding apart once more—but this time, they only open one inch before slamming shut again.

"What's wrong?" Andy demands shrilly, almost with tears in his eyes now. "Why won't you open?"

He grabbles at the doors, trying to force his fingers in between them to pry them apart, but to no avail.

He steps back, panting, staring at the doors as they attempt to open a third time, then a fourth and a fifth, but every time they're slammed shut, as though some invisible force is outmuscling the electrical system.

As soon as Andy thinks the thought, he realizes this is exactly what's happening, and he backs away, his heart pounding in his throat.

It's her ... she won't allow me to leave ...

He wheels around, expecting to see a ghost girl standing there, but he's still alone.

The building is completely silent—except for the strained opening and shutting of the doors behind him.

Andy steps forward tentatively as he looks in all directions, scanning the library for any windows. They're all way up high, too high for him to reach. For a moment, he considers running to the bathroom and locking himself in there, but it's small and has no windows, and the thought of him being stuck in there is claustrophobic.

There is only one way out of the library, and that way is being blocked; which means he's trapped.

A new flood of fear rushes through his body, sending out icy darts of adrenaline all the way to his fingertips.

"Who are you?" he whispers to the empty air, his voice shaky. "Why are you keeping me here?"

Andy holds his breath and listens. There's no answer, except for the roaring of his own pulse.

"What do you want from me?" he demands a little louder.

Still, no reply.

The doors behind him have given up the fight and stopped trying to open. Andy moistens his lips with a clammy tongue and swallows dryly.

Why doesn't she answer me? Or show herself?

Maybe she can't. Maybe the only way she can communicate is ...

He goes back towards the armchair, walking slowly, all his senses poised. He's ready to turn and run at the slightest indication of something ghostly showing itself. But nothing ghostly does, and he finds the book exactly where he left it.

Andy sits back down, his back and buttocks drenched with sweat underneath his clothes, his fingers cold as icicles as he picks up *Solaris*. The text on the page is yet again normal, and the dialogue between the two characters plays out exactly as you would expect it to, no mention of the name Lisa.

Andy clears his throat, then whispers. "Can you ... can you hear me?"

He expects the text to change right in front of his eyes, the letters morphing into some other message.

But the text stays the same.

Andy frowns. To his surprise, he's both relieved but also a little disappointed that he didn't get an answer.

Maybe she can't do it while I'm looking.

The sudden impulse makes Andy shut the book then open it again. And there, on the middle of the page, one single line, completely out of context, screams up at him like a drop of blood on a clean bedsheet.

»yes«

Invisible ants appear on Andy's lower back, crawling up along his spine and spreading out over his shoulders. He glances around, looks behind the armchair, but finds no one.

He's completely alone.

And yet he's not. Someone is here. Talking to him.

"What ... what do you want?" he croaks, the words barely audible.

He closes the book and opens it again.

»talk«

Andy blinks at the word. He had expected something a little more dramatic than that.

"You just ... you just want to talk? Okay. I guess we can talk a little."

He clears his throat, wondering how to small-talk with a ghost.

"So, uhm ... did you talk with anyone else than me?"

He closes and opens the book.

»no«

For someone wanting to talk, Lisa Labowski comes off as awfully curt. Perhaps, Andy wonders, it's not easy for her to talk through the book. Afterall, it must take some effort to change the words on the page. He decides that he should probably be the one doing most of the talking.

"So, have you always been here?" he asks. "Ever since you died, I mean."

»yes«

Andy ponders that reply and exactly what it entails.

How many times has he visited the library? How many hours has he spent here? Every time he has been carelessly strolling around the shelves or sitting here reading a book, an invisible ghost girl has been very close by. Watching him. Maybe she has even touched him. It's a crazy thought.

Another question pops into his mind. "Haven't you been awfully lonesome? I mean, all those years since you died, with no one to talk to."

For the first time, Lisa offers Andy more than a single word reply.

»no time«

He's pretty sure what the answer means, that time stands still when you're dead, or at least moves very differently. Maybe those eighteen years Lisa Labowski has been here in the library haven't felt like eighteen years at all.

But that answer begs still another question. "Where are you exactly? I don't get it ... If you're dead, how can you be here in the library and in the books?"

He shuts the book and opens it again. Lisa's reply makes no sense at first.

»church bells«

Then he hears it. The bells from the church across the street are ringing out.

Andy checks his phone, but the battery is dead. He looks instead up at the clock on the wall. "Oh no, it's six already! I've got to go. It's my mom, she'll worry if I'm out too long. But ... I'll be back again tomorrow. Maybe, you know, I mean, if you feel like it—we could talk some more then?"

Andy's hands are shaking a little as he closes and opens the book—but this time, it's not so much from fear.

»yes«

"Cool," Andy says. "I'll come right over from school."

He brings the book with him as he leaves the library.

Andy notices nothing of the world around him all the way home. More than once, a car honks at him, as he's about to make a turn or cross the street without looking. His thoughts keep going back to the conversation he had with Lisa Labowski.

It's difficult to grasp there was a real girl behind the short lines. At least real in a sense. Not living, but still somehow able to communicate with him from somewhere ... from where, exactly? That last question didn't get any answer.

Andy imagines how Lisa must be able to enter the books in order to change the text. Maybe she sees the universe of the book exactly like he sees the real world. Like a space traveler who can jump from one dimension to another.

This image in his mind spawns a host of other questions. Like, is it only the books at the library, or can Lisa visit any book in the world? Could she be in his backpack right now? Andy doesn't think so. He believes Lisa is somehow tied to the library.

There are also more far-reaching questions to be answered. If Lisa Labowski is really living some sort of afterlife, is she the only one? Could there be others? Do all people get to live on in books when they die? Or could it perhaps be only people who love books and read a lot, like Andy himself? And are there other people out there who have encountered a dead person living in a book?

The more he thinks about it, the crazier everything seems. Like something a child made up in his imagination. Still, his belly feels bubbly with anticipation at the thought of going back to the library tomorrow. He is almost—

Andy's thoughts are abruptly disrupted as he turns into the driveway of the house. The front door is yanked open and his mom comes rushing out. She runs to him and pulls him into a crushing embrace, almost tipping him over, her breath coming in rapid gasps.

"What ... what's the matter, Mom?" Andy asks. "What's wrong?"

Mom's hands are fondling his back, squeezing his sides, checking his arms, and Andy realizes this isn't a hug.

"Are you okay?" she breathes in his ear. "Are you hurt? Did anything happen to you?"

"I'm fine," Andy says, trying to pull back. But Mom grips him firmer, strokes his hair and checks his skull as though looking for bumps or bruises. Andy shoves her back. "Relax, Mom. I told you, I'm not hurt."

She grabs him by the shoulders, and as their eyes finally meet, Andy sees that his mom is not simply worried; her face is contorted in an awful grimace, causing her to look almost like a stranger to him. "Where have you been? Where have you *been*, Andy? We were worried sick! I spoke with all the neighbors, and your father is out looking for you, and I was just about to call the police ... Where have you *been*?"

Andy gapes at her. "But ... but I've just been at the library, like I alwa—"

"Don't you dare lie to me!" Mom exclaims, tightening her grip around his upper arms, her voice growing half an octave higher. "We've been at the library and you weren't there. So where were you, Andy? Did you go home with anybody you don't know? Did you talk to any strangers? Did anyone give you a ride in their car? I've told you over and over again never to say yes to anybody who—"

"Mom, please!" Andy almost yells to outshout her. "I was only at the library. I promise! You must have been there right after I left."

"Then why don't you answer your phone?" Mom's voice is close to a pitch of hysteria, and her grip is hurting him. "I called you like ten times—why didn't you pick up?"

"My battery is dead," he says.

"Your battery is always dead! Or your phone is in your bag, so you didn't hear it, or it's on silent, or you forgot it at home, or ..." She sighs, shaking her head violently. "Sometimes I think you do it on purpose."

"I'm sorry, Mom."

"Sorry doesn't cut it. You're not—"

"Helen? Oh, I see you found him."

Andy turns his head to see Paul Herbert come trudging across the street. The old widower lifts his dingy old cap, exposing the bald head for a second. "Where was he?"

"He came home on his own," Mom says, straightening herself, but only lets go of one of Andy's arms—like she's afraid he might take off. "He says he was at the library. We must have just missed him when we were there."

Paul Herbert raises his thick, white eyebrows in a look of relief. "I see. Well, I'm glad he's fine."

Mom nods, absentmindedly brushing her bangs aside. "I'm sorry we got you worried too, Paul."

"Don't worry about that," Paul Herbert says, sending Andy a brief smile. "And don't be too harsh on him now, Helen. Boys his age so easily forgets time, and—"

"Thank you for your concern, Paul," Mom says, turning to go back inside, hauling Andy along.

The Silence is extra oppressive that evening as the family sits down to eat dinner. Andy feels Mom glancing at him every few seconds, almost like she expects him to disappear into thin air if she takes her eyes off him for too long.

Cindy is home and has joined the family for dinner—both of which happen still less often. Andy still hasn't gotten used to her new haircut: Cindy's hair is long on one side, buzzcut on the other. She also wears a lot more makeup around her eyes than she used to, and her clothes are mostly black and worn-looking. She pokes at her food with her fork for five minutes, then excuses herself and takes her plate to the kitchen. A moment later, Andy hears her running up the stairs. Sometimes, Andy wonders if Cindy has even noticed Rebecca is gone. In a way he envies his older sister for her ability to simply not care. Since Rebecca disappeared, Cindy has seemingly been more concerned with her looks than mourning their little sister. Andy hasn't seen her cry even once.

Suddenly, Mom puts down her knife and fork and says: "Well, let's talk about it."

Dad looks up from his plate. "About what, hon?"

"What do you think, Henry? About your son's behavior."

"Oh, right." Dad looks at Andy. "It wasn't very smart, Andy. You had us all very worried. From now on, we need you to keep better track of time, okay?"

"Okay, Dad."

Dad nods, then resumes eating.

Mom glares at Dad. "Is that all you're going to do about it?"

Dad looks up once more, shrugging. "What do you want me to do, Helen? The boy knows he messed up. He promised not to—"

"Yeah, well, apparently we can't count on his promise, can we? He promised to follow Rebecca home from school, and look what happened."

Andy feels like Mom just punched him in the gut. A moment of thick Silence slugs its way through the dining room, until Dad finally says something.

"Helen," he sighs. "Please think about what you're saying ..."

"I'm not the one who needs to think!" Mom exclaims. "How can we ever feel at ease if we can't know whether our son will come home again or not? Or don't you even care? Don't you care if Andy also disa ... disa ..." Mom can't get the word out. Her lips start to quiver.

"Calm down, hon," Dad tries and reaches across the table.

Mom moves her hand away and breathes sternly a few times. Then she looks at Andy. And there it is again, that strange expression on her face, and suddenly, Andy can see it very clearly, that it's no longer his Mom. Not really. The eyes are all wrong.

"If your father won't be strict with you, I'll have to," she says coldly. "You're grounded for the entire weekend."

Andy shrinks at the thought of two whole days as a hostage in the looming Silence. And what's worse: He won't be able to keep his promise to Lisa.

"It's about time you learned to think about other people, Andy," Mom goes on, her voice lower and less angry, but somehow that's even worse. She looks him straight in the eye, a look of anguish on her face. "Your actions have consequences. Can't you see how terrified you make us when you don't come home on time and we can't reach you? After what happened to your sister ... don't you ever think about that?"

Andy looks down at his plate, his chin begins to jump up and down. He fights back the tears with all his might, but they squeeze out anyway. He feels like jumping up and running upstairs.

But he doesn't.

He just sits there, his head lowered as he starts to sob. He doesn't run to his room, for in a way he understands the punishment is just.

What he has sensed ever since that terrible day, what has been hovering over his head like a heavy cloud, what he has been reading off of the faces of everybody in his life, has finally been stated outright by his mom.

I promised to follow Rebecca home from school, and look what happened.

The words echo in his mind, causing his face to burn and the tears to flow faster.

It's my fault Rebecca disappeared. It's all my fault.

Later that evening there's a knocking at Andy's door. He's on his bed, reading *Solaris*—though he can hardly concentrate on the story, as his thoughts keep going back to Rebecca.

The door opens and Dad looks at him. "Can I come in?"

"Sure." Andy sit up and discretely wipes his cheeks, but the tears from earlier have dried up.

Dad closes the door after himself and goes to sit down at Andy's desk. "Your mom didn't really mean what she said—you know that, right, Andy? She's just afraid, that's all. Afraid of losing you and afraid that Rebecca won't come home."

Andy nods, digesting the words. He believes the second part to be true, the part about his mom being scared. He's not convinced about the first part though.

Quietly, he asks: "Do you believe Rebecca will come home, Dad?"

"Of course I do," Dad says promptly. But to Andy, he doesn't sound very sincere.

He broods for another moment, as he feels the words bubbling up from deep inside, and then he finally says it outright: "I know it's my fault. I shouldn't have gone into the library that day."

The confession hangs heavily in the air. Dad doesn't reply right away, just stares into empty space.

Andy badly wants him to say something, anything. He can even agree with what Andy said—as long as he doesn't just keep quiet. Anything is better than silence.

But Dad doesn't say anything.

"Dad?"

Dad blinks. "Yeah?"

"What if Rebecca doesn't come back?"

"Don't think about that, Andy. She'll turn up."

"Yes, but ... what if? What will happen then?"

Dad looks to the window and the dim evening sky outside. He sighs deeply and says: "Then I guess we'll just have to live on without Rebecca."

Then, as though the conversation is over, he simply gets up and leaves the room with no more words, not even looking at Andy before closing the door again.

For several long minutes, Andy just sits there on his bed, feeling his heart beat heavily in his chest.

How could Dad say it like that? How could he even pretend like everything will eventually return to normal if Rebecca never comes home? Of course it won't. Nothing will ever be normal again without Rebecca.

The thoughts keep going around and around, and Andy feels fresh tears building up in his eyes. He's just about to give in and begin to cry, when something changes.

Something inside of him.

It's like a shift, subtle but significant.

A feeling he hasn't felt before arises and fills him up, strong enough to drown out the impending sobs and force back the tears; it even pushes aside the guilt. Andy is not quite sure what the feeling is, but he's suddenly reminded of Lisa Labowski.

And then he finally recognizes what's going on inside him.

He has a strong impulse to act instead of just feeling sorry for himself. If he can talk with a dead girl in a book, then anything is possible. And since it's his fault Rebecca disappeared, it's also his responsibility to find her again.

Andy gets out of bed and begins planning.

DAY 58

He is awakened by his alarm at exactly 0:00. The ringtone is dialed all the way down; that way, he doesn't risk waking anyone else in the house.

Andy gets up and gets dressed. His clothes are laid out and ready. So is his backpack, which he puts under the blanket and arranges it just like he practiced earlier. With a little effort he manages to make it look exactly like he's still in bed. He goes to the door and looks back at the bed, making sure it looks right from over here—which is where Mom or Dad will be looking from, in case either of them gets up to take a pee and decides to check on him.

As the final touch, Andy takes his phone and starts the recording he made. It's a three-minute-long audio file of him snoring discretely. He sets it on loop and hides the phone next to the pillow. Then he steps back to get the full impression.

It looks totally realistic—in fact, with the added sound effect, Andy gets an eerie feeling of really looking at someone sleeping in his bed.

"Perfect," he whispers to himself, realizing he is smiling. He can't recall the last time he smiled. He can't recall the last time he felt this good, either. He's not exactly happy, but he feels motivated, which is a big step up from sadness.

Now for the second part of the plan, he thinks to himself as he turns to the door. *Getting out of the house unnoticed.*

He leaves his room and slips downstairs. He knows which steps give off screeching sounds, so he deftly avoids them. In his jacket pocket is his own key to the house, and he uses it to lock the front door after he steps outside.

The night air is cool and crisp and quiet. Andy goes to the garage, unlocks his bike and takes it outside. He rides down the street, stops at the nearest light post and finds the map he printed out.

The town is not that big; he doesn't know the exact population figure, but besides the church there is a mall, a drugstore, a nursing home, and of course the school and the library.

He pulls out his marker, locates his own house on the map and puts a tiny X. He does the same with Paul Herbert's house.

"Two down," he whispers. "Only the rest of town to go."

He puts away the map and marker, turns his bike lights on and heads down the street.

Andy spends two hours riding around town.

Surprisingly, he's not sleepy at all. On the contrary, his senses seem somehow heightened, and his lungs welcome the chill air. He only meets a couple of late drivers; besides that the streets are quiet and empty.

He checks every driveway. Every single house gets an X on the map. Where there are closed-off garages, he peeks in through windows or opens the doors slightly—if they aren't locked, of course. If they are locked—or if he is for some other reason unable to get a visual of the car—that particular house gets a dot on the map; which means "scheduled for a later checkup."

A few places he's surprised by automated lights turning on, almost causing him to trip over his own bike in a frantic attempt to get out of sight.

And at one house, a large dog chained up in the carport starts barking at him furiously, probably waking up half the street. By the time the owners could get out to see what the dog was barking at, however, Andy was long gone, riding his bike like a desperate fugitive.

He can't skip even a single house; he needs to cross them all off the map. If he misses one, he might miss the one where the yellow van resides.

Half past three Andy rides back home. He's dead tired and a little disappointed. He honestly didn't expect to find the yellow van on this first night of searching, though; that would be too much luck to ask for, as he has only cleared a very modest portion of the town. He's still determined to spend as many nights as it will take.

When he comes home, he puts the bike in the garage, lets himself inside, sneaks upstairs, throws himself on the bed and immediately falls asleep.

DAY 60

Andy spends all Saturday and Sunday in his room. They are the longest days of his life.

He has finished *Solaris* and reread another book, though he had a hard time concentrating on the reading, since his thoughts were constantly darting back and forth between Rebecca and Lisa Labowski. The thought of her waiting for him at the library is plaguing him. He keeps imagining her standing behind the glass doors, gazing out, a frail ghost girl with a look of sadness in her eyes. Or maybe not sadness—maybe something else. Disappointment? Frustration? Anger, even? How will she react to him standing her up like this, when he promised to be back the next day?

At the same time, Andy is fighting a constant battle with his thoughts which keep telling him Lisa Labowski isn't waiting for him, that she was never really there, that it was all just a trick of his imagination.

Andy finds that idea even worse. For some reason, the prospect of talking with a ghost fills him with great excitement—even though he knows absolutely nothing about her or her intentions.

Which is why he decides to Google her.

It's a pretty rare name, not exactly the kind of name you hear every day. And he's in luck: He finds an article from a local newspaper about a thirteen-year-old girl by the name of Lisa Labowski who died in a car accident right by the intersection of Low Banks and Glenmore Ground—which is the one next to the library building.

So Lisa was hit and killed by a car right outside the library. Perhaps that's why her spirit ended up in the books? Maybe, on its way to heaven after leaving her dead body, it got entangled somehow in the world of the books, which enabled her to live on even though she should be dead.

The only other thing helping Andy to keep his spirit up is his nightly excursions.

In three nights he has crossed off more than two hundred houses—and yet there are still so many left. Being awake half the night is also starting to take a toll on him during the day.

Finally, Monday arrives and Andy is back in school. He fights his way through the lessons, struggling to keep his eyes open.

As soon as he hears the bell, his energy shifts completely, and he bolts out the classroom and makes for the bike shed.

Just as he rounds the corner, Sheila steps out right in front of him. Andy has no time to react, so he bumps into her, nearly knocking her over.

"Watch where you're going, Fatty!" she yells at him, shoving him hard in the chest. Andy is so surprised he loses his balance and trips, falling to the asphalt. He breaks the fall with his left hand, scraping it pretty badly and even drawing blood.

Sheila just scoffs and walks away.

It all happened so fast and unexpectedly, Andy is still befuddled as he gets back up, carefully dusting dirt off his bleeding palm.

Sheila has never done something like this before. Usually, she just taunts him.

He looks in the direction she left and sees her standing not far away, joined by Kimmie and Stacey. Sheila smiles and points to him, making the older girls laugh out loud.

Andy frowns. *She did it on purpose. She was waiting for me.*

Now that he thinks about it, Sheila actually darted him menacing looks more than once during the day, when their eyes incidentally met. He was too tired to read anything into it, but now it's clear to him that Sheila was just waiting for the right time to strike.

I don't get it, Andy thinks, as the mean trio turns and walks away, still sniggering. *What did I do to piss her off?*

He can't think of an answer, so he unlocks his bike and hurries on towards the library.

Regan isn't at work that afternoon; instead Andy is greeted by Stanley, an older librarian with a meticulous grey beard always dressed in shirt and tie. Stanley is chatting with a younger man by the autobiography section as Andy slips by them and heads for row B.

He pulls out *The Wendigo* and brings it to the armchair, which luckily is unoccupied. He makes sure no one is within earshot, before he whispers to the book. "Lisa? It's me, Andy."

He opens to a random page and reads the lines, but they all seem normal.

Maybe she didn't hear me.

He clears his throat and says a little louder: "Lisa Labowski? Can you hear me? It's Andy Wisler."

He scans the page—still nothing.

Perhaps she's in a different book right now?

He gets up and picks another book at random. He whispers to it, opens it and checks—but finds no reply from Lisa.

A sinking feeling settles in Andy's stomach. Is Lisa Labowski not real after all? Was it all just make-believe?

Then something occurs to him.

He gazes at the book, biting his lip, before speaking softly. "I'm sorry I didn't show up when I said I would. I didn't mean to stand you up like that. My mom grounded me because I came home late."

He holds his breath and with shaky hands he opens the book once more. This time, one of the lines pops out at him.

»hello«

Andy feels a jolt of excitement. But it's quickly dampened by a feeling of guilt. Somehow, he senses a lot of different feelings in that single word on the page; sadness, hesitation, anger. The thought of Lisa being trapped in the world of the undead all alone with no one to talk with for eighteen years—and the first time she reaches out, she's almost rejected. He realizes he needs to say something more.

"I ... I thought of you all day. I was really looking forward to speaking with you again."

There's no answer this time. But Andy feels that Lisa heard him, and he gives her a minute before he opens the book again. This time, there's a question:

»hand?«

Andy looks to his left hand and remembers the scrape. It's not bleeding anymore, but it still throbs a little. He discretely closes it. "It's nothing," he mutters, aptly changing the subject. "There's something I've been thinking about: How can you see me? I mean, are you, like, looking out from the book? Like it's a window or something?"

Lisa's reply is both cryptical and very fascinating.

»worlds behind worlds«

Andy imagines being inside the world of the book, to be able to hear all the sounds of the story, smell all the odors, being able to touch the characters and perhaps even talk with them. He imagines it must feel completely real. And still, there's another reality—*his* reality, the reality of the living—right under the surface. Like two photographs blended together.

The thought almost makes him dizzy. "So, does that mean you're actually in both worlds at once?"

This time, he gets no answer. He tries again, but still Lisa is silent.

"Lisa?" he asks tentatively. "Is something wrong?"

The lines remain unchanged. For a moment, Andy fears he might have said something insulting, something to make her upset. But he can't imagine what that would be, and he—

"Andy?"

The voice is right next to him, and Andy jumps in the chair.

Stanley is standing there, a pile of books under his arm, looking from Andy to the book in Andy's lap. "Are you ... talking to the book?"

"I ... uhm ... yeah, well ... it's just ..." Andy stutters, searching frantically for a plausible excuse. "I guess I got a little carried away ... by the story, you know." He tries for a smile, which feels more like a grimace.

Stanley stares at him for a long moment. He's far more old fashioned and rigid than Regan, always talking slowly and deliberately. Andy halfway expects him to wrinkle his nose and walk on, but to his surprise, a faint smile tugs at Stanley's mouth. "It's amazing when a book can make you forget everything else around you. Sorry to disturb you, Andy."

Stanley gives him a nod, then walks to the nearest shelf and begins putting books in their places. He whistles low as he makes his way around the shelves, disappearing out of sight.

Andy's pulse takes a minute to calm down. When it finally does, he asks the book: "Lisa? You there?"

And when he opens the book, Lisa says:

»yes«

Andy thinks for a moment. Lisa got quiet when Stanley was here. But why? Didn't she want him to see what she was saying? Perhaps she wants only Andy to know about her. That at least seems like a logical explanation—and it makes Andy feel special.

On the other hand, it also somewhat fans the flame of the creeping doubt at the back of his mind, the doubt about whether the ghost of Lisa Labowski is real or not.

If she's simply a figment of his imagination, it would make perfect sense that Andy imagines her not wanting anyone else to come in contact with her—just like she avoided Regan the first time Andy saw the strange lines in the book—as that would cause the illusion to break down.

In order to know if she's real or not, Andy decides he needs to know more about her.

"There are so many things I'd like to ask you," he tells her. "Like, did you live here in town? When you were alive, I mean."

He shuts the book and opens it again.

»yes«

"Right. And who were your family? Do they still live here?"

Andy closes and opens the book again, and this time, Lisa's reply takes him by surprise.

»my turn«

"Oh! Sure. I mean ... you want to ask me something? Go ahead."

Closes and opens.

»siblings?«

"Uhm, yes, I've got two sisters. One older sister called Cindy, but she's hardly ever home. I don't even feel like I know her anymore, and I can't remember the last time we talked. My other sister's name is Rebecca. She's younger than me. She's ..." Andy stops himself short. "Right, my turn to ask. I want to know about your family. Are they still in town?"

Lisa doesn't answer his question; instead, she poses another one of her own:

»rebecca?«

Andy frowns. "I thought we were supposed to take turns? You already asked a question."

He closes and opens the book a few times, but the line doesn't change and doesn't go away. It's obvious Lisa wants to hear about Rebecca.

Andy sighs. He doesn't want to argue with a ghost. "All right. Rebecca is ten. She can be a real pain in the butt, but also very sweet. If, for instance, she already ate all her candy and I still have some left, then she's *really* sweet. Let me see, what else? Oh, she's good at drawing. She likes to draw birds. We used to go looking at birds together back before she—"

Andy realizes at the last moment what he's about to say and closes his mouth. He closes the book, too, then opens it again, looking for a reply from Lisa.

But there isn't one.

Andy can sense her waiting; can sense the question still hanging in the air.

He breathes deeply, then begins talking in a low voice. "Rebecca is missing. It happened two months ago ..."

He tells Lisa everything. For the first time since Rebecca disappeared, he allows himself to go through everything that happened that day. It makes him sad to talk about Rebecca like this, but it also somehow makes him feel lighter once he's done.

He closes the book and opens it again. This time, Lisa speaks.

»sorry«

Andy smiles sadly. "Thank you. I guess it's even harder on my parents. They almost never speak anymore. But once I find Rebecca, it'll be all right again. I'm looking for her, you see, at night. Or rather, I'm looking for the yellow van I told you about. As soon as I find that, I'll find Rebecca."

»police?«

Andy shakes his head. "I already told them about the van, but they don't believe it's got anything to do with Rebecca. But I know it was her knocking. I just know it."

This time, Lisa doesn't reply.

Andy waits for a minute, then tries again.

Still nothing.

He says her name a few times, but still Lisa remains silent. He looks around to see if anyone could be within earshot, but he's all alone with the book.

Then, finally, Lisa speaks.

»saw it«

Andy feels a tug in his intestines. "What did you see? The yellow van?"

»outside«

Andy's heart speeds up. "Did you see the yellow van go by right outside the library? When was it, Lisa? Do you remember? And did you get the license plate?"

His hands shake as he shuts the book and opens it again.

»no«

Andy feels his heart sink, but only a little. Now he knows the yellow van drove by the library at least once, which means it probably belongs to someone here in town or nearby. It makes him more optimistic about finding it.

He sits for a few minutes, brooding. Then he decides to turn the conversation back to Lisa by saying: "I read an article about you. I know how you died. What's the last thing you remember from being alive? What's your last memory?"

Half a minute passes, before Lisa says:

»blinding sunlight«

An image comes to Andy immediately of Lisa sitting on a porch in the afternoon sunlight, enjoying the warmth on her face. The thought makes him smile. "That's a beautiful memory. You want to ask me something now?"

»tired«

"Oh, okay," Andy says, feeling embarrassed. "Well, I was about to head home anyway. I guess ... I guess I'll see you around?"

Lisa doesn't reply.

Andy feels his cheeks burning without really knowing why. Is Lisa tired of talking with him? Does he bore her? Or is she really exhausted? Maybe it takes great effort for her to talk.

He gets up and goes to put the book back in place. Just before he does, he checks it one last time. There's a line from Lisa.

»took rebecca«

Andy's insides turn to ice. He whispers: "Do you know, Lisa? Do you know who took her?"

He almost doesn't dare to close the book and open it again, but he forces himself. The new line screams up at him:

»wendigo«

Andy suddenly finds it hard to breathe. He never mentioned the wendigo to Lisa when he told her about Rebecca. Now he's reminded of the ominous dream he had where the demonic creature abducted his sister.

"The wendigo ... isn't real," Andy croaks. "It's just made up ... like vampires and werewolves."

Lisa replies right away, repeating herself:

»met it«

Andy almost can't squeeze out the next question, and it comes as barely more than a breath: "Where?"

The reply from Lisa, on the other hand, comes promptly:

»library«

DAY 61

The next morning, Andy rides his bike to school as usual. And although it seems like a day like any other, to Andy it feels like everything has undergone a shift of sorts.

He's more hopeful than he's been for months.

He's also scared and dead-tired—the latter due to the fact that he was out again last night for three hours straight looking for the yellow van—and the fear comes from what Lisa told him yesterday.

That the wendigo took Rebecca. That she has even seen it, because it visited the library once.

Andy never seriously considered the thought that something other than a human could have taken Rebecca. But now it all makes sense. How he chose that exact book, the story about the wendigo, on the day Rebecca disappeared. What his nightmare meant. And why the police can't find out who took Rebecca. How would they ever do that if they're only looking for a person?

Andy has always seen a clear distinction between what could exist in real life and what could only exist in books. But then again, ghosts have firmly belonged in the latter category, and that conviction has certainly been put to the test.

Somehow, the more he talks with Lisa, the more he becomes convinced that she's real. That he has met her for a reason. In books, nothing ever happens by accident—there is always a deeper meaning—and Andy is getting a growing sense that the real world has somehow been mixed up with the world of books.

He is riding through the park, so wrapped up in his thoughts, that he doesn't notice the strange sound until the third or fourth time he hears it, even though it's quite loud in the cool quiet morning air. It's a brief, sharp rapping.

dakka-dakka-dakka!

Andy stops his bike and looks in the direction of the sound. Apparently, it came from the trees at the bottom of the park. A few seconds pass by until the sound repeats.

He recalls Rebecca often talking about the woodpeckers residing in the park. She always hoped to see them, but as far as Andy knows, she never succeeded.

dakka-dakka-dakka!

There it is again. It's almost like the noise is calling for him. He puts his bike on the stand and steps out onto the wet grass. The sound keeps repeating with short intervals, guiding him, leading him to the trees. As he crosses the tree line, large, cold drops of dew fall from the branches, hitting his hair and his jacket. Andy hardly notices; he's too focused on the sound. He's getting closer. He's almost—

And then, right beside him: *DAKKA-DAKKA-DAKKA!*

Andy spins around, staring at the tree he just passed. There are no leaves on the branches, since the tree is dead. He can tell from the white bark the tree is a birch. But he can't see the woodpecker anywhere.

Slowly, he walks around the tree. He scans the thick trunk up and down, scrutinizing every branch, but sees no birds.

And then he sees it.

The hole.

It's right in the middle of the trunk about ten feet up. Perfectly round, no larger than a ping-pong ball. The rapid tapping sound comes again. It comes from inside the hole.

Andy has an idea. He purses his lips and whistles.

Almost immediately, a small head peaks out from the hole. It's black-and-white and has a pointy beak. The woodpecker looks down at Andy, turning his head slightly to do so.

For a couple of seconds they just stare at each other.

Then the bird loses interest. It pulls its head back in. And a moment later the rapping continues.

Andy's heart is racing. Rebecca loved birds. He needs to show her the woodpecker's home right away. She will be ecstatic when she—

Then he remembers that Rebecca is gone, and his excitement dissipates. He's struck by a deep sadness—until he recalls he has someone new he can share his discovery with.

"It's building a home for itself," he tells Lisa that same afternoon. "I think it wants to put its eggs in there. Maybe it will even hatch them out and have babies! I really wish you could see it. Wait a minute—you can! I could just bring the book to the park."

He closes and opens the book, and the reply from Lisa shouts at him:

»NO«

"Okay, okay," Andy mutters, his cheeks reddening. "It was only a suggestion." He broods for a moment, then asks tentatively: "What happens if you leave the library?"

»death«

Andy stares at the single, ominous word, feeling a cold shiver run down his spine. What does "death" mean? Lisa is already that—but then again, not really. Part of her is still alive in the books.

If she leaves the library, she will die for real.

The thought of Lisa really dying fills Andy with an unexpected sense of dread. He wouldn't want to risk losing his opportunity to talk with her. Already he feels a strange bond with the dead girl, having exchanged but a few words with her and still knowing next to nothing about her.

Andy senses Lisa saying something, and he opens the book.

»rebecca?«

"I'm still searching for her every night," he says, yawning at the mere thought of being up half the night. "I haven't found her yet, but I will. I just need to find that yellow van."

»brave«

Andy feels heat go to his cheeks. "Me? Oh, I think anyone would do the same if someone in their family disappeared."

»not me«

The line befuddles Andy at first. Then it starts to make sense. He frowns. "Lisa, did you ... also disappear?"

»I«

The line seems cut short, as though Lisa interrupted herself.

Andy closes and opens again. This time, there's nothing.

"What is it, Lisa?" he whispers. "What is it you're trying to tell me?"

A couple of minutes pass by. Andy keeps closing and opening the book. Finally, a new line appears.

»gone«

Andy sinks back in the chair. It's obvious to him that Lisa almost remembered something important, but then lost it again. He bites his lip, then says: "You told me the wendigo once visited this library. Do you remember what it came for?"

This time, Lisa replies right away.

»book«

"You remember which one?"

This time, no answer.

"Lisa?"

Still nothing.

Andy waits patiently. Several minutes pass. He checks for an answer now and then, but Lisa thinks for a long time.

At last, she speaks again. What appears on the page is the longest line Lisa has ever spoken to him.

»anatomy of the human eye«

Andy feels a rush of adrenaline. "Okay!" he bursts out. "Okay, hold on a minute. I'll try to find it."

He puts down the book and eagerly goes to search for the book Lisa just named. Judging by the title, he assumes it's a nonfiction, so he goes to that section.

He finds plenty of books on the subject of the human body and different parts of it, including one or two about the eye and the vision, but he finds none with that specific title.

Andy goes to the terminal and makes a search for the book, but gets no hits.

He returns to the armchair and asks Lisa: "There seems to be no book by that title—are you sure you remember it correctly?"

Andy closes then opens the book, but receives no reply from Lisa. He waits half a minute then tries again. Still no answer. He waits again several minutes this time, but still Lisa doesn't say anything.

Finally, Andy concludes that Lisa is tired. She probably spent the last of her strength giving him the name of the book, and she has no more energy to speak today.

Andy is left with a mixture of excitement and disappointment. He was really hoping to find the book the wendigo has read. He's not sure why, but something tells him that book would provide him with a vital clue; perhaps even lead him to the wendigo—and by that, to Rebecca.

DAY 78

The days begin to look alike. Andy's life falls into a certain routine.

In the morning, on his way to school, he checks in on the woodpecker. The bird is working away tirelessly building its home, the rapping sound growing more and more hollow with each day, as the hole inside the tree apparently grows steadily larger.

After school he goes by the library to visit Lisa. Some days he's not alone and they can't really talk. Other days Lisa is more talkative than others.

Andy tries a few times to get her to remember something more about the wendigo—anything that might help him find it. But whenever he brings up the subject, Lisa becomes oddly quiet, as though talking about it to her is either strenuous or uncomfortable. So mostly, they talk about ordinary stuff.

In truth, Andy is doing most of the talking, telling Lisa about his life, sharing his fondest memories and also his ideas for stories he wants to write someday, when he hopefully becomes an author.

When at home, Andy keeps to himself in his room, avoiding The Silence as best he can.

He goes to bed right after dinner and is awakened by the alarm around midnight, enabling him to sneak out of the house to go look for the yellow van. He has several hundred houses crossed off his list by now, but there are still even more to go, and progress slows down with each night as he needs to go still farther away from home in order to find new houses to check off.

Mom has become even more strict about the time that Andy must be home from school—five o'clock sharp—so Andy does his best to maximize the time he can spend at the library. He packs his bag two minutes before the bell sounds. He keeps his jacket ready by his side. And he bolts out the door the minute class ends. It takes him only four minutes riding his bike from school to the library, and only six from the library and home; this gives him a total of fifty minutes in which he can speak to Lisa.

This routine gives Andy a certain amount of comfort. He feels safe knowing what the day will bring, he enjoys the excitement of talking with Lisa, and he's satisfied with the progress—however slow it may be—he is doing at night. There is also a touch of pride in his work; at least he's doing *something* to find Rebecca, unlike everyone else.

Then suddenly one day, something happens which breaks the routine.

One morning, on his way to school, Andy stops by the woodpecker's tree as always. He stands still and listens. And then he hears it. Tiny chirping voices calling from within the tree. Andy breaks into a smile. The sound can only mean one thing.

At that moment, something comes whooshing over his head. The woodpecker lands by the opening in the tree, holding something in its beak. Before Andy can make out what it is, the bird disappears inside the tree. The chirping noises grow more eager. A moment later the woodpecker pops back out and flies off to find more food for its babies.

Andy just stands there, awestruck.

"The babies have hatched," he whispers to the book as soon he sits down in the armchair at the library that same afternoon, still panting from riding his bike as fast as he could all the way from school. "The woodpecker, I mean. I heard them—it was so amazing, Lisa."

He opens the book, but finds no reply from Lisa.

He checks to see if anybody could be within earshot; no one is. In fact, he's the only one here right now. Maybe Lisa simply waits for him to go on—so, he does.

"I saw the parents fly off and come back with food. And I made a recording of the sounds so you could hear them. Here, hold on a minute."

He takes out his phone and finds the recording. He's just about to hit play, when he suddenly feels a cold shiver run down his back for no discernable reason.

Andy looks at the book. "Lisa? Is something wrong?"

He closes and opens the book. The line from Lisa make the tiny hairs at the back of Andy's neck all stand on end.

»it's coming«

He knows immediately who—or rather, what—Lisa is referring to. He darts a look at the window, but can't really see anything from where he's sitting.

"Is it coming in here?" he whispers, his ears stiff, listening for the sound of the automated doors.

He closes and opens the book a few times, but Lisa has gone silent again.

Andy gets up, his legs shaky, and goes to the window. The parking lot in front of the library is empty. So is the sidewalk as far as Andy can see.

Then, it comes into view. Andy's heart feels like it explodes in his chest.

The yellow van drives right past the building.

Before he can even think, Andy is running for the exit. He almost clashes with the glass doors, squeezing out as soon as they're far enough apart. He stares down the street, but the van is already out of sight.

"Damnit!"

Andy runs to his bike, jumps on it and heads off, pedaling harder than he ever did. He spends twenty minutes searching the nearby streets, checking every possible turn the van could have taken. But he doesn't find it.

Andy rides back to the library, trudges back inside, his thigh muscles aching from the effort, and slouches back down into the armchair. "I didn't catch it," he sighs, wiping sweat from his brow. "It was so close. If I had just come a little bit closer, I could have glimpsed the license plate ..."

Lisa doesn't say anything, so Andy just sits there in silence for a while, feeling the sour sting of disappointment.

"My plan isn't working," he mutters. "It could be months before I find that stupid van if I have to keep searching like this. I'm still only halfway. If only there was a quicker way ..."

He senses Lisa saying something, and he opens the book.

»memory«

Andy sits up a little straighter. He can feel the hesitation of the word, feel how Lisa is concentrating not to lose the memory again. He says nothing, gives her time. Then, he closes and opens the book again.

»kidnapped«

Andy stares at the word. His tongue is like sandpaper. He can't talk, so he just closes the book, then opens it once more.

»yellow van«

Andy's heart is knocking against his ribcage. He closes and opens the book several times, but Lisa says no more.

"Who did it, Lisa?" he finally asks. "Who kidnapped you?"

No answer.

"Was it the wendigo? Was it the same one who's taken Rebecca?"

No answer.

"Please, Lisa. Say something. Do you remember anything else?"

This time, Lisa answers him.

»blinding sunlight«

Andy reads the line a couple of times, trying to figure out what it means. Lisa mentioned the memory of the sunlight blinding her before, but he must have misinterpreted it since she brings it up again.

What does it mean? Why is Lisa's last memory of blinding sunlight?

Andy feels like he's very close to a breakthrough. For some reason, he knows whatever happened to Lisa has something to do with Rebecca. He just needs the last few pieces of the puzzle.

"You got to give me something more, Lisa," he tries. "I can't figure it out."

He holds his breath as he closes and opens the book.

»tired«

That's the last word Lisa speaks to him that day.

DAY 79

The follow morning, Andy wakes up exhausted.

He was out again last night, spending three hours riding around looking for the yellow van. Part of him knew he wasn't going to find it, but another part of him felt optimistic since seeing it yesterday.

He plans on going straight to the library after school as he always does. He can't wait to find out if Lisa remembered anything else which might help him.

On his way to school, he rides through the park as usual, wanting to check in on the woodpeckers, and maybe snap a picture of one of the parents to show Lisa.

As soon as he enters the park, though, he becomes aware of a sound quite unfamiliar. It's a loud rumbling, almost like a car engine revving away, except angrier.

Andy stops and stares at the sight which meets him. Many of the trees are tipped over. Two men in bright-orange vests and chainsaws are busy cutting more of them down.

Andy feels his stomach tighten up into a painful knot of fear. He can't see the woodpecker's tree anywhere.

He drops his bike and runs over to the place it used to be. Sawdust is everywhere, the smell of freshly cut wood thick in the morning air, mixed with petrol from the chainsaws.

Andy stops dead in front of the old birch.

It's lying flat on its side. The woodpecker's hole is pointing up into the sky.

Andy's heart turns to stone. He feels nauseous and dizzy as he slumps down on the trunk, burying his face in his palms, fighting the tears.

He can't believe it. They cut down the tree and killed all the baby woodpeckers. The thought makes him want to scream.

At that moment, the chainsaws stop. Silence falls over the park. Andy can hear the men talk with each other; their voices lighthearted. One of them even laughs.

How could they? How could they cut it down and kill those poor babies like that?

Then, suddenly, Andy hears a chirping. He stares at the hole next to him, his eyes widening.

One of the babies is still alive in there! Then, another one chimes in. And a third.

Andy jumps to his feet. He can't believe it: the woodpecker babies have survived the crash!

A loud chirp makes him spin around. In one of the trees still standing, high up on a thin branch, sits one of the parent woodpeckers. It has brought food.

Andy backs away. He's no more than a few yards distance from the birch, when the woodpecker swoops down, lands on the tree and dives down into the hole. The babies tweet eagerly inside.

Andy looks in stunned amazement as the woodpecker reappears and flies off. A few minutes later, the other parent comes, bringing more food.

Andy hardly believes what he's witnessing. The woodpeckers seem to pay little heed to the fact that the tree has been cut down. Apparently, they're still firmly determined to feed their babies.

"Hey, kid!"

Andy turns around.

One of the men is waving at him. "Better not play around here right now. It's not safe. We're cutting up the trees."

Andy points at the birch. "You cut down a tree with a family of woodpeckers inside!"

The man frowns and comes to him. He's younger than Andy took him for, maybe only twenty years old. He lifts his helmet, revealing a pimply forehead.

"Jesus," he mutters. "Looks like you're right, kid. And they're all still alive in there, judging from the sound."

"Yes, and the parents are still bringing them food," Andy says.

As though to prove him right, one of the woodpeckers lands on the birch at that exact moment and slips into the hole.

"Jesus," the guy says again, smiling broadly. "I'll be damned. Hey, Tommy! Come over here a second."

The other guy joins them. He's very overweight and sports a thick moustache. He heaves as though he just ran half a marathon. "What's up, Cliff?"

"Check it out," the young guy says, pointing to the hole. "That's a woodpecker's hole. There's a whole bunch of younglings in there—just listen!"

Tommy looks at the hole, breathing through his mouth. "You're right. Shoot, what a shame we didn't see it before we cut it down. We could have left it standing. Now they're probably not going to make it."

"They will!" Andy exclaims. "The parents are still feeding them."

Tommy looks at him, raising his bushy brow. "You sure about that?"

"It's true," Cliff says. "I saw one of them just a minute ago."

Tommy scratches his neck thoughtfully. "Well, whaddaya know."

"You think we can do something?" Cliff says. "If we just leave it here, the guys will come tomorrow and chop it to chips like the rest."

Andy lets out a gasp of horror at the thought of the woodpecker babies suffering such a terrible death.

"I don't know," Tommy says. "We could move it out of the way, I guess, except it's way too heavy."

"What if we cut out the middle part?" Cliff suggests, snapping his fingers. "We only need to move the part where the hole is, right?"

Tommy shrugs. "I guess it's worth a shot."

Andy feels his hopes rising. He takes a few steps back as the men puts their helmets and earmuffs on.

"Better cover your ears," Cliff tells Andy, then he pulls the string, and the chainsaw roars to life.

The men go to work cutting out about three feet of the birch trunk. The chainsaw bites into the tree eagerly, causing the sawdust to spurt into the air. Meanwhile, Andy notices both woodpeckers waiting and watching in a nearby tree.

The men turn off their chainsaws again. By working together, they raise the piece of the trunk upright. The babies are chirping away inside.

"At least the noise didn't kill 'em," Tommy remarks, looking around. "Right, if we drag it over there ..."

The men pull the tree stump across the soft ground and prop it up between two younger trees which have been spared.

"I hope we didn't scare off the parents," Cliff says, looking around. Andy can't see the woodpeckers anywhere.

The three of them step back a little and wait. The minutes go by. No sign of the parents.

"Hmmm," Tommy growls. "Don't look too good. Maybe we shouldn't have moved it."

Cliff doesn't answer; he glances at Andy.

"Well, there's really nothing more we can do," Tommy says. "We'd better get back to it, Cliff."

"I hope they'll be back," Cliff says, darting Andy a smile. "At least the babies have a fighting chance now. Good thing you spotted the hole, kid."

Andy stays behind as the men go back and resume their work.

He looks at his phone. It's half past eight. He should have been at school more than half an hour ago. He doesn't care, though. He needs to make sure the woodpeckers will keep bringing the babies food.

At that moment, something comes whooshing over Andy's head. The woodpecker flies to the piece of the birch tree and lands on the ground in front of it. It looks around, as though checking out the new surroundings.

"Go on," Andy whispers. "It's okay. Go on!"

The babies chirp from inside the hole.

The woodpecker looks around one last time. Then, it flies up and slips through the opening.

"Yes!" Andy shouts, throwing his fist to the sky. "Yes, yes, yes! They're going to make it!" Without really thinking, he shouts out: "Cliff! Hey, Cliff!"

Cliff is wearing his earmuffs, but still he hears Andy call to him, stops and looks over at him. Andy points to the birch and holds up a thumb.

Cliff smiles broadly and returns the gesture.

Andy feels very relieved as he hurries back to his bike.

He's almost an hour late for school.

He runs down the hallway and reaches his classroom. He's just about to knock, when the door is opened.

Their math teacher Otto looks at him in surprise. "Oh, hi, Andy! Didn't think you'd come today."

"I'm sorry," Andy mutters. "I was just a little late."

"That's okay," Otto says, smiling. "I'm glad you're here now. I just called your mom."

Andy freezes. "What? Why?"

Otto shrugs. "I was worried about you. You need to call in sick if you can't make it to school, remember? And since I hadn't heard from you, I decided to call and check. Your mom sounded pretty worried, so I think I'll call her back and tell her you're here now."

Otto goes to his pocket when a voice cries out: "Andy! Oh, thank God!"

Andy's stomach curls up. He turns around as though in slow motion to see Mom come running towards him, her hair fluttering. She grabs him and hugs him tight.

"Oh, dear God," she breathes. "There you are ... there you are ... oh, God, I was so scared ..."

"Mom, calm down," Andy says, trying to pull free. "I'm fine. I was just a little late."

Mom pulls back, and as Andy looks into her eyes, he can tell right away it's New Mom. "A little late?" she repeats shrilly. "Otto calls me because it's been almost an hour and no one knows where you are! You call that 'a little late'? Where were you, Andy? Where *were* you?"

"I ... I was at the park," Andy says, glancing through the open classroom door. Several of his classmates have come to look at the scene. Andy feels the heat rise to his cheeks.

New Mom doesn't seem to care one bit how many are looking. She just stares right at Andy, her pupils contracted. "The park? What on earth were you doing in the park?"

"I had to save the woodpeckers, Mom," he murmurs. "They had cut down the tree, and ..."

"Woodpeckers?" New Mom exclaims. "You're on your way to school, and you go looking for birds? My God, what's wrong with you, boy? Don't you ever think anymore?"

Otto clears his throat. "Well, Andy is here now. I'm sure he'll be more careful about the time in the future."

Mom looks at Otto briefly, as though only now noticing his presence. "Thank you for calling me, Otto. I'm terribly sorry about this."

"Don't be," Otto says, looking at Andy. "Come with me now, Andy."

Andy is very thankful to Otto. The teacher obviously senses how embarrassing the situation is for Andy. And if Otto hadn't interfered, New Mom could easily have worked herself up into hysteria. Andy tries to walk away, but New Mom grips him by the arm.

"Hold on," she says. "Since you can't be trusted to go alone anymore, I'll drive you to school from now on, and I'll pick you up afterwards."

"No, Mom," Andy says, shaking his head in horror. "I'll go straight to school from now on, I promise. You don't need to—"

"I don't care about your promises," New Mom interrupts harshly, pointing to his face. "This is the way it'll be. Got that?"

Andy stares at her, and he can tell there's nothing to do. The frustration bubbles up inside of him. He's painfully aware that both Otto and his classmates are watching him, awaiting a reaction. Andy feels like screaming. His face is burning.

"Okay, Mom," he mutters.

New Mom's expression softens a bit. She releases him and sends Otto a smile which is really more of a grin. "Please don't hesitate to call me again if anything else like this happens."

"I will," Otto says, forcing a smile.

Andy hurries into the classroom, cutting through the masses blocking the doorway and heads for his desk. Somewhere in the crowd he can hear Sheila laughing scornfully.

And from the doorway, he hears Mom's voice: "See you at two o'clock, Andy. I'll be parked by the bike shed."

Andy doesn't answer.

The humiliation is complete.

DAY 80

"It's the most embarrassing thing I've ever experienced," Andy tells Lisa. "And I can only come here with her as my warden now." He nods at the window. "She's parked right outside, waiting. Once my ten minutes is up, she'll come and get me."

Lisa doesn't answer him.

Andy sighs heavily. "And now Sheila will have something new to bully me with—it's just great."

This time, there's a reply from Lisa.

»sheila?«

Andy realizes he has never told Lisa about Sheila. "It's just a girl in my class. She's a real pain in the butt. She's always badgering me. I don't know why, though, but it got a lot worse after Rebecca disappeared. She's even started hurting me. Remember that day I had a scratch in my palm? That was her. She shoved me so I—"

Andy shuts up as he suddenly becomes aware of what he's saying. He sounds like a complete wuss, complaining about a girl bullying him.

Lisa says something.

Andy opens the book.

»fight back«

Andy is very surprised by Lisa's answer. "What do you mean? Should I … shove her back? No, I can't. She's a girl."

»bring her here«

Andy bursts into laughter at how unexpected the line is, then he looks around guiltily. Luckily, no one is around to hear him.

"Why?" he asks, smiling at the book. "Why would I bring her here? What would you do to her if I did? Beat her up? You're only a ghost, remember?"

As soon as the words leave his lips, Andy hears how mean they sound. He didn't mean for them to come out like that, not at all, he's just in a bad mood.

"I'm sorry, Lisa," he sighs. "It's just—"

Andy stops as the chair begins shaking. At first, he thinks it's his own legs, but then the shaking grows more intense, and the chair almost tips over.

"Holy crap!" Andy exclaims, jumping to his feet. He stares at the trembling chair. "What the …? Lisa, is that you?"

Suddenly, it's not only the chair shaking, but all the shelves around him. Books begin raining down, thudding to the floor, the noise growing deafening. It's like an earthquake going through the building, two of the shelves even tipping over with a couple of loud crashes, books spilling out everywhere.

Then, it stops.

It's over just as suddenly as it began. A few more books slide to the floor, then complete silence falls over the library.

"Oh my God," Andy whispers, looking around at the devastation. "Why did you do that?"

He opens the book still clutched in his hand. Lisa doesn't answer him.

Andy realizes that while the room is no longer trembling, his entire body is shaking. He's terrified. Suddenly, he doesn't want to be here anymore. He feels like someone is standing very close, staring at him with eyes full of rage.

"I ... I have to go," he says to the empty air. "The ten minutes are up. I'll ... I'll see you around."

He turns and leaves the library in a hurry.

DAY 81

The next day, Mom drives him to school as promised.

As they pass by the park, Andy almost crawls out of his seat to look for the birch tree.

"What are you doing?" Mom says. "Sit down, Andy."

He sits back down with a sigh. "I can't see them from the street anyway."

"See who?"

"The woodpeckers."

He can feel Mom eyeing him. "We can stop by the park on the way home," she says.

Andy looks at her, but now she's looking straight ahead.

"As long as you keep our agreement and comes straight out to the car as soon as class ends," she adds, still not looking at him.

"Fine," he mutters.

They reach the school and Mom drops him off. Andy looks around the parking lot as soon as Mom drives off, hoping that no one was around to see him. But of course, someone was.

Sheila is coming towards him, flanked by her two faithful cronies, Kimmy and Stacey.

Oh, crap ...

"Well, look! The baby just got dropped off at the daycare," Sheila taunts right out the gate.

Andy sighs heavily. Normally, he would avoid looking her in the eye and head in another direction in a hurry. But something keeps him from moving. Lisa's line from yesterday suddenly appears in his mind's eye.

»fight back«

Andy stays where he is. He feels the old, familiar fear come rushing up from within; but instead of reacting to it, as he's so used to doing, he brushes it aside.

"I'm not in the mood today, Sheila," he hears himself saying—his voice surprisingly firm.

Sheila stops in front of him, widening her eyes dramatically. "Uh, whaddaya know? The baby talks!"

"Don't call me that."

"You don't tell us what to say," Kimmie brays.

Andy doesn't even look at her; he holds Sheila's gaze. "I mean it, Shelia. I'm done with this."

Andy's heart is pounding away like a jackhammer, trying to make its way into his throat. But to Andy's great surprise, he finds himself not caring anymore. He doesn't care about the fear, and he doesn't care about Sheila. He's not the old Andy any longer, the nervous, submissive Andy who would let Sheila walk all over him because he was afraid. He's still afraid, mind you, but he's even more angry. And those words are still flashing in his brain, like a silent fire alarm.

»fight back« ... »fight back« ... »fight back«

The cronies are both cackling now, yet Andy doesn't hear a word of it; he's still just staring at Sheila, who's staring back at him, a devilish smile on her lips.

"I wonder," she says, her voice playfully soft and sinister. "What will happen if we keep you here until class begins? You think the teacher will call your home again? You think Mommy might come running again? You'd like that, wouldn't you, you big baby?"

Cries of shrill laughter come from Kimmie and Stacey.

"I'll only tell you this once," Andy says, his voice still firm. "I'm going to go to class now. And don't you try and stop me."

Sheila's eyes grow narrow. "You don't talk to me like that. You don't have the right to—"

Andy simply walks right by her, cutting between her and Stacey.

Sheila is so surprised, she doesn't even have time to react.

"Hey!" she shouts after him. "I'm talking to you!"

Andy walks towards the entrance. He wants to run, but he forces himself to walk. He doesn't want it to look like he's fleeing.

He can hear Sheila come running after him.

"You stop right there!" she hisses, grabbing his arm. "I'm not done talking with you!"

Andy doesn't turn around, but he jerks his arm free with such force, he almost sends Sheila flying. She struggles to keep her balance, then she just glares at him in stunned disbelief. Her cronies come running to the rescue, shouting angrily at Andy. He just walks on towards the entrance.

Sheila doesn't try to catch up with him again.

Andy heads down the hallway, his pulse still beating like a heavy metal band, his armpits are drenched from sweat. But a tentative smile is lurking at the corner of his mouth.

I did it ... I really did it!

He can't believe it. He stood up against Sheila, and he won! It's almost too good to be true.

In fact, it *is* too good to be true.

As he steps into class, most of the students are there. A few of them look at him, and Andy feels like he can tell a difference on their faces. He feels like a whole new person, and he's pretty sure his classmates can tell. He straightens his back and goes to his desk.

Just as he puts down his backpack, Sheila comes into the classroom. She's no longer accompanied by her cronies, but her expression makes it clear immediately that the matter isn't settled yet. Her eyes seek out Andy and fire lightning at him.

"There you are, you fat piece of shit," she snarls. "You just think you can walk away from me like that? Who the hell do you think you are?"

Heavy silence falls on the room. Everyone freezes up and looks from Sheila to Andy.

Andy doesn't answer. He ought to sit down, but his body doesn't obey; it just stands there, next to his desk, firm like a soldier in line.

Sheila breaks eye contact to look around for something. She goes to the whiteboard and grabs the pointer stick out of the holder. It's a three-feet-long, thin aluminum spear, and in Sheila's hand it looks like a nasty weapon.

She turns to Andy, and now she's once again smiling. She waves the pointer stick back and forth like a windshield wiper as she walks towards him.

"What are you going to do with that?" Andy asks in a low voice.

The bell sounds right at that moment, and Andy feels a jolt of hope. He might be saved by the bell, quite literally. The trouble is, sometimes it takes five minutes before the teacher shows up. And Sheila doesn't even react to the bell.

"I just want to ask you a question," Sheila says, stopping a few paces away from him. "That's all. Just one simple question."

As they stand in front of each other, Andy is both taller and broader than Sheila by a significant margin, yet Sheila's voice clearly betrays that she feels like the one in control—and that she enjoys that feeling.

"Fair enough," Andy says. "Ask it then."

"Why are you so fat?"

A couple of the other students snigger nervously.

Sheila breaks into fake laughter. "That was just a trick question! I already know why you're so fat: you eat too much."

"Stop calling me that."

"Why should I? It's true. You *are* fat, Andy."

Andy glances towards the door. Students are coming in at a steady pace, yet no sign of the teacher. The classroom has turned into an arena, everyone looking at Sheila and Andy, the newcomers quickly realizing what's about to go down and joining the circle.

"All right, here's my real question," Sheila says. "But I warn you ..." She taps him on the shoulder with the pointer stick. "If you don't answer correctly, I'll have to punish you."

"If you hit me with that," Andy says through gritted teeth, biting back the rest of the sentence.

"Then *what*?" Sheila hisses, stepping close to him and staring up into his face. Andy can smell her perfume. "Then what, you fat moron? Are you going to run home to your Mommy crying?"

Andy can't reply. He can't get any more words out. His blood is boiling. Every muscle is seething. He manages to shake his head once.

Sheila smiles. "Good. Here's my question, then. It's about your sister."

A rush goes through the room, then everyone falls even more quiet. Sheila just mentioned Rebecca, whom no one talks about.

Andy feels something brewing in his chest. It feels like thunder.

"Now, I know the police say she's disappeared," Sheila begins in a lighthearted tone. "But isn't it the truth, simply, that you ate her?"

No one laughs this time. The silence is as thick as sand.

Sheila stares at Andy, smiling and holding the pointer stick ready to strike. "What do you say, Andy? Did you eat her? Is that what really happened to poor little Rebecca?"

Andy forces his jaw to unclench, enabling him to whisper: "Fuck you!"

Sheila's smile vanishes. "Wrong answer." She swings the stick. It hits Andy on the thigh, hard enough to produce a loud smacking noise. Andy doesn't feel anything, though. He doesn't even flinch.

Instead, he draws back his right arm and hurls it at Sheila, connecting his open palm to her cheek with brutal force. The slap is much harder than he anticipated. Sheila's head is flung sideways, she stumbles and halfway falls over a desk. The pointer stick lands on the floor with a metallic sound.

Then, a few long seconds of silence.

No one moves.

Sheila straightens up, wobbles briefly, then lifts her hand to her cheek, which is already a fiery red. She stares from her hand to Andy, her face a mask of shock and confusion. Then the mask crumbles and she breaks into tears, right before she whirls around and runs out of the classroom.

In the doorway she almost collides with Otto, who enters at that exact moment.

"Wow, Sheila, where are you going? Class is about to begin …"

Sheila just squeezes past him and disappears out of sight.

Otto looks to the rest of the class. "Was she crying? What happened in here?"

No one seems to want to answer. The students just exchange hesitant glances. A few of them look at Andy.

Andy is suddenly able to move again. He sits down in his chair. The rest of the class follows his example and finds their seats.

"Well," Otto murmurs, shrugging. "I guess I'll find out if it concerns me, won't I? Right, let's get to work …"

DAY 84

Andy is certain punishment awaits him. He's sure the principal will show up, telling him they need a talk. Maybe he'll even get expelled. And of course, once Mom hears about it, he'll be grounded for life.

Or maybe Sheila won't even tell on him. Maybe she'll simply take matters in her own hands and show up with a gun at recess to shoot him. Andy almost prefers that outcome; at least it'll be over quick.

But to Andy's utter amazement, none of the scenarios come true. In fact, nothing further happens.

The rest of the day proceeds in a surprisingly normal fashion. Sheila doesn't turn back up. Apparently, she left school when she ran out of class.

The only difference is how his classmates are looking at him. To begin with, their eyes are anxious, almost scared. But then, little by little, as they find out Andy hasn't turned into a raging monster, they become softer, warmer even—and by the end of the day, a few of them have even smiled at him. That hasn't happened since Rebecca disappeared. In fact, being completely honest, Andy can't remember any of his classmates having *ever* smiled at him.

Mom shows up after school. They go by the park as she promised, and Andy checks on the woodpeckers. He can still hear them in there, chirping away.

Afterwards, they go by the library. Andy had actually decided to tell Mom they could skip the library today—after what happened last time, he was afraid to show himself, much less talk with Lisa. But now he's not remotely scared anymore.

Regan greets him with a smile when he steps inside. "Hello, Andy! Gosh, did you hear what happened? Apparently, an earthquake hit the library yesterday."

Andy stops dead in his tracks. "An ... earthquake?"

"Yeah, I know, it's insane! Come look at this."

She shows him into her office and finds a videoclip on the computer. "Now, I'm really not supposed to show you this—it's from the surveillance cameras."

Andy feels his skin on his scalp tighten all over.

"But since no one is on the recording, I think it's fine," Regan goes on. "The angle is a little off; the camera moved slightly just as the shaking began, but we fixed it. Well, here it is, are you ready?"

She runs the clip, and Andy sees a black-and-white overview of the library exactly where he sat yesterday—except the angle is just far enough to the side that the armchair isn't in the shot. He sees how the shelves start to shake and books fall out.

"Holy crap," he whispers.

"I know," Regan says. "Luckily, no one was here—I checked in the system. They're sending someone from a local news station later this afternoon to talk with me about it. Isn't that crazy? I mean, there's never been an earthquake within five hundred miles of here!"

"That *is* crazy," Andy admits, swallowing dryly, trying to think. It isn't true that no one was here yesterday—*he* was. He let himself in using his card. But why doesn't that show in the system?

And who moved the camera so that I wasn't in the shot?

Andy feels goose bumps pop out all over his back.

Regan talks some more, and Andy tries to nod at the right places. Then a woman comes to ask for Regan's help finding a book, and Andy is released.

He goes to the armchair. The shelves have been fixed and all the books are back in place—it must have taken Regan hours to sort it out.

Andy takes a random book and sits down. For a moment, he just sits there, the book on his lap. He doesn't really know what to say. He can sense Lisa is there, waiting.

Then, finally, he says: "I fought back."

He waits a moment longer, then opens the book. A single word from Lisa.

»good«

That evening, Andy waits for someone to call Mom; either from school or maybe Sheila's parents. But part of him knows it won't happen.
   And that part is right; Mom's phone never rings.

DAY 87

Sheila doesn't come to school the next day. Or the day after that.

Andy begins to think she'll never show up; that she maybe moved to another school. But on the third morning, right after Mom drops him off, he sees her standing in the schoolyard, waiting, alone.

Andy hesitates for a moment. He can tell Sheila has already seen him, but she just stands there, her expression blank.

Okay, this might be it, Andy tells himself, breathing deeply. *Round two is about to begin. Be tough. Don't let her get away with whatever she's going to try.*

He walks towards her, stopping a few yards away. His fists are buried in his pockets, clenched firmly. For a moment, they just stare at each other, like two cowboys in a western.

Then Sheila says: "Hey." No anger in her voice.

"Hey yourself," Andy retorts, a bit uncertain.

Sheila rubs her arm and looks away. Then she takes a few steps closer. Andy stands his ground, thinking it's a trick. He darts a quick look around, suspecting Kimmie and Stacey to be sneaking up on him; but no one else is around.

Sheila looks at Andy's feet as she says: "Look, I'm sorry for what I said about Rebecca."

She sounds so sincere, Andy is taken completely off guard. "That's ... that's okay."

"No, it really wasn't. It was very mean."

Andy has no idea how to react or what to say. The situation is so unexpected, almost surreal. Part of him is still suspicious, expecting this to be some sort of devious ploy to get him to lower his defenses so that Sheila can really hurt him when he's most vulnerable. But something tells him she's being honest.

"I guess I'm sorry I slapped you," he says.

Sheila scrapes the ground with her shoe. "I probably deserved it; I hit you first."

"It didn't really hurt."

"So ... we're friends, then?"

"Uhm, yeah, sure."

Sheila looks up at him briefly, before she turns to walk away, but then seems to think better of it and turns back around. "You know, my older sister died."

"Oh," Andy says stupidly. He had no idea Sheila even had a sister.

"She was about Rebecca's age when it happened," she goes on, her voice very low, almost a whisper, and Andy must strain to hear her.

"I'm ... very sorry," Andy manages. "How did it happen?"

"She drowned. One day, she just vanished. The police never found her, but they found her clothes and her bag in the stream down in the park. They think her body

...." Sheila breaks off as her lower lip begins to quiver. She bites it to make it stop, but Andy can see tears in her eyes now. "Her body must have been taken by the stream out to the ocean and eaten by fish. I was only six back then, but I still remember how we used to play." A single tear runs down Sheila's cheek, and she quickly wipes it away, then looks him straight in the eye. "I hope Rebecca comes home."

Sheila turns around and leaves.

DAY 95

Following the episode with Sheila, the days go back to normal and begin to look very much alike again.

Andy is still looking for the yellow van at night; he feels his efforts might be in vain, but he doesn't know what else to do, and at least doing *something* is better than nothing.

The trips have grown longer, since he needs to go farther away from home to find streets he hasn't crossed off the map yet. There are only a few hundred homes left by now, and with each night, Andy's hope of finding the yellow van dwindles.

One night, as Andy returns home at about 3:30 AM, he puts his bike in the garage and lets himself in through the front door, making as little noise as possible.

By now, he's done it so many times—slipping in and out of the house like a burglar—that he hardly thinks about it. That's why the surprise is so much bigger when the lights in the hall suddenly flick on.

Andy spins around.

In the door to the kitchen he sees Mom. She's dressed in her robe. Her hair messy and her eyes puffy. Behind her, on the counter, is a glass of water.

For several long seconds, the two of them simply stare at each other.

Andy has no idea what to say or do; his mind is blank with shock. On Mom's face, however, a terrifying transformation begins, as she turns into New Mom in front of Andy.

"Where ... have you ... been?" she breathes, barely moving her lips.

Andy tries to answer, but he can't.

New Mom steps closer. "I asked you a question, boy." Her voice rising ever so slightly. "Where have you been?"

"I ... I was just ..." Andy gropes for the words. Perhaps he can still get out of it. An idea pops into his head. "I just remembered I forgot to turn off the lights on my bike. I went out to check, just in case I—"

New Mom is at him in three longs strides, grabbing both his ears before he can even react.

"Don't you dare lie to me!" she screams. "I saw you from the kitchen window! I saw you come riding on your bike! Where have you been?"

Andy tries to get loose, tries to pull away, but his back meets the wall. "Auv, Mom!" he howls. "Let go!"

"What is this?" New Mom lets go of one of his ears to snag the map out of Andy's hand. She stares at the crumbled paper. "It's a ... a map," she says, breathless with horror. "Have you been all over town? In the middle of the night?"

"I was just—"

New Mom drops the map and twists Andy's ear all the way around. The pain is intense. Andy can feel the spit hitting his face as New Mom screams at the top of her lungs: "*Have you gone insane, boy!? Have you gone completely insane!? Do you want to disappear like your sister!? Do you!? Is that what you're trying to do!?*"

"No, Mom!" Andy cries. He's on his toes, grabbing her wrist with both hands, trying desperately to relief the pain from the twisted-up ear.

She grabs him by the hair with the other hand and shakes his head back and forth, still screaming into his face: "*Do you want to disappear!? Do you!? Do you!? Answer me! Do you want to disappear!?*"

Andy no longer understands the words; the world is an inferno of pain and fear. He hears himself crying and shouting over and over: "I'm sorry! I'm sorry!"

Then, a new voice cuts through: "**Helen!**"

Andy is able to turn his head just enough to see Dad's legs coming down the stairs. "What are you doing?" he shouts in disbelief. "Let him go!"

New Mom doesn't let go. She just turns on him like a hawk, spitting: "Your son has been out riding around all over town! He's been making fools of us, Henry! He's gone insane! He's—"

"Let go of him, Helen! He's crying!"

Only when Dad rushes to grab Mom does she finally release Andy, and the pain lessens somewhat. He stumbles sideways, his hand going to his ear, feeling warm blood.

"What the fuck is going on?"

A new voice from the staircase. Cindy is standing there in her nightclothes, glaring around at the scene with eyes big from shock.

New Mom is still standing in the middle of the hall. The halogen spots in the ceiling cause her to look more like an animal than anything else. She's breathing heavily, her lips wet from spit, her eyes wild. Her right hand is red from Andy's blood. "He ... he lied to us," she hisses between ragged breaths. "He's been making fools of us all ... he's going to disappear ... just like Rebecca ... he's going to disappear ... he's going to disappear ..."

Dad comes to Andy; his eyes are worried and alive—*really* alive. Like they used to be before Rebecca disappeared. "Are you all right, Andy? God, you're really bleeding."

Andy can't answer, he's still crying too much.

"Disappear ... disappear ..." New Mom keeps saying. "He's going to disappear ..."

"Helen, damnit," Dad says, turning around. "You've almost—" His voice changes abruptly. "Helen?"

Andy looks past Dad just in time to see New Mom turn her eyes up, then collapse to the floor.

Cindy screams.

"It looks a lot better already," Dad says, squeezing the Band-Aid back in place on Andy's earlobe. "It's no longer bleeding."

They are in Andy's room. Andy is sitting on his bed; Dad is standing in front of him.

"What about Mom?" Andy says. "What happened to her?"

"She just got a little too riled up," Dad says. "She's sleeping now."

"Did the ambulance come by? I thought I heard someone talking downstairs."

"I called them just to be sure. But they said everything will be all right. Mom just needs to rest for a few days. She's under a lot of pressure right now. You understand that, don't you?"

Andy nods. There's a dull throbbing in his earlobe.

Dad sits down next to him. "You need to tell me what you were doing riding around town, Andy."

Andy takes a deep breath. "I was looking for Rebecca."

Dad squeezes his shoulder. "That's thoughtful of you, Andy. But you don't need to go looking for her. The police are doing that. They'll find her."

Andy throws out his arms. "But they have no idea where to look. I saw the van, Dad. The yellow van. That's the one I'm looking for. If I find it, I'll find Rebecca."

Dad sighs. He sounds exhausted. "You can't go on like this, Andy."

"But you went looking for her in the beginning. You told me so yourself."

"That's different. I'm a grown-up."

"But I—"

"Listen to me, Andy. You can't be riding around town in the middle of the night looking for some van just because you think it's got something to do with Rebecca. We need to trust the police and wait."

And there it was. The magical word.

"I don't want to wait, Dad! Waiting isn't doing anything for Rebecca. I want to *find* her! It's my fault she disappeared, so it's my responsibility to find her again."

"We went over this already, Andy. It's not your fault that—"

"But it is! It *is* my fault! And you know it—I can tell by your face."

Dad is quiet for a while. He looks down on the floor. Andy's heart is pounding away in his chest.

When Dad looks up at him, his eyes are once more dull and blank. The aliveness has gone away again. "No more excursions, all right? Please give me the map."

Andy realizes it's over. Dad is no longer on his side. He hands Dad the paper.

Dad gets up and trudges to the door. He looks back to say: "I'll be locking the door to your room at night from now on, Andy. Just until this is over."

PART TWO
RECBECCA WISLER

DAY 1

Rebecca glares at Andy as he crosses the street.

Does he really think she's going to wait out here in the freezing cold while he goes looking for a stupid book? Well, if so, he'd better think again. Rebecca decides to give Andy a good scare.

He parks his bike by the stand and looks back over at her one last time, his expression hilariously forbidding, like he's trying to browbeat her from across the street. Rebecca sends him her sweetest smile and a little wave.

He huffs, turns around and marches into the library.

As soon as he's out of sight, Rebecca runs down the sidewalk, her bag jumping up and down. By the entrance to the park are two large elm trees, and Rebecca hides behind the nearest.

She peeks out and holds her breath in excitement. From here, she has a good view of the entrance to the library, yet Andy won't be able to spot *her*. Once he comes out, he'll think she went on homewards, and then he'll hurry to catch up with her.

Rebecca smiles at the thought of tricking Andy like this.

This is what you get for being a jerk.

A minute passes, but Andy doesn't come out.

Rebecca needs to pee really bad. Typical Andy, taking his sweet time.

"Come on," she whispers, shifting her weight from one foot to the other. "Come on, stupid Andy!"

Still, the glass doors don't open.

Then, she hears it.

dakka-dakka-dakka!

Rebecca spins around, staring into the park, her eyes scanning the trees. She immediately knows what made the sound. It's the woodpecker. She's heard it a few times before, and every time she and Andy walk through the park, she keeps an eye out for it, yet she never managed to actually see it.

dakka-dakka-dakka!

There it was again!

Rebecca can even tell which direction the sound came from. This might be her greatest chance to get to finally have a look at the woodpecker.

She forgets completely about teasing Andy and heads into the park, running with excitement. The sound came from the far end of the park, where there's a large area of younger trees. She can't see the bird in the first trees, so she ventures farther in. It's still early spring and only a few of the trees have leaves, so the woodpecker will be easy to spot on the naked branches—provided it hasn't flown off yet. Rebecca scans every treetop meticulously as she goes on.

dakka-dakka-dakka!

She lets out a gasp. The sound was closer and a little to the right. She changes direction and speeds up.

The trees are bigger and stand closer together now, making everything a little dimmer, but Rebecca hardly notices. She reaches some bushes and pushes her way through, then she almost trips over an old, rusty bike someone left here several years ago.

Rebecca looks up as she walks on, listening intently, but now the woodpecker has fallen silent.

She's amazed at how far the trees go on; come to think of it, she's not quite sure what's on the other side of the park. But she needs to see the woodpecker, so she presses on. If only she could—

"*Help me!*"

Rebecca stops abruptly. She holds her breath and listens.

Was that a voice? Someone calling for help?

Now there's only the slight breeze, pushing at the treetops and causing the old leaves on the ground to stir and rustle. She picks up something on the wind, a foul smell; probably a dog turd, except it's even worse than that.

She turns to look back but suddenly she can't tell exactly which way she came from; the forest has grown too thick to see very far, and it looks the same in every direction. She can't even hear the sound of traffic anymore.

Am I even still in the park?

She feels a faint trace of budding panic.

Of course she is still in the park; where else would she be?

Rebecca isn't normally very easily scared. She's not afraid of the dark, not afraid of spiders, and she can even watch scary movies without having nightmares afterwards.

But this is different. She can't put her finger on it, but something is wrong here. She wants to get out of the forest as fast as possible. She doesn't even care about seeing the woodpecker anymore. In fact, she wishes she had never left Andy. She considers for a moment taking out her phone and calling him for help, but Andy will no doubt tease her for getting lost.

Besides, she's not *that* scared. Not yet.

She pulls herself together. She just needs to pick a direction, that's all. Whichever way she chooses will eventually lead her out of the trees. She knows the town pretty well and can easily find her way home from wherever she might end up.

That awful smell again, stronger this time. It smells like something rotting.

Rebecca is just about to move on, when the voice comes again.

"*I'm hurt. Please help me.*"

This time, she can tell it really is someone calling and not just the wind. A girl, probably around her own age. She sounds like she's about to cry.

Rebecca turns towards the sound but can't see anything between the trees. Or can she? She squints.

Rebecca's eyesight is perfectly fine—not like Andy, who needs glasses—and she glimpses something far off. Something yellow. She walks closer.

Rebecca reaches an almost overgrown dirt road obviously no longer in use. An old, mustard yellow and rusty van is parked right in the tire tracks. Rebecca can see through the dark windshield that no one is behind the wheel. She goes around to the back. The back doors are open. She hesitates. The stench has grown stronger still.

"Ugh, what *is* that?" she whispers, wrinkling her nose.

"*It really hurts,*" the voice whimpers—coming from inside the car. "*Won't you please help me?*"

"Sure, I'm coming," Rebecca says, instinctively responding to the pleading tone of the voice, as she steps over to the van, grabs the handle and opens the door.

There is no girl in the car.

There's not even a human being.

The creature staring out at her might *look* like one, but Rebecca can tell right away the face belongs to something very different.

Something monstrous.

Everything happens very fast, too fast for Rebecca to react.

The creature lunges at her. She's pretty sure she fights to get free; she might also be screaming. The only thing she knows for certain, though, is the feeling of the creature's cold, strong fingers.

Then she's lying in the dark, dazed and terrified, as the engine roars to life and the car begins moving. Branches are scratching along the outside of the van, screaming against the metal. Besides the terrible, rotting stench, she can also smell oil and dog in the stuffy air.

She tries to get up, but loses her balance and falls down again right away. She feels something, a car wheel. She recalls briefly having seen it before the light went out and left her in complete darkness.

Except it's not complete darkness.

Rebecca stares at a thin, vertical line of daylight. She crawls towards it. The car makes a turn, causing her to roll sideways, bumping hard into the wall. It hurts badly enough to make her scream out in pain, but there's no time to sulk, she knows that. She needs to get out, while the car is still in the forest. If they make it onto the real streets, it will be too dangerous to jump out.

Her thoughts are going a million miles an hour, flickering around her head like a murder of scared crows, each one trying to out-shout the next.

I'm being kidnapped! What does it want with me? Maybe it wants to kill me! I've got to get out!

Rebecca reaches the strip of light separating the two back doors. She fumbles for a handle but finds nothing.

The car makes another turn, but this time she's more ready for it, and manages to keep upright. She feels the ground smoothing out underneath the car as they speed up.

Oh, no! We're driving on asphalt now!

But they must still be in town. Which means they can't go very fast. Rebecca just still might be able to jump out without hurting herself too badly. Even if she should break an arm or bruise herself bloody, it would still be a thousand times better than being taken by the creature.

The problem is, though, the doors can't be opened from within. She pushes and struggles, but nothing helps.

I can't get out!

Rebecca begins to scream. The sound is ear-piercing inside the confined room of the car, yet she's not sure it can be heard from outside, due to the rumble of the engine. She places her mouth to the strip of light and screams at the top of her lungs: "*Help! Help me! I'm being kidnapped! Heeelp!*"

Suddenly, the car stops, sending Rebecca sprawling backwards, landing hard on her back. She sits back up and listens. The engine is still going, but the car isn't moving.

Then, the sound of the front door opening. The car tilts slightly as the driver gets out. She counts four quick footsteps. Then the light strip is blocked out by a shadow on the other side, and next the doors are yanked open.

Rebecca isn't prepared for the daylight, and it blinds her. She only just has time to glimpse the tall, skinny figure, as it reaches in to grab her. Rebecca fights back, but the creature pulls her in, and again she feels the hard, cold hands as they turn her around so that she faces away from the open doors.

It's going to kill me!

She screams again, but something soft is jammed into her mouth, followed by a sharp, unpleasant taste. Rebecca chokes and tries to spit out the thing in her mouth, but the creature swiftly wraps something thin and hard around her head and tightens it. A shove in her back and Rebecca falls to her hands and knees. Before she can get up, the doors are already shut, and she's once again left in the dark.

Rebecca tries to scream, but no sound comes out this time. She fumbles over her face and feels the cloth in her mouth. A strip of what feels like plastic is tied around her head and keeps the cloth tightly in place. Her fingers find what feels like a knot at the back of her head, but she can't loosen it.

The car moves again.

Rebecca crawls to the light strip and puts her eye close to it. She sees a residential street unfamiliar to her. But at least they're still in town. She screams with hardly any sound and begins banging on the doors.

The car just rolls leisurely through town. The creature is obviously not in a hurry; it knows Rebecca can't get out and now she can't scream for help, either.

As they ride through town, Rebecca peers out at a world which feels miles away. She sees pedestrians, cyclists and people in other cars, and every time she screams for help and hammers away on the doors until her fists ache—but none of them hear her.

Then, suddenly, she remembers her phone. Instantly, her hand goes to her pocket, but she finds it empty. A sinking feeling in her stomach as she recalls how the creature's fingers dug into the pocket. Her bag is also gone.

The car jerks sideways, almost throwing Rebecca to the floor again, and the horn blares angrily. Rebecca looks out of the thin strip and sees—

Andy!

She can hardly believe it. Andy is standing on the sidewalk with his bike, a stunned look on his face as he stares after the van which apparently almost ran him over.

Rebecca screams as loudly as she can into the cloth which is soaked with saliva, and hammers away on the doors with both hands.

To her surprise, the car slows down and comes to a full stop. Rebecca stops banging. For a moment, she is sure the creature will jump out and run to grab Andy, too, but she can't hear the front door open.

She stares at her brother. He looks right back at her. His expression one of confusion and—suspicion?

He's listening! He heard me!

Rebecca starts banging again, just as the car revs up and gets moving again, turning left. The view changes and Andy disappears from sight.

*But he heard me! He **heard** me!*

But what good does it do her? Even if Andy did hear her, he can't catch up with the van now, not on his bike. And if he calls the police, the van will be long gone by the time they show up. It doesn't work like in the movies, where police cars always seem to be parked right around the corner whenever someone dials 9-1-1. It could be several minutes. And by that time, the creature will have taken her far away, maybe all the way out of town, and it could have stopped at a rest stop, and it could have killed Rebecca in the most horrible way imaginable.

Rebecca keeps banging on the doors, but now her effort is weak. She begins to cry. The car drives on. Within a few minutes, it reaches the town limit and speeds up. It heads out onto the highway as Rebecca sees the last houses grow distant.

Still, she keeps banging until her legs give in and she sinks to the floor, sobbing.

She has no idea how long they drive for. Time feels odd in the darkness. Sometimes it seems to move very fast, others it stands almost still.

To begin with, she noticed every time they made a turn, trying to print the route into her memory. But by now they've turned so many times she's lost count.

Every time the van slows down, Rebecca is certain the creature will pull over, come around the back and kill her. But every time she draws a sigh of relief, as the van only slowed down in order to make a turn.

Then, suddenly, the ground turns to gravel. Rebecca can hear it rumble beneath the tires. A few more minutes pass. Then, they finally come to a full stop. The engine is still going. The front door opens and the creature gets out.

This is it! It's going to kill me now!

Her heart feels as though it explodes in her chest. She jumps to her feet and steps away from the doors, as far back as she can. She tries to ready herself for the doors to open, tells herself to not become blinded this time, to get ready to fight for her life.

But surprisingly, the doors don't open. The footsteps don't come around the back, but head away from the van in the opposite direction. She listens intently.

Someplace not far from the van she picks up the sound of metal rattling. Then, the footsteps come back towards the car. It rocks gently as the creature gets back in behind the wheel, then they are moving again.

Rebecca goes to the doors to peek out. They have just passed through an open and very tall wrought-iron gate, and now they enter a large gravel courtyard. Old buildings appear on each side.

The van stops again. This time, the engine dies with a few, dry coughs. Rebecca can hear her heart pound away in the silence that follows.

The creature once more gets out of the car. Steady footsteps through the gravel. Rebecca backs up and readies herself again, staring at the strip of light. But the doors are still not opened. Instead, she hears the metal rattle once more.

It went to close the gate.

Rebecca listens as the footsteps move farther away from the van. There's a sound of a door opening. Then, silence.

Rebecca breathes quickly through her nose. Her jaw is aching, and her cheeks are burning from where the plastic strip is gnawing at the skin. She can hardly fathom she's still alive. But it might only be a matter of minutes. The creature probably went inside the building to find something to kill her with.

I need to get out of here before it comes back! This could be my last chance ...

She kneels down and feels her way across the floor, searching for something, anything she can use to pry open the doors. All she finds is the tire, a roll of rope, an empty cardboard box and a crooked metal pipe of some sort. None of it can be used as a door opener.

Suddenly, she hears the footsteps return—two pairs of them, now. One pair of long, steady steps, and one much smaller, much faster.

Rebecca picks up the pipe and backs away from the doors. She's not sure how hard she'll be able to swing the pipe, as it's very heavy in her hands, but she's determined to do her best.

The strip of light disappears.

The lock turns.

The doors open.

Rebecca squints at the bright daylight and holds up the pipe, ready to swing at anything which might come at her.

But nothing does.

She blinks as her eyes adjust to the light. She sees a slice of the courtyard, but the creature is nowhere to be seen. In the gravel, however, a few yards away, sits a small dog that looks up at her with a look of curiosity, its tail wagging gently.

Rebecca holds her breath to listen. *Is it a trick? It has to be ...*

She swallows hard and fights to hold back the tears. It's hard; she's never been this scared before, has never been in a situation like this. She shifts her weight from foot to foot, the pipe growing slippery with sweat from her palms.

The dog gives off an impatient whimper and moves its head a little. A tiny bell hanging from the collar rings briefly as the dog looks at her like it's trying to say: "Why are you just standing there? Come on out here. It's okay."

Rebecca can't take it anymore. She drops the pipe and makes a run for it, jumping out of the open doors. The dog pulls back in surprise as Rebecca comes flying out. But she never lands on the gravel. A long, slender arm shoots out and catches her midair.

Rebecca squirms, kicks and punches. The creature wraps its arms around her, pinning her against its boney body in a crushing embrace, preventing her from moving. It's way too strong; way stronger than a human. It can easily break every bone in Rebecca's body. The stench from it fills her nose as she is carried towards the building. She screams into the cloth until she almost can't breathe.

The creature brings her inside what looks like a quite ordinary, yet very messy, home. The air is stale and stuffy, smelling heavily of dust and cigars.

The creature carries her upstairs, down a hallway and into a tiny room with old, nicotine-brown wallpaper. Then, it throws her facedown onto a bed without any sheets.

Before Rebecca can get up, a hand is placed right between her shoulder blades, pushing her down into the mattress, squeezing the air out of her lungs.

As Rebecca struggles in panic to breathe through her nose, she vaguely notices her shoes and socks being pulled off. The pressure on her back eases off just enough for her to lift and turn her head sideways, heaving in long, whining breaths through her nostrils. Then a cold, strong hand locks around her ankle, and she hears a strange whistling noise which reminds her of the sound a hot stove gives off when you spray water droplets onto it.

Then comes the pain.

It's sudden and sharp and shoots up through the ball of her foot.

Rebecca screams and tries to kick, but the grip around her ankle is like iron, and the creature presses her back down as she tries to wriggle sideways.

The pain in her foot eases slightly as the seething noise stops. Still keeping her pinned to the mattress, causing Rebecca to once again feel like she's suffocating, the creature shifts its grip to the other foot, and then the noise and the pain come again, just as bad as before.

Rebecca screams, cries, coughs and wretches all at once, fighting to get air in through her nose and trying not to throw up into the cloth, which would definitely cause her to choke.

Then she's abruptly turned onto her back.

Rebecca flails her arms aimlessly, trying to tear at the creature, sensing only a blurry outline of it through teary eyes.

It grabs both her wrists, seemingly with little effort, and pins them both atop her head. Rebecca squints her eyes, anticipating pain and tries to turn her face away, but the creature's cold fingers clamp down on her chin and turns her head back to neutral. She tries again to scream, but manages only a muffled sigh, as the creature's fingers go to her left eye and force it open. Through tears, Rebecca gets a glimpse of its greyish face soaring above her with the brown ceiling as a backdrop. Then she feels a drop of cold, thick liquid in her eye, blurring her vision even more. A second later, it begins to burn and sting. The creature moves to the other eye and repeats the procedure.

During the whole operation, the creature is completely silent. Rebecca can't even hear it breathing—only her own, panicked noises.

Finally, it rolls her over on her side and lets go of her wrists. Rebecca's hands immediately go to her stinging eyes, rubbing them, but that only makes it worse. She feels the creature fumble at the back of her neck. There's a snap. The pressure around her head disappears, as Rebecca is able to spit out the soaked-through cloth and heave in deep, freeing breaths.

She tries to open her eyes, but they burn too badly, so she simply scrambles to the far end of the bed, pushing up against the wall. Her feet are burning, and her eyes sting like mad. She forces herself to breathe quietly, allowing her to listen.

The room is quiet. It sounds like the creature left.

But no. Rebecca can smell it. The rotten stench and the sour odor of cigar. Only now, it's mixed with the scent of something burned.

She manages to pry open one eye a few millimeters, and she gets a glimpse of the ragged figure standing there, next to the bed, staring down at her, what looks like a lit cigar dangling from its lips.

Rebecca knows the creature only just got started. She knows it's only taking a short break from torturing her. Any second, it will resume.

"Lea ... leave me be," she whimpers, her mouth still wooly from the cloth. "Please just ... leave me be ..."

The creature doesn't answer. Rebecca doesn't know if it understands her; if it even talks. Then she recalls the small, whimpering voice of the girl from the car, and she trembles even more. She blinks and tries to look at the creature, but it's painful having her eyes open.

Then, it suddenly speaks. The voice is nothing like the one it used to lure Rebecca to the van. It's low and rusty, like it's very rarely used.

"Welcome home, Alice," it says.

Rebecca sobs. "I ... I want to go home ... if ... if you take me home ... I promise not to tell anyone ... I promise!"

She halfway sees, halfway hears the creature turn around and walk out of the room, closing the door gently behind it.

Rebecca doesn't move for a while. The stench of burnt skin, smoke and fear is heavy in the air.

She tells herself to get up and try to get out. But her eyes are still stinging, and the pain from under her feet has grown worse. She carefully feels the ball of her feet with her fingers and finds two small wounds on the soft skin. They're no bigger than a penny, but they're bleeding.

While it happened, Rebecca thought the creature cut her with a knife, but now she can piece it together: the circular shape of the wounds, the smell of burnt skin, the cigar.

It burned me.

Rebecca begins to cry again, her thoughts going back to Andy. Did he really hear her knocking from inside the car? Yes, he must have. He turned his head to look straight at her.

Even if Andy didn't hear her, by now he must have realized Rebecca is missing. He probably already told Mom and Dad. They must be out looking for her. Did they call the police yet? If Andy heard her knocking inside the van, he will tell the police—maybe he even had time to see the license plate.

Rebecca feels a faint hope at the thought.

They'll come for me. Andy heard me. They'll come for me.

She keeps repeating it in her head. It keeps all the scary thoughts somewhat a bay. She's very exhausted from being terrified for so long. Now, as the immediate danger seems to be over, the fear drains away slowly, leaving Rebecca to drift off into something close to sleep.

DAY 2

Rebecca awakens abruptly and sits up with a jerk.

What comes back to her first is the pain in her feet. It has turned into more of a hot, pulsating sensation, but it's still painful. Her eyes, however, are a little better; they don't burn or sting as much as they did before she drifted off. But her eyesight is still somewhat blurry, even after she has blinked several times and rubbed at her eyes.

The dusty taste of the cloth is still in her mouth, and she can feel dried-up saliva on her cheeks. She's terribly thirsty.

She looks around the room. It seems to be a child's room, most likely belonging to a girl, judging from the old-fashioned dolls on the shelf on the wall. Aside from the bed, which is placed under a slanted wall, the only pieces of furniture are a bookcase, a desk with a wooden chair, an old chest and a tall, built-in closet. The floor has a worn-down rug and the ceiling hangs very low, like it's about to fall.

Rebecca has no idea how long she was out for. The room is dimmer now, outside the single window the sky is dark grey. She slept very deep with no dreams; in fact, it felt more like she was unconscious. For all she knows, she could have been gone for hours, perhaps even a whole day.

She swings her legs over the edge of the bed and carefully puts her feet to the floor, immediately sparking darts of pain from the burn wounds.

She manages to get up and wobbles to the window. The view is blurry, almost like the glass was wet from rain, but she can make out a large garden encircled by a tall, thick hedge, and on the other side are open, naked fields. No other houses are visible for as far as Rebecca can see. Out by the horizon lies a brownish belt, most likely a forest. For a hopeful moment, Rebecca thinks it might be the forest next to the park, but then she remembers how long they drove to get here; it must be another forest.

She turns and staggers across the room to the door, her feet throbbing worse with every tentative step. She tries her best to only put weight on her heels, but it's difficult walking like that. She reaches the door and tries the knob, expecting it to be locked, but it turns willingly.

Rebecca peers down a long, dark and narrow hallway with no windows and three doors, all closed. At the end is the staircase leading down.

She can neither see nor hear the creature; it could be lurking right behind any of the doors, or maybe at the bottom of the stairs. She breathes through her nose, sensing faintly the rotten smell in the air.

Rebecca's heart is beating in her chest. The hallway reminds her of a river in Africa, and she's a gazelle who needs to cross it, not sure if a crocodile is waiting just below the surface, ready to strike.

Rebecca bites her lip. *Do I make a run for it? What if it catches me? What will it do to me?*

She decides not to risk it, not like this. She can't run on her aching feet, which means she'll have a very poor chance of outrunning the creature if it comes after her.

So, she closes the door again and limps back over to the window. She's on the second floor, and there's a long way down to the lawn. Below the window is a tiled terrace. Rebecca is okay with heights, but jumping from this high up will undoubtedly result in something fracturing—if that happens, she'll have zero chance of escaping.

She moans and sits back down onto the bed, relieved to take the pressure off her feet which are really hurting now.

Perhaps she needs to wait, just a little while. Only until her feet are better. Hopefully, her eyesight will get better, too.

Besides, she's sure help is on its way. The police will come. Andy heard her—she knows he did. He told them about the van. They're probably working hard to trace it right now. Maybe they're even on their way out here. She imagines three police cars racing down the highway, sirens blaring. It's a very comforting image. She hopes they'll shoot the creature dead once they get here.

Rebecca's gaze fall on the basket sitting on the desk. It's about the size of a shoebox. She frowns.

Was that here before? Or has the creature been in here while I slept?

The thought gives her the shivers.

She goes to look in the basket. There's a packet of Band-Aids. A roll of gauze. A tube of cream and a tiny, brown bottle.

Rebecca strains her eyes to read the inscriptions on the labels. There are some difficult words, and she needs to spell her way through them.

Burn gel, it says on the tube.

And *Chlorhexidine – for disinfection*, on the bottle.

The basket is a first-aid kit, Rebecca realizes with surprise. The creature put it here, so she could tend to her wounds.

Next to the basket is a big glass of water. Rebecca sniffs it, not really sure she can trust to drink it. Maybe the creature put poison in it.

But why would it do that? If it wanted to kill her, it could just as easily come in here and do it itself. She would be powerless to stop it.

So, she drinks the glass of water, gulping down every last drop. It washes away the dry taste in her mouth and feels wonderful in her throat.

She brings the basket to the bed and uses first the chlorhexidine, then the burn gel on the wounds. The first one stings badly, but the second one soothes the pain again. She uses the gauze to bandage her feet.

Afterwards, she lies back down, feeling a little better, staring up into the blurry ceiling. She recalls the image of the police cars and feels even better still.

They'll come for me soon. Andy heard me, and he told the police about the van. I just need to wait. They'll be here any minute ...

Rebecca dozes off again.

DAY 3

The next time Rebecca awakens, the room is dimly lit by a faint daylight. She notices right away the pain in her feet is less intense, and as she blinks her eyes open, her sight is almost back to normal, only a small fuzziness around the edges.

She lies still for a moment, listening. She had a dream that policemen were storming the house, shouting and shooting downstairs. The sound of the firing guns and the men's voices were so real, she believes for a second it might not have been a dream at all. But the house is completely quiet, which probably means the police haven't come yet.

That's okay, she tells herself. *They will soon.*

She sits up and feels the bandages. One of them has come a little loose, and she spends a minute fixing it. As she works on the bandage, she becomes aware of a pleasant smell. She looks around the room, noticing she's able to perceive a lot more details now, and she sees a plate on the desk. Which means the creature was in here again.

Her stomach rumbles from hunger. It's amazing, actually, that she can be hungry in a situation like this, but she is. So, she stands up carefully. It's still painful, but with the help of the bandages she's almost able to walk normally.

She goes to the desk and sits down. Sniffs the plate. It's mashed potatoes with small brown lumps, which look like bacon.

She considers again if the creature might want to poison her, or maybe give her something which puts her back to sleep so it can do things to her. But again: why would it make the effort, when it can do what it wants to her already? Besides, there was that thing it said.

"Welcome home."

And then some name, Rebecca can't recall what it was. But apparently, the creature thinks Rebecca lives here now.

"Well, it's wrong," Rebecca whispers to herself. "I'm going back very soon to my real home. The police will be here any minute now."

Meanwhile, she might as well eat something. She lifts the fork and takes a tiny bite. There is nothing alarming about the taste. She takes another bite, then another, and soon she's shoveling down the meal.

Once the plate is empty, she wipes her mouth with her sleeve, then gets up and goes to the door. Again she finds it unlocked.

Rebecca feels a lot braver now, with her stomach full and her head well rested. Still, her heart rate immediately speeds up as she slips out into the hallway. She steps as carefully as she can, but the ancient, worm-eaten floorboards give off tired moans nonetheless. She flinches every time there's a new stab of pain from the wounds. The hallway seems like it's a mile long.

Finally, she reaches the staircase, her mouth dry and her armpits clammy, and she halts for a moment, holding her breath and listening.

Is that someone talking?

It is. And it's not the voice of the creature. It's a man's voice, deep and calm. Someone else is downstairs—maybe the police really have come after all!

Rebecca feels her hope go up. She begins to descend the stairs one step at a time while grasping the greasy banister for support.

She stops four steps from the bottom and crouches down. From here she can see a tiny kitchen bathed in a grey daylight. The stove is really old and greasy, and there seems to be no fridge. The counter is stuffed with plates, newspapers and garbage. But other than that, the kitchen is empty. Yet the voice of the man is still audible.

Who's talking?

Rebecca spots the radio on the windowsill, and immediately, her spirits sink. No one has come for her. She's still alone in the house with the creature. And what's worse: she has no idea where it currently is.

Only one door leads out from the kitchen, and it's open. Rebecca can make out another dim hallway out there.

She gets moving again. Her feet are hurting now, but she ignores the pain and pushes on, hoping to reach the front door and get out of the house before the creature shows up.

Halfway through the kitchen, a subtle ringing makes Rebecca stop in her tracks. She turns to look. In the corner is an old wicker basket. The dog is looking up at her with a curious expression. She completely forgot about the dog. It's a brown dachshund.

"It's okay," Rebecca whispers, afraid the dog might bark to alarm the creature. "I just want to get out of here."

As though the dog understands her, it sighs, then rests its chin on the edge of the basket.

Rebecca presses on. The hallway leads to several other rooms. One of them is a living room. Another is the scullery. At the sight of the front door, Rebecca's heart jumps.

She moves quickly, hardly sensing the painful jabs from the souls of her feet. She is just about to grab the knob, when something tells her not to. Instead, she looks down and sees a dog hatch at the bottom of the door. It's too narrow for her to squeeze through, but she crouches down to have a look. With her hand, she flips up the hatch and peers outside, the cool, early evening air seeping in.

She sees a section of the courtyard and one half of the garage, in which the yellow van is parked.

Then the creature comes into view, and Rebecca almost screams.

The figure trudges across the gravel on its long, thin legs, dressed in blue overalls. It has something which might be a pair of large hedge shears in one hand. It's only a brief glimpse, then the creature is gone from view again. Rebecca can hear the crunching footsteps disappear out of earshot. She carefully closes the hatch again and goes into the living room.

Just like the rest of the house, everything in here is as old as Rebecca's grandma. The furniture looks worn and forgotten. There's a heavy couch, a rocking chair, a piano and a tall grandfather clock. There's also an open fireplace completely black from soot, and through a row of dirty windows Rebecca can see the terrace.

She limps to the garden door and turns the handle. This one opens with a squeak. Rebecca looks back across her shoulder as she hears the bell chime. The dachshund has followed her into the living room and is now standing there, eyeing her expectantly.

"I'm leaving now," she tells it. "You want to come with me?"

The dog tilts its head, but doesn't move.

"All right," Rebecca says. "Bye, then."

She steps outside and closes the garden door. The terrace is obviously never used: the garden table is green from moss and weeds are growing tall between the tiles.

Rebecca staggers out on the lawn and continues toward the hedge. She squeezes through the branches and comes out the other side. From here, she has a clear view over the open fields and forest in the distance. She stands for a moment, hesitant, not sure which direction to go in.

Does it matter? As long as I get far away from here ...

She begins walking, and—

And steps directly into something.

"Ouch," she moans, steps back and rubs her nose and forehead. She stares at the chain-link fence right in front of her. She didn't see it before, because the thin, grey metal bands blend in perfectly with the overcast sky.

The fence is ten feet tall, and at the very top sits a row of barbed-wire, making it impossible to climb over. Rebecca begins walking sideways, following the fence all around the outside of the hedge, her hope of finding a way out dwindling with every yard.

Finally, she reaches the front of the house, where the hedge ends and the open courtyard begins. She stops and peers out from the corner of the hedge. The fence runs all the way around the courtyard, too; the only place it's interrupted is by the gate where they came in with the van. Even from here, Rebecca can see the chain holding the gate shut and the metal spikes pointing to the sky on top of the gate.

She turns to go back to look for another way out, and there, between the hedge and the fence, is the creature.

It has snuck up on her completely silent, the cigar between its thin lips, the garden shears in its hand.

Rebecca screams. She ought to flee, but the shock has locked her in place. Instead, she holds up her arms in an effort to protect herself, as the creature comes towards her.

But it doesn't grab her.

It simply walks right by her.

Rebecca blinks and turns to look, as it trudges out onto the courtyard and into the garage.

Why didn't it hurt me? Why didn't it pull me back inside the house?

Slowly, things begin to fall into place for Rebecca. There really is only one logical conclusion as to why the creature didn't mind her being out here: it knows she can't get away.

Rebecca panics. She runs back along the fence, ignoring the pain from her feet, searching desperately for an opening or even a tiny hole to squeeze through. But she finds nothing. And less than two minutes later, she's back by the courtyard, only on the other side of the house.

Rebecca grabs the fence and tries to climb it. She's pretty good at climbing trees, and she manages to reach the top. But as soon as she tries to grab hold of the barbed-wire, she cuts her hand, screams and falls to the ground.

She jumps back up and begins shaking the fence. "*Help!*" she screams. "*Help me! I've been kidnapped! Hello! Can anybody hear me? I need he—*"

She is cut short as something grabs her from behind. The creature drags Rebecca into the house, upstairs and into the room with the brown wallpaper. It throws her down on the bed and then repeats the procedure of burning her feet and dripping the thick liquid into her eyes. Rebecca screams and fights back all the way through. But the creature is simply too strong.

Afterwards, it leaves the room.

This time, it locks the door.

DAY 4

Early next morning, before the sun is up, the door is suddenly unlocked.

Rebecca is already up, sitting by the window, looking into the blurry darkness outside, when she hears the key turn. She turns to look at the door, which is fuzzy to her, expecting it to open—but it doesn't. Instead, she hears faint footsteps from the hallway as the creature walks downstairs again.

Rebecca gets up from the chair, then flinches at the pain in her feet. The new wounds hurt worse than the old ones, making it even harder for her to stand up now. In an effort to dull the pain, she wrapped her feet in plenty of gauze, turning them into clunky lumps. She also bandaged the hand she cut on the fence.

She goes to open the door and finds the hallway empty and almost completely dark. The stench of the creature is still in the air, but so is something much more inviting: the smell of food.

Rebecca is starving, but the last thing she can think about is food. She hardly slept last night; she just sat by the window, watched the moon rise and set again, and waited for the sound of sirens which never came.

She doesn't get it. What's taking them so long? She's been here for three days now. They must have begun looking for her by now, so why aren't they coming?

Rebecca doesn't feel like waiting anymore. She's going to do something about it.

The stairs are too big of an obstacle for her throbbing feet, so she has to sit on her buttocks and climb down one step at a time, like a toddler would do it. It takes a little longer, but it gets the job done.

Once she reaches the bottom, she limps out into the kitchen, supporting herself against the wall. She immediately sees the creature; it's sitting by the table, eating from a plate, its back to her. A second plate is laid out across from it. She can't tell what's for breakfast using her eyes, but the unmistakable smell of eggs and bacon makes her mouth water.

Rebecca has no intention of joining the creature. She stays in the doorway and stares at the blurry outline of its bald head, her heart throbbing in her throat—both from fear, but also something else.

"Sit down, Alice," the creature says with its rusty voice, not turning to look at her.

"I'm not Alice," Rebecca says, feeling anger arise. "And I'm not going to eat your nasty food. I don't want to be here. I want to go home."

The creature doesn't reply. It just keeps eating calmly.

"You'll go to jail for this, you know," Rebecca says. Tears are starting to form in her eyes, and her voice trembles. "Once the police find me, you'll go to jail for the rest of your life."

The creature still doesn't look at her, but it hesitates a second before it continues eating. "Sit down and eat your breakfast, Alice," it says.

"I'm not Alice!" Rebecca shouts. "Now take me home!"

"No."

"Take me home!"

"No!" The creature only raises its voice slightly, but it's enough to startle Rebecca.

"Fuck you!" she retorts, and turns to leave.

The creature reacts with frightening speed. Rebecca hears the chair screech across the floor, four quick footsteps, and then it grabs her from behind.

Rebecca screams as she's lifted up, then put down onto the chair.

"Sit," the creature growls in her ear, pressing her down so hard it hurts. "Now, eat."

It lets go of her, and Rebecca immediately goes to get back up, but the creature slams her down once more, this time hard enough for Rebecca's teeth to clamber.

"Eat your breakfast, Alice," it demands.

This time, Rebecca stays seated as the creature has made its way back to the other side of the table. It sits down across from her, picks up its fork and resumes eating like nothing has happened.

Rebecca fights back tears, breathing in through suppressed sobs. She looks down at the plate in front of her, her appetite completely gone now.

She just sits there, defiantly not touching her meal, while the creature finishes its own. Rebecca doesn't want to look directly at it, so she keeps her gaze low, listening to it chewing.

When it's done, it looks across the table, sees her plate still full, and asks with a mild tone of surprise: "Not hungry, Alice?"

"No," Rebecca says firmly. "I'm not hungry. And I'm not Alice."

The creature is looking right at her, and despite her fuzzy vision, Rebecca can see its demeanor change. "Watch your tone, Alice," it says in a low voice.

Rebecca crosses her arms, trying not to show how scared she feels. "Can I go now?"

The creature looks at her for a moment longer, then it says: "Yes. You can go, Alice."

Rebecca gets up and limps upstairs, her feet sending painful jolts up through her legs with every step. She slams the door to the room, throws herself on the bed and cries into the pillow.

Her feet are hurting worse than ever. She can feel the fresh wounds bleed again. She cries and cries as she thinks about her family and Andy who heard her knocking from the van, she knows he did, and he'll tell the police, and the police will find her, she's sure they will, but maybe it'll be a little while, and she cries because she doesn't want to spend another minute in this house, but she can't get away, not on her own, because there's no way she can climb the fence.

Her thoughts go on like that for a while, until they finally lose speed and without knowing it, Rebecca drifts into sleep.

In her dream, Rebecca sneaks out into the garden, which has suddenly grown much, much bigger—in fact, it looks more like the park. But it's still hemmed in by the fence, and the fence is way too high for her to scale it.

She looks up at the house—except it doesn't look at all like the house, more like a big, black castle, like the one Dracula lives in. She can't see the creature in any of the windows, yet she knows it's in there somewhere and that it might look out any minute to see her trying to escape, which means she needs to hurry, so she turns to the fence, and to her surprise sees Andy standing there right on the other side, holding his bike and waving at her.

"Come on, Becca!" he calls to her. "Come out here!"

"I can't! The fence is too high, and there's barbed-wire at the top."

"You don't go *over* it," Andy says, grinning and shaking his head the way he always does when he finds her silly. "You go *under* it!"

Rebecca looks down and sees a small hole in the lawn right up against the fence. It looks like a cat or maybe a fox has dug its way under the fence.

She throws herself down and begins widening the hole by digging eagerly with her fingers. It's a lot easier than she thought; the ground is very soft and comes away in big chunks.

Soon the hole is large enough for her to crawl through. And so she does, squeezing under the fence and jumping to her feet.

"I did it!" she exclaims with joy, looking around. "I did it, Andy! ... Andy? Hey, where did you go?"

Her brother is nowhere to be seen. Suddenly, the day seems a lot darker, as heavy, black clouds have covered the sky above.

"What are you waiting for, Becca?"

Andy's voice makes her turn around. To her astonishment, she sees Andy grinning at her from the other side of the fence.

"Quit messing about, Becca," he says, his smile faltering a little. "Come on out here."

"What are you talking about?" Rebecca says. "You're the one who—" She stops talking when she realizes she's still in the garden. She must have crawled back by accident somehow.

She gets down, squeezes through the hole, gets back up, and ...

And is still in the garden.

"Seriously, Becca," Andy says from the other side—he's starting to sound scared now. "It's not funny anymore. Just come out here, okay?"

Rebecca crawls under the fence again. And again. Each time she does, she ends up right back in the garden.

"Hurry up, Becca!" Andy shouts suddenly, pointing towards something behind her. "It's coming for you!"

Rebecca doesn't have time to react before a strong, cold hand grabs her shoulder, and she

awakens with a gasp. She sits up in bed, breathing heavily, as she remembers where she is.

In the room with the brown wallpaper. In the creature's house.

Outside, the sun is setting. She feels like she was only gone for twenty minutes or so, but once again she slept most of the day. The pain in her feet has lessened. Instead, her stomach aches from hunger.

She rubs her eyes and looks around to test her vision. It's better, but not perfect. She sniffs at the smell of food and sees the plate on the desk.

She gets up, but sits back down again right away, as lightning shoots up from her feet. She can't walk, so she gets down on her hands and knees and crawls to the desk, climbing up onto the chair.

Rebecca eats the whole meal. It's mashed potatoes with bacon bits just like yesterday, and it lands heavy in her belly. There's also a big glass of milk. It's lukewarm, but she downs it all in one go anyway.

Then, she leans back in the chair and sighs deeply. Somewhere in the house a melody is playing; it's probably the radio.

She recalls the dream she had. She can't remember it exactly, but it was something about Andy. She spoke with him. His voice sounded so real in her mind. She bites her lip to keep back the tears.

There was something else in the dream. An idea. It's floating around right at the outskirts of her memory, threatening to dissipate forever. She concentrates hard.

What was it? Something about the fence, I think.

She slips down from the chair and crawls to the window, pulling herself up by the arms. There is no moon or stars out this evening, as the sky is cloudy, so everything is very dark out there. But she can still make out the hedge separating the garden from the surrounding fields. And she knows the fence is right on the other side.

I had an idea. A way to get past the fence. What was it?

Then it comes to her. She dreamed she crawled under the fence instead of over it. She dug a hole—no, a tunnel, actually, just like inmates would do in old-school movies when trying to escape prison—and then squeezed through it.

Rebecca feels invigorated. It's a good idea. It just might work.

But not yet. Not until tonight. When it's sleeping.

Rebecca stares out of the window a little while longer, then she crawls back to bed, heaves herself up and rolls onto her back.

She just lies there, waiting for night to come, listening for the melody playing downstairs. Now she doesn't feel quite as hopeless. Now she has a plan.

DAY 5

She must have slept some more, because when she suddenly sits bolt upright, it's even darker in the room. And the house is completely silent.

It's time.

She swings both feet to the floor, gently putting weight on them. The feet immediately object with painful jabs, and it makes her hesitate. The mere thought of making her way through the house, downstairs and out into the garden is enough to almost make her postpone the plan. Maybe it's better to wait a few days—just until the wounds have healed enough for her to walk again.

"No," she whispers, gripped by a sudden determination. She won't spend one more night in this house. Even if it means she has to crawl out of here.

So, she gets to her feet and limps to the door. She opens it tentatively and looks out into the dark, empty hallway. She walks to the stairs, leaning on the wall as she does so, then scales the stairs using her toddler-method.

She heads for the scullery, walking slowly and stepping carefully, trying to make as little noise as possible. As she crosses the hallway, she picks up a whistling snore from a door standing ajar. She peeks in, holding her breath, and sees a large bed with a thin figure lying under a blanket. At the foot of the bed is a dark lump which suddenly comes to life and lifts its head. It's the dachshund, looking over at her.

Rebecca puts a finger across her lips in a silent shushing. The dog probably doesn't understand the gesture, but it stays put anyway and doesn't make a sound.

Rebecca's heart is pounding away by now. The creature is probably very easily stirred awake, so she needs to be extra careful.

She slips out into the scullery and places her hand on the knob. It won't move. Instead, she turns the lock very slowly. It clicks with a sound like a gunshot. Rebecca freezes and just stands there for ten seconds, listening.

Nothing happens. No sounds from the bedroom.

Once she's satisfied the creature is still sleeping, she opens the front door and is met by a breath of fresh, cool night air. She steps outside and closes the door behind her.

The sky is no longer cloudy, and the moon shines bright enough for her to see.

As she steps out onto the gravel, her bare feet—which are hurting plenty by now—give off renewed shots of pain as the pebbles press up into the bandages. But there's no way back now.

She looks to the gate. It's closed and probably also locked, although she can't see the chain from here; still, she knows it would be a waste of valuable time to go check it.

Instead, she heads for the garage.

The walk across the gravel is the closest thing to torture Rebecca has ever experienced. She attempts to place the weight on her heels, but it only reduces the pain a tiny bit.

When she finally reaches the garage and steps onto the cold concrete floor, her feet are turned into a couple of burning lumps, and tears are running down her cheeks.

She wipes them away and looks around in the dark, blinks and strains to see. There is a lot of junk in here, and a long table filled with tools, but she can't see what she came for. Perhaps it's not here. Perhaps the creature doesn't even own a—

Then she sees it. It's hanging on the wall right next to her along with a few other garden tools. Rebecca reaches out and carefully takes the shovel off the hanger.

She limps back out of the garage and around the back. This time, she can use the shovel as a cane, leaning on it to take some the weight off her feet.

The lawn is wet with dew, and the bandages quickly soak through and turn icy cold. She doesn't mind, though, as it actually sooths the pain from the wounds.

Rebecca already chose the spot from the window. It'll be behind the large bushes down in the farthest corner of the garden.

She walks determined across the lawn, darting a look back for every ten steps. She halfway expects one of the windows to light up and the silhouette of the creature to appear. But the house remains dark. And once she limps around the bushes, she disappears from sight.

There are a few yards between the bushes and the fence—more than enough room for Rebecca to work on. She places herself close to the fence and puts the shovel to the ground. It's difficult to get it to sink in, because the ground is pretty hard. She tries to use her foot to press down the shovel, but it hurts too badly, so she simply leans on the shovel. With a little effort, it gradually goes in.

But the task turns out a lot harder than she had imagined. It takes a lot of strength just getting the shovel into the ground, and the hole only grows very slowly deeper. With this speed, she won't be out until sunup.

Yet Rebecca is firmly determined to get away, so she bites down and keeps working. Sweat begins to run down her forehead. A couple of blisters form in her palms. But the hole grows deeper, and the ground becomes softer.

I'll make it, I'll make it, she repeats to herself over and over. *I'm getting away from here. I'll make it.*

Once the hole is about two feet deep, the shovel meets something hard, giving off a sharp CLANG!

Damnit, I must have hit a stone.

She kneels down, brushes away the dirt and reveals something white. Feeling around the surface of the stone, she can tell it's bigger than a softball and very smooth to the touch. Rebecca scoops it up and is about to put it aside, when she gets a closer look at it.

That's funny, she thinks to herself, turning the stone over. *It looks almost like a—*

Rebecca screams as she sees the two large, empty eye sockets and the grinning mouth. She drops the skull and stumbles backwards, wiping her hands frantically on her pants.

She breathes fast, wanting to run away, but forces herself to stay, as she stares at the skull grinning up at the stars.

Questions race around her head.

Is it a human skull? Why is it so small? Is it from a child, maybe? What is a child's skull doing buried here? How did the child die? Was it killed? Did the creature kill it, then bury the body here? Was it—

Rebecca's thoughts are interrupted as she senses a movement out of the corner of her eye. She turns her head and gasps at the sight of the creature standing there. Once again, it has come sneaking up on her completely without a sound.

"Alice," it croaks.

"I ... I wasn't trying to ..." Rebecca fumbles for an excuse, but of course the creature has already gathered why she's here; it's staring at the hole. She ought to run away, she knows that, but there's nowhere to run.

"Alice," the creature says again, still speaking very low, shaking its head like a disappointed parent would. It's still looking at the hole and not at Rebecca. "Oh, Alice," it says, the voice sad and almost whiney now, like a child about to cry.

And then it suddenly hits her. The creature isn't addressing *her*.

"Who ... who was that?" Rebecca says, hardly aware she's speaking.

The creature snaps its head around, and even in the darkness and even despite her still slightly blurry eyesight, Rebecca can see the black eyes lock on her.

"Alice," it says again.

This time, the voice is thick with rage.

The creature drags Rebecca back inside the house and up to her room. For the third time, it drips liquid into her eyes and burns her feet. But this time, it keeps going until Rebecca's feet are completely covered in burn wounds and she is halfway unconscious from pain and fear, having screamed herself hoarse.

Only then does the creature leave the room, leaving Rebecca alone in the silence. She produces a sound, not quite crying; she has no more strength left to cry. She can't move, either. She just stares with her burning eyes into the watery darkness in front of her.

There are no more emotions, no more thoughts. Only emptiness and pain.

And then, in the silent space, a realization appears.

Rebecca has just met Alice.

DAY 10

Several days pass before Rebecca is able to walk again.

She spends those days lying in bed. Sometimes she sleeps, sometimes she's awake. Days and night melt together. Now and then she hears the door open, as the creature brings her food. Every so often she will hear the melody playing downstairs, repeating over and over. Other times, the house is silent.

The pain from her feet is really bad, but the creature only gives her disinfectant and gauze—no burn gel to help the pain. The best way to alleviate it is to sleep.

The entire time Rebecca lies in bed she hopes the next time she wakes up, it will be to the sound of police cars approaching. More than once she dreams that Andy has come. Yet every time she wakes up to find she's still alone.

Her sight returns a little more with each day, but it doesn't go all the way back to normal; everything still appears as though through a thin veil.

As far as she can see, the burn wounds on her feet have healed over, but the slightest touch or movement makes them bleed again.

Even after the pain has lessened considerably and the wounds are healed enough for her to stand up again, Rebecca stays in bed. She has realized escape is impossible. The creature has some supernatural sense, alerting it if she tries to run away. And the next time it will probably hurt her even more badly; perhaps even kill her.

Now her only hope is to wait for rescue. And she plans on staying in bed until that happens. And of course it will happen. It just takes a little longer than she expected. The police apparently have had some trouble tracking her down. But they will. Missing persons always get found.

Don't they?

DAY 11

Suddenly, one afternoon, she hears a scraping at the door.

Rebecca sits up in bed and listens. The scraping continues, very discretely. Is it the creature? If it wants in, why doesn't it just open the door? Is it some sort of game?

Then there's a whimpering from the hallway.

Rebecca gets up and limps to the door. She opens it, and the dog looks up at her with mild bemusement in its dark eyes, as though it wants to say: "How long are you going to stay in there?"

Rebecca leans out and peers down the hallway. No sign of the creature. She's not sure how, but she can somehow tell the creature is not in the house. It's almost like the atmosphere is different.

So, Rebecca decides to finally leave the room.

She slips down the hallway and stops by the next door. It's ajar, and she can make out an empty room. She steps inside and walks across the dusty carpet to the window. From here she can see the courtyard and the garage—the van isn't there.

Rebecca's heart speeds up a little. The creature really isn't home.

She leaves the empty room again, almost stepping on the dog, who's waiting for her just outside. She steps past it and limps over to the stairs, scaling them one painful step at a time, then heads straight for the scullery. She grabs the front door, but finds it locked. And it's one of those old-fashioned ones where you need a key from both sides. She considers trying the dog hatch, but she can tell it's too small.

Instead, she heads for the living room and the terrace door—but that one is also locked.

"Damnit," she whispers and looks around for another way.

She tries the living room windows, but they can only open a few inches due to short safety chains.

She goes to the kitchen, but the windows here also have chains. She searches the entire ground floor—even the creature's bedroom, where the smell is so bad, she has to hold her nose—and finds all windows impossible to open.

The dog follows her along wherever she goes, the tiny bell on its collar chiming softly, until finally, Rebecca goes back into the living room and sinks down on the couch with a sigh. Her feet are throbbing painfully, so she pulls them up to give them a rest.

She looks around. There are no signs of anyone else living here besides the creature. The carpet has several big stains and is worn right down to the wood in more than one place. Every window is dusty and tarnished, making it hard to see through. From the ceiling hangs large cobwebs and the wall paintings are big, faded landscape portraits in heavy wooden frames. There are a few decorative items, like porcelain animals, embroidered pillows and brass candlesticks. There's also a single photograph, standing on a tiny, dust-covered table next to the couch.

Rebecca reaches over and takes the frame. Her eyesight is still blurry, but by holding it close, she can just make out the face in the picture. It's a girl with platinum blond hair—just like Rebecca always wanted, but Rebecca's hair is raven-black. The girl is wearing a yellow shirt and white pants, sitting on a chair, smiling nervously at the camera, almost like she has a secret with whoever took the picture.

Something sniffs her knee. Rebecca looks down to see the dog.

"You want up?" she asks.

The dog is obviously no stranger to being on the couch, because it willingly lets her lift it up and immediately curls up next to her.

"I never found out your name," Rebecca says, searching with her fingers in the dog's fur for the old collar. "Boris," she reads. The dog's ears move slightly. She smiles. "Hi, Boris. I'm Rebecca."

Boris looks up at her, friendly, but not particularly interested. Its pupils look cloudy, and Rebecca is pretty sure that means it's almost blind; just like her.

"Do you know who this is?" she asks Boris and shows him the photo. Boris just sighs and puts his head back down. "Nah, me neither," she mutters and studies the blond girl and her shy smile. The picture could be very old. Maybe the girl is grown up by now. Maybe she's very old, or even dead. Maybe—

Suddenly, it hits home.

Rebecca can't explain why, but she knows for a fact that the girl in the picture is Alice, and she feels goose bumps come crawling all the way up her back. She quickly puts the photo back—all of a sudden, she doesn't want to touch it; it feels wrong, somehow. Like it creates an unwelcome connection between her and the dead girl.

Then she hears a faint rumble, like a car driving on gravel.

Rebecca jumps to her feet and limps to the kitchen. Through the window over the sink she can see the courtyard and the rear-end of the yellow van as it drives into the garage.

It's back!

Rebecca goes back to the living room, scoops up Boris and hurries out to the staircase. She's not sure why, but she doesn't want the creature to know she's been snooping around the house. So she hurries up to the room and closes the door. She sits down on the bed and listens.

A few minutes pass by.

Then the stairs give off their unmistakable creaky sounds as the creature comes upstairs.

The door is opened slowly. The tall, gangly figure towers in the opening. It's too tall to look into the room unless it bends its neck slightly. The arms and legs are also long, unnaturally so, and the way it moves them sometimes makes it look like they each have an extra joint. Like a spider.

The creature steps into the room, but doesn't go more than a few steps. It just stands there, staring at her.

Rebecca doesn't want to look right at it, so she keeps her gaze at its feet. "What do you want?" she asks, her heart pounding in her throat, making her voice jumpy.

The creature doesn't answer, just stands there, breathing slowly.

Boris grows restless in her arms and gives off a small bark. Rebecca realizes the creature isn't looking at her, but at the dog. She doesn't want to let Boris go, but she's also afraid to keep him if the creature wants him, so she bends over and puts him on the floor. She expects the dog to run to its owner. But to her surprise, Boris sits down between her feet.

She glances towards the creature. "I think ... I think he wants to stay with me."

The creature just stands there for another long moment. Then, it turns around, leaves and closes the door behind it. She hears it walk downstairs again.

Rebecca breathes out in relief. She bends over and pats Boris. "Thank you," she whispers. "I'm glad you chose me. But we can't become too friendly, you know. I'm not staying here for much longer."

Boris just sighs, as though he doesn't really care, then makes himself comfortable between Rebecca's banded-up feet.

"I don't care if you believe me," Rebecca says. "They'll come for me. Soon. You'll see."

She's not sure if she's telling the dog or herself.

DAY 18

The days go by.

Rebecca waits.

No one comes for her.

Gradually, she learns the routines of the creature. It eats the same three meals every day: scrambled eggs, ham sandwich and mashed potatoes with bacon bits. Every night, before it goes to bed, it sits down by the piano and plays the same melody over and over—that's what Rebecca initially took for the radio. She knows the song, but she can't quite place it at first.

The worst part of the routine is the burning of her feet and the liquid it puts in her eyes. It does it every third day now. In the evening, before bedtime, it comes to her room, the lit cigar between its grey lips.

Rebecca fights it every step of the way, even though it makes no real difference. She can't help it, though; she can't just let it harm her without offering resistance.

The weird thing about it is, the creature doesn't seem angry at her at all. It doesn't make a sound during the procedure, and it doesn't seem to derive any kind of pleasure from it. It's almost like it simply needs to be done. Probably, Rebecca figures, to keep her from doing any more attempts of escaping. By keeping her halfway blind and unable to walk properly, Rebecca has a very bad chance of running away.

The creature also changes its attitude towards her; it begins demanding things.

First, it stops bringing her food. If she wants to eat, she has no other choice than joining it in the kitchen. Rebecca tries to avoid it by waiting until the creature is done, then sneaking down to the kitchen to find something to eat. But every time she does so, the creature appears, staring at her menacingly, causing Rebecca to slink away again.

The third time it happens, she tells it, with as much defiance as she can muster: "I want something to eat."

The creature shakes its head and answers: "Not time for eating now, Alice."

Rebecca knows what will happen if she proceeds. She stares at the fridge for a few seconds, feeling her stomach rumble with hunger.

Then she turns on her heel and leaves the kitchen, scoffing: "Fine. I wasn't really hungry anyway."

But she was. And the next time a meal is served, Rebecca goes to the kitchen.

She tries to take the plate and leave, but of course, the creature won't let her: it gets up and grabs her with incredible speed, forcing her back down.

Rebecca tries a few more times to find a way to eat alone, but the creature is relentless. She has even tried eating while the creature went out one day. She took two eggs from the fridge and fried them on the stove instead of scrambling them, as the creature would always serve them. Then she ate the eggs with great relish, happy with finally having outsmarted the creature.

But as soon as it came home and found the two eggs missing from the fridge, the creature came up and burned her badly.

So finally, Rebecca resolves to join it for those three meals a day, not look at it, not speak to it, just chow down the food, then go back up to her room. She can do that, even though she doesn't like it. But it's a matter of survival.

The creature makes other demands, some of which are quite harder for Rebecca to come to terms with.

For instance, she wakes up one morning to find her clothes and her shoes, which she always puts right next to her bed, missing. The creature must have been in here while she slept and taken it.

She has been wearing the same outfit ever since she got here, and by now it is turning pretty smelly, since Rebecca hasn't showered even once, so her first thought is that the creature took it to wash it.

But that turns out to not be the case.

Rebecca never sees her clothes again. Instead, she finds a bunch of clothes on the desk. It's six identical outfits of yellow shirts and white linen pants; the exact same clothes as the girl in the photo down in the living room.

Rebecca really doesn't like the thought that some dead girl once wore the clothes, but she dislikes the thought of walking around in her underwear even less, so she has no real choice.

DAY 20

A few days later, Rebecca learns that the clothes were only a small sacrifice, as she wakes up to find a plastic bag on the floor next to the bed. She looks inside and finds a hair bleach kit.

At first, Rebecca almost laughs at the idea that the creature apparently wants her to dye her hair. But then, the more she thinks about it, the fun of it evaporates.

The girl in the photograph—Alice—has blond hair. And Rebecca is already wearing her clothes.

"It can't be serious," she tells Boris. "I'm not going to dye my hair—no freaking way."

She throws the bag in the downstairs trash can.

The next morning, it's there again, next to her bed.

Rebecca hides it away in the back of her closet.

The next morning, it's back again, and the creature is there, too, staring at her.

Rebecca sits up with a jerk. Boris wakes up with a confused whimper.

"Get out of here," Rebecca tells the creature in a hoarse whisper.

It just stares at her, holding out the plastic bag.

Rebecca shakes her head. "I'm not going to do it. I won't dye my hair. You can't make me!"

But of course, the creature can.

It reaches out and grabs Rebecca by the arm, pulling her out of bed. Rebecca screams and fights to get free. It drags her out into the bathroom, puts the bag in the sink, then leaves and locks the door.

Rebecca is left alone, kicking the door. She rubs her arm and forces back angry tears.

"Fuck you!" she shouts. "I'm not doing it!"

She waits for an answer, but can only hear the sound of the stairs, as the creature walks calmly downstairs.

Rebecca sits down on the toilet and breathes deeply. She can't do it. She can't change her appearance like that—wearing the strange clothes is one thing, but dying her hair—she'd rather starve to death.

And that seems to be exactly what will happen.

The creature comes back a few times to check on her; just a brief look, before it closes the door and locks it again.

Rebecca drinks water from the sink and tries to make time go by without thinking about her hair or the hunger, which becomes more and more intense.

She stays in the bathroom all night, sleeping in the tub.

The following day, the creature again checks in on her a few times.

When noon comes around, Rebecca is so hungry, she can't take it anymore.

"It's just hair," she tells herself in the mirror. The Rebecca staring back at her looks thin and pale and has dark circles around her eyes. "It's just hair, it doesn't mean anything. Besides, I always wanted to be a blonde."

She tries to smile, but it turns into tears, as she opens the bag with trembling fingers.

She follows the instructions of the packet, finishing off by washing her hair in the tub.

Just as she reaches for the towel, she sees the door in the mirror. It's open. The creature is standing there, smoking its cigar, looking in at her.

"What are you looking at?" Rebecca snarls. "Isn't this what you wanted?"

The creature takes a long drag on the cigar and blows out the smoke. "Good, Alice," it whispers. Then, it simply turns and walks away, leaving the door halfway open.

"I'm not Alice!" Rebecca shouts. "My name is Rebecca!"

She takes one last look in the mirror. She did a pretty awful job; the roots are still dark, and some places are whiter than others. But she doesn't really care anymore. She just wants something to eat.

When she comes downstairs, the creature has prepared an extra-large ham sandwich for her.

For once, Rebecca is allowed to eat alone.

DAY 21

The following evening, after dinner, as Rebecca has gone up to her room with Boris, the creature comes and opens the door without knocking.

"Downstairs, Alice," it tells her from the doorway, then turns and leaves without waiting for a reply.

Rebecca's pulse immediately rises. This is something new, and she has a bad feeling about it.

She considers staying here, or even trying to hide. But she knows that won't work. Also, she can feel the creature's patience becoming thinner and thinner the more she resists; anymore disobedience, and she'll likely get punished severely. Her feet are aching from the last burn. So, she decides the wiser course is to simply follow the creature downstairs and find out what it wants.

She picks up Boris and brings him for moral support.

All the way down to the living room, her fear and dread for what's to come rises steadily, until her knees feel shaky.

She clutches Boris to her chest and peers into the dimly lit living room. She spots the creature by the piano, the cigar it in its mouth and its back to her.

Slowly, it turns its head and lifts one boney hand to wave her closer.

Rebecca approaches the piano but stops a few paces away.

"What ... what do you want?" she asks, her voice thin.

The creature doesn't answer her. It takes out the cigar and places it in an overfilled ashtray on top of the piano. Then it begins playing, and Rebecca immediately recognizes the melody she has heard many times. What she at first took for the radio must have been the creature playing.

She watches in silent wonder, almost forgetting her fears, at the gangly figure producing those soft, melancholy tunes. And she realizes she knows the song. It's the lullaby Mom used to sing when Rebecca was little. She hasn't heard it for years, but she can still remember the lyrics, and her eyes fill with tears, as she whispers along to the melody.

Once the verse is over, the creature plays the melody over again. Then, the third time around, it says: "Sing, Alice."

And Rebecca finally realizes why the creature brought her hear. It doesn't want simply to play to her; it's wants to play *with* her, to hear her sing.

"No," Rebecca croaks, almost sobbing now.

"Sing, Alice," the creature repeats, staring over once more.

Rebecca doesn't want to sing, but she knows what will likely happen if the creature needs to tell her a third time, so she begins singing softly along with the melody:

"Hush-a-bye baby

On the treetop,
When the wind blows
The cradle will rock.
When the bough breaks,
The cradle will fall,
And down will fall baby
Cradle and all."

The creature starts over, and Rebecca sings the verse again; it's the only one she knows. The creature doesn't seem to mind, and it plays the melody over five or six more times, accompanied by Rebecca's low singing.

Finally, it stops, takes the cigar and heaves a deep drag, blowing out the air slowly and watching it drift to the ceiling.

"Can ... can I go now?" Rebecca whispers, her cheeks wet from tears, Boris sleeping in her arms.

The creature doesn't answer, but it turns its head slowly and gives a tiny nod. Rebecca hurries back upstairs.

As she lies in bed a few minutes later, trying to sleep, she feels a weird mixture of feelings. She misses her family more than ever, but she's also afraid. In a strange way, singing with the creature was worse than getting her feet burned. Rebecca can't figure out why, but she feels terrible inside.

"I hope that was the only time it wants me to sing," she whispers to Boris, who's snoring at the foot of her bed.

But it wasn't.

Every evening from then on, the creature comes to get her after dinner, uttering those same two words from the doorway: "Downstairs, Alice."

And every evening, Rebecca goes downstairs to sing the lullaby while the creature plays the piano, feeling awful afterwards.

DAY 23

The creature also demands other, smaller things from Rebecca. Some of them rather peculiar.

Like, one morning, at breakfast, it suddenly tells her: "Other hand, Alice."

Rebecca, who's shoveling down eggs, looks across the table at the open newspaper, which the creature is holding.

"What?" she asks.

"Other hand," the creature repeats.

She just stares at the newspaper for a few seconds, before it begins to dawn on her what it means.

She puts the fork in her left hand. "Like this? But I'm not left-handed."

She continues eating with her right.

"Other hand, Alice," the creature says, its voice rising. And this time, it lowers the newspaper enough for its tiny black eyes to stare at her.

Rebecca immediately looks down on her plate and shifts the fork. Eating with her left hand seems like a very little sacrifice, so she doesn't make a fuss about it.

In the days to come, she forgets about it almost every meal, but the creature reminds her patiently from across the table: "Other hand, Alice," and Rebecca slowly gets used to eating left-handed.

Rebecca knows the reason for these things, of course. She knows the creature wants her to be Alice, to be like the dead girl it once knew.

She tells herself it's no big deal, that she can do it in order to survive, that it's simply a matter of keeping her head down until she can get away from here.

But from a deeper part of her, a sense of growing dread gets a little bit bigger each time she voluntarily adjusts her own behavior. It goes against who Rebecca is in her heart, and it scares her.

The weirdest thing is, other than those areas, the creature seems oddly non-interested in how Rebecca spends her time—as long, of course, she doesn't act disrespectful or try to escape.

And so long as Rebecca does what it wants, they fall into an almost peaceful coexistence.

Besides for the burnings and the blindings every third night.

DAY 28

More days go by; still no one comes for her.

Rebecca begins to venture out of her room more and more. She prefers to do so whenever she can sense the creature is outside, working in the garden or fixing something in the garage. Whenever it drives off in the van, it always locks the doors beforehand, trapping Rebecca in the house.

Her fear diminishes as she realizes the creature isn't going to kill her or do anything worse than burn her feet and blind her eyes—which is bad enough, of course, but she also somehow gets used to the pain; or at least, she learns to get through it.

It provides her with a sense of comfort knowing what to expect from the creature. She can predict approximately when it'll leave and when it'll be back again, when it's safe for her to walk around the house, when the meals will be served, when it goes to bed, and so on.

Whenever it's at home, Rebecca stays mostly in her room; not so much because she's afraid it'll harm her if it sees her, she just doesn't like being around it when she doesn't have to. She can never really tell where in the house it is, as it moves very quietly.

Boris sleeps in Rebecca's room every night, curled up by her feet. Whenever she wakes up from a nightmare, she's thankful the dog is there.

Every evening, after they have played and sang together, and Rebecca has gone to bed, the creature comes up to her room to say good night.

The scene is always the same: Rebecca lies in bed. She hears the stairs creak. The door opens. From the doorway, the creature whispers: "Sleep tight, Alice," right before closing the door.

Rebecca never answers; she's grown wary of correcting the name, which the creature seems determined to call her. Until one night, when Rebecca is in a bad mood.

"I'm not Alice," she says loudly. "Alice is dead."

The creature freezes in the doorway. Though the lighting is dim and Rebecca's eyesight is blurry, she can tell the tall figure is shaking its head.

"No," it whispers. "No, no, *no!*" The voice turns into a thunderous roar, causing Rebecca to sit up and Boris to begin whining.

For one fearful moment, she's sure the creature will come at her. It actually looks like it struggles to keep itself back, trembling in the doorway, clutching the frame with both hands.

Then, it simply shakes its head once more, and repeats calmly, "No," then closes the door.

For the first time, that night, the creature doesn't go to bed at the usual time. Instead, it stays up, playing the piano over and over again for almost two hours, that same lullaby.

And as Rebecca lies in bed, listening, she can't help but whisper along, while thinking about her mom and her dad and Andy and Cindy, and she cries deeper than ever before.

And while she does so, it's as though something shifts inside of her—or rather, falls into place. It's a realization which makes her scared, but even more sad.

Rebecca realizes that no one will come for her right now. That it could be many days, perhaps even months, before she gets found.

Which means, that for now, this house is her new home.

DAY 76

Rebecca is sitting on the chair in the room with the brown wallpaper and staring out of the window at nothing in particular, hardly noticing the open fields or the orange evening sky above.

She has no idea how long she's been here; she long since gave up counting the days. But when she came here, the fields had tiny, green sprouts, and now the wheat is knee-high. The weather is warmer, too, and the days longer.

She's spent many hours right here, on the chair in front of the window. Down in the living room she can hear the grandfather clock. Rebecca counts twelve chimes. She hates that clock. No matter where she is in the house, she can hear it. Every hour it reminds her that time is moving. And it reminds her of the church bells she could hear from her room. The sound makes her homesick.

"Duuip!"

A cry from a bird in the distance. The sound makes Rebecca straighten a little.

It's them. They're back.

She leans forward and listens. Another cry, closer this time. She can't see the birds yet. She opens the window and listens. Another couple of cries, before the birds finally come into view.

"Duuip! Duuip!"

Although Rebecca doesn't have her bird book or access to the Internet, she still remembers the names of most of the local species, and these are without a doubt lapwings.

The birds circle above the house, disappear out of sight for a moment, then reappear and land on the lawn. They mince around on their skinny legs, looking for food in the grass. From this far away, Rebecca can't make out any details, but she still smiles to herself. She leans her cheek against the cold window glass and watches the birds.

Then, suddenly, they take flight, soaring close by the window, and Rebecca listens as their cries disappear into the distance. She wishes she was a lapwing herself and could go with them.

The stairs creak. The familiar sound of footsteps.

Rebecca gets up and waddles to the bed where she sits back down. The door opens. The creature looks in at her.

Rebecca doesn't like looking, but she doesn't like not looking, either, so she fastens her gaze on the greyish hand resting on the doorknob. She can't make out the long, skinny fingers very well, but she knows the touch of them intimately; they're rough and chapped and very cold. The smell from the creature fills the room.

"It's time, Alice," it whispers. "Lie down."

"My name is not Alice," Rebecca says, still staring at the hand. "It's Rebecca."

She has said it hundreds of times, perhaps even thousands. The creature doesn't care; it just keeps calling her Alice, as though it doesn't even hear her.

The hand lets go of the knob and goes to the collarbone, where it scratches the skin through the shirt. Rebecca stares at the hand because she doesn't want to look at the face, which always gives her the shivers. It's too narrow and the forehead is too high, topped off with white tusks of dying hair. The nose is a thin, sharp edge, running from the grey upper lip to the brow protruding like a cliff, hiding the eyes in a permanent shadow.

And they are the worst.

The eyes.

Small, black, circular and gleamy. No life behind them. Glass-like.

She only looks the creature in the eye when she absolutely can't help it.

The hand stops scratching and goes to the front pocket. The long fingers pull out a cigar and places it between the cracked lips. Rebecca watches as the creature finds the lighter and lights up the cigar. The smoke fills the room almost instantly.

The creature repeats the command: "Lie down, Alice."

Rebecca hesitates for another few seconds, then lies down on her back, her legs slightly apart and her arms at her sides. The creature comes over and sits down at the foot of the bed, making the springs creak.

Rebecca clutches the bed linen with both hands, breathes through her nose and looks up into the ceiling. She tries to imagine she can hear the lapwings somewhere in the distance. That she has X-ray vision and is able to see them fly around above the roof.

The creature sits for half a minute, pulsing on the cigar. The wait is always the worst.

Then she feels its rough hand grab her ankle and lift up her bare foot. Rebecca squeezes her lips together tightly, but she doesn't close her eyes—for some reason, the pain is worse with eyes closed.

The low seething sound comes first, boding the pain which follows half a second later. Rebecca gives off a whimper, as burning needles force their way up through the sole of her foot and spreads out into the toes. There's a long second of rising pain, reaching almost an unbearable level, then it subsides. The creature lies her leg back down on the bed and takes the other one.

"Now the other, Alice."

The same exact words, the same exact tone.

The creature takes a long drag off of the cigar, firing it up again, before repeating the procedure with the other foot. The needles sink in, the pain increases until the point where she almost screams out—and then it goes away again, turning into a dull throbbing.

Rebecca goes limp all over, feeling the sweat on her forehead and her heart pounding dully in her chest.

The creature lets go of her ankle and goes on to the eyes. They are a lot easier to deal with than the feet; the pain is nowhere near as bad.

Rebecca holds her breath so as to not breathe in the stench from the creature as it leans over her. She turns her eyes sideways, staring into the wall and not at the figure looming over her. The creature breathes calmly as it administers the cool drops to Rebecca's eyes. She blinks as the liquid runs down her cheeks like sluggish tears. A slight sting, and she blinks it off.

The creature gets to its feet. "It's done. You did well, Alice."

It doesn't wait for an answer, it just heads for the door.

"My name is not Alice," Rebecca automatically replies, wiping the excess liquid from her cheeks. "It's ..."

She pauses, and for a terrible moment, the name is gone. Her mouth is open, but no sound comes out.

"It's ..." she says again, trying to force it to appear. "It's ..." And then it comes. "Rebecca!" she blurts out, feeling a deep sense of relief. "Rebecca Wisler! My name is Rebecca Wisler."

She lifts her head and looks to see if the creature is still here. It is. Standing in the doorway. And through the blurry haze, she sees its face in the light of the cigar, and she is almost certain she sees a smile on its lips as it whispers: "Sleep tight, Alice." Then it closes the door and leaves Rebecca to the silence.

She feels like crying. She decided a while back that she wouldn't cry anymore, that she wouldn't give in to it, that she would act brave; but she's not brave, not at all. She misses her family so much and she's scared. Scared of the creature, scared that she'll never be found, scared that she'll eventually forget her name.

She gets up, wipes the tears from her still stinging eyes and wobbles to the table with small gasps of pain with every step. She can feel the burn wounds bleeding, but she doesn't care; she's so used to the pain by now, she hardly registers it.

The table is stuffed with pieces of paper, drawings of birds, mostly lapwings but also other kinds. She found the pencil and the paper in a drawer downstairs, and the creature apparently didn't mind her bringing it to her room.

She grabs the pencil and a blank piece of paper and writes in big, bold letters:
REBECCA WISLER

She stares at the name, then writes it again. And again. Smaller and smaller as she runs out of blank space. Writing her name alleviates some of the fear.

Afterwards, she looks at the paper and realizes it's no good having it around. The creature will not stand for it. It will confiscate it as soon as it finds it—and it *will* find it, no matter where she hides it. It searches the room now and then, and if it finds something it doesn't like, it'll punish her with an extra-long and drawn-out round of feet-burning.

Like the time she had written a letter for help which she planned on taping to the back of the van, in the hope that the creature wouldn't notice it the next time it went for a drive.

Or when she stole a knife from the kitchen, planning to cut the creature as it came up to say good night. She wasn't sure she could really go through with it, but she was so pissed off that day, she was willing to try.

She never got the chance, though, because right on that same day—just like on the day she had written the letter and hidden it under the carpet—the creature came to search the room and found her secret.

Because it knows. Somehow, it always knows if Rebecca has done something she shouldn't have.

Writing her real name all over a piece of paper will almost certainly spark its fury.

*But I need to write it down **somewhere**,* Rebecca thinks to herself, looking around the room. *Or I might forget it.*

She limps to the window, bends down and examines the windowsill. The lower part protrudes a few inches from the wall. There is just enough space for her to write on.

She glances at the door, then kneels down and writes her full name on the underside of the windowsill. She writes it again and again, tracing the letters and pushing the pencil harder each time, until there's a slight crevice in the board and the tip of the pencil is worn flat.

She looks at the name, feeling better now.

Back in the beginning, Rebecca had hoped the cigars would kill off the creature. Mom often told her how smoking is bad for you and can cause a lot of diseases. Lung cancer, for instance.

When Rebecca sometimes lies awake at night, thinking about her family, fighting the tears, she desperately hopes for the creature to fall ill and die. If that happens, she will leave the house, unlock the gate and run down the gravel road as fast as she can, not looking back and not stopping until she reaches another house or meets a passing car.

Unfortunately, the creature doesn't seem ill in anyway. And Rebecca has long since rejected the hope that she will outlive it.

"My name is not Alice," she whispers as she goes to the desk and picks up the paper. "My name is Rebecca, and I'll never forget it."

She tears up the paper into tiny pieces.

That night, somewhere around midnight, Rebecca wakes up and notices the light. It's coming from the closet; a thin, white strip streaming out from the crack in the door.

The closet across from the bed is built into the wall. The door is made of dark wood with a cut-out ornament which makes Rebecca think of leaves and butterflies.

At first, Rebecca is confused as to what causes the light, and she even suspects this might be a dream. But no, she feels awake.

She pushes the blanket aside, waking up Boris, who looks at her from the foot-end of the bed with sleepy eyes. Rebecca gets out and slips over to the closet. She places her hand in the stream of light, as though to check it's real. She lets her fingers play with the tiny, fine flecks of dust in the air. Then, she carefully opens the closet door.

On the shelves, her clothes—white pants and yellow shirts—are neatly folded up, just like Mom taught her. Rebecca washes her clothes in the sink and hangs them out to dry on the line in the garden, so they don't get to stink.

The light is coming from the top of the closet. There's a crack in the boards, and this is where the light comes in.

Rebecca reaches up. She can't quite reach the opening, but she can feel the cool breeze coming in.

And she realizes the crack is a hole in the roof, and that the light is moonlight.

Why haven't I seen this before? Why doesn't the sun shine in through here too?

The answer is obvious, of course. In the day, everything is bright, and the stream of light wouldn't be visible. But now, when the room is completely dark, the strip of moonlight is free to show itself off.

Rebecca closes the closet and goes to the window. She leans against the glass and can just make out the moon high above. It's only one-third full, but its white light shines down over the house and the garden.

For some reason, Rebecca thinks of Andy. She imagines him sitting in his room, looking out the window and up at the moon, just like she is now.

Could he be thinking about her? Is he wondering where she might be? Or did he forget about her? Do they all assume she's dead? Maybe Mom and Dad even decided to have another child. If it's a girl, it can have Rebecca's room.

The thought makes her so sad she begins to sob quietly. She sits there for a long time, crying by the window, bathed in the moonlight, thinking about her family, wondering if she will ever see them again.

DAY 89

One morning, as Rebecca wakes up and gets out of bed, Boris doesn't jump to the floor as he usually does, eager for Rebecca to let him out for his morning pee, then feed him breakfast. Instead, he just stays snuggled up at the bottom of the bed.

"Hey, sleepy head," Rebecca yawns, nudging him gently. "It's morning. Time to wake up now."

The dog doesn't react at all. Rebecca knows he's pretty old and doesn't always hear too well, but him sleeping this heavily is quite unusual.

"Boris? Wakey-wakey."

She strokes the back of his neck, surprised to feel how cold he is. She nudges him harder. Still no reaction.

"Oh, no," Rebecca whispers, as she realizes with a sinking feeling what's wrong. "Boris!"

She grabs him and shakes him, but he's all limp, his eyes are closed and his mouth open. She lets go of him again with a gasp, and he just slumps back down onto the bed.

"Oh, no, no, no," Rebecca whimpers, putting both hands to her mouth. The shock is overwhelming; Boris had shown no signs of illness, so how can he just have died overnight? The thought of losing her last friend is too much to bear, and Rebecca buries her face in her hands and starts crying loudly.

A moment later, she senses the smell and looks up. Through tears she sees the creature standing in the open door.

"He's ... he's dead," she sobs. "Boris is dead."

The creature comes into the room and stops by the foot of the bed. Rebecca just looks at Boris and sniffles. The creature picks up the dog, gently, then carries it out of the room. She hears it go downstairs, and a minute later, the sound of the front door.

For a minute or so, Rebecca hopes that the creature will fix Boris. Maybe he wasn't really dead after all. Maybe the creature has some sort of supernatural power which can bring him back. She almost begins to hope.

Then something draws her attention towards the window. She gets up and goes to it. Down in the garden, she sees the creature walking with Boris under one arm and the shovel under the other. It goes behind the hedge at the place where Alice is buried.

Rebecca starts crying again and throws herself onto the bed.

She stays in the room for the rest of the day and the days to come.

It feels like she lost more than just a good friend. It feels like she's lost everyone and is left completely alone in the world. She misses Boris badly, particularly in the morning when she wakes up and finds the foot of the bed empty. The only sound in the house that could make her happy was the low ringing of the bell in Boris's collar, telling her the dog was somewhere nearby, and that she wasn't alone with the creature. But now there is only the silence and that damned grandfather clock and the creaks from the floorboards as the creature moves around.

Rebecca can't bring herself to leave the room; she's too depressed. The creature brings her food while she sleeps. Rebecca has hardly any appetite and struggles to eat.

The only consolation is that the creature stops burning her feet and dripping her eyes for a few days. Yet Rebecca doesn't really care. She would have almost welcomed the pain. Anything would be better than the emptiness left by Boris.

She's never felt this lonely in her life.

DAY 91

One evening, as Rebecca leaves her room and goes to pee, she suddenly hears a sound from downstairs.

It's the ringing of Boris's bell.

She feels her heart open like a flower, and for a moment she imagines Boris has returned, that he wasn't really dead after all, that the creature didn't really burry him, but instead took him to the vet who has now fixed him. But of course, it's a silly thought.

Then what's making the ringing?

Rebecca goes downstairs and peeks into the living room. Her eyes are a little better because the creature hasn't given her the liquid for almost a week, and she immediately sees the puppy sitting on the floor, playing with a sock. It's a dachshund, the exact same color as Boris, and it's wearing Boris's collar, even though it's too big for the tiny neck.

The sight of the puppy is so unreal, Rebecca feels like she's looking at Boris reincarnated. She steps into the room.

The puppy looks up and sees her. It yelps happily and runs to greet her on its stumpy legs. It jumps up and down in front her, whining impatiently as the bell rings.

Rebecca kneels down and picks it up. The puppy licks her chin and bites her hair. Rebecca can't help but snigger.

"Who are you?" she asks, holding out the puppy to study it. It just looks back at her with a silly expression, mouth open and the pink tongue hanging out.

Rebecca checks the name tag on the collar. It still says BORIS.

"Oh, so your name is Boris too," she smiles, rubbing her nose against the puppy's snout, then laughing as it tries to lick her nostrils. "Are you going to live here now?"

The puppy yelps again, squirming joyfully in her hands, and Rebecca feels her heart beating warmly in her chest.

She has been so taken in by the puppy that she hasn't noticed the creature until now. It's sitting in the armchair over at the corner, halfway hidden in shadow, only its skinny legs visible, and of course the orange glow from the cigar. It's been sitting completely quiet, watching her.

Rebecca feels a cold shiver run down her back. She doesn't like how the creature saw her reaction to the puppy, saw her laughing happily. It's almost like she's been exposed. She quickly puts down the puppy, then rushes out of the room and back upstairs.

Later, as she lies in bed, trying to sleep, she can't stop thinking about the puppy downstairs. Once or twice she hears it yelp. She wishes now that she had brought it up with her.

She awakens during the night because she dreams Boris is licking her cheek. The sensation is so real, she can even smell his fur, and she smiles dreamily.

As she becomes more awake, she blinks and rubs her eyes, and the warm feeling from the dream turns into sadness when she remembers once more that Boris is dead and gone.

But then she hears someone breathing right next to the pillow, and she turns her head. The puppy is looking at her with small, sleepy eyes, before licking her cheek one last time, then lying down with a sigh.

Rebecca stares at the door. It's closed. Which means the puppy can't have ventured in here on its own. Besides, how would it have climbed the stairs? Old Boris could only just manage the steps, and he was three times as big. That can only mean …

Rebecca doesn't care at all for the thought that the creature has been in here while she slept—she hates when it does that. But she is happy that New Boris is here. She places her hand on its back, feeling its rapid breathing and tiny heartbeat.

She falls asleep and sleeps well the rest of the night.

DAY 97

Rebecca instantly becomes best friends with New Boris. He sleeps in her bed every night—not by her feet, like Old Boris would, but right up against her pillow.

In the daytime, they play in the room or out in the garden when the sun is shining. Rebecca feeds him twice a day like she did with Old Boris, taking the food from the bag in the scullery. She's not entirely sure how much food the puppy needs, so she gives him plenty. After all, he needs to grow.

Rebecca doesn't feel quite as sad about Old Boris being dead anymore. She has a new friend now. And yet something about the thought of Old Boris keeps nagging her whenever she remembers him. She's not quite sure what it is, though.

One day, Rebecca realizes the puppy is actually a she. She has brought it out into the garden to pee—she's seen it pee many times, but watching it now, it suddenly occurs to her that it doesn't pee quite like Old Boris did. Whereas Old Boris would raise one hindleg up high, New Boris simply bends both hindlegs.

Rebecca picks up the puppy and turns it over to make sure. It checks out. New Boris is definitely a she.

That same evening, after mulling it over, Rebecca decides to make it right.

She brings the puppy down to the kitchen, where the creature is sitting by the table, reading the newspaper and smoking. Even though its back is turned, it apparently senses Rebecca standing there, because it stops reading and turns around on the chair. It doesn't say anything, just looks in her direction, as though waiting for her to speak.

"You need to buy a new name tag," Rebecca says. "It can't be called Boris. It's a girl."

The puppy yaps in agreement.

The creature, however, shakes its head slowly and says simply: "Boris."

"No, she can't be named Boris," Rebecca says patiently. "Boris is a boy's name."

"Boris," the creature repeats, still shaking its head.

"She's a girl," Rebecca persists, stepping a little closer. "Look. She doesn't have a—"

The creature slams both hands onto the table with in a sudden ferocity and bellows: "*BORIS!*"

Rebecca staggers backwards, almost dropping the puppy, who jerks and begins whimpering in her arms. Rebecca turns and flees upstairs.

As she closes the door to the room and clutches the puppy to her chest, she can't really tell if it's her own or the dog's heart that's beating faster.

That evening, for the first time since Old Boris died, the creature begins burning her feet and giving her the eye-liquid again.

Later on, as she lies in bed with the puppy snoring softly next to the pillow, Rebecca can't fall asleep. She just stares up into the blurry ceiling, as thoughts keep going around her head, and her feet throb painfully under the fresh bandages.

Rebecca turns her head sideways and strokes the puppy's back as she broods. Now she understands what was bugging her about the thought of Old Boris.

As she lies in bed now, in the dark room, it all comes into place in her mind, and she finally realizes no one will come for her. It's been way too long now.

In fact, she has known it for a while, she just didn't want to face it. But losing Old Boris somehow brought it to the surface.

The truth is, if she wants to get away from this place, she needs to do it herself. Or else she will spend the rest of her life here, without ever seeing her family or even another human being again. And one day, if she turns fatefully ill or the creature grows tired of her and decides to kill her, she will end up in a hole in the ground out behind the hedge next to the bones of Alice, and the creature will go on to find a replacement, just like it did with Boris.

The thought makes her both angry and very sad. The creature tries to forget that Old Boris is dead, that he was even really here. But he was. Rebecca remembers him, and she always will.

"Your name isn't Boris," she whispers to the puppy. "From now on, your name is ... Doris."

Rebecca smiles and breathes deeply through her nose. Something has changed within her. Something has been brought back to life. Something which had almost gone away forever.

She's scared at the thought of fleeing—terrified, actually—but somehow, weirdly, she also feels relief. Even if it should fail and the creature catches her and punishes her, the punishment can't be worse than staying here, waiting to die.

"I'm going to try," she tells the sleeping puppy. "I really am. And I'm bringing you with me, Doris."

Rebecca closes her eyes then and falls asleep with surprising ease.

And for the first time in a long time, she dreams about Andy and the rest of her family waiting for her back home.

DAY 98

Rebecca spends an hour the next day, when the creature is out, going around the house, looking in every room, thinking.

It's the first time she goes through the house like this, and she finds something quite unexpected in the creature's bedroom. In the closet, which she presumed only contained the creature's clothes, she finds a shelf full of different shoes, including Rebecca's own. They're all around the same size, and all seem to be girl's shoes. Some of them are very old. She counts at least six pairs.

She considers for a moment taking her own shoes, but that would of course be a blatant mistake; the creature would find out and punish her for it. Besides, she's quite used to walking around in her socks by now, even when she's outside.

She leaves the shoes and goes on investigating while she ponders the plan. There are a lot of questions she needs to answer.

Should she do it in the day or in the night? Should she try while the creature is sleeping or wait for it to leave in the van? If it's out, it will lock the doors, meaning Rebecca needs to smash a window to get out of the house. But even if she does, the biggest obstacle will still be the fence. She can't climb it because of the barbed-wire, that's too dangerous. Which means she needs to go either *under* it or *through* it.

There is, of course, the beech. It's a big, old tree by the side of the house, and it has long branches reaching out over the fence. If she could somehow climb up there, she might be able to climb over the fence and jump down on the other side.

The problem is, though, that the lowest branches of the beech sit very high, too high for her to reach them, even if she brought a chair to stand on. She would need a ladder. She knows there is one in the garage—she saw it one day, when she was out playing with the puppy and it ran into the garage—but it's firmly chained to the wall; as though the creature predicted the ladder might be used to scale the fence. So, the beech is not really an option, either.

Later, in the afternoon, Rebecca goes outside and checks the garage. The creature has returned home and is taking a nap in its bedroom.

She finds a pair of pliers which might be big enough to cut the fence—if Rebecca has the strength, that is. She picks up a piece of wire from the floor and tests the pliers. She manages to cut the wire, but it takes a lot of effort, and the fence is even thicker. Besides, she needs to cut it in at least ten places in order to make an opening big enough to squeeze through; probably more like twenty. How long will that take her? Will she tire out before she's done?

There is also still the option she already tried once: digging her way under the fence. The biggest problem with that option is how long it'll take. The first time she tried it, the creature had time to sense what she was doing and showed up. Which means, if she chooses to dig her way out, she needs to do it while the creature isn't home.

But then the next question pops up: what does she do if she makes it past the fence? Where does she run to? There are open fields in every direction and she has no idea which way town is. Of course, she can follow the gravel road until she reaches the highway, but if she flees while the creature is out, she runs the risk of it returning and seeing her on the road.

It might be better to just choose a direction and make a run for it. At some point, she's bound to meet a house or a town.

Then how much of a head start will she need? If the creature sets after her, which she feels pretty certain it will, she better make sure she's far enough away that it can't catch up with her. Even more so if the creature follows her in the van.

Unless she sabotages it, of course. She's seen in the movies how people will cut a wire or something in the engine of a car, and then it won't start. Maybe she can do the same before she makes a run for it?

There are so many things to consider, Rebecca's head is spinning, but she wants to make sure she doesn't overlook anything, so she prepares herself mentally for staying another couple of days, just until she has got it all figured out.

Then, suddenly, a completely unexpected chance shows itself.

DAY 99

Rebecca hears it already from very far away, as she's out playing with Doris in the garden. She immediately recognizes the sound of tires on the gravel, and at first, she thinks it's the creature who has left in the van. But she hasn't heard the engine start up or the rattling of the chain at the gate.

So, she picks up the puppy and goes around to the courtyard. The yellow van is still in the garage.

Some distance up the gravel road, she can make out a red car coming this way. The gravel is very dry and creates a tall, narrow cloud of dust rising towards the blue sky.

Rebecca feels her heart rate rising. She turns and looks at the house. The creature is in there somewhere. Has it heard the car yet? Why hasn't it come out? Perhaps it's napping—it sometimes does that around this time of day.

Rebecca looks toward the approaching car again. It's driving along at a leisurely speed, with no hurry.

Who is it? Someone who knows the creature and wants to pay it a visit?

Rebecca never even considered the possibility of the creature having relatives or friends, and it seems highly unlikely.

She stands there in the courtyard, uncertain what to do, watching the car come closer. Still no sign of the creature as the car reaches the gate. It stops but doesn't turn off its engine.

Rebecca can't see through the windshield due to the reflection of sunlight. The driver's door is opened and an older gentleman steps out. As soon as Rebecca sees his face, she understands he's not a friend of the creature.

"Hello?" he calls out, waving at Rebecca. "Hello, there! Could you please help me, darling?"

Rebecca is completely unprepared for the man's thick accent. It's British, as far as she can tell, like the way old, fancy people from Europe talk in movies. The man sounds very nice, and he's smiling at her and waving her closer.

Rebecca glances back at the house again. The front door is still closed. The creature would have heard the car by now. Perhaps it really is napping.

She bites her lip. *Should I go for it?*

The old guy is still waving and calling for her.

Rebecca can't open the gate, and neither can the man, since it requires a key, which the creature has. And if she tells the man to call the police or go for help, and the creature shows up to see her talking with him, she will no doubt be punished. In fact, just standing here looking at the guy might be considered a disobedience by the creature. Perhaps she ought to simply go inside the house.

On the other hand, this might be the chance she's been waiting for. Rebecca decides to take it.

She runs to the gate.

"Hello, sweetheart," the old man says, holding out a brochure of some kind. "What a lovely little dog you've got there. Listen, I'm looking for this motel, you see, but I've been going 'round for hours on end now, and I just can't seem to—"

"You've got to help me," Rebecca interrupts. "You need to call someone."

The man's smile falters. "I ... I'm sorry, sweetheart, I'm not quite sure I follow?"

Rebecca grabs the cold metal bars of the gate. "Help me!" she says earnestly. "Help me get out of here!" She darts a look back towards the house.

The old man follows her gaze, frowning. "What ... what's wrong, darling? Are you all right?"

"No! I'm not all right! I'm being held hostage. Call the police!"

The man raises his eyebrows. "The police? But, really—"

"Yes! The police! Call them now!"

The man hesitates for a moment longer, looking from the house to Rebecca, then seems to decide to believe her and goes to his pockets. "Shoot, where's my bloody cell phone?"

He goes back to his car.

Rebecca's heart is pounding away in her throat, Doris is shaking in her arms.

And then she hears it. The front door.

She turns her head like in slow motion to see the creature come out of the house. It looks right at her, but weirdly, it's walking in a different direction; it's headed for the garage.

The old man has found his phone and is coming back towards the gate, fumbling with a pair of reading glasses.

Rebecca reaches her arm out through the gate, pointing frantically. "Hurry up! Call them! It's coming! The creature is coming! Call them, just call them!"

"Now, hold on a minute," the old man says, and then he says something more, which Rebecca doesn't pick up, because she's looking back to see the creature coming back out from the garage, holding the shovel and coming this way.

"Call the police!" Rebecca screams. "Call them now! Please!" She lunges for the phone, but the old man steps backward with a look of utter confusion.

He looks to the creature and says: "Good afternoon, sir. Could you please explain to me why this young lady seems to be terrified? What exactly is going on here?"

"*Call the police! Call them!*" Rebecca screams, as the creature grabs her and drags her aside. It produces the key and unlocks the chain.

Rebecca is still screaming, the old guy is still talking to the creature, but now he's also backing away towards his car, the cell phone still in his hand.

"*Run!*" Rebecca screams to him. "*Get out of here!*"

Finally, the seriousness of the situation dawns on the old man, and he turns and makes for his car. The creature has just pulled the gate aside and is still far enough away that the old guy can actually make it—but his shoe slips on the gravel, and he grabs the door so as to not fall down.

It gives the creature the five seconds it needs to get to him and raise the shovel.

Rebecca doesn't actually hear the blade of the shovel connecting with the old guy's skull, because her own scream drowns it out.

She doesn't see it, either, because thankfully, the creature is blocking the view.

But she does see the man fall to the gravel and she sees the creature swing the shovel three times more and she sees the man's bloody face.

Then, she only sees the blue sky and finds herself lying flat on her back, Doris barking somewhere nearby.

I guess I fainted, she thinks curiously, looking at the white clouds drifting by.

She tries to lift her head and is surprised to find she actually can. She sees the creature come walking across the courtyard, dragging along the old man by one leg.

Rebecca feels very faint and weak, but she uses her last strength to turn her head towards the gate. The old guy's car is still right outside, his cell phone lies in the gravel, only a few yards away from Rebecca.

But the creature has closed and chained-up the gate once more, so the car and phone might as well be on Mars.

Then, Rebecca rests her head on the gravel and looks back up at the clouds.

That was my chance, she thinks. *Now the creature will kill me.*

She drifts off.

PART THREE
AMBROOS VAN DE GOOR

DAY 103

The creature doesn't kill her.

It burns her feet until they're both like one giant, oozing wound. It drips the liquid in her eyes and blinds her. It doesn't feed her for three days. And it keeps her locked in the room the entire time.

But it doesn't kill her.

Rebecca lies in bed for a week as her feet slowly heal and her eyes recover somewhat.

The pain is so bad the first couple of days that she barely sleeps. She drifts in and out of feverlike dreams, where she witnesses over and over again the creature beating the old man to death with the shovel. She hears crunching on gravel, her own scream and the sharp thud of a metal blade connecting with a skull.

But she also sometimes dreams about Andy and the rest of her family; they call to her from behind a thick window. She can't hear their voices, but she can see them waving and banging the glass.

Rebecca reads Andy's lips. He keeps repeating the same three words:

"Come home, Becca!"

On the fourth day, the creature brings her a bucket to use as a toilet and starts bringing her meals again. It doesn't look at her or talk to her, though.

As Rebecca slowly recovers in bed, she gradually becomes able to think straight again. And she realizes the thought of trying to escape is even worse, now that she knows what the creature is willing to do to keep her here. She harbors no illusions that it will kill her without hesitation if she tries to run and it catches her.

And why wouldn't it? After all, Rebecca is pretty replaceable. The creature could easily find a new Alice. Maybe it even has done so before.

The way the creature simply replaced Boris makes Rebecca wonder if she is the first one to get caught by the creature? It would explain the many girl's shoes she found.

How many Alices have gone before her? How many exactly are buried around the garden?

So what happened to them? Did they simply grow too old? Or perhaps they refused to toe the line. Perhaps they refused to forget their real name or their family. And finally, one day, they tried to run away. And the creature caught them. And now, their bones lie buried in the ground out back, their flesh eaten away by maggots.

The thought brings out a deep dread in Rebecca.

Though she feels terrified at the thought of trying to flee, she has also already made up her mind to do it. At least it will offer her a chance to see Andy and Mom and Dad and Cindy again, even if the chance is slim. If she does nothing, however, she won't see them for sure.

She also realizes, as she spends the week in bed, how she will do it. It comes to her in a half-dream in the middle of a night full of pain, as she suddenly opened her eyes and stared right at the solution.

Actually, the idea has already occurred to her several days back, maybe all the way back to the night she first saw the moonlight shining in from the closet; she just hadn't realized what it meant until now.

It's obvious, really, when she thinks of it.

It's like a sign from heaven.

Her way out.

And besides, what other way is left? Now that the creature won't even let her out of the room, all of her other options are gone.

She will escape through the closet. The hole at the top leads right onto the roof. And from there, she can make it to the tree. And via the tree, she can climb over the fence and jump down on the other side.

That's the plan, anyway.

If it's doable, she has no idea, and she doesn't really concern herself with the question. She's going to try—that's all that matters. In a couple of days. As soon as her feet are healed enough for to walk again.

There is only one last thing she needs to figure out: how will she bring Doris?

She hasn't seen her since the old man came. The creature won't allow her into the room anymore. Rebecca hears her several times a day, whining from the bottom of the stairs.

Rebecca won't run without Doris. She won't leave her here with the creature.

So, she begins to think out a plan. That's how Andy would do it. Andy is brainy and very meticulous when it comes to problem-solving. He loves riddles and always finds a solution to difficult challenges, using only his mind. Rebecca tries to think like Andy would.

It's going to be difficult getting Doris up here since she can't leave the room, and the only time the creature unlocks the door is when it brings food and empties her toilet-bucket.

Rebecca spends an entire afternoon sitting by the window, gazing down into the garden as she broods. Once or twice she sees Doris, as she comes out through the dog hatch in the terrace door, strolls about the garden, pees, then goes back inside.

Slowly, an idea starts to form.

DAY 104
The next day, Rebecca sets her plan into motion.
She begins to leave a small portion of each meal. A bit of scrambled egg, small pieces of sandwich and three bits of bacon. She hides it in a sock which she places under the mattress.
She spends a few hours by the window every day. As soon as she sees Doris in the garden, she whistles three times, then drops a little food from the open window.
To begin with, Doris has trouble catching on, and she doesn't notice the food right away. Then, the fourth time Rebecca does it, the dog looks up and sees the food falling. After that, she quickly figures out what the three whistles mean.

DAY 107
Rebecca continues the training the next day and the day after that. By the third day, she can get Doris to come running out from inside the house by whistling three times.
Rebecca also spends the days on another part of her plan: making a rope.
She collects all sorts of things: the string from the blinds, the wire from the desk lamp and a thick thread from the carpet in the corner where it's already unraveled. She binds everything together to form a single, long piece, until she's confident it can reach all the way down to the ground. It's very thin and definitely not strong enough to carry Rebecca's weight—but it's not supposed to carry *her*.
Finally, there's only one last piece to the plan: the bucket. The one Rebecca uses as a toilet.
The creature empties it every night as it brings dinner. Five minutes later, it comes back and drops the bucket on the floor. It's been rinsed out and smells of sanitizer.
Rebecca worries the smell might scare off Doris. She can only hope the smell of the bait is more prominent.
Rebecca hides the makeshift rope under the mattress as the creature comes on the third day to bring her evening meal. It puts the plate on the desk, takes the bucket and closes the door again behind it without even looking at her.
Rebecca immediately goes to eat, plucking away three bits of bacon and devouring the rest of the meal.
When the creature returns with the cleaned-out bucket, Rebecca has already stuffed the bacon away and is sitting on her bed, looking innocent.
Normally, the creature would have found out. It would have looked at her closely and figured out she was hiding something. But because it's still punishing her and hasn't spent any time with her lately, its ability to sense that something is up seems to have weakened.

Yet this time, it suddenly hesitates in the doorway. Rebecca doesn't look over at it, but she senses how its eyes rest on her.

"Alice," it whispers.

Rebecca doesn't move. Sweat is prickling her back. Did the creature figure it out after all? Did it hear her whistling for Doris through the window? Or has it been in here when she slept and found the rope? Does it know she's planning to flee?

"Alice," it whispers again.

Rebecca turns her head halfway towards the door and, for the first time ever, she answers to the false name by saying: "Yes?"

She's surprised at how sincere her voice sounds.

The creature doesn't say anything else. It just stands there, staring at her. Then, it closes the door and goes downstairs.

Rebecca begins breathing again. *What did that mean? Was it a warning?*

The creature didn't sound either angry or threatening—in fact, there was almost warmth in the voice. Maybe it didn't figure out her plan after all. Maybe it just wants to make peace.

Rebecca can't tell for sure. But she knows she needs to make the plan happen now, tonight.

DAY 108
Never before has time gone by so slowly.

Andy twists and turns. He keeps checking his phone. Every time he does so, only a few minutes have passed since he last looked. If time would just hurry up so he could get going.

Finally, he can't wait any longer. It's only 0:23 AM, and he meant to wait until 1:00 AM, but he's pretty certain both Mom and Dad are sleeping by now.

So, he gets up, gets dressed and arranges the bed like he has done hundreds of times before.

But this time is special. This time might be the last.

He checks his phone. The address is a fair way outside of town—way too long for him to have ever found it on his nightly outings, anyway—almost twelve miles. It will take him most of the night just to reach it. His legs are in pretty good shape, but he'll probably still get very sore muscles tomorrow.

Andy doesn't care if he'll walk sideways for the rest of his life. Rebecca is at the end of the twelve miles, and that's the only thing that matters.

He takes out his bag from under the bed. It's loaded with crackers, a Mars bar, a water bottle, *The Wendigo* and a boxcutter.

He's not exactly sure why he brings the book, but he somehow feels braver knowing it's with him. He picks up the boxcutter and slides out the blade. It shines up at him. Andy swallows dryly. He really hopes he won't need it, but he might end up in a position where he has to defend himself or Rebecca, and it was the best weapon he could find in Dad's toolbox.

He zips up the bag and swings it over his shoulder. Then, he crawls out of the window, uses the drainpipe to slide to the ground, runs around the house and remembers to duck as he passes his parents' bedroom window, even though the curtains are drawn.

He sneaks into the garage but leaves the lights off. He knows the surroundings well enough to locate his bike in the dark. He pulls it out to the driveway and is just about to head off, when he notices something is wrong. He looks down to see the back tire completely flat.

"Oh, crap," he whispers. "Not now!"

He gets back off the bike again and looks at it for a moment. He doesn't know how to fix a flat tire—Dad always does it for him. Which means he needs to postpone the whole thing till tomorrow.

The thought of waiting another day makes him very ill at ease. He goes back into the garage and takes out his phone, using its flashlight to look around.

Mom's bike is dismantled because Dad is in the progress of fixing the gears. Dad's bike is too big for Andy. And Cindy doesn't own a bike.

Andy moans and feels like kicking something out of frustration. He feels so close, but now he has to wait.

Then he sees Cindy's scooter.

Andy hesitates for a moment. He did actually try it once, last summer, where Cindy let him have a go on it without Mom and Dad knowing about it. He even knows how to start it—and he knows where to find the key, too.

Andy decides to do it.

He sneaks into the house. In the entrance hall the key for the scooter hangs from the rack among other keys. Andy steps over and carefully takes it, when suddenly, there's a sound from the bathroom.

Andy freezes. Steps are coming this way. There's nowhere to hide.

The door opens, and Cindy appears. She jumps a little when she sees him. "Oh, you scared me, Andy. What are you doing up at this hour?"

Andy tries to reply, but only a dry croak comes out.

Cindy looks down and notices Andy is fully dressed, shoes and all.

She sighs. "Goddamnit, Andy. Are you still sneaking out at night? Mom will kill you if she finds out."

"I ... I have to, Cindy."

"No, you don't, actually. You need to move on. Rebecca won't come back, okay?"

The words connect with Andy's stomach like heavy blows. He forces down a deep breath, reminding himself that Cindy means well. And she doesn't know what *he* knows.

He keeps the key for the scooter hidden behind his back and hopes she won't notice it missing from the rack.

"Come on upstairs with me, Andy," she says pleadingly, stepping closer. "You can sleep in my room if you like."

For a moment, Andy is so surprised at the offer, he almost feels tempted to go with Cindy. He hasn't slept in her room since he was very little. Before Rebecca was born. Back then, he and Cindy still played together.

"Cindy," he says, not even considering what he's about to ask her. "Why aren't you sad that Rebecca's gone?"

The answer is obvious from Cindy's face right away, as she struggles to not let it crumble.

Instead, she shakes her head. "How thick are you, Andy? Of course I'm sad. I cry myself to sleep every night. I just ... I just don't wear my emotions on my sleeve."

"I ... I didn't know," Andy says, feeling stupid.

Cindy sighs again. "How would you? We're all wrapped up in our own shit right now, aren't we?"

"I guess so," Andy says, looking at Cindy in a completely new light.

The haircut, the makeup, the new clothes. It all happened after Rebecca disappeared. And maybe it wasn't at all about Cindy's looks after all.

"I'm sorry, Cindy," he says, realizing his sister might have been suffering just as much as he has over the loss of Rebecca.

"It's fine," Cindy says, managing a smile. "Come on upstairs with me, won't you?"

Cindy makes as though to go, putting a hand on Andy's shoulder, but Andy stays firm.

"I need to go, Cindy," he whispers.

Cindy is about to answer, when she looks at him and sees the tears in his eyes.

"This will be the last time," he says. "I promise."

Cindy eyes him, a look of deep sadness coming over her face. "All right," she mutters, nodding.

"You won't tell Mom, will you?"

"I guess I should, but ..." Cindy shrugs. "If this is your way of dealing with things, then who am I to tell you otherwise? Just promise me to be careful. Put the lights on your bike, okay?" She squeezes his shoulder, then heads upstairs.

Andy breathes out. His entire body is trembling. The key is sweaty in his clutched hand.

* * *

Rebecca can't sleep.

She lies awake, staring at the ceiling. She knows this will be the last time she lies here. The last time she sees this room. One way or another.

The hours drag on. She doesn't have a watch, but she listens to the grandfather clock downstairs, counting the chimes. Finally, she decides it's time.

She sits up, already dressed. She finds the rope and the sock full of food, moving as quietly as possible. She ties the rope to the handle of the bucket and empties the sock into the bucket. There's almost an entire meal. She hopes it'll be enough to tempt Doris.

But first she needs to take care of something else.

Rebecca slips over to the closet and opens it. The moon is full and its light is streaming in through the crack in the roof. Rebecca steps up onto the lower shelf and reaches up with one hand. It takes some medaling, but she manages to pry one of the roof tiles loose. It's very heavy. She carefully lowers it and places it neatly on the floor, before stepping back up and loosening the next one.

When three tiles are gone, the hole is big enough for her to fit through. A rectangular piece of black, starry sky is visible, and the cool night air seeps in, inviting her.

Rebecca steps out of the closet and closes the door again. Her heart is thumping away; the creature might open the door to the room at any point and ruin everything. But so far, it hasn't. And Rebecca moves on.

She opens the window and picks up the bucket. Then, she whistles three times. It sounds very loud in the silence. She waits a minute or so, but Doris doesn't show up. Rebecca knows the puppy is sleeping in the living room right below her, and the creature's bedroom is way over at the far end of the house. But which of them sleeps deeper?

Rebecca whistles again, a little louder.

Still, no Doris.

She whistles a third time, as loudly as she dares.

And then she hears the dog hatch open. Doris comes trundling out, shakes her fur and looks up at Rebecca with sleepy eyes.

"Hey, Doris," she whispers and waves.

The tail starts wagging.

"Don't make any noise now," Rebecca instructs her. "The creature mustn't hear us."

Doris sits down and waits patiently for her treat.

"I've got something special for you this time," Rebecca whispers and lets the bucket slip out of the window, lowering it carefully with the rope.

Doris looks curiously at the bucket as it comes closer. Rebecca lands it gently next to the dog. Then she makes a few sideways jerks with the rope, causing the bucket to tip over on the side.

Doris steps a little back. She whimpers and sniffs the bucket suspiciously. She can obviously smell the food, but isn't quite sure if it's safe to dig in.

"Just go for it," Rebecca whispers. "It's okay, just take the food, Doris."

She glances back. The door is still closed.

After a little more sniffing around, Doris decides to chance it and tentatively reaches into the bucket. Rebecca can hear her eating.

"Just a little farther," Rebecca breathes, staring at the dog and the bucket.

Doris takes another step forward. She's halfway inside the bucket now. Still not enough. If Rebecca tries to lift the bucket now, and Doris slips out, she's afraid the puppy will be too scared to go near the bucket again. She only gets one shot.

"Just a liiitle more ..."

Finally, Doris steps all the way into the bucket, only her tail is showing now.

Rebecca jerks the rope upwards. The bucket tilts back upright and lifts off the ground. Doris gives off a little yelp of surprise. Rebecca hauls the bucket up quickly. Doris jumps to get out, and the bucket sways dangerously. For a terrible moment, Rebecca is sure the puppy will fall out and hurt herself badly on the stone terrace below.

But Doris falls back into the bucket and a moment later, Rebecca grabs the handle and pulls it into the room.

"You did so good," she whispers and lifts up Doris. "Good girl, good girl."

The puppy licks Rebecca's face and whines happily at the reunion. It's been several days since they last were together.

"Sssh," Rebecca shushes. "We need to be very quiet now."

She buttons down her shirt and places Doris inside it. The puppy is warm against her stomach, and it settles in immediately, giving a satisfied yawn.

"That's right, you rest. I'll do the work."

Rebecca goes to the closet. So far, so good. Now comes the tricky part. She breathes deeply, opens the closet and climbs up the shelves. She sticks her head up through the hole and surveys the roof for a moment. It's steeper that she thought, and it's also wet from dew.

I can make it. I just need to be careful.

Rebecca steps up onto the top shelf and raises herself up onto the roof. She's really high up. Luckily, she has never been scared of heights. Still, a fall from up here might results in several broken bones.

She tests the roof with her foot, the socks slipping easily. She takes them off and tries with her bare feet. The burn wounds hurt a little, but the soles of her feet have a little more grip without the socks.

Slowly, she begins the climb. The tree is on the other side of the house, which means she needs to scale the rooftop. A few times she almost slips, but then she figures out a method where she grabs the edge of the tiles. They are pretty sharp and rough on her fingers, but she ignores the pain.

Doris is sleeping calmly against her stomach.

Rebecca reaches the top of the roof and moves along the ridge until she's right next to the beech. Now, she only needs to get down to the branches.

The biggest problem with her plan, she realizes now, is that the tree is right outside the creature's bedroom, and she will be climbing right over it. Which means she needs to be extra silent.

Rebecca begins the descent. It's a lot harder than going up. After only a few feet, she loses her grip and slips. She almost screams out as she slides down the slippery roof, her buttock giving off small bumps with every tile, moving faster and faster, the branches rushing towards her, and then she meets them, groping wildly for something to catch on to. One or two of the thinner branches break off, and she is very close to sliding right through, when, at the last moment, she grabs a branch thick enough to halt her.

Rebecca sits still, clutching the branch, her heart racing. Doris moves under the shirt.

"It's okay," she whispers. "We're okay. Go back to sleep."

Rebecca listens for noises from inside the house. The bumps from her wild ride might have been enough to wake up the creature.

Then get a move on!

Rebecca climbs onto the tree. It's more difficult than she imagined, the branches aren't very thick and are also slippery, but she manages to make her way to the trunk of the tree.

She stands still for a moment and looks down. She can see the window to the creature's bedroom. It's dark in there, but the window is open, letting the night air in.

Rebecca looks out over the branch that reaches across the fence. From here, it looks a lot thinner and less supportive than it did from the ground. And there are several feet down. She feels so close to freedom, but she still needs to cross one final, dangerous stage.

And suddenly, unexpectedly, Rebecca is gripped by the most overwhelming fear she has ever felt in her life. For a moment, she wants to drop everything. To climb back up onto the roof and slip back inside her room. Lower Doris back down onto the lawn and go to bed.

Would it really be so bad living here? Is it really worth risking her life to get away? If she just does as the creature asks of her, she has really nothing to fear. She could live here for many years to come.

But she knows she can't do that. She knows there's only one way for her, and that's out over that fence, no matter how scared she is.

She breathes deeply, forces her hands to let go of the trunk and begins walking. Rebecca is pretty good at balancing. The first half of the way, she has other branches to hold onto for support. But then they run out, and she needs to walk on her own. The branch isn't much wider than her feet, and it bobs gently under her weight. The burn wounds at the soles of her feet begin stinging badly, but she ignores the pain, steps slowly, one foot at a time.

She's almost above the fence now.

Two more steps. She is very close.

Two more. One.

And then she's over.

Rebecca kneels down and grabs the branch with both hands. Out here, it's not much thicker than a broomstick. She shivers all over. Now she just needs to make the jump. There's almost ten feet to the ground. She's never made a jump this high before. She could swing herself down and hang from her arms, that way making the jump shorter, but she's afraid the shirt might open and Doris could fall out if she stretches out like that. So she needs to just jump.

Come on, you can do it. It's the last thing you need to do, and then you're free!

Rebecca closes her eyes. Then she jumps.

She wooshes through the air, faster and faster. The fall seems to go on forever.

Then she hits the wheat and the soft ground below and rolls to her back to soften the blow on the feet. Her ankles hurt a bit, but it soon wears off. She didn't break anything. Doris wakes up and moves around.

Rebecca gets to her feet and looks around. The wheat is knee-high, but she can see very far.

I ... I did it ... I'm free! I—

A movement above her. Rebecca looks up and sees something white swoop through the air. A large, snowy owl lands in the beech and looks down at her with big, round and yellow eyes.

Rebecca stares back at it, dumbfounded.

The owl blinks at her. Then turns its head to look at the house.

Rebecca follows its gaze. And freezes when she sees the creature.

It's standing right on the other side of the fence, glaring at her.

"Alice."

The word comes creeping through the night air. The voice is low. Ominous. Furious.

Rebecca shakes her head and begins backing away through the wheat. She can't take her eyes off the creature. She's certain it will take off and scale the fence in one giant leap at any moment. But it just keeps standing there.

"Alice," it says again, a little louder.

"No!" Rebecca says, and the sound of her voice is like a spell-breaker. Suddenly, she can turn around and run.

She looks back and sees the creature move along the fence. It's headed for the courtyard and the gate. Which means it's can't scale the fence after all. That should give Rebecca courage, but something about the way the creature moves scares her more than anything. It doesn't run, it just walks with long, casual strides.

Like it knows it doesn't need to hurry.

Like it's got all night.

Like Rebecca's flight is doomed to fail.

The owl takes flight and glides noiselessly over her head before disappearing into the darkness.

Rebecca runs for her life.

* * *

Andy gives it full throttle as he races along the dark highway.

To begin with, he rode carefully, but now he's got the hang of it, and he feels comfortable about going at full speed. The road is mostly straight, and the light from the scooter helps him see the dew-wet asphalt ahead. He's been riding for close to half an hour now.

Now and then he stops to check his phone and make sure he's on the right track.

Until he got out of town, he was afraid of getting stopped by a police car. He only met a few late drivers, though, and none of them paid any attention to him. He's wearing Cindy's helmet, so hopefully no one can tell he's only thirteen.

Out here in the country, the chance of getting stopped is obviously a lot smaller, and he hasn't met a single car yet. Only the stars above keep him company.

Something dark appears ahead.

It's a forest, Andy realizes as he gets closer. It fits with what the map told him: the house he's looking for will be on the other side of the forest. Which means he's close now.

The road cuts right through the trees. The darkness grows thicker around him as he enters the forest, and there are leaves on the asphalt, making it slippery, so he lets off the gas a little. Crashing with the scooter would be almost as bad as getting caught by the police. Just the thought of having to call home, admit the whole thing and ask them to come get him ... Andy shivers. That mustn't happen. But as long as he's careful—

Suddenly, he sees it.

It appears out of nowhere, like a jack-in-box, completely unexpected.

He stops the scooter and puts his feet to the ground. He pulls off the helmet and stares open-mouthed at the yellow van parked at the roadside.

Although it's been almost four months since he saw it, there's no doubt in his mind he's looking at the exact same van.

He squints, adjusts his glasses and tries to look through the windshield. As far as he can tell, no one is behind the wheel. He looks around in the darkness, peering in between the trees.

No figures in sight. He feels alone, but ... how can he be sure?

Andy shuts off the scooter's engine and puts it on the kickstand. Then he quickly takes off the bag, opens it and reaches in for the boxcutter.

He steps a little closer to the van, holding his breath as he listens.

The night is absolutely quiet.

Not a breeze stirs.

Not a leaf rustles.

Only Andy's heart is buzzing in his ears.

He walks closer to the van, clutching the boxcutter, ready to push out the blade, in case he's walking into a trap.

He walks around the van. All the doors are closed. Andy tries to open the back door. It's locked.

"Rebecca?" he whispers. "You in there?"

No reply.

Andy's intuition tells him the car is empty. He goes around to the front and places his hand on the hood; it's a trick he learned from a detective's novel. It's still warm. The van can only have been left here a few minutes ago.

Andy suddenly gets a strong feeling that someone is looking at him, and he spins around.

No one to see. Except—

He looks up and sees the owl eyeing him from the nearest tree.

That does it. The owl must be a sign. There's still almost one mile to the house, but now Andy knows Rebecca is nearby.

"Where is she?" he asks the owl. "Tell me!"

The owl blinks. Then it takes flight and swoops over his head without a noise, headed into the forest and quickly disappears in the darkness.

Andy stares after it and sees the trail snaking between the trees. It's too narrow for a car, so whoever came in the van has probably parked it here and continued into the forest on foot.

Andy swallows dryly. He's suddenly very much aware that he's standing in the middle of nowhere all alone in the dead of night. No one even knows he's here, and now he's about to go pursue a dangerous monster with only a boxcutter to defend himself.

If I'm afraid, how must Rebecca feel?

The thought makes him breath hard through his nose.

"I'm coming, Becca," he tells the night.

* * *

Rebecca isn't really aware that she's headed for the forest until it's right in front of her. She just runs across the field as quickly as she can. It's hard, because the wheat keeps trying to trip her, and her pants are completely soaked through from dew.

The full moon lights up the land, allowing her to see a little ahead despite her blurry vision. A few times she stumbles, but quickly gets back up.

She keeps looking back, expecting to see the creature come running for her, but so far that hasn't happened, and by now the house and beech tree have turned into nothing but a tiny, dark blotch.

Yet she knows it's coming.

She knows it won't just let her leave.

She sees the forest and stops to catch her heaving breath. Doris moves under the shirt, whimpering.

"I know," Rebecca pants. "But you can't get out yet, Doris."

She considers for a moment if it's wise to go into the forest. On the one hand she'll be less easy to see once she's no longer out in the open. On the other, she has a feeling the forest is where the creature moves most naturally. After all, it was in the park forest it was waiting for her when it took her. Perhaps it's better for her to run around the forest. Maybe she ought to—

The wind whispers at her. It's only the slightest breeze.

"Alice."

The name is just barely audible.

Rebecca spins around and looks in every direction. She's still alone in the field. But suddenly, she doesn't *feel* alone.

She runs into the forest, clutching the puppy against her stomach as she zigzags between the trees. It's extra hard to see in here, because most of the moonlight is drowned out by the treetops, their leaves and branches creating flickering shadows all around. The forest floor is uneven and overgrown in ferns, causing her to almost stumble.

She reaches a clearing and stops, looks around, panting, straining her eyes.

The shadows from the trees play with her imagination, making it seem like one of them could step forward at any minute, revealing itself as the creature.

No, it can't be here already, Rebecca tries to tell herself. *I had a good head start and I ran as fast as I could all the way over. Unless, of course ... unless it **drove** here ...*

The thought sends icy chills down her sweaty back. What if the creature knew she was headed for the forest? What if it just casually walked to the van and drove over here? Perhaps it's already here. Perhaps it's even waiting for her ...

The feeling of being watched creeps up on her from every side. She wants to run, she feels exposed in the middle of the clearing, but she doesn't know which direction to take.

"Hello?" she whispers, spinning slowly. "Is anybody here?"

No answer comes. At least not from a human voice. But the breeze stirs again, floats through the clearing, causing the ferns to rattle, and carries the creature's squeaking little-girl-voice to her.

"*Alice ...*"

The breath is pulled from Rebecca's mouth. She wants to scream, but can't. Her entire body is trembling, her knees threaten to buckle. She turns and turns, desperately trying to get eyes on the creature.

"Where are you?" she croaks.

"*Alice,*" the wind whispers.

"*Where are you!?*" Rebecca screams.

The sound throws an echo and a flock of sleeping crows take flight from the treetops. Their shrill shrieks fill the air, and their flickering shadows flow across the clearing, before the birds are gone and silence once again descends over the forest.

Rebecca holds her breath and listens. The breeze is gone now. Everything is quiet. Rebecca feels a faint hope. She can't hear the voice anymore. Maybe the creature got distracted by the crows. Maybe it's—

"Alice."

This time, the voice comes from right behind her.

Rebecca spins around with a scream, just as the creature steps out from the shadows. As the moonlight hits it, Rebecca sees to her utter horror that it's fully naked. The pale, greyish skin covers the thin limbs and gives it a sickly look. It moves in a strange, almost dreamlike fashion on the long, spiderlike legs, and the black eyes lock Rebecca in place.

She wants to turn, to run, to get away, but she can't move a muscle, can only stand there like a statue and stare at the creature sweeping towards her, and she knows that this is it, knows without a shadow of a doubt that the creature will kill her now.

Rebecca notices very faintly a distant sound growing louder. At first, she takes it for her own pulse buzzing behind her eardrums. But once the sound grows louder, it reminds her more of an angry wasp coming this way. And then the sound rises even further, turning into an angry roar.

The creature hears it too, because it snaps its boney neck and looks to the side, just as a sharp, white flash lights up everything for a brief second.

Rebecca turns her head in a slow, dreamy movement. She catches a glimpse of the scooter as it comes crashing into the clearing, bumping wildly over the forest floor. She also sees the creature caught in the headlight like a surprised animal. It raises its arms and lets out a hoarse scream, but the sound is cut short as the scooter collides with it and sends it sprawling backwards. The scooter does a somersault and the driver flies off before it lands and both the headlight and the engine die.

Rebecca blinks and stares at the driver, who has landed right in front of her. With a moan of pain, the person comes to their feet and pulls the helmet off.

Andy looks at her.

He's taller, thinner, and his hair is longer. But it is Andy. He smiles, and the smile is exactly the same.

"Hi, Becca," he says, a little out of breath.

Then his smile goes away as he turns to look at the creature. Rebecca follows his gaze and sees the thin figure on the ground starting to stir.

"Come on," Andy says, grabbing her by the arm. "We've got to go."

The feeling of his hand on her arm wakes Rebecca from her trance. She follows him to the scooter, which he lifts up with a groan. He turns the key, and the engine sneers and comes to life.

"Hop on!" Andy says, getting on the scooter himself.

Rebecca jumps up behind him. She puts her arms around his waist and squeezes him so tightly that Doris is almost flattened between them.

Andy revs up the engine and turns the scooter around. In the movement, the glare from the headlight sweeps across the clearing, and Rebecca gets another glimpse of the creature, who's already halfway back to its feet. It clutches its side as it stares at them in a wordless sneer.

Then, it's gone, and the scooter is bumping through the forest, and Rebecca tries her best not to fall off.

* * *

It feels like forever before they finally reach the road.

Andy is pumped up on the adrenaline still coursing through him. He barely felt any pain when he collided with the creature, even though he went flying head over heels. He'll probably find a host of bruises all over his body later, though, but for now he only feels exultant.

Rebecca is squeezing him tightly, and he still can't believe it's really her—that he really found her!

She doesn't really look like herself, though. She has lost some weight, and there are dark patches under her eyes. Also, her hair has been dyed blond for some strange reason.

But nonetheless, it *is* her.

The forest floor is very uneven, yet Andy gives it almost full throttle, biting down hard to prevent his teeth from chattering. Without the helmet it's actually easier for him to see.

Suddenly, the ground changes into asphalt, and Andy hits the brake, stopping the scooter in the middle of the road. They've come out at the exact same place he went in: a few yards from the yellow van.

"That's how I found you," Andy says over his shoulder. "When I saw the van, I knew you were in the forest somewhere."

"We have to get away from here, Andy," Rebecca says in his ear. "It's going to follow us."

"I know," Andy says, getting off the scooter and putting it on the stand. "But we need a head start."

He goes to the van, kneels down and studies the tire. He finds the valve and tries twisting it. With a little effort, he manages to loosen it, and the valve gives off a hissing as it lets out the air.

Andy makes sure the tire is completely flat before he runs back to the scooter. He notices Rebecca eyeing him with something close to awe, and he feels a wild sense of pride. He jumps up and revs the engine.

"Right, hold on."

They speed along the road headed for town. Andy can feel how Rebecca keeps turning to look back.

"I think it might have gotten hurt when I hit it," Andy says. "Maybe it doesn't have the strength to take up pursuit."

"I wouldn't count on it," Rebecca says grimly, adding: "It's not human."

"I know," Andy says.

Rebecca is silent for a few seconds, then she asks: "How do you know?"

"From a book," Andy says. "It's a long story, but I think it's a wendigo."

"A what-now?"

"A wendigo. It's a monster from old stories, like vampires and stuff like that. It's—" Andy feels something move against his back. "What's that?" he asks, looking back.

"It's just Doris. It's a puppy I brought with me from the creature's house."

"Oh, okay."

They drive for some time without speaking. Andy feels Rebecca looking back a few more times, then she stops. As they get out of the forest and the shadows, the moon and stars light up the open landscape around them.

"I didn't think anyone would come for me," she suddenly says in his ear. Andy can tell she's almost crying. "That's why I ran. I thought you had all given up on me."

"I didn't give up on you," Andy says firmly. "Never."

"Then why didn't the police come for me?"

"They said there was nothing more they could do. And Mom and Dad, well ... they believed it, I guess. But I didn't. I knew we could still find you and get you home."

"Is that why you came alone? On Cindy's scooter?"

"Yeah. Mom and Dad don't even know I'm gone." He breaks into laughter. "Imagine their faces when we show up!"

Rebecca is quiet a little while. "How did you figure out where I was?"

Andy begins explaining, and once he starts, the whole story comes out. Everything from the book to the woodpeckers to New Mom to *Anatomy of the Human Eye*. He even tells about Lisa.

Rebecca listens while he talks. Andy can't recall she's ever listened for so long without interrupting him.

When he's finished, she simply says: "So, ghosts are real then."

"I guess so. At least this one is." Andy can feel Rebecca's arms tremble. "Are you cold?"

"Yes, very."

"It's only ten more minutes to town. Hang on a little longer, Becca. Can you do that?"

Andy expects her to scoff and says something like: "What do you think?" or "Of course I can, I'm not a baby." That's what the old Rebecca would have said.

Instead, she answers meekly: "Okay."

Andy feels a stab in his heart. What was it the wendigo did when it caught someone? It broke down the person's mind and spirit, sucked the life force out of them, until they weren't even a human anymore.

Andy really hopes the wendigo didn't suck too much life force out of Rebecca. He really hopes she's still Rebecca.

The sky has started to lighten, and the moon and stars have lost some of their shine, when they finally see the town up ahead. The night is turning into morning, and very soon the traffic will set in.

They have just passed the town limit, when the scooter gives a jolt.

Andy looks to the dashboard. A red light next to the fuel-indicator is blinking.

"Oh, crap."

"What is it?"

"It's out of gas."

The scooter jerks again and loses speed. Andy pulls onto the sidewalk just as the engine dies and they come to a halt.

"We have to walk the rest of the way," Andy says, putting the scooter on the stand, before helping Rebecca down. It's only now he notices she's barefooted. "Where are your shoes?"

"I had to leave them," she simply says, cupping the bundle on her stomach.

"You want me to carry you?"

"No, that's okay."

They begin walking down the sidewalk. It feels unreal to Andy, strolling alongside Rebecca again. She limps a little.

"So, what was its name?" she asks, glancing at Andy.

"The wendigo?"

"Yes, you said you knew right away when Regan found the name."

"Here, let me show you ..." Andy finds his phone and types in the name.

Rebecca reads the name, then frowns. "What a strange name."

"I know. But try to sound it out."

Rebecca does so. "Ambroos van de Goor ..." At first, she doesn't seem to get it. Then she squints her eyes and repeats it. "Van de Goor ... it sounds a lot like 'wendigo.'"

"Exactly!" Andy says, smiling. "I guess it made up its own name, trying to pass off as a human being. It must have had a social security number and everything, since it could take a book from the library."

"Maybe it was a human being once," Rebecca says, her tone distant, as Andy can tell she's thinking back on something.

"Why do you say that?"

"There was a picture of a girl at its house."

"A girl? What girl?"

Rebecca shakes her head. "I don't know. Someone the crea ... the wendigo loved. I'm pretty sure she's dead now."

Rebecca falls silent, and her eyes seem to stare at nothing as they walk on.

Andy glances at her once more. "Did it ... did it hurt you, Becca?"

Rebecca keeps looking straight ahead. "It burned the soles of my feet with a cigar and dripped something in my eyes which made them sting."

"That monster," Andy whispers, feeling shivers run down his spine, and anger well up in his chest. He looks at Rebecca again. "I can tell your eyes are kind of pink—can you see all right?"

"Not really. Everything is blurry."

"I'm sure it'll pass."

"It did so in the beginning, but not anymore."

Andy clenches his fist. He feels so bad for Rebecca, but he also feels furious at the police, at Mom and Dad, at himself, at everyone for not finding Rebecca sooner. Now she might have permanent eye damage due to what the wendigo did to her.

"What about your hair?" he asks.

"It made me dye it."

"Did it do anything else to hurt you?"

Rebecca is silent for a long time.

Andy begins to think she won't answer.

Then, she says very quietly: "It kept calling me Alice."

"Alice?"

"Yes. I told it over and over my name was Rebecca, but it just kept calling me Alice."

"Why would it do that?" Andy asks, frowning.

Rebecca keeps looking forward as she says blankly: "It wanted me to forget my real name."

Andy notices her face tremble slightly as they walk on. He can see thoughts going through her head, and he can tell how badly it has affected Rebecca's mind being trapped by the wendigo for that long.

"But you didn't forget your name, did you?" he asks tentatively.

Rebecca hesitates just a second, then shakes her head. "No. I wrote it down."

"Good. That was clever."

"It also ... it also killed an old man," Rebecca goes on. "I saw it."

Andy swallows. "Who was he?"

"I don't know, some guy who came by looking for directions. It beat him to death with a shovel."

"Holy crap," Andy mutters, then thinks of something to change the subject: "How did it catch you? I mean, how did it get you into the van in the first place? 'Cause you *were* in the van, right? When I heard you knocking from the inside?"

Rebecca nods. "I was, and I saw you through the crack between the doors."

"How did it happen? Did it just scoop you up outside the library?"

"No, I went to the park."

"The park? Why?"

"I wanted to give you a scare. You know, because I was mad at you."

Andy shakes his head. "Well, that's just typical you, Becca. You should have stayed and waited for me like I told you."

He sounds a lot more accusatory than he meant to, and he immediately regrets saying it.

"I know," Rebecca says, breaking into sudden tears. "I know I should have waited, and I'm sorry, Andy, I'm so sorry!"

She stops, turns and puts her arms around him.

Andy is so surprised to see Rebecca cry, at first, he just stands there, dumbfounded, as she holds him in an awkward, sideways embrace.

Then, he puts his arms around her. "It's okay, Becca."

"It's not okay, it's my fault, I should have stayed!"

"No, it's *my* fault," Andy says, tears coming to his eyes now. It breaks his heart to hear Rebecca blame herself, but at the same time, it makes his own guilt easier to bear, and it enables him to say what has been on his lips ever since he saw Rebecca again: "I'm so sorry I left you, Becca. If I had never gone into the library that day, none of this would have happened. Can you ever forgive me?"

Rebecca tries to say something, but it drowns in sobs, and Andy just holds her as she cries uncontrollably into his chest. He hears someone whisper soothingly, and realizes after a while it's himself.

"It's okay. It's okay now. You're back. You're safe now. It's okay."

Finally, Rebecca's crying dies out, and she wipes her eyes. "I'm so glad you came for me, Andy."

Andy smiles, discretely blinking away a single tear. "I'm just sorry I couldn't have been there earlier. You've been really brave."

Rebecca looks down. "My feet are really hurting. I think I'd like you to carry me now."

"Sure, hop on the Andy Express."

That's what he used to call it when Rebecca was very little and wanted a piggy-back ride.

He kneels down, allowing Rebecca to climb onto his back. They haven't done this for years, but luckily, Rebecca isn't very heavy.

Andy begins walking, and they move through the still sleeping town, the streetlights casting their yellow glare from above.

"What do you think will happen to it?" Rebecca asks. "The creature, I mean."

"It'll be arrested for sure. As soon as I give its name to the police, they'll track it down and put it in jail. Or maybe they'll even kill it once they find out it's not human."

"Good," Rebecca just says.

"Look, we're almost at the library," Andy says, nodding ahead. "Ain't that weird? It was right down there we spoke and saw each other last, right before you disappeared."

Rebecca doesn't answer right away. Instead, she says: "Do you hear something?" A note of tension in her voice.

Andy stops and listens. He *does* hear something. It's a rumbling *ga-dunk, ga-dunk, ga-dunk*, growing both louder and faster, and it's coming from behind.

Andy turns and feels his stomach drop.

The yellow van is approaching fast, tilted to one side and flapping away on the flat tire, but still going very fast.

"Oh, shit!" Andy exclaims. "It's coming!"

"*We've got to run, Andy!*" Rebecca screams into his ear—quite unnecessarily, as Andy has already spun back around and is running as fast as he can, Rebecca bopping up and down on his back.

The street ahead is empty; there are no side streets, no driveways or other places to turn, and no people to call for help, either. Andy can't do anything but run straight ahead.

Rebecca shouts something, but Andy doesn't register the words. He can hear the yellow van gaining on them fast. He darts a look back and sees it now driving with two of the wheels up on the sidewalk. Behind the dark windshield he glimpses the pale face staring out at them, and he realizes with a jolt of cold fear that the wendigo is going to run them both over.

There is still nowhere to get off the street, only fences and hedges, but they have almost reached the library now, and if he can just make it another twenty feet or so, he can cross the street and run into safety behind the bike rack on the parking lot. But the sound of the van is so close now, Andy has no choice but to make a dash for it, so he turns out onto the street. The turn proves a little too sharp, however, and the already spent muscles in his legs give way, causing him to stumble and fall to his knees with a painful thud.

"*Watch out, Andy!*" Rebecca screams.

Andy looks up at the last moment, just as the sharp headlights swallow up everything in his visual field. It's too late to lunge forward, too late to go back, too late to get out of the way.

Andy does the only thing he can; he throws Rebecca off.

Then the van hits him.

* * *

Rebecca lands halfway onto the sidewalk, scraping her palm and hurting her knees, but hardly noticing either.

She immediately turns her head to look back at Andy. And she sees it all happen. Just like the time the creature killed the old man, everything turns to slow-motion.

The van isn't going quite as fast as it did, but it's still moving at a considerable speed when it collides with Andy and sends him flying across the asphalt.

He rolls over several times before coming to rest on his back, his legs and arms splayed out to the sides, his head tilted sideways so Rebecca can see his face. His glasses are hanging from one ear, his eyes are closed and his mouth is open. A dark stream of blood runs from the corner of his mouth. She stares at his chest. It's not moving.

He's dead, a thought tells her from somewhere very far off. *Andy is dead.*

She can't take her eyes off Andy's face; everything else disappears around her. She just stares at him, willing him to open his eyes, to begin breathing again, to make him lift his head or move a hand. But Andy just lies completely still, not breathing, not opening his eyes and not moving anything.

Something stirs under Rebecca's shirt, and she vaguely remembers the puppy.

Somewhere nearby she hears the sound of a car door opening, slow steps coming across the sidewalk. The tall, gangly, naked figure of the creature comes into view. It stops next to Andy. Stands there for a moment, staring at him, in the middle of the empty street.

Leave him be, Rebecca thinks, trying to turn it into words, but failing.

The creature bends over, scoops Andy up and carries him back to the van.

Rebecca's thoughts are broken. She feels distant and dizzy, black dots are dancing in front of her eyes and she blinks to try and keep herself awake, but it's a losing battle.

Call for help, she thinks, but still can't find her voice. She couldn't call out any more than she could take flight. She can't even get up or turn her head. Out of the corner of her eye, she sees how the creature opens the back doors of the van and puts Andy's body inside.

When the creature comes to take her, she can't do anything to fight it. She feels the cold hands grab her and lift her up, and then the blackness comes rolling in, rushing over her like a wave of tar, drowning out the last of her conscious mind.

Rebecca faints.

* * *

Andy wakes up very gradually from a very deep sleep.

At least, so it feels.

But something is different. He feels so much lighter, like his body has turned into warm air. And when he opens his eyes, something is different with his vision as well.

He stares at a dim sky with faint stars overhead, but everything appears like he's looking through a window wet from rain.

He sits up, realizing where he is, but remembering nothing about how he got here. He's outside the library, in the middle of the street, and it's either late evening or very early morning, judging from the dark skies overhead.

Even though he recognizes the surroundings, they look simultaneously very strange, somehow more fresh and vibrant, almost like he never really saw them before. Everything is shimmering slightly, the road, the houses, the library, even the air around him.

"*I must be dreaming*," Andy thinks—or maybe he actually speaks it out loud, because the words seem to reverberate around him for a few seconds, before drifting away.

He gets to his feet, amazed at how easily he can move—it's like he simply forms the intention to move, and then it happens without any effort on his part. He feels weightless, like he is mostly part of the air around him, like he isn't really there.

"*I'm not really here*," he think-speaks, listening to the words, trying to understand them.

He looks at his hands, turning them over slowly, studying them as they flicker and blur in front of his eyes, the edges constantly trying to bleed out into the air, as though his body is reacting to an unfelt breeze, almost taking off.

"*What a strange dream this is.*"

The words float around him for a while, then dissipate.

Then, new words appear: "*It's not a dream.*"

Andy turns around—at least he thinks he does, but it feels more like the world around him revolves, spinning like a giant disc—until he faces the library, from where the new words seemed to come. The darkish building is swimming before his eyes, and a bright figure comes floating towards him, touching the ground but not really walking. It's a girl, wearing blue, her long, dark auburn hair floating around her head and constantly moving as though she were underwater.

Andy tries to focus, tries to look at the girl more closely, but discerning her features is like pinning down a piece of soap you dropped in the sink.

"*Who are you?*" he asks the figure with his mind.

"*I'm Lisa,*" the girl replies, hovering in front of him. "*You remember me, Andy.*"

That's not true, Andy doesn't remember anything. He didn't even remember his own name until the girl mentioned it just now.

But then he does remember, very vaguely.

He remembers having talked to a girl named Lisa sometime very long ago in a distant place far from here.

"*I do remember you,*" he says in his head and out loud. "*You're the dead girl at the library.*" Suddenly, more memories return, and they turn into speech. "*You died right here outside the library.*"

"*So did you,*" the girl tells him, her voice betraying no emotion. It's funny how the words sound, like birdsong in the air. "*We're both dead.*"

Andy bursts into laughter. Somehow, that seems like the appropriate response to someone telling you you're dead. Of course he isn't dead. Dead people don't speak, don't hear, don't experience anything.

"*I'm not dead,*" he tells the girl. "*I'm just dreaming. You're in my dream.*"

"*Look closer, Andy.*"

Andy stops smiling and looks closer. He notices something behind the girl, something in the sky above the library. The background is changing, turning into something else. It's a bright purple sky with foreign planets drifting around; then it shifts again into something else. This time it's a desert, and then it's an old castle, then an open flowery field, an active volcano spewing lava, a battlefield strewn with dead soldiers, a schoolyard full of children.

The sky keeps changing, the scenes bleeding into each other, all of them trying to appear at the same time, and Andy notices he can call forth new ones, open up the ones he wants to look at. And he recognizes some of them.

There is the Shire.

There is Hogwarts.

There is the space station of Solaris.

He feels something different with each reality appearing in front of him, just like he did when he read the books.

"*Worlds behind worlds,*" he speaks, not really sure where the words come from or what they mean.

The girl in front of him doesn't say anything; she simply hovers there.

Andy forces himself to look away from the shifting universes above and fixes instead on the girl's face, trying hard to see her for real.

He remembers her now, at least partly. She's Lisa Labowski, the dead girl who spoke to him through the books. And he desperately wants to see her face. But the traits keep drifting in and out, bleeding and flickering. He can only make out the auburn hair, the pale skin and the darkness around the eyes.

For some strange reason, Andy feels a pang of fear. He doesn't understand; why would the girl scare him? She is his friend, he knows that.

"*I wanted you to come in here so badly, Andy,*" she says. "*I wanted to be with you forever.*"

Lisa moves then, or maybe it's the surroundings spinning again; either way she floats around him, disappearing from sight, speaking again from behind him.

"*I've been alone for so long. I just wanted someone to talk to.*"

Andy is stricken by a deep sadness. He wants to help Lisa, wants to make her happy again. He doesn't want her to be all alone.

"*I'm here now,*" he tells her, turning around, but not seeing the girl. "*You're not alone anymore. I'll stay here with you.*"

"Help her, Andy," a voice inside his mind tells him. "She needs you."

Andy turns and turns, trying to find Lisa, but he can't. The fear comes creeping back. "I want to help you," he says out loud. "I want to help you, Lisa! Where are you?"

No answer from the girl.

Andy is alone in the street.

The universes above the library are still changing, displaying one marvelous scenery after the other, offering so many different moods and feelings, Andy's eyes are drawn to them.

"*I'll stay here with you,*" he whispers. "*We'll live inside the books together.*"

He walks towards the library, moving his legs but not really using them. The glass doors of the library open, a warm orange glow welcoming him, dispelling the darkness around him and the fear in his heart.

"*Help her, Andy!*" the voice tells him again.

"*I will,*" Andy whispers and is about to step through the open doors and into the glow.

Then suddenly, the dead girl is right in front of him, and for a split second, he sees her face clearly, and he can tell she really is very dead.

Andy recoils, the fear overwhelming him for a moment, and he wants to flee, wants to throw himself into the library and the many worlds awaiting him, but Lisa Labowski blocks the way, and she's suddenly grown very tall.

"**Help her, Andy!**" she bellows, her voice shaking the world. "**She needs you!**"

"I can't!" Andy cries out, covering his ears and trying to look away. "I can't help her! I'm scared!"

He doesn't want to look, but he can't help it, and he sees the dead girl in front of him. She's no longer towering over him, but has shrunk to her regular size again, the size of a thirteen-year-old girl.

"We're all scared, Andy," Lisa tells him, her voice calm and dreamlike once more. "But the things we're scared off are never real. Not really. They're just stories."

The girl looks up, and Andy follows her gaze. The sky above them has stopped shifting and has come to rest showing a single scenery. It's a dark forest, four men clad in old-fashioned hunter's uniforms walking between the tall trees.

"*The wendigo,*" Andy says. "*The wendigo is real. It took Rebecca.*"

"*Then you take her back,*" Lisa tells him, her voice rising again as she moves closer, very close, close enough for Andy to feel a breath of cold air on his face.

He shuts his eyes, waiting for Lisa to shout at him.

But instead, he hears her voice very gently inside his mind: "*It's okay to be scared, Andy. You simply go on anyway.*"

And when Andy opens his eyes again, Lisa is floating backwards towards the library, the doors opening once more, the tempting orange glow surrounding her like a halo.

"Don't go," Andy says, almost crying now. "Don't go, Lisa."

"*Go, Andy,*" Lisa tells him. "*Help her.*"

Then she sinks into the orange light and it swallows her up as the glass doors slide shut.

Andy looks up at the sky still portraying the scene from *The Wendigo*. The men have now set up camp, and darkness is falling upon the forest. Andy remembers the story; he knows what comes next: very soon, the wendigo will come creeping and take one of them.

"Not this time," Andy says, and he turns away from the library and the breathtaking scenery.

* * *

Rebecca wakes up with only a vague notion of being inside a car. She can hear the rumble of the engine and the *ga-dunks* from the flat tire below. She can also smell motor oil and the stink of the creature.

She has no idea how long she has been out, but her head feels heavy. There is almost complete darkness around her, but Rebecca is used to not seeing well, so she instinctively feels around with her hands. She finds someone lying next to her and she lets out a gasp as her memory comes rushing back.

"Andy!"

She bends over, finds his face and puts her ear close to his mouth, praying to hear him breathing. But he doesn't. There is no air flowing in or out of Andy's slightly open mouth.

"Oh, Andy," Rebecca moans, starting to cry. "Oh, Andy, wake up! Please, wake up!"

She hugs him and shakes him, begs him again and again to wake up.

And then, suddenly, he does. A single, faint breath.

Rebecca stares at him, sensing only a dim, blurry outline of his face.

"Not this time," Andy whispers almost inaudibly. Then he takes another breath. He doesn't open his eyes, though, and he's still not conscious, but Rebecca doesn't care; her heart is almost bursting with joy at the thought of Andy being alive!

She hugs him again, gentler this time, so as to not hurt him. She just lies there next to him for several minutes, listening to him breathe, feeling his chest rise and fall, thanking God and heaven that Andy didn't die when the creature ran him over, that she isn't left alone with the creature.

Then she hears something sniffing next to her ear, and she reaches out and feels Doris. She pulls the puppy into her arms and hugs her, too.

She is so exhausted from being afraid that she begins to nod off, the soft rocking of the car almost lulling her to sleep, when it suddenly stops.

Rebecca hears the rattling of the metal chain and knows exactly where they are. The van rolls on into the courtyard, and the creature shuts off the engine, then gets out to close the gate again.

Rebecca stares at the crack where a faint daylight is coming in, feeling a dreadful sense of déjà vu from the day the creature caught her the first time.

This time around, it also opens the back doors to the car, but it makes no attempt to hide. Its boney, still-naked frame is visible in the opening against the now dimly lit horizon. Before Rebecca has time to react, the creature reaches in and grabs Andy's ankle.

"*No!*" she cries, as the creature pulls Andy towards it.

Rebecca throws herself on top of Andy, but the creature shoves her aside like it would an annoying fly over its dinner, and she bangs against the inside of the car, knocking the wind out of her.

Somewhere, Doris begins to bark angrily.

"Stop!" Rebecca croaks, fighting to get her breath back. "Let go of him!"

The creature doesn't listen. It lifts Andy up like he weighs no more than a doll, then slings him over its shoulder like a bag of potatoes. Andy gives off a moan.

Rebecca scrambles to her feet and throws herself at the open doors, but the creature steps aside, and Rebecca falls onto the gravel.

"Come back!" she screams, her lungs working again. "*Don't you hurt him!*"

She sees the creature walk towards the garden, still carrying Andy, and she jumps up and runs after, ignoring the pain from her feet.

She catches up with the creature and grabs Andy's leg, but only manages to pull off his shoe. She grabs hold of Andy's pantleg, but the creature is way too strong and simply drags Rebecca along as it strides across the wet lawn. Instead, Rebecca begins punching the creature in the back.

"*Stop it! Put him down!*"

The creature ignores her. It carries Andy to the place behind the hedge, then drops him on the ground. Andy moans again and rolls onto his back. He mutters something and looks like he's trying to open his eyes.

Rebecca throws herself down next to him, hardly noticing the creature stepping back.

"Andy?" she says, her voice trembling. "Are you okay? Can you hear me?"

"Becca?" he murmurs, sounding very weak. He opens his eyes halfway but can't seem to get them to focus. "Where ... are ... we?"

"We're back at the—"

Rebecca stops talking as she notices the creature coming back into view from the side. She turns her head and gasps.

It only stepped away to pick up the shovel, which was lying a few feet away. Even in the dim morning light, Rebecca can see the blade shining as the creature raises the shovel high above its head.

"*Nooo!*" Rebecca screams, and without thinking, she throws herself over Andy, readying herself for an intense pain in the back as the shovel will probably shatter her spine—but the pain never comes, because the shovel never comes.

Rebecca glances up and sees the creature hesitate, the shovel still halfway raised.

"Move aside," it whispers hoarsely.

"N ... no," Rebecca says, shaking her head defiantly. "You can't hurt him."

"Move aside."

"No!"

The creature bends over, grabs her by the neck and pulls her aside. But Rebecca scrambles back as soon as it lets go and raises the shovel again, once more covering Andy with her body.

"Becca," Andy mutters dully below her, apparently not really aware of what's going on.

"Don't worry," Rebecca tells him, her voice trembling. "I'll make sure it doesn't—"

She's interrupted as the creature grabs her again and flings her away. This time, she rolls around a couple of times, then jumps back up and half crawls, half lunges herself over Andy once more, a split-second before the creature can let the shovel fall.

It gives off an irritated grunt, then throws down the shovel.

Rebecca feels a brief, intense rush of victory.

It gave up!

But then the creature grabs her hard by the arm and drags her back towards the house. And Rebecca realizes what it intends: it'll lock her in the house, then go back outside to kill Andy with no more interruptions. Then it'll use the shovel to bury him next to the bones of Alice and the still-fresh grave of the old, British guy.

Rebecca begins fighting to get free, heaving and kicking, but the creature is simply too strong. It's like being dragged behind a car. She strikes it, kicks it, even tries to bite its hand, but it just pushes her head back using the free hand. All the while, it pulls her around the house, across the courtyard, into the house and up the stairs.

Rebecca is very close to panic now. If the creature locks her in the room, it's over; there will be nothing more she can do.

She begins begging. "Stop! Please, stop! I'll do anything! I'll never run away ever again; I promise! Just please don't hurt him!"

No reaction from the creature; it just drags her down the hallway.

"I'll ... I'll stay here!" Rebecca says. "I'll stay here for the rest of my life! I swear!"

Still, no reaction. They reach the room, and the creature opens the door.

Rebecca searches frantically for the right words. And then, just as the creature shoves her inside the room and is about to close the door, they come to her.

"*I'll be Alice!*"

It's like a magic formula.

The creature freezes, the door halfway closed. It turns its head slowly to look at her.

Rebecca breathes quickly, blinking in an effort to see more clearly. Through a veil of tears she can almost make out the expression on the creature's face. It stares at her, waiting.

"I'll be Alice," she repeats. "Forever. If you just don't hurt him."

The creature looks at her for several seconds. The only sound is Rebecca's own, ragged breathing.

"Alice?" it finally whispers, a question in the word.

"Yes," Rebecca whispers back, nodding. "Yes, I'm Alice from now on."

Then something incredible happens. The creature simply turns and walks away, leaving the door open. Rebecca slips back out of the room, seeing the creature walk downstairs. She follows it. It goes outside and back to the garden.

The morning is lighter now, the sun is peeking over the horizon, coloring the sky orange and purple.

Rebecca follows the creature back to the place where they left Andy. Her brother has fainted again, lying on his side. Rebecca is ready to jump in and protect him again, if the creature still wants to hurt him. But somehow, she knows it won't.

It simply bends down, picks up Andy and walks back to the house. Rebecca follows at its heels, as it carries Andy upstairs and into the room next to Rebecca's. It puts him down on the bed and turns to leave.

As it passes by her, it briefly reaches out and strokes her cheek, the touch surprisingly tender. Rebecca is completely unprepared for the gesture and it's all she can do not to recoil.

"Alice," the creature whispers, and the warmth in the voice is the most terrifying thing Rebecca has ever heard.

Then it walks out of the room and leaves Andy and Rebecca alone.

DAY 113

Rebecca opens the door very carefully and slips inside the room.

Her eyesight still hasn't recovered from the last treatment, and her feet are still sore from the fresh burn wounds.

To her surprise, the creature didn't punish her particularly bad this time, despite her attempt to run away. Probably because she made a promise to be obedient from now on. To be Alice.

Andy's room is bathed in a golden evening light streaming in through the drawn curtains. Her eyes as usual go to the bed in the corner, and to her surprise, she sees Andy sitting up this time, wearing his glasses.

"It's just me," she says, closing the door softly behind her. "I have your dinner." She brings him the plate.

Andy takes it, but just puts it on his lap. "I'm not hungry," he mutters.

"You need to begin eating."

"I can't. My head hurts too bad."

"What about the pills? Are they still not helping?"

"Not really, no."

Rebecca sits down next to Andy on the bed. It's weird; part of her knows she has plenty of reason to be scared and worried, and yet she feels a lot safer now that Andy is here. He hasn't been able to do anything but lie in bed, sleep, throw up and complain about the headache and his busted-up leg, but just having him here is a great comfort.

She knows, of course, that even if Andy had been in fine shape and not hurt at all, he still wouldn't have been able to help her escape. She has come to terms with that. She is Alice now—in a way, at least—and her last chance of getting away is gone, which means she will likely spend the rest of her life here. Still, the thought is much more bearable with Andy around. At least she won't be alone anymore.

"How are your feet coming along?" Andy asks.

"Better. They still hurt, but I can walk again."

She made sure to bite down hard and not scream during the latest burning, because she knew Andy was in the room next to her and could hear if she cried out. She didn't want to worry him.

It's amazing how quickly things have gone back to normal. The creature has taken up its usual routines and acts like nothing really happened.

The only exception, really, is that Andy is here now. The creature doesn't speak to him and never enters his room. It's obvious it doesn't care about him, but it doesn't stop Rebecca in caring for him, either.

So, she brings him food and helps him to the bathroom. She also asked the creature for painkillers to help with Andy's headache—she did it with no real hope of getting it, she just couldn't take Andy's painful writhing anymore—but to her utter astonishment, the creature actually brought her some.

There is one other thing that's different now: the way the creature acts around Rebecca. It looks at her differently. At first, she couldn't figure out what it meant, but now she gets it.

There is affection in its voice now. Warmth.

It touches her now and then, always briefly, always when she doesn't expect it. Rebecca still has to control herself so as to not draw back—she fears it'll enrage the creature if it sees her flinching away from its touch.

But even though the creature seems to have warm feelings towards her now that she has agreed to become its Alice, she can still feel how closely it watches her. How those black eyes follow her around whenever her back is turned. How it keeps an eye on her every time she takes Doris outside to pee. How it checks her room discretely whenever it comes to say good night.

Rebecca holds no illusions: The love the creature shows her is conditional. It'll only treat her this way as long as she stays obedient. Just below the surface, a constant, unspoken threat lures.

Rebecca is pretty sure this is her very last chance. If the creature catches her doing anything she shouldn't, there will be no more leeway. It'll kill both her and Andy and go find a new Alice.

"How is your leg?" Rebecca asks.

Andy bends his knee. "It doesn't hurt as bad anymore. I don't think it's broken after all. It probably just got busted pretty bad when the van hit me."

There are still black and blue bruises running up Andy's calf and thigh, but they are lessening day by day.

If the leg isn't broken, that's great news, and it means Andy will be able to walk again. Unfortunately, his head was less lucky. Rebecca can still recall seeing it bounce off of the asphalt as Andy fell. Already the following morning, he had a huge, red swelling behind his left ear and he started throwing up all the time.

Rebecca had a concussion once. She was very young. It was the first time her family went skiing. An older boy on a snowboard knocked her to the ground, and she hit her head pretty badly. She's pretty sure Andy now has a concussion and she remembers how painful it is.

A low scraping from the door. Rebecca goes to open it, and Doris slips inside, runs across the floor and jumps up into bed.

The dog has also changed since they tried to run away. Now, it'll only be with Andy and Rebecca, and it growls whenever it sees the creature.

Andy picks a piece of bacon out and offers it to the dog. Doris swallows it eagerly.

"We've got to make a plan," Andy says, looking at Doris.

Rebecca sighs. "We've been over this, Andy. You can't even walk yet."

Andy doesn't seem to hear her. "Does it go to work?"

"Work?"

"Yeah, I mean, does it ever leave for work?"

"I ... don't think so."

"But it leaves sometimes, right? It has to. It needs to buy stuff, groceries and stuff."

Rebecca considers it for a moment. "I think it goes to town once a week, maybe, but you know it locks the door before it leaves. And it's hard to tell how long it'll be gone; sometimes, it's only half an hour."

Andy gives Doris another piece of bacon. "So it knows about the hole in the roof now, right? It knows how you got out?"

"Yes. It sealed the roof."

"That means we need to find another way out."

Andy is still looking at the dog, frowning slightly as he concentrates.

It's the first time Rebecca has seen him act like his old self. In one way, it makes her happy—but in another, it's also heartbreaking, because he looks so determined, so confident. He clearly hasn't accepted the reality of their situation yet.

"The windows up here are too high, and there is nothing to climb down," he goes on. "So either we need to pick the lock to the door, or we have to smash a window downstairs."

"Andy, listen. I really don't think—"

"It'll probably take too long to pick the lock," Andy interrupts. "So I think the better choice is busting a window. Is there anything inside the house heavy enough to smash a window?"

He finally looks at her.

Rebecca looks back at him. Even despite her blurry vision, she can tell how adamant he looks.

"Andy," she says softly. "It's not going to work, no matter how we do it."

Andy's frown grows deeper. "Why not?"

"It won't allow us to flee again. It just won't."

"Of course it won't allow it, but it's not up to it. We decide, Rebecca. We'll find a way to—"

"No, Andy. That's not what I mean. I told you this already. It watches me now. Everything I do. It's always nearby, listening. Like it's just waiting to see if I try anything again."

"Right," Andy says, closing his eyes and rubbing his forehead as the pain obviously comes back. "Then we just need to ... need to be more clever ... we have to outsmart it."

"But if we fail ..." Rebecca takes his hand and lowers her voice. "If it catches us again, Andy ... it will kill us. This time, it won't be merciful."

"Merciful," Andy repeats, almost sneering. "You think it's been merciful keeping you here like a prisoner? Was it merciful of it to burn your feet and damage your eyes?"

"No, but—"

"So what do you think, we should just stay here for the rest of our lives?"

"Maybe ... maybe someone will come by and find us."

"Like who? Some random stranger who the creature will just kill and bury? That's not going to work."

"Then maybe the police."

"The police," Andy scoffs. "They've probably already given up. They couldn't find you, remember? And even if they are still looking for me, how would they find me? They have absolutely nothing to go on. When you disappeared, at least they had a witness—me!" Andy stabs himself in the chest with a thumb. "The problem is, they didn't listen to me! And now, they have nothing—*nothing*, Becca!"

Rebecca doesn't know what to say. Andy is too upset to listen to reason, and she doesn't want to argue with him, so she gets up and is about to leave the room, when Andy grabs her wrist and pulls her back down.

"We need to run away," he says, talking low, his face close enough for her to smell puke on his breath. "As soon as possible. We can't give up. And we can't count on help from the outside. You did it once, and you can do it again. I'll figure out the plan, but I'm going to need your help. You know this place and you know the wendigo. You need to come up with an idea for a way to escape—however small it seems. When you got something, come to me, and I'll do the rest. All right? All right, Becca?"

Rebecca breathes deeply a few times. Andy looks so desperate; she can't bring herself to say what she thinks. That's it no use. That they'll never find a way. That trying to flee is suicide. And that she's not going to risk their lives.

So, instead, she forces a smile, then lies to him: "All right, Andy. I'll come up with an idea. Just give me time."

DAY 114

"Hello?"

Regan blinks and comes to. For a moment, she has no idea where she is, and she looks around to find herself behind the desk at the library. On the other side is a girl around seventeen, looking at her with mild bemusement.

"I'm sorry," Regan mutters and smiles at the girl. "I guess I just drifted off for a moment. What did you say?"

The girl holds out a book. "I found this book ..."

"Sure, you want to borrow it? Just run it through the terminal over there. Do you need me to show you how—"

"I don't want to borrow it," the girl says. "It was just lying around on the floor, so I didn't really know what to do with it."

"Oh, okay. Thank you," Regan says, taking the book.

The girl goes back to browsing the shelves.

Regan stares at the girl for a while without really seeing her; she's already lost in thoughts again.

She can't stop thinking about Andy. He's been on her mind ever since they officially reported him missing yesterday—no, even before that. Ever since the first day Andy didn't show up at the library. Of course, it's happened before that he skipped a day or two, but Regan still had a weird feeling this time. A feeling that something bad had happened.

And when Andy didn't come the day after that, her feeling grew stronger.

And by the third day, when they began talking about him in the news, she already knew her feeling was right.

She almost went to the police; had actually gone to her car twice to drive down to the station, but both times she changed her mind. Because what could she tell them? That she had had a hunch Andy would disappear? How would that help them find him?

She had no idea where Andy was now or what had happened to him. And the police seemed to have no idea either. Their spokesperson on television kept uttering phrases like "ongoing investigation" and "still looking into leads" and "keeping all possibilities open"—and that was exactly what they kept saying when Andy's sister went missing in the spring.

It's so terrible. First Rebecca and now Andy.

Rumors were already circulating town. She heard a couple of old ladies talk together just yesterday, right here at the library. They were certain that Andy had run away from home because he was still devastated over losing his sister.

Regan knows better. While it's true Andy was still sad about the loss of Rebecca, he wasn't devastated. In fact, he had seemed very eager the last time she spoke with him. Almost like he ... like he *what?*

"It's got something to do with Rebecca."

Regan has played their last conversation over and over in her mind. Something about it keeps bugging her. Something her brain tries to tell her. It keeps pulling her back to that one thing Andy said.

"It's got something to do with Rebecca."

The glass doors open as an older gentleman enters the library, the sound pulling Regan out of her thoughts once more, and she decides to get on with what she was actually doing: putting back returned books.

Perhaps she needs to stop brooding about it. There's nothing she can do anyway. The thought that Andy is missing makes her deeply sad, and what good is that to anybody? She can't go on like this, spending the days lost in gloomy thoughts, barely able to function.

She takes a deep breath and goes to the book cart, when she notices the book still in her hand—the one the girl handed her. She completely forgot about it.

"It was just lying around on the floor."

Regan stares at the faded, anonymous leather cover. She knows this book. It's *The Wendigo*—the one Andy spoke so highly about. She's seen him sit around the library reading it a ton of times.

The funny thing is ... she also picked it up from off the ground yesterday, when she found it lying in front of the shelves, as though someone had taken it out and just dropped it.

Regan goes to row B, finds the empty slot and is just about to slide in the book, when a strange feeling comes over her. It feels almost like she can sense someone talking to her, but without any sound.

She looks around discretely to make sure no one actually did talk to her, but finds herself alone in this part of the library.

Regan bites her lip, considers for a moment, then she opens the book and leafs through the pages, skimming the text, not really sure what she's looking for.

Why was Andy so obsessed with this book? He must have read it a hundred times. Is it really that exciting?

She stops on a random page and reads a bit. The language is fluent and picturesque, and the storyline seems appealing. But it doesn't tell her anything about what fascinated Andy so much about the book. She closes it again with a sigh, puts it back and turns to go back to the cart.

She's only taken three or four steps, however, when there's a sharp thud behind her.

Regan stops and turns back around.

The book is lying on the floor. Regan stares at it.

How did that happen? I thought I put it in properly.

Apparently, she didn't. She must have spaced out again and didn't push the book all the way in. She goes back and picks it up once more, noticing her heart beating a little too fast. She puts the book back a second time, this time making sure it's all the way in.

Then, she takes a few steps back, keeping an eye on the book, like she halfway expects it to fall to the floor again. Of course, it doesn't.

Regan shakes her head. *I must be really losing it. I need to get a grip.*

She leaves row B and goes back to the cart. Just as she takes the first book, she hears it again. The thud.

Regan's heart leaps into her throat, and she needs to swallow hard to force it back down. She puts the book down and goes back to row B.

The Wendigo is once again lying flat on the floor.

She just stands there, staring at it. She doesn't really want to go near it, is almost afraid to do so.

Must be something about the cover. Maybe the leather is too slippery, or ... or maybe the shelf is sloping outwards slightly. But then why wouldn't the other books fall? It could also be something like static electricity that pushed it out ...

Regan listens to her thoughts' desperate attempt to come up with a rational explanation, while a deeper part of her knows there isn't one. That something else entirely is going on here.

She goes and picks up the book. Brings it back to the desk, places it on the table and stares at it.

What are you trying to tell me?

Andy. It has definitely got something to do with Andy. She can sense it. Sense something buzzing around just outside the reach of her mind. Like when you hear a fly but you can't see it.

"It's got something to do with Rebecca."

Why would Andy say that? What could he have meant? What was he trying to do? To find Rebecca? How could a nonfiction book about the human eye have anything to do with Andy's sister disappearing?

And then it finally hits home.

It wasn't the book Andy was interested in. It was the last person who borrowed it. And Regan helped him find it. She broke the rules because Andy asked her so urgently. Like it was absolutely crucial that he got that name.

But why? What did he need that name for? He didn't say anything, he just stared at the name for a minute, then thanked her and went back to reading *The Wendigo*. Like it wasn't a big deal after all. But now, thinking back, Regan can tell he was only playing cool so as to not draw any more attention to himself.

You clever little rascal ... what did that name tell you?

Did the person know anything about Rebecca's disappearance? That was too far a stretch. If the person really had some information about Rebecca, the police would have been here a long time ago, asking to have a look in the system. Andy is thirteen years old. Could he have unraveled a mysterious disappearance that the police had given up on? Of course not. Things like that only happened in movies. Or in books.

But the timing ...

Andy went missing that same night. Could it just be a coincidence? What if he didn't get kidnapped, and he didn't run away either; what if he went out voluntarily to look for Rebecca? What if he really believed the person behind that name she helped him find had something to do with it? And what if he was right?

It actually made sense. Except it was ludicrous.

But what if it wasn't?

What if this was a chance to find Andy—maybe the only chance there would ever be? Regan's mind is trying to tell her it's all make-believe, a shot in the dark at best, but her gut keeps insisting she's onto something.

Two girls at around Andy's age enter through the glass doors. They're wearing schoolbags, and don't even look at Regan as they pass by the desk, since they're wrapped up in a whispering conversation. Regan catches a few lines.

"Think they'll find him?"

"No. They never found his sister."

Then the girls are gone between the shelves, and Regan is left with a sinking feeling in her stomach.

She looks at the book still in her hand. The book that keeps falling to the floor on its own accord.

And she turns to the computer and begins typing.

DAY 115

Andy is at the library, and he's all alone. He has come to talk with Lisa—there's something vital he needs to tell her, although he's not really sure what exactly it is.

He finds *The Wendigo* and begins talking to the book, but Lisa doesn't answer him.

He leafs through the pages, faster and faster, back and forth, searching desperately for a line from her, but finds nothing. With rising panic he grabs another book from the shelf and looks through it, then, still finding nothing, drops it and takes a new one.

He shouts for Lisa, pleading for her to answer him, and when he looks up, he finds the shelves have grown high as towers, too high for him to even see the tops. And suddenly, the books start coming down over him, hundreds of them, thousands even, hitting him over the head, on his shoulders, and he tries to get away, but he's already up to his waist in books, and they just keep coming, hitting his head again, and it's really painful, his head is throbbing now, throbbing badly, more books hit him, and the pain is causing him nausea, and it feels like he's about to ...

Andy barely has time to roll over on his side before breakfast comes bubbling up through his throat and spills down into the tub next to the bed. He pukes for a few seconds while an avalanche of pain rumbles away inside his skull.

He spits one last time, then wipes his mouth on his sleeve, which is already crusty from the many previous throw-ups. He really needs a shower; he reeks of old sweat and vomit, and his skin and his hair are all greasy.

He rolls onto his back, sighing with relief as the headache subsides. It wasn't as bad this time, and it didn't last as long, either. That's a good sign.

He reaches out and finds his glasses, puts them on, then blinks and glances towards the window and can tell it's still daytime from the light seeping in. Rebecca will probably soon come with lunch, or maybe dinner—he's not sure what time of day it is.

He isn't sure how many days have gone by, either. Five, maybe, or six. It feels like a month to Andy.

When he first woke up here in this bed, he was very confused and couldn't remember anything of what had happened. He only vaguely recalled the van chasing them. Then there was a dream where he spoke to Lisa, and then Rebecca was lying on top of him, screaming.

Once he started coming a little more to his senses, Rebecca explained everything to him; how the van had hit him and almost killed him, how the creature had wanted to murder him with the shovel, and how she bargained to save his life.

What a great rescue, an unpleasant voice in his head says. *Not only did you not save Rebecca, you also managed to get yourself caught,* **and** *you got a nice big concussion to go with the failure. Nice work, Andy.*

The voice sounds like Sheila used to talk, mixed with a taint of the icy cold tone of New Mom. Andy hates the voice and tries not to listen to it. It has haunted him ever since he came here.

He tries instead to tell himself that all hope is not lost yet. That at least he found Rebecca, and now they can figure out a way to escape together.

The problem is, it'll be a while before Andy is fit to run.

And there's also the bigger problem. The problem of Rebecca.

Andy can feel she's reluctant to the idea of trying to flee again. It's like she has spent all her courage on that last attempt, and now she has nothing left to try again.

Andy doesn't care about the deal she made with the wendigo, not one bit. He knows Rebecca only did it to save his life, but he can also sense part of her has accepted the deal.

He can't blame her, of course. She's been very brave, living alone with the wendigo for all this time, constantly fighting to not give in.

Andy isn't sure he could have done it. But Rebecca is very strong and stubborn—at least, she used to be—and if she hadn't been, she would no doubt have succumbed to the wendigo already, losing herself completely and accepting her new life here. Or rather, her non-life. Andy can tell how dull her eyes look, how little of the old Rebecca is left.

It's not too late, though. Rebecca still found the will to flee only days ago. She can still be saved. But it'll be up to him. He needs to be the brave one now. He needs to be the one fighting the wendigo.

Andy is terrified at the thought of the monster. He only dimly remembers seeing its face with those tiny, black eyes; he glimpsed it in the forest right before he rammed it with the scooter, and then again when he briefly gained consciousness out in the garden, with Rebecca lying atop of him and the wendigo towering over them, its grey head silhouetted against the dark sky. He hasn't seen it since. It doesn't come in here. Which is both comforting and disturbing.

Why hasn't it burned his feet or blinded him, like it did with Rebecca? Maybe it simply doesn't care about him. Maybe it knows Andy is still too weak to do anything.

Yet he knows the wendigo wants him dead despite the agreement it made with Rebecca. And maybe it already plans on killing him. It could make it look like an accident, so Rebecca won't realize it was murder. It could easily poison his food. Or Andy could wake up anytime in the middle of the night to see it standing over him ...

Andy shivers at the thought.

How would it go about it? How would it kill him if it came in here? Probably with the shovel.

He doesn't want to think about it, but he can't help it. Somehow, he feels he needs to think it through, he needs the fear to motivate him. So he tries to imagine how it would feel to get bludgeoned to death with a shovel.

The pain will be intense—if he even had time to feel it. Maybe the first strike, then it'll probably knock him out. But the wendigo will keep going until it hears his skull crunch ...

The nausea comes back, and Andy swallows hard to keep it down.

Concentrate on something else. Figure out a way to get out of here.

The problem is, he has only seen a small part of the house outside of this room. He knows Rebecca's room is next door, and he knows the bathroom is down the hallway. The last time Rebecca helped him to the bathroom, he tried to persuade her to take him downstairs, but she refused because the wendigo was down there.

Andy can't go exploring on his own; he's not strong enough yet. But as soon as he is, he'll be able to check out the house while the wendigo is out, and he's sure he can find a way to escape. He's tired of lying around here, being in pain and feeling useless.

His hand goes to his pocket where he feels the boxcutter. It's a small miracle he didn't lose it when he was run over. The wendigo obviously didn't check his pockets, because if it had, it would have no doubt confiscated the knife like it did his backpack. Now it's Andy's secret weapon. He's not sure how effective a boxcutter is against a mythical creature, but he's going to find out if he has to. If it comes to kill him, he won't give in without at least trying to fight back.

The thought gives him the motivation to get up. He carefully swings his legs out and places both feet on the floor, pushing himself up with his elbow. He tries to lift his butt, and he actually manages to stand. He smiles. Just getting up on his own feels like progress. He feels dizzy, but there is no pain.

He walks back and forth a few times, then sits back down. The room spins for a couple of seconds, but still no headache.

Andy feels very uplifted. It won't be that many days until he's ready to act. But until then, the best he can do is rest. So, he lies back down and closes his eyes.

He has barely drifted off to sleep when he hears quick footsteps come down the hallway, and then the door opens. Andy sits up a little too fast, making his head spin.

Rebecca comes in, closes the door behind her and turns around. Her eyes are big and frightened, and for a terrible moment, Andy is sure the wendigo is coming to kill them both.

"What is—" he begins, but Rebecca cuts him off.

"A car. There's a car coming," she breathes.

Andy's heart leaps, and he stands up, ignoring the dizziness. "You sure?"

Rebecca nods emphatically. "I saw it from my window. It's coming up the gravel road right now."

Andy goes to the window, grabs hold of the windowsill and presses his cheek against the glass in order to look down into the courtyard. He can only see part of the gate and the gravel road beyond. Up ahead, still far away, a car really is headed this way, making its way slowly down towards the house.

Andy squints, looking through the cracked lenses of his glasses. He can tell the car is turquoise. Not a police car, then, which is what he was hoping. But there is something familiar with the car, it occurs to Andy. It's not his parents' and it doesn't belong to any of the neighbors, either. Still, he has seen it before; he's almost sure of it. That color is very recognizable.

Rebecca says something, but Andy doesn't hear her. He just stares at the tiny car coming slowly closer, his heart thumping in his chest, causing a slight headache to sprout behind his forehead, but Andy doesn't even feel it; he just concentrates hard on the car.

Where have I seen it before?

And then it comes to him: Outside the library. Because the car belongs to ...

"Regan," Andy whispers, his breath fogging up the glass.

"What?" Rebecca asks.

"It's Regan coming," Andy says, his brain filling in several blanks in the brief moment it takes him to turn around and look at his sister, who is staring back at him. "She's found us, Becca. She's come to help!"

No trace of joy nor hope appears on Rebecca's face, only fear. "It's going to kill her," she whispers. "As soon as it sees her ..."

Andy feels a lump of hot coal appear in the pit of his stomach, as he recalls what Rebecca told him about the old British guy.

"Where is it?" he asks. "Do you know?"

"Downstairs, somewhere. In the living room, probably."

"Did it hear Regan's car yet, you think?"

"I don't know."

Andy looks out the window again, briefly. "We've got to warn her," he says.

"We can't," Rebecca says, shaking her head. "If we talk to her, the creature will punish us. I promised I would be good."

"Listen to me ..."

"I promised, Andy! I promised, and if I break that promise, it'll kill us both!"

Andy grabs Rebecca by the arms, hissing into her face: "We can't just stay here and watch it kill Regan!"

Rebecca's lips are quivering.

Andy can tell she's fighting something internally. He eases off his grip slightly.

"You have to do it, Becca. I'm not fast enough. She'll be by the gate in thirty seconds. You need to go down there and warn her."

"No," Rebecca croaks, trying to pull back, shaking her head wildly. "No, I can't, Andy. I can't!"

"Of course you can!" Andy almost shouts, but manages to keep his voice down. He shakes her firmly, once. "You are brave, Becca. All you need to do is run down to the gate and tell Regan to call the police—she'll understand."

"But ... what if the creature comes?"

"Then you run away. Hide somewhere in the garden. As soon as Regan calls the cops, it'll get something else entirely to worry about, and it won't bother finding you."

Rebecca looks like she just might throw up. "What ... what about you, then?"

"Don't worry about me," Andy says, trying to sound assuring. "I'll be fine. I can defend myself if it comes for me. Now go, Becca! There's no more time!"

He shoves her towards the door, and Rebecca staggers along hesitantly. She looks back at him one last time, looking as though she's about to say something.

"You can do it," Andy tells her. "And if you get the chance, run and don't look back."

Rebecca blinks once. Then she turns and leaves the room. A moment later, Andy can hear her run downstairs.

He turns back to the window and sees Regan's tiny, blue car reach the gate and stop. Then the door opens, and Regan steps out.

The sight of her makes Andy catch his breath, and he realizes faintly that this is probably the first time he sees Regan outside of the library. She looks up at the house, shielding her eyes with her hand.

"You found us," he whispers.

Then a smaller figure comes into view. It's Rebecca, running across the courtyard while looking back at the house. And because she's so busy looking back at the house, she doesn't see the garage door opening.

But Andy does.

And he sees the wendigo, too, as it comes striding out on the courtyard, headed for the gate.

In one, boney hand it's clutching the shovel.

* * *

Rebecca has never been this scared in her life, and the fear drowns out everything else; she doesn't even feel the painful stabs from running on the gravel.

This situation is somehow much worse than when she ran away. Because this time, it's not only her life at stake, but Andy's too.

Andy who never gave up on her.

Andy who kept looking when the police didn't.

Andy who found her.

The thought of the creature killing Andy scares Rebecca more than anything. But it's too late now: she's already made a run for the gate.

The creature can appear any moment. And this time, it won't forgive her. This time, she has promised to be good, to be Alice, and it will realize it can never trust her again.

She's almost at the gate now, and she darts one last look back at the house; still no sign of the creature.

"Rebecca? Is that really you?"

Regan has come out of the car and is now staring at her through the metal bars.

"Yes," Rebecca says, stopping in front of the gate. "It's me. Andy is here too. But you need to get away, Regan. Right now. Drive off. Or the creature will come and kill you."

"The creature?" Regan says, frowning and looking from Rebecca to the house. "Who are you talking about, Rebecca? Where is Andy?"

"Just call the—"

Andy's voice screams from the house: "*Becca! Watch out! It's coming!*"

Rebecca spins around, just as she hears the footsteps coming across the gravel from her right.

Rebecca can't run.

She can't do anything at all.

She just stands there, frozen in place, staring at the creature coming at her with long strides, holding the shovel. Behind her, Regan says something, her voice shrill.

The creature reaches out its hand and shoves Rebecca aside hard enough to almost knock her to the ground. It pulls out the key and unlocks the chain.

Andy is still screaming from the house: "*Run, Regan! Get out of here!*"

Rebecca looks at everything like in a trance, and she sees it all play out.

Regan, who has already caught on to the danger of the situation, is getting back into her car. The creature swings open the gate. Regan slams the door, and Rebecca hears the lock clicking. She sees Regan find her phone and put it to her ear. The creature walks to the car, pulls back the shovel and swings it full force at the side window. The glass explodes with a bang. And then, suddenly, events speed up. Regan screams. The creature reaches in and grabs her by the shirt, pulls her out through the window. Regan falls to the ground, tries to get up, but the creature is faster. It raises the shovel. Regan screams again, covering her face at the last second. The blade connects with her arm, giving off a loud crack. Regan's scream turns into pain. The creature raises the shovel again. Regan's arm is obviously broken, and she can no longer protect her head.

Rebecca knows then, that it's all over.

That she will now get to see Regan die the same way the old guy did. And as soon as it's over, the creature will go upstairs and kill Andy. Then it'll bury them both in the garden. And if it's merciful, it will kill her too. All she can do is hope that she will pass out soon.

Then something completely unexpected happens.

Something tiny and brown comes shooting past her leg. Rebecca blinks dazedly and looks down to see Doris, as the dog sprints for the creature and clamps down hard on its bare ankle.

The creature gives off a grunt, lowers the shovel and shakes the leg to get the dog off. But Doris is not intent on letting go; she growls and bites down harder.

The creature bends down to grab the dog, but Doris sees the hand coming and lets go, only to attack the other ankle. Rebecca can see tiny, bloody marks from the dog's teeth. And she sees Regan reach up and climb into the car, her broken arm all crooked and useless, her glasses gone, but she still fights her way up into the seat.

The creature catches Doris by the neck. The dog whimpers briefly before the creature flings it aside. Then it turns its attention back to the car, which Regan is trying to get into reverse.

She won't make it.

The thought does something to Rebecca. Or maybe it was seeing Doris attack the creature which did it. Whatever the cause, she's suddenly able to move again. And before she knows what she's doing, she jumps forward and kicks the creature on the calf, just as it's about to reach in and grab Regan for the second time. The kick is hard enough to make the creature spin around, and the black pin-drop eyes fix on Rebecca.

For a long moment, they stare at each other, as the creature's face slowly contorts into rage.

Then the car revs up its engine.

The creature snaps its head around just as Regan guns it and the car lunges backwards, gravel spurting from the tires. Both Rebecca and the creature stare after it as it heads back out of the driveway.

"if you get the chance, run and don't look back."

Andy's voice jolts her into motion, and she begins running.

The creature notices her at the last second and grabs for her just as she passes it, its thin fingers missing her hair by less than an inch, and then she's past it.

She runs as fast as she has ever run, pumping her hands up and down, her feet barely touching the gravel road. The car in front of her sways back and forth as Regan backs away from the house as fast as she can without losing control.

"Regan!" Rebecca shouts and waves. "*Wait for me!*"

Whether Regan hears her or sees her, Rebecca can't tell, but the car slows down enough for Rebecca to catch up with it. She runs to the passenger side, opens the door and jumps in.

Regan speeds up again, turning in the seat to look back, clutching the broken arm to her chest.

"The road is too narrow," she gasps, sweat running down her cheeks like tears—or maybe it really *is* tears. "I can't turn the car around."

Rebecca looks out the front window and sees the gate grow smaller as they quickly move away from the house. The creature is still standing there, in the middle of the open gate, staring after them. Rebecca feels like it's looking straight at her. Then it turns around and marches back inside the courtyard.

"Andy," Rebecca breathes. "Regan, it's going to kill Andy!"

Regan gives a moan of pain. "We can't go back, Rebecca."

"But it's going to kill him! We need to help him!"

"If we go back, it'll kill all of us!" Regan shouts, her voice breaking. "We need to get away, we need to call for help."

"But ... but ..." Rebecca is on the verge of tears.

"Find my phone," Regan says, wincing from pain and breathing fast. "I dropped it somewhere in the car."

Rebecca looks for the phone on the floor as her eyes fill with tears. She knows Regan is right. And she remembers Andy telling her to not worry about him. And part of her feels immense relief that she has actually made it, that she managed to escape. But the thought of leaving Andy behind like this, with the creature probably already headed up the stairs to kill him, is just too—

Rebecca's train of thoughts get interrupted as something causes her to look up. She stares out the front window, her mouth opening.

"Regan," she hears herself whisper.

"What? Did you find it?"

"No," Rebecca croaks. "It's coming for us."

Regan turns her head to look for a brief second and gives off a tiny scream just as the yellow van comes bolting out the gate like a big, old, hungry predator.

Rebecca's stomach turns to stone.

She thought for a second she had made it. She was naïve enough to think she could escape this easily; that the creature would simply let her go. She thought the only one still in danger was Andy.

She turns her head and looks back. The gravel road goes on for as long as she can see. The highway is still way too far away.

* * *

Andy sees it all from his window; it feels like being a spectator to the scariest horror movie.

He tried to shout to warn them, but it was too late. If it hadn't been for the dog, the wendigo would have killed Regan.

But now he sees her climbing back up into the car, even though she's obviously hurt badly.

I can't just stand here—I've got to do something.

Andy goes to the door, opens it and heads for the stairs. Looking down the steps, everything grows hazy for a moment, as a wave of dizziness floods him, but he bites down hard, forces his eyes to focus, then descends the stairs.

It's easier than he thought. Soon he's in the scullery. He opens the front door and looks out, afraid of what he will see.

Over by the gate, the wendigo is standing, facing away from the house. It's staring after Regan's car, which is speeding backwards out the driveway. Rebecca is running after it.

They got away!

Andy can hardly believe it, and he is filled with wild excitement.

But he quickly finds out that it's not over, as the wendigo turns and strides to the garage.

It's going to follow them.

Andy feels a pang of panic. He looks out the driveway, and he can still see Regan's car, which has now picked up Rebecca—it hasn't gotten much farther away, though, because it can't go very fast in reverse. The wendigo will quickly catch up with them in its van.

Andy knows what he must do. He steps out the door and crosses the courtyard. He reaches the garage and hears the driver-side door slam shut. Andy grabs the handle to the backdoor and opens it just as the van starts up its engine with a roar. He's about to climb up as it shoots backwards, almost running him over for the second time, but he manages to jump up and land inside the van, the door slamming behind him, but the sound is drowned out as the van backs out onto the crunching gravel. It stops, turns and shoots forward, almost sending Andy sprawling in the dark. He grabs for something to hold onto as the nausea comes rolling up his throat. He forces it back down and makes an effort to see the inside of the van

The only thing visible is a square somewhere above him: a small opening, Andy realizes, separating the cabin from the back. There's a hatch to close it, but right now, the hatch is open, and daylight is streaming in.

Andy crawls towards the light as the van speeds up, the gravel rumbling underneath. They're probably already headed up the road.

Andy manages to get up by supporting himself against the wall, and he looks through the opening. He sees Regan's car still backing away as fast as it can, but the van is gaining on it fast. Rebecca is sitting in the passenger seat.

Andy looks down and sees the arms and hands of the wendigo clutching the wheel.

What do I do? Think! In a minute it will catch up with Regan's car, and it's probably going to ram it off the road. I need to do something!

Andy looks for something, anything he can use. Then he remembers the boxcutter and goes to his pocket. The blade shines in the darkness as he pushes it out.

A new sound reaches him, a hoarse mumbling, and he realizes the wendigo is talking to itself, uttering curses. The van is still gaining speed.

It no longer wants Rebecca, Andy realizes with icy clarity. *It's going to kill them both.*

In less than ten seconds, the van will smash into Regan's car, sending it off the road, maybe even causing it to flip over. The van is double the size, and it's going really fast now, almost flying along the gravel road, stones banging against the undercarriage like gunshots.

Andy reaches the boxcutter through the opening followed by his entire arm.

The wendigo doesn't notice; it's leaning forward now, the bald head visible to Andy. It's mumbling louder to itself as it stares at Regan's car only a few seconds away now.

Andy screams and slashes at the head of Ambroos van de Goor.

* * *

Rebecca stares at the van coming closer way too fast. The closer it gets, the faster it seems to be going.

Soon she can make out the creature behind the dark windshield. The tall, thin, pale figure is hunched over the steering wheel, and she can almost feel the hate emanating from the black eyes fixed on her.

Next to her, Regan gives off another choked scream; it sounds like a mixture of pain, fear and crying. She's leaning sideways, her eyes darting back and forth between the front and back window, the bad arm presses against her chest, and Rebecca only now notices the piece of white bone protruding through the sleeve at the place where the arm bends.

"We won't make it," Regan says, almost crying now. "It's going to hit us! Buckle up, Rebecca!"

"What about you?"

"There's no time!"

But Rebecca has already leaned over and reached across Regan's shoulder, grabbing the seatbelt and pulling it over. Once Regan is secured, Rebecca buckles up too.

Then she looks out the front window again, and now the view is almost blocked by the van as it's about to collide with them within the next few seconds, and—

Rebecca is just about to close her eyes and prepare for the crash, when she sees a face inside the van, right next to the creature.

It makes no sense.

It's Andy.

* * *

In the split second before the blade reaches its target, the wendigo snaps its head around and stares right at him. Instead of slashing open the back of its head, the boxcutter cuts along the jawline, opening a thin, dark gash.

The wendigo screams out and lunges sideways, hitting the wheel and causing it to spin violently. The tires jerk to the side way too sharply, and the van goes flying. Andy is thrown up into the ceiling, then to the side, and then he's lying flat on his back.

Everything becomes quiet. The world sways for a moment, before coming to a stop.

* * *

"Holy hell," Regan whispers and slows down the car as she stares out at the tipped-over van lying halfway in the ditch. "He drove off the road …"

"It was Andy," Rebecca hears herself saying. She unbuckles, opens the door and jumps out.

"Rebecca! Wait! Come back!"

Rebecca isn't listening. She runs to the van, jumps across the ditch and looks in through the windshield. Behind the wheel is the creature, bunched up in an awkward position. Its face is visible, and Rebecca can tell its eyes are closed, a dark gash running down its jaw and another bleeding on its forehead. But Andy isn't in there.

She runs to the back and grabs the handle. The door resists for a moment, then opens. Andy is lying right inside. He rolls to his side, looking up at her, blinking with obvious effort. His expression is hazy, like someone just waking up.

"What … what happened?" he croaks.

"You crashed," Rebecca says simply, taking him by the arm. "Come on, Andy. Quickly. I don't think it's dead."

That last part seems to strike a chord with Andy, and he suddenly looks more coherent. He lets her help him out, but gives off a cry as he tries to stand.

"My knee," he winces. "It's hurting really bad …"

"I'll help you," Rebecca says, placing Andy's arm across her shoulders, supporting him as best she can, as Andy jumps across the ditch on one leg and heads for Regan's car.

"Oh, my head," Andy suddenly moans, stopping and bending over. He wretches and throws up onto the gravel road. It's mostly just spit.

Rebecca hates stopping. They're only halfway between the van and Regan's car. She looks to the latter and sees Regan behind the wheel talking on her phone. Then she looks back and sees the van's driver's door swing open.

"Andy," she says, starting to pull him along. "We need to keep moving—it's coming!"

Andy is still throwing up, but he limps on ahead. They reach the car, and Rebecca opens the back door to help in Andy, who has finally stopped puking.

"Hurry up!" Regan calls, and for a moment Rebecca thinks she's talking to them, then realizes she's still on the phone. She ends the call and gasps aloud. "Rebecca, look out!"

Rebecca is just about to get in, when she turns her head and sees the creature.

It's standing in the middle of the road. Staring right at her.

Regan shouts something.

Rebecca throws herself into the car.

Regan guns it and the car lurches backwards.

Rebecca stares out at the creature, expecting it to run after them—but to her surprise, it doesn't move an inch; it just stands there, staring after the car.

"I think it finally gave up," Regan says, once she realizes the creature isn't taking up pursuit. She slows down only a little. "Thank God. Are you okay, Andy?"

"I think so," Andy mutters, but Rebecca can hear him moan and hold his head in his hands as though it's throbbing. "Thank you for coming to save us, Regan."

"I'm sorry I didn't come earlier, but I didn't figure it out until yesterday, and I ... oh, my arm!"

"You need to get to the hospital," Rebecca says. "You both do."

At that moment, they reach the highway. Regan turns onto the asphalt, stops, and uses her good arm to put the car in drive.

Rebecca looks back up the driveway, and can still see the creature standing there; now it's only a thin, grey line next to the tipped-over van.

Just as they begin to roll down the road, Rebecca sees the blue lights up ahead. "Is that ... the police?"

Andy lifts his head. "The police? Already?"

"Yeah," Regan moans, stopping the car again. "They traced my call the first time, so they had already sent someone out when I called them the second time."

She leans back her head and closes her eyes.

Then, Rebecca turns to look at Andy.

He's very pale and still looks nauseous. Yet he looks up at her and manages a smile, as he whispers: "We did it. This time, we really did it, Becca."

EPILOGUE

"You ready yet?"

Rebecca looks at him from the open front door. Doris is pulling at the leash impatiently, eager to get going. The puppy has grown quite a lot since the first time Andy saw it.

"Hold your horses," he says, fumbling with his laces. "I can't get this knot untied—it's all tangled."

"You're so clumsy," Rebecca sighs and steps over to him. "Let me do it."

She kneels down, shoving his hands aside. With a few brisk movements, she unties the knot and ties his shoe.

Andy looks at her, smiling. When they first got home, he was afraid the wendigo might have sucked too much life force out of Rebecca for her to ever become herself again. And it seemed like it to begin with; Rebecca was very anxious and restless and would often cry. She also rarely spoke and had trouble sleeping at night due to bad dreams.

But it's been nearly two months now, and Rebecca has already changed back to her old, familiar self in most ways: She doesn't cry anymore, and she talks a lot again. And when Andy tripped in the driveway the other day and fell down, she laughed out loud. Andy didn't even get mad at her; he was just so happy to hear Rebecca laugh again.

Now she gets up and says: "There. That wasn't very hard, was it?"

"Thank you," Andy says, smiling at her, his eyes lingering on her face for a moment.

Rebecca squints. "What are you looking at?"

"Your glasses."

"Don't tease me."

"No, they look good on you."

Rebecca crosses her arms, but doesn't say anything.

Andy can't help it, and he goes on: "Remember all the times you called me four-eyes when you got angry with me? Well, now that's come back to bite you in the butt, missy."

Rebecca sighs. "Right, can we get going? Doris is about to pee on the floor."

"I'll just tell Mom we're going." Andy goes to peek into the living room. "Mom? We're leaving now."

Mom is reading a book while eating an apple. She stops chewing and sends him an alarmed look; Andy can see the words building up.

Then Mom thinks better of it, and instead she asks: "You got your phone on you?"

"Sure do."

"Good." She forces a smile. "Have fun."

Andy returns the smile and closes the door to the living room again. Rebecca is not the only one who has changed back to her old self, and it makes Andy happy to see Mom feeling better every day.

Those first weeks were tough, though; she wouldn't let either Andy or Rebecca out of sight, even demanding they all sleep in the same room. But after she went to see a therapist, she slowly began to relax. Now and then she can still fall back to the habits of New Mom and become harsh and overprotective, but Andy feels confident she just needs time.

Dad is also his old self again—in fact, even more so than before. It's almost like his work doesn't mean as much to him any longer. He's cut down on his office hours and spends a lot more time with Andy and Rebecca in the afternoon, which he only rarely did before.

Even Cindy seems different. She eats home every night and she talks a lot more with Mom and Dad than she used to. She has also forgiven Andy for busting up her scooter. Actually, Andy suspects she might even be glad he did, since she used the money from the insurance to start saving for a car. Also, she has stopped dying her hair.

Andy follows Rebecca out into the driveway, where a fresh fall breeze and a golden sunshine greet them. Doris runs around, eagerly sniffing everything.

They walk through town without saying much. It's a quiet Saturday afternoon. All the cars, cyclists and pedestrians move slow, like none of them are in a hurry to get anywhere, but prefer to simply enjoy what will probably be one of the last warm days this year.

A car rolls by, and Andy recognizes the girl in the passenger seat. He waves, and Sheila waves back. Then she's gone.

"Who was that?" Rebecca says, pushing her glasses up her nose.

"Just someone from class," Andy shrugs.

Sheila has begun smiling at Andy whenever their eyes meet. She even talks to him now and then. Andy is pretty sure she's grateful to him that Kristy was finally found.

After the police arrested him, Ambroos van de Goor confessed to kidnapping six girls over the years and killing at least five people. Once the police began digging up his garden, they found plenty of bones—including Sheila's older sister's.

Kristy didn't drown in the stream in the park like the police had originally reasoned. Her clothes and schoolbag had only ended up there, because Ambroos van de Goor had dumped them after he kidnapped her. In reality, she died in his home two years after he took her. She got appendicitis and he didn't take her to the hospital.

Ambroos van de Goor also confessed to being responsible for the death of Lisa Labowski. He kidnapped her six months after he had buried Kristy in his garden. Lisa was kept as a prisoner for four months, but much like Rebecca, she never really stopped trying to escape, and he couldn't leave her home alone, so whenever he had to go to town, he brought her in the back of the van.

One day, Lisa managed to pick the lock and open the back door from the inside. But it happened so unexpectedly that she fell out while the van was still driving. A car coming the opposite way struck Lisa before she could get to her feet and killed her instantly. It happened right outside the library.

Andy can still recall what Lisa had told him.

"kidnapped"

"yellow van"

"blinding sunlight"

Back then, those fragments didn't make much sense to him, but now he can fill in the blanks and vividly imagine Lisa in the back of the van, scared and alone in the dark, fumbling with the lock, and when she suddenly got it and the doors swung open, the sunlight streaming in must have felt very intense. Maybe it even blinded her. Maybe that's why she fell out.

Unfortunately, no one noticed Lisa falling out of the van, so it was never uncovered how she suddenly appeared in the middle of town after having been gone for four months. And no one apparently read too much into the fact that Lisa's hair color had changed from auburn to blond; it only confirmed the suspicion many people had that the girl had run away from home in some sort of teenage revelry and didn't want to get found.

Andy, of course, figured out the truth: the wendigo had forced Lisa to dye her hair blond just like it did to Rebecca.

After the final fight with the wendigo, Andy spent a week in the hospital. He suffered a bad concussion, a twisted knee and two broken ribs.

As soon as he got home, he went to the library to tell Lisa everything. But once he stood there, holding *The Wendigo*, Lisa was oddly silent. He tried several other books, but she still didn't answer, and she hasn't spoken to him since.

Although he could sense Lisa was no longer in the library, it still took Andy some time to accept she was gone for good. Gradually, he grew to understand she had only lived in the books on borrowed time to begin with, and that she had now gone on to whatever awaits after death.

It still strikes him as odd, though, that Lisa would disappear right after Rebecca came back. The explanation could be that she lingered in the books to help Andy find Rebecca and get her own murderer thrown in jail. That would make sense, Andy figured; after all, ghosts probably have a reason for sticking around. Something that hasn't been resolved. And as soon as it is, they move on.

But there is also another explanation. One that Andy cares a lot less for.

Perhaps the ghost of Lisa Labowski was never really there. Perhaps it all took place in his imagination. All the lines, all the conversations he had with her—it could all be make-believe.

They pass the library, and Andy stops for a moment. It's Saturday, so Regan won't be at work, and the turquoise car isn't parked outside the building.

In the weeks after the fight, Regan wore her arm in cast, and Andy got to sign it with a marker. He wrote: *Thank you, Regan*, and Regan teared up. Their friendship has grown even stronger than before. Every time they meet, Regan hugs him, and she even came over for dinner a couple of times. Mom and Dad couldn't stop thanking her, and Mom bought a huge bouquet of flowers for her.

Andy didn't get any flowers, and he guesses that's only fair. After all, he wasn't actually the one who freed Rebecca, although he played a vital part. Everyone at school has told him how brave he was, but in the media, it's Regan getting all the fame.

Young woman rescues two kidnapped children—risked her own life!

Andy is okay with Regan taking the glory. To him, the most important thing is that Rebecca is home.

"You think they'll ever let him out?" Rebecca asks, pulling Andy from his thoughts.

He looks at her and sees her staring at the library. It's weird standing here with her, on the exact spot where they once split up.

"They say he'll get life in prison," Andy says.

"But that's only about twenty-five years. I Googled it."

"By that time he'll be dead from old age."

Rebecca looks at him critically, and Andy knows exactly what she's thinking. The things they are saying about Ambroos van de Goor in the media are quite disturbing. Something about his DNA being all wrong, and that he seems to be suffering from some hitherto unknown genetical disease, which causes him to age much slower than normal. The medical examiners reported him being at least a hundred years old, and they noted his body temperature never seems to rise above 70 degrees. The weird DNA also explains why the police investigators could never track him down, although they found DNA from him on both Kristy's clothes and Lisa Labowski's body.

But Andy knows better. He knows it's no genetical disease which has messed up Ambroos van de Goor's DNA. The explanation is much simpler: Ambroos van de Goor is not a human being.

It should be obvious simply from looking at him, really. But somehow, other people can't seem to tell right away that the wendigo isn't human; they apparently just see a boney and very tall old man with sharp features, unhealthy, greyish complexion and very dark eyes.

Originally of European descent, he had lived way up in Canada until forty years ago; that's when he came down here and began taking girls.

"Even if they do let him out," Andy says, shaking off the gloomy thoughts, "they'll be watching him closely. He'll never get to kidnap anybody again."

"I hope not," Rebecca says.

"Come on," Andy says, placing a hand on her shoulder.

They go on to the park, where the trees have started to take on yellow colors.

"You think we'll get to see them this time?" Rebecca asks, a growing excitement in her voice, and Andy can tell she has put Ambroos van de Goor out of her mind once more.

"If we're lucky," Andy says, smiling. "Keep your eyes and ears open."

Rebecca lets Doris off the leash, and the dog immediately begins running around in circles, taking in all the exciting smells. Andy and Rebecca stroll alongside each other while they listen and look up into the trees.

Andy glances towards the graveyard and is struck by a strong déjà vu from the day he saw Lisa Labowski's gravestone. He can't help but wonder once more if the ghost was real or not. He was the only one who ever spoke to Lisa, after all. Wouldn't that suggest he made it all up in his mind?

Then suddenly something occurs to him.

The book. *Anatomy of the Human Eye.*

It was Lisa who gave him the title of the book that Ambroos van de Goor took out from the library and never returned. The police found it in his home, and he confessed to having used the book to figure out a poisonous mixture which would blind the girls without taking away their vision completely.

How could Andy possibly have known the name of that book? He couldn't. And that's why the ghost of Lisa Labowski had to have been real.

"There!" Rebecca exclaims, pointing. "You see it?"

Andy follows her finger to a nearby tree and searches the trunk until he sees the hole. And at that exact moment—as though it heard them talking—the woodpecker pops out its head to look down at them.

Rebecca lets out a joyful gasp, and Andy smiles as he closes his eyes for a moment.

***

This story was very hard for me to write, and I almost gave up several times. I kept changing the viewpoints and format until I couldn't tell if it was even a good story any longer.

Luckily, something about that brave boy kept pulling me back, so after several years, I finally managed to get the plot right, and I was able to give Andy the ending his story deserved.

I'm particularly happy that this story got a second chance. Because back when I published it as an independent book, it totally flopped. I had no idea why. I figured the story just wasn't that good. Which made me really sad, not only because of all the time and hard work I'd put into it, but also because it's very dear to me. It's easily one of my personal favorites out of all the stories I've ever written.

Then, when I launched this collection you're reading right now, *The Girl Who Wasn't There* got a second chance to reach new readers. At the time of writing this, it's only been a few months, but I've already heard back from a lot of readers telling me that it's one of their favorites, too. Which proves to me that it wasn't because of the story that it didn't do well the first time around. It was probably the cover. Or the timing. Who knows? It doesn't really matter now. What matters is that Andy's story got a second chance and you got to read it. I truly hope you liked it.

I've written another story about the Wendigo. It's called *Human Flesh*, and it's coming up later in this collection. It takes a different approach to the mythical creature. It's less, shall we say, romantic. More brutal.

CHILLS & CREEPS 2
Eight scary stories

Contents

1. Babysitter #
2. Deadly Dreams #
3. Ghost Tennis #
4. When I Snap My Fingers ... #
5. The Teacher from Outer Space #
6. The Scarecrow #
7. Lord of the Crabs #
8. Under the Ice #

Babysitter

Julie jumps off her bike outside number 18, glancing at the mailbox which clearly states: *The Livingstons*. She looks up at the house, a big, modern bungalow; there is no grass or plants in the front garden, just tiles and gravel. A small fountain trickles peacefully, and a row of small lamps are turned on in the early evening twilight.

Geez, Julie thinks to herself as she parks her bike in the carport. *They must be stinking rich.*

This isn't Julie's first job—she has babysat many times before—but it's the first time she is babysitting for the Livingstons. She doesn't know them, in fact, she's never even met them; she just answered the advert on the bulletin board in the local mall.

Seeking young girl for babysitting job.
We have two small children, they're very well behaved and quiet.
Please call for further information.

Julie called the number as soon as she got home.

A friendly female voice answered: "*You've reached the Livingstons. We're not able to answer your call at the present time, but please leave a message, and we'll get back to you.*"

So, Julie left a message, explaining her interest in the job. She briefly described her earlier experiences, and she gave her name and number.

The next day she received a text message.

Hello Julie. Thank you for your call. You sound like a nice girl. We would like to hire you. Can you start Friday night? We're going to the theatre. Sincerely, Livia and Steve.

Julie was surprised, she had expected for them to at least want to meet her first. But apparently, they trusted her to be an honest person.

She wrote back and told them Friday was good, and they exchanged a few texts back and forth, agreeing on a time and a salary. They offered three times as much as Julie was used to.

Now, as she strides up the tiled path to the front door, she checks her watch. Five to eight. Five minutes early. Perfect.

The door is made of smooth, black wood, and next to it is a tall, narrow window. She glances at herself in the reflection of the glass, fixes her bangs, practices her smile, then rings the doorbell. A melody plays on the other side of the door.

Half a minute passes. A minute. No one comes to open it.

Julie rings the bell once more. Still, no answer. She listens, but can't hear anything from inside the house. She's about to ring the bell a third time when, finally, she sees the note. It's right in front of her, it's a wonder she hasn't noticed it before. It's a classic yellow Post-It, the text is written in a beautiful shorthand, identical to the one on the advert.

Hey Julie.
We had to leave half an hour early. The kids are already sleeping. You'll find their rooms on the second floor.
The password for the door is 0107. The alarm system turns on automatically once you let yourself in.

Julie notices a small panel underneath the knob and enters the password. She opens the door and steps into a large entrance hall. The lights turn on by themselves. The jackets are all on hangers and the shoes are neatly placed on a rack.

Julie takes off her own shoes and jacket and brings her bag into the next room. It's the kitchen. Again, the light turns on by itself. Everything is made of steel and glass and is very shiny. The room looks like something out of a catalogue. There's a discrete smell of food, but mostly it smells like cleaning products.

With a home like this they can probably afford a housekeeper.

The fridge has two doors, the right door containing an ice dispenser, the left one has a Post-It. Julie goes to read it.

Please help yourself to a snack. There are soft drinks and fruit and other things.

Julie smiles. How nice of them. She's about to turn around, when she sees the envelope on the counter. There's yet another Post-It stuck to it.

Here's your salary for the first 4 hours. We thought you should have them in advance. As we agreed, we are expecting to be home at midnight. In case we're late, you'll of course be compensated.

Julie opens the envelope. The sight of the money makes her smile even wider. Quickly, she puts it away in her bag.

Then she goes to check out the living room. And again, everything is picture perfect: the couch is black leather, the floor is shiny, the television is big as a cinema screen. In the middle of it is a fourth Post-It.

They really love writing notes, Julie thinks and reads it.

Just turn on the television if you get bored. But maybe keep down the volume a bit, or you'll wake up the kids.

Julie takes a look around and sees four, no, five more notes scattered around the room. There's one on the terrace door, one on the coffee table, one on the bookcase, one on a mural, even one on the big plant in the corner.

She reads them all one at a time. They are friendly but kind of redundant.

You're welcome to take a look in our bookcase, maybe you'll find something you like.

If you want to go out on the terrace, you have to use this password to open the door: 0208.

Put your feet up, it won't ruin the table.

Always ending the note with that little smiling face.

Julie shakes her head. Judging from the handwriting, she's guessing it's Livia who wrote the notes. She must be a bit of a control freak.

Julie takes a quick look around the rest of the ground floor. There are of course more notes. She also notices the many paintings which decorate every single wall. She finds a bathroom, an office and an art studio. There's a half-finished painting on an easel. It depicts a face, but it has no eyes yet.

One of them must be an artist. Maybe that's why they're so rich.

Her phone vibrates in her pocket. She takes it out. It's Amber.

"Hey, sweetie. How's it going? Are the rug rats behaving?"

"I haven't met them yet."

"*But weren't you babysitting tonight?*"

"Yeah, but the children were already asleep when I got here."

"*Oh, I see. Lucky you. Let's hope they don't wake up.*"

Julie can hear loud music in the background. "You're at a club?"

"*You bet. We're at Click right now. Everybody's here.*"

Julie sighs. "I wish I could be there."

"*Well, you can still make it. You get off at midnight, right?*"

"Yeah, but I have no way of getting downtown." She goes back into the living room and looks out the terrace door.

"*Can't you grab a cab?*"

"And spend most of my hard-earned money before I even get home?"

"*All right, you cheapskate. We'll come and get you then. Simon isn't drinking. He doesn't mind picking you up. Right, Simon?*"

Simon shouts something in the background.

"Let's wait and see," Julie says, gazing out into the garden. The sun has set now, and she can hardly make out the contours of a shallow hedge which separates the gardens between this house and the next. There's light in the neighbor's windows. "Maybe I'll be too tired by that time."

"*Aren't you just going to be eating popcorn and watching bad horror movies? I mean, if the kids are just going to be asleep anyway ...*"

"I'm not watching any horror movies—you know I hate those. I actually brought some homework. I have an essay I need to finish."

"*You're always so responsible, it's almost nauseating. Oh, Dennis just got here. I'll tell him you said hey.*"

"Don't," Julie says coldly. "Flip him off instead."

Dennis is Julie's ex. She broke up with him because she caught him cheating, that bastard.

"*I'm talking to Julie,*" Amber blurts out to someone in the background. "*Yeah, she says to flip you off.*"

Amber laughs shrilly, as Dennis apparently says something, then disregarding the fact she is talking to Julie, she begins a friendly chat with Dennis. Julie can only make out Amber's part of the conversation.

"*No, she's working ... Yeah, she's a babysitter ... Over in the wealthy part of town ... I think she said Pine Street ... Hello? Julie? What was the name of the family you're babysitting for?*"

Julie moans. "Jesus Christ, could you stop telling Dennis every little detail of my life, please? It's none of his business what I'm doing."

"Oh, all right, sorry, I just wanted to ... What's that, Dennis? ... He's asking if it's the Livingstons?"

Julie frowns. "How does he know?" She immediately regrets asking. "No, never mind, Amber ..."

But Amber is already asking Dennis.

"*He says he knows them. Oh, he just left. I guess he had something more important to do. Listen, don't worry about him. Just come when you're done working, sweetie.*"

Julie is about to answer, when she suddenly sees a face staring in at her through the window. She gasps and steps back.

"*What's wrong?*"

"There is ... there is someone out in the garden ..."

"*There's **what**?*"

Julie squints her eyes to see more clearly. It's the face of an old lady. She realizes the lady is standing on the other side of the hedge.

"Oh, it's just the neighbor," she sighs. "I've got to go, Amber. I'll talk to you later, all right?"

She disconnects and goes to pull the curtain. Once the view to the garden is blocked, she feels better. A note has appeared on the wall where the curtain was.

Had enough of Rosamunde? We've gotten used to her by now. She's old and senile—and very curious. We can't sit in the living room at night without her keeping an eye on us. Creepy, right?

Julie gets an involuntary shiver. If it was *her* house, she would build a tall fence.

She notices a picture on a shelf. It's a young couple with two children. All four of them are smiling. The mother is pretty and has fair hair, the dad has a reddish beard. Both children have kind of long hair, making it difficult to tell which one is the boy and which one is the girl.

Julie remembers she still hasn't seen the upstairs yet and decides to go check it out. Walking up the wide staircase, she comes to a hallway with several large skylights and five doors.

The first one is ajar; it's the bathroom. The next one is the parents' bedroom. A huge bed is made up beautifully with tons of pillows.

The third door has big blue letters on it, spelling out the name VICTOR. And on the door across the hall, red letters say: REBECCA. There are Post-It notes on both doors.

Victor is afraid of the dark, and prefers sleeping with the night-light on.

Rebecca needs music to fall asleep. We usually leave it on, in case she wakes up during the night.

From the boy's room she hears a faint snoring. From the girl's room comes a low, soothing melody.

Julie opens Rebecca's door carefully a few inches. The room is dark; she can only just make out the shape of the furniture. There's a small figure lying underneath the bedcovers, and the music is playing very gently from a small device on the nightstand.

Julie also checks on Victor. His room is a little brighter, due to the night-light. The boy is sleeping with his back to the door, the blanket pulled all up. She can just make out the top of his hair. Julie smiles and silently closes the door.

She goes down the hallway to the last door, but finds it locked. There is—surprise, surprise—a Post-It on it.

Oops! This is our private room.
The children aren't allowed in here, and neither is the babysitter.

Julie feels embarrassed. It's almost like Livia and Steve have caught her snooping around. But she is also somehow intrigued. Why do they have a private room? Is there something valuable in there? Or something secret?
Well, it's none of my business anyway, she tells herself, slipping downstairs again.
At the end of the staircase, she sees something on the wall which she overlooked on the way up: a small console with a loudspeaker. Right beside it a note explains:

This is an intercom. Victor and Rebecca have transmitters in their rooms. They might use them to call you, in case they wake up. You can check on them by pressing the buttons. 1 is for Victor, 2 is for Rebecca. Saves you the walk up and down the stairs.

The intercom looks pretty straightforward: three buttons, marked 1, 2 and 3. She holds down the first and hears Victor calmly snoring. When pushing button number two she hears the music from Rebecca's room.
Julie is about to push the third button, but hesitates. The note doesn't mention this one. She doesn't know where the last transmitter might be. Maybe it would be better to leave it. On the other hand, what harm could it do?
She holds down the third button.
There's only silence coming from the speaker.
Julie feels a bit disappointed. She runs her hands through her hair and looks at her watch: 8:13. Three hours and forty-five minutes left.
Julie is sitting in the living room working on her essay. The topic is *identity theft*, and for once, it's actually a pretty interesting assignment.
Suddenly, she hears a sound, like someone whispering.
Julie sits up, looks out into the kitchen. Now it's quiet again. It was probably nothing—she's just not used to the noises of the house. So, she gets back to her essay.
But a minute later she hears the whispering again. It's louder, but still too subtle to make out any words.
"Hello?"
Julie sets aside the laptop, gets up and goes to the kitchen. No one's there. As she passes the staircase, her gaze falls on the intercom. She goes and holds down the different buttons one at a time. Victor is still snoring, and Rebecca's music is still playing, the third one is still silent.
Julie checks out the other rooms, just to be sure, beginning with the studio. It's empty, and she's just about to close the door when she notices the painting. Apparently, she was wrong the first time: the person in the picture *does* have eyes. They're just closed. Actually, the face on the painting is quite creepy.
Julie goes back through the kitchen, finding the refrigerator door open. She probably didn't close it properly when she helped herself to a Coke. She goes to close it and finds a note next to the handle.

The refrigerator door tends to open by itself.
The repair man is coming next week to fix it.

Julie is surprised she didn't notice this note earlier. It's almost like they are appearing on their own. But of course, that's nonsense—there are just so many of them, she hasn't noticed all of them.

She closes the fridge and returns to the living room and the essay, but she can't really seem to concentrate anymore, so she turns on the television. A late news program is on. The reporter talks about a gang that has been robbing houses in the area. So far, they've hit four homes. That story doesn't exactly calm Julie's nerves, so she changes the channel and finds a random comedy.

She has only been watching a few minutes before the whispering returns. She grabs the remote and hits mute. Listens. The house is completely quiet. She turns the sound back on.

She finds herself not really watching the movie, but instead listening for noises. She's pretty sure she hears the whispering several times, but as soon as she puts the television on mute, it's all quiet again.

She has just decided it must be in her head, when she hears a voice coming from the hallway. "*Julie? Please come.*"

It's a child's voice, whispering.

Julie quickly gets up, expecting to see one of the children on the staircase, but there's no one there. Maybe they called her over the intercom. She rushes up the stairs, goes to Rebecca's room and gently opens the door. The tiny figure is still lying under the blanket.

"Rebecca?" Julie whispers. "Was it you calling me?"

Rebecca doesn't answer. She seems to be sleeping.

Julie closes the door and opens Victor's room instead. He's also lying in bed, still under the blanket.

"Victor?" Julie whispers. "Did you call me?"

The boy is snoring softly.

Julie closes the door again, and for a moment, she just stands there, wondering, before going back downstairs. Perhaps one of the kids called her, but was too shy to talk to her and pretended to be asleep.

Just as she reaches the bottom of the stairs, a voice comes from the intercom. "*My music stopped. Can you please turn it on again?*"

Julie realizes she didn't hear any music when checking on Rebecca. She hurries back upstairs. "Hi, Rebecca," she says quietly, entering the girl's room. "My name is Julie. But I guess you already knew that."

There's no answer from the girl, not even the slightest movement. She just lies with her back to Julie. Julie can only see the top of her head. She's probably shy.

"I'll turn the music back on now," she says, pushing play on the player on the nightstand. The gentle music flows once again from the speakers. "There you go. Isn't that better?"

No answer. The girl is lying completely still.

Has she already gone back to sleep? Or is she just pretending?

Julie puts her hand on the blanket and strokes it briefly. "Sleep tight," she whispers. "If you get scared again, just call me, all right?"

The girl still doesn't answer. Julie leans a little closer, tries to get a look of the face, but it's halfway hidden by the girl's hair. It's hard to tell in the darkness whether Rebecca's eyes are open or—

A sudden sound behind her makes Julie turn around.

Just the door closing. Probably did it on its own.

Julie leaves the room and goes back downstairs. She feels kind of uneasy and decides to call Amber just to have someone to talk with. But her phone is very low on battery. Luckily, she brought the charger. She gets it from her bag and finds an outlet in the kitchen next to the coffeemaker.

Then, she returns to the living room, slumps down onto the couch and takes a deep breath, staring emptily at the television for a few minutes.

It takes her a while before realizing she's not watching the same movie anymore—it's not even the same channel. This one is a horror flick.

Julie reaches for the remote, but her hand stops abruptly midair.

There is a cup of coffee right there on the table. Julie touches it. It's lukewarm.

Her heart starts beating faster. She's almost a hundred percent sure the cup wasn't there before.

Stop yourself. Of course it was—you just didn't see it. But how come it's warm? Maybe Steve had a cup of coffee just before they left.

Julie looks at her watch. It's almost ten. She's been here for two hours. A cup of coffee can't possibly stay warm for that long.

Julie stares around the room. Suddenly, she doesn't feel like she's alone anymore.

All right, just calm down. Do you really think someone sat here and had a cup of coffee while you tended to Rebecca? Someone who ran away and hid somewhere as soon as you came back downstairs? Just listen to yourself. That's ridiculous.

There has to be a logical explanation. She just didn't notice the cup before, and she forgot that she herself changed the channel, or maybe she pushed the remote by accident when she got up. Yeah, that's probably it.

Julie has almost managed to calm herself down when she hears a gargling sound from the kitchen.

Oh, come on ...

She gets up and slowly walks out there. She stops and stares at the coffeemaker. It's brewing. The pitcher is almost full of freshly made coffee. She turns it off. The machine gargles a little longer before falling silent.

Julie looks around the kitchen. The room suddenly seems a lot bigger with a lot of places someone could be hiding. Under the table. Behind the fridge. In the corner behind the—

Stop. I probably turned on the coffeemaker by mistake. I pushed the button when I put in the charger for my—

Julie stares at the outlet. Her charger is still there, but the phone is gone. At that moment, someone laughs.

"... ha-ha-ha-ha ..."

Julie can't tell if the laughter came from the living room or the hallway. It sounded like a child's laughter. Something falls into place. Julie feels a surge of relief rush through her. She even manages to smile.

It's the kids playing tricks on her. They pretended to be asleep when she checked on them. But now they're up and are sneaking around.

My God, I've been so paranoid. They just want to play.

"Hmmm," Julie says out loud as she walks into the living room. "I wonder who took my phone?"

She looks behind the couch. Under the table. Behind the curtains. She doesn't find anyone.

"... ha-ha-ha-ha ..."

This time, the laughter is definitely coming from the hallway.

"Hey! I think I heard something," Julie says with exaggerated surprise and hurries out there. The door to the studio is ajar. She's sure she closed it earlier. She smiles knowingly. "I think I know where the phone thieves are hiding ..."

She pushes the door open and looks around the room, but to her astonishment, she doesn't find anyone. The kids must have been in here earlier, but decided to find a better place to hide.

Julie is just about to leave, when the painting catches her gaze.

Chills run down her back. The last time she looked, the man in the painting had eyes, but they were both closed. Now one of them is slightly open. And he has a crooked smile. Like he's smiling at her.

"What the hell is going on?" Julie whispers, the sound of her own voice startling her.

But not as much as the voice coming from behind her: "*Julie?*"

She turns around, expecting to see one of the kids there. But again, there's no one.

"*Julie?*" the voice asks once more. It's coming from the intercom.

She goes and pushes the button. "Rebecca, is that you?"

She waits. Silence. She's about to push the button again.

Then the girl whispers, very faintly, and on the verge of crying: "*Please come up here, Julie. He was in my room. He said he wants to hurt us.*"

A clammy fear enrobes Julie's entire body. She holds down the button and says hoarsely: "Who?"

"*I've never seen him before. I'm really scared, Julie.*"

Julie has to force out the words. "Rebecca ... listen to me ... if this is a trick, it's not funny."

The girl sniffles, she's really crying now. "*You have to come up here. I think he's in Victor's room. I'm scared he's going to hurt him ...*"

"All right," Julie says, looking around, not knowing what she is looking for exactly. "All right, I'm coming. Lock your door right now, Rebecca. And don't open it unless I tell you to."

Julie walks up a couple of steps. She listens. It's completely quiet up there.

What am I going to do? I don't have a phone, so I can't even call the police.

But it could all still just be a misunderstanding. Or maybe the kids are playing a mean prank on her. Rebecca did sound very scared, though. She definitely wasn't acting. But she could have simply dreamed the stuff about some stranger being in her room.

*Do I go and check? What if there really **is** someone in the house?*

It would explain all the weird stuff that's been happening: the coffee, the teasing laughter, and someone stealing her phone from the charger.

Suddenly, she remembers something she saw on the news. About that gang that's been robbing houses.

Maybe I should run over to one of the neighbors and borrow a phone.

She could do that, but what if the whole thing turns out to be nothing? It would be so embarrassing, and she certainly wouldn't be able to babysit for the Livingstons again, once they hear how she panicked and abandoned the kids.

Julie decides to go investigate. If someone really is up there, and that someone is intent on hurting the kids, she can't just run away. But she's not going up there unarmed. In the kitchen she grabs the biggest knife she can find. Then, she sneaks upstairs, stopping at the top to peek down the hall. No one in sight, and not a sound. Both doors to the children's rooms are closed.

Julie tiptoes down the hallway, holding the knife ready, her hand trembling slightly. She tries to open Rebecca's door, but it's locked. Good. At least the girl is safe. Julie can't hear any music from in there.

"It's just me, Rebecca," she whispers through the door. "I'm going to check on Victor now."

She turns towards Victor's door. Takes a deep breath. Then reaches for the door handle.

But at that moment, she hears her phone ringing. Instinctively, her hand goes to her pocket before she remembers it's not there. She follows the sound down the hallway, stops in front of the door to the private room. The phone is ringing from inside. She tries to open the door, but it's locked, and she needs a password to unlock it. The phone is still ringing.

Julie glances at the note she already read once, then looks a second time, as something seems different. Now, it reads:

This is our private room.
The password is 0406.

Julie feels a strong shiver.

The password wasn't there the first time—was it? No. She's almost certain the note said something about the children not being allowed in there, but definitely no password. Someone switched out the note.

She types in the four numbers. The lock clicks, and Julie opens the door, revealing a small office. There's a desk with a laptop and not much else—except for Julie's phone, still ringing. She walks over and grabs it.

It's Amber calling. Julie doesn't know what else to do, so she answers the call. "Hello?" she whispers.

"*Hey! Why don't you answer your phone? I called you like three times.*"

The sound of Amber's voice calms Julie down a little. She closes the door to the office. Somehow, she feels safer in here. "Someone took my phone. I think someone is in the house, Amber."

"*What do you mean? Who is in the house?*"

"I don't know, a stranger. Someone took my phone, and I found a cup of coffee, and ... and I heard someone laughing."

"*Are you sure it's not just the children who—*"

"I really don't think so. Amber, I'm scared. I even have a knife with me. Do you think I should call the police?"

"*The **police**?*" Amber sounds surprised. "*Well, did you check the entire house?*"

"Yes. Except the boy's room."

"*Maybe you should check it out before calling?*"

"But I think the intruder might be in there."

"*Well ... who do you think it is?*"

"I don't know! Maybe one of those thieves they talked about on the news."

"*They all got arrested. I just read it on Twitter like five minutes ago.*"

"They did?" Julie is very relieved.

"*Yes. Listen, I actually called you because Dennis was asking for your number. He wanted to stop by and see you.*"

"When did he say that?"

"*I don't know, I guess about an hour ago. He was kind of weird. I think he was really drunk.*"

"Wait ... didn't you say earlier he knows the family I'm working for?"

"*Yeah, I think it's his uncle or something.*"

Julie bites her lip.

Amber reads her mind. "*Do you think it could be Dennis who's playing with you?*"

"I don't know. Maybe ..." Julie is just about to say something else. She's sitting on the corner of the desk. Accidentally, her hand touches the mouse, and the computer screen lights up. She turns her head and lets out a gasp.

"*Julie?*" Amber asks. "*You still there?*"

Julie gapes at the screen. "I ... I'll call you back."

"*Is everything all right?*"

Julie hangs up. Everything it *not* all right—in fact, something is obviously *very* wrong.

On the screen are live feeds from all the rooms. Apparently, hidden cameras are placed all over the house. At the bottom of the screen is a window with different programs, including:

Coffeemaker

Television

Alarm system

It looks like everything can be controlled from the computer. On the right is a whole catalogue of different sound files, all named things like:

Children's laughter

Rebecca's music

Victor's snoring

Rebecca is scared

Julie clicks on the last one, and immediately Rebecca's petrified voice comes out of the speaker. "*Julie? ... Julie? ... Please come up here, Julie. He was in my room. He said he wants to hurt us ... I've never seen him before. I'm really scared, Julie ...*"

As she listens, goose bumps crawl all the way up her legs and spread out all over her back. She stops the recording.

What the hell? Did someone record Rebecca when she spoke to me through the intercom ...?

She clicks on the file titled *Children's laughter*. It's the exact same laughter she heard down stairs, a low, teasing: "*— ha-ha-ha-ha —*"

Now it's all coming together in her mind.

It wasn't Rebecca she was talking to over the intercom—it was a pre-made recording. The same goes with Victor's snoring. An utterly insane thought hits her: *Are the children even real?*

Julie lets out a muffled snort of joyless laughter.

*Of course, they're real—I **saw** them!*

But did she really? She tries hard to remember. What did she see, *exactly*, when she was in Rebecca's room? The top of someone's head. That's all. The rest was hidden under the blanket.

Suddenly, she just wants to get out of the house. She doesn't even care what's going on anymore. All she knows is, someone is playing an insane game with her, and she might be in danger.

She picks up the knife and phone and brings them to the door, which she opens slowly and peeks out into the hallway. It's empty. She slips quickly past the children's rooms and downstairs on legs shaky with fear. She walks quickly through the house, forcing herself not to run, while trying to look in all directions at once. She reaches the entrance hall and grabs the handle of the front door. But it's locked. There's a note.

Are you leaving already? Just when the fun is about to start?

Julie senses something behind her. She spins around, wielding the knife.
She's alone in the entrance hall. Her heart is in her throat and she swallows to force it back down. There is no more doubt in her mind: someone else is definitely in the house with her. She feels it.
She turns again, grabs the door handle and tries to pull the door open, yanking it with all her strength, but it's not budging.
What's the stupid password?
She racks her brain trying to remember, but she can't. She's too scared. It doesn't really matter anyway, because whoever is doing this probably changed it since she came.
Maybe I can get out through a window?
She goes back to the kitchen. As she passes the studio, the door is suddenly wide open, and she can see the painting from where she's standing. The man's eyes are fully open now, the mouth spread wide in a menacing grin.
Julie wants to scream, but squeezes her lips together firmly.
She tries one of the windows in the kitchen, but it can't be opened. Neither can the windows in the living room.
Suddenly, the television turns on, making Julie scream and whirl around once more, only to yet again find no one.
But it didn't turn on by itself. It was turned on by someone at the computer. He's sitting there, watching me right now.
Julie looks up at the corners of the room, spotting a tiny, almost invisible camera. Before she can stop herself, she yells out: "Are you having fun? You psycho! Just so you know, I'm calling the police!"
The words offer her a little spout of courage. She pulls out her phone, dials 9-1-1 and makes the call. It rings twice, before a female voice answers: "*You have reached 9-1-1. Please hold.*"
Julie waits as several seconds pass, not taking her eyes off the camera.
Then, suddenly, a different voice comes on. A voice Julie knows all too well.
"*Amber, I'm really scared. I even have a knife with me. Do you think I should call the police?*"
Julie glares at the phone, mouth open in stunned surprise. She disconnects and instead calls up Amber.
Again, it's her own voice answering: "*I think someone is in the house, Amber.*"
"No," Julie moans, almost crying, dropping the useless phone onto the coffee table. "No, no, no ..."
An audible thump from upstairs.
He's still up there ...
Julie clutches the knife with both hands and takes a deep breath. She can't get out. She can't call for help. She doesn't know if the children in the rooms are real. All she knows for sure is that she's not alone in the house. And whoever made that noise from upstairs is the one doing all of this to her.

I have to go up there. I have to find out what's going on.

Julie's legs feel like rubber. One step at a time, she walks back up the stairs, holding the knife ready at all times, peering around, wide-eyed, her breath wheezing between her dry lips.

The hallway is empty. She checks out the rooms one at a time, starting with the private room. No one's there. The parents' bedroom. No one. Rebecca's room. It's locked. There's only Victor's room left. There's a new note on the door.

Please, come in.

Julie turns the knob. The door glides willingly open. The room looks exactly as it did the first time she was in there. A figure is lying underneath the blanket. The night-light is on, casting a faint glow over the room.

Julie reaches in and feels around for a switch. Finds it. Flicks it. Nothing.

She steps into the room, looking it over, finding no one, except for the person in the bed. The figure is snoring softly.

No, he's not, she reminds herself. *It's a recording. It's all one big trick. Nothing in his house is real. But it ends now.*

Slowly, Julie walks over to the bed. She grabs the edge of the blanket with one hand, holds the knife ready to strike with the other. She counts to three in her head.

Then, she pulls the blanket aside swiftly and lets out a loud gasp.

***

I wonder if it's possible to write a babysitter story where you never see the children ...

That was my thought when I got the idea for *Babysitter*. I imagined how, in the last scene, the babysitter would walk into the children's room, pull aside the blanket and gasp aloud, but without it being revealed what she sees—just like the scene you've just read.

What do you think Julie finds under Victor's blanket? It's up to you, really, since I don't have an answer—honestly, I don't. There are plenty of plausible explanations; choose the one you like best.

If you're one of those people who hates open endings, I apologize. This one is undeniably open. It's not usually something I do with my stories, but this one just felt right. I've grown to like open endings and cliffhangers myself quite a lot, even though I used to find them frustrating.

Deadly Dreams

It's a typical winter morning, dark and cold outside the windows. Inside, the students are bored out of their minds. The teacher is babbling on about fractions at the blackboard, even though nobody is paying any attention.

Daniel feels like he's about to fall asleep, wishing badly he was in his bed, when suddenly, the door opens and Alfred comes barging in. His beanie is almost covering one eye, his bag hangs by the elbows, and he looks confused.

The teacher turns around and sends the boy a prissy look. "Good morning, Alfred. Nice of you to join us. Please take your seat."

Alfred mumbles something that sounds like "sorry," then shuffles down to his table, throws his bag on the floor and sits down.

Christian jabs a finger in Daniel's side and whispers: "Look at him. He still has his beanie and jacket on."

Daniel looks over at Alfred. It's true. Alfred seems not to have noticed, as he's busy staring at his hands, apparently muttering to himself.

"Are you cold, Alfred?" the teacher asks sharply.

Alfred looks up. "Uhm ... no. Why?"

"Would you like to take your jacket off then?"

"Uh ... yeah, sure ... I mean, I'm sorry ..."

Laughter spreads throughout the classroom.

Alfred stands up, takes off the jacket and the beanie and goes to hang them on the rack by the wall.

Daniel whispers to Christian: "What's up with him today? He seems like he's gone completely mental."

"I think he's just playing that game."

"What game?"

"*Deadly Dreams*. Haven't you heard about it?"

"No."

Alfred walks back over to his seat, almost tripping over a bag on the way, causing more laughter.

"That's enough!" the teacher demands. "Alfred, sit down, and please try to act normal for the rest of the lesson, would you?"

Alfred sits down. Daniel can see him pulling his phone out under the table.

"Yeah, he's definitely playing," Christian whispers. "Once you start, you can't stop."

"What's it about?"

"Daniel and Christian!" The teacher points at the blackboard. "Is it by any chance this equation you gentlemen are discussing? If not, please be quiet and pay attention."

"I'll tell you at recess," Christian breathes out of the corner of his mouth.

Daniel keeps a close eye on Alfred for the rest of the lesson.

He is completely lost to the world, fumbling with the phone between his thighs, once in a while making a fist, as if to say: "Yes!" Other times he mutters audibly: "No!" or "Damnit!"

The teacher tells him off several times, but Alfred doesn't really seem to care—whatever he's doing on that phone is obviously much more important.

Christian gets up as soon as the bell rings. "Come on. Let's see how he's doing."

They walk over to Alfred.

"Hey," Christian says.

Alfred doesn't hear him, so Christian bangs his hand onto the table.

Alfred gives a startle and looks up. "What? Oh, is it recess?" Then he looks back down. "Nooo, I died! For fuck's sake ..."

"What level are you on?" Christian asks.

"Level three," Alfred answers. "The last one—the *hardest* one. I've got to practice."

"It sounds like a cool game," Daniel says. "What's it about?"

Alfred doesn't answer—he's already gone again.

Christian snatches the phone from him.

"Hey!" Alfred whines. "Give it back!"

"Oops, now you died again," Christian says. "Sorry. Can you please take a break? We want to talk to you."

"Talk to me about *what?*" Alfred snaps, not taking his eyes off the phone in Christian's hand.

"About the game you're playing," Daniel says. "You're completely obsessed with it."

Alfred sends him a quick frown. "Well, you would be too, if it was you. Give me the phone, Chris. I need to practice."

"Just relax for five minutes," Christian says. "You look like someone who hasn't slept for days."

"I haven't. Not really, anyway."

"Tell Daniel about the game."

Alfred sighs deeply. "I wish I never started playing it. It was my cousin who introduced me to it. He warned me, you know, but I was too curious. And now I can't stop. You can't stop until you complete the game."

"But it's only three levels?" Daniel asks. "Are they difficult?"

"It depends on how much you practice. I already completed the last level a few times."

"So, you completed the game then?"

"No. You're not done until you've completed the other half of the level. The *real half.*"

Daniel is confused. "What do you mean?"

Alfred breathes a little faster. "It happens at night. It's like a dream, but not really."

"*What* happens at night?"

"The game. It becomes real. I've already completed the first two levels. Tonight, I'm playing the third. That's why I have to practice." He tries to grab the phone back, but Christian holds it out of reach.

"You sure you're not just dreaming about playing the game?" Daniel asks.

Alfred shakes his head. "It's not just me. A lot of people have played it. I think it started in China or Korea. It's actually more like a virus—the game sort of infects your brain or something; I don't know how it works. All I know is, I should never have downloaded it."

"Why is it so important to complete the final level?" Daniel asks.

Alfred looks at him, his eyes gleaming with fear. "Because if you die in the game, you die *for real*."

Christian snorts. "Listen to him. He really believes in that crap."

Alfred stares at him angrily. "It's true! You don't know because you haven't tried it."

"And I'm not going to. But I do know you can't die from losing a stupid game on your phone. It's just some shit they made up to make more money."

"It's free," Alfred says immediately. "And there are already people who died from it. Another one went yesterday, down in South America, somewhere. You can read about it online. There's a list …"

"Get a hold of yourself, dude," Christian says. "It's a fucking scam. A bunch of nerds having a laugh."

Alfred shakes his head. "You don't get it. It's *real*. Ninety-nine out of a hundred people make it, and I'm sure as hell not going to be that one poor guy who doesn't." He leaps forward and wrenches the phone out of Christian's hand. "Those who died are the ones who didn't take the game seriously. Now, go away, please. I have to practice."

"Come on," Christian shrugs, slapping Daniel's arm. "Let the gamer get some peace to do his thing."

As they turn to walk away, Alfred says: "Daniel?"

Daniel turns around. "Yeah?"

Alfred looks at him. "Don't do it. You'll regret it."

Daniel's cheeks turn warm. He shrugs. "I'm not thinking about playing. It sounds like a stupid game."

Alfred looks at him a little while longer. "Okay. I'm just warning you." Then he concentrates on his phone again.

***

But of course, Daniel is curious.

At the next recess, he locks himself in the bathroom and searches for the game online. He finds it in English, but also a lot of other different languages. *Tödliche Träume*, it's called in German. *Rêves Mortels* in French. All of the sites he finds have warnings posted on them. There are pictures of people who reportedly died from playing.

He finds the list that Alfred mentioned: 8,014 have completed the game so far; 72 have died.

Daniel feels his stomach flutter with butterflies. Can it really be true? Alfred at least seems to genuinely believe in it.

Daniel finds the download page. A message pops up:

Download? Yes/No

Daniel hears Alfred's voice: "*Don't do it. You'll regret it.*"

Quickly, Daniel puts away the phone. His heart is pounding.

***

The next day, Alfred doesn't come to school.

Daniel grabs Christian's arm. "You think he's dead?"

"Who?"

"Alfred, of course."

Christian smiles. "Oh, you mean because of the game? Come on. He probably just overslept. Wouldn't be the first time."

"Maybe," Daniel mumbles.

Christian slaps his shoulder. "Hey, you don't believe it's true, do you? I told you, it's just a load of bullshit."

Daniel bites his lip. "Then why don't you want to play?"

Christian shrugs. "Because it's childish."

Daniel can't stop looking at Alfred's empty chair.

***

After school he passes by Alfred's house and rings the doorbell. He has to ring it three times before someone answers.

Alfred is standing there in his underwear with messy hair, squinting his eyes. "What do you want?"

Daniel is a little relieved. "I just wanted to see if you … I mean, that you didn't …"

Alfred raises his eyebrows. "That I didn't die?"

"Yeah."

"Well, I didn't. But I'm pretty goddamn tired." Alfred yawns and rubs his forehead. "It's been three crazy nights. Luckily, my mum let me skip school today. She believed me when I said I was ill."

"So, you completed the game?"

Alfred nods. Apparently, he's not going to say any more about it, so Daniel has to ask.

"What did you have to do?"

"I had to fight against alien invaders. But it varies."

"Yeah, it's different from person to person, right?"

Alfred looks at him curiously. "How do you know?"

"I read about it online," Daniel admits.

Immediately, Alfred looks wary. "You're not going to play, are you?"

"No, no. I was just curious. Was it difficult?"

Alfred sighs. "It was harder than I expected. Maybe because I knew my life was at risk."

Daniel has a thousand questions. "How does it work? Do you get transported to another world, or …?"

Alfred scratches his head. "It's hard to explain. It's like a dream, but not really. Listen, Dan, I'm pretty drained …"

"Yeah, because I tried to find something about it online, but no one really seems to want to talk about it."

"I get that," Alfred murmurs. "I also just want to forget this ever happened." He yawns loudly. "Is it all right if we talk tomorrow at school?"

"Tomorrow's Saturday."

"Oh, right. We'll talk Monday, then."

"Sure." Daniel tries to smile, but he's very disappointed. "See you. And congratulations, or whatever you're supposed to say."

Alfred smiles weakly. "Thanks."

***

Daniel is constantly thinking about the game.

He checks the list at least once every hour. Now it's up to 8,017, three more have completed since yesterday. One of them must be Alfred. The death toll is still the same.

Daniel finds a few people who wrote about what happened in their game. One person had to avoid being bitten by werewolves. Another had to find a vampire hiding in an old castle and drive a stake through its heart. Every person gets a challenge that fits exactly him or her.

Daniel gets goose bumps by the mere thought of playing. It just sounds so exiting—he wonders what *his* game would consist of. He feels tempted. Should he try it? Most people seem to do all right. If he just makes sure to practice, it's probably not that dangerous. Besides, he's still not a hundred percent convinced that you die for real if you don't complete one of the levels. It sounds pretty far-fetched. Supernatural, almost.

He opens the download page on his phone several times, but he never goes further than:

Download? Yes/No

When he wakes up Saturday morning, the first thing to pop into his head is the game. It's a lovely morning; the sun is shining; the birds are chirping away in the garden. Suddenly, it all seems so silly. It's just a game! And he *wants* to play it, in spite of Alfred's warning. So, he picks up the phone and finds the page.

Download?

Daniel hits Yes.
The download starts.
8 % ... 14 % ... 22 % ...
Someone knocks hard on the window.
Daniel gives a start and sits bolt upright.
Christian is standing outside with messy hair and big, frightened eyes, signaling for Daniel to open the window.
Daniels glances at his phone.
87 % ...
He hits Cancel. The download is discontinued. Then, he opens the window. "What are you doing here?"
Christian crawls in. "I started playing the game."
Daniel's heart speeds up, as he slumps down on the bed.
Christian starts pacing restlessly back and forth. "I played the first level last night. I didn't think it was going to be real, but as soon as it started ..." He shakes his head. "It was insane. Suddenly, the whole world changed. I was *in* the goddamn game. But I still knew who I was, and I could move just like normal. It was like dreaming, but at the same time you're awake. Does that make sense?"
"I think so. But why did you do it?"

Christian throws out his arms. "Because I wanted to prove it was bullshit, of course. I thought Alfred was joking. But he wasn't. It's real. The game is real. It's insane. I should have never started playing ..." Christian is breathing rapidly now, tugging at his hair.

"But you completed the first level?" Daniel asks.

Christian darts him a furtive look. "If I hadn't, I wouldn't be standing here right now. But check this out ..." He pulls up his sleeve, revealing a couple of large Band-Aids on his lower arm. He gently removes one of them, showing Daniel three bloody puncture wounds.

Daniel feels his stomach tighten. "Are those ... *teeth marks*?"

Christian nods gravely, pulling his sleeve back down. "It bit me."

"*What* bit you?"

"A lizard. It happened so fast, I almost didn't see it coming. I was just lucky it didn't get a real good bite, the teeth just grazed me."

"Does it hurt?"

"Like a motherfucker. I bled all over my sheets, I had to wash them when I woke up. If my mom notices the wounds, I'll have to tell her a dog bit me."

"But you got away from it?"

Christian swallows and nods. "I ran as fast as I could. I found the blue door."

"The blue door?"

"Yeah, that was the goal. I remembered it from playing on my phone."

"Wait, wait, just tell me everything from the beginning. And sit down, you're stressing me out!"

Christian sits down on the bed, placing his face in his hands. "Shit! This is really fucked up. You have to help me, dude. I don't want to play the next two levels. I don't want to face those monsters again. We have to find some way to terminate the game. I tried deleting it, but ..."

"That's not possible," Daniel says. "The game can't be stopped, no matter what you do. Everyone who's played it says so. You *have* to complete it."

Christian looks like he is on the verge of crying.

Daniel puts a hand on his shoulder. "I'll help you."

"Really?"

"I'll do whatever I can."

Christian smiles. "Thanks, man."

"Tell me about the game."

"I think it's easier if I show you." Christian takes out his phone.

Daniel involuntarily pulls a little back.

Christian looks at him. "What?"

"Nothing," Daniel mumbles.

"It's not dangerous for you. It's only me who can play. See for yourself." He hands Daniel the phone.

Daniel hesitates, but then takes it, and sees a black screen, red letters are blinking:

Start Level 2
Play

Daniel looks at Christian. "Are you sure?"

"Positive. My brother wanted to try it after I played yesterday. He couldn't start it."

Daniel hits Play, but nothing happens. He tries again; still nothing.

Christian takes back the phone and hits Play—the game starts at once.

"Now, follow closely," he mutters. "I haven't completed this level yet."

Daniel comes closer, staring intensely at the screen as Christian starts playing.

They're inside a sewer pipe. Green slime is dripping from the ceiling, and the floor is covered in muddy water. The pipe divides, turns, and goes on forever in a crazy labyrinth. Here and there, light is shining down from grids in the ceiling, but most of the time it's very dim.

Huge, flesh-eating lizards are lurking in the darkness, circling their prey, using their sense of smell, coming closer and closer. You can hear them growling. A splash from behind, pink tongues whistling close by, tails disappearing around a corner, shiny scales glistening in the dark.

Christian is getting more and more panicky. He's trying to navigate the sewers blindly. One wrong turn could mean death.

And suddenly, it happens. Something grabs his ankle. He screams and hits the phone with his finger wildly. "*It was hiding in the water! Fuck! Fuck!*" His avatar falls down. The water splashes. Screaming. Roaring. Blood. Black screen.

And then, in red letters:

> Game over.
> Try again?

"Try again," Daniel says, and Christian starts over.

The level loads once more; they're back in the sewer. The boys both stare at the screen while muttering to each other.

"Was it left here?"

"No, straight ahead."

"Wait, that's a dead end."

"Are you sure?"

"Yeah, I recognize the spider web right there."

"Right. I said *right*!"

"Okay, dude, chill!"

"Look out!"

"Fuck!"

"That was close!"

"What do I do now? What do I do now?!"

"I don't know! You didn't make it this far the last time."

Without warning, a gate springs open and a lizard jumps out. The boys both scream, Christian turns around, but another lizard pops up behind him. He's surrounded. They attack him from both sides, foaming mouths with sharp teeth, blood everywhere, then ...

> Game over.

"For fuck's sake, it's impossible!" Christian cries, throwing the phone onto the bed.

"No, we'll get it," Daniel says, picking up the phone. "We have as many tries as we want, right?"

"Yeah, but ... but I don't remember what way to go! My memory sucks! I was never good at solving mazes and shit like that."

Daniel gets an idea. He takes out his own phone. "Then we'll write it down. Start the game again."

They play the level from the beginning, and this time, they reach a little farther before the lizards get them. Daniel makes a note every time they make a turn, and he marks where the lizards are hiding. They die a few more times, but for every time they play, they reach a little farther still.

Until suddenly, they see the blue door.

Christian lets out a gasp. "There it is! We did it!" He runs over, opens the door and steps through it. The screen goes black, and red text appears:

> Congratulations! You've completed the first half of the level.
> Tonight, the second half will begin.
> Try again?

"Start over," Daniel says.

"Why?" Christian grins. "We just completed it."

"Yes, but don't you want to know it by heart?"

Christian looks at him, then nods. "Yeah, you're right."

They complete the level again. And again. And again.

Finally, Christian is able to complete the level without Daniel's notes. Daniel looks at the time—it's almost twelve o'clock. He feels dizzy and he's starving.

"What are we going to do tonight?" Christian asks.

Daniel mulls it over. "I'll spend the night at your place. I probably can't do anything other than stay awake and see what happens. If it looks like you need help, maybe I can wake you up."

"Is that even possible?"

"I don't know."

Christian nods, slowly at first, then more convinced. "It's a good idea. I'm sure I'll feel safer, knowing you're sitting next to me, keeping watch."

"All right." Daniel gets up, his stomach rumbling. "Want some breakfast?"

They spend the night in Christian's room, watching a movie, eating candy and trying to forget about what will happen come nightfall.

At bedtime, they blow up an air mattress for Daniel.

"You really think you can stay awake the entire night?" Christian asks, starting to sound nervous.

Daniel takes out a thermos from his back. "If not, I have my magic potion."

"Is that coffee?"

"Yeah. I made it extra strong."

***

It takes a while for Christian to fall asleep. He keeps twisting and turning and constantly asks Daniel if he feels sleepy.

Daniel is sitting with his back against the wall, watching a movie on his laptop while sipping coffee. It tastes horrible, but he's already feeling the effect: he is not sleepy at all; in fact, his eyes feel strangely reluctant to even blink.

Finally, Christian starts snoring, and Daniel checks the time. Twelve thirty. He puts on another movie.

An hour passes, and nothing happens.

An hour more, still nothing.

Daniel finds a third movie. He is starting to feel a bit drowsy, but the coffee has given him quite a nasty heartburn, so he decides not to drink anymore.

It's getting close to three o'clock. Daniel needs to pee really bad—he has been holding it in for the past half hour, and his bladder is about to burst, so he gets up and slips out to the bathroom. The relief is enormous, and he keeps going for what seems like forever.

When he finally returns to Christian's room, his friend is mumbling in his sleep. Daniel sits down on the bed, closely examining Christian's face.

He breathes rapidly while moving his head from side to side. "Where am I? ... What's that smell?"

Daniel bites his lip. *He's playing the game. Should I wake him up? No, I'll wait and see. Maybe he'll be all right.*

But Christian is getting more and more scared. He starts to sweat; his body is twitching. "No," he whispers. "No, I don't want to! ... Get me out of here ..."

Daniel decides to wake him up. He nudges him gently. "Christian? Wake up. You're dreaming."

Christian doesn't wake up. His skin is cold and clammy to the touch.

Daniel shakes him. "Christian! Hey, wake up!"

It's not working. Christian twists and turns, throwing off his blanket, still whispering, his voice filled with fear. "Leave me alone! Go away! No! Ouch!"

He covers his face with his arms, like he's trying to protect himself. Three deep cuts appear on the skin of his arm. They immediately start bleeding. Christian whisper-screams in pain.

Daniels gasps and jumps up. *Fuck! What do I do?*

He runs to the bathroom, finds a bowl in the cupboard under the sink, fills it with cold water—hissing frantically to the tap: "Come on, come on!"—then, hurries back into the room.

Christian is throwing himself around on the bed, flailing and shrieking hoarsely, but amazingly enough still asleep and still dreaming. The bed is covered in sweat and blood.

Daniel pours the cold water over him. Christian spits and splutters—but he *still* doesn't wake up!

"Help!" Christian whispers. "Someone! Help me!"

Daniel changes strategy. He grabs Christian's shoulders, holding him down as best he can and puts his mouth close to his ear. "I'm right here, Christian. Listen to my voice. You're in the game. Do you understand? You have to complete the level. Concentrate! You know what way to go!"

Christian calms down a little, then a little more. He is still breathing fast, but now his body is more relaxed.

"Good," Daniel whispers. "Keep going. You can do this."

The gashes on Christian's arm are still bleeding, but luckily it doesn't seem as though he has been cut anywhere else. Daniel pulls the case of the pillow and wraps it tightly around the cuts, making the bleeding stop.

Daniel stays right next to Christian, looking and listening carefully to every expression and word he mutters. Five minutes pass, then ten.

And suddenly, Christian sits bolt upright, eyes wide open. Daniel draws back in surprise.

"Are you ... awake?" he croaks. "Did you complete the level?"

Christian looks at him, for a moment he looks like he doesn't recognize him, then relief comes over his face, and he whispers: "I found it ... I found the blue door!"

The boys manage to get the bloody bedsheets stripped off and smuggled down to the washer without Christian's mom noticing.

But Christian can't hide the cuts on his arm.

"What happened?" cries his mom when she sees them. "Chris, what did you do?"

Christian lies and says he doesn't remember. "I must have done it in my sleep," he says. "Maybe I scratched myself."

But the cuts are way deeper than anything possibly caused by human fingernails. Christian's mom takes him to the emergency room.

Daniel goes home, feeling completely exhausted.

***

In the afternoon, the doorbell rings. Daniel is home alone, so he answers the door.

Christian is standing there, looking strikingly like Alfred did on Friday: red eyes, messy hair and pale skin. The only difference being his arm is all bandaged up.

"I got twelve stitches," he mumbles.

"What about the third level?"

Christian gets out his phone, using his left hand. "I've already practiced a bunch of times on the way home from the emergency room."

"Good. At least now we know I can't wake you up."

Christian shrugs. "So, what do we do?"

Daniel thinks. "I actually have an idea. I looked it up online. A guy from Scotland invented a trick."

Christian's eyebrows pull together. "A trick?"

"It's a method to pull someone else into the dream. He used his sister; she played the game alongside of him."

Christian cheers up immediately. "That's awesome! Yes! We have to do that, Dan!"

Daniel hesitates. "I don't know if it's a good idea."

"Why not? My parents aren't home tonight, they'll be spending the night at my grandma's place. It's perfect!"

"But we don't know how it works, and honestly, I'm not sure I want to risk my life."

Christian looks taken aback. "So, I'm just on my own then? You promised you'd help! Thanks for nothing, asshole! Some friend you are."

"You're the one who wanted to play the game, remember? Not me."

Christian points a shaky finger in Daniel's face. "You can't just ... You have to ... It's not fair!" He looks like he is going to say something else, but instead he lets out a long sigh, and his shoulders sink down. "I'm scared out of my mind, dude. Please, will you help me?"

Daniel looks into his friend's fearful eyes, and he knows he can't turn him down. "Okay," he says quietly.

***

It's almost twelve o'clock. Daniel is in his bed, and Christian is lying on the couch by the window. The table lamp provides the only light in the room.

"You ready?" Daniel asks.

"As ready as I'll ever be," Christian says. "Who's making the call?"

"You are."

Christian gets out his phone. A moment later, Daniel's phone starts ringing. He answers the call.

"All right, now be careful you don't hang up," Daniel instructs.

The boys put their phones on the floor.

"Dan?"

"Yeah?"

"Do you think it'll work?" Christian's voice is hoarse.

"I hope so."

Daniel reaches out and turns off the light. Then, he closes his eyes and folds his hands on his chest. He can feel his heart beating. He doesn't feel particularly sleepy, although he's exhausted after playing the second level over and over again all day.

Gradually, Daniel drifts off ...

***

... and is immediately jerked awake by a strange noise.

He sits up and looks around. He's not in his bed anymore; in fact, the whole room has disappeared. Instead, he's in a damp and smelly swamp at nighttime. The fog is hanging close to the ground, thick and white, making it hard to see.

It worked, he thinks to himself. *I'm in the game.*

He gets to his feet, his pajamas already soaked from the wet ground, and looks around. The swamp stretches as far as the eye can see in all directions. There is no sign of Christian.

Then, a voice behind him says: "Dan?" He turns around and sees his friend standing there, smiling nervously: "You're here too."

"Yeah. It worked. Come on, we need to get going. Do you remember the way?"

Christian glances around in the darkness. "No. It all looks the same to me."

"What about the tree? There was a tree that had fallen over, remember? We have to try and find it."

The boys choose a direction. There are puddles all over the place, and they are difficult to see due to the soupy fog. They step from mound to mound, trying not to touch the black water.

"Be careful where you step," Daniel whispers over his shoulder. "Some of the mounds are really treacherous. It's like they—"

He breaks off abruptly, as the mound he's about to tread on suddenly comes alive. A big, grey lizard rises from the water, mud covering its shiny green scales.

Daniel stumbles and falls over, landing with a splash, getting water up his nose and in his eyes.

"Fuck!" Christian yells somewhere above. "There's more!"

Daniel splutters as he manages to get back up, wiping the muddy water from his eyes and trying to find steady footing on the soft, slippery swamp bed. Everywhere around them, lizards are rising up from the water.

"*Run!*" he screams, climbing up on the nearest mound. His suggestion is quite redundant, as Christian has already spun around and is fleeing head over heels. Daniel follows, jumping from mound to mound as fast as he can without falling over again.

The lizard snaps at him with every step. He runs, jumps, turns, stumbles, slips, one foot in the water, pulling it up again, jumps again, keep going, just keep going. More than once, he's dangerously close to getting bitten or torn—he can even feel the cold tongues brushing up against his bare arms.

Then, it happens.

A sharp pain shoots up his foot. One of the lizards caught it between its razor-sharp teeth and is pulling. Daniel screams and jerks his leg free, feeling how the teeth rip his skin. Luckily, the sock takes the worst of it, slipping off and enabling him to escape, turn and run away limping, leaving the lizards behind for now.

He pants heavily as he looks around for Christian, who is nowhere to be seen. He's afraid to yell out, as the lizards might find him again.

He stops, tries to catch his breath, while scanning the water, making sure there are no yellow eyes watching him. It looks like he is safe, for now at least. But the worst possible thing has happened: they have separated. And Daniel has no way of knowing which way to go.

I should never have joined him. Now we're both going to die!

His foot is throbbing and bleeding, the skin is ripped pretty badly, but he can still walk.

He's just about to go on when he sees it and freezes for a moment on the spot.

The dead tree. It's leaning to the side, looking like a crooked skeleton in the darkness. The blue door isn't far away! Daniel runs to the tree, climbs up the trunk and looks out over the foggy landscape.

"Christian!" he calls out, his voice echoing over the bare land. "Where are you?"

No answer. He calls again. And again.

He's just about to give up, when he hears Christian's voice calling back from far away: "... *here! I'm here!* ..."

"I found the tree!" Daniel calls back. "Follow my voice!"

Daniel keeps yelling, guiding Christian, and suddenly, he sees him coming through the fog. Christian is soaked from head to toe, his hair sticking to his forehead, his face white as snow. His pants are ripped, and he's bleeding from several smaller cuts on his legs.

"You made it," Daniel says, jumping down to meet him.

"Barely," Christian pants. "I thought I was going to die."

"Me too. But now we're going to make it. We just need to follow the tree."

Christian briefly glances up at the tree, then starts walking in the direction the tree is leaning.

"No, wait!" Daniel grabs his arm.

"What?"

"Did you forget? There are three big lizards lurking that way. We have to turn left first."

"Oh, right."

They follow the route they've practiced, and it seems to be working, because they don't encounter any lizards—even though Daniel is afraid every step might be his last.

At one point, Christian whispers in his ear: "Look! They're watching us ..."

Daniel sees the yellow eyes shining in the dark water a few feet away. They're lying between the mounds, waiting, hoping. If the boys had gone straight forward, they would have walked right into the trap.

Daniel shivers all over. They continue, keeping a safe distance from the lurking lizards. And then they see the door. It's not supported by walls or anything else; it's just standing on its own in the empty air.

"We made it!" Christian shrieks, running towards the door.

Daniel is a few paces behind him, that's why he has time to see the lizard come sprinting out of the dark, its stumpy legs splashing through the water, the yellow eyes fixed hungrily at Christian.

No, that can't be right, Daniel has time to think. *It wasn't in the game!*

"Chris!" he screams.

Christian doesn't hear him. Just as he reaches the door and pulls it open, the lizard charges him with a roar. Christian turns his head in the last second, his eyes growing wide, then both he and the lizard tumble through the doorway and disappear.

Daniel just stands there for a moment, frozen, unable to fathom what just happened.

Did he ... did he make it? Where did the lizard go?

He gets his body moving again, walks to the door and checks behind it. No sign of either Christian or the lizard. From somewhere far away, he thinks he can hear someone scream. Daniel steps through the doorway and

***

into Christian's room.

The scream is coming from his friend, who is lying sprawled on the floor, fighting a losing battle against the lizard on top of him, biting and scratching away at him.

Daniel doesn't have time to think. He grabs the nearest object—a pen lying on Christian's desk—and stabs it hard at the back of the lizard's neck, sinking it in deep right below the skull.

The animal collapses like someone pulled its plug and slides sideways of off Christian, the muddy legs twitching a few times, then it stops moving and dies.

Daniel stares at his bloody friend on the floor; it's hard to even tell it's Christian. He isn't screaming anymore, he is not even moving, his eyes staring emptily up at the ceiling.

He ... he's dead ...

Daniel stumbles as his legs give way and he almost falls down, grabbing the desk for support. His mind is a tornado of thoughts. He hears a noise from somewhere below, a faint melody, and he looks down dreamily to see himself standing on his phone, the screen alight.

He bends down slowly and picks it up. The words on the screen scream up at him:

Download completed.
Start level 1
Play

"No, it ... it was an accident," he mutters, shaking his head. "I didn't mean to ..."

It's okay, I'll just uninstall it.

But he knows he can't. Everyone on the Internet said so. He tries anyway, but to no avail.

"No!" he yells at the phone. "I can't walk! How am I supposed to play *if I can't walk*?"

Daniel stands there for several minutes, swaying and panting. He feels like puking; his mind is blank and his foot throbbing. He has never felt more exhausted in his life. His eyes keep darting glances at his dead friend.

He sits down on the bed, takes a deep breath, then starts playing the first level.

***

Remind you of *Squid Game*? I've had the idea for *Deadly Dreams* a long time. In fact, it's been kicking around in my head for so long the game was originally supposed to be played on a Game Boy. There was supposed to be ten levels to the game, but I realized it would become boring to read about that many levels, so I decided to cut it down to three.

Ghost Tennis

"It's just the right house for us!" Mom exclaims, looking around the living room. "Lots of space, two children's rooms—it's perfect!"

Dad is standing by the window, adding: "And there's a big garden."

"Oh, yes. The kids are going to love the garden, aren't you, Joe?" Mom sends Joseph a beaming smile, her hands resting on her bulging stomach.

Joseph is not sure what to answer; he hasn't really gotten used to the thought of having a little brother, so he just mutters: "I guess."

The real estate agent smiles. "I thought you would like it."

"Do we!" Mom says. "I know it's only the second time we've seen it, but it already felt right the first time. And the price is just amazing."

"Yes, well, the owners are very eager to sell."

"Is that why they already packed up?" Dad asks, pointing to the stacks of filled moving boxes in the corner. Joseph notices the pictures have been taken down.

"Well, I think they—"

Mom interrupts, exclaiming: "Isn't this just perfect? Tell me where to sign!"

The real estate agent blinks in surprise. "Uh ... well, I didn't bring the papers ..."

Dad looks at Mom. "Shouldn't we at least think it over, honey?"

"What's there to think about? This is our dreamhouse—can't you feel it? It just feels so *right* ..."

The real estate agent clears his throat. "That's lovely, but wouldn't you like to see the garden first?"

They go to the hall, where Dad helps Mom get her shoes back on—she can't really bend over because of the tummy.

Joseph has just put on his jacket, when Mom puts a hand on his shoulder. "You didn't get to see the room we thought you should have, sweetheart. It's just down the hallway." She points and smiles encouragingly. "Go on, go take a look. You can catch up with us outside afterwards."

Joseph walks down the hallway and opens the door. The room obviously belongs to a girl: the walls are pink, the bed is hidden behind a see-through veil, and there's a distinct smell of perfume. Most of the things are packed into boxes and ready to go.

Joseph feels like an intruder as he gazes around and tries to imagine how his own stuff will look in the room. He steps inside and goes to the window, from where he can see the backyard. There's a greenhouse and what appears to be a tennis court at the far end.

A noise behind him.

Joseph spins around, staring back and forth, but he seems to be alone in the room.

"He ... hello?" he croaks, his heart in his throat. "Is anybody here?"

A movement by the bed catches his eye. A shadow rises behind the veil, and Joseph is just about to scream, as a girl sticks her head out, wearing a pair of headphones and glaring at him in silent surprise.

"Who are you?" she asks, taking off the headset.

Joseph tries to answer, but his throat is all closed up. His brain is still trying to comprehend that the girl isn't a ghost.

"What are you doing here?" she asks, getting out of bed. She's a year or two older than Joseph.

"I ... we ... were ... uhm ... seeing the house," Joseph stammers.

The girl sees something outside the window, and Joseph follows her gaze. Mom and Dad and the real estate agent are crossing the lawn.

"Oh!" the girl says, her expression clearing up. "Now I get it. You are the buyers. My mom said you wouldn't be here until tomorrow." She talks with a hint of an accent Joseph can't really place.

"The plans were changed," he tells her.

"Yeah, I figured."

There's a moment's awkward silence.

Joseph makes for the door, when the girl says: "You can look around if you want. I don't mind, just don't touch anything."

Joseph feels indecisive. It would almost be impolite to leave now that he already disturbed the girl, but it's also very weird to look around the room while she's present.

The girl doesn't seem to mind, though; she just sits down on the bed again, and starts looking at something on her phone.

Joseph doesn't know what do to, so he looks out the window once more. Mom and Dad are inspecting the greenhouse, Mom clapping her hands in excitement. She has been talking a lot about growing her own vegetables.

Joseph looks down at the tennis court. It's halfway hidden behind some bushes.

"That's the reason we're moving, you know."

Joseph turns and looks at the girl. "Huh?"

"Weren't you looking at the tennis court?" She gets up and comes over, glancing up and down at him. "Are you from around here?"

"No."

"What's your name?"

"Joseph."

The tip of her tongue plays briefly in the corner of her mouth. "Do you believe in ghosts, Joseph?"

"Nah."

"Well, you will. If your folks buy this house, that is."

"How's that?"

"Because that tennis court out there is haunted."

Joseph snorts with laughter, gaining a bit of courage. It's obvious the girl is trying to punk him. "I've heard about haunted castles and graveyards, but never a haunted tennis court."

The girl doesn't smile. "It began right after we moved in. We've only been here a year, but my folks can't take it anymore—if the house isn't sold by the end of the week, we'll move to a hotel."

Joseph shakes his head. "Sorry, I'm not buying it."

"Suit yourself."

There's a knocking at the window, and Joseph almost has another heart attack.

Mom is waving at him. "Aren't you coming out here, Joe?"

"Sure!"

Mom doesn't seem to notice the girl, she just turns and follows Dad and the real estate agent, as they disappear around the corner.

Joseph is about to leave, when he notices the girl's face. Her eyes are distant, and she mumbles, almost to herself: "The noises are the worst of it. You can't sleep once they begin. That fucking sound ... it's a tennis ball, being hit back and forth, back and forth, sometimes all night long. He doesn't have anyone to play with, you see. I guess it's kind of sad really."

"Who are you talking about?"

The girl blinks. "The ghost, of course. It's a boy, he was eleven when he died. His name is Dennis Cornwell."

"How do you know?" Joseph asks, trying for what he hopes is a confident smile. "You talked to him?"

"I found it online. There's an article—it's probably still there. You can Google his name if you want." She finally looks at him. "Just don't piss him off. Whatever you do, *don't* make him angry."

Joseph suddenly doesn't feel like talking to the girl anymore. "Right, whatever. Thank you for letting me see the room." He goes to the door.

The girl says something.

Joseph stops and looks back. "What was that?"

The girl glances at him. "I said, if you blink, you can see him."

Joseph feels a trail of goose bumps work its way down his back. He leaves the girl's room, closing the door behind him.

***

They buy the house and move in already that same weekend. The previous owners are out of there like a gunshot; they don't even get to meet them.

Mom and Joseph spend the first day painting his new room green, while Dad puts up shelves and pictures all around the house. The moving guys take care of the furniture. Everything goes very fast, and Sunday evening they sleep in the house for the first time.

"You think you can fall asleep?" Mom is sitting on the edge of Joseph's bed. "You're not scared, are you?"

"Mom, I'm not a baby."

She smiles. "All right, I'm just making sure. I'll leave the window open, or it'll get too hot in here. Dad and I are right in the next room if you need us. Okay?"

"Sure."

"Sweet dreams, honey." Mom kisses his forehead, turns off the light and closes the door behind her.

Joseph shuts his eyes and soon he drifts off to sleep.

He wakes up while it's still dark outside, confused at first as to where he is, but then he remembers.

He lies and listens to the silence for a few minutes. There are no sounds at all, not even traffic, like he is used to from the apartment. He is just about to drift off again, when he hears a noise.

FONG! ... *dum-dum-dum*

Joseph is suddenly wide awake. Was that ...?

*No! It was **not** the sound of a tennis ball being hit by a racket. It was something else entirely. A waterpipe, maybe. Or the house settling.* Mom said it could do that, because it's old.

But the sound came from the backyard, not the house. Joseph turns his head to look. The curtain moves slightly in the breeze.

*I'm **not** going over there.*

The sound probably wasn't even real. It was his imagination. Maybe he was already dreaming, or maybe—

FONG! ... dum-dum-dum

The sound definitely comes from the backyard.

Joseph sits up, his heart pounding like he just ran a mile. He gnaws at his lip as he tries to decide what to do. *All right, I'll go over there. But not to look—I'll just close the window.*

He pushes off the blanket and places his feet on the floor, slipping across the room and catching the curtain. Just as he reaches to close the window, he looks out, and just as he does so, the sound comes again.

FONG! ... dum-dum-dum

This time, he also sees the ball. A small, bright lump, floating through the darkness, across the net and landing on the other side of the court. It jumps a few times, rolls and stops. The night is moonlit, so most of the yard is visible. The tennis court is empty; no one is out there.

Joseph can't move, can't take his eyes off the ball. He holds his breath as his heart tries to make its way out of his chest.

For a few seconds, nothing happens.

Then, the ball suddenly rises straight up into the air. It hovers about three feet over the ground, exactly as though someone is holding it. It rises even higher, quickly, as someone throws it upwards. On its way down, an invisible racket hits it with an audible

FONG!

and the ball flies back over the net, landing on the other side.

dum-dum-dum

Joseph suddenly jolts back to life. He grabs the window, closes it and turns the lock. Then he pulls the curtain shut and jumps back into bed, burying his head under the blanket.

It's too hot under the blanket. Only a few minutes later, he starts sweating profusely. But he doesn't care; he doesn't want to hear the sound again.

***

At the breakfast table, Mom suddenly asks: "Did you guys also hear something last night?"

Joseph gives a startle and looks up.

Dad takes a bit of his toast. "Nah, I slept like a log."

"Of course you did." Mom sips her coffee. "I just thought I heard a noise from the backyard. How about you, Joe? Did you hear anything?"

"No," Joseph mutters, not really sure why he's lying.

"Every place has new noises," Dad says. "You'll see, honey, in a few nights you won't even notice anymore."

"I guess you're right."

Mom and Dad start talking about their plans for the rest of the summer holidays.

Joseph feels light-headed. He couldn't really get back to sleep last night after the episode. But now with the sun shining outside, it actually seems a little silly; like nothing more than a bad dream.

"Thank you for breakfast," Joseph says, feeling a little better as he gets up from the table. "I think I'll go outside."

Outside the birds are singing and the air is already warm. Joseph goes around to the backyard and immediately feels his pulse rising as he sees the tennis court. Still he walks closer, wanting to convince himself he has nothing to fear.

The court is in a very poor state; the red gravel is rugged, tufts of weed are growing several places, the lines are almost gone and the net is slack and full of holes. The only thing implying the court has been used recently is the ball. It's lying in the middle of the court. It was probably yellow once, but now it's brown and shaggy.

"Hello?" Joseph whispers. "Is anyone here?"

No answer. A bee buzzes by lazily.

Joseph gathers his courage and steps onto the court. The gravel crunches beneath his shoes as he walks to the ball and picks it up. He throws it onto the ground a few times; it's not very bouncy anymore.

Joseph breaks out into a smile. He feels silly. What was he afraid for? It's just an old tennis court, for God's sake. He must have dreamt the whole thing. The girl's story was what caused him to dream about it.

Joseph drops the ball and turns to leave—when he suddenly remembers something the girl said.

"*If you blink, you can see him.*"

Joseph considers for a moment. Then, he blinks and darts a look around. Nothing happens. The court is still empty. He blinks twice. Still nothing. He feels more courageous, so he blinks many times.

And suddenly, he sees the boy. It's only in a flash, and only out of the corner of his eye, but there is no mistaking it. The boy is standing right on the other side of the net. He's about the same height as Joseph, and he's dressed in white shorts and a polo shirt. In his hand he's holding a racket.

Joseph screams and jumps backwards, staring at the place where the boys just was. Now he sees nothing. But suddenly he doesn't feel alone on the court anymore.

He turns around and sprints back up to the house.

Joseph Googles the boy's name, and after a little digging around, he finds the article the girl mentioned.

Dennis Cornwell, born in 1936 in England, dead 1947 in the USA.

There is even a photo. It's black-and-white and shows a family—a father, a mother, a little girl and three boys, the youngest being outlined by a ring.

Joseph reads the article.

The family came to the States right after the Second World War. The British are known to love tennis, and the Cornwells were no exception, so as soon as they had settled in the house, they made a court in their new backyard. On a warm summer afternoon, the parents went to town, bringing the two older boys and the younger girl, while Dennis stayed at home to play with a friend from school. They were going at it on the tennis court, when Dennis suddenly had a heart attack and collapsed, probably due to the heat. His friend tried to revive him, but to no avail. Once help arrived, it was all too late.

Joseph sinks back in the chair, brooding.

Can it really be Dennis Cornwell haunting the tennis court? If so, what does he want? Is he friendly or hostile? And is it possible to make him go away?

Joseph wishes he could have another word with the girl who used to live here. She might know more about the ghost.

***

Joseph decides not to tell his parents. What good would it do? They wouldn't believe him anyway, and even if they did—what could they do?

He stays away from the tennis court the rest of the day, but keeps an eye on it from his room. The tennis ball is still lying where he left it, and it doesn't move an inch.

At bedtime, Mom comes into his room.

"Do you want me to open the window?" she asks.

"No, that's okay, Mom. I actually feel a little chilly." That's a lie; he's already sweating. But he doesn't want the window open.

Mom gives him a kiss and leaves the room.

Joseph lies awake for a long time, staring at the ceiling, listening for the noise, watching the glowing numbers on his alarm clock shift. Eleven. Half past eleven. Twelve. Still no noises from outside.

Joseph has kicked off the blanket, the sweat is streaming off him, the room is like a sauna.

Maybe if I open it just slightly ...

He gets up to open the window, sighing with relief as the cool night air seeps in. He glances out at the tennis court—the ball is still there.

Joseph feels a tentative optimism as he goes back to the bed. But just as he lies down—

FONG! ... dum-dum-dum

Joseph stiffens. He doesn't want to go back to close the window, afraid of what he might see, so he just lies there, listening to the sounds from the yard.

FONG! ... dum-dum-dum ... FONG! ... dum-dum-dum ... FONG! ... dum-dum-dum

The ball goes back and forth, back and forth, tirelessly.

It takes a long time for Joseph to fall asleep—and even in his dreams he hears the sound of the ghost playing tennis.

It goes on like that for some days.

Joseph tries his best to pretend like nothing is wrong, tries to make the hours pass during the day; he plays computer, helps Mom clean the windows, helps Dad clear out the basement, practices soccer in the yard—far away from the tennis court.

But every night the ghost plays tennis, and every night Joseph is lying in his bed, twisting and turning, slipping in and out of a restless doze, sweaty and scared. When he manages to drift off properly for a few minutes, he has nightmares about the ghost.

Just before sunrise the noise finally ceases. By morning, Joseph is completely weary.

Mom notices at the breakfast table. "You look a little pale, Joe. You're not getting sick, are you?"

"I'm just not sleeping well," he mumbles.

"Is it the noises from the yard? Because I also hear them now and then."

Joseph needs to do something; it can't go on like this. Either he loses his mind from insomnia, or Mom will decide to investigate the nightly noises. He's not sure how she will react if she sees the tennis ball playing by itself, but he has heard about some pregnant women experiencing a shock great enough to send them into early labor right on the spot. Joseph can't risk that happening.

So he comes up with an idea.

That same afternoon, he goes to the tennis court and starts blinking. He goes on like that for almost a full minute, but he doesn't see Dennis Cornwell.

Perfect. He's not here. Now is my chance!

He grabs the ball and runs back into the house. He already picked out a hiding place: behind the washer in the basement.

Joseph goes to his room and looks out at the tennis court, smiling. "That'll give us some peace and quiet."

***

That night, when midnight comes around, no noise is heard from the tennis court; and Joseph's window is even open all the way. He falls asleep and snores deeply.

But he's woken abruptly at around three o'clock. It's not a sound waking him—more of a sensation. He can sense someone in the room with him.

"Mom?" he mutters. "Is that you?"

No answer. Joseph sits up, rubs his eyes and looks around. The room is empty. He's eyes are drawn to the window, which is still open, but now the curtain is pulled aside, almost like—

Like someone has climbed in!

Joseph's skin is covered with invisible ice. He starts blinking, expecting Dennis Cornwell to turn up somewhere in the room, but nothing happens. Then, Joseph notices the door being opened. There's a noise from the hallway.

Joseph is too scared to get up, but he's also too scared to stay put. If the ghost has entered the house, he needs to know. So, he gets up and slips to the door, his legs wobbly with fear.

The hallway is empty. At the other end is the door to the basement, and it's ajar. Joseph tiptoes down the hallway and peeks down the stairs. Someone is rummaging around down there. Things are being thrown to the floor.

Then a sudden silence falls over the basement.

Joseph holds his breath. He can't see anything down in the basement, but he gets the sense that someone is looking at him. He blinks quickly three times.

Dennis Cornwell is standing at the foot of the stairs, staring up at him. Even though it's only a short glimpse, Joseph has time to make out two things: the tennis ball in Dennis's hand, and the hate shining from his eyes.

Then, he's gone. Loud footsteps come running up the stairs.

Joseph spins around and flees down the hallway, yanking open the bathroom door, slamming it behind him and turning the key. He holds his panting breath and listens. Vaguely, he can hear footsteps coming down the hallway, stopping briefly outside the bathroom, then continuing.

In his mind, Joseph keeps hearing the girl saying, "*Just don't piss him off. Whatever you do,* **don't** *make him angry.*"

He waits a couple of minutes before unlocking the door and stepping out into the hallway. He blinks just to make sure, but sees nothing of Dennis Cornwell. Joseph can somehow sense the ghost has left the house.

He checks the basement. Everything is thrown about or tipped over. The washer has been pulled out from the wall, and the tennis ball is gone.

Joseph pushes the machine back into the wall and tidies up most of the mess. Then, he sneaks back upstairs and goes to bed—but not before closing the window, because outside, the ghost is playing tennis.

***

Several nights pass by, the ghost is playing more loudly than ever, and Joseph hardly gets any sleep. He doesn't know what to do. He almost becomes desperate enough to steal the tennis ball again—it would be easy, since it just lies around the court all day—but this time, he will burn it. The problem is, he still remembers the angry look on Dennis Cornwell's face all too well, so stealing the ball is out of the question.

The summer holidays come to an end and Joseph is to begin at the local school. He feels quite welcome and falls in well with the class. He likes going to school—it gives him something else to think about during the daytime.

But at night, the problem still haunts him, and it's getting worse. Mom is also hearing the noises regularly now. Joseph can tell she isn't sleeping well at night either.

"Joe," she says one evening at dinner. "Were you outside last night?"

Joseph looks up from his plate. "No. Why?"

"I just thought I heard something."

"Are you talking about those noises again?" Dad asks.

Mom doesn't seem to hear him. "It's almost like ... like someone hitting a tennis ball."

Joseph freezes.

Dad laughs. "Really? You think someone is playing tennis in our backyard in the middle of the night?"

Mom shakes her head. "I don't know. But I got up to take a look, and ..."

Joseph holds his breath, staring at Mom. She frowns, but doesn't say anything.

"And?" Dad prompts her. "Did you see anyone?"

"No. The apple tree is blocking the view, but the longer I listened, the better I could hear it."

"Are you sure you weren't just dreaming?"

Mom bites her lips. "Maybe. It just felt very real."

Dad begins to talk about work.

Joseph can see that Mom isn't really listening. He knows he has to do something.

He spends the evening working out a plan. He will try to talk to the ghost. Maybe they can make some sort of deal. It's worth a shot, even though Joseph is terrified at the thought.

***

That night he stays awake until twelve o'clock, his nightlamp burning, window open, listening for the familiar sound.

Like clockwork, it begins a few minutes past midnight.

Joseph gets out of bed, legs shaky with anticipation. He gets dressed and climbs out the window.

The ball is going back and forth on the court. Joseph goes to the edge and stops. "H ... hi," he says.

The ball lands, but this time, it's not picked up.

Joseph can feel the ghost; he knows it's here. Waiting. Listening. He swallows and starts blinking.

He immediately sees Dennis Cornwell standing by the net, racket in hand, looking suspiciously at Joseph. Then, he's gone again.

"It's ... it's kind of hard to get any sleep with you playing out here," he says. "You think ... you think you might want to ... only play when we're not home, maybe?"

No answer.

Joseph blinks again and gets another glimpse of the ghost. It has moved; now it's by the ball. Joseph sees the ball being picked up. He assumes Dennis will hit it, but that doesn't happen. Instead, the ball comes closer. And closer. And closer.

Joseph starts backing up. "Uhm ... if you ... if you don't like the idea ..."

He's just about to turn around and run, when the ball stops a few feet away. It just hangs there, hovering in the empty air.

Joseph tentatively holds out his hand. The ball drops into his palm.

"You want me to ... play with you?"

Suddenly, it clicks. He recalls the girl's voice: *"He doesn't have anyone to play with."* Obviously, the ghost must be very lonely, out here on his own every night.

Joseph blinks. Dennis Cornwell is right in front of him, smiling.

"All right," Joseph mutters. "I guess we could play, but ... I don't have a racket."

When he blinks again, the ghost is gone.

"Hello?" Joseph asks. "Where are you?"

A noise from the bottom of the yard makes him turn. The door to the shed swings open, and a moment later, a racket comes soaring out. It flies over to Joseph, and he takes it.

"Thank you."

He steps out onto the court, faces the net and blinks. Dennis Cornwell is on the other side, racket in his hand, looking eager and ready.

This is insane, Joseph thinks, looking at the ball in his hand. *I'm about to play a game of tennis with a ghost ...*

He throws the ball into the air and hits it with the racket. It goes over the net and immediately comes flying back. Joseph misses the shot and has to pick up the ball from the grass. He hits it back over to the ghost, and again it's returned hard. But this time, Joseph is ready, and he hits it back.

They play for twenty minutes. Joseph isn't familiar with the rules, but it's pretty obvious Dennis Cornwell is winning by a stretch.

Joseph is sweating and panting in the chill night air. "All right," he gasps. "I can't play anymore now. I have to go back to bed." He puts down the racket and is about to leave, but an invisible hand grabs his arm. "Let go!" he exclaims. "Let go of me!"

But the ghost doesn't let go. Its grip is firm and very cold.

Joseph quickly thinks up something. "Listen, we'll play again tomorrow. All right?"

The grip loosens a little.

"I promise. Tomorrow after school, I'll come out here again."

The ghost lets go of him. Joseph leaves and climbs back into his room. He darts one last look out on the court. The ball is lying peacefully on the gravel.

No more tennis is being played that night.

***

The next morning Joseph wakes up feeling unusually well rested—he even smiles as he gets up.

Joseph plays tennis again that afternoon. And the day after. And the day after.

Dad is at work, and Mom is busy doing things in the house, so none of them notice Joseph playing against an invisible opponent—Mom just thinks he's practicing on his own.

He begins to sleep well at night. Mom doesn't mention the noises anymore either.

And slowly, Joseph actually starts to enjoy the game. Little by little, he also gets better at it—still not as good as Dennis, but he scores a few points now and then. He reads about the rules online and orders a new racket and three new balls. It makes all the difference. Once a week he fixes up the court by raking and sweeping it.

The days go by as though everything is normal. The nights are quiet, the family is happy. Mom's tummy is steadily growing to the point where it looks ready to explode. His new brother will arrive any day now.

But there is still one thing nagging Joseph. What if he suddenly becomes unable to play with Dennis? Will the ghost start playing at night again? Imagine if Joseph has to go to summer school, or if he gets an injury which prevents him from playing—Dennis Cornwell might be furious. And from what the girl told him, no one will be able to stop him releasing his anger on the house or the family. The thought of the ghost hurting Mom—or even worse, his new little brother—is enough for Joseph to decide that things need to change. They cannot live under the threat of potential disaster.

So, he comes up with a new idea. It's a good one, but also a little risky. He decides to give it a go.

***

"Dennis?" he asks on the court that same day, just as he is about to serve. "I've been thinking. There is something I need to ask you."

No answer from the other side of the net, but Joseph knows Dennis is listening.

"I want to make a bet with you. If I win this game, you go away. You leave this place forever, and you never come back. But if *you* win, I'll keep playing with you, every day for the rest of my life."

Joseph waits for Dennis to answer, hoping he'll take the bet.

"How about it?" he says, bouncing the ball a few times, trying to look casual. "You're in?"

Joseph blinks and gets a glimpse of the dead boy. He's standing with his thumb pointing up and a confident smirk on his face.

Joseph's heart picks up its pace as he nods. "Great. Let's play then."

Joseph plays the best he can, and he's actually doing better than he hoped. Over the last few weeks, he has played badly on purpose, has been letting Dennis win and giving him the false sense that he is far better than Joseph. But now Joseph gives him a real challenge.

And he takes the first set.

Joseph can hardly believe it. He's winning! The plan is working.

Then Dennis pulls himself together. Joseph gets overwhelmed and loses the second set.

"Shit," he pants, wiping sweat of his forehead. *All right, I can still win. I just need to give it everything.*

And Joseph does. He plays as though his fate depends on it—which isn't far from the truth.

Third set is nerve-rackingly close. They fight doggedly for every point. Joseph sprints back and forth, jumping, sliding and yelling out with every swing of the racket.

And yet, Dennis gets a match ball. Defeat is hovering just above Joseph's head. But Dennis blows it and Joseph fights his way back. Now *he* has the match ball.

He serves a perfect serve. Dennis returns it. Joseph feels like it's out, so he doesn't swing on it. But the ball hits the ground just inside the line with less than half an inch. It's a point for Dennis. But Joseph throws up his arms. "Yes! It was out! It was out! I win!"

Someone pushes him hard in the chest, almost knocking him over.

"Don't do that! It was out, I tell you."

Another hard push.

"Stop pushing me. It's not my fault. You lose!"

This time, Dennis doesn't push him. Joseph awaits his reaction, his heart pounding away.

"You ... you have to leave now. That was the deal."

He prepares for another shove, but it doesn't come. He can feel he's suddenly alone. To be sure, he blinks. The court is empty.

Dennis Cornwell has gone.

Joseph feels a little nervous. The rest of the day he walks around darting glances all over, blinking constantly, and checking the tennis court at least once an hour. But he doesn't see the ghost anywhere.

***

As Joseph goes to his room after dinner, he gets a big surprise. On his bed, the girl who used to live there is sitting, her legs crossed, casually going through one of Joseph's school books.

He stops in the doorway, frozen with amazement. "What ... what are you doing here?"

She looks up, sending him a sad smile and putting aside the book. "I told you not to piss him off."

Josephs shuts the door behind him without taking his eyes off the girl. "You mean the ghost?"

"Who else?"

"I didn't piss him off. I just won a bet. I got him to leave."

The girl looks at him, giving off a deep sigh. "No, you didn't. He will never leave."

Joseph feels scared, and that makes him angry. "How do you know? Why did you even come here? You can't just walk into other people's houses—we live here now!"

"I've lived here far longer than you," the girl says quietly.

"That doesn't matter!" Joseph splutters. "We own the place now!"

The girl suddenly gets up. "Well, if you're going to take that tone with me, I might as well leave."

"Please do!" Joseph says, gesturing to the door. "And the next time, if you want to visit, use the doorbell or something."

The girl stares at him angrily. "He was right, you really are arrogant. Stupid American boy." Her accent suddenly becomes more audible—she seems to notice so herself, because she clears her throat and says, very calmly, and almost without a trace of the accent: "I came here to give you one last chance, but you blew it."

"How nice of you," Joseph sneers. "Now, please get out."

The girl leaves without a word and closes the door gently behind her. Joseph is left to the silence, his heart is pounding, but he can't tell if it's because of anger or fear.

***

Joseph spends the rest of the evening in his room, feeling oddly tense and uneasy, constantly darting glances out at the tennis court and listening intently for any noises.

But nothing happens.

At bedtime, Joseph slips under the covers, feeling not the slightest bit sleepy. He lies awake until midnight. Still no sounds from outside. Joseph finally starts to relax. It worked! The ghost has left the place. The girl's weird warning was just a load of crap.

Joseph drifts off into sleep.

A few minutes later, the window slides open ever so slowly. An unseen figure climbs in, pushing the curtain aside, slipping across the floor and stopping next to the bed.

Suddenly, the door is flung open. "Joseph!" Dad yells. "Wake up! Mom has gone into labor!"

Joseph sits up with a jolt. "What? Who?"

"We have to go to the emergency room, right now! Hurry up, get dressed." Dad rushes down the hallway.

Joseph quickly finds his clothes. He's feeling groggy, he had a dream about tennis. He can hear Mom yelling somewhere in the house, and in the driveway he hears the car engine start up. Joseph feels excited—he finally gets to meet his new brother! Maybe they can play tennis one day. Joseph can teach him how to serve, and they can—

Joseph is going for the door when it suddenly slams shut, apparently all on its own.

Joseph stares at it for a second, but before he realizes what is happening, it's too late. Something comes flying out of the air, hitting him squarely in the face. There is a crunching noise, which might come from either Joseph's nose bone or the racket, because they both break. Joseph falls to the floor, halfway unconscious, tasting blood and staring up at the ceiling. He blinks dazedly.

And he sees Dennis Cornwell. The dead boy is hovering above him, face contorted in rage, eyes glowing with hate. Joseph's heart fills up with fear, as it dawns on him what is going on.

Then he sees another figure behind the ghost. It's the girl again! She's looking down at him with a pitiful expression. Joseph feels a flash of hope. "Help me," he croaks, his eyes filling with water, as he reaches his hand up towards her.

"I'm sorry," she says softly. "I tried to warn you not to piss him off." Her accent is more clearly audible now, like she isn't trying to hide it anymore. Joseph still can't place it, though. "You see, I never wanted to play tennis," the girl goes on, placing her hand at her shoulder. "So, Dennis has been waiting patiently all this time for someone to play with him. And then you came along, and he was finally happy again." The girl looks at Dennis for a moment, her eyes warm and kind. It's odd, she almost looks at him like he ... like he's family or something. Her eyes grow sad once more, as she looks down at Joseph. "But you just had to piss him off, right? You betrayed him, you tried to cheat."

"No, I ..." Joseph whispers, his voice thick because of the blood spilling from his nose, but he stops as Dennis steps forward with a furious but silent sneer.

The girl grabs hold of Dennis's arm and holds him back. "Not yet, Dennis. I don't think he gets it yet."

"Gets *what*?" Joseph snorts, almost crying now, his nose still gushing blood and throbbing painfully.

"Who I am," the girl says, tilting her head. "I can't believe you haven't figured it out—you even saw me in the photograph." Her accent is now very pronounced, and Joseph can tell she's British. Then finally, it falls into place.

"You ... the girl ... his younger sister ..."

The girl smiles and nods. "I had the same heart defect as Dennis. I died a few years later." She looks at Dennis again, who is still glaring at Joseph. "All right," she says very gently. "You can do it now."

"No, please don't," Joseph begs, as Dennis descends upon him.

***

"What's taking him so long?" Mom is in the backseat, breathing fast. "Are you sure you woke him up?"

"Yes, damnit!" Dad says, honking the horn.

Joseph doesn't turn up.

"Go get him!" Mom demands in a shrill voice.

Dad unbuckles and jumps out, running into the house. "Joe! Come on! What's the holdup?" He paces quickly down the hallway, tearing open the door to his son's room. "Joe, honestly, why are you—"

Dad stops dead in the doorway, staring at Joseph who is lying on the floor. His face is blue, his eyes are bulging, glancing at nothing. It's hard to tell what caused Joseph to suffocate—the blood, pouring from his nose, or the tennis ball, which is stuffed down his throat.

***

Most of my ideas come from ordinary everyday situations, and this one is no exception. Last summer, I was playing tennis on my own, practicing my serve. Suddenly, I saw a figure out of the corner of my eye, standing right on the other side of the net. When I turned my head abruptly, there was nothing. It was probably just my imagination, but I didn't really *feel* alone on the court anymore, and I got the chills even though it was really warm. Later, on my way home, my imagination started going, and I came up with the idea for a haunted tennis court. It turned into the story you just read.

When I Snap My Fingers ...

"Come on, Rach. Mom and Dad are waiting."

"This is the last one, I swear!" Rachel pleads, pointing at the tent. "Please, Calvin, I really want to go."

The fair is buzzing with people, the sun is shining, kids are laughing, music is playing, and the air smells like beer and candy floss.

"We promised to be back at two o'clock," Calvin reminds her. "You know Mom will be pissed."

"I'll take the blame," Rachel promises. "I'll tell her we forgot the time. Come on, Calvin, please-please-please!"

Calvin sighs and glances at his watch. It's already five minutes past two, so they'll be late anyway. "Fine," he says.

Rachel jumps with excitement and grabs his hand. "Thank you, Calvin. You're the best brother in the world."

She pulls him towards the tent, while Calvin discretely looks around and hopes no one he knows sees him holding hands with his little sister.

Rachel stops and looks up at the sign above the tent. "Madam ... Spinoza," she reads aloud. "Hyp-no-tist ..."

"You know it's not real, right?"

"I still really want to try." She sticks her head in the opening. "It's all dark ... Hello? Is anybody here?"

"It looks like they're closed," Calvin remarks. "Maybe we'd better—"

"Step closer," a hoarse voice whispers from inside the tent.

Rachel gives a little startle, looks up at Calvin and grins. Then, she slips inside, pulling Calvin along. As they leave the bright sunlight and enter the cool darkness, Calvin can't see a thing. The sounds of the fair also fade away to a faint echo.

"I can't see anything," Rachel says.

A match is struck with a dry crackle, and a small flame flares up, revealing a wrinkly face floating in the dark. It's hard for Calvin to determine whether it's a man or lady. Grey tufts of hair are protruding from under a purple bandana, and a large silver earring dangles from one ear.

"Welcome," the person says with a smile, showing a row of yellow teeth. "Please, be seated."

Calvin can make out a couple of stools in front of a small table. The hypnotist is sitting on the other side, and on the table are laid out several objects: an old tape recorder, a pocket watch, a silver coin and a thick, white candle, which their host lights with the match.

Nicely done, Calvin thinks. *It almost seems real.*

He actually feels a little shiver, but it's probably only the cold.

Rachel has already sat down, and Calvin joins her.

"My name is Griselda Spinoza," the old lady begins. Calvin notices she has a strange accent. "I'm 105 years old. My family have been hypnotists since the beginning of time. Now, who of you would like to be hypnotized?"

"Me," Rachel says at once. "I've always wanted to try it. I think it's very exciting."

"It is," Madam Spinoza says. "But it can also be dangerous."

"How's that?"

The old lady smiles. "Do you believe in life after death, Rachel?"

"Uhm ... I don't know."

The hypnotist looks at Calvin. "How about big brother?"

"Nah, I think ..." He's about to say he doesn't believe anything happens after death, but then he remembers Rachel is listening, so instead, he says: "I think you go to heaven."

"You're wrong," the hypnotist snubs. "Heaven is only for the few lucky; most of us are condemned to live forever, only in different bodies. I myself, for instance, have lived at least seven lives that I can remember."

Rachel lets out a gasp of astonishment.

Calvin rolls his eyes. *Yeah, right. That's pretty lame, but as long as Rachel is entertained ...*

"Now we will see who you have been in one of your previous lives, Rachel," Madam Spinoza says, pointing at Rachel with a thick, yellow fingernail. "But first, the money. It's five bucks."

Calvin hands her the money. It quickly disappears into a pocket.

"Are you ready, Rachel?"

"Yes," Rachel whispers breathlessly.

The hypnotist presses the recorder, and the tape starts turning. She picks up the coin. "Keep an eye on this." She lets it wander across her boney knuckles. At first, it's very slow, but soon it picks up speed, dancing faster and faster, the silver blinking in the glow of the candle flame. "Keep looking at the coin," Madam Spinoza whispers. "Don't take your eyes off it. Look how it moves. And feel your body relaxing."

Calvin realizes he is becoming drowsy; in fact, he's close to falling asleep. He straightens up and blinks a few times. Then, he glances at Rachel. Her eyes are almost closed.

"Keep your eyes on the coin, Rachel," the hypnotist whispers. "In a moment you'll fall asleep. Once you're sleeping, I want one of your previous lives to come forward. And only when I snap my fingers, will you wake up as Rachel again. Is that clear?"

Rachel nods and mumbles: "Yes ..." right before her eyes close.

"You're sleeping," the old lady croaks, putting down the coin and folding her hands on the table. "Now, who will come forward?"

Calvin stares at Rachel; she really looks like she's sitting upright sleeping, chin resting on her chest, breathing softly.

"She's not saying anything," Calvin mutters.

"Sssh!" Madam Spinoza hisses, not taking her eyes off Rachel. "Who will come forward?"

A few more moments pass. Calvin can smell the smoke from the candle.

Then, suddenly, Rachel says: "It's me. Elmer Hedrick." The voice is completely different, deeper and rawer.

"Hello, Elmer," the hypnotist says without hesitation. "How old are you, boy?"

"Ten," Rachel says, not lifting her head or opening her eyes. "It was my birthday yesterday."

"Really? Did you get any gifts?"

"No."

"Didn't your parents buy you anything?"

"No."

"How come?"

"They're dead."

"I'm sorry to hear that. When did they die?"

"Yesterday."

Madam Spinoza raises her thin eyebrows, showing the first sign of surprise. "They died on your birthday? Both of them?"

"Yes."

"Was it a car crash?"

Rachel sneers. "A *what*?"

The hypnotist smacks her dry lips. "What time are you living in, Elmer? What year is it?"

"Nineteen oh three, of course."

"I'll say," Madam Spinoza mutters, seemingly talking to herself. "It's very rare I get one this far back ... How did your parents die, Elmer?"

"They got their throats cut open with a knife."

"Goodness! Did the police catch the killer?"

"No."

"I'm sure they'll get him."

"I don't think so."

"Why not?"

Rachel doesn't answer. Calvin notices her face tic. But he can't really make out the details anymore; it's like the air has turned foggy.

"Elmer?" the hypnotist asks. "Why don't you think the police will catch the one who murdered your parents?"

Rachel lifts her head ever so slightly and opens her eyes, staring straight at the old lady and hisses: "Because I made it look like someone else did it."

Calvin feels his stomach tighten.

Madam Spinoza looks befuddled. "Close your eyes, Rachel. You're not supposed to open then until I—"

"Rachel isn't here," she interrupts. "My name is Elmer."

"Is this part of the trick?" Calvin asks.

The hypnotist looks at him briefly. "Uhm ... I think we better ..."

Rachel turns her head and glares at Calvin. For a moment he's sure her eyes are brown—which of course is nonsense, because Rachel's eyes are blue—it has to be the smoky air playing a trick on his senses, but he still gets the chills.

"Who are you?" she sneers at him.

"That's enough for now," Madam Spinoza interjects. "Rachel! Look at me."

Rachel looks back at the old lady, her face contorts into an angry grimace. "I told you, I'm not Rachel. Stop calling me that. My name is Elmer, and I—"

The hypnotist reaches across the table, grabbing hold of Rachel's arm. "Listen to me! When I snap my fingers ..."

Suddenly, daylight comes streaming in, as the tent door is torn open. Calvin turns to see a heavyset man stare in at them. "Get out of there!" he yells. "Right now!"

"Close the door!" Madam Spinoza hisses. "We're in the middle of a séance!"

The man's expression is one of disbelief. "Haven't you heard us calling? The tent is on fire, damnit!"

Calvin realizes the air is full of smoke. It feels like waking from a dream—now he can also feel the burning heat and hear the crackle of the flames. He also feels very dizzy.

"Come on, hurry up!" the man roars. "Get out, get *out!*" He steps in and grabs Rachel, pulling her back.

Calvin gets to his feet, coughs and stumbles towards the light. He reaches the opening, the sun is blinding him, there are people with scared faces all around. His eyes sting, and his throat feels raw. He hears someone cough right next to him and sees the man still holding on to Rachel.

Calvin looks back and lets out a loud gasp. The tent is one big bonfire, the orange flames reaching hungrily for the blue sky, smoke coming out of every opening. The heat is intense enough to make him stagger backwards.

"Was there anyone else in there?" someone shouts.

"I certainly hope not!" another voice answers. "Because it's way too late now ..."

As though the words make it happen, the tent collapses, the flames roaring even more fiercely, sparks flying all around. The onlookers pull back.

Calvin goes to Rachel. "Are you all right? Are you hurt?"

Rachel doesn't answer, she just stares at nothing.

"Rachel!" He shakes her.

She blinks, looks at him and starts to cry. "What ... what happened, Calvin?"

He hugs her. "The tent caught fire. It's all right, we got out in time."

Calvin and Rachel are taken to a medical tent, where a medic takes a look at them.

Suddenly, their mom pops her head in, sees them and runs over. "My God, are you two okay?" She attempts to hug and examine them at the same time.

"They both got off lightly," the doctor says. "But it was a matter of seconds before the tent would have collapsed."

"Oh, thank God," their mom sighs, always on the verge of tears. "Why didn't you come? We've been looking all over for you!"

"Uhm ... we just wanted to ..."

"It was my fault," Rachel sniffs. "I talked Calvin into it. I just really wanted to get hypnotized, Mom."

At that moment, their dad enters the tent.

"They're unharmed," their mom says. "Nothing happened."

"Don't ever scare us like that again," their dad says, looking demandingly at Calvin. "I thought you were more responsible, Calvin. How could you forget the time like that?"

"It was only ten minutes," Calvin murmurs defensively.

"Ten minutes?" their mom exclaims, her voice shrill. "Do you know what time it is?"

Rachel bursts into tears. "Sorry, Mom ..."

Mom hugs her and strokes her hair. "It's all right, honey. I was just so afraid something horrible had happened."

"We almost called the police," their dad tells Calvin in a lowered voice. "You have been gone for three hours."

"No," Calvin says, shaking his head. "We were only in that tent for five minutes or so."

"Really?" Dad holds his watch so Calvin can see it.

Calvin stares at the time. It's almost half past five. He doesn't get it—how can the time have gone by so fast? Perhaps he lost his sense of time due to the shock of the fire.

***

The following evening, another strange thing occurs.

They're just about to sit down for dinner—they're having curry, Rachel's favorite dish—when she sees the pot and sneers. "Yuck, that stinks!"

"But you used to love curry," her mom says.

"No, I hate it," Rachel says, pushing her plate away. "It tastes like old farts."

"Watch your tone, please," her dad says.

"You watch your tone!" Rachel shouts.

They all freeze up around the table. Rachel never talks like that to anyone, especially not her dad. But she doesn't even seem remorseful, she just crosses her arms and looks at him defiantly.

"Well, you can go to bed on an empty stomach, then," her dad says.

"I'd rather," Rachel scoffs, getting up and leaving the room.

Mom looks at Dad, her eyebrows raised. "What got into her?"

Dad shrugs. "She's becoming a teenager, I guess."

"She's only seven!"

"Well, I don't know."

Calvin starts eating and doesn't really give the episode a second thought—at least not until next day.

It's Sunday, and they always tidy up their rooms on Sunday, so that Mom can vacuum the whole house. Calvin is done in ten minutes, but Rachel refuses to do her room, even when Mom tells her a third time. But the more Mom asks, the more stubborn Rachel becomes. Finally, Dad has to drag her into the room and shut the door.

"And you don't come out until that room is tidy!" he yells, and as he walks away, Calvin can hear him mutter: "Christ, what's wrong with that girl?"

Calvin listens by the door to Rachel's room as she's rummaging around in there.

When Dad comes back ten minutes later and opens the door, he lets out a gasp. Calvin looks past him and sees the room completely ravaged. Everything is tipped over or thrown about.

Rachel is sitting on her bed, swinging her legs and smiling malevolently.

The smile gives Calvin the creeps.

***

Rachel is grounded for a week. But it doesn't help; during the next days, she only becomes worse. Calvin can hardly recognize her anymore, it's like her personality has completely changed. Even her voice sometimes sounds a little deeper, and her eyes can in brief glimpses appear brown instead of blue.

Calvin overhears his mom and dad talking one evening. They think the change in Rachel has something to do with the fire at the fair. Rachel must have some sort of delayed reaction. They decide to take her to see a shrink.

That doesn't help either. Rachel refuses to talk to the shrink, so he can't help her. Finally, after three visits, they give up.

Calvin knows what's wrong with Rachel, although he's afraid to admit it at first, but it has started to become obvious. She is still hypnotized. The séance was interrupted before Madam Spinoza could snap her fingers.

Calvin tries to tell his dad about the hypnotism.

"That was just a trick, Calvin."

"But she became a completely different person, Dad. I saw it myself."

"That sort of thing only happens in movies."

Calvin gives up.

More days pass by, and Rachel becomes more and more mean. She doesn't just talk back anymore; she will also hit or even bite. She tips over things on purpose, slams the doors, kicks the furniture, she's even mean to the cat.

Calvin starts to become really worried.

But the worst thing is the threats. Whenever Dad yells at her, or Mom tells her off, she will squint her eyes and mutter something about they better be careful.

***

One evening, Rachel drops her plate on the floor because Mom serves her broccoli. Dad grabs her arm. "That's it, young lady!"

"Let go of me!" Rachel screams. "I'll kill you!"

Complete silence falls over the room.

Dad glares at her. "What did you say?"

Rachel shows her tiny teeth in something Calvin can't decide whether is a smile or a sneer, but she doesn't say anything, she just gets up and goes to her room.

Calvin recalls something from the séance.

"How did your parents die, Elmer?"

"They got their throats cut open with a knife."

Calvin feels invisible ants crawl up his spine. It finally sinks in just how serious the situation is. He has been secretly hoping things would go back to normal on their own, but now he cannot sit idly by anymore; he has got to do something.

***

Later that evening he searches for Elmer Hedrick online. He doesn't really get anything of interest before he adds "killed parents."

He finds a reference to a book called *Young Killers of the Century*.

Calvin hurries down to the library, finds the book and leafs through the pages until he finds the chapter on Elmer Hedrick. With a thumping heart, he reads the text.

Elmer Hedrick is one of the youngest killers in recorded history, being only ten years of age when he murdered both his parents. He wasn't sentenced until three years later, though, since another boy was initially blamed for the crime.

On the night of the killings, Elmer was found by the police, sobbing and petrified, telling them the boy next door had done it. And the police accordingly found the bloody knife in the room of the neighbors' child.

The innocent boy was sent to a correctional facility, and Elmer went to live with a foster family, with whom he soon developed a strained relationship. At the age of twelve he tried to kill his foster parents, but this time he failed and was caught red-handed.

The near-murders prompted the police to reopen the old case of Elmer's biological parents. The neighbor's boy had never confessed to the crime, but kept blaming Elmer for planting the knife in his room, framing him for the murders.

During interrogation, Elmer finally admitted everything. He was sentenced to juvenile prison, but he never served a day of his punishment; he fell ill from tuberculosis and died a few days later.

Calvin reads the chapter three times over. Suddenly, everything makes sense to him—although it's almost too horrifying to believe. Rachel has been Elmer Hedrick in a previous life, and now his soul has been brought back to life—in her body!

"It's insane," he mutters.

"Are you going to borrow that book?"

Calvin gives a startle, and looks up at the librarian.

"You'd better get a move on; the library closes in five minutes."

"Uhm, no, that's okay. I don't need to borrow it."

Calvin puts the book back and goes back home, brooding all the way, trying to decide what might be the best course of action. He decides to simply confront Elmer dead-on; letting him know that Calvin is on to him. Perhaps he can even scare him away.

So, he heads straight for Rachel's room once he gets home and knocks on the door.

"Scram!" Rachel yells.

Calvin enters anyway.

Rachel is lying on the bed. "What do you want?" she sneers.

"We need to talk, Rachel."

"I don't want to talk to you. Fuck off, will you?"

Calvin doesn't go anywhere. His heart is racing. "I know who you are."

Rachel's eyes grow suspicious. "What are you on about?"

"Your name is Elmer Hedrick. You were alive more than a hundred years ago. You killed your own parents. Then you died from tuberculosis."

Rachel snorts. "You're out of your goddamn head."

"Rachel would never talk like that. You're not Rachel."

"Yes, I am. Now get out of my room."

"I'm not going anywhere until I speak to Rachel."

She sits bolt upright, glaring at him. "And what if Rachel is gone?"

Calvin swallows. "Then I want her back."

"That's not possible."

Calvin steps a little closer.

Rachel frowns. "What are you doing?"

"Rachel," he says. "Listen to my voice."

Rachel grins maliciously. "That's not going to work."

"Rachel," Calvin goes on. "When I snap my fingers, you'll wake up as yourself." He holds out his hand and makes a loud snap.

Rachel freezes, her expression goes blank. Then, she blinks and looks around. "Where ... where am I?"

Calvin's heart feels ten pounds lighter. "Is it really you, Rachel?"

She looks at him. "Calvin? What happened?"

"You were hypnotized. Don't you remember?"

"No."

He bends down and hugs her. "Never mind, it's over now. You're back."

Rachel returns the hug, holding him closely. She moves her mouth to his ear, as though to whisper something. Then, he feels a sharp pain when Rachel bites down hard on his earlobe.

"Ouch!" he yells and pulls away.

Rachel smiles grimly up at him, a trickle of blood on her lower lip. "You're such a jackass."

Calvin stares at the person on the bed, while gently touching his throbbing ear.

"You know, I've always wanted an older brother," Rachel says, wiping the blood from her lips. "Perhaps we can make it work, you and I. What do you say?"

Calvin can't say anything; he just shakes his head.

"I just need to take care of the folks," Rachel goes on. "Once they're off our cases, we can do whatever we want."

"You ... you're a psycho," Calvin whispers.

Rachel's face grows dark. "Don't call me that. Unless you want to end up the same way as them."

Calvin points a shaking finger at Rachel. "Don't you dare touch Mom or Dad. You hear me? I'll call the police on you."

Rachel throws back her head and laughs heartily. "The police? What are they going to do? Arrest your sweet little sister?" Rachel tilts her head, blinks innocently and says with a soft tone, imitating Rachel's real voice: "I would never think of doing anything like that."

Calvin can't take it anymore. He spins around and rushes out of the room.

***

Calvin tries once more to make his dad understand. He finds him in the garage.

"Dad? I really need to talk to you about something."

Dad looks up from the open hood, a streak of oil on his cheek. "Sure, what's up?"

"It's about Rachel."

Dad grabs his rag and wipes his fingers. "What about her?"

"She's not herself anymore. She's a boy named Elmer."

Dad sighs. "Come on, Calvin. I thought we went over—"

"She will try to kill you!" Calvin cuts him off. "I just heard her say it. She's going to murder you and Mom if she gets the chance."

Dad frowns. "She doesn't know what she's saying. It's the shock from the fire. The shrink told us—"

"All right, fine, it's shock. But we still need to take it seriously! What if she attacks you guys while you sleep?"

"Calm down, Calvin. Rachel would never do anything like that, shock or no shock. Besides, we already called the doctor; Mom will take her there tomorrow."

Calvin feels a little bit better. Maybe the doctor can see that something is seriously wrong with Rachel.

"Stop worrying about it," Dad says, bending down over the engine once more. "She'll be fine."

***

The doctor gives Rachel a prescription for some pills.

They seem to work; at least Rachel acts a little better the following days. In fact, she almost seems like herself again. She is once again happy and polite, and she doesn't scream or break anything. Dad and Mom seem very relieved.

But Calvin can't quite celebrate yet; he still has a nagging feeling that something isn't completely right. It's the brief glances Rachel darts him. And although she's smiling, the eyes are somehow wrong. Calvin is pretty sure it's still Elmer in there—and that he's merely pretending like the medicine is working.

His suspicion is confirmed one evening, just as he is about to go to sleep. He brushes his teeth and goes to say good night to his mom. He finds her in the kitchen, rummaging through the drawers.

"Oh, hi, Calvin," she murmurs. "Have you seen the carving knife?"

"No."

"That's weird. I used it just this evening, and now it's gone."

Goose bumps spring out all over Calvin's body. He leaves the kitchen without a word and goes straight to Rachel's room. She's already sleeping, but he opens the door without knocking and turns on the light.

He lets out a horrified gasp.

Rachel isn't sleeping; she's sitting upright in bed, grinning broadly, as though she knew he was coming.

"Where is it?" Calvin asks darkly.

Rachel shrugs, still grinning.

Calvin searches the room. He checks under the bed, in the drawers, under Rachel's pillow, behind the curtains, all the while keeping a close eye on Rachel, who just sits there, following him with her eyes, smiling.

He checks the clothes cabinet and feels something hard between Rachel's blouses. He carefully pulls out the long carving knife and turns towards the bed.

Rachel's smile is finally gone. "You shouldn't have done that. You just made the list, you know."

Calvin goes to the kitchen, where his mom is still searching for the knife. While her back is turned, he opens a random drawer and says: "Is this the one you're looking for?"

Mom turns around. "Yes! Oh, thank you, Calvin."

Calvin says good night and goes to bed, even though he's sure he won't be sleeping tonight. He knows his mom and dad won't believe him, so it's up to him to fix this. And he has an idea that just might work.

He searches online for Griselda Spinoza, but only gets results on people from Latin America. He tries Madam Spinoza instead, and finds an article from a local online paper. The headline reads: *Hypnotist charged with breach of safety.*

Madam Spinoza—whose real name is Gretchen Spooner—has been charged a legal fine after the fire, because candles were forbidden at the fair. Spooner, however, claims she has lost her memory due to shock and that she recalls nothing about lighting a candle. The article concludes by noting that this is not the first time Spooner is in legal trouble, but has had several run-ins with the law on account of fraud and tax evasion.

Calvin makes a search for Gretchen Spooner and finds an address here in town. It's not that far; he can make it on his bike.

Now, he just needs to wait. He opens his door slightly ajar, lies down on his bed, listening intently for any sounds. If he hears anything from Rachel's room or sees her in the hallway, he'll be ready.

But Rachel doesn't leave her room.

At half past eleven, he hears his mom and dad go to bed. He waits a little longer, till he's certain they are asleep. Then, he gets up and slips through the house and out into the garage. He finds his dad's duct tape and brings it back to Rachel's door, which he gently opens. He can hear her snoring softly in the dark. He sneaks over to the bed and looks down at her sleeping face.

He yanks a piece of tape off the roll, making a slight noise. Rachel moves. Calvin presses the tape hard across her mouth. Rachel opens her eyes and starts writhing and fighting to get free. But Calvin is stronger. He holds her down and tapes together her hands and feet. Finally, Rachel stops squirming and stares up at him, panting behind the tape.

"Sorry, Rachel," he whispers. "I had to do it."

He leaves the room and closes the door behind him.

***

It's a twenty-minutes bike ride to Gretchen Spooner's house. The city is mostly sleeping, only a few cars on the roads.

It's a small, terraced house with dark windows. He checks the name on the mailbox before he knocks on the door. No answer. Calvin knocks again, louder. Still, no one opens.

Calvin doesn't intend to give up. He bangs on the door repeatedly.

Suddenly, the nearest window lights up. A moment later, someone fumbles with the lock, and the door opens. A wrinkly face with messy hair peers out at him. "What's going on? Who are you? Whadda you want?"

Calvin notices the accent is gone.

"Do you remember me?" he asks. "You hypnotized my little sister a few weeks ago, right before your tent burnt down."

The old lady shakes her head. "You have the wrong house, kid."

She's about to close the door, but Calvin puts his foot in the crack. "Aren't you Madam Spinoza?"

"No. That's just a character I play."

"You need to help me. My sister is still hypnotized. She thinks she's Elmer, that boy you brought forth in her. She's planning to hurt my parents. I've tried to wake her up, but it doesn't work."

Gretchen Spooner eyes him through the gap. "Hypnosis isn't real, it's just trickery. There are no such thing as previous lives. Your sister just got a fixed idea."

"No," Calvin says firmly. "I can see it in her eyes. You did something to her, and you're the only one who can undo it. If you're not going to help me, I'll go to the police."

The old lady's eyes grow a little wider. "The police?"

"I'll tell them you lied about your memory. I'll tell them you remember exactly what happened, and that you were the one lighting the candle."

Gretchen Spooner stares at him for a moment. Then, she opens the door with a sigh. "Come on in, kid."

Calvin steps into a hall reeking of cigarette smoke. The woman is dressed in a worn-out robe. He follows her as she trudges out into the kitchen, slumps down on a chair and lights up a cigarette.

Calvin looks at her with mild disgust. "So, it was all just an act?"

"It's a show," Gretchen Spooner says, blowing out smoke and coughing. "I entertain people."

"You deceive them. You pretended to be from a foreign country."

The woman laughs dryly. "Well, I'm actually born and raised right here in town. And I'm only sixty-two, I just smoke too many cigarettes."

"It's a dangerous thing you're doing."

"I know, but it's really hard to quit."

"I'm not talking about the cigarettes; I'm talking about the hypnosis! You're messing with people's heads."

Gretchen Spooner purses her lips. "It's not my fault people are naïve."

Calvin is furious, but he bites his tongue; he still needs her help. "Are you coming, then? We don't have all night."

"Coming where?"

"To my house. You have to snap your fingers, so Rachel can wake up."

The lady groans.

"If you don't come, I'll call the police," Calvin says, showing his phone.

Gretchen Spooner eyes him crossly, before stubbing out the cigarette. "Fine. But afterwards you'll leave me alone."

Gretchen Spooner has an old, smelly car, which they drive to Calvin's house.

He unlocks the door and whispers: "Be quiet, we can't wake up my parents."

Gretchen Spooner nods. She is wearing her costume on Calvin's demand. It has got to seem real to Rachel, or it might not work.

"Remember the accent," he tells Gretchen over his shoulder. "She needs to believe you really are a hypnotist."

"Yeah, yeah," Gretchen hisses. "I know the role, don't worry, kid."

He leads her to Rachel's room, opens the door and—

He freezes on the spot.

Rachel is gone. Only bits of tape are spread around the bed.

"Oh, no ..." He steps into the room, looking around. Rachel is nowhere to be seen.

"Where is she?" Gretchen asks, coming into the room.

"I don't know, she's not here. She must have escaped. She's probably—"

"Are you guys looking for me?"

Calvin spins around to see Rachel standing in the doorway, smiling. She's wearing Calvin's T-shirt for some reason, and she's holding something long and shiny in her hand. It's the carving knife.

"Rachel," Calvin croaks. "Don't do anything stupid, all right? We've come to help you."

"I don't need your help," Rachel sneers, stepping into the room. "In fact, I already fixed everything all on my own."

"Put down the knife, Rachel."

To his astonishment, Rachel actually drops the knife and steps back.

Calvin leaps forward, bending down and grabbing the knife. Not until he holds it in his hand does he realize it's covered in blood. A sharp pang of fear shoots through him. "What ... what did you do?"

"I didn't do anything," Rachel smiles innocently. She pulls off the T-shirt and throws it at him. "But you, on the other hand ..."

Calvin catches the T-shirt, realizing that too is drenched in blood. Something flies through his mind. Rachel—or rather, Elmer—saying: "*I made it look like someone else did it.*"

And suddenly, he hears the sirens in the distance. Calvin looks down at his hand holding the bloody knife, his prints are all over the handle. And the blood ... where is all that blood coming from?

"I won't have anything to do with this," Gretchen says, bolting for the door. "I wasn't even here." She squeezes past Rachel and runs down the hallway. A moment later, the front door slams, and a car engine roars in the driveway.

Calvin just stands there, staring at Rachel, as the sound of the sirens grows steadily louder. Rachel casually walks past him, lying down on the bed and pulling the blanket over herself.

"It was you," Calvin hears himself mutter. "You called the police."

"Of course, I did," Rachel says. "You tried to kill me, like you killed them."

Calvin finally drops the knife. He staggers down the hallway to his parents' bedroom, his legs wobbly, his eyes watering. He's afraid to open the door, but he has to, he can't help it.

Calvin turns the handle, pushes open the door and begins to scream.

The sound is mixed with the sirens, as the police cars turn up into the driveway.

***

I have never really believed in hypnotism, but I always thought it was creepy. I probably wouldn't try it myself if I got the chance. Even though most hypnotists are just entertainers who can make people walk and talk like a chicken, they might by accident trigger something deeper and darker. Who knows what might come forth? Who knows who I might have been before ...?

The Teacher from Outer Space

A short letter shows up in the mail one day.

To Tommy and his parents,
It has come to our attention that certain rumors are circulating the school. The nature of these rumors is quite sinister, and we regret very much to find that Tommy is the one behind them. The school has a very strict non-tolerance towards matters such as this. Therefore, we hereby summon Tommy and his parents for a school-home conversation tomorrow at five.
Kind regards,
The teachers.

Dad looks at Tommy. "Do you know anything about this?"

Tommy reads the letter with growing disbelief, shaking his head. "I have no idea what rumors they are talking about, but I sure didn't start any. I swear."

"It must be a mistake," Mom says. "Tommy would never do such a thing."

It's true; Tommy is a really good student. He hands in his assignments on time, he raises his hand before speaking in class, he plays by the rules at PE, he doesn't bully anyone and he has never started a rumor.

***

The next day, he tells Nathan about the letter.

"Don't go," Nathan says, his eyes growing wide. "Don't you remember Johan?"

"Johan?"

"Yes, Johan. That kid with the chipped tooth."

"Oh, right. What about him?"

"He was also called in for a school-home conversation."

"And?"

"And then he disappeared! The next day he was gone—poof!—just like that. No one ever saw him again."

"Please, Nate," Tommy says. "That's ridiculous—he just moved to another school."

Nathan darts a glance around the schoolyard, as if to make sure no one is listening. Then, he stares at Tommy again. "That's what they *said*. But really, something much worse happened to him."

"And what's that?"

Nathan shakes his head slowly and with emphasis. "I don't know; no one knows. All I know is Johan isn't the only one. My older brother says a boy from his class also went missing after he was called in."

Tommy scuffs. "That's all in your head, Nate. You don't even know why they called me in."

"Yeah, I do." Nathan lowers his voice. "Don't you remember? What we drew on the blackboard?"

Tommy thinks for a moment, then he recalls the incident. One day at recess, he drew an alien on the blackboard. Nathan came in to the classroom, saw the drawing, laughed out loud and drew an arrow pointing at the alien. At the end of the arrow, he wrote: Edgar. That's their math teacher. Tommy intended to erase the drawing before recess ended, but he forgot.

Edgar came in, whistling as always, and saw the drawing. The short, heavyset man turned red in the face and rushed out of class, only to return shortly with Principal Liz. They talked together in hushed voices for a moment, then Liz turned and asked sharply who drew the alien.

Tommy was just about to raise his hand, but Nathan grabbed his arm.

No one said anything.

Finally, Liz had left again, and Edgar erased the drawing with brisk strokes and started teaching—although he seemed even more weird than usual.

"But it was just a drawing," Tommy said. "And the teachers don't know who drew it."

"Someone must have told. And it wasn't just a drawing, dude—it was *the truth*."

Tommy wrinkles his nose. "What are you talking about? Do you seriously believe Edgar is an alien?"

Nathan shushes him and darts another look around before leaning closer and whispering hoarsely: "That was what Johan discovered. Didn't you hear him talking about it? He went about telling everyone that Edgar was an alien from outer space."

"And how would he know?"

"I don't know; he probably saw something."

Tommy's mouth is suddenly very dry. "You're messing with me," he murmurs.

Nathan looks scared. "I wish, dude. Everyone one who knows about the secret disappears. The teachers get rid of them."

"Come on," Tommy says, attempting to laugh. "This can't be real, it's just some crazy—"

Nathan grabs his arm, squeezing hard. "You have to deny it. When they ask you. Pretend like you drew it as a joke. Make them believe you're not suspicious about Edgar. Maybe you're lucky and they believe you. Maybe they won't make you disappear." He swallows audibly. "But no matter what you do ... don't tell them I was the one who wrote Edgar's name on the blackboard. Okay?"

Nathan eyes him for a second, searching for his voice. "Why did you do it? If it's really that dangerous?"

"I didn't believe it was true, just like you don't. But then my brother told me about Johan."

Tommy is pretty sure Nathan's big brother has played a trick on him. And if so, Nathan has fallen for it hook, line and sinker, because he looks genuinely terrified. "Promise not to mention my name," he pleads. "No matter how hard they press you ..."

Tommy promises.

***

The next day, Tommy and his parents arrive at the school five minutes to five. It's late spring, the sun has already gone down, and the school yard is only dimly lit. The windows to the teachers' room, however, are fully lit up, and Tommy can make out a few figures in there.

"I hope we won't have to stay for long," Mom says, shuttering in the cold.

"I'm sure it's all just a misunderstanding," Dad says.

Entering through the main entrance, they find the hallway empty and dimly lit. It's a weird feeling for Tommy, being at the school after hours. They stop by the door to the teachers' lounge.

"Well," Mom says, looking at Tommy. "You'd better go first. Don't forget to knock now."

Tommy steps forward, hesitantly, and raises his hand to knock, as the door is torn open. A tall, boney lady stares down at him through a pair of halfmoon-shaped glasses.

"Hello, Tommy," Liz says, the shadow of a smile flickering across the tight lips. "Please, come in."

She steps aside, making room for Tommy to enter, and he steps past her. A huge, oval table, laid out with cookies and coffee, takes up most of the room. The teachers are all perched around it—all of them. Not just two or three, as Tommy might have expected; every single one, including the janitor and the school nurse. And they are all turning their heads to look at him simultaneously.

Tommy forces a cramped smile, as his mom and dad shake hands with Liz behind him.

"You can put your coats on the rack," the principal says, pointing.

Tommy and his parents obey.

"That's a lot of people," Dad says, looking around.

"We all wanted to be here for this," Liz says. "We do take matters such as these very seriously. That being said, I'm sure we can find a way to work it out. Please, be seated."

It's no trouble deciding where to sit, since there are only three empty chairs, and Tommy is glad that he gets the middle one, between his mom and dad.

"All right then," Liz says, sitting down at the end of the table. In front of her are a few items meticulously placed: a closed laptop, a shiny black folder and a pen. Liz rests her elbows on the table. "We all know the reason for this meeting ..."

Dad clears his throat. "Actually, it's not quite clear to me yet. I know it said in the letter it's about some rumors, but Tommy assures us—"

"Rumors, yes," Liz interrupts. "We'll get to the details in just a moment, but first we need to make sure no errors have been made." She opens the folder and looks at the first paper. "Can you confirm that your names are Penny and Rupert Halloway, the parents of Tommy?"

Mom and Dad exchange a look. "Uhm ... well, yeah," Mom says.

"You reside at 2811 Sycamore Road?"

"Yes."

"Do you have other children besides Tommy?"

"No."

"Is Tommy your biological son? He's not adopted or placed in foster—"

"Of course he's our biological son," Dad exclaims. "Excuse me for asking, but what's the point of all these questions?"

Liz doesn't answer, she simply turns her attention to Tommy. "Your name is Tommy Halloway. Your social security number is ..." She reads out the numbers. "You attend fourth grade at this school. Edgar Sherwin is your math teacher. Correct?"

"Yes," Tommy says meekly. He darts a look around and finds Edgar sitting opposite the table from him. The math teacher is hunched over on his chair, fumbling with his pen, looking as though he's trying to avoid any attention.

Liz licks the tip of her red-nailed index finger with an equally red tongue tip and flips the page. "Now, concerning the rumors." She takes out the page, studies it briefly with a look of disgust on her face, then puts it down on the table and pushes it in front of Tommy and his parents.

It's a collage of photos showing the blackboard with Tommy's drawing on it from different angles. Tommy's stomach tightens up.

"Is that all?" his dad mutters.

"Bullying!" Liz erupts, eyeing Dad fiercely. "Bullying of the worst kind. That drawing is malicious and hurtful. Not only does it imply that our dear Edgar belongs to a foreign species, but also that he originates from another planet. And that he ..." Liz glances at the photos, a row of thin wrinkles appearing atop her nose. "That he has four arms and an extra eye in the middle of his forehead." She straightens up. "I don't think any of us would appreciate being depicted like that."

A brief choir of confirming muttering and nodding from the rest of the staff.

Liz folds her thin hands, resting them on the folder. "I will ask you now, Tommy, and you will be wise not to lie." She stares at him penetratingly. "Did you make that drawing?"

Tommy is at a loss. He knows he's not supposed to lie, but the situation is completely surreal, it's like being in a cross examination. The entire staff is staring at him, their eyes gleaming with morbid anticipation. What will they do if his confesses?

Suddenly, he recalls Nathan's voice: "*And then he disappeared! The next day he was gone—poof!—just like that. No one ever saw him again.*"

He looks at Mom, then at Dad. Then, he breaths deeply and says: "Yes. I did it. I made the drawing."

A rush goes through the room, and the teachers start mumbling and exchanging grave looks.

"Is that true, Tommy?" Mom asks.

Before Tommy can answer, Liz demands: "Silence!"

Complete stillness settles over the room. Everyone is looking at the principal, awaiting her judgement.

She looks at Tommy, a measured smile on her face. "I'm pleased you confess, Tommy. That will save us quite some time and effort. Your honesty will not be forgotten as we now mete out your punishment."

"His *punishment*?" Dad asks. "Do you mean detention?"

"I don't mean detention," Liz says calmly. "The penalty for bullying is a lot more severe than that. I'm afraid we will have to move Tommy to another school."

"*What*?" This time, the outburst comes from Mom. "Is that really necessary? I mean, it's only a drawing ..."

"Only a drawing?" a new voice chimes in—Osmond, the biology teacher. "That thing is the most horrendous piece of filth I've ever seen, and you people keep talking about it like it's nothing!"

"That's right!" Claire, the art teacher, interjects. "And it's not even very well done. The golden ratio is way off."

"Look, there's no reason to get so upset," Dad tries. "Tommy didn't mean anything by it ..."

Dad goes on, but the rest is drowned out by more of the teachers voicing their opinion. Dad raises his voice, and so do the teachers, making Mom start shouting too. Liz calls for order, but no one hears her.

Tommy is suddenly afraid; very afraid. He's afraid that Nathan might be right. That the teachers might make him disappear. He has to put this right. He stands up and screams: "*I didn't draw the arrow!*"

The heated discussion dies down at once. Everyone shuts up and looks at Tommy.

Liz leans forward. "What did you say, Tommy?"

"The arrow and the name," Tommy says, pointing to the page with the photos. "That wasn't me, they were added later. I only drew the alien, but I wasn't trying to depict Edgar or anyone else—it was just an alien!"

A wave of uncertain murmurs floats through the room.

Liz doesn't take her eyes off Tommy. "Is that true?"

"Yes!"

She smacks her lips, then consults another page in the folder. "The drawing was done on Monday November 11 at the nine o'clock recess. Several witnesses saw you draw it."

"I know, I already confessed to that. But I didn't draw the arrow." Tommy emphasizes every word by tapping his finger onto the table.

Then, he and everybody else look at the principal for a reaction.

Liz drums the table thoughtfully with her bloodred nails as she surveys the crowd. "If that's true, if Tommy really didn't draw that arrow or write Edgar's name, then he isn't really the defendant in this case. Although it's not exactly considered proper behavior to draw at the blackboard as a recess pastime activity, no rules specifically prohibit it."

Tommy breathes a sigh of relief.

The teachers exchange hesitant glances, some of them even look embarrassed.

"Great," Dad says, getting up. "Are we free to leave then? Actually, I believe you owe my son an apology. This charade was more like a court trial than a home-school conversation, to be honest."

Liz looks at Dad with narrow eyes. "We withdrew our charge; that will be enough of an apology."

Dad snorts. "Come on, let's get out of here."

Tommy and Mom stand up.

"The meeting has not been adjourned!" Liz's voice cuts through the room like an axe.

Dad turns to face her. "Why not?"

Liz turns her neck and looks at Tommy, her eyes like ice. "Because Tommy still hasn't told us who the true culprit is."

Tommy feels the relief seep out of him. "How ... how should I know?"

"Please, sit back down."

Tommy glances at his mom and dad. They all three obey reluctantly.

"You confessed to making the drawing," Liz goes on. "How long did it take?"

"Uhm ... I don't know. A couple of minutes, I guess."

"A couple of minutes." Liz jots down a note with her pen. "The nine o'clock recess is twenty minutes. What did you do in the remaining eighteen minutes?"

Tommy shrugs. "I really can't remember. I ... I guess I was just ... walking around."

"Inside or out?"

Tommy tries to recall. "Outside, I think."

"Are you sure? Because the weather wasn't really that good." Liz reads from a page. "Heavy rain before noon, strong breeze to high wind. That's the weather forecast for that day."

"All right, I guess I was inside, then," Tommy murmurs.

"In your classroom?"

"Maybe. I can't recall."

"Do you usually eat lunch at the nine o'clock recess?"

"Sometimes."

"A witness saw you eating a tuna fish sandwich in the classroom at around 9:17."

Tommy can't believe this is real, the whole scene is completely ludicrous. He considers if he might be dreaming ...

"Christ, did you interrogate the whole school?" Dad asks.

Liz doesn't reply to that. "At this time, the witness claims the drawing was complete, arrow, name and everything. That means you must have been in the classroom when the arrow and the name was drawn. So, I ask you once more: Are you certain you don't know who did it?"

Of course Tommy knows; he remembers the situation quite clearly. He was eating his sandwich when Nathan entered the classroom, saw the drawing and laughed. "You did that, Tommy? It looks just like Edgar!" He went to the blackboard, drew the arrow and wrote the name. "There! Perfect."

"Tommy?" Liz's voice pulls him back. "Tell me who drew the arrow."

"I ... I don't know," Tommy says.

"Yes, you do. Tell me."

"I don't know."

"Tell me!"

"I can't!"

Another rush of excited murmur.

Liz—her voice now perfectly calm once more—asks: "And *why* can't you tell me?"

"Because you'll make him move to another school!"

"So, it's a boy," Liz says, making a note. "And we can be fairly certain he's in your class, or you wouldn't have felt the need to protect him. That narrows it down quite a bit." Liz suddenly gets up and goes to the door.

For a brief moment, Tommy hopes she will ask them to leave. But instead, she flips the switch and turns off the lights. Then, she comes back to the table and turns on the screen on the wall. She sits down, opens the laptop and hits a few keys.

On the screen, Tommy's class photo appears.

"Two of the students have moved since this picture was taken," Liz begins, using the touchpad to cross out two faces with thick, red lines. "And we can get rid of all the females."

More red Xs appear on the screen. Now only seven faces are left, counting Tommy.

Liz slowly draws a circle around Tommy. "Who of your six friends drew that arrow, Tommy? Look closely at them."

Tommy's eyes glide across the screen, his heart doing a little jump as he looks at Nathan. He hurriedly looks away.

"Give us the name of the culprit, Tommy," Liz goes on. "And you can leave."

Tommy is sweating. His thoughts are running rampant, desperately looking for a way out. He suddenly has an idea. "Uhm ... I need to pee. May I be excused?"

Liz blinks and straightens up. "Very well. I expect we might be here for a little while longer, so I guess it's only reasonable to take a short break. We will meet back here in five."

***

Tommy immediately gets to his feet, his pants drenched, his knees soft, as he hurries out into the hallway.

Mom and Dad join him.

"They're out of their damned minds," Dad mutters. "I say we bolt."

"We can't," Mom hisses. "That will only make matters worse."

Dad points to the door to the teachers' lounge. "She is not going to stop until Tommy gives her that name, you know that, right?"

"Yes. And that's why I think Tommy should tell her."

Both Dad and Tommy are appalled by the notion.

"Honestly, Mom."

"You can't be serious, honey, you don't rat out your friends."

Mom plants her hands at her hips. "And why not? It's better they find the culprit than Tommy taking the fall."

"The culprit," Dad sneers. "Listen to yourself, honey. You sound like her."

"I'm just saying—"

Tommy can't listen to his mom and dad fighting right now, so he turns and leaves, striding down the hallway.

Tommy finds the toilets empty, going down to the farthest booth and locking the door. He doesn't really have to pee, so he just sits down on the lid.

His thoughts are racing back and forth. *Should I give them Nathan's name? What will happen to him if I do? What will happen to me if I refuse? And for how long—*

The stream of thoughts is interrupted as someone enters the toilet. The person is whistling a tune Tommy knows very well. It's always the same tune.

That's Edgar!

Tommy sits dead still and listens.

Edgar chooses the booth next to Tommy's, apparently not noticing the next one being locked. The sound of a zipper, and then Edgar starts to pee with a sigh of relief. At first, everything sounds normal. But then the noise rises. And rises. Until it's deafening, splashing and spurting, as though Edgar has a firehose in there.

Christ, he really needed a pee ...

Tommy bends his head down to the floor. He can see Edgar's brown shoes standing in front of the bowl, but something is wrong; the shoes are facing the wrong way. It looks like Edgar is peeing standing up—but with his back to the toilet.

Before Tommy can figure out what is going on, the noise dies out.

"Aaah," Edgar sighs.

The zipper again, then the toilet is flushed. The lock turns and the door opens. Tommy follows Edgar's shoes as they walk to the sinks. He bends down a little farther, curious to see Edgar's face for some reason.

The math teacher stops in front of the mirror. For a moment he just stands there, looking at himself. Then he puts his hand to his face, pressing a finger under the eye. He goes on to push up his nose, as though to check the inside of the nostrils. Finally, he sticks a couple of fingers in his mouth, pulling out the cheek to the point where it looks like it's about to burst, revealing the back molars. Edgar studies his mouth for a moment, then lets go of the cheek, making it snap back into place.

Tommy completely forgets to be discrete; he's lying with his face against the floor, eyeing Edgar in stupefied amazement.

The teacher proceeds to wash his hands. The display of weird behavior is apparently over, and Tommy is just about to pull his head back up, when he notices something moving on Edgar's back underneath the shirt. It wriggles downwards and pops out just above the belt.

Tommy can't believe what he's seeing.

A blue tentacle, like on a giant squid, is working its way out from under Edgar's shirt. It just keeps coming, inch after inch, reaching almost a full five feet. Then, it reaches down into his back pocket, pulls out a comb, and starts combing Edgar's hair.

Edgar just keeps washing his hands, whistling once more, as though nothing out of the ordinary is going on.

Tommy gapes as everything falls into place. Nathan's brother was right. Johan was right. Tommy is not looking at a human being, only a clever disguise. Edgar is really an—

At that exact moment, Edgar looks at Tommy in the mirror. The teacher gives a startle, the tentacle twitches and drops the comb. Tommy's heart leaps in his chest, and he pulls up his head, but it's too late. Edgar saw him.

Tommy doesn't know what to do. He just sits there, frozen, for a couple of really long seconds, holding his breath, listening to the running water.

Then, it stops. A series of footsteps rush across the floor. The door out into the hallway is ripped open and closes again.

Then there's silence.

Tommy bends down once more, peering out. He can't see Edgar's shoes anywhere. Only the comb is still lying on the floor. Edgar—or whatever it was—has left the toilet.

**

Five minutes later, Tommy steps out into the hallway on legs still shaking with shock.

He has been trying desperately to convince himself that he didn't see what he saw, but to no avail.

There are no other explanations. Edgar really is an alien.

A host of new questions are pestering Tommy's poor brain. Do the other teachers know about this? They have to, why would they defend him so vehemently if they didn't? Is it only Edgar then? Or are any other of them aliens too? Perhaps all of them?!

Tommy is cold and clammy all over from sweating profusely. What should he do? For a minute he considers climbing out the window and simply bolting. But then he remembers Mom and Dad and decides to go get them first.

He goes back to the teachers' lounge and finds the door ajar. As he approaches, a sudden blue light shines out through the opening, then disappears again. He thinks he heard something too, almost like a distant scream. But now he can only hear the teachers talking with each other.

Tommy has an excuse ready. He can't say anything that will arouse Liz's suspicion, so he will tell her he has fallen ill and that they will have to end the meeting for now.

Just as he's about to enter the teachers' lounge, he hears Liz hissing: "You have got to be more careful!"

"I said I'm sorry." That's Edgar's voice.

"No wonder we have all these problems. Now look what we had to do."

"But it's not my fault—"

"Sssh!" someone hushes loudly. "Stop talking. He'll probably be back soon."

"Right. Pretend like nothing happened."

Before Tommy can do anything, the door is suddenly ripped open. Liz grabs his arm and pulls him inside.

"Now, where were we?"

Tommy looks around timidly. All the other teachers are looking back at him. Mom and Dad's chairs are empty.

"Where ... where are my parents?" he asks.

Liz pushes him towards the table. "We felt it was better the rest of the meeting was just between you and us, so we sent your parents home. Take a seat."

Tommy stares up at her, as Liz shoves him down onto the chair. "*What*? Did they just leave without me?" He notices something on the floor. It's a broken coffee cup. He turns and points. "Why are their coats still here?"

"They forgot them," Liz says shortly. "But don't worry about them, this is about you, young man. You were about to tell us the name of the culprit."

Tommy darts a nervous glance around, the many accusatory faces all staring back at him. His eyes meet Edgar's for a brief moment, before the math teacher looks away.

Something is really wrong ...

Finally, it dawns on Tommy that Edgar told Liz what happened at the toilet. They all know that Tommy knows the secret now. And Mom and Dad ... Mom and Dad have ...

Tommy doesn't finish the thought. He jumps up and leaps for the door.

"*Stop him!*" Liz shrieks.

The sound of many chairs being pushed backwards as all the teachers get to their feet simultaneously.

Tommy doesn't turn to look, he just yanks open the door, jumps out into the hallway and makes for the exit at full sprint.

Behind him the teachers take up the pursuit. He darts a quick glance over his shoulder and sees them as they almost trip over each other to get out from the teachers' lounge. Most of them are old or in poor shape, but Johnson, the PE teacher, is young and strong and very fast. He runs so fast his tie is flapping over his shoulder.

Tommy ups his speed even more; he runs faster than he has ever done before. He runs for his life. He turns at the last second and throws himself at the glass door, pushing it open and tumbling out into the cool evening air. He charges across the schoolyard, looking back to see Johnson still at his tail, but looking very winded and losing speed.

Tommy feels a pang of wild excitement.

He's tired! I made it! They can't catch me now!

He turns around the corner of the bike shed and crashes into Agnes, the home economics teacher, although it feels more like a hippopotamus—as Agnes weighs roughly around the same as one. Tommy has the wind completely knocked out of him, and he falls to the ground, panting in pain.

Agnes bends over—with great difficulty—grabs his arm and shouts: "*He's here! I've got him!*"

Tommy tries desperately to tear himself free, but Agnes's grip is very strong, and in just a few seconds he's surrounded by the teachers. They're all panting and eyeing him maliciously in the light from the bike shed.

"Nice job, Agnes," one of them says. "Good idea to stand guard out here."

"Let me go," Tommy begs, looking up at their hard faces. "I didn't see anything. I swear!"

"He's lying." Edgar's voice is somewhere in the ring of teachers. "He saw my ... extra arm."

Liz steps forward, her hair messy from running. "We can't let you go now, Tommy. We are obliged by a contract, you see. It's a deal we've made with one of them out there." She points up at the stars. "They have one of ours, as we have one of theirs. It's like an exchange project—we're trying to learn from each other. But that secret can never get out, or there will be widespread panic."

Tommy only barely comprehends what the principal is telling him—all he can think about is what is going to happen to him. Then, suddenly, he has an idea. It may be his last chance. "It was Nathan!" he blurts out. "He drew the arrow and wrote the name! Nathan! Take him instead of me!"

Liz looks at him. "Nathan, you say?" She smiles. "You see, that wasn't so hard, was it? You could have simply told me."

For a moment, Tommy thinks she will let him go.

Then strong hands grab him from both sides.

"Hold him down," Liz says, producing a weird instrument which looks kind of like a toaster. It beeps and sends out a bright, blue light.

"*No! Stop! Let me go!*"

Tommy twists and turns, but to no avail.

Liz pushes a button and holds the instrument above Tommy's head. The blue light envelopes him, blinds him, a terrible scattering noise fills his ears. Tommy screams and closes his eyes as he feels a strong pulling sensation in his stomach.

Then, he's gone.

***

Nathan writes a lot of messages to Tommy that night.
Call me when you come home.
Is the meeting over?
How did it go?
Why aren't you answering my calls?
Come on, man. It's not funny.
Just call me, will you?
Hello?

He gets no answer and no calls from Tommy. Finally, he gives up and tries to go to sleep. Tommy probably just misplaced his phone and can't find it. Or maybe he's pulling a prank on Nathan, pretending the meeting went bad and that he has disappeared.

But it can't be true. Tommy can't be gone.

Nathan finally drifts off.

He wakes up next morning feeling sick to his stomach. Mom lets him stay home from school and leaves for work. Nathan is home alone all day. He keeps checking the windows and tries to call Tommy a bunch of times.

Suddenly, a letter comes through the mail slot.

To Nathan and his parents,
It has come to our attention that certain rumors are circulating the school. The nature of these rumors is quite sinister, and we regret very much to find that Nathan is the one behind them. The school has a very strict non-tolerance towards matters such as this. Therefore, we hereby summon Nathan and his parents for a school-home conversation tomorrow at five.
Kind regards,
The teachers.

***

My old math teacher was quite possibly an alien. At least he often acted very oddly. I never saw any proof, like a tentacle or something, but my friend and I were still convinced the guy must have been from outer space, and the very clever disguise didn't fool us for a second.

Kids have the silliest fantasies. Because it *was* only a fantasy.

At least I think so.

The Scarecrow

"Oh, come on! Not again!"

Miles looks up from his plate with mild surprise, as Tom's mom comes rushing through the kitchen.

She opens the garden door, jumps out onto the lawn, waves her arms and shouts: "Get out of here! Shoo! Shoo!"

Miles looks at Tom, one eyebrow raised. "Has your mom lost it?"

"Nah, it's the birds," Tom says, taking a bite off his sandwich. "They eat her vegetables. I don't know why she reacts like this, though …" Tom glances out at his mom, who is still yelling. "I say let them. At least they *like* all that nasty stuff … spinach and kale and shit."

"I heard that!" his mom calls, before screaming at the birds once more. "Get lost, goddamnit!"

Miles stretches his neck and sees a flock of crows sitting amongst the row of newly sprouted vegetables. They don't seem bothered by the yells of Tom's mom, though, barely looking in her direction. Not until she runs down there do they lazily take flight.

Miles also sees a scarecrow. It's sitting on a pole, not looking particularly scary. It's made out of old clothes stuffed with hay, and the head is an old pillowcase with a badly drawn smiley face on it.

"Doesn't the scarecrow work?" he asks Tom.

Tom snorts. "Would you be scared away by that stupid thing? It doesn't even resemble a human."

"Who made it?"

"My dad, and he isn't exactly the creative type."

Tom's mom comes back into the kitchen. "Stupid birds," she hisses, closing the door behind her. "If they keep coming, there'll be nothing left."

"Can't I just shoot 'em?" Tom asks. "Grandpa says I can borrow his rifle …"

"You're not touching that rifle," Tom's mom says, pointing at him. "But if you really want to help, why don't you build a scarecrow that actually works? Maybe Miles could help you."

Tom looks at Miles. "You want to?"

Miles shrugs. "Sure, why not?"

It's the fourth week of the summer holidays, and the boys are already getting bored, so Miles is actually mildly enthusiastic about the idea of something to do.

When they're done eating, they go down to Tom's dad's workshop.

"Right, where do we begin?" Tom asks, looking around. "I guess we need some wood first of all." He goes to a pile of wooden boards in the corner.

"Don't you usually make a cross?" Miles suggests. "And then you kind of dress it up."

"That's what Dad did," Tom says. "That doesn't seem like a good recipe. It needs to look *realistic*. How do we make it look like a real person?"

Miles takes out his phone. "Let's ask Google."

The boys sit down next to each other on a couple of boxes each with their phones.

Miles finds some instructions: How to build a scarecrow. It has drawings and all, but it's also based on a cross and doesn't look that good.

"Hey, check this out," Tom says, holding out his phone. "Doesn't that look neat?"

He has found a very creepy illustration of a scarecrow come to life.

"Nasty," Miles mutters. "I bet *that thing* would keep the birds away."

"I know. If you could only make a living scarecrow ..."

"You could dress up," Miles suggests teasingly. "I'm sure your ugly mug would scare anyone from coming near the vegetables."

Tom doesn't answer. He's reading something on his phone. Then, he looks up. "Wow, look at this ..."

He has found a website with the headline: *Living scarecrows – how the old European witches did it.*

"It's about witchcraft," Tom mutters and starts reading: "In the medieval times, witches were able to summon their scarecrows to life by using blood, since blood was believed to hold life-giving powers. The witches would kill an innocent person and drain them for blood. Then they would fill up the head of the scarecrow—which was made by a hollowed-out pumpkin—with the blood. The following night, the scarecrow would come to life, and the witch never again had to worry about birds or thieving neighbors, with the scarecrow protecting her entire property ..." Tom looks up, grinning. "Wouldn't that be sick if we tried it?"

Miles raises one brow. "Yeah, very sick."

"No, I mean like, it would be awesome. What if works?"

"Of course it doesn't work."

"I know, but what if?"

That was one of Tom's mantras, whenever he got a crazy idea. What if? What if you could learn to walk on the walls? What if the teacher was an alien? What if ...?

"So who would you kill to get the blood?" Miles asks.

Tom's smile fades a little. "Oh, right ... damnit, I really wanted to try."

"I guess we'll have to settle for a normal scarecrow then. Look, I found one where the arms are designed to move in the wind. That's a little realistic, right?"

Tom grudgingly accepts the model, and the boys starts working. They spend all afternoon in the workshop.

Late that evening, as he's just about to hit the sack, Miles gets a call from Tom.

"Hello?"

"Hey, man. I've got something you need to hear."

Miles can tell right away how excited Tom is. He must've gotten one of his what if-ideas.

"I know how we can get the blood."

"What blood? Oh, you're still thinking about that crazy witch-stuff?"

"Yeah. And we don't need to kill anyone."

"How so?"

"We can use our own blood!"

"No thank you. I don't feel like getting drained."

"It's not dangerous and it doesn't even hurt."

"Christ, man, I hope you're not actually thinking about cutting your wrist open or anything, 'cause that would be a really goddamned stupid—"

"Fuck, no! What do you think I am, a psycho?"

"Sometimes."

"Shut up." Tom lowers his voice. "We'll use one of my dad's syringes."

"What syringes?"

"He has to take a blood sample once a month, because of his diabetes, you know, and Mom helps him—I've seen her do it a bunch of times, it's really easy-peasy. And they have all the gear and a ton of syringes. I'm sure they won't notice if one or two goes missing."

"Your mom is a nurse," Miles reminds him. "She is trained to do that kind of stuff."

"Everyone can do it," Tom guarantees. "She even explained it to me. The trick is just to find the vein."

Miles wrinkles his nose. "That sounds a little too fucked up for me."

"Are you scared?"

"No, I just don't feel like it."

"Right, I'll do it myself then." Tom sounds offended. "But you won't get any of the glory if it turns out to be a success."

Miles can live without the glory. They say goodbye, and Miles goes to bed and dreams about living scarecrows.

Miles goes to visit Tom again the next day. Tom's parents are at work, and they have the house to themselves.

"Come see," Tom says, gesturing eagerly for Miles to follow him down to the workshop. He goes to an old fridge in the corner, opens it and carefully takes out a large plastic bottle. Something dark is slushing around the bottom of it. "I've almost got twenty ounces!"

Miles can't believe his eyes. "Is that seriously your blood?"

"It sure is. The finest vintage you'll ever find." Tom grins and pulls up his sleeve, revealing a tiny, red dot on his skin. "I got it right the first time, only needed one try."

Miles shakes his head. "You're not right in the head."

Tom just laughs. "Come on, are we going to finish it or what?"

They continue working on the scarecrow, and after a few hours, it's ready. It looks kind of like a human, except for the missing head.

"I know what you're thinking," Tom says, finding a plastic bag and pulling out a pumpkin. "Ta-daa! We just need to hollow it out."

They cut off the top of the pumpkin and start working on it with two large spoons, scooping out all the soft insides.

"How about a face?" Miles asks.

"I don't think it's a good idea, I think the blood will just spill out if we cut out a face. Besides, he will be more scary without one. Here, hold it for a moment."

Tom takes the bottle, and Miles looks at the pumpkin with disgust as Tom pours the blood down the hole in the top.

"There," he says, when the bottle is empty. "Now we just need to put it up."

Tom carries the head, and Miles takes the body.

In the garden they find the crows once more having a feast on the vegetables; a couple of them are even sitting on the shoulders of the scarecrow, as though to taunt them. They take flight as they see the boys coming.

Tom carefully puts down the pumpkin and takes down the old scarecrow. They put their own scarecrow up on the pole, and finally, they help each other place the pumpkin on top of the shoulders, securing it with duct tape.

Finally, they step back and admire their work.

"He actually looks pretty mean," Tom says excitedly. "Don't you think?"

"Kind of," Miles admits.

A sudden gust of wind rips through the garden, making the shirt of the scarecrow move and the head tilt slightly to the side.

"Shit, did you see that?" Tom whispers. "It looked just like he nodded at us. Like he was saying hello."

"It was just the wind," Miles observes.

Tom doesn't seem to hear him. "Now we just have to wait for midnight."

"Why's that?"

"Don't you remember the article? It said you had to tell the scarecrow what you wanted it to do by whispering to it by midnight."

"Come on, you're actually going to ..." But Miles stops himself as he glances at his friend. Tom is clearly not listening; his eyes are gleaming as he looks up at the scarecrow. For a moment, it actually looks like Tom honestly expects this crazy idea to work.

Miles spends the night at Tom's place. The boys stay up late, playing video games and waiting for the clock to turn twelve.

"It's time," Tom says, getting up. "Only five minutes to midnight. Are you ready?"

Miles puts down the joypad and yawns. "Can't you do it without me? I don't feel like going outside."

"Come on, you lazy bastard," Tom says, shoving him.

Miles sighs and gets up. "I can't believe I'm actually indulging your fucked-up ideas."

"Yeah right, play hard to get, but you know you want to," Tom says, smiling wryly.

The house is dark and quiet, as Tom's parents are already asleep. The boys slip out to the entrance hall, bringing their jackets and shoes to the kitchen.

Tom stops in front of the garden door for a moment. "There he is," he whispers. "Doesn't he look great in the moonlight?"

Miles gazes out, and he has to admit—yes, the scarecrow looks pretty creepy, bathed in the blueish light from the full moon, which is bright enough for casting shadows.

Tom opens the door, and they sneak out into the garden and across the lawn towards the scarecrow. Miles somehow can't take his eyes off of it. He knows it's silly, but part of him expects the thing to start moving any minute.

"Are you going to do it?" Tom whispers.

"Nah, you go ahead," Miles says, trying to sound casual.

Tom nods, swallows audibly and steps in between the rows of vegetables. He stops in front of the scarecrow and glances back at Miles, grinning. "Fuck, it's scary!"

"Just get it over with, will you? I'm freezing, I want to go back inside." Of course, Miles can't admit he's actually kind of scared.

Tom stands on his tiptoes, leans closer to the scarecrow and whispers something into where its ear should be. Then, he steps backwards and looks at the scarecrow, as though he expects something to happen. But of course, nothing does. The thing just sits there.

"Do you think it worked?" Tom whispers.

"I don't know. Can we please go back now?"

Tom reluctantly pulls himself away and they go back inside. From Tom's room they have a clear view of the vegetable garden. The scarecrow is still sitting there, looking exactly like before.

"I hope it worked," Tom says.

"Don't get your hopes up."

"Don't be such a buzzkill."

"Come on, man, you don't actually think that stupid thing is going to come alive, do you?" Miles feels more confident now, being back inside the house.

"You never know," Tom says, smiling.

"Well, I guess we'll see for ourselves," Miles says, starting to become annoyed with Tom.

"No, we won't."

"What do you mean?"

"The article said the scarecrow only moves while no one is watching."

Miles yawns and pulls off his shirt. "Whatever, man. I'm pretty tired, can we please go to sleep now?"

Tom doesn't answer, he just stares out of the window.

"Suit yourself," Miles grunts. He slips under the blanket and falls asleep almost right away.

Miles wakes up just before sunrise. He can hear the birds already singing outside, and that reminds him of the scarecrow.

He sits up and rubs his eyes. Tom is still snoring. Miles gets up and goes to the window. The garden is calm and dewy in the early twilight. The scarecrow is sitting where they left it, but Miles can make out something black and ruffled at its feet. It almost looks like ...

He needs to know for sure, so he sneaks out to the kitchen and out through the garden door. Bare-footed, he walks across the wet lawn, approaching the vegetable garden.

Already several paces away he can see that the black thing really is what he thought it was: a dead crow. It has lost a few feathers, which are scattered around it, its beak is open and the dead, beetle-black eyes are staring up at the sky.

Miles feels his stomach tighten. He looks up at the scarecrow. It sits completely still, exactly as they left it, the faceless pumpkin-head seeming to stare down at him.

Tom must have placed the bird. He's playing a sick joke on me. It can't be—

A hoarse shriek comes from above. Miles looks up and sees the crows perched on top of the old birch tree. They seem to be looking down at him, almost warningly, as though they saw what really happened to their fellow being.

"Miles?"

He turns around abruptly.

Tom is approaching him, his eyes wide and his face pale. "Is that ... is that a dead crow?"

"You tell me," Miles says. "You're the one who put it here, right?"

Tom frowns briefly at him, before staring at the dead bird. "Why the fuck would I do that?"

"To scare me, of course."

"I didn't put it here. Shit, is it really dead?"

"Oh, yeah, it's dead all right. So, you didn't come out here after I fell asleep?"

"No, I fell asleep right after you did."

"You sure about that? If this is a prank, it's not funny, Tom."

Tom looks at him earnestly. "I haven't been outside, okay? How would I even catch a bird and kill it? Shit, it must have been the scarecrow ..."

"Maybe it ... maybe it just died of old age," Miles mutters. "Hey, what are you doing?"

Tom has gone to the bird and is now crouching down, picking it up. "Its neck is broken," he whispers, holding up the crow for Miles to see. The head is hanging limply to the side.

Miles pulls back a little. "Well, it probably flew into something, and that's how it broke its neck. Birds do that all the time."

"Flew into *what*?" Tom says, stretching out his arms and looking around.

There is nothing nearby tall enough for the bird to have flown into.

"I don't know," Miles says, hearing the trace of annoyance in his own voice. "Maybe it hit the house but didn't die right away, so it flew back over here. How should I know? All I know is, that thing didn't kill it." He points at the scarecrow.

Tom doesn't seem to be listening. "Holy crap, I think it really worked. Do you know what this means, Miles? Witchcraft is *real*!"

Miles scoffs. "Get a grip, man. You've been watching too much Harry Potter."

"We can be famous," Tom goes on, unabashed. "We can make millions of dollars on this. We can—"

Miles grabs his arm hard. "Snap out of it, will you? You're a moron if you really believe that thing killed the bird. That kind of shit simply doesn't happen."

Tom's expression changes to one of mild insult, and he rips himself free. "Fine, then. We'll just have to wait and see if it kills any more birds."

"And how will you do that? It's only supposed to move when no one is watching, remember?"

"Oh, right." Tom thinks for a moment, then he grabs Miles and pulls him back into the house.

"What is it?" Miles asks, as Tom shuts the garden door behind them.

"We don't need to watch it," Tom says, smiling eagerly and pointing at his computer. "We can just record it!"

The boys put up the webcam in the window, making sure the scarecrow is in full view, and start the recording.

After breakfast, they decide to go to the park and practice baseball. They spend a few hours at the park, swinging away, laughing and not thinking about dead birds.

At lunchtime they go back to the house, and as soon as they open the front door, the raised voices of Tom's parents meet them from the kitchen.

"I'm telling you, I didn't use poison," Tom's dad says, sounding annoyed.

"Well, how do you explain it, then?" Tom's mom asks accusatorily.

"I can't explain it! For all I know, one of the neighbors might be going around shooting the damn things."

"Did you hear any shots fired? Because I didn't."

"No, but—"

The conversation stops abruptly as the boys enter the kitchen.

"Tom," his mom says. "Do you know anything about the birds?"

"What birds?" Tom asks, darting a quick glance at Miles.

"The dead birds in the vegetable garden. I found five of them. I had to bury them."

Miles feels an involuntary shiver, and Tom is apparently too stunned to answer. His mom doesn't notice, though, as she turns again to Tom's dad.

"What if it's some sort of disease? Like bird flu, or something. Isn't that dangerous? Maybe we should call someone."

"Let's not overreact," Tom's dad says. "We don't know what it is, so we might as well wait and see if it happens again …"

Miles doesn't hear any more of the conversation, as Tom grabs him by the arm and pulls him through the house and into his room, locking the door behind them.

"Fuck, fuck, fuck," he mutters, running to the computer. "I can't wait to watch it!"

"Do you … do you think it actually caught it?" Miles asks, not sounding nearly as critical as he hoped.

"Of course it did. Come look!"

Miles stands beside Tom, as Tom starts the recorded movie. It's a little over four hours long. The first few minutes, nothing happens; the scarecrow is just standing there, the shirt moving seamlessly in the breeze.

"Can you fast-forward?" Miles suggests.

Tom ups the speed of the movie. Half an hour passes, an hour—and suddenly, something grey appears on the ground.

"Stop!" Miles says, pointing. "What's that?"

"I don't know, I didn't see what happened."

"Go back."

Tom jumps back a couple of minutes. The grey lump disappears. He starts the movie again at normal speed. Miles becomes aware he's shaking slightly, as they both stare intensely at the screen.

A pigeon lands on the lawn. It waddles about a bit, nipping at the grass. Then, it wanders into the vegetable garden. It is just about to eat off the lettuce, when—

The movie cuts.

The next instant, the pigeon is transformed into the dead, grey lump.

"What?" Tom exclaims. "What happened?"

"It was a glip," Miles says. "Try running it again."

Tom jumps back and plays the scene again, but the same thing happens.

"Damnit," Tom says. "Something must have happened with the camera. Stupid thing!"

"Go to the next bird, then," Miles says.

Tom fast-forwards until a dead blackbird appears. But when he goes back to play the previous minute, the same thing happens as with the pigeon: the bird is alive, the recording skips a few seconds, and the bird is dead.

"It can't be!" Tom shouts angrily. "What are the odds? Two glips with the worst possible timing."

Miles is starting to feel pretty sure they won't see any of the birds dying.

Tom finds the next bird, another pigeon. Same problem. The last two birds are magpies, and they die simultaneously in another glip.

Tom sinks back in the chair, disheartened, and says exactly what Miles is thinking: "It can't be a coincidence—it must be the witchcraft doing it."

"So, we can't see the thing moving directly, and we can't film it either," Miles concludes. "Any other ideas?"

Tom bites his lip. "Well," he says slowly. "Maybe we could just ask it for a proof?"

Miles frowns. "Do you really think that would work?"

"It's supposed to do our bidding, right? We'll simply wait for midnight and command it to give us proof that it's alive."

Miles looks out the window at the scarecrow but doesn't answer.

Miles spends another night at Tom's place. At midnight, they once again leave the house through the kitchen door, and Tom once again whispers into the nonexistent ear of the scarecrow. Miles is shaking all over as they go back into the house, and it's not just because of the cold night air.

"How do you think it will give us the proof?" Tom says as they crawl back into bed.

"I have no idea," Miles says, feeling sure he won't get any sleep this night.

But he does fall asleep, and he is awakened a few hours later, while it's still dark.

Was that a noise?

He turns his head on the pillow, listening to the quiet of the room. There's a soft creak nearby, as someone steps carefully on the floor. Miles is still halfway asleep, but then he remembers the scarecrow and is instantly thrown into full wakefulness.

He lifts his head and looks to Tom's bed, where he can just make out his friend, snoring with an open mouth.

Another creak from the floor. Miles sits up with a jolt and stares into the darkness. His eyes can't make out the details, but he's pretty sure someone is standing there.

"He ... hello?" he croaks. "Who's there?"

A long pause. Miles's heart is thumping wildly. Then, another creak, closer this time.

Miles can't take it anymore. He jumps to his feet, throws himself at the light by Tom's bed, fumbling to find the switch, and—

Miles thinks his heart is going to explode.

Right in the middle of the room, by the foot of Miles's mattress, the scarecrow is standing. It looks all wrong, like a badly Photoshopped picture, except it's not a picture. Miles can smell the hay and the old clothes and dirt.

"What are you doing?" Tom grunts. "Why did you turn on the—oh, shit! How did that come in here?"

Miles tries to answer him, but his mouth is too dry.

"Can you ... can you speak?" Tom asks, getting out of bed. For a brief moment, Miles thinks he's talking to him, but he's looking at the scarecrow. "Please answer me if you can speak."

The scarecrow doesn't answer, and it doesn't move an inch. It's simply standing there, completely still, balancing on its fake feet. Tom steps a little closer.

"Careful," Miles manages to hiss.

"It didn't come here to hurt us," Tom reminds him. "It just came to prove it's alive."

"Then why did it come sneaking in like that?"

"Because it didn't want to wake up the whole house. We are the only ones who are supposed to see it." Tom walks around the scarecrow a couple of times, admiring it. Then, he grins widely at Miles. "Well, what more proof do you need?"

Miles just shakes his head. "How do we get it out of here? I'm not touching it."

"We don't need to," Tom says confidently. "We just turn our backs. Go on, look the other way!"

Miles eyes the scarecrow. The last thing he wants is to take his eyes away from it, offering it a chance to move. But Tom, who is standing with his back to the scarecrow, looks at him encouragingly.

Miles forces himself to look down at his feet. Almost instantly, he hears a rustle of hay, a series of fast-paced footsteps leaving the room, and the sound of the door closing. When he looks up again, the scarecrow is gone.

Tom turns around and laughs. "Holy shit, it really worked!" He goes to the window and points. "Look at that! It's already back on the pole." He turns and looks beamingly at Miles. "Wasn't that just the coolest fucking thing you ever saw?"

Miles stares at him in disbelief, realizing he is shaking all over. He barely recognizes his friend anymore. "Cool?" he says. "You think that was cool?"

"Yes, of course, I—"

"That was fucking unnatural, that's what it was," Miles says loudly.

"Keep it down," Tom says. "My parents—"

"I don't give a fuck about your parents," Miles interrupts. "We should call the fucking police—no, better yet, we should go out right now and burn that nasty thing!"

Tom's expression hardens. "Why would you do that?"

"Because, we've made something that's not supposed to be alive! It's fucking dangerous! It knows how to kill things. And didn't you hear how fast it moved? It's like a predator or some shit …"

"Come on," Tom says. "You sound like a pussy. What are you even afraid of? It's not going to harm us; we are its masters."

Miles shakes his head, starting to put on his clothes. "You've fucking lost it, man. I'm not taking any more part in this."

"Fine," Tom says immediately. "But you won't get any of the credit."

"Keep your fucking credit," Miles sneers and leaves the room, slamming the door behind him. He is so mad, he walks all the way home.

Miles doesn't hear from Tom for several days.

It's weird. They've had arguments like this before, whenever Tom gets obsessed with a crazy idea, but he usually calls Miles as soon as he cools down to make friends again.

Miles is actually starting to worry. So finally, he swallows his pride and calls up Tom.

"*Hello?*" Tom answers, sounding tired.

"Hey," Miles says testily. "What's up? How's it going?"

"*Not so good. I can't make it work anymore.*"

"How come?"

"*No idea. It has just stopped doing what I tell it. It just hangs out there on its pole all day. It's not even killing the birds anymore. I don't know, it's like the magic has run out or something.*"

"That's weird," Miles says, but actually feeling a great deal of relief. Perhaps this whole deal is over, and they can forget it ever happened. Of course, he knows Tom isn't going to let it go that easily.

"*I'm going to try with more blood,*" he says. "*Maybe it's dried up, and it just needs a refill.*"

"Hmmm," Miles says. "You sure it's a good idea?"

"*Sure, why not? It worked once.*"

"I suppose so."

"*I'm doing it tonight,*" Tom says, a slight hesitation in his voice. "*Do you … want to come over and help?*"

"I think I'll pass. But … I can come by tomorrow? You can tell me how it went."

"*Okay,*" Tom says brightly. "*See you then, buddy.*"

Miles can't fall asleep that night. He has a nagging feeling in his chest, a feeling that something bad is going to happen. He can't quite put his finger on it though.

He twists and turns, keeps checking his phone, like he expects Tom to call him up anytime soon. It's almost twelve o'clock, which means Tom has probably already filled up the head of the scarecrow with the new portion of his own blood and is just about to sneak outside to whisper a command to it.

Should I have gone there? Was it a mistake to say no? If something bad is going to happen to Tom, maybe I could have helped him.

Miles tries to tell himself he's being silly. That Tom is probably all right.

But he can't convince himself, and finally he gets up and gets dressed.

He takes his bike and rides to Tom's house. Already at a distance he can see the blue lights blinking. An ambulance and two police cars are parked in front of the house.

Oh, no!

Miles runs around to the backyard. A lot of policemen are standing around. The vegetable garden has been sealed off with yellow tape, the scarecrow is sitting on its pole, looking innocent.

"What are you doing here, kid?" An officer grabs his arm.

"I was looking for my friend, Tom."

The officer frowns. "Who's Tom?"

"He lives here in this house."

"Oh, you mean that guy?" The officer points towards the vegetable garden. And suddenly, Miles can see the person lying on the ground in front of the scarecrow. The officer lets go of his arm, and Miles walks closer, afraid of what he's about to see, but unable to stop himself.

It's Tom. He's lying splayed out on the ground, his neck is obviously broken, and the eyes are staring right up at Miles.

Miles starts to scream and—

—sits up in bed.

He looks wildly around the room but finds nothing out of the ordinary.

"A nightmare," he pants. "Only a nightmare."

He finds his phone. No messages from Tom. It's half past two.

Miles lies back down, trying to go back to sleep, but his mind is racing, and he can't forget about the dream. It had seemed so real; almost like a premonition.

Suddenly, he remembers something and sits up again.

"No, that can't be true," he whispers to the empty room. "It didn't say ..."

Miles grabs his phone and finds the website with the article about how the witches made the scarecrows come alive. He scrolls down over the text, stopping at the small paragraph at the bottom.

Some witches would use their own blood, but that turned out to be a horrible mistake. Although at first it seems to work, the scarecrow will soon stop following commands, and on the sixth night it will be able to break free of the spell by killing the person from which the blood came, thereby gaining its own freedom.

Miles stares at the text for a few very long seconds, as he tries to remember how many days have passed since they built the scarecrow. He's not sure, but it could be six.

He jumps out of bed, feeling a strong sense of déjà-vu as he gets dressed, leaves the house and rides his bike to Tom's house.

But this time, no ambulances or police cars are in the driveway. Miles feels a faint hope, but he still needs to know for sure if Tom is all right, so he goes up to the house, finding to his surprise the front door open.

Miles carefully pushes it open and enters the house. He goes to Tom's room, stopping in front of the door, his heart pumping right under his chin. He turns the knob and opens the door very carefully, trying not to make the slightest sound.

He can make out Tom's figure in bed and feels a stab of relief.

He's okay ...

As he enters the room and is about to shake Tom awake, he glances out the window and sees the pole in the vegetable garden empty. Miles stops in his tracks.

Where did it go?

The thought makes him turn around, but no one is in the room, and the house is dead quiet. In fact, he can't even hear Tom snoring. He glares at Tom's figure under the blanket, only the top of the head is visible. Is Tom even breathing?

Miles remembers the front door being open. Had someone left the house right before he came? Someone ... or something?

Miles suddenly can't move his feet. Instead, he croaks: "Tom?"

He gets no answer.

"Tom!" he says loudly, hearing the fear in his own voice. "Wake up!"

The person in the bed doesn't move an inch.

Miles's eyes fall on the night-light. He reaches out his hand and finds the switch. And right before he presses it, a weird sense of clear-headedness comes over him.

He already knows what the light will show him. He has already seen it in the dream. Tom's face will be white. His eyes will be staring dead up at nothing. The neck will be broken, just like the birds.

Miles flips the switch, sees his dead friend and opens his mouth to scream.

But at that moment, he catches a reflection in the black glass of the window and turns his head just in time to see the tall, human-shaped figure step out from behind the door and approach him from behind with unnatural speed.

He doesn't have time to turn around, though, before the scarecrow grabs his head and twists it violently halfway around. The crackle of his vertebras breaking is the last sound to ever reach Miles's ears.

Everything turns black, his body goes limp and collapses onto the floor.

The scarecrow just stands there for a minute or two, apparently surveying the two dead boys. Then, it lifts its faceless head and strides across the floor, pushing open the window, climbing out and disappearing into the night.

***

This one is also an idea I've had for a long time. That image of a living scarecrow with a pumpkin head just kept returning to me, haunting me year after year, demanding to become a story—until finally, I wrote it.

I guess the message in the story is, don't mess with forces you don't understand. It's a lesson as old as time; and yet, the main characters (or their crazy friends) never seem to learn, do they? I have to admit, though, had it been me stumbling across an article like the one in this story when I was a kid, I too would be very much tempted to try it out.

Lord of the Crabs

Alex hates being on holiday with his mom and dad, and yet they invariably drag him along every single year. Honestly, who goes for a vacation by the ocean *in winter*?

Alex is thirteen, making him perfectly able to stay home alone—except his mom doesn't agree. So for two long weeks in January Alex bores himself half to death in a stupid house next to a freezing beach far away from his friends. And this year proves no exception.

As soon as they arrive, Alex leaves the car and heads straight down to the beach. After seven hours in a heavily over-loaded station wagon with his parents mindlessly chitchatting, he thoroughly needs some alone time.

Small piles of snow are scattered around in the dunes, perfect for kicking, turning them into clouds of glittering powder dissolving in the wind. The ocean is steely grey under a heavy sky, and the rolling waves are topped with frosty white foam. The wind is biting his face, making his eyes water.

He bends down and picks up a stone, weighing it in his hand.

"So fucking unfair," he mutters. "I don't want to be here."

He throws the stone into the water. It makes a tiny plop and disappears.

Alex seems to hear a ringing, but when he takes out his phone, he has no new texts. It was probably only the sound of the wind. He picks up another flat stone, turning it between his fingers.

"Why don't I get a say in the matter? I'm old enough."

It's not even four in the afternoon, and yet the sun has almost set. Within half an hour, it will be pitch darkness and he will have to go back to the house. Just the thought of spending the evening with his parents is enough to make him—

A sharp pain in his finger abruptly interrupts his train of thought.

"Ouch, damnit!"

He glares stupidly at the stone, not comprehending what he sees for the first second or two. The stone has somehow managed to grow an arm with a claw at the end of it, which is clamping down on his finger.

"Let go of me!" he yells and waves his hand up and down, causing the crab to lose its grip and fall down on the sand. It immediately starts running sideways away from him.

Alex stares at his finger. A tiny red blush is visible, but the crab's claw didn't puncture the skin.

He looks down and sees more than one crab, in fact there are several of them, maybe even a hundred. They are all around him, all running in the same direction towards the dunes, like a mini-invasion.

"Fuck, that's nasty," Alex sneers, raising his foot. "Consider this payback for my finger …"

He is just about to stomp down, crushing at least a handful of crabs, when a deep, hoarse voice cuts through the air.

"Hey, you! Don't do that!"

Alex spins around in surprise, finding an old man in a heavy coat standing just a few yards away. A thick woolen beanie is pulled down over his ears, a few tufts of white hair protruding on each side. He is leaning sideways onto a walking stick, making it all the more impressive how swiftly he has appeared out of nowhere.

"What do you think you're doing?" the old man demands before Alex has time to say anything.

"Uhm ... well, I ... I was just ..."

"You were about to step on my crabs, that's what. Who do think you are exactly?"

Alex is at first too stunned to utter a word. "Calm down, they're only crabs," he mutters.

"Only crabs?" The old man snorts. "You have no idea what you're talking about." He looks lovingly down at the tiny creatures running along between their shoes.

"Well, it pinched me," Alex says, regaining a little composure.

"Of course it did. You wanted to throw it. How would you like being picked up by a giant and tossed into the ocean?"

"The crab didn't know I was going to throw it."

The old man sends him a knowing look. "You'd be surprised what they know. Crabs are very clever."

It's Alex's turn to snort. "Yeah, right. Whatever." He looks down at them, amazed that they are still coming, a seemingly endless stream of them. "Do you know where they are going?"

"Yes. To my house."

Alex bursts into laughter, certain the old man just made a joke, but he stops laughing when he sees the expression on the man's face. "Are you serious?"

"Of course I am. I called them myself."

"You did *what*? How?"

The man puts his hand in his jacket pocket and pulls out a small bell. "With this."

Alex finally realizes the man is a nutcase, and he suddenly doesn't feel like talking to him anymore. "Well, I'd better be off now." He starts to walk away.

Then he hears the bell chiming, and he stops and turns around. The old man is ringing the bell, and the crabs are no longer in a rush to get to the dunes; instead, they are gathering around the man's boots.

"Awesome," Alex murmurs and can't help but smile. "How does that work? Is it something about the sound? Like that special whistle you use for training dogs?"

The old man shrugs. "It hasn't really got anything to do with the bell—that's just how I call to them. I'm their lord, you see."

Alex raises his eyebrows. "Oookaaay ... so, they come whenever you call?"

"Absolutely. And they only obey me."

"Right ... so if I were to ring the bell, they wouldn't come?" Alex asks slyly, certain he has caught the old prick.

But the man just holds out the bell invitingly. "Try it for yourself."

Alex hesitates for a moment, then steps closer, being careful not to step on any of the crabs, and takes the bell. He walks away a few steps and rings the bell.

The crabs don't come; they stay huddled around the old guy. Alex chimes the bell louder, but the crabs don't seem to care about the sound.

"What the fuck?" he mutters, looking at the bell.

"You see?" the old man says, gesturing for Alex to come closer. "Give it back, please. I want to get back before dark."

Alex hands him back the bell.

The old man rings the bell once and starts walking. He's not particularly careful about where he puts his feet or his walking stick, and he doesn't need to be; the crabs move out of the way automatically, following him towards the dunes.

Alex stays for a moment, looking after the weird old guy and the crabs. It's dark now, and he ought to go back to the house, but he's awfully curious about what he just witnessed.

"Hey, wait up!" he calls.

The old man turns and looks back as Alex runs to him. "Is this ... I mean, is this for real? You're not just jerking me around? Are you honestly able to control the crabs with that bell?"

The man smiles crookedly, causing even more wrinkles to appear on the weather-beaten face. "You can join me for supper, and I can tell you more about them."

Without waiting for an answer, the old man walks up.

Alex thinks for a moment. Would it be a good idea to take the invite? This is one of those situations his mom always warned him about, going home with a stranger.

But he gets angry at the thought of his mom behaving like he's a baby who can't take care of himself, and he decides to prove her wrong. So, he follows the old man.

A small wooden cottage appears right on the other side of the dunes, reeds growing on the roof, a dim light burning in the small window. Leaning against the wall is a large woodpile, and behind the cottage Alex can make out a tiny fishing boat.

The man opens the door—which isn't locked—and steps inside. The crabs, however, stop on the doormat. There is no step or any other visible obstacle preventing them from going in; it looks more like they are simply waiting.

"Go on now," the old man says, ringing the bell.

Instantly, the crabs swarm into the cottage.

"Awesome," Alex mutters. "You taught them to wait for permission to enter."

The man apparently doesn't hear him, he just waves at Alex impatiently. "Come on, before we let out all the heat."

Alex steps inside and closes the door behind him. The cottage is very sparsely furnished: there is a small dining table with a single stool, an old rocker in the corner and a dresser. Right inside is a gas stove, and at the far end is a wood burner, a warm fire crackling inside, and behind the door is a bed. The floor is made of wood boards, although they are hardly visible for the many crabs, their tiny feet clicking against the wood.

Clickety-clickety-clickety ...

There is a lovely smell of spicy food in the air, and Alex sees the pot on the stove. Something is bubbling under the lid.

"Well, this is where I live," the man says, hanging his coat on a nail, revealing a thick woolen sweater which only makes him look even thinner.

"It's ... nice," Alex says, noticing the sound of the wind pulling the roof and wondering how much the tiny cottage can withstand before blowing away.

"You're a liar," the man says, shuffling over to the rocker and sitting down with a deep sigh. "But at least you're polite. Sit down."

Alex looks around, unsure where he is supposed to sit, then deciding on the only stool, pulls it carefully from the table and sits down.

"You hungry?" the man asks, unfolding a newspaper. "The soup will be ready soon."

"I could eat some," Alex says, inhaling the smell and feeling his stomach growl.

Silence falls over the cottage, except for the crackling of the fire, the howling of the wind and the clicking of the crabs.

Clickety-clickety-clickety...

Alex studies the tiny animals. They come in a wide variety of color and size. Blueish, reddish, greenish, whiteish. Some big as a fist, others tiny as a dice.

"Do they sleep here with you?" he asks.

The man answers through the paper. "Yes. But they always disappear before I wake up. They leave through the cracks in the floor."

"So, how did you train them?"

The old man lowers the paper, gazing at him through a pair of crooked spectacles. "Train them? I didn't train them. I'm their lord, I told you that already. They obey me and only me."

"All right. How did you become their lord then?"

"I inherited them."

"From whom?"

"From my granddad."

"Was he their lord before you?"

"That's right." The man has lifted the newspaper once more, seemingly not that interested in talking. But Alex pushes on for answers.

"How did your granddad become their lord then?"

The man puts down the newspaper again, sighing. "He inherited them too. The line goes back a long, long way. No one remembers how it started. I'm only the most recent lord, and soon my time will be done, and someone new will have to take over."

"Will it be your grandson then?"

"I don't have a grandson. I don't have any family. But it doesn't need to be a family member; anyone can become the new lord."

Alex looks down at the crabs. "What's the point?"

"The point?"

"Yeah, I mean, what do you do with a giant army of crabs?"

"They can be really useful. But it's really not about what they can do for you. It's just as much about *you* taking care of *them*. It's a big responsibility to be lord of the crabs."

"So you have to feed them and such?"

"No, they take care of that on their own. But in the winter, I provide them with shelter for the nights. Although, if I'm completely honest, it's mostly for my own sake; I enjoy the company." The man reaches down a hand, caressing the backside of the shell of one of the crabs. Others quickly budge in, trying to get a piece of the attention. The man stares down at them, his eyes suddenly far away. "They saved my life more than once, you see," he mutters.

"They did? How?"

The man starts talking in a slow, distant voice. "The first time was many years ago. I was young and stupid back then. I went out to sea right before a storm, and my boat capsized. Luckily, I had the bell in my pocket, and I was able to call for them. They came and brought me ashore."

Alex stares at the man's face, listening intently. "And how about the other time?"

The old face wrinkles up as the man frowns. "It's probably better I don't tell you."

"Why not?"

The man looks directly at him, smiling. "Because you don't want to lose your appetite, do you?"

The soup is ready a few minutes later, and the man gets up from the rocker with a loud moan as he goes to serve the food. He offers Alex the bowl, and even though the thick, orange soup smells delicious, Alex declines politely. Afterall, he has only known the guy for half an hour.

The old man simply shrugs before sitting down on the bed and starting to slurp down the piping hot soup in big, greedy gulps.

Alex's mouth is watering; he is really hungry now, so he takes the second bowl and fills it with soup. Apparently, the old man doesn't use spoons, so Alex follows his lead and takes a sip directly from the bowl.

The soup tastes wonderful, it's creamy and spicy, with pieces of carrot and celery, and also sort of soft, white meat.

"This is a really nice soup," he says, taking another gulp. "What kind is it?"

"Crab," the man says.

Alex swallows audibly. "Come again?"

"It's crab soup," the man says, sounding quite jovial. "The best kind there is, if you ask me."

Alex stares from the small animals on the floor to his bowl to the old man. "Do you ... do you *eat* them?"

"Sure. It's pretty much the only thing I do eat."

"But I thought you were supposed to protect them?"

"I only eat the ones who died from old age. There really isn't any point in that lovely meat going to waste, is there?"

"So ... they don't mind?" Alex glances down at the crabs and realizes he is whispering, like they can understand him.

"Nah," the old man says, producing a pipe. "They are very good natured. The only thing they don't tolerate is me turning my back on them. A good lord never abandons his flock."

Alex forces himself to finish the rest of his portion, although the soup doesn't taste quite as good anymore. The old man has got the pipe going, and the cottage is quickly filled with a sweet-smelling tobacco smoke.

The crabs are less active now; the clickety-clickety has stopped, as they seem to have settled all around the cottage for a good night's rest.

"So, did you find an heir?" Alex asks.

"No, not yet."

"You don't have anyone in mind?"

He gets no answer; the old man just studies his pipe and doesn't seem to want to explain any further.

"How about that second time they saved your life?" Alex tries. "I'm done eating now, so you can tell me about it."

The old man looks at him, raising one of his bushy white eyebrows. He doesn't say anything right away, and Alex doesn't think he will. But after a few moments, he starts talking.

"I had a break-in last year. Can you believe it? I mean, who the hell breaks in to an old cottage by the sea? A couple of damned misfits, that's who. Probably drugs addicts or something. They weren't from around here, I promise you that. Anyway, I was in my bed, taking my afternoon nap, and I never really lock the door, since no one ever comes around. They snuck in and tied me up with duct tape. They threatened me with a knife, wanting to know where I kept my money." The old man snorts. "Like I have any damned money—do I look like a wealthy person to you? Well, I just shook my head, so they started tearing up the place, searching for anything of value." He points to a tiny table next to the bed. "I always keep the bell right next to me when I'm sleeping, and luckily, they had tied my hands in the front, so I could still use them. I grabbed the bell and started ringing—I don't even think the burglars noticed, they were so busy ransacking my home. But they did notice once the crabs started swarming in." The old man's eyes take on a distant look. "At first they didn't understand the danger they were in; I even remember them laughing as the crabs started pinching at their shoes. But my friends just kept coming, more of them than I've never seen in one place. I'm telling you, there were millions. They were crawling over each other to get at the burglars, who now had to brush them off their pants. But there were simply too many, and the burglars started shouting in pain as the crabs pinched their legs bloody. They tried to run, but one of them tripped and fell. The crabs were instantly on him. He tried to scream—I say 'tried' because his voice was muffled, as the crabs made their way into his mouth and down his windpipe ..." The old man suddenly blinks and comes to. He looks at Alex inquisitively. "Do you want to hear the rest, or should we end the story here?"

Alex manages to nod. "I want to hear the rest."

The man puffs on his pipe. "The other one wasn't so lucky. He put up more of a struggle. Even though his legs were all torn up, he stayed on his feet, fighting his way through the sea of crabs, reaching the door. And he almost got it open, but then the crabs rose up in a wave in front of him, blocking the door and crashing down over him. Still, he manages to stay standing—you'll have to give him that much, he really fought for his life. But now the crabs were everywhere on him, their pinchers clipping at his fingers, his neck, his ears, his lips, his nose, and even his eyelids. The blood was spilling out of him, and he finally collapsed and died."

The old man stops talking, and Alex becomes aware his mouth is open wide. "Did the police come?" he asks breathlessly.

"The police? No, why would they come? It was all over, you see. The crabs tore the tape and released me."

"But ... what about the burglars?"

"You mean the bodies? The crabs took care of them too."

Alex swallows something. "Are you saying ...?"

"Crabs are scavengers," the old man says in an eerily calm voice. "They only left the bones, all picked clean. I buried them out back, by the woodpile."

Alex studies the old man for a moment, then he says: "How about me?"

"You? What about you?"

"Could I become your heir?"

"I don't think that's a good idea, son."

"Why not? I promise to take good care of them."

The old man doesn't answer.

Alex is starting to become annoyed. "At least give me a good reason why I can't be lord of the crabs!"

The old man glares at him. "I'll tell you why. Because you're just like every other young person nowadays: spoiled and entitled. You're not mature enough to handle such a big responsibility."

Alex feels the heat rise to his cheeks. His whole body is burning with anger. He hates being talked down to. He feels like getting up and leaving without a word, but something makes him stay.

"Well," the old man says, stretching his boney arms and sounding like nothing happened, like he didn't just deliver a mean insult. "I think I'll hit the hay. I trust you can find your way home." He gets up with an audible series of cracks from his knees and shuffles over to the bed.

Alex stays seated for a moment or two, trying to think of something to say, something to convince the old moron that Alex is the right choice for an heir, that he is mature enough—but nothing comes to mind. He gets up with an angry snort, striding towards the door, the crabs moving aside with every one of his steps.

Then, just before reaching the door, Alex stops and looks back. The old man pulls his ragged blanket over himself with a satisfied sigh.

Alex realizes he is standing right next to the stove. He glances across the room to the fire, which is still burning. For a moment, he just stands there.

Do it, a voice says.

No, I can't, another voice answers.

You want to be the lord of the crabs, don't you?

Yes, but that doesn't mean I—

Remember what he called you? Spoiled and entitled.

Alex feels the anger rising once more. He reaches out and turns the knob ever so slightly. There is a barely audible hissing sound as the gas starts seeping.

Alex turns and opens the door, but just before he leaves the cottage, he glances back once more. The old man has turned to face the wall, apparently already sleeping, but the crabs are all turned towards him, Alex, and he gets the eerie sensation that they are staring at him, that they somehow know what he just did.

Of course they don't. They're just stupid animals.

Alex closes the door and runs all the way back to the house, his heart pounding wildly.

***

That night, Alex dreams about crabs.

He wakes up before his parents—which usually never happens—and immediately remembers what happened last night. He sits bolt upright, horrified. It's like a charm has been lifted while he slept. As he went to bed, he was still furious at the old man and the way he had insulted Alex, but now he regrets turning on the gas.

What have I done?

He gets up, gets dressed and chows down a bowl of cereal before leaving the house.

The sun has barely set on a heavy grey sky, and the wind is cold. Yet Alex isn't bothered by it; in fact, he hardly notices as he walks hurriedly through the dunes, his mouth dry and his pulse beating in his ears.

Why did I do it? Why did I do it?

The question keeps repeating in his mind.

Then, suddenly, he stops abruptly as he sees the old man's cottage. He excepted to find it burned down, only the smoldering ashes remaining, but the cottage is still standing exactly as he left it the night before.

Alex is immensely relieved. The old man must've noticed the gas before it could fill up the cottage and reach the fire in the wood burner. But Alex can't relax completely until he is sure the old man is okay, so he goes to the cottage and knocks on the door.

No one answers.

He knocks again, harder.

Still no answer.

Alex goes around to the window, wipes clean the glass with his jacket sleeve and looks in. He can make out most of the cottage. There is no sight of the crabs, but the old man is still lying in bed. But something about the way the old man is lying makes Alex nervous: exactly as Alex left him, facing the wall. Like he hasn't moved all night.

Alex goes to the door and opens it, stepping inside the cottage. "Hello?" he asks.

No response from the bed.

The cottage is very cold, the fire has long since burned out. Alex checks the stove and feels a jolt in his stomach. The gas is still open, but there is no more hissing sound. As he breathes in, he can smell a faint metallic odor in the air.

Oh, fuck ... please don't tell me ...

Alex strides to the bed, grabs the old man's shoulder and shakes him. "Wake up! Hey? You hear me? Wake up!"

The old man rolls to his back, and the sight of his face makes Alex scream out loud. The skin is completely white, almost blueish, and the mouth is open, revealing the old, yellow teeth in a horrible, ghostlike smile.

Alex backs away, bumping into the table, but hardly noticing.

Maybe it's not too late ... maybe it's not too late ...

His hand reaches for his pocket and pulls out his phone.

***

The ambulance arrives within half an hour.

Alex can't stand being inside the cottage, so he waits outside, striding back and forth, trying to keep warm, but trembling all over nonetheless.

The medics—a man and a woman—are in no hurry once they have taken a look at the old man. They don't even try to resuscitate him, but simply lift him on a stretcher and carry it to the ambulance.

"Did you make the call?" the male medic asks him.

Alex nods quietly.

"Were you related to him?"

"No. I just ... came by."

"You didn't know him?"

"No. I only spoke with him once before."

"Do you know his name?"

Alex thinks for a moment. "No. He didn't tell me."

The female medic comes out from the cottage, shaking her head. "I couldn't find anything."

"Not even a wallet?"

"Nope."

The man snorts. "I'll be damned. Well, we'll have to leave it to the police to figure out who he was, then." He sends Alex a quick thumbs-up. "Thank you for calling."

"Wait up," Alex says as the medics are about to leave. "What ... what did he die from?"

The man shrugs. "Old age, I presume."

Alex blinks. "Oh. All right."

The medics leave, and Alex just stands there, looking after the ambulance as it makes its way down the beach, his eyes watering in the cold wind.

***

The next couple of days Alex feels kind of empty. He doesn't tell his parents about the old man, even though it's pretty much all he can think of.

He was very old, he tells himself. *He was going to die soon anyway.*

He tries to forget about it, tries to tell himself he didn't really murder the guy, tries to find something else to occupy his mind.

But he keeps going back to thinking about the crabs. What will they do know? Who will become their new lord?

At long last the final day of the vacation arrives, and Alex packs his suitcase already in the morning. But they are not leaving until noon, so he decides to go for a walk to pass the time.

Without really thinking about it, he goes down to the dunes and stops by the old man's empty cottage. He looks at the woodpile leaning up against the wall, and recalls something the old man said.

"They only left the bones, all picked clean. I buried them out back, by the woodpile."

Of course, the story can't be true. The old fool was just joshing him. But what if he wasn't? What if the bones of the two men really are buried right underneath the sand? The shovel is even standing right there, like a murder weapon left on the crime scene.

Alex goes over and grabs the shovel. He starts digging.

This is crazy, he thinks as he throws sand aside. *Why am I even doing this? What do I expect to find? There is nothing here ...*

CLONK!

The shovel hits something hard. Alex freezes for a moment, then he digs around it. Soon, a white, football-sized stone appears. Except it isn't a stone. Two large, empty eye sockets glare up at him.

"Oh, fuck," Alex gasps, stumbling backwards. He stares down at the skull for a moment, his mind racing. Then he starts digging furiously again, covering up the hole he just made.

When there is no trace left, he throws aside the shovel and steps back, panting.

I can't believe it, he really did it ... he buried the remains of two guys out here after the crabs had killed them.

Alex stares at the cottage, getting the distinct feeling of it staring right back at him. He remembers the bell. Is it still inside?

Alex goes to the door, his heart thumping in his chest, and opens it. The inside of the cottage looks exactly as the last time he saw it, except, of course, the old man isn't there anymore.

His heart makes a jump as his eyes fall on the tiny bell sitting right on the nightstand. He goes and picks it up, very tentatively, like it's some sort of rare diamond. Holding it gives him a weird sense of power.

Maybe if I ring it, they will come. Maybe I can be their new lord ...

He holds the bell up higher and is just about to shake it when a great bolt of fear suddenly shoots through his stomach. What if the crabs saw him turn on the gas?

What if they understand he caused their lord to die? Will they seek vengeance on him?

Alex carefully puts the bell back down, but his hand is shaking too much, and just as he lets go, the bell tips to the side and rolls onto the floor, chiming shrilly, almost as though it calls out for help.

"No! Fuck! Shut up!"

He bends down and grabs it, squeezing it in his hands to muffle the sound. He holds his breath, listening for a beat. Nothing but the sound of the wind. He darts a look towards the doorway, but finds nothing.

He puts down the bell once more, using both hands this time and succeeding. He turns quickly around, wishing only to leave the dusty old cottage, leave the crime scene and never come back, but—

He stops abruptly.

The crabs have come. Hundreds—no, thousands—of them. They are blocking the doorway, all standing perfectly still, eyeing him silently.

Alex glances down at the bell, and before he can think about it, he starts talking to the crabs. "Uhm ... no, you guys misunderstand ... I didn't ... I didn't call you. It was a mistake."

The crabs don't move a leg or a claw.

"Do you hear me?" Alex says a little louder. "I didn't call you. All right? Now, please go away."

Still no reaction from the crabs.

Alex starts to feel annoyed, although he is also pretty scared. He takes a few steps forward. The crabs finally move, scrambling to get out of his way. Alex walk out through the doorway, the crabs swarming around him, but keeping a few inches of distance.

"I'm leaving now," he says, feeling stupid talking to the crabs. "And I'm not coming back. You guys are not coming with me. I'm not your lord, all right?"

As he utters the words, something the old man says flies through his mind.

"The only thing they don't tolerate is me turning my back on them. A good lord never abandons his flock."

The crabs start moving about restlessly, stepping back and forth on their tiny legs. It almost looks like they are unsure what to do.

Suddenly, Alex just wants to get far away from them. He runs as fast as he can away from the cottage, stumbling through the dunes. As he looks back, he can't make out the cottage or the crabs.

But he doesn't slow down.

"Where have you been?" his mom asks as Alex comes charging into the driveway in front of the house. Both his parents are standing next to the packed-up car, ready to go. "And why are you running like that?"

"I just ... I just ... went for a run," he gasps. "Is it noon already?"

"Ten minutes past, actually. Get in the car, please."

Alex has never been happier to get in a car with his parents for a seven-hour-long drive.

***

That night, Alex can finally crawl into his own bed again. It feels great being back in familiar surroundings, and he almost looks forward to going back to school tomorrow morning.

Now that he is far away from the beach and the cottage, it all just seems like a stupid dream. Like something someone else has experienced. There never was an old guy who died, and if there was—who cares? He had no family, no one knew of him. Even the medics couldn't identify him. The bottom line is, what happened didn't really hurt anybody, and it wasn't anybody's fault.

Alex yawns and drifts off to sleep.

But just before he dozes off completely, there is a faint noise.

Clickety-clickety-clickety ...

Alex opens his eyes abruptly and sits up. He looks around the room and listens.

What was that?

It sounded like ... like the crabs. That's crazy, of course. The small animals couldn't travel that far in that short amount of time. Still, a prickling sweat appears on his back.

His room is empty—as far as he can see—and the noise doesn't come again. He listens for a moment longer, but the house is completely silent, his parents must have gone to bed too.

He sits up and takes his phone, activates the camera light and searches the floor. Nothing except the pile of clothes he has left next to the bed.

Alex's heart finally slows down—he hadn't really noticed it had started racing—and he gives off a sigh of relief.

It was just a dream ...

He needs to pee, so he gets up and walks to the door. The noise of the tiny steps of the crabs are still lodged in his memory, and just to erase any trace of doubt, he turns on the light in the room and looks around.

Nothing.

Of course nothing.

It was just a dream.

He turns off the light and slips down the hallway to the bathroom. He pees, washes his hands and goes back to his room. He yawns loudly as he crosses the floor, but just as he is about to lie down, the yawn turns into a shriek of surprise.

On his pillow sits a large, dark crab. It's not moving at all, only opening and closing the giant claws very slowly.

"What the fuck ... are you doing here?" Alex croaks, his heart pounding in his throat and making it hard to get out the words. "Get out of my bed ..."

Then he hears the noise once more, and this time, he is definitely awake.

Clickety-clickety-clickety ...

It comes from the hallway. Alex spins around, staring at the door which he left ajar. It slowly pushes open, as the crabs start swarming into the room, their legs clicking against the floorboards.

Clickety-clickety-clickety ...

There are many of them. Way too many.

Alex feels his heart stop. *They've found me ...*

His eyes darts to the corner of the room, where his baseball bat is leaning against the wall. Alex runs over and grabs it, turns towards the crabs now closing in on him, forming a half-circle around him.

"Fuck off! Out of my room! I'm your lord! Obey me!"

The crabs don't obey, they just come in closer, tightening the half-circle.
Why didn't I bring that stupid bell?
"*Mom!*" he cries. "*Dad!*"
The parents' bedroom is upstairs, at the other end of the house. They probably can't hear him.

Alex takes a step forward, swinging the bat at the crabs, who move aside swiftly, causing the tip of the bat to only scrape the floor.

Alex draws back the bat, ready for another swing—but he doesn't notice the giant crab on his bed. It has jumped down onto the floor and is now making its way towards him along the wall panel, creeping up on his hindfoot. Just as Alex swings the bat again, the giant crab opens its claw and cuts deeply into Alex's Achilles' tendon.

Alex lets out a wail of pain, drops the bat and falls down on his knee, clutching his ankle.

The crabs seize the opportunity. They are at him before he can get back up. They are everywhere, crawling on his body, pinching and cutting, tearing through his skin. It's like being stung by bees all over. They are in his hair now, down his pants, even on his face, blinding him by going for his eyes. He thrashes wildly and flails his arms in an attempt to brush them off, but they cling on like mousetraps. The pain is almost too much now, he can't even feel it anymore.

Alex realizes his only chance is getting out of the house, so he crawls forward, lashing out blindly. He feels his fist connecting with several crabs and crushing them against the floor, and he gets a sick jolt of brief pleasure knowing he at least got some of them.

But he also hears the sound of thousands of tiny legs rushing into the room as the crabs just keep coming, the sound filling his ears and drowning out everything, as he can't keep in the agony any longer, opening his mouth and letting out a scream, which is instantly silenced as the crabs rush into his mouth and force their way down his throat.

Clickety-clickety-clickety-clickety-clickety-clickety-clickety-clickety-clickety ...

***

Growing up by the sea, I've always felt there was something really atmospheric about the beach in wintertime. In the summer, there is so much life and warmth and color. But come November, everything turns cold, grey and dead. It is a perfect scenery for a scary story, and once I got the idea of the human-killing army of crabs, well ... that was just too good not to write.

Under the Ice

Reggie can't sleep; it's simply too quiet.

There is no knocking, no low rapping noises from the other side of the wall. The room next to his is now empty. The thought makes him very sad, but he doesn't want to cry anymore. He's been crying every night for three months.

Reggie turns onto his side, tugging his hand down the crack between the wall and the mattress and finding the small piece of paper. He pulls it out and unfolds it. The alphabet is written out in three columns, and next to every letter is a combination of lines and dots.

Reggie has looked at the paper hundreds of times, and he doesn't really need it anymore; he has memorized every letter in the alphabet. He puts his hand against the wall and starts tapping meticulously.

Knuckle. Pause.

Knuckle, knuckle, knuckle. Pause.

Knuckle, palm. Pause.

E-V-A

He waits. Listens. Hopes.

Of course, no answer comes. There is no one there anymore. No Eva to knock back "Reggie." Reggie is once again an only child.

Still, he keeps knocking for a while.

What are you doing? he knocks. And: *Are you still awake?*

After a few minutes, he hears footsteps coming down the hallway, and his door opens. Dad pops his head in, his eyes are tired, his cheeks sunken. "Are you knocking on the wall again, Reggie?"

"Yes."

"Could you please stop? We can hear it from our bedroom."

"Sorry, Dad."

"It's all right. Just go to sleep, okay?"

"Okay."

"Good night."

"Good night, Dad."

Dad closes the door, and Reggie turns onto his back, staring up at the ceiling. "We," Dad said. "We can hear it ..." But Reggie knows it's really only Dolores who is annoyed by the noise. Dad never used to mind when Eva was alive and they would knock back and forth for hours on end every night.

But that changed once Dolores moved in. A lot of things changed.

Outside, the wind has started howling, throwing the snowflakes at the window. It's been snowing all day, and Reggie is reminded of that day last winter, where he and Eva built a snowman down in the park. Perhaps he will build one tomorrow. Alone.

Reggie's eyes fill up with tears.

***

School ends at three o'clock. He trudges home through the streets, the sidewalks slushy with grey, half-melted snow. It has been thawing just a bit, and the snow is perfect for building a snowman.

As he reaches the park, he finds only a few kids playing in the snow, so Reggie puts down his bag and starts rolling a couple of balls, one slightly bigger than the other. With a fair amount of difficulty he gets the smaller lifted onto the other, and he starts rolling the third ball as the sweat starts trickling down his back.

When the head of the snowman is in place, he goes to the trees at the bottom of the park and finds a couple of branches to serve as arms. Although it's not even four in the afternoon, the sun has already started to set, the sky turning dark purple above the tops of the naked trees, as Reggie mounts the snowman's arms and steps back to admire his work.

The left arm is a little crooked; it almost looks as though the snowman is pointing at something. Reggie looks in the direction and his stomach tightens. The snowman is pointing towards the lake.

Reggie has avoided going anywhere near the park for three months, but now he realizes what he really has avoided is the lake. Even this far away, the ice looks ominous, black and shiny, reflecting the sky above, a single star blinking.

Reggie looks up to the sky, trying to locate the star, but is not able to do so. Yet it's still blinking in the ice. He frowns, looks up again, but the star is nowhere to be seen in the darkening sky. There are no other lights in that direction, no streetlamps—which are lit by now—and no houses, either.

Reggie is mystified. The more he stares at the light in the icy lake, the weirder it seems, like it doesn't really belong.

A cold wind sweeps by, making him blink, and he suddenly becomes aware of how dark it has gotten. He checks his phone. It's almost six o'clock. Reggie hurries home.

Dolores is in a foul mood when he comes home.

"Can't you tell the time?" she snarls as Reggie enters kitchen.

Reggie slinks to his seat and sits down.

Dolores lands a plate of food in front of him. "Here you go. It's cold, but that's your own fault."

Reggie looks at the mashed potatoes, then up at Dolores. "Can't I just heat it in the microwave?"

"It's broken," Dolores snaps, turning her back—and then glancing back at him, demanding: "Eat."

Reggie sighs without any sound. He knows the microwave is working just fine. If his dad had been here, Dolores would never force Reggie to eat cold food. She's always sweet and joyful when his dad is around. But his dad is probably in the garage, where he spends most of his time.

Reggie slowly chews his way through the food, while his thoughts drifts back to the strange light in the ice. For some reason, he can't stop thinking about it.

The next morning as Reggie rides his bike to school, he decides to go through the park, even though his dad has forbidden him to do so, not wanting to risk another accident.

The morning is still dim, and the air turns into white clouds before his face with every breath.

Already at a distance he notices the light still blinking in the lake. Reggie stops his bike to look at it. The light looks really weird, almost unnatural. Some of the blinks are longer than others. It kind of reminds him of ...

Reggie lets out a gasp.

The light is sending out a Morse code! Reggie tears off his gloves and plunges his hand into his pocket, pulling out his phone without taking his eyes off the lights. He opens a new message and types in the rhythm of the light. It turns out to be a sequence of three repeating themselves over and over. The first one is:

Long, short, short.
Long, long, long.
Short, long, short, short.
Long, long, long.
Short, long, short.
Short.
Short, short, short.

Reggie stares at the code, unable to believe what he is seeing. The light really is blinking in Morse code, and Reggie knows the code well enough to read the first word without needing to look it up.

DOLORES.

Reggie is suddenly sweating heavily under his jacket, even though his hands are cold as ice.

"Hi, Reggie! What are you doing?"

Reggie jumps and instinctively hides the phone behind his back as Crystal and Justine from his class come by on their bikes, smiling and slowing down to say hello.

"Uhm ... well, nothing," he mutters, slipping his phone into his back pocket.

"Aren't you coming to school?" Crystal asks.

"Sure."

"Do you want to ride with us?"

Reggie can't bring himself to say no, so he picks up his bag and rides with the girls to school, the three of them chatting casually all the way, yet Reggie isn't really listening; his thoughts keep going back to the light, and his phone is burning in his pocket.

***

As soon as they reach school, Reggie runs into the classroom, barely noticing a couple of his classmates greeting him as he finds his seat and pulls out his phone. He looks at the two remaining words.

The first one reads:

Short, long, long, short.
Long, long, long.
Short, short.
Short, short, short.
Long, long, long.
Long, short.

Again, Reggie has little trouble decoding the word, which is POISON.

He feels his mouth drying out as he scrolls down to the third and final word. Beginning with the same two letters as the former word, it reads:
Short, long, long, short.
Long, long, long.
Short, long, short, short.
Short, short.
Long, short, long, short.
Short.
"Reggie?"
He looks up as someone says his name, only to find Susan, their teacher, standing in front of his desk.
"Would you mind putting away your phone, please?"
Reggie looks around dreamily and realizes the class has begun. Everyone is staring at him, and his ears turn red. "Sorry," he mutters, shoving his phone into his pocket.
"Are you all right, Reggie?" Susan asks, eyeing him. "You look a little pale."
"I'm fine," he says, swallows and musters a faint smile.
Susan looks at him for a second or two, then she goes on to start the lesson.

***

Reggie can't really concentrate for the rest of the day. The three words, which the light in the frozen lake sent out, keep repeating in his mind.
DOLORES ... POISON ... POLICE
On his way home, Reggie slowly rides his bike through town absentmindedly, a thousand questions tumbling about in his head.
What produces the light in the lake? Or who? Why does it blink in Morse code? What does the message mean? And who is it addressed to?
Reggie would like to believe the message isn't directed at him—Dolores is, after all, a quite common name, he's sure there must be at least a few other Doloreses in town—but he has a pretty strong feeling it's him, Reggie Griffin, the light was communicating to. And he has a pretty good guess who was behind the message.
"It's insane," Reggie mutters to himself. "Things like that don't happen in real life."
But no matter how much he racks his brain, he really can't find another explanation, and slowly he starts accepting the truth.
Eva sent the message. He has no idea how, but his dead sister is trying to tell him something from the place she died, through the form of communication the two of them used almost every day when she was still alive. As to what Eva is trying to tell him, well, there is really no doubt about it.
Dolores killed her and Reggie needs to go to the police about it.
Reggie reaches the park, his legs starting to become shaky the closer he gets to the lake, and yet he forces himself onwards; he needs to see it once more, needs to know he didn't just imagine it.
And he sees it as soon as he gets close enough—even though the light is harder to see in the grey daylight. And something is different. Reggie can tell right away. The rhythm of the light's blinking has changed. He stares at it, trying to decode it.
It looks like there is only one word repeating now, a short one, only four letters.
Long, short, short, short.
Short, short.
Long, short, long.

Short.
BIKE

Reggie's eyes grow wide, as the word connects in his mind. He steps on the pedal and rides all the way home as fast as he can.

***

Reggie enters the house through the garage and turns on the lights.

The garage has turned into his dad's sanctuary since Eva died, it's the place he spends most of his time at home, and he always wants to be alone.

Reggie's eyes find the bike immediately—it's hard not to notice, as it's hanging on the wall, all clean and shiny, looking brand new, even though Eva had used it for almost a year when she died.

Dolores has told Dad more than once how it's morbid of him to keep the bike and has asked him to get rid of it. But for once, Dad doesn't listen to her.

Reggie looks at the bike, recalling how it looked as it was lifted out of the lake, all muddy and gooey. Dad has done a fine job cleaning it.

Reggie shakes the image out of his mind and steps closer. He studies the bike closely, eyeing every bolt and gear to see if something might betray what he is supposed to see.

What am I looking for? What is it Eva wants me to see?

A noise behind him makes him start and turn around.

Dolores is standing there, in the doorway in to the house, glaring at him. "What are you doing here?" she asks, like Reggie has no earthly business in the house at large.

"I'm ... uhm ... nothing," Reggie mumbles, feeling very guilty even though he hasn't done anything wrong.

Dolores squints at him. "Nothing? That's a funny place to be doing nothing." She steps a little closer, darting a glance up at the bike. "Are you turning into your father? Are you also going to be standing down here, ogling that nasty thing for hours on end?"

Reggie has no idea what to answer, the three words are flashing across his mind.

DOLORES ... POISON ... POLICE

Suddenly, the woman in front of him seems like a complete stranger.

"Are you deaf?" she asks a little louder, coming even closer still, crowding him. "I would like to know what you think you are doing down here."

Reggie gets a sudden idea, shooting a glance up at the wall next to the bike. "It wasn't the bike I was looking at," he says, pointing. "I just wanted to check if we had any poison left."

Dolores stops in her tracks, looking up at the shelf where Dad keeps his dangerous chemicals like cans of spray paint, Round-Up and bug spray. Dolores frowns. "Poison?"

"Yeah, you know, for rats. I think I saw one in the front yard as I was coming in."

Reggie has no idea where the words are coming from, but the memory of his dad putting out poison for the rats a couple of years ago suddenly jumped into his head. And Dolores seems to be buying it.

"We don't have rats anymore," she says. "It was probably just a mouse you saw. Those are pretty harmless."

"Oh, okay, but ..." Reggie makes an effort to sound casual. "If it was a rat, and if it should come back ... do we have any poison then?" His heart is beating hard enough to make his temples pulse, but he keeps looking at Dolores.

"Of course we don't have any poison," she snaps, her eyes flickering for just a fraction of a second. "And if we do get rats again, you certainly aren't going to be the one dealing with them. Now go to your room and do your homework."

Reggie leaves the garage, but he can't forget how Dolores's eyes had flickered. She lied. She lied about the poison.

***

That night, as Reggie lies in his bed, he starts tapping the wall.

Eva, he taps. *Can you hear me?*

He gets no answer. Instead, Dad shows up, looking tired as usual.

"Are you knocking on the wall again, Reggie?"

"Sorry, Dad. I forgot."

Dad is just about to close the door again.

"Dad? There is something I want to talk with you about."

"It's late, Reggie; can't it wait for tomorrow?"

"I'd prefer to talk about it now."

Dad sighs, nods, and comes into the room. He sits down on the edge of Reggie's bed, rubbing his forehead. "All right, what is it?"

Reggie thinks hard for a moment. He needs to choose his words carefully. Earlier he actually considered telling his dad everything, from the blinking light and the message, to his suspicion towards Dolores. But he quickly came to the conclusion that his dad of course wouldn't believe him because of a blinking light in the frozen lake. He needs hard evidence.

"I was just thinking about the day Eva died," he begins.

Dad nods very slowly. "I think about that very often too."

"I think it's weird, that she just drove into the lake, you know. It wasn't like the ground was icy or slippery or anything. I mean, how could she have ridden right into the water?"

Dad shrugs limply. "You know Eva. She was probably busy doing something else, like texting one of her friends, not paying any attention to where she was going."

"Or maybe ... maybe she was ill."

"Ill?"

"Yeah, I mean ... like dizzy or something."

Dad puts a hand on Reggie's shoulder. "Don't worry yourself with stuff like that, son. It's no use. You were at camp, remember? You couldn't have done anything to prevent it."

"I know, it's just ..." Reggie decides to jump the gun and ask the crucial question. "Do you remember if Eva seemed ill the day before?"

Dad thinks for a moment, then shakes his head. "She seemed perfectly normal. We had soup for dinner, and she had a very healthy appetite."

"What about when she went to sleep? Did you notice anything odd about her then?"

"No, she just said good night and went to her room, exactly like she always did." Dad's eyes grow distant. "And that was the last time I saw her. I had to go to work early the next morning, so Dolores made Eva breakfast and sent her off to school ..."

Dad clears his throat as his voice starts shaking. "Well, I think you need to go to sleep now. I'll see you in the morning."

Dad gets up and leaves the room.

Reggie is left to the silence. His mind starts going at a hundred miles an hour.

Dolores was the last person to see Eva alive. If she had poisoned her, could she have done it in the morning? Maybe she put something in her breakfast, but the poison didn't kick in until Eva reached the park, and that was why she crashed into the lake? So she didn't really drown, it just looked that way, and the police didn't check for any poison in her body, because, well, why would they? The cause of death seemed obvious.

Reggie's heart is beating like an old steam engine in his chest.

It makes sense. It could be what really happened. But something is missing, one piece doesn't fit the puzzle: How could Dolores know exactly when the poison would kill Eva? If she had died anywhere else on her way to school, the police would definitely have checked for a cause of death, and the poison would probably have been discovered.

Reggie bites his lip, thinking hard. He is convinced Eva didn't drown, but instead was poisoned by Dolores. He just doesn't see how she did it.

If he could only get another clue.

Of course he can get another clue.

***

In the morning, he goes through the park, stopping by the lake once more. The light is still blinking faithfully under the ice, and once again, it's a new rhythm.

Reggie stares at it, counting in his head, decoding the letters one at a time.

The word is:

TREEHOUSE

***

Reggie isn't able to focus all day at school; the lessons pass by before him in a haze. More than once someone talks to him without him noticing.

There is only one thing on his mind. The treehouse in the yard. The one built when Reggie and Eva were both very young.

Finally, the bell rings. Reggie shoots out of the building like a bullet from a gun, grabs his bike and rides through town. He doesn't enter the house, but goes straight around to the yard, looking at the old apple tree leaning over the tiny treehouse.

Reggie strides across the frozen lawn, when something makes him stop abruptly. He suddenly has the distinct feeling of being watched. He turns and almost lets out a scream.

From the living room window Dolores is peering out at him, her face pale behind the glass, the eyes staring fixedly, as though she had read his mind and knows exactly what he is up to.

For a long time, Reggie just stands there, unable to move.

Finally, Dolores opens the window. "What do you think you're doing?"

"I ... uhm ..."

"Hunting for rats again?" She sends him an unpleasant smile.

Reggie can't find any good excuse, so he simply walks back around the house. Dolores is waiting for him in the hall. "You didn't answer me," she demands. "What were you doing in the yard?"

"Nothing."

"You looked pretty determined for someone doing nothing. What were you doing out there?"

"Nothing," Reggie repeats, hearing the desperately obvious lie in his own voice, but still not able to come up with anything better. He takes off his jacket and tries to slip by Dolores, but she grabs him by the arm.

"I'm getting really tired of you skulking around all over the place like you're up to something. Tell me what you were doing in the yard. You were going to that disgusting old treehouse, weren't you? You haven't been down there since she died, so why the sudden urge?"

Reggie hates when Dolores mentions Eva; she never says her name outright, but she always has a distinct sneer in her voice. He tears himself free of her grip with a sudden violent jerk. "Let go of me! I don't have to tell you anything."

Dolores's face goes blank. "What did you say?"

"And her name is Eva! Did you forget that already? You never say her name, but her name is Eva!"

Dolores is obviously taken aback. He expects her to start shouting, but when she talks, her voice is lower than usual. "So that's why you've been acting weird. You miss her."

The surprise in her words makes Reggie even more angry. "Of course I miss her! But you probably don't get that. You couldn't stand her!"

Dolores looks almost genuinely hurt. "What kind of a thing is that to say? Of course I—"

"Oh, stop lying! You were always mean to her when Dad wasn't around. But she never toed the line no matter how much you bullied her, and you couldn't deal with that. That's why you decided to—" Reggie breaks off abruptly, as the words almost fly out of his mouth.

Dolores's eyes grow big for a moment, before they become very narrow. "Decided to do what?" she asks in a very low, very ominous voice.

Reggie runs past her and up to his room. He slams the door behind him and listens for a moment, expecting Dolores to come running after him. But she doesn't.

***

Reggie stays in his room until four o'clock—that's when Dad comes home from work.

Dolores turns into her usual happy self as soon as Dad enters the house, bustling about and smiling cheerfully. But whenever her and Reggie's eyes meet, he feels a shiver down his spine.

He tries to get out to the treehouse more than once, but Dolores is keeping an eye on him. As the sun goes down, he decides to wait until tomorrow, as he won't be able to see anything out there anyway.

The conversation with Dolores has only made him even more certain. Something is definitely out there in the treehouse, waiting for him to discover it. Something which will tell him what really happened to Eva.

Reggie tries several times the next day to make it out to the treehouse, but Dolores is watching him like a bird of prey. Twice he manages to leave the house, but as soon he reaches the yard, he finds her staring at him from the window.

She is clearly on to him, and since she doesn't have a job, she never leaves the house other than to do grocery shopping once or twice a week, but that always only happens while Reggie is at school.

Reggie bides his time, trying to think up a solution.

A couple of days more pass by. He hopes Dolores might forget about it, but she doesn't; she stills eyes him suspiciously every time they meet. Neither of them speak, however. It's almost like a game of chess, each of them waiting for the other to make the move.

Reggie gets more and more anxious. Every day, as he passes through the park, the light in the frozen lake keeps blinking the same message over and over.

TREEHOUSE ... TREEHOUSE ... TREEHOUSE

Eva is begging him to go out there.

But he can't. Not as long as Dolores is guarding him.

Then suddenly, something happens.

**

Reggie is sitting in his room one evening. Glancing out through the window, he can just make out the treehouse.

"Reggie!" his dad calls from the kitchen. "Dinner's ready!"

Reggie gets up and leaves the room. Just as he enters the kitchen, he stops dead.

The table is laid out for three, the soup has already been served, and Dad and Dolores are both eating.

"Mmmm," Dad says, slurping away. "It's a really nice soup."

"Thank you, dear," Dolores smiles. She turns her head and looks at Reggie, still smiling sweetly. "Please sit down, Reggie. Eat the soup while it's hot."

Reggie manages to stagger over to the table and slump down on his seat. The soup is steaming and smells very inviting, but Reggie doesn't dare inhale the steam, much less taste the soup. He recalls what Dad told him.

"We had soup for dinner, and she had a very healthy appetite."

Reggie notices Dolores watching him. "Is something wrong, Reggie?"

"Uhm ... I'm really not hungry."

"You don't have to finish it all, just eat as much as you can." Dolores continues eating, looking at Reggie between every spoonful.

Reggie picks up his spoon, willing his hand not to tremble. He glances at Dad, but Dad is pouring down the soup, not noticing Reggie's discomfort. Should he tell? Should he blabber the whole deal to Dad, right here and now? Would Dad believe him if he did?

"Reggie?" Dolores says inquiringly. "Eat your soup, please."

"I ... I feel kind of sick," he mutters.

"A little soup will do you good."

"I can't," he says, shaking his head. "I'm sorry, but I can't." He is not exaggerating; he really couldn't squeeze down even a single slurp, as his throat is utterly clammed up.

Dad finally looks up from his bowl. "That's all right, buddy. Maybe you'll feel better later on."

Reggie feels immensely relieved. "Can I leave the table then?"

"Couldn't you at least try it?" Dolores says, cutting Dad off. Her smile is gone now. "I've spent a long time cooking. I think it's quite rude not to at least taste the food."

"He's not feeling well," Dad says.

Dolores puts down her spoon. "So the lovely soup is just going to go to waste then, is it?"

"Don't worry, dear, I'll eat his portion." Dad has already emptied his own bowl and now reaches for Reggie's.

Reggie is just about to protest, but Dolores beats him to it: she snatches the bowl and gets to her feet. "No, no, if it's going to be like that, we might as well chuck it."

"What? Oh, come on now, honey ... No, don't do that!"

But it's too late: Dolores has poured the soup into the sink. "There!" she says angrily, sitting back down, and resumes eating without another word.

Reggie looks at Dad, and Dad just shrugs, helping himself to a second serving from the pot.

Reggie quietly leaves the kitchen.

***

Back in his room, Reggie paces the room, his heart pounding frantically.

Dolores just tried to poison him! It's insane, but he just knows that was what just happened.

He's out of time. He has to do something. Dolores is clearly trying to get him out of the way. She knows Reggie is suspicious towards her, and she can't risk him finding out what happened to Eva.

He stops in front of the window. I have to get out there. Now. Tonight.

***

Reggie keeps himself awake that night. It's not hard, as his whole body is trembling with a mixture of fear and excitement.

He watches the numbers on his alarm clock turning eleven, then twelve, then one.

He's afraid that Dolores might be awake still, lying silently in bed, listening for any sounds. But finally, at two o'clock, he feels confident she must have drifted off. So, he gets out of bed, putting on his socks. He doesn't dare leave through the front door, as that would mean sneaking all the way through the house and risk waking Dolores up.

Instead, he opens his window and climbs out, bringing his cell phone.

The night is freezing cold, the grass crunches below his feet. He runs across the lawn, stops in front of the treehouse and looks back, halfway expecting to find Dolores glaring out at him from the living room window.

But the window is black and empty.

He opens the door to the treehouse and steps inside, closing the door behind him. For a moment, he is surrounded by complete darkness. Then, he turns on his cell light. The inside of the treehouse looks exactly as he remembers it. The table, the two chairs, the curtains by the window. There are old cobwebs in the corners.

Reggie examines everything thoroughly, his teeth clattering with cold. But he doesn't find anything out of the ordinary. He starts wondering if Dolores might have been out here, getting rid of whatever Eva wanted him to find. Maybe he's too late. Maybe—

Then he sees it. It's a very discrete detail. But one of the screws in the floorboards is shining up at him as the light hits it. It's completely clean, no dust or dirt is covering it like the rest of the screwheads.

It has been unscrewed recently ...

Reggie's pulse rises. He needs to get to the garage, where Dad keeps his tools. He turns off the cell light and leaves the treehouse. He runs back across the yard and climbs back in through the window.

This time, he has no choice: he needs to walk through the house, passing right by Dad and Dolores's bedroom, in order to get to the garage.

Reggie waits a few minutes, until his body stops shaking with cold. Then, he takes a deep breath and leaves the room. He knows the places where the floor is creaking, so he steps carefully as he makes his way down the hallway. He has never felt more scared in his life, but he forces himself to think of Eva, and it gives him a little courage.

He stops briefly in front of the bedroom door. He can hear his dad snoring on the other side, but no sound of Dolores.

Reggie continues down the hallway, reaching the hall and slipping down into the garage. He reaches his hand inside, searching for the light switch. For a moment, he imagines Dolores standing right in front of him, waiting with a knife.

But the garage is empty. Reggie goes to the cupboard, looking around for a screwdriver and finding one. He brings it along, remembering to turn off the light again as he leaves the garage and sneaks back through the house.

Safely back in his room, Reggie lets out a deep sigh of relief. He is almost there. The hard part is over. He climbs out the window and runs back down to the treehouse.

Closing the door behind him, he uses the light from his phone to locate the shiny screw. He drops down to his knees and starts unscrewing it. It takes almost a minute, but finally he can lift up the board.

He peers down into the hole. There is nothing but solid, frozen ground. But he can tell it has been recently dug up. He starts prodding at the ground with the screwdriver. It's not made for digging, but after a while he gets through the frozen surface and reaches softer ground. He is able to reach down a hand and finds something hard.

He pulls out a clear plastic bag, staring at it in the light from his phone. Inside the bag is only one item. A small, clear plastic bottle with no sticker or writing of any kind. He unzips the bag, takes out the bottle and unscrews the lid. Carefully, he sniffs the opening of the bottle. It smells like acid.

Can it be the poison Dolores used to kill Eva?

A noise behind him.

Reggie turns his head and sees the door opening, revealing Dolores dressed in her robe and staring at him, her eyes black as the night.

"You stupid little brat ..." she hisses, her voice thick with fury. "You just had to keep looking, didn't you?"

Reggie can't get a word out. Not that he has the time. Dolores steps inside and closes the door behind her, before she throws herself at Reggie.

"No! Don't! Stop it!"

Reggie struggles to get her off, but Dolores is surprisingly strong, apparently getting fueled by her rage. She pins him down, grabs his hair and slams his head against the floor, making Reggie dizzy with pain.

He tries to scream for help, tries to call for his dad, for the neighbors, for anyone, but Dolores muffles his cries by slapping her palm across his mouth, using the other hand to take the bottle from him.

"Now you do as I say," she seethes somewhere above him, her breath warm against his cheek. "Or I swear I'll make this painful for you."

The hand moves away from his mouth, and the bottle is forced in between his lips. "Now, drink it!"

Reggie bites down hard, thrashing his head from side to side. He can taste the acid on his lips, making him spit and sputter. He gropes blindly with his hands, searching for anything, finding Dolores's hair. He grabs it and tugs at it, hard. Dolores lets out a hiss of pain and punches him twice in the face before once again forcing the bottle to his mouth.

"Drink it, I say! Drink it, you piece of filth!"

But Reggie once again closes his mouth just before she can get the bottle across his teeth.

Dolores keeps swearing at him, as she reaches her fingers into his mouth and squeezes his teeth hard, causing him great pain and forcing him to open up a little.

"There's a good boy," she snarls hysterically, once more lifting the bottle.

Bite her.

It's Eva's voice, loud and clear, yet cool and calm, somewhere in his head.

Reggie doesn't think about it, he just does it: he opens wide, surprising Dolores, who is still pressing down on his teeth, causing her fingers to slip into his mouth, and before she can pull them out, Reggie bites down on them.

He feels the skin on Dolores's fingers puncture. He clamps down even harder, and there is a snapping noise as one of the fingers breaks.

Dolores lets out a scream of pain, trying to pull out her broken fingers, but Reggie keeps biting down as hard as he can, now tasting the warm blood filling his mouth.

"Let go of me!" Dolores screams, slapping him with her free hand. "Let go of me, you fucking animal!"

She keeps hitting him, making his eyes water and his ears ring, but Reggie keeps his jaws locked for as long and hard as he can. He doesn't think about anything else than not letting Dolores get back her hand, as he listens to Eva's voice, telling him calm but firm: *That's right, Reggie. Just hold on. Just for a little longer now. Just hold on.*

And Reggie holds on, as the sound of Dolores's anguished screaming becomes fainter and the pain from her punches gradually fades away. He holds on until a booming voice suddenly breaks through to him.

"Dolores! What the hell are you doing?"

Reggie finally releases his jaw and Dolores's fingers slip out of his mouth, the weight of her lifting from his body.

Reggie opens his eyes and looks up at Dad's face staring down at him with great concern. "Oh my God ... what happened?"

"She ... killed ... Eva ..." Reggie whispers, fighting to stay conscious, his mouth sticky with blood.

"You lying little bastard!" Dolores shrieks somewhere nearby. "Look what he did to me! I'm bleeding!"

But Dad keeps staring at Reggie. "What did you say, buddy?"

"Poison ..." Reggie says, not sure if the words are audible. "Poison ... in the bottle ..."

Dad's face shifts out of focus. The world starts growing black. The last thing Reggie hears before he drifts away is Dolores's voice, shrill with hysteria.

***

Winter turns into spring. The cold retreats and everything starts slowly thawing, including the lake in the park.

Reggie goes down there one Saturday morning in the early summer. The sun is shining warmly, and a couple of kids are playing baseball on the grass. A mother duck with four ducklings are floating around in the lake.

Reggie stops by the edge, looking down into the blue water, searching for the light. But of course, it's not there. It hasn't been since the night Dolores was arrested. Faced with a first-degree murder charge and attempted murder, Dolores had no choice but to plead guilty. Dad has assured him she will never get out of prison.

Eva's body was dug up and the police performed an autopsy. The results showed the same kind of chemical as they found in the bottle in the treehouse. A deadly poison which is symptomless but works within a few hours.

After eating the poisoned soup, Eva had been dead shortly after she went to bed that night. At around midnight, Dolores got up, dressed Eva's body, packed her schoolbag, her lunch and everything. Then she lifted her out into the car and put her bike in the trunk. She drove to the park and threw Eva into the lake along with the bike.

Reggie stares at the calm surface, feeling very sad and very relieved at the same time. And then he sees something. It's a tiny thing, just on the brink on the other side. He goes over and picks it up.

It's a bike light. Eva's bike light. He tries to turn it on, but the batteries are dead.

Reggie puts the light in his pocket, drawing in a deep breath and looking up at the sky. As he turns and walks away from the lake, he notices a smile on his face—the first one in a long time.

***

This story is inspired by two other great stories which I love. First off, the short story *The Lake* by Ray Bradbury, and secondly, the novel *The Lovely Bones* by Alice Sebold. I highly recommend you check them out if you haven't read them already. Both are heart-wrenching.

The idea for *Under the Ice* came to me one winter evening. I was walking through a park, passing by a frozen lake, and just like Reggie in the story, I saw a blinking light in the ice which I couldn't explain, as there were no stars or anything else to cause the reflection. I figured the light must have come from somewhere below, assuming it was a bike light someone had thrown in the water, but I never found out the truth.

Perhaps I should have looked a little closer. Perhaps someone was trying to tell me something.

DREAMLAND

Imagine you could visit a world
where everything was exactly the way you wanted;
where you had it all to yourself
and where everything was possible.
And imagine if all you had to do
to get there was to sleep.

Would you ever want to wake up?

Louie had always had lifelike dreams, but he'd never had a dream continuing over several nights, like chapters in a book—not until he visited Dreamland.

Of course, he didn't know the name of the place at first. To him, it was just a normal dream, except it felt more real. He could feel the wind and smell the grass—those kinds of details usually didn't register in his dreams.

It was so real, in fact, that if it hadn't been for the sky, Louie probably would've had a hard time discerning whether he was actually dreaming or not. The sky in Dreamland was the only sure telltale sign, because it was always a wrong color.

In the beginning there weren't any other people around. The dreams took place in a town where Louie would wander about all by himself. It was actually kind of boring.

But then the man in blue started showing up.

Louie would notice him now and again, but never up close and always just in brief glimpses. Sometimes he was standing on the corner of a street, sometimes by a tree in the park. There wasn't anything threatening or scary about him; he was just a regular guy, always smiling and always dressed in the same outfit: a sky-blue suit.

The first time Louie spoke to the man was in a playground. The sun was shining, the bugs were buzzing, the grass had been newly mown, and the sky was pink like candy floss.

Louie had just sat down on the swing when a voice behind him said: "Hello, Louie."

Louie gave a startle and almost fell off the swing.

The man had just appeared out of nowhere, like he had dropped down from heaven.

"How do you know my name?" Louie asked.

"I'm part of your dream, Louie. I know all the things you know."

"You seem familiar. I think I know you from somewhere."

The man went and sat down on the swing next to Louie. "Well, of course you do. You've been here in Dreamland before."

"Dreamland?"

"That's what I call the place."

"Oh. But, no, I mean before that. I think I know you from the real world."

The man tilted his head. "Is this world not real?"

"It can't be real, it's just a dream world—you just said so yourself," Louie pointed out.

"I never said dreams aren't real."

Louie looked at the man, swinging gently from side to side, trying to figure out if he was being serious. "You talk funny," he remarked.

"It's quite normal to talk a funny when you live in Dreamland."

"Do you *live* here?"

"Yes."

"All alone?"

"Yes."

"Don't you ever get lonely?"

"A little. Luckily, I have a visitor."

"But when I wake up, do you just stay in here?"

The man nodded. "I stay in here and wait for you to come back." He breathed deeply, got up and straightened his jacket. "Well, it was nice to meet you, Louie. I hope we can continue our talk the next time you come by."

"Why not continue now?"

The man shrugged and said as if it was self-evident: "Because you're waking up now."

Louie opened his mouth to answer, but realized he was suddenly in his bed. It was morning.

"Mom," he said at breakfast. "Do you want to hear about a strange dream I had last night?"

"Mmmm," his mom said. She was busy rummaging through her purse.

Louie stirred his cornflakes. "I dreamt I was in another world. There was a town but no people, except this one guy dressed in a blue suit."

"That sounds exciting, Louie. Listen, have you seen my lip balm?" Mom started going through the drawers.

"I haven't seen it," Louie said. "Do you think dreams can be real, Mom?"

"Sure."

"You do?"

Mom looked up. "What? Real? No, of course not. It's just dreams. Darn it, how can a lip balm just disappear like that?"

"Perhaps it's still in one of the boxes?" Louie suggested, pointing with his spoon at the two big cardboard boxes by the wall.

Mom considered for a brief moment, then she went to look in the boxes.

"The man in my dreams reminded me of someone," Louie went on. "He's tall and has brown hair. He smiles a lot, and he has a space between his front teeth."

Mom stopped searching and looked at him. "He has *what*?"

"A space between his front teeth." Louie grinned. "Like me."

Mom came closer, eyeing him thoughtfully. "Who did you say that man was?"

"I don't know. But I think I saw him somewhere. What is it, Mom? You look worried."

Mom sat down next to him. "Louie, do you remember how your father looked?"

Louie thought for a second. "Nah, not really."

"But you've seen pictures of him, right?"

"Yes, you showed me one a long time ago. Why?"

Mom's eyes moved for a second. "I just thought you might …" She sighed and stroked his hair. "Forget it, Louie. Eat your breakfast."

Louie ate his breakfast. But out of the corner of his eye he noticed his mom wasn't looking for the lip balm anymore. Instead, she just stood gazing out the window.

"Do you miss your father, Louie?" she asked without turning.

Louie was surprised; Mom never spoke about Dad. "I don't know," he said hesitantly. "Do you?"

"Sometimes. But it's no good living in the past, right?"

"No, Mom."

Louie knew that was the only correct answer, whenever his mom told him it was no good living in the past. It was curious, though—she almost sounded scared, when she said it. Louie didn't really get how you could be scared of the past.

Mom went out in the hallway. Louie heard the door to her bedroom close.

He finished his meal and rinsed out the bowl before going to his room. He got his bag and sat down on the bed, from where he could see out into the hallway.

A few minutes later, Mom came out from her room. She turned her head and saw him. Her expression was for a moment strange. Then, she smiled. "Don't forget your swimwear. It's Tuesday."

"I remembered, Mom."

She looked at her watch. "It's time to go. I just need to pee, then we leave." She went to the bathroom and closed the door.

Louie got up and slipped into his mom's bedroom. He looked around and noticed the bottom drawer of the dresser being ajar. He went to open it very carefully. It contained only towels. But when he lifted the top one, he found a framed picture lying face down. Louie took it and turned it over.

It was his parents' wedding picture.

Louie stared at it.

Although his suit was white and not blue, there was no mistaking it: Louie was looking at the man from his dreams.

Louie now knew who the man in blue was, and he planned on telling him so as soon as he saw him again.

He got the opportunity a couple of nights later. He arrived in Dreamland on an evening where the sky was the color of desert sand. He met the man in blue at a cobbled square next to a big fountain.

"Good evening, Louie," he said as he came walking over. "Welcome back to Dreamland."

"I know who you—" Louie began, but interrupted himself as his courage suddenly failed him.

The man looked inquiringly at him. "Who I what?"

Louie was afraid to say it. He didn't know how the man would react.

"I know who you remind me of," he said.

"And who might that be?"

"My dad. In fact, you look just like him."

"I do?"

"Yes. I've seen a photo of him. By the way, I never got your name?"

"That's right, you didn't. My name is John."

Louie gasped. "My dad's name was John!"

The man raised his brow. "Really?"

Louie bit his lip, then decided to take the chance. "Maybe ... maybe you *are* my dad." He added quickly: "My dad died when I was little."

John smiled. "In here, everything is really two things, Louie. What you see and what you want to see. For instance, have you ever seen a fountain where the water turns into marbles?"

Louie turned around and stared. The man was right: water spurted up into the air, but on the way down the droplets turned into tiny, see-through marbles, which glimmered in the light of the setting sun before dumping back into the water and sinking to the bottom.

"Wow, how did you do that?"

"I didn't do anything. You're just seeing what you want to see."

Louie admired the magical fountain. Then, he looked back at the man in blue. "So, you just *look* like my dad? Because I want you to?"

"Does that disappoint you?"

Louie shrugged. "A little."

They stood in silence for a short while.

"Let's take a walk," John said. "I want to know what happened since the last time we saw each other."

"You do?" Louie asked with mild surprise. "Well, there's really nothing exciting to tell. I've just been to school."

"Tell me about school, then. What's your favorite subject?"

"Science," Louie said immediately, as they started walking across the cobblestones. "I'm also fairly good at math, but it's just not nearly as fun."

"What's your least favorite subject, then?"

Louie thought about it and said: "English. We always have to do grammar. Our teacher's name is Josephine, and she only picks the most boring stories for us to read. And she always asks questions, like: 'Why would the main character say that?' or, 'How do you think he's feeling on the inside?'" Louie shrugged. "How should I know? I didn't write the story."

"Maybe Josephine is trying to teach you to read between the lines."

"What does that mean?"

"It means finding stuff that's not being stated outright, but is still there. Those things are often the most important part of the story."

Louie chewed on it. "I think I get it. You're a lot better at explaining than Josephine."

The dreams about the man in blue continued. Sometimes a few nights passed from one visit to the next, but Louie always ended up going back to Dreamland sooner or later.

He somehow never got bored in the company of John, although John spoke very little. Louie, on the other hand, talked like a waterfall. Whenever he would finish, John had a new question. Louie had never met a grown-up who would listen so intently.

The more time he spent with John, the more he reminded him of his father. Not just from the wedding photo, but also the small things he would do. How he moved his lips just before he spoke. How he always blinked twice.

It seemed odd that Louie was reminded of a person he didn't remember. But he was.

About a month later, Louie once again told his mom about the man in blue, and this time she reacted even more strangely than before. They were sharing a pizza in the car on their way home—it was one of those days where his mom had to work late, and Louie had waited at the after-school center.

"You sure it's the same dream?" she asked.

"It's not the same dream. Well, in a way, I guess. But something new always happens."

"But it's the same guy? This man in blue?"

"Yes."

"How many times would you say you've dreamt about him?"

"Mmmm. I don't know."

"Five times?"

"More."

"Ten times?"

"More."

Mom took her eyes off the road to look at him. "Twenty times?"

Louie took a bite of his slice. "More or less."

For a moment neither of them spoke.

"Do you know his name?" his mom asked.

"It's John. Like Dad."

"So, it *is* your father."

"No, he just has the same name. And he kind of looks like him. But he says he's not him."

They stopped at a red light. An old couple crossed the road. The light changed, and his mom set the car in motion, when a teenage girl walked out into the crosswalk. She was wearing a headset and stared at her phone, oblivious to the world.

"Goddamnit," his mom said, stopping the car abruptly. "Watch where you're going, young lady!"

It wasn't until his mom gave a short honk that the girl looked up and realized the light was red. She hurried back onto the sidewalk.

"Some people are a danger to themselves," Louie remarked.

Mom turned her head and looked at him. "What did you say?"

"I meant *her*, Mom. Not you."

"Where did you hear that expression?"

"John said it. I told him about that time Ron climbed onto the roof of the bike shed to show off in front of the girls and then fell down and broke his wrist."

Mom drove on. She seemed to be trying to study Louie's face and the road at the same time.

"I've got a question for the guy in your dreams," she said. "If you dream about him again, would you ask him something for me?"

"Sure. What is it?"

"Ask him who Capella is."

"Who is it?"

"Just ask him, please."

"Okay."

Louie didn't really get why his mom was suddenly interested in his dreams, but he was going to do as she asked.

That same night he got the chance.

"Capella is your mom," John said with a twinkle in his eye.

Mom dropped the electric kettle, causing steaming hot water to pour out over the kitchen counter. She spun around and looked at him. "*What* did he say?"

"He said you were Capella," Louie repeated hesitantly.

"What else?"

"Nothing, really."

"He didn't explain to you what the name means?"

"No. Mom, the water is running to the floor ..."

Mom took a dishcloth and mopped up the water.

Louie fondled the edge of his T-shirt. "Is something wrong, Mom?"

"No, no. Everything's fine."

"I thought you dropped the kettle because of what I said."

She came over and knelt down in front of him. "You didn't do anything wrong, okay? I'm not mad at you. But I need you to tell me something. Did you already know that your dad used to call me Capella?"

Louie shook his head. "I never heard that name before in my life, Mom."

"You sure?"

"A hundred percent."

"All right, sweetheart." She smiled briefly and got up. Apparently, she didn't want the tea anyway, because she just went straight to the bedroom and locked the door.

As Louie lay in bed that night, he somehow knew he would visit Dreamland again.

From the bathroom he could hear his mom talk on the phone. She always went to the bathroom to talk whenever it was something she didn't want him to hear, or when she wanted to smoke. She said she didn't smoke, but Louie found cigarette butts in the toilet now and then.

He only picked up some of the words, but it was pretty clear his mom was angry. It was probably Aunt Tina she was talking to; Mom was often angry with Aunt Tina.

"... I told you, there was no one else ... no, not Mom, either ... you sure? ... then where could he have heard it from? ... I swear, if you're lying to me, Tina ..."

Louie let his eyes wander across the empty bookcase. From the ceiling hung a naked lightbulb. The books and the lampshade were still in the boxes in the corner. Louie wasn't sure it was worth the effort to unpack. They had already stayed here for four months, which was longer than most places.

He turned onto his side and studied the pattern in the wallpaper. He had looked at many different wallpapers. In this one he could make out a cloud and a tiger and a motorcycle with only one wheel. His eyelids started to get heavy.

A moment later he found himself in the park in Dreamland.

It was a lovely afternoon; the sun was shining and the sky was the color of rye bread. Louie saw the man in blue sitting on the bench underneath a big chestnut tree.

He went and sat down next to him.

"Hello, Louie. Nice to see you again."

"Hello, Dad."

John smiled at him, curiously. "Why do you call me that?"

"Because you *have* to be my father. Only my dad called my mom Capella."

"I'm part of your dream, remember?" John said, extending his arms. "It's all taking place in your brain."

"I thought so at first," Louie admitted. "But *I* didn't know the name. So you couldn't have gotten it from my brain."

John smiled. "You're a clever boy, Louie. I would have waited a little while longer before telling you. I wanted to be sure that *you* were sure. Like I said, it can be difficult to tell the difference between what you see and what you want to see."

"So ... it's true? You really are my ...?"

John nodded.

Louie didn't know how to react. He had often wondered what it would be like to meet his dad, and now he was sitting right next to him. In a way.

"You told me so much about yourself," his dad said, getting up. "Perhaps you want to know a little about me?"

Louie followed him, as he wandered to a lake where a swan couple was floating around amongst the waterlilies.

"How did you die?" Louie asked.

"Your mom didn't tell you?"

"I think it was some kind of disease. She said something once about the last days being really tough."

Dad nodded. "I died from cancer. I got the diagnosis when you were only ten months old, and I died shortly after you turned one." He looked like he remembered something. "Do you want to hear one of the last memories I have? Your mom baked a cake and brought it to the hospital. I had to blow out the candle for you, but when I did, you started laughing like crazy, so your mom lit the candle again, and I blew it out once more. I think we did it like ten times. You laughed until you were red in the face." Dad chuckled.

Louie looked shyly down into the grass. That was such a nice memory—why had his mom never told him about it?

"Did it hurt to die?" he asked.

"I didn't feel anything. I was very weak and slept most of the time. Sometimes I would sleep for days on end." Dad seemed to be slipping away into memories. He was almost talking to himself now. "That was when I started having the dreams."

"What dreams?"

They came to a wooden bridge leading to a small island in the middle of the lake. A flock of ducks were lying in the reeds, basking in the sunlight.

Dad stepped out onto the bridge and leaned against the railing. Louie followed him and looked down into the water. It was clear enough to see the bottom and the goldfishes which were swimming about.

"Dreams about your grandmother. My mom. She started showing up in my dreams, always wearing a pretty blue dress." Dad glanced at him. "Do you know how your grandmother died?"

Louie shook his head.

"It was a car accident. I was only fourteen back then. I always missed her a lot, so when she suddenly came to me in my dreams, I was very happy. I spent a lot of time with her. It was a relief, too, because here in Dreamland I wasn't sick or afraid.

"Towards the end I started preparing for death. It was incredibly hard to have to say goodbye to your mom and you. I didn't feel like my life was over, not by a long shot. It was all very unfair. But then your grandmother told me something amazing one day."

Dad produced a lump of bread from his pocket and tore it into halves, handing one to Louie. They started crumbling the bread and letting small pieces fall into the water. The ducks got up and waddled down to the brink.

"She told me I could live on if I joined her in here. You have to understand: at that time, I slept almost around the clock, and I spent more time in here than in the waking world. I somehow felt more at home in here—that's why I made the decision." Dad was out of bread. He brushed off his hands. "I felt ashamed because I left you and your mother before it was time, but I was afraid of dying."

Louie realized he too was out of bread. The ducks grabbed the last pieces and looked eagerly up at him. He turned to his father. "So you didn't really die. You just went to this place."

Dad leaned his back against the railing. "I died all right, but only in the waking world. Here in Dreamland I have lived on for eleven years."

"How about Grandma? Is she in here too?"

Dad shook his head. "Sadly, she disappeared shortly before I met you for the first time. I don't think she will be back."

"Then why did you and I meet? I mean, how did it happen?"

"Suddenly one day I just saw you. I understood right away who you were, but I decided it was better to hold off on telling you all of this until we knew each other a little better."

"But why am I here? I'm not sick."

"Apparently, you don't need to be sick to visit Dreamland." Dad shrugged. "I don't know the rules, and I don't know who makes them."

A whole bunch of questions tumbled about in Louie's brain. Mom had often told him that clever kids would think before they asked any questions, and he had already asked a lot of questions. So, he just stood for a little while with his dad looking at the ducks and the goldfishes.

The light was beginning to dwindle when Louie looked up and noticed the first, bright star burning on the horizon.

"That's not a star," his dad said, as though he had read Louie's mind. "It's a planet."

"A planet?"

"Venus. She's beautiful tonight. Do you want to see her up close?"

Between them was suddenly a large telescope on a tripod. Louie put his eye to the ocular and gasped at the sight of the planet. It was beige and had the form of a sickle.

"Did your mom ever tell you I had my own observatory?"

"No."

"I made it in a small chamber in the attic underneath a skylight. It had a telescope, a chair, a computer, and everything. Your mom thought the equipment was too expensive, but the night sky was my great passion, so I had to have it." Dad smiled and looked up. "I was up there almost every night, even if I had to get up early in the morning."

Louie tried to imagine his dad's observatory. He tried to imagine Mom and Dad together, talking with each other, laughing. But it was difficult.

"Mom never really told me anything about you," he said. "I don't think she wants to talk about you."

"Every time she remembers me, it breaks her heart a little," his dad explained. "We loved each other very much."

Louie thought about it, and suddenly he got why his mom would move so often. He'd always had a sense that she was looking for something, but maybe it was the other way around—maybe she was trying to get away from something.

"But she doesn't need to feel sad anymore," Louie said. "Now I can tell her that you're still alive—sort of."

"I think it's better if you don't tell her about me anymore, Louie."

"Why's that?"

"She hasn't visited Dreamland herself, so she can never understand. It would only make her even more sad if you told her you are spending time with me."

"Can't she come here?" Louie suggested. "So she can meet you?"

"Like I said, Louie: I have no idea how this place works, or how you get to come here."

Louie lowered his head.

"Perhaps, one day, your mom will show up," his dad said, placing an arm around his shoulders. "Until then, it can be our little secret. What do you say?"

Louie looked up and smiled. "Sure, Dad."

"You look like you had a good night's sleep," his mom remarked as Louie joined her for breakfast.

It was Saturday, so Louie didn't have school. Mom was working on her laptop.

Louie rolled up his sleeves, like his mom had taught him, and hummed to himself as he buttered up his toast.

"Did you dream anything last night?" his mom asked casually.

"Yes, I ..." Louie stopped and thought for a moment. He didn't want to tell a lie. "I dreamt I was walking in a park and feeding ducks in a pond."

"How nice." Mom sipped her coffee. "Phil will be joining us for dinner tonight."

"Okay. Is he spending the night?"

Mom's cup froze midair. "Why do you ask me that?"

Louie shrugged. "He often eats dinner here, so I just figured you guys might be ... like, dating."

"Louie Taylor, are you accusing your own mother of fooling around with boys? You know you're my only love." She leaned over and tried to kiss him.

Louie pushed her away, laughing.

Mom closed the laptop. "Listen, Louie, I'm sorry if I scared you a little yesterday. I just didn't understand how you could know that Capella was your father's nickname for me. But the more I think about it, I realize you must have heard it somewhere."

Of course, I did, Louie thought. *I heard it when Dad told me just the other night.* But he simply said: "Don't worry about it, Mom."

"It's actually a star ..."

"I know. The third brightest in the night sky. I Googled it. I think it's a pretty name."

Mom smiled. "I think so too." She seemed to remember something. "I spoke with the housing association. Like I expected, they didn't believe me about the mouse droppings at first, but finally they agreed to send an exterminator on Monday."

Louie knew where this was going—they would soon be moving again. It always happened like this: his mom would get a whim that something was wrong with the place—dampness, leaky windows, ants, whatever—and when caretakers and craftsmen and pest fighters had visited several times and assured her the apartment was in excellent condition, she came to the conclusion that they were wrong, and that she didn't want to live in such an unhealthy environment.

A question popped into his head. "Mom? Where did we live when Dad was alive?"

"We lived in a house."

"Here in town?"

"Yes, but out at the other end. At Park Road, the big red one. Haven't I pointed it out to you?"

"No, you haven't," Louie said. And when his mom's eyes grew distant, he quickly asked: "Is it okay if I go visit Marc?"

Louie rode his bike right past Marc's house and continued until he reached a part of town he had rarely been in. On a corner he asked a woman with a stroller for directions.

"Park Road? That's close by," she said, pointing. "Two blocks more and then left."

Louie rode on and soon reached Park Road. It was a calm street with big houses on both sides, but none of them were red—not until the very last one, at the end of the street, where it met the tall trees of the park.

The grass in the front yard was overdue for a trimming, and the windows were dirty. Next to the mailbox was a FOR SALE sign. The house had obviously been empty for a while.

He put his bike on the kickstand and went up the garden path. Knocked carefully three times on the door. When nothing happened, he daringly turned the handle. The door was locked.

He went around to the backyard, where the grass was even taller. Large apple trees stood with small, green fruits, and a flock of birds hopped around on the terrace.

Louie had no memory of this place. He hadn't even been two years old when they moved out. It was strange to think that his mom and dad had sat here in the summertime, drinking iced tea. The only picture he could come up with in his imagination was an artificial one of a young, cool couple, who looked suspiciously like a couple he had seen in a perfume commercial.

Louie put his hands to the glass and looked through the terrace door. The living room was big and empty, the walls naked and the floor dusty.

Why was the house abandoned? Didn't anyone want to live here? Had there even been other residents since Louie and his mom had moved out?

Louie went farther around the house and reached a back door leading into a garage. He grabbed the handle without really expecting any luck—but the door opened.

Cautiously, he stepped into a dim, oil-smelling room with shelves full of old tools and paint buckets. Was that his dad's old stuff? Had his mom just left it here when they moved out?

The door leading into the house was ajar. Louie pushed it open and peeked into an empty, shadowy hallway. He stepped inside, the floorboards creaking and the noise echoing between the walls. Everything felt a lot bigger than the apartments he was used to.

He met a staircase and went up the steps. On the first floor he went through the empty rooms one at a time. In one of them he found candy wrappers and empty beer bottles—some older kids seemed to have had a party in here.

By the end of the hallway was a ladder leading up to a hatch in the ceiling. Louie climbed up and gave the hatch a push. At first it didn't move, but he pushed harder and managed to get it up, dust raining down on him.

As he stuck his head up into the attic, he immediately realized he had found what he had been looking for most of all.

The sunlight was streaming in through the skylight and bathed the dusty armchair in a golden glow. The chair was the only furniture in the small attic, but Louie knew his dad's telescope and his computer had been up here, too.

He went to sit down in the armchair and looked out at the blue sky. It was odd. He was in a strange house, yet he had never felt more at home.

Phil came at around five thirty, bringing a bottle of wine.

Phil was a tall guy with very short hair who smiled a lot. Louie liked him.

At dinner his mom started telling Phil about how they might soon have to move out, due to her suspicion about the apartment being infected with mice and possibly also rats. Phil said he sure hoped they wouldn't move too far away, but Mom assured him they would find another apartment somewhere in town—if it even came to that.

"Mom, I've been thinking about something," Louie said during a short pause in the conversation. "I would like to get a telescope."

"A telescope? That kind of equipment is terribly expensive, Louie. You need to start saving."

"I thought about that, too. What if I stop swimming? Then we can use the money we save from that. It would only take about five months until we could afford a decent one."

"That's not how it works. Swimming is a leisure activity, something you do in order to learn. You can't just trade that away for a toy."

"It's not a toy," Louie said. "A telescope is also a leisure activity. It would teach me about the stars and planets."

Mom raised one eyebrow. "You certainly thought this through, didn't you? So, you're going to be an astrologer all of a sudden?"

"It's called an astronomer, Mom. An astrologer is one who makes horoscopes."

"Well, pardon my professional ignorance," his mom said, smiling at Phil.

Louie said casually: "If the new apartment has a skylight, I could even fit out my own observatory."

Mom's fork slipped and made a loud screeching noise against the plate.

Phil looked at Louie. "An observatory? That's a great idea. Maybe you could discover a comet or something, and get it named after you. Louie's Comet—huh? How does that sound?"

"It sounds awesome!" Louie said and laughed. But when he met his mom's eyes, his smile faded. She was staring at him across the table.

"Ellen?" Phil said. "Is something wrong?"

Only when Phil put his hand on Mom's arm, did she come to. She blinked and forced a smile. "Sorry, I was lost in thought for a second." She cleared her throat. "We'll see if we can afford a telescope, Louie."

Louie could tell from her voice that the matter needed to rest for now.

Phil put down his fork. "I have a little surprise." He reached into his pocket and produced two small pieces of cardboard which he handed to Louie. "It's tickets for a hockey game tomorrow. Panthers versus Red Wings. I thought it might be something for you, Louie. Have you ever seen a hockey match live?"

Louie shook his head.

"It's really cool. The seats are very close to the ice, so we'll be able to see everything. What do you say? You want to go?"

"Wow," Mom said. "Wouldn't that be so neat? Watching ice hockey together is like a real guy thing. I totally envy you." She smiled at Phil, and Phil smiled back. Then, they both looked at Louie.

He couldn't very well do anything else than smile and say yes.

That night, Louie didn't dream about his father. In fact, he didn't dream at all.

In the morning, he opened his eyes and looked at his Batman alarm clock. It was 6:54. Early sunlight was coming through the blinds, but the room was still dim. He stretched and yawned and closed his eyes again, intending to sleep a little longer.

Suddenly, a voice whispered: "Louie? Can you hear me? I have something very important to tell you."

Louie sat up abruptly and looked around the room. For a moment it was as if his eyes failed him, because the room looked completely wrong. Then he blinked, and the surroundings became normal again, although the room seemed a little brighter than before. He had heard the voice quite clearly, as if someone had stood right beside the bed. But he was alone.

"Hello?" Louie murmured. "Phil?"

Phil was the only guy he could think of, but as soon as he said the name out loud, he realized how silly it was. As if Phil would suddenly appear from underneath the bed or step out from behind the boxes in the corner. That was just absurd.

But who had spoken then?

Louie turned and placed his feet on the ground, and as he did so, it felt like his head became clearer. He looked at the watch. It was now 7:23. More than half an hour had passed. He had slept without knowing it. The whispering voice, therefore, must have been something he had dreamed.

In the kitchen he found the table laid out for breakfast. He sat down, poured himself a bowl of cornflakes, and started eating. A minute later, his mom came out from the bathroom. She looked unusually pretty this morning, and Louie got a whiff of perfume as she bent down to kiss him on the forehead.

"Are you going to work today?"

"No, it's Sunday."

"Oh, right."

"Phil will be here to pick you up at one, so if you go out, make sure to be home before noon."

"Okay, Mom."

Louie had just put the bowl in the dishwasher when the doorbell rang.

Mom was in her bedroom, so Louie went to open.

"Hi, Louie," Marc said. "You want to go to the zip wire? My mom says I've been playing on the computer for too long and I need to spend the rest of the day outside."

Marc wore glasses that had a habit of sliding down. He didn't use his finger to push them back up, but lifted them by grimacing.

"I can only be out until noon," Louie said. "I have to go somewhere else."

"Where?"

"I'm going to see ... an ice hockey game."

Marc didn't have time to answer, because Louie's mom joined them at that moment. "Hi, Marc. So, are you guys playing here today?"

Louie felt a pang of panic. Marc could easily reveal to his mom that Louie hadn't been at his place yesterday.

"We're going to the zip wire," Louie said, grabbing his jacket. Before his mom could remind him, he added: "I'll keep an eye on the time."

The hockey game was a mixed experience for Louie. It was fun seeing all the people jumping and shouting and cheering. The game itself didn't really capture him, though—it went so fast he could hardly see where the puck was. For the last half hour, he was so bored he had to hide a yawn several times.

Phil was very engaged, jumping to his feet along with the rest of the crowd whenever something exciting happened on the ice. He kept asking Louie questions like: "Are you having fun?" and "Can you see well enough?" and "Do you want a soda or anything?"

In the car on the ride home, Phil asked him what he thought about the game.

"It was exciting," Louie said.

"Ice hockey isn't really your thing, is it?"

Louie turned his head in surprise. "Not really," he admitted. "I'm sorry, Phil."

Phil burst of laughing. "Don't apologize, Louie. *I* invited *you*. I've always loved ice hockey—I played it myself, when I was young. But I understand it's not for everyone. If you want to hang out with me again sometime, we'll find something else to do."

"I would like that."

"Cool. Do you have anything in mind?"

"Hmmm ... not really."

A moment's silence in the car.

Phil snapped his fingers. "I know! The planetarium. Have you ever been there?"

"What is the planetarium?"

"It's like a museum, only it's about space. I went with my class many years ago. They've probably gotten a lot of new stuff since then. You want to go?"

Louie nodded with emphasis. "Sure!"

"It's a date, then," Phil said.

That night, Louie visited Dreamland once more. This time, he arrived at an old train station on a cool and foggy morning, where the sky was green like moss.

Louie's father wasn't there at first, so Louie jumped down onto the tracks and played a balancing game on them. Of course, in the real world, it would have been dangerous, but here in Dreamland he knew no real harm could come to him.

Louie tried to beat his own record, which made him go farther and farther away from the train station and towards the city limit where the open fields began.

Suddenly, he felt a chilly wind. Puzzled, he stopped and looked around. The sun was shining, the fog had lifted, and the air was warm. But a short distance away, the tracks disappeared into shadow, as if an invisible cloud was hanging above them. It was a strange sight.

Another cold breeze rustled his hair. It almost sounded like the wind was singing. It had a melody. Beautiful bright tones.

Louie listened intently. He couldn't hear the birds anymore. Everything was quiet except for the wind. He stared out into the shadow—that was where the wind came from. He wanted to hear it more clearly, so he stepped closer.

"... *Louuuuie ... Louuuuie ...*"

It sounded like the wind was singing his name. He was only a few steps away, and somewhere out in the darkness he could make out something white moving and swaying from side to side. He reached out his hand.

"Louie!"

He blinked and turned around. Dad was standing on the tracks, waving. Louie smiled and ran to him.

"Where were you going?" his dad asked.

"Nowhere," Louie said. "I just thought I heard someone singing. Are you sure we are the only ones here?"

"Absolutely," his dad said, putting his arm around Louie's shoulders. "Come on, let's go back."

"That guy Phil sounds like a really nice guy," his dad said when Louie had told him about the hockey game.

They were sitting on a bench by the train station.

"He sure is," Louie said. "And we're going to the ... what was it called now? It's like a planet museum ..."

Dad raised his eyebrows. "The planetarium?"

"Exactly! The planetarium. From what he told me, it sounds really cool."

"It is," his dad said. "I went there many times while I was alive. I never got tired of walking around looking at the satellites and lunar rocks and the big models of the planets. It's a great place for space geeks like us. I only wish I could be the one to ..." He fell silent, looked sad for a moment, then smiled. "I'm sure you'll have a great time with Phil."

Louie too felt a pinch of sadness that they couldn't go to the planetarium together.

"Is Phil also into astronomy?" his dad asked.

"Not really. I think it's mostly for my sake we're going."

"That's nice of him. He's almost ..." Dad broke off once more.

"Almost what, Dad?"

"Nothing. I was just reminded of something completely different."

Louie waited as his dad seemed to drift away into memories.

Then, he suddenly lit up. "You know what, Louie? I just remembered something. I don't think your mom ever got rid of my telescope. She always threatened to sell it off to someone while I wasn't at home, but after I died ..." Dad looked up at the sky, like he did whenever he was wondering about something. "I think she kept it. She might even have forgotten she still has it."

Louie jumped to his feet. "You really think so?"

"I think there's a fair chance."

"Then I don't need to save for one!"

The conversation turned to planets and stars. It was exciting for Louie, since his dad knew so many things. Louie asked a lot of questions, and his dad answered and explained as best he could. They practiced the names of the constellations and the order of the planets. Dad pulled out a star map from his jacket pocket and taught Louie to navigate from coordinates.

"So the numbers on the map correspond to degrees in the sky," his dad said.

"I'm not sure I get it," Louie said. "It would be a lot easier if I could see the stars."

"Funny you should say so. I think it's getting dark."

Louie looked around at the platform. It was high noon and the sun was shining. "Uhm, Dad, I don't think ..."

But at that moment, something happened to the light. The shadows started moving, grew longer. And when Louie looked up, he saw the sun race across the sky, headed for the horizon. It was like watching a movie being fast-forwarded. Shortly before the sun disappeared, it colored the horizon pink. Then, it was gone, and Louie immediately felt the temperature drop. A flock of pigeons who had been waddling about the platform took to their wings and flew up on the roof of the station building, where they settled in for the night. Darkness descended and the stars lit up above.

Louie was speechless.

"There," his dad said. "That's much better. Now we just need to turn off the last light." He pointed at the nearest lamppost and snapped his fingers. It turned off. He looked at Louie. "You want to try?"

"Yeah!"

Louie pointed to the next lamppost and snapped his fingers. The light went out.

"Awesome! It's like having magical powers."

"I guess so. Now, where were we? Oh, wait a second; we have another small problem." He pointed up at the sky, where a few clouds had gathered, blocking the view of some of the stars. "Would you care to handle it, Louie?"

"How?"

"Well, you could try blowing them away."

Louie sniggered nervously, got up, pursed his lips and blew up at the skies. He didn't really expect anything to happen, but the clouds moved like feathers in the wind. He inhaled deeply and blew again, making the clouds scatter in all directions. He blew again and again, pushing them all the way to the horizon, where they disappeared.

When the sky was all clear, Louie felt dizzy. He almost lost his balance, but his dad caught him by the arm, and they both laughed.

"Now we just need the telescope," his dad said. "Ah, there it is."

Louie turned to see the telescope they had already used once before.

Dad and Louie looked at stars all through the night.

"I have a riddle for you, Louie," his dad said at one point, lifting a finger. "You remember we saw Venus the other day?"

"Yes, of course."

"The riddle is about Venus. Are you ready?"

Louie nodded.

"Why can't you see Venus at night?"

Louie frowned. "You can't? But we saw—"

"We saw it in the *evening*. Venus is only visible in the morning and in the evening. It disappears in the night. Why is that?"

Louie pondered. For a long time. Finally, he shook his head. "I don't know the answer."

Dad smiled. "Sure you do. It will come to you. Just be patient."

"Okay, Dad."

Louie heard a strange, whirring noise.

"What's that?" he asked, looking around. "Is that a train?"

"That's you waking up." Dad rustled his hair. "I really enjoyed our night together, Louie. I'll see you soon."

The noise grew to a terrible roar, and now Louie recognized it. It was his alarm clock.

Louie rolled to the side and reached for the snooze button.

I was with Dad the whole night, he thought, lying for a moment in silence. He had never spent that much time in Dreamland before.

He shoved the cover aside and sat up, yawning and rubbing his eyes. He didn't feel particularly well rested; in fact, his head was dull and his body felt heavy.

Louie got up and went to pee. As he was standing in front of the toilet, he suddenly remembered the telescope and what his dad had said about it.

Had his mom really kept it? And if so, where could it be?

The answer was obvious: the basement. Where the moving stuff was. The moving stuff was all the things they always brought along when they moved, but which never got unpacked. Books, an old television, cast-off clothes, and even pieces of furniture they didn't use anymore.

Louie stood for a moment and listened. From the living room he could hear the morning news, which meant his mom was up. She probably sat in the kitchen eating her breakfast while working on her laptop.

He considered postponing until after school. Mom came home late on Mondays, so he would have plenty of time to go exploring. But the problem was, he really couldn't wait that long.

Quickly he got dressed and slipped down the hallway. The kitchen door was closed, so he was able to pick the key from the peg, open and close the front door very carefully, and then run down the stairs to the basement.

The long row of rooms behind the wooden bars reminded Louie of prison cells. He couldn't remember their current apartment number—since it changed on a regular basis—so he had to look at the key. Fourteen, second on the right.

He found the corresponding room, unlocked the door, and started going through the stuff. There was a lot of it. He didn't get why his mom couldn't just get rid of it.

He had looked for several minutes when his eyes caught a metal suitcase by the back wall. He remembered having noticed it before, yet he had never wondered what was in it. He pulled it out and fumbled for a moment with the lock. It opened with a click. Louie held his breath.

The telescope lay in a recess of black foam rubber. It was dismantled into several parts, and the flashy metal and the thin mirror discs shone up at him, looking brand new.

"Wow," Louie whispered.

He was almost afraid to touch it. He imagined himself assembling it and putting it on the tripod stand. He would place his eye against the eyepiece, just like his dad had shown him in the dream, and …

The sound of footsteps. Someone was coming down the hallway.

Louie spun around, just as his mom stopped in front of the room.

"What on Earth are you doing down here, Louie?"

"I just wanted ... I just had to ..." Louie searched for a lie, but his mom had already seen the open suitcase.

"Is that ... your father's old telescope?" she asked with amazement, stepping into the room. "Where the heck did you find that?"

"Right here, with the moving stuff. It has been here the whole time, Mom. Ever since Dad died."

Mom looked from the suitcase to Louie. "But how did you know it was down here?"

"I just ... guessed it."

Mom placed her hands on her hips. "How did you even know your father had a telescope? Who told you?"

Louie briefly considered making something up, but he didn't think his mom was going to accept a half-baked lie. Besides, she guessed the answer before he could say anything.

"You've been dreaming about your father again, haven't you?"

She made it sound like an accusation.

Louie nodded guiltily. "I didn't want to tell you, because you always ... you always ..." He couldn't find the right words.

"*What*, Louie?" demanded his mom, her voice getting higher. "I always *what*?"

"You become like this!" Louie exclaimed, pointing at her. "You always freak out whenever I mention Dad. You don't want to me to dream about him, but I can't help it."

Mom blinked with surprise. "Louie, listen to me. I'm only worried about you. You can't—"

"Dad told me about the telescope," he interrupted. "He said it was probably still here somewhere."

Mom's hand went up to her temple, as though her head was suddenly filled with thoughts. Louie could tell she made an effort to talk calmly. "Your father's dead, Louie. Who is telling you all these things?"

"Dad."

"Stop lying. You know I won't stand for it."

"I'm not lying! You want to know what Dad told me? He told me that you often threatened to sell off the telescope because you thought it had been too expensive, and that was also why you didn't want him to buy it in the first place. But after he died, you couldn't bring yourself to sell it anyway, so you just forgot about it."

Mom backed away from him with a terrified look on her face.

"It's the truth, Mom," Louie said. His heart was in his throat. He expected his mom to start yelling.

But she only said: "Please put it back and come with me back upstairs. You need to eat your breakfast, or you'll be late."

Louie tried to determine his mom's face and tone. He didn't think she would do or say any more about the telescope or his dad. She would probably just pretend like nothing happened. He could live with that. But he was afraid she might get rid of the telescope while he was at school.

"Are you driving me today?" he asked.

"You can ride with me, sure."

Louie nodded, satisfied with the knowledge that he would be home before her.

He shut the case, and his mom locked the room before they left the basement together.

Louie ran all the way home from school, the books bouncing around inside his bag, a side stitch poked him viciously in the ribs, but he ignored it.

As soon as he reached the block, he went straight for the basement and gave a sigh of relief when he found the suitcase. Just to be sure, he opened it to confirm the telescope was still there. It was.

He carefully picked up the case and carried it outside to his bike. But as he looked at the luggage carrier, he immediately realized the suitcase was too big to fit on it. Instead, he brought it to the bus stop around the corner.

A couple of older boys sent him and the metal suitcase some curious glances as Louie got onto the bus. He went all the way to the back and sat down with the case on his lap, clutching it.

Twelve minutes later Louie stood in front of the house on Park Road, the sky above him had turned heavy with clouds threatening to start raining any minute. Louie hurried to the back and entered through the garage door. The inside of the house seemed dimmer today, since the sun wasn't shining, and the only light making its way through the windows was grey and flickering with dust.

He lifted the suitcase upstairs. The muscles in his arms and back were starting to complain. The ladder was an even bigger challenge—the ladder was very steep and the rungs very narrow, and he had to take two breaks along the way up. Just before reaching the hatch in the ceiling, he came close to dropping the suitcase, but he caught it in the last second. He had no idea if the telescope could survive a drop like that, and he had no desire to find out.

Finally, he was sitting securely in the attic, sweating and resting. He could hear the rain starting to drum on the roof tiles and the skylight. Louie checked the time. No worries—he could easily be home before his mom.

He put his jacket on a nail protruding from a beam and opened the suitcase. Louie had always been good at playing with Legos, and the telescope turned out to be much less complicated than it looked. He unfolded the legs, clicked the joints into place, tightened the thumbscrews—and soon the telescope was standing in all its glory in the cramped and dusty attic.

Louie felt the excitement bubble in his stomach. He had an unbelievable urge to try it out, but firstly he couldn't see anything through the rain clouds, and secondly, it was still daytime, so neither the stars nor planets were visible.

"If only I could do like we did in Dreamland," he murmured to himself. "Just turn the time forward and blow the clouds away."

He noticed water seeping in through a tiny crack beneath the skylight. He went down to the garage and found a piece of plastic and a blanket. The plastic he stuffed into the crack and the blanket he put over the telescope to protect it from dust. He ran his hand over it in a gentle caress.

"I'll be back one of the next days," he promised. "I can't wait to see what you will show me."

Some days passed before Louie went to Dreamland again. Those days brought some other remarkable events.

Mom told him she had made an appointment with the school psychologist for him. She explained to him that a psychologist was a doctor of the mind and that it could never hurt to have a professional to share your thoughts with. Louie knew, of course, it was because of the dreams, but he said nothing.

Louie visited the house on Park Road one evening his mom had to stay at work late. He waited with excitement in the attic as the sun set outside. But just as the first stars appeared, the alarm on his phone told him the last bus would go in ten minutes. Disappointed, he had to put the blanket back over the telescope, leave the house, and run to the bus stop.

On his way home, he sat looking out through the window at the yellow streetlights gliding by and wondered how he could get a chance to visit the house after dark. He couldn't stay out later than five o'clock, so his only hope was darkness coming earlier, which of course would happen in the coming winter. But it was still just mid-September, and the days only very slowly got shorter.

Not until around Christmas would darkness come early enough, and there was no way Louie could wait that long.

He had to figure something out.

One day, Phil came by for a cup of coffee and asked Louie if he still felt up for a trip to the planetarium, because he was thinking they could all three go this weekend.

The visit at the planetarium went well. Louie was completely taken in by the many things he could look at and read about.

At one time, he noticed his mom had tucked her arm under Phil's. It seemed quite natural, as if she hadn't even thought about it. And she was smiling.

It made Louie happy.

A few days later Louie was in his room when he heard his mom talking on the phone. He had found an online calendar outlining when the planets, comets, and different meteor showers would be visible and he was writing down the dates. He also noted the lunar and solar eclipses, even though the next one wasn't until next year.

Mom's voice came from the bathroom, and he could hear her snigger. "... not really sure, Phil ... can't be home alone, not old enough yet ... just not comfortable with it ..." A short pause, then his mom laughed again. "Oh, really? ... think so? ... better be careful what you wish for, mister ..."

She sounded almost giggly, and Louie felt a little ashamed about eavesdropping. He got the point of the conversation, though: Phil wanted his mom to spend the night at his place, but his mom couldn't because she didn't want to leave Louie alone all night.

Louie realized this was exactly what he needed. If he could spend a night alone, he could ride his bike to the house on Park Road and stay for as long as he wanted.

The only question was: How could he convince his mom it was a good idea to sleep at Phil's place?

The next day Louie made dinner. He peeled the potatoes and baked them in the oven, washed and chopped the salad, seasoned the lamb chops and fried them. He did all this while his mom was at the library.

When he heard the front door, he turned to see his mom standing in the kitchen doorway, staring at the laid-out table.

"Hi, Mom," Louie said. He was standing at the sink wearing the yellow rubber gloves, scrubbing the skillet. "Dinner's ready."

"Louie," his mom said, putting down the library book. "Did you do all this on your own?"

"Sure," he said, pulling off the gloves. "You told me we were having lamb chops, and I remember how you used to make them. Let's eat while it's still warm."

Louie was talking eagerly during the meal. He suggested they start taking turns cooking dinner. And that his mom could teach him to operate the washer in the basement, so he could start doing his own laundry.

"Hold on a second," his mom interrupted. "Are you practicing moving out?"

He laughed. "Of course not, Mom. I'm only twelve. I just want to"—Louie searched briefly for the right word—"be a little less of a burden."

Mom reached over and squeezed his hand. "You're definitely not a burden, sweetheart. But I'm grateful you want to help out."

Afterwards, Louie cleaned off the table and finished the last of the washing up. Mom emptied her wine glass and watched him with a smile.

"Louie," she said softly. "Would you mind spending a night alone sometime?"

Louie froze for a second, but tried his best to hide it. He glanced casually over his shoulder. "No, that would be totally fine. Why? Are you sleeping at Phil's?"

Mom pointed at him with the wine glass. "You can use the dishtowel to wipe that smile off of your face."

Louie pretended to wipe his mouth, and they both laughed.

"I still think it's too soon for him to spend the night here," his mom said. "Not that ... I mean, we don't know how it'll work out, and ... you know ..."

"I think it's a great idea, Mom." Louie smiled. "I promise to be good while you're not home."

Already the following night his mom slept at Phil's place.

Louie packed his sleeping bag, a pillow, and a flashlight along with some juice and biscuits for a late-night snack. He managed to fit it all into his schoolbag and brought it to the bus stop. He gazed up at the clear sky with a smile as he got off the bus at Park Road—it looked like it was going to be a starry night.

In the attic he got comfortable in the armchair, which he had thoroughly dusted off. He knew from the calendar that three bodies would be visible tonight: Jupiter, Saturn, and the moon. As darkness descended, he got ready.

Mom called to say good night, and Louie told her he was lying on the couch watching a movie.

"*Don't you fall asleep without brushing your teeth now,*" she demanded. "*And we agreed on no later than eleven o'clock, remember?*"

"Sure, Mom. I'll be going to bed soon anyway, I'm pretty tired." Louie was anything but tired, yet he faked a yawn.

The moon was the first one to rise. It was in its first quarter. With his heart thumping in his chest, Louie adjusted the telescope and put his eye to the ocular. It took him a while to find anything other than black sky.

The fuzzy lightshow which finally met his retina was confusing at first. He feared the telescope might have suffered some sort of damage and wasn't functioning properly. Then he realized he just needed to focus. It had never been necessary in Dreamland; the telescope in there just did it by itself.

As he turned the knob and the visual field came into focus, he pulled back his head in sheer amazement. He had expected to see an enlarged view of the moon. What he saw was a mess of hills and craters. It felt as though he was soaring right above the surface of the moon—he was almost close enough to reach out and touch it. The feeling was supported by the fact that the image was slowly sliding sideways, which meant he constantly had to adjust the telescope in order to follow the moon as it moved across the sky. Louie went exploring in the many beautiful surface formations.

At one point something strange happened.

Louie reached down towards the floor, searching for the juice box, but not willing to remove his eye from the ocular. The juice box was out of reach of his groping hand, but as though by the help of some magnetic force, it suddenly came closer, sliding steadily across the dusty floor, until Louie's fingers caught it.

Louie did not notice the odd phenomenon.

He admired the moon for almost an hour. When it was close to nine o'clock, he tore himself loose and decided to go looking for the planets. He consulted his notes with the coordinates.

"Saturn will be just above the southern horizon, close to the hind leg of Leo," he muttered and found the constellation after a bit of searching. Dad had told him that the planets looked like stars to the naked eye, so he rotated the telescope and aimed for the "stars" which fit the coordinates approximately.

It turned out to be extremely difficult to capture and focus on the stars. They were way too tiny and way too many. Louie realized he was searching in vain—he would need a miracle to find Saturn this way.

Disappointed, he shrank back in the chair. He had come all this way, but he couldn't take the final step. He had already emptied two juice boxes and needed to pee.

He left the attic and went down the stairs to the toilet. There was water in the bowl, but it smelled sour. The tap didn't work, so he couldn't wash his hands afterwards.

He caught a movement and looked at himself in the mirror. The light from the flashlight made him look pale and ghostly. He realized he probably ought to be scared—here he was, alone in a big, abandoned house, late at night, without anyone knowing—and he even intended on spending the night.

And yet, he wasn't afraid. The house didn't scare him. On the contrary, it felt almost protective in some way. Besides, what could harm him? He didn't really believe in ghosts, and he didn't think it likely that anyone would break in, since there was nothing of value to steal.

When he returned to the attic, he took the star map, intent on giving it another shot. But he had only just sat down in the chair when he realized the telescope was pointing in a new direction, although he hadn't touched it.

Louie looked at it for a moment, puzzled. Then he put his eye to the ocular.

Saturn was dazzlingly beautiful with its patterned surface and the mighty rings. Louie felt an overwhelming excitement, and he completely forgot about the strange fact that the telescope seemed to have self-adjusted while he was gone.

He followed the path of Saturn across the night sky until he fell asleep in the armchair with the sleeping bag wrapped around him.

He had no dreams that night.

He awoke early to the sound of the alarm and took the first bus home.

The following night Louie met with his dad in a parking lot. He sat down next to him on the hood of a red Toyota that gleamed with dew in the early morning sun.

"Did you figure out the riddle?" was the first thing his dad asked him.

"No, not yet."

"Do you want a hint?"

"Yes, please."

"All right, here it comes." Dad paused, then said: "The same thing goes for Mercury."

"Is Mercury also only visible in the morning and in the evening?"

"Yes. And that's the only two planets it applies to. So, what makes these two special?"

Louie thought long and hard. He had read quite a bit about the planets. Mercury was the closest one to the sun; it was small and very hot. Venus was the Earth's neighbor; it was named after the Roman goddess of love, because of how clearly and beautifully it shone. But what did they have in common?

"I don't think I know the answer, Dad," he finally said.

"I know you know it, Louie. It's a lot simpler than you think." Dad got up and clapped his hands together. "Well now, I've been looking forward to hearing about what you've been up to since the last time I saw you."

Louie immediately told him the biggest piece of news: "I saw the moon, and after that I also saw Saturn! I saw them both in the telescope. It was amazing!"

"Really? Cool! So, you managed to assemble the telescope and everything? Where did you put it?"

Louie realized he had completely forgotten to tell his dad about the house. So, he did.

"That old house on Park Road?" Dad looked slightly uneasy. "Are you sure it's a good idea to play around in there?"

"Yeah, sure. No one is living there anymore."

"But is it for sale? I mean, it has to be the property of someone, and it's probably being displayed to potential buyers now and then. You risk getting into trouble with the real estate agency. That's not really a problem to put on your mom."

"I really don't think anyone wants to buy it. It has been empty for many years. I've been there four times now, and I've never seen anyone."

"What if you hurt yourself then? It's a big house with lots of loose floorboards and ... and nails protruding everywhere. Imagine you fall down the stairs and you break your leg or you step in some broken glass and cut yourself. And who knows what kind of rodents or bugs are living there? You could get bitten by a rat." Dad was obviously upset.

"I'll be careful," Louie murmured.

Dad shook his head. "I really don't like it, Louie. An abandoned house is not a good place to play."

Louie lowered his head. He thought his dad was exaggerating. He didn't see why the house was any more dangerous just because it was abandoned.

"I just wanted the telescope at the same spot as when you were alive. This way, your observatory is still being used."

"I understand, Louie. But the house isn't the same as it once was." Dad put a hand on his shoulder. "I'm only saying this because I care for you. Will you promise me to bring the telescope home and not visit that nasty house ever again?"

Louie met his dad's eyes, which were no longer upset, but filled with warmth and compassion. Louie smiled. "Sure, Dad."

Dad rustled his hair. "Thank you, son. I wouldn't be able to live with myself if anything happened to you. Well, I'm not really alive anyway, but ... you know what I mean."

He laughed, and Louie laughed too.

"When you get the telescope back home, you could let your mother take a peek through it," his dad suggested, once they had finished laughing.

"Actually, I haven't told her about the telescope," Louie admitted. "As far as she knows, it's still in the suitcase in the basement."

Dad looked surprised.

"I think it's best she doesn't know I'm using it," Louie explained.

"Are you afraid she will take it away from you?"

"It's more that I'm afraid she will get sad."

Dad considered it. "I see your point. But I don't like you keeping secrets from your mom, Louie. It's important you can trust each other."

"How about *our* secret, then?" Louie asked promptly. "It was your idea not telling her anymore about Dreamland. Weren't you also afraid she would get sad?"

"Yes, but …" Dad sighed. "You're right, Louie. I can't expect you to be better than me. How will you keep her from finding out about the telescope, then?"

"That's easy," Louie said. "Whenever I'm not using it, I'll just disassemble it and put it under the bed."

As the words left his mouth, it dawned on Louie they weren't actually true. He didn't want to risk his mom discovering the telescope and for some reason taking it away from him, which meant that he couldn't bring it home. He was going to leave it at the house on Park Road, so he could keep visiting it, and he would simply not mention the house to his dad again.

Louie and his dad spent the day together. They walked around the vacant town, ate soft ice, looked at shop windows, and talked about all kinds of stuff.

When evening came and the stars lit up, his dad took him to a hill outside town and magically made the telescope appear.

"Ah, I can see Jupiter," he announced after a quick glance in the ocular. "You want to see it, Louie?"

"Yes!" Louie said and looked. He saw Jupiter, all right, with all its orange belts. "Wow, it's really pretty! I can't wait to see it in real life."

"Is this not real enough?" Dad smiled, but sounded a bit hurt.

"Yes, well, I just meant … it's kind of different in here."

"How's that?"

"Well, in here all the planets are always visible," Louie said. "That's never the case in the real world. And in here, you can see Uranus and Neptune, even though they are way too far away for such a small telescope—you told me so yourself. So, the things we see in the telescope can't really be real, right?"

Dad didn't answer right away, and Louie was afraid he would become angry or disappointed with him. But he finally just smiled secretively. "You're right, Louie. But you forget something: this is Dreamland. So when you look through the telescope, what do you think you see?"

"What I want to see?" Louie guessed.

"Exactly. Now, what do you prefer? A telescope that only shows what it shows you? Or a telescope that shows you exactly what you want?" Before Louie had time to answer, his dad spread out his arms. "In here, dreams are real, Louie. In the waking world they are only dreams."

Later on, they sat on a couch and watched the stars as they ate popcorn and drank soda. They took turns in making a shooting star by pointing and drawing a line.

"How are they, by the way?" his dad asked suddenly. "Your mother and Phil, I mean."

"Actually, Mom has …" Louie hesitated, then said: "Mom has spent a night at Phil's place."

"She must really trust him, then. She hasn't had a boyfriend since I died, has she?"

"No. But she seems really happy with Phil."

"She deserves to be happy. It's about time she moved on. And Phil seems like the perfect …"

Louie looked up at his dad, and noticed his eyes had turned distant. "Dad? What are you thinking about?"

For a moment, his dad just sat there, staring into nothing. Then, he came to. "I was just thinking, that even in the waking world it can sometimes be hard to tell the difference between what you see and what you wish to see."

"What do you mean by that?"

"I believe a part of your mother wants to move on, to find someone new to share her life with. I just hope that doesn't make her blind."

"But ... Phil is a nice guy. You said so yourself."

"Phil seems really nice, for sure. You just don't always know people as well as you think."

Louie suddenly felt worried. "What makes you say that, Dad?"

"Did your mother ever tell you about Elise?"

"No, who's Elise?"

"It was a woman my dad married after my mom passed away." Dad started to talk, slowly and thoughtfully. "I went to high school at the time, so I was kind of too old to get a new mom, but Elise was really nice and helped me with my homework and often talked to me about my dreams of becoming an astronomer. In fact, she was the perfect mom, and it was impossible not to like her.

"Then, Elise started to change. It was as though she just dropped a mask. She never had time to talk anymore, and she was always irritable. Sometimes she would yell or even throw things at me. When I tried to tell my dad, he got upset with me, because he thought I was lying. He couldn't see that she was the one changing, because she was still nice and smiling whenever he was around. Me and Dad ended up fighting a lot. One day he got so mad he threw me out."

Dad stopped talking. Louie saw darkness in his eyes.

"What did you do then, Dad?" he whispered.

"I moved in with a friend of mine until I was old enough to get my own apartment. I never really spoke with my dad again. He and Elise stayed happily married. Elise's plan had been to get my dad all to herself. And I felt in some way it was my fault that she had succeeded. I was angry with Elise, but I was even more angry at myself for letting her come into our lives."

Silence as his dad's story ended.

"I'm sorry, it wasn't my intention to ruin the mood like that," his dad said, putting his arm around Louie's shoulders. "I just got carried away by my silly memories. Phil really is a nice guy, and your mom is very picky when it comes to guys."

They talked for a while, but Louie felt absentminded. His thoughts keep going back to the story his dad had told him. The story about Elise, who in the beginning had been the perfect stepmom.

He couldn't help but visualize Phil's face.

Phil, who was always smiling.

Whenever his mom slept at Phil's, Louie slept at the house on Park Road. Mom was glad that Louie could spend the night on his own, and she was always in a fantastic mood when she got home.

Dad taught Louie to read coordinates and to adjust the telescope properly, and that made things a whole lot easier. Louie didn't tell his dad the telescope was still at the house; instead, he lied and said he had put it in a tool shed at the end of the block. During the nights, he saw planets, stars, and even a comet.

The first time he saw Jupiter, he was enchanted by the sight of the mighty king of the planets. In his mind he heard his dad say: "*Is this not real enough*?"

Now, as he was looking at the real Jupiter, he could actually tell the difference, although it was slight. The sight was pretty much the same, but the *experience* was somehow different. Maybe it was because he had waited a long time to finally see Jupiter. In Dreamland you never had to wait or worry about the weather or even know how to use the telescope.

Perhaps these challenges were exactly what made it worthwhile.

Louie was home alone one day when someone knocked on the door. He opened it and met Phil, who was standing with his hands behind his back.

"Oh, hi, Louie. Is your mom home?"

"No, she's still at work."

Phil produced a huge bouquet of flowers. "I wanted to surprise her. Will she be home soon?"

"It could be a while," Louie said, making room for Phil to enter. "Do you want a cup of coffee?"

Phil looked surprised. "Do you drink coffee?"

"Nah, but I know how to make it."

"You're a polite young man, Louie. Did your mom teach you to be so nice to people?"

Louie smiled shyly.

Phil entered, and Louie showed him the moving box where his mom had her vases. Phil filled one of them with water, while Louie made coffee.

"Your mom told me she's looking for a new apartment. How do you feel about moving?"

"I've tried it before."

"Are you happy about living in an apartment like this one?" Phil turned and looked around. "Wouldn't you like to live in a real house? With a garden and lots of space to play?"

Louie could hear that Phil was fishing for something. "Do you have a house like that?" he asked.

"No, but I would like to. A big house with a garden, and maybe even a lake, so you could make a hockey field in the winter." He winked at Louie. "In a house like that you could easily find room for an observatory."

Louie smiled and winked back, thinking: *I already have an observatory.*

Phil's phone rang. He found it and answered. "Hi, Liz." He glanced in the direction of Louie. "Actually, it's not a good time right now. Can I call you back?"

The coffee was done. Louie made a cup of hot cocoa for himself. Phil sat down at the kitchen table, as Louie brought the cups.

"Do you have children?" Louie asked, sitting down across from Phil.

"Nope," Phil said, shaking his head.

"Why not?"

"I've been busy with other things. And I never met the right woman before it was too late."

"Too late? What do you mean?"

Phil laughed. "I'm forty-one, Louie. If I have kids now, people will think I'm their grandpa."

"But did you want kids? I mean, before you turned forty-one?"

Phil shrugged. "I never really thought that much about it. When I was little, I often wished for a brother. I only had a sister, and she always played with dolls. I missed someone to have fun with." He leaned his elbows on the table. "Actually, I've had a lot of fun with you lately, Louie. I hope we can keep doing things together."

Suddenly, Louie heard his dad's voice: "*Phil seems like the perfect ...*"

"Do you smoke, Phil?" The question just burst out of him.

"No, are you crazy? It's unhealthy and disgusting."

"Would you date someone who smoked?"

Phil blinked. "Why are you asking me that, Louie?"

"My mom smokes. But only when she thinks no one notices. She doesn't want anyone to know."

Phil obviously didn't know what to say.

"I just thought you should know," Louie said. "Mom told me never to lie. I guess that goes for her, too."

"I guess," Phil muttered.

Louie sipped at his cocoa and pretended like he had already forgotten about the subject. But out of the corner of his eye he noticed Phil didn't drink anymore of his coffee; he just kept turning the cup.

Mom came home ten minutes later. She smiled with surprise when she saw Phil, and her cheeks turned red at the sight of the bouquet.

"My God, Phil, you really shouldn't have," she cooed, smelling the flowers. "They're so beautiful."

Phil stood up, his hands in his pockets. "I thought you would like them."

Mom slipped her arms around him. "I do." She kissed him.

Phil pulled back a little. "You smell of smoke."

Louie noticed his mom's eyes flicker for a split second. "I do?"

"Yes. I thought you didn't smoke?"

"I don't. It must have been Mariann. I ate lunch with her today, and she smokes like a chimney."

Phil looked at her for a moment. "Well, I have to go. There's a couple of things I need to take care of. But I just wanted to give you the flowers and say hi."

"Okay," Mom said with a confused smile. "Well, hi, then."

Phil walked towards the hall. "See you, Louie," he said with a quick glance over his shoulder, and Louie waved at him.

A moment later, the front door opened and closed.

Mom came over and kissed Louie on the forehead. "Tell me, is it just me, or was he acting a bit weird? He brings a huge bouquet of flowers, but as soon as he sees me, he runs out the door."

Louie got up. "I'm going to do my homework."

The following Monday Louie went to see the psychologist after school. He found her office at the end of the hallway. She was a friendly old lady with grey hair and grey teeth.

"Your mom told me you've been dreaming quite a lot about your dad recently," she began as they sat down by the window facing the schoolyard, where the last students were scrambling towards freedom. "She also told me your dad died when you were only one year old."

Louie wasn't sure whether it was a question.

The psychologist folded her tiny hands over her knee. "Would you like to tell me a little about your dreams, Louie?"

"It's just dreams," he began hesitantly. "Although they're kind of special, I guess. Since they take place in the same world. It's called—" He almost said "Dreamland," but decided not to share the name. "It's like the same dream continuing, sort of."

"So it's the same dream you're having, over and over again?"

Louie shook his head. "It's the same dream, but new things happen. I can't explain it any better."

The psychologist nodded slowly, as though she understood. "And what happens in the dream?"

Louie realized his chair could turn from side to side. He felt like spinning all the way around, but didn't. "Not much, actually. It's mostly just Dad and me, talking."

"What do you talk about?"

"All kinds of stuff."

"Could you give me some examples?"

"I guess we mostly talk about planets and stars and things like that. Dad is very into astronomy, and so am I."

The psychologist made an exaggerated expression of interest and typed something on a small laptop in her lap.

"We also talk about Mom and Phil. I do most of the talking, to be honest. Dad just listens. Except for when he teaches me things. My dad is very smart."

The psychologist asked questions and nodded while Louie answered. Was Louie ever afraid in the dreams? Did the dreams make him sad? How often did he think about his dad during the day? Did he miss his dad? Did he miss him more now that he had started dreaming about him? Did he have any memories about his dad? And so on. Towards the end of the session Louie noticed the questions ever so discretely turning in a new direction.

"Have you ever met anyone else you know in the dreams?"

Louie shook his head.

"Do you ever dream about anyone else from your family? Your mom, for instance?"

Louie shook his head.

"Can you see why your mom would worry about you dreaming about your dad?"

"Not really. I mean, of course I understand why she worries, but there's really no need."

"Why do you think she worries?"

"Because she's afraid of the past."

The psychologist kept the same, encouraging expression, but a new gleam suddenly appeared in her eyes. "What do you mean when you say she's afraid of the past, Louie?"

"Well, she's still very sad about Dad dying. She tries to forget the sorrow and the pain. And she's afraid I might bring back some memories that will make her feel bad again."

The psychologist nodded. "I think you're absolutely right, Louie. You are a very thoughtful boy, since you understand how your mom thinks."

Louie turned back and forth on the chair.

"But I also think your mom might be scared on *your* behalf," the psychologist continued.

She was about to go on, when Louie said: "She's afraid I might have suppressed a deep grief from losing Dad, even though I can't remember it. She thinks that that grief might come back up now, like delayed, and that it's causing the dreams. That's why she wants me to speak with you."

This time the surprise in the psychologist's face was genuine. "I must say, Louie. I don't think I ever met a twelve-year-old boy as clever as you." She squinted her eyes and smiled. "Have you by any chance talked to another grown-up about this?"

Louie shrugged. "Just my dad."

The psychologist didn't answer, but she eyed Louie for quite some time before she spoke again. "How would you describe your mom, Louie? And remember, like I told you in the beginning, I have a duty to keep everything you tell me a complete secret, even to your mom. So please feel free to speak your mind."

Louie weighed his words for a moment. "I think Mom is a good mom. She's very loving and she takes good care of me. She can be strict, but I guess she has to, since she doesn't have a husband. She often says I'm her only love, but I've always felt she was lonely. I'm happy she met Phil."

The psychologist ended the conversation, thanked Louie for his time, and shook his hand as she led him to the door.

Later that evening Louie was lying on the couch watching a show about whales. It was only about eight o'clock, but his eyes were already heavy. He was just about to doze off, when his mom entered the living room.

"Make room, will you?" she said, moving Louie's legs before sitting down next to him. "What are you watching? An animal program?"

"Something about whales," Louie yawned.

They sat for a while in silence. Mom bit her thumbnail.

"Is something wrong, Mom?"

Mom came to. "Hmm? Oh, no. Not at all."

"Did you talk to Phil today?"

"Yes, but he has been acting kind of weird lately. It's like he doesn't really have the time to talk."

Louie didn't answer.

"I've been thinking," his mom said. "I'll terminate the tenancy by next month. We can't live like this, with vermin crawling everywhere. And I've been looking for a new place, but I can't find anything. So Phil offered us to stay with him for a few days—but only if it comes to that, and only until I find an apartment. Would you mind that?"

"Nah."

Mom smiled with relief. "Thank you, Louie. I'm sure something will turn up."

Louie felt a bubbling unease in his stomach. His plan of telling Phil about his mom's smoking habit hadn't really slowed things down like he had hoped. Mom and Phil already planned on moving in together.

"I just hope it doesn't make her blind."

Mom got up to leave the room.

Louie racked his brain. An idea popped into his head, and he said: "Mom, who is Liz?"

Mom stopped in the doorway. "Liz? Why do you ask?"

Louie shrugged. "I just heard Phil talk to someone named Liz over the phone the last time he was here."

Louie sensed his mom's eyes fasten on him. He looked at the whales. A nerve-racking moment of silence past.

"Liz is Phil's ex-wife," his mom said. "They got divorced last year."

Louie felt his heart thump. He knew he had hit the spot. He strained to sound casual, as he said: "Oh, then I get it."

"Get what? What were they talking about?" Something stiff in his mom's voice.

"Something about Phil stopping by, I think. I didn't really hear it all, because he hurried out into the hall."

Mom stood there for a moment longer. Then she left the room without a word.

Louie was left with an empty feeling. He didn't want to hurt his mom. But he had to put on the brakes before things got out of hand. Phil had entered their lives way too fast. And you didn't always know people as well as you thought.

The dreams about his dad now came almost every night, and they lasted the whole night; from the moment he fell into sleep to the moment his alarm woke him up.

Whenever Louie had visited Dreamland, it was difficult for him to awaken properly again. He felt sluggish and exhausted, and had a hard time concentrating. One time he put his T-shirt on backwards, another time he poured milk on his yogurt.

Some days the tiredness lasted several hours, and during the first few lessons at school he almost fell asleep on his desk. Not until noon would he finally feel normal and clearheaded again.

Every time the alarm called him back from Dreamland, he had the peculiar feeling of the night having lasted much longer than usual. But the time was always only 7:10.

One day, as Louie was sitting in art class, fighting to keep his eyes open, something odd happened. He rested his forehead on his palms, so Bridget, their teacher, wouldn't notice if his eyes closed for a minute or two, while he listened absently to her exposition on perspective and golden ratios.

Gradually, Bridget's voice faded and disappeared. Louie smiled. He appreciated some quiet.

Then, he heard a whisper: "Hello? Can you hear me, Louie?"

Louie lifted his head and looked around. He was alone in the classroom. At first, he thought he had missed the bell and the rest of the class had gone out for recess, but then he noticed something else was amiss: everything was turning blurred and shimmering. The surroundings seem to be changing.

"Answer me if you can hear me, Louie. It's very important!"

"Yes, I hear you," Louie muttered and got up. "Where are you? Where am *I*?"

By now the room had changed enough for himself to answer the latter question: He was in the living room of the house on Park Road. The dusty wooden floors appeared, as did the naked walls and the sad, grey windows which faced the garden with the fruit trees.

"Listen carefully, Louie," the voice whispered. "Don't—"

A hand landed on Louie's shoulder.

He winced and blinked his eyes, and suddenly he was back in the classroom—and this time it wasn't empty. All his classmates were sitting and staring at him in silent fascination.

"Are you all right, Louie?"

Louie looked dreamingly up at Bridget, who was standing at his side.

Her face was worried. "I think you were sleepwalking. Do you feel awake now?"

"I ... I think so," Louie murmured, although he wasn't quite sure.

"Do you need a glass of water?"

"How about a cup of coffee?" Jack shouted, and a tornado of laughter broke out and rolled over Louie from all sides. The noise was so loud, it was all he could do not to flee out the door. But his brain was becoming a little more lucid by now, and he somehow managed to sit back down on his seat without making a further fool of himself. He pulled his shoulders up to his ears and wished he could turn invisible.

The episode was soon over, Bridget went back to teaching, and the rest of the class continued being bored out of their minds.

Louie, however, felt very much awake now. That strange voice had spoken to him again. Where did it come from? Who was trying to tell him something? And why had he suddenly been in the house on Park Road?

At recess Louie was invited to go on a ghost hunt by Marc, who came running at him in the hallway.

"My older brother and one of his friends want to visit the haunted house—have you heard about it? It's an old, creepy house—well, it's more like a castle, really, like the one Dracula lives in. It's been empty for almost a hundred years, ever since the Middle Ages, I think, and once there lived ..." Marc stopped speaking and pulled Louie aside as a group of girls passed by. He waited till they were out of earshot and lowered his voice. Louie could smell tuna on his breath. "There once lived a man in the house, who slaughtered his whole family with an axe because he went insane. And now he hunts the house in his search for more victims. No one's ever dared to enter the house after dark, because that's when he appears."

Louie eyed his friend with fascination and skepticism. "So why would your brother want to visit that house?"

"To prove the ghost is real, of course. Are you in?"

Louie sent a text to his mom asking for permission to go home with Marc and spend the night. Mom had no objections.

Marc's brother, on the other hand, did. Marc hadn't asked if he could bring a fourth guy, so Jean had to take a close look at Louie in order to make sure he was made of the right stuff and wouldn't tattle or run away if things turned ugly.

"Can you run fast?"

"Yes."

"Are you scared of the dark?"

"A little."

"Have you ever seen a ghost before?"

"Only in a movie."

Jean ceased the cross-examination and let his gaze glide up and down Louie a few times. Finally, he nodded. "All right, you'll be our sentry. You stay outside and keep watch, and you don't enter until me and Troy have made sure the coast is clear."

Those conditions were acceptable to Louie.

After dinner the three boys left the house and rode their bikes through town.

Jean and Troy, being the heads of the operation, led the way. They reached the park and rode along the winding gravel paths among the trees, whose leaves had turned yellow and soon would start to fall. By a large bush the boys hit the brakes and made sure that no dog-walkers were in sight before dragging the bikes into the shrubbery.

"All right, sentry, you wait here and guard our bikes," Jean ordered.

"Is it here?" Marc asked, confused, and looked around.

"It's on the other side of the bushes," Jean said and pointed. "Didn't you listen when we went through the plan of operations? No one will notice us because we go in through the backyard."

"Oh, right."

"Come on. The sun has almost set. Remember the flashlights!"

Marc gave Louie an excited look, before he followed the two older boys and crawled deeper into the shrubbery. Louie squatted down and kept looking after them till they disappeared out of sight.

For a while he sat alone in silence. A bird chirped somewhere. A couple of joggers ran by out on the gravel path. The boredom became too much for Louie, and he decided to take a look at the house.

When he stuck his head out of the bush, his mouth dropped open in surprise. He was staring at the backside of the house on Park Road. Louie laughed out loud. He crawled out of the bush and walked across the lawn to the garage, where the other boys had left the door ajar.

Right inside stood Marc. He spun around with a loud gasp when Louie said his name.

"Louie! Jesus, I thought you were the ghost! Why are you here already? Jean hasn't giving the signal yet. You'd better go back outside, before he—"

"This is no haunted house," Louie interrupted. "This was where my parents lived."

"What?"

"Don't you remember I told you about that? I've spent the night here many times. There are no ghosts here, I promise you."

Marc was a living question mark. "That can't be true—are you sure this is the same house? Everyone knows about this house. Many people have experienced—"

"I'm absolutely sure, Marc. I can show you the attic—that's where my telescope is. Come with me!"

Louie ignored his friend's protests and went into the house. Marc followed him through the hallway and across the living room. Louie walked with a stern stride, while Marc took short, uncertain steps. The house was rather dim, but Louie was familiar with the surroundings and wasn't at all bothered by the creaking floorboards or the shadows creeping along the panels.

At the foot of the stairs, Troy jumped out and blinded Louie with his flashlight. "Stop! Identify yourself!" And a breath later: "Oh, it's you guys. What the hell are you doing in here? I was about to knock you out cold."

Louie noticed the baseball bat in Troy's other hand.

"I couldn't stop him," Marc pleaded. "He says his parents used to live here."

"It's true," Louie added. "I've been here before, and the house isn't haunted."

Troy stared from one to the other, as though they had tried to make him believe that monkeys could fly. "Jean is checking out the second floor," he said, hesitantly. "When he comes down, you can talk to him."

"But I'm telling you," Louie began.

He was interrupted by a shrill screaming from upstairs. All three of the boys stiffened and looked up the stairs. The scream was immediately followed by running footsteps, and a second later Jean appeared at the top of the stairs. His eyes and mouth were dark circles of terror in his pale face as he stopped and glared down at them.

"I ... I saw him," he croaked, the words so full of dread that Louie got goose bumps all over. "I saw him in the mir—"

Jean was abruptly interrupted, when someone shoved him hard sideways—that's how it looked, anyway. The boy was flung into the wall with a loud crack, making him stumble with dizziness dangerously close to the staircase. Then came the sound of loud, fast, invisible feet rumbling down the steps.

"*He's coming for you!*" Jean shrieked. "*Run!*"

The footsteps were about halfway down the stairs when it got too much for Troy and Marc. They spun around on their heels and fled wailing through the living room.

Louie was too stunned to move a muscle, much less run away, so he simply shut his eyes. He heard the steps coming towards him fast and prepared for the collision of whatever would hit him. But the only thing hitting him was a warm breeze. He turned around as he opened his eyes again, and he caught a brief reflection in the large terrace windows of a blurry figure rushing through the living room.

Troy and Marc had already reached the hallway; Louie heard them knocking each other over trying to get to the garage and the salvation of the back door. In a matter of seconds, they had left the house.

Louie listened to the silence that followed.

No movements, no sounds.

At the top of the stairs Jean had disappeared.

Louie walked up the steps and called out his name. He noticed an open window in one of the rooms and went to look. Down in the backyard, Troy and Marc were helping Jean across the lawn. Jean seemed to have injured his foot as he had jumped from the window.

"Hey, guys!" Louie called. "Where are you going?"

The boys stopped shortly and looked back, their faces pale with fear. They didn't notice him before he waved his arms.

"Louie!" Marc yelled.

"What are you doing? Get out of that house, you maniac!" Jean yelled, almost crying. "We are not waiting around for you!"

And they really didn't; they simple disappeared into the bushes at the far end of the yard.

Louie sensed something behind him and turned around.

The door to the room was ajar, but now it slowly opened all the way, inch by inch, until it gently bumped into the wall.

Louie stared intensely at the empty doorway, half-expecting something to appear. The shadows in the hallway suddenly seemed heavy.

"H-hello?" he said. "Is someone there?"

He got no answer. Cautiously, he slipped over to the doorway and peered out into the hallway. He saw no one. He looked up at the hatch to the attic, was for a brief moment tempted to crawl up the ladder to check on the telescope, but decided not to. Instead, he walked downstairs and left the house.

He found his bike in the bushes. The others were gone.

On the ride home Louie was mulling over the events. There clearly was a ghost in the house on Park Road; the rumors were real. But he didn't exactly think it was an axe murderer who haunted the place.

Louie needed to talk to someone about it. But when he reached Marc and Jean's house, the boys had locked themselves in their rooms, and neither of them would open for him.

"You can't spend the night here," Marc told him through the keyhole. "You have to go home."

"Why? What's going on?"

At first, Marc didn't want to spill it, but Louie kept demanding an answer. Finally, his friend whispered: "It's not safe for us to sleep in the same house as you. You're in cahoots with the ghost."

Louie shook his head and told Marc how ridiculous that idea was. But Marc didn't budge. After a while Louie gave up, took his bag, and went back out to his bike.

As he was yet again riding through the streets, Louie asked himself how Marc had gotten such a crazy notion. But little by little he realized it wasn't that crazy after all. Why had the ghost pushed Jean and chased the other two boys, but done nothing to Louie? It had had plenty of opportunity when he was alone in the upstairs room, and yet he hadn't felt anything malevolent from the ghost—on the contrary, it had felt more like …

"Like we knew each other," Louie whispered underneath his breath.

When Louie let himself into the apartment, he heard muffled sobs from the living room. Puzzled he went in to see who was crying.

Mom was sitting on the couch only wearing her dressing gown. On the television a movie was playing with a couple dancing slowly to romantic tunes. She blew her nose, crumbled up the napkin and threw it on the coffee table, where a small pile of used napkins had gathered next to an almost empty bottle of wine.

"Mom? Is something wrong?"

Mom turned her head. Louie had never seen his mom like this. For a moment he thought she had a bad case of hay fever; her nose was running, and she was red and swollen around the eyes.

"Louie? What are you doing here? Weren't you sleeping at Marc's?"

"I changed my mind," Louie said and came closer. "What's the matter, Mom?"

She turned away, yanked a new napkin from the box, and used it to dab her eyes. "Nothing, sweetheart. I'm just a little ... sad."

Louie was completely unprepared for this. He stood for a moment without any idea of what to do or say.

Mom sent him a smile and reached for him. "Come over here, my sweet boy."

He stepped hesitantly closer and let himself be pulled into a squeezing embrace. Mom smelled of perfume and wine.

"Don't look so worried, Louie. It's nothing serious, I just need to cry a little."

"Why are you crying then?"

His mom gave a sniffle and let go of him. "It's silly, really. Phil and I had a fight. I went over to see him. It was stupid of me, I know. I was in a bad mood after what you told me about Liz." She shook her head, took a napkin and wiped her nose. "I guess I was too accusatory. Of course, he got mad. He said I was lying about smoking, and we ended up shouting at each other ..." Mom started crying again and hid her face in her palms.

Louie placed a hand on her shoulders. On the inside he was a living chaos of thoughts. He almost burst out confessing his lie.

But he managed to keep it in. If he told his mom that he had caused the fight, she might never forgive him. Perhaps she would tell Phil, and they would both hate him. He couldn't run that risk; that was exactly what he had been trying to prevent!

No, I've got to keep my mouth shut ...

So, Louie just sat there, comforted his mother as best he could, and pretended like he had nothing to do with her tears.

As he lay in bed that night, listening to his mom speak on the phone with his aunt Tina, he wondered how everything would work out. He could see a couple of possible outcomes.

Either his mom and Phil patched things up and continued where they had left off. If so, he would only have delayed things, given them a break, a chance to think.

Or else it was over between his mom and Phil. The thought gave Louie a bad taste in his mouth. He hadn't wanted to ruin it—just to make them slow down a bit.

On the other hand, if their relationship broke down over a few small bumps in the road, it would probably have happened sooner or later anyway.

But it wasn't small bumps. Louie had intentionally turned his mom and Phil against each other by lying. He knew that, if he was honest with himself. And now it was too late. The damage was done. He could only wait and see.

For the first time in months, Louie had trouble falling asleep.

From that day on, his mom didn't sleep at Phil's place anymore, which meant that when Louie wanted to use the telescope at the house, he had to tell her he spent the night at Marc's.

It wasn't really a problem, though, since his mom didn't seem to care. In fact, she didn't seem to care about most things. She had an empty look on her face, and she hardly ever smiled.

Louie tried his best to cheer her up, but it was no use. It was as though she waited. Waited to see if things would be all right. If Phil would come around. If she would get the courage to call him.

Louie waited, too.

If his mom and Phil's relationship really was over, things might go back to how they had been. Just Mom and Louie. He would be her only love again. He could live with that; he had been happy.

But had his mom?

One night, Louie was on his bed with his computer. It was almost nine o'clock and he was terribly tired, yet he wanted to keep awake for just a short while longer, since he suspected he would be going straight to Dreamland as soon as he drifted off. And while he did enjoy spending time with his dad, his dreams now lasted more than one night. When he woke up, of course, it was only the next morning—but it *felt* like he had been gone for much longer.

He had had a large glass of iced tea, and he needed to pee. On his way to the bathroom he heard something that surprised him. He peered out into the kitchen and saw his mom doing the dishes while she listened to the radio and hummed along.

She noticed him and smiled. "Hi, Louie. Did you do your homework?"

"Yes."

"That's good. So, what's up?"

"Nothing."

"Okay, then why are you looking at me like that?"

"You were humming."

"I was? Well, it's a catchy song."

Louie thought for a second. "Have you spoken to Phil?"

"Nope."

"But ... you guys are going to work it out, aren't you?"

Mom sighed and gazed out the window. "I don't know."

"Maybe you should try calling him?" Louie suggested. "He might be in a better mood, too. Then you can start seeing each other again."

"Do you miss him?"

Louie considered his answer. "I miss seeing you happy."

Mom came over and hugged him. "Sometimes I forget how sweet you are, Louie. I don't think I need anyone else than you. By the way, did I mention I got the tenancy prolonged for three months? That way we have time to find something else."

Louie decided to ask her point-blank. "Don't you want to be with Phil anymore?"

Mom took a deep breath. "Honestly, I don't know what I want, Louie. Can we please not talk about it for now?" She handed him the trash bag. "Do you mind taking this down for me?"

Louie took the bag. He couldn't come up with anything more to say, so he went to the hall and slipped into his jacket. In the kitchen he heard his mom starting to hum again.

Louie went down the stairs and out into the parking lot. A cold wind blew past him, biting his cheeks. He shuddered and hurried up towards the container. As he opened the lid and threw in the bag, someone got out of a car parked just a few yards away.

"Hi, Louie."

Louie turned around and saw Phil. "Hi! We just talked about you." The words flew before he could stop them.

"You did?" Phil smiled and locked the car.

Louie noticed he had a small gift in his hand. "Have you come to talk to Mom?"

"Yes, I have. How is she doing?"

"She ... she's actually not in a good mood."

Phil raised his eyebrows. "Oh."

"Yeah, she's still very sad about ... you and her."

Louie couldn't believe what he was saying.

Phil smiled and showed him the gift. "It's a good thing I've come to make it up, then. Let's go up, Louie."

"I ... I don't think it's a good idea."

"Why not?"

"Well ... Mom is still pretty mad at you. A lot, actually. On account of Liz and all that."

Why was he lying? Just a few minutes ago he had been sad by the thought of his mom never seeing Phil again—yet now he felt a mild panic by the thought of Phil talking to his mom.

"No problems are too big to solve," Phil said. "Aren't you coming, Louie? It's freezing."

Phil started walking, but Louie cut him off. "Wait! I ... I ..."

Phil eyed him. "What's the matter, Louie? What are you trying to tell me?"

Louie searched desperately for an excuse to not let Phil go with him up to the apartment. But he didn't have time to come up with anything before Phil spoke again.

"I have to say, Louie, it feels almost like you don't want me to come up." He tilted his head. It looked like something changed ever so slightly in his face. "Wait a minute ... was that why you told me about your mom's cigarettes? And you heard me talk to Liz on the phone that day I brought the flowers ..."

Louie couldn't move a muscle. All of a sudden it wasn't Phil in front of him, but a completely different person. The mask had come off.

"Go away," Louie heard himself whisper, as he started backing up. "You're not coming up."

"Listen to me, Louie. I understand if it's difficult for you ..."

"Keep away! You're mean!"

Phil glared at him. "Christ, relax, will you? I just want to—"

"*I'll tell her you hit me!*" He turned his back to Phil and ran for the door.

"Louie, goddamnit! What's gotten into you?"

Louie slammed the door behind him—although he knew he couldn't prevent Phil from using the door phone or simply just calling his mom. He peered out at the narrow windowpane next to the door.

Phil still stood in the middle of the parking lot, looking at a loss. He took a few steps towards the door, then stopped, flung out his arms, hesitated for a moment longer, before finally going back to his car.

Louie was trembling all over.

Louie spent the next days waiting.

He winced every time his mom's phone rang, or whenever he heard the front door. He had even prepared a cover story in case his mom spoke to Phil: He would tell her that Phil had hit him at the hockey game, because Louie had spilt his soda on him. Then, Phil had threatened him not to say anything about it. And that was why Louie had lied about the cigarettes and Liz. He had been scared and couldn't see another way.

The reality was, of course, quite different. In reality it was Louie who had threatened Phil. But Louie felt confident his mom would believe him over Phil if she had to choose.

He hoped so, anyway.

Mom didn't hear from Phil.

As several days passed by, Louie began to relax. The threat had seemed to work. Phil was no longer in their lives.

Louie started visiting the house on Park Road once more.

One day, as he sat in the bus, he fell asleep with his head leaning against the window. Once again, he had the strange experience of suddenly finding himself in the house and hearing a strange voice.

"Can you hear me?"

The words were spoken close to his ear, but very low and soft, as though the voice tried to talk to him without anyone else hearing it.

"Yes, I hear you," Louie said, looking around. "But I can't see you."

"Don't worry about that. We don't have much time. You need to listen to me."

"Who are you?"

"I'm your father, Louie—your *real* father."

In his sleep, Louie frowned. The bus slowed down and turned at an intersection, making Louie's head rock gently, but didn't wake him up.

"I don't have time to explain any further," the voice whispered. "You'll wake up in a moment. When you do, I need you to write something down. You have to write it *as soon* as you wake up. It's very important."

"All right."

"Write this down ..." The voice paused for a beat, then it said: "Don't trust the man in blue."

"*Hey!*" cried a shrill voice, and Louie jerked upright in his seat. "That was my stop! You missed my stop!"

An old lady was standing in the aisle next to Louie and waved angrily at the driver, who realized his mistake and quickly brought the bus to a halt.

"My apologies," he called back and opened the door.

The lady mumbled something under her breath as she left the bus, dragging two full grocery bags along.

Louie sat for a moment staring at nothing. He tried to remember what the voice in his dream had said. It was something which filled him with a nagging unease. But the memory was already fading away.

*"You have to write it **as soon** as you wake up."*

Louie searched frantically for his phone, found it, opened a new text message and stared at the screen as his thumbs hovered above the letters.

What was he supposed to write? It was important. What *was* it?

Come on, come on! Something about the man in blue ...

Louie grunted with frustration. The words had escaped him. The old lady had confused him in the first few precarious seconds after he woke up, and now the message from the dream was gone forever.

The only thing that remained was an unshakable feeling that something was wrong.

That night Louie returned to Dreamland, and he met his dad on a tennis court underneath a lemon-yellow sky. They sat down on the bench and Louie told him about the strange visions and the voice who had whispered to him three times now.

"It always comes just as I'm about to drift off to sleep, or right before I wake up."

"A voice, you say? What did it tell you?"

Louie flung out his hand. "I don't remember! It disappears as soon as I wake up. But this last time I got a feeling that ..." He frowned and searched for the right words. "A feeling that the voice tried to *warn* me about something." He shook his head. "Maybe it's all just my imagination, or maybe ..." Louie fell silent when he saw the serious look on his dad's face. "What's wrong, Dad?"

Dad got up and brushed off his jacket absentmindedly. He seemed worried but also adamant, as he said: "Come with me, Louie. There's something I need to show you."

Louie got to his feet. "Where are we going?"

"To the outskirts. It's about time you learn what's outside Dreamland."

Dad held out his hand, and Louie took it. They left the tennis court, crossed the parking lot, and walked down the street. Louie wondered where they were going.

Then something strange happened; they sped up. Or rather, the surroundings sped up. For every step, Louie and his dad traveled several hundred yards. Louie felt dizzy and had to close his eyes as he held on firmly to his dad's hand.

"We're here," his dad said and stopped. "You can open your eyes now."

Louie blinked at the sight that met him. They had left town and were standing on a cornfield, the wheat smelling sweet and summerly. But not far ahead was an invisible barrier. On the other side, everything was different. The wheat lay withered on the black ground, and the sky was covered with thick grey clouds. Even the sunlight stopped at the border. Louie could sense that the air was colder on the other side; it was like looking from summer to winter. Or from day to night. No, even more than that: from dream to nightmare.

Louie gave a shudder. "I've seen it before," he muttered. "At the train station. But it was so foggy, I couldn't really see it."

"Dreamland is merely a small part of the dreamworld," his dad said. "All around us is this. I call it the outskirts. That's where nightmares come from."

Louie stared out into the wasteland and felt a growing discomfort.

"Something lives out there," his dad went on, his eyes searching the horizon. "Once in a while they come close enough to the border to be glimpsed. And if you listen carefully, you can hear their voices."

Louie held his breath and listened. The silence on this side was deep and calm, only interrupted by bird song now and then. On the other side a cold wind howled.

"Do you hear them?" his dad asked.

"I only hear the wind." But as he said it, he realized the wind *was* the voices. It was a chanting choir of faint fragments; whispering, giggling, alluring.

"... hi, Louuuuie ..."

"... how sweet he is ..."

"... come out here ..."

"... we've been waiting for you ..."

"... visit us, Louuuuie ..."

They kept saying his name. The sound made him shiver. The voices seemed to rise and fall with the wind, but at the same time it seemed like they came from *inside* his head. There was something drawing, almost hypnotic about them. Louie wanted to step closer, just so he could hear them a little more clearly ...

"Louie?"

Dad's voice pulled him back, and he looked up.

"Don't listen anymore. If you listen for too long, you end up taking the bait. The reason I show you this is so that you can understand where the voice you heard is coming from. It's the creatures out there who have been trying to reach you through your dreams."

Louie stared out into the darkness and tried to see the creatures. He thought he saw a group of glowing, wavy figures in the dark. They stood side by side, twisting in a hypnotic dance. He stepped a little closer to his dad. "What do they want with me?"

"They want to drown you in bad dreams until your mind breaks down. They will try to lure you anyway they can. They will lie and tell you anything to make you follow them. And if you do ..." Dad caught Louie's eyes. "There's no way back if they catch you."

Louie's mouth felt completely dry. He did his best not to listen to the voices, but they grew louder and more insistent. "But what if they get in here?" he asked. "If they cross the border and take us?"

Dad gave his shoulder a reassuring squeeze. "Don't worry, Louie. We're safe in here; nothing can reach us. Dreamland is our oasis of pleasant dreams."

His smile made Louie a little less frightened.

"Come on, let's go back," his dad said, and they turned around.

Louie darted a last glance over his shoulder.

"... stay, Louuuuie ..."

"... we just want to talk ..."

"... you're so sweet ..."

"... come to us, Louuuuie ..."

"Louie!"

Dad's voice made him startle.

Louie turned around, irritated. "What?"

"You started walking towards them."

Louie realized he was closer to the border. The voices were louder in his ears. Although they whispered, it sounded like shouting.

Dad came and took his hand. "We'd better go together."

Louie shook his head. "It's not necessary, Dad. I wasn't going there, I just wanted to ..." But he didn't know what to say.

"Come on, buddy," his dad said softly, and they walked back across the field, hand in hand.

Louie felt a strange urge to look back, to stay and listen just a little bit longer. But his dad's grip was firm, and the farther they went away from the outskirts, the more distant the voices grew.

Finally, Louie's head cleared up. He realized to his terror how close he had gotten. Had he gone to the outskirts on his own, the nightmare creatures would have lured him to cross the border. He would have listened to their singing voices and walked right out into the darkness to meet them.

Monday morning, after Louie had once more visited Dreamland, he wasn't awakened by the alarm, but by his mom shaking him.

"Louie? Wake up!" Her voice had a tinge of panic. "Are you awake? Louie?"

"Yeah, I'm awake," Louie grunted, shoving her hands away. "Stop yelling, Mom."

"Thank God! You were sleeping so heavily I almost couldn't wake you up. Didn't you hear the alarm?"

Louie rolled to his side and tried to open his eyes to look at the Batman-clock, but someone had dipped his eyelids in glue. He was terribly, terribly tired. He was reminded of that time he woke up from the anesthetic after having his tonsils removed; all he wanted was to go back to sleep.

Mom got up and pulled the blinds, causing a bright sunlight to stream right into Louie's face. He squinted and managed with great effort to sit up.

How long had he spent with his dad this time? He wasn't sure, but it must've been several days.

Mom said something about breakfast and left the room.

The duvet was heavy as wet sand, and Louie had to use all his strength to push it aside and stand up. He wobbled for a moment, blinked repeatedly and forced his eyes to focus. Little by little he became somewhat more awake, but only enough for him to stagger to the bathroom and splash water in his face, get dressed, and find his way to the kitchen.

"You don't look too hot," his mom remarked as he slumped down on his chair. She came over and put her hand on his forehead. "Are you coming down with something?"

"I think so," Louie mumbled.

"You don't feel particularly warm. But maybe it's best if you stay home today."

Louie nodded, got up and trudged back to his room. He could only think of getting back into bed, closing his eyes, and drifting away. But as he stood by the bed, he stopped and hesitated briefly, as his head suddenly felt clear.

If he went back to sleep now, would he travel to Dreamland? How long would he stay this time? There was something unnerving about the fact that each visit to Dreamland seemed to be longer than the previous.

But he didn't really have a choice. If he didn't sleep now, he would definitely fall asleep at school. Louie went to bed and slept instantaneously.

A moment later he opened his eyes on a soccer field underneath a violet sky. The sun was shining and a butterfly landed on his shoe. As if by a stroke of magic, the sleepiness was gone, his thoughts felt light and fresh.

"Hello, Louie. Are you back already?"

Louie turned and saw his dad coming towards him with a soccer ball under his arm.

Louie slept the whole day.

At dinnertime his mom managed to wake him up just enough for him to drink a glass of water and eat some of the soup she had made. She helped him to the bathroom so he could pee. But Louie didn't really become fully conscious at any time. He could only mumble and move like a sleepwalker.

He slept on through the night.

In Dreamland it was more than just a day and a night. Louie spent six days with his dad—longer than ever before. The days slipped into nights, the nights into new days. They talked and laughed and made fun, ate ice cream, and enjoyed the sun, gazed at the planets, the comets, and the stars.

The only thing they didn't do was sleep; after all, they were already in Dreamland.

On Friday, his mom brought Louie to the doctor.

"I've seen him sleep a lot when he has a fever," she explained when they came in to the office. "But this seems completely unnatural to me. It's been going on for weeks now, and it's only getting worse. He only went to school three days this week."

The doctor examined Louie's pupils, reflexes, and tonsils. She took his temperature and called an assistant to draw a blood sample from him.

She pulled off the latex gloves and sat down on a stool in front of them. "I can't find anything obviously wrong, but I would like to test his blood for a few different viruses. My best guess would be mono. But I will say, it's actually not unusual for boys at Louie's age to go through periods of sleepiness and exhaustion. It could all simply be hormonal changes, growing pains, or other things associated with the onset of puberty. I see no immediate cause to worry. Make sure he gets enough fresh air and sunlight, and—do you give him vitamins?"

Mom nodded.

"Great, continue doing that. There are other supplements to consider, but I would prefer a balanced diet, low carbs, vegetables, go easy on the sugar. You'll hear from the clinic once the test results are in."

Louie awoke pretty early the following Saturday feeling somewhat rested. For once he hadn't been to Dreamland in his sleep. As soon as he woke up, he realized he had unfinished business he hadn't been able to take care of.

Mom, on the other hand, slept in. She had had a couple of friends from work over the night before. When Louie opened the door to her bedroom, the blinds were still shut, and the air smelled of booze.

"Mom? Mom?"

He had to give her a slight push before she woke and rasped: "What's the matter, Louie?"

"Can I go to Marc's place?"

She lifted her head an inch from the pillow. "Are you feeling better today?"

"A little."

Mom eyed him for a moment. "All right. But call me if you need anything."

Louie rode to Park Road. In the early daylight the house didn't seem at all ghostly. He went to the living room and looked around.

"Hello?" he asked, his own voice answering back with the same question. "It's me again. Do you remember me? I've come to talk with you."

No answer came. Out on the terrace landed a couple of blackbirds; one of them eyed him curiously through the glass door.

Louie went upstairs. He checked in all the rooms, not quite sure what he hoped to find, and found nothing anyway. The house felt exactly as usual. He climbed the ladder to the attic, opened the hatch, and found the telescope like he had left it, covered by the blanket in the dusty sunlight.

He started to climb back down. Suddenly, there came a loud crack as the topmost rung snapped under his weight. Louie screamed and prepared for the pain.

But it didn't come.

Louie blinked in surprise. He looked down and saw he was standing on the next rung. He had felt something grabbing hold of him just as he started to fall, a brief, firm grasp in his back. He looked over his shoulder, but saw nothing.

Louie climbed down fast and stood for a moment shaking. Something started to dawn on him.

He went to the stairs and looked down the dusty steps. Considered. Put his hand on the banister and tiptoed all the way out, so that his toecaps were protruding a few inches over the edge.

What am I doing? I must have lost my mind ...

Yet something told him he had nothing to fear. So, Louie let go of the banister, balancing right on the edge of the neck-breaking fall. Even the slightest push would tip him over.

Louie closed his eyes and leaned forward. His stomach clenched violently as he felt the free fall begin, and he couldn't help but scream.

But the sensation only lasted a second.

Louie opened his eyes and would have gasped, had he had the breath to do so. He was still standing on the edge of the stairs, leaning forward, but his body had stopped at an impossible angle; he was tilted about forty-five degrees out into empty air.

Louie stared around, trying to find a logical explanation—a string holding him, or a knob which might have caught his jacket. But there wasn't anything. He was simply supported by nothing. The air had caught him.

And when the air pushed him back upright, Louie almost screamed once more.

Louie was shocked, but also ecstatic. He stared intensely out into the air, trying hard to see what was in front of him, because he knew there must be *something*.

"Hello?" he whispered

Complete silence. Like every room in the house were holding their breath.

"Who are you? And why are you protecting me?"

A door slammed shut right behind him.

Louie spun around. Dust was twirling in the air. His heart was pounding away. But as soon as the shock subsided, he understood that he had gotten some form of an answer.

"What are you trying to say?" he breathed, prepared for a new loud noise.

The noise this time came from his pocket; the phone started ringing. Wide-eyed, Louie picked it out of his pocket. For a moment he was sure it was the ghost calling. It was just his mom.

"*Louie? Where are you?*"

"At Marc's."

A strange pause of his mom merely breathing. "*I want you to come home right away, Louie,*" she said.

"But we're right in the middle of a game, Mom. Can't it wait till we ...?"

"*Are you really?*" The voice was cold as ice. "*That's funny, because Marc was just here asking for you.*"

Louie's stomach turned to stone. His thoughts groped for a lie. "It's because we ... uhm ..."

"*I don't want to hear another word, Louie. Come home ... right now.*"

All the way home on his bike he brooded over what to tell his mom. The pedals felt dull and heavy, and yet the trip was over way too fast.

Louie dragged himself up the stairwell. He was just about to touch the handle, when the front door was yanked open.

Mom was wearing her robe and her hair was untidy. She stared at him for the longest time without speaking. Then, she stepped aside and pointed towards the kitchen. "Get in."

Louie skulked past her.

Mom slammed the door. "Do you know what Marc told me? He told me that you haven't slept at his place since the summer holidays. So what are you lying for? Explain yourself! Where have you been all these nights when you pretended to sleep at Marc's? And you'd better tell the truth."

Louie squirmed. "The house on Park Road."

"*What?*"

"I've been in the house on Park Road," he repeated, keeping his gaze on the floor.

Mom shook her head. "What are you talking about? Do you mean ... *our* house? The one we used to live in?"

"Yes. It's empty. I've been sleeping there in my sleeping bag."

Mom's face was a perfect picture of fear and disgust. "So you've been sleeping alone in an abandoned house ... Are you out of your mind? What in God's name were you thinking?"

Louie didn't speak.

"Answer me!" his mom demanded. "Why did you go to that filthy old house?"

"It's not filthy."

Mom didn't hear him. "I can't even imagine the horrible things that could have happened ... abandoned houses attract homeless people or teen gangs or ... or ... stray animals ..."

Louie shook his head. "None of those things are there. It's a nice place."

"A nice place?" Mom's voice grew even more shrill. "Is that why you slept there? Because it's a nice place? Have you gone completely insane, Louie? Have you even ...?"

"At least no one's shouting at me there."

Somehow Louie's mouth spoke on its own accord. And the way it spoke made his mom stop talking abruptly. Louie still didn't look up.

Mom glared at him. "Are you talking back at me?"

"I'm just saying, you don't need to yel—"

"I'm yelling because you lied to my face! You slept all alone in some strange place without telling anybody. Don't you see how dangerous that was?"

"It's not dangerous, I keep telling you," Louie began, but then his mom grabbed his arm and forced him to look her in the eye.

"As if it wasn't enough that you've behaved rotten. You also seriously think you can convince me there's nothing wrong with spending the night in an abandoned house, which ..."

Louie freed himself with a violent yank. He was overwhelmed by a sudden anger. "I'd rather be alone in that house than here with you!"

Mom looked stunned for a moment. Then the anger returned. "That may be, but you're living here with me, and you—"

"No!" Louie shouted. "We don't belong in this stupid apartment or any of the other places you drag me along to! But you don't really care where I am, as long as I'm not in the way, isn't that right? You were glad I found somewhere else to sleep, so *you* could sleep with Phil!"

Mom's face turned to stone. "How dare you?" She tried to keep her voice firm, but Louie could tell she was rattled. "I've never ..."

"You never cared about me! Even Phil spoke more with me, and he only did so just to squeeze himself into our family." Louie couldn't hold back. The anger made him play his highest card. "Dad would have listened to me instead of yelling at me. That's right, I still dream about Dad. I dream about him every night, and there's nothing you can do about it!"

Louie crossed his arms and held his mom's gaze. This time, she was the one averting her eyes.

"Go to your room," she said hoarsely. "And don't come out till I say so."

"Fine," Louie said, turning on his heel.

Louie stayed in his room all day. At first, he wandered about restlessly, muttering angrily to himself. He was furious with his mom and the way she had spoken about the house.

Did she honestly think she could keep treating him like this without him giving back the same? He wasn't a little child anymore, and he wasn't her slave.

Dad never talked down to him, he never told him what he could or couldn't do. Instead, he explained things, listened attentively and gave Louie advice.

Louie no longer intended to tolerate his mom's tyranny. He had proven he could get by on his own just fine. Mom was the childish one; she had thrown herself into a relationship with a man she barely knew, had even planned on moving in with him. Louie had been the sensible one, he had seen things more clearly. He no longer felt bad about sabotaging his mom and Phil's relationship.

After some time when his thoughts had run in angry circles, he was so exhausted that he threw himself on the bed and fell asleep.

Immediately he arrived in Dreamland at a warm beach, where blue waves washed in over the sand and seagulls tripped in the shallows.

Louie took off his shoes and socks and picked up pebbles and practiced playing ducks and drakes until he heard a cheerful whistle. Dad came walking along the shore, impeccably dressed as always in his blue suit, except he was barefoot.

"Hello, Louie. Nice to see you again."

"Hi, Dad."

"Are you up for a swim? I think the water's warm enough. If not, we can always crank it up a few degrees." When Louie didn't answer, his dad looked curiously at him. "Is something up, Louie? You look serious."

"I had a fight with Mom."

Dad frowned. "Do you want to talk about it?"

Louie thought about it, then nodded.

Dad put his hand on Louie's shoulder. "Come on, son."

Together they went up into the dunes and settled between the patches of reeds. Dad didn't say anything, just waited for Louie to start.

"It was kind of my fault we got into the fight," he admitted, and then he came out with everything. How he had sabotaged his mom's relationship with Phil. How he had led his mom to believe he could be home alone at night. How his mom had discovered his lies about sleeping at Marc's. The only thing he wasn't open about was his visits to the house, which he replaced with the tool shed. "She was livid when I got home. And I can't really explain why, but suddenly, *I* became angry, too. Normally, I'm never angry with Mom. I guess I'm just tired of her trying to control me, like I'm some stupid little kid." When he finally stopped talking, he looked anticipatively at his dad, awaiting his reaction.

Dad had been listening in silence, while he collected handfuls of sand and made it run slowly through his fingers. It glittered like gold in the breeze. Finally, he said: "You remind me of me at your age."

That was about the last thing Louie had expected. "I do?"

"I'll admit, when I first met you, I sometimes found myself thinking: 'Is this really my son?' I couldn't recognize myself in you; you were different than I had expected."

"How's that?"

"You were polite, thoughtful, well behaved, calm. You were a really pleasant guy to spend time with." He brushed his hands and folded them over his knee. "I wasn't at all like you when I was twelve. I had a temper. I was impatient. I didn't put up with anyone trying to tell me what to do. I could even get furious and yell at people."

"That was what I was like with Mom."

"How do you feel about it?"

Louie looked at the reed he had picked and was now tearing into smaller pieces. "I guess I'm embarrassed. I know it's not the right way to behave."

To his surprise, his dad shook his head. "It's never wrong to express your feelings, Louie. Even if you're feeling anger or frustration. It's a lot worse to keep them bottled up inside, where they'll just stay and eat away at you. Didn't you feel relieved afterwards?"

Louie thought back. "A little."

"I was afraid you were burying yourself, that your mother had taught you to hide your feelings, the way she's doing it. That's not a healthy way to live. I regret a lot of things in my life, but never being honest and standing my ground."

Louie chewed on it. It made sense. The new, strange thoughts and feelings that had appeared. It came from his father.

"But I also lied," he said. "About Phil."

"Who says it's a lie? Maybe Phil really has something going with that woman. Otherwise, he wouldn't need to keep it hidden from your mother, would he?"

Louie bit his lip. "Even if it wasn't a lie, my intention was to turn them against each other."

"What you did was take control," his dad said, drawing a line in the sand with his finger. "Your mother hasn't been able to create the safe environment that you both need. She's not giving you a steady home, but expects you to follow along wherever she decides to go. You were like a doll, Louie. A doll who wasn't asked and didn't have a choice. Nobody can live like that. You seized the opportunity to influence your own life."

Louie nodded. At first slowly, then more firmly. He smiled. "Thank you, Dad."

"Don't thank me, the achievement is all yours," his dad said. "You did it completely without my help."

Louie didn't agree. He thought his dad had a lot to do with the changes in his life lately. All the new things he was learning. Suddenly he felt an overwhelming urge to jump over and give his dad a hug. And so he did. "I'm really happy I met you, Dad."

"Me too, son."

It got still more difficult for Louie to wake up in the morning. In fact, most days he didn't succeed; he just walked around like a zombie, perceiving almost nothing of what went on around him. He constantly yawned, and if he sat still for more than ten minutes, he would fall asleep.

The dreams about his father had become even longer—by now Louie was gone for more than one week at a time. And when he opened his eyes in his bed in the morning, the room seemed somehow strange, as if he had been gone on a holiday.

He still enjoyed being in Dreamland, and it didn't really cause him much concern that the dreams seemed to drain energy from his waking hours. The days had started to feel like something that just needed to be done with so he could go back to bed, anyway.

Mom received an answer from the doctor; the test results didn't offer any clue as to Louie's excessive tiredness. She walked around in the kitchen, talking on her phone, while Louie was in the living room, nearly dozing off on the coach.

"Yes, this is Ellen Taylor, I'm calling on behalf of my son, Louie. He recently submitted a blood sample, and ... no, I already got the answers ... yes ... but they told me there were no viruses or other things ... no, on the contrary, I'm actually pretty concerned ... all right ... all right, yes, I'll make an appointment with the secretary. I just have one question, though."

Mom paused for a beat, and Louie heard her coming towards the living room. He closed his eyes almost shut and saw her dart a glance at him from the doorway before disappearing again. Now she spoke more quietly, so he had to sit up and strain his ears to hear.

"You see, I lost my husband John eleven years ago. He died from cancer in the brain. In the weeks leading to his death, he became very tired and slept for days on end, just like Louie is doing now. I know it might sound crazy, but I can't help but see a correlation. I'm not saying I think Louie has cancer, but isn't it possible that John had some undiagnosed disease which has been passed on to Louie? Maybe something genetic?"

Mom was quiet for a minute or so, as the doctor apparently answered her question.

"All right ... all right ... well, it was just a thought ... yes, I'll try not to worry too much. Thank you for your help."

Mom made a new appointment and ended the call. Louie lay back down and pretended to sleep.

For a long time, there was only silence coming from the kitchen. He imagined his mom standing there, staring out of the window. Was she thinking about his dad?

Louie hadn't visited the house on Park Road since his mom caught him lying about it—she didn't let him leave the apartment for anything but school—so he hadn't used the telescope in a while. Not that it made that much of a difference, really, since he was almost too tired to function. His thoughts were languid, his senses dull.

One morning on his bike on his way to school, he saw Venus. She had risen about an hour ago and was now hanging above the rooftops on the dark blue sky.

Louie was groggy and absentminded and had almost run a red light, making a car honk angrily at him. As he stood waiting for green, slouching over the handlebar, he looked up and noticed the glowing spot in the horizon, and then something clicked in his tired brain.

"Venus is closer to the sun," he muttered. "The same goes for Mercury. They can never be on the nightside of Earth, because that will always be the side facing away from the sun. That's why you'll never see them at night."

He smiled, and the smile turned into a yawn. He looked forward to telling his dad the answer to the riddle.

That afternoon, his mom suddenly opened the door to Louie's room and said: "Please join me in the living room. We need to talk."

Louie didn't get up from his desk, where he was doing his homework. "About what?" he asked curtly.

"About you and me."

Louie followed her hesitantly into the living room. They sat down on opposite ends of the couch.

"You've changed since you started dreaming about your father," his mom began. "Would you like to talk about him?"

Louie eyed her with surprise. "Do *you* want to talk about Dad?"

Mom took a deep breath. "You probably have a lot of questions, and I've been avoiding them. I thought I was protecting you, but perhaps it wasn't the right thing to do."

For a long moment they looked at each other.

Then, Louie nodded. "All right."

"Good." Mom turned her palms up. "What would you like to ask me?"

Louie thought carefully, then asked: "What's your fondest memory of Dad?"

"There are so many. Let me just think." It took her a few seconds. "I think my favorite memory is from an evening when I was pregnant with you. We were watching a movie, and suddenly I got a craving for strawberry ice cream. We didn't have any in the house. It was pouring down outside, and we didn't own a car, but your father insisted on riding his bike downtown to get me ice cream. When he came back, he told me they had been out of strawberry ice cream, so he had to buy something else. He went to the kitchen and came back with a big plate of vanilla ice cream, fresh strawberries, lit sparklers, and hot waffles." Mom laughed and shook her head. "I have no idea where he got all of that from, because it was pretty late at night. He must have driven all around town, that silly fool."

Louie realized he was smiling. He thought about his next question. "Did you ever have a really bad fight?" He hesitated, then added: "Like the one you had with Phil?"

Mom thought for a moment. "I don't think so. Of course, we argued about things from time to time, but I don't recall us ever fighting." After a brief pause, she went on: "When your father died, I was certain I would never find another man like him."

"What's your worst memory about Dad?" Louie asked.

Mom's eyes grew distant. "It was your one-year birthday. I had baked a cake which I brought to the hospital, so he could watch you blow out the candles. He slept when we arrived. He slept most of the time. Normally, I couldn't wake him, and neither could the nurses, but that day he must have heard us coming, because he suddenly opened his eyes. As soon as I saw him, I knew he was in a bad mood." Mom tried in vain to blink away the tears that had formed in the bottom of her eyes. "I held you on my arm and had the cake in the other hand. I went over to the bed and asked him if he wanted to help me turn the candle. Next thing I remember, the cake is on the floor and you are crying." Her voice almost became a whisper now. "Your dad had knocked the cake out of my hand. He pointed at me and said something about me not being right in the head to wake him up for something so stupid. He was sick, and he needed to sleep. I couldn't answer. I just left with you."

"That can't be true," Louie muttered.

Mom nodded. "Sadly, it is. I know it's hard to hear, Louie, but your father was often in that kind of a mood towards the end. And it wasn't just his mood—he *changed* somehow. The doctors kept saying it was the illness, that the tumor in his brain was affecting his personality. But by the end I couldn't even recognize him. One wrong word would make the hate flare up, and he ... he accused me of the most horrendous things. He said I had put something in his food and that was why he was sick." The tears started streaming now, and his mom didn't wipe them away. "The episode with the cake was the last time I ever spoke to him. After that, he was always asleep when I came, and I couldn't wake him anymore."

"You're lying," Louie said. "Why are you telling such mean lies about Dad?"

"I'm not lying, Louie. I wish I was, but ..."

"Yes, you are. Dad told me about that day, and it wasn't at all like you just said. You were both happy, and I blew out the candle, and we ... we all laughed, all three of us."

Mom shook her head softly. "I don't know who told you that, but that was not what happened. Why would I lie to you?"

"Because you're trying to turn me against Dad. You didn't even love him, and you were happy when he died." Louie's mouth was once again doing the talking on its own.

Mom put her hand to her mouth. "How dare you ..."

"That's why you twist the truth about Dad. You want me to forget about him. You're afraid I'll find out he loved me more than you ever have!"

"Louie!" Mom's eyes were suddenly shooting lightning. "Stop talking like that, or you'll—"

"*I wish you had died instead of Dad!*"

For a moment, they were both stunned.

Then came the hand. The slap rang out in the living room.

Louie touched his cheek and stared at his mom. "You see?" he whispered. "Dad would never hit me."

He turned around before his mom could see his tears. He ran to his room, locked the door, and threw himself on the bed. His cheek was tingling painfully, and he gently caressed it.

"Louie?" Mom's voice through the door, soft as birdsong. "I'm sorry. I'm really sorry. I shouldn't have hit you."

A pause. She probably waited for an answer. Louie wasn't going to give her one.

"Could you please come out, Louie? We need to talk."

"I'm never talking with you again," Louie muttered under his breath. "I hate you."

"Did you say something, sweetheart? Please open the door."

Louie got up and went to the window. He thought about jumping. It was a long way down, but he would land on the grass. He had once seen a movie where a guy made a rope out of his bedsheets. Louie pulled off the sheet and tried to mimic the trick from the movie. It actually worked. After only a short hesitation, he climbed out the window and lowered himself towards the ground. Thirty seconds later he was safe on the ground.

Louie couldn't get to the basement for his bike without the key, so he had to do it on foot. It took him almost two hours to walk to the house. More than once he had to stop and rest.

When he finally let himself into the garage, he was so exhausted he immediately collapsed on the floor and fell asleep.

Louie opened his eyes in a green forest with mushrooms and birdsong, soft moss and the sweet smell of rind.

"Dad?" he asked, turning all the way around. All he saw was trees in every direction.

"What's up, Louie?"

The voice made him spin around.

A few yards away was his dad in his usual blue suit. His expression was one of concern. "You look like you've been crying."

Louie looked down. "It was Mom. She hit me."

Dad came closer. "Why in God's name would she do that?" When Louie didn't answer, his dad put a finger under his chin and gently lifted his head. "Did you guys have another fight?"

"We ... we were talking about you, and she ... she told a lie." He shook his head. "I don't get it. How can she be so mean? I hate her."

"Don't say that, Louie."

"I do. I hate her, Dad."

Dad gave a sigh and kneeled down. "Come here, buddy."

Louie let himself be embraced. "I never want to see her again."

"What are you saying, Louie?"

"I want to stay in here with you, Dad."

A sudden shiver went through his dad's body. At the same instant, a brisk wind blew through the woods, making the leaves rattle and the trees sigh. It was a drawn-out, quivering sound, oddly humanlike, filled with relief. Like someone who can finally relax after great exertion.

Louie pulled back and glanced around. "Did you hear that, Dad?"

Dad didn't answer. Louie looked at him. Dad got to his feet, opened his mouth wide, and took a deep breath. He closed his mouth and distended his cheeks, holding his breath like that for several seconds. A vein started appearing in his forehead. When he finally let out his breath, it was like a whirlwind, blowing back Louie's hair and making him gasp for breath. Dad lifted his arms, folded his hands behind his head and dropped backwards. A black armchair materialized out of nothing and caught him. Dad just sat there, eyes closed, breathing softly.

"Dad? Is something wrong?"

Dad didn't give any answer, and he didn't even open his eyes.

Louie was suddenly gripped by a cold terror. The wind started blowing again, but now it was only a soft whisper creeping around the trees and rustling the leaves. Louie realized the light was fading, as if a big cloud was blocking out the sun, and—

And then he heard them.

"... at last! ..."
"... been waiting forever ..."
"... wasn't easy to lure ..."
"... finally ours ..."

This time the voices weren't talking to him, but to each other, and that was somehow worse. Louie's breath got shorter and harder. He turned around and grabbed his dad's arm.

"They're here, Dad! The nightmare creatures! I can hear them! We need to get out of here!"

Dad still didn't open his eyes, but he whispered something Louie couldn't make out.

"What, Dad? What are you saying?" He put his ear closer to his dad's mouth.

Dad breathed a single word: "Finally."

Louie recoiled. Dad opened his eyes and looked at him. He smiled, and it was a hungry smile.

"All that energy I spent on you, kid." The voice was wrong. Hoarse and shrill. And it mixed with the whispering voices from the nightmare creatures, which got louder. "I thought you'd never give in."

"Wh-what do you mean?" Louie croaked, his throat tight with fear. He tried to back up, but his legs wouldn't obey. "Why are you talking like that, Dad?"

"Did you forget?" Dad slowly got to his feet. He suddenly seemed way too tall, so tall, in fact, that he blotted out the last remnants of daylight. "Everything in here is two things, Louie. What you see, and what you want to see."

"You're ... you're one of them," Louie gasped.

He suddenly got back control of his body. He spun around to flee, but realized the forest had changed. Everything green was gone, the ground was bare and black, the branches swayed nakedly in the cold air, the trees were silent, threatening giants. And between them, in the twilight, glowing figures were slinking. They slid in and out between each other, weightless like smoke dancing in the wind. Their voices had become an excited whining, completely devoid of any melody and repeating the same two phrases over and over again.

"... OURS AT LAST ..."
"... AT LAST OURS ..."
"... OURS AT LAST ..."
"... AT LAST OURS ..."
"... OURS AT LAST ..."
"... AT LAST OURS ..."

To his utter terror, Louie realized he was surrounded by the nightmare creatures on all sides, and that he no longer was in Dreamland, but somewhere in the outskirts.

He turned around and stared up into what had just a moment ago been the face of John Taylor, but now bore no resemblance to a human. It was a contorted mask, something only a nightmare could produce.

"Come with us, Louie," the creature screeched. "You're ours now."

"No! No! I want to go back! I want to wake up!" Louie hit himself on the forehead, slapped his cheeks, pinched his arm.

The creature smiled hideously. "It's too late for that, Louie. Way too late. You belong in here now. You said it yourself."

And as it reached out a long-fingered hand to grab him, Louie lost the last shred of coherent thought. If he had been awake, he would have fainted, but this was the world of dreaming, and in here fainting wasn't a way out. Instead, he collapsed on the forest floor, stiff and trembling, crimping and whining. He screamed when he felt their hands—soft and scaly at the same time. Then, he was lifted off the ground.

For a long, long time, he was carried through the dead forest. The chanting voices entered his mind and filled the world.

Louie had never known fear like this. He knew the creatures could at anytime tear him limb from limb or eat him alive or scratch out his eyes or a thousand other unimaginable things.

Louie knew he was about to die.

Ellen sat outside her son's room for almost twenty minutes, patiently waiting while trying to talk him into coming out.

"Are you ever going to answer me?" she finally asked.

Still not a sound from the room.

Ellen got to her feet with a sigh. He had probably fallen asleep. No wonder; he looked like someone who hadn't slept for days. So, she decided to let him rest and instead went to the kitchen, where she started making dinner.

She was sitting on the couch finishing up today's work on her laptop, when she suddenly realized it was dark outside. She checked the time. Six o'clock.

"Goddamnit," she murmured and rushed to the kitchen.

The lasagna was a little burned, but not inedible. She laid out the table and thought of Louie. She went to his room and knocked on the door.

"Louie? Dinner is ready. Hello?"

She knocked harder.

No reaction.

She knocked so hard her palm started to hurt. Could he really sleep through a noise like that? Or was he awake in there and just didn't answer?

"I made lasagna. I know you must be hungry." After a brief pause. "Louie, come on. I said I'm sorry. Please come out so we can talk about it." When Louie still didn't answer, Ellen said: "Suit yourself. Your dinner will be cold."

She ate in the living room, alone, while watching the news. The volume was turned down very low, and the door to the hallway was open, so she could hear it in case Louie unlocked his room.

When it was almost nine o'clock and Louie still hadn't shown himself, she started to get annoyed. It was obvious he was punishing her. She might deserve it, but it wasn't like him to take it this far.

And when it was almost bedtime, she told him through the door that she would go to bed now, and if he intended to spend the whole night moping, it was fine with her.

But as soon as she lay in the dark and listened to the silence, she regretted saying it. Was he really stubborn enough to keep a hunger strike all through the night? Unwelcome thoughts started to appear. Had something happened? Would he maybe go so far as to hurt himself? The thoughts made it impossible for her to go to sleep, and she tossed and turned until finally, at half past two, she got up and went to Louie's door.

Still only silence. It was almost ten hours since he locked himself in there, and she hadn't heard a single noise from him.

Ellen had to fight a sudden violent urge to bang the door and shake the handle. Something was wrong. She could feel it.

She persuaded herself to go back to bed. He would come out tomorrow morning. And if he didn't, then she would bang and shake.

Louie didn't die.

He realized, however, that the voices were gone; suddenly, there was only deafening silence. Slowly, he came back to consciousness and managed to open his eyes. His vision was blurred as he stared into a grey darkness. He blinked and tried to force the world into focus. He had expected to see a night sky, but instead a wooden ceiling materialized.

Tentatively, he moved his body to find out if he was hurt. It didn't seem so; there was no pain. Apparently, he lay flat on his back on a hard, level surface.

"Louie?"

The voice came from somewhere far away.

A face came hovering into his field of vision. Not the terrible face of the nightmare creature, but a human face. A friendly face. Dad's face.

"Can you hear me, Louie?"

This time the voice was clearer.

Then, Louie remembered. A wild panic seized him. He rolled to his side and crawled clumsily in a random direction. He didn't go very far, though, before he banged into a wall.

"There's nothing to fear, Louie," his dad said behind him. "I won't hurt you."

Louie stared around wildly. He knew this place. He was in the house on Park Road. On the floor, a few yards away, sat his dad. But he was very different. The blue suit was gone. Instead, he wore an old hospital gown. His features were the same, yet his eyes were new. They beamed with a wealth of emotions, and Louie found it hard to look away.

His dad smiled gently and held out a hand. "I'm your father, Louie. I know you're scared, but you can trust me. I'm a prisoner here, just like you."

Louie breathed rapidly, but didn't answer.

"Did they hurt you?" his dad asked with concern. "Are you okay?"

Louie glanced down at himself. His clothes were filthy, and his chest felt sore, as though his heart had been working overtime, but physically, he was fine.

"Do you recognize this place?" his dad asked.

Louie nodded.

Dad shrugged his boney shoulders. "I don't know why they chose this house as our prison. Perhaps it holds some special meaning."

Louie still didn't speak, but he studied his dad's face intensely as he spoke.

"I don't even know why they keep us here. I think they are getting something from us. I mean, if they didn't, they would probably just kill us. I've been here for eleven years now, and they've never done anything to me."

"You've been here ... for eleven years?"

Dad nodded. "Although it feels like much longer, to be frank."

"So, I'm dead?" Louie looked at his hands. They were a little paler, but otherwise they looked normal to him.

"No, I think you're still alive. You're still in color."

Louie didn't understand. But when he looked around a second time, he realized that everything was grey. The walls, the floor, even his dad—he had been too dazed to notice before. The only thing that had color was Louie himself.

"But it probably won't be long," his dad sighed. "You've already started to fade. I'm so sorry, Louie … I tried to warn you, I really did. But I couldn't reach you when they were looking, and they almost constantly keep watch …"

Louie shook his head in confusion. "Did *you* try to warn me?"

"Yes, I spoke to you when you were on the verge of sleep. You heard me a couple of times, but I never got the message properly through."

"The whispering voice," Louie muttered. Could it really be so? Dad—the fake dad—had told him the voice came from the nightmare creatures.

"It was me," his dad nodded. "It was also me who was here in the house with you, when you came to use the telescope."

"Are you … the ghost?"

"Yep."

Louie felt the pieces started to fall into place. "So you're the one who scared Jean."

Dad smiled palely. "Your friends came to see the ghost, and I didn't want to disappoint them. Besides, I don't like when people come here. I know it's silly, but I guess I still feel like it's my house."

Suddenly, it was clear to Louie why the house had been empty all these years. "But you didn't scare me," he said.

"Of course not. The more time you spent here, the better I could reach you. And I also enjoyed your company."

Louie looked down. He had a hard time processing everything. For a moment he felt dizzy. At first there had been the dad whom he had formed a bond with, whom he had grown to love, and who had turned out to be a terrible, malevolent monster. And now there was this dad, who claimed he was the real dad.

Gradually, the picture started to make sense. He had been deceived. The creature who had pretended to be his father had lied about the memories, twisted them, thereby making Louie angry with his mom and pushing him away Phil. It had all been a big hoax to gain Louie's trust. The creature had even tried to keep him away from this house.

"How did they get you?" he asked and look at the man in the hospital gown.

"The same way they got you. The only difference was, I was already sick and dying. I began dreaming about my mother, and she lured me to spend more and more time with her in Dreamland. It drained all my energy, made me irritable and hostile towards everyone—even your mother." A wave of shame floated across his dad's face, and he looked down. "At that time, it was all too late. My mother promised me I could get away from the pain and the illness and live forever with her, if I only wished so. I told her yes. And a second later I realized it was a terrible mistake." He let his eyes wander across the walls. "I thought I was going to spend eternity in here, alone. But then suddenly, you came to the house. I was thrilled to see you. But I also sensed something was wrong. I could feel you were in danger. I knew the sirens were after you now, and they were using me as bait."

"The sirens?"

"That's what I call them. They remind me of the sirens from Greek mythology. Perhaps you heard about them in school?"

"No."

"Well, they were monsters disguised as women, and they would lure sailors close to the coast with their beautiful song, making them wreck their ships on the cliffs and causing the sailors to drown."

Louie shivered. That description fit the nightmare creatures very well.

"I don't think we're the only ones," his dad went on. "I have a feeling others may be trapped like us. But I'm just guessing, of course."

"But why us then?"

"I don't know why they chose us. Maybe it was random, or maybe something made us vulnerable."

"We have to get out of here," Louie said and got up. "We have to find our way back to Dreamland."

Dad shook his head. "I don't even think there is a Dreamland, Louie. It was all just a big fata morgana."

"But everything was different," Louie argued. "The sky, the sunlight, the bird song ..."

"We saw what we wanted."

"But ... I don't get it—where are we?"

"I've thought a lot about it. I think we're somewhere in between."

"In between what?"

"We're not really dead, but we're not really alive. Don't you see? We're ghosts, Louie."

Louie had no words.

"Did she bring you to the outskirts?"

"She?"

"The siren."

"Oh. Yes."

"She brought me too. It was part of the trick. We needed to feel safe in Dreamland, to form even stronger bonds to her."

"But ... but ... there has to be a way out of here." Louie started towards the hall. "If I'm not dead yet, I can maybe get back. I need to tell Mom what happened."

"You can't leave the house," his dad called after him. "The door is locked, and they are watching."

Louie stopped and turned around. Dad gestured towards the terrace door. Louie peered out through the dusty glass. He couldn't make out anything but darkness, so he stepped a little closer. He saw the lawn and the apple trees, leafless and dead. At the bottom of the yard were the glowing figures, performing their rhythmic dance.

Louie stepped back. "Why can't we hear them?"

"Because they're no longer singing. Not to us, anyway."

Louie went through the whole house. He tried the front door, checked all the windows, even the one in the attic, where the telescope was. None of them could be opened, and everywhere he looked out, he saw the swaying figures. As he climbed down the ladder, his dad was standing there with a look of regret.

"I've been looking for a way out for eleven years. I've even tried digging my way out through the basement. It's just not possible."

Louie realized to his horror that he really was trapped. Suddenly, the house didn't seem like such a friendly place anymore. Now the grey surroundings filled him with dread. His gaze fell on the staircase, and he remembered something.

"Were you the one protecting me? While I was in the house?"

Dad smiled wanly. "I couldn't let you get hurt. By the way, I also helped you adjusting the telescope a few times, but I don't think you noticed."

Louie looked at the man in the tattered hospital gown. He only sensed sincerity from him. His movements were slow, his eyes had given up. He didn't have the strength to pretend anything, he probably couldn't even tell a lie. He was a prisoner, a lost soul, who should have been released from his destiny a long time ago.

"Why didn't you show yourself to me? Jean said he saw you."

"I didn't dare risk you telling the siren about me. If she found out we were spending time together in the house, she would find a way to stop you from coming here."

Louie remembered how the man in blue—the siren—had reacted when he told about the house.

"I've wished so many times I could meet you, Louie," the man said, a deep sadness in his voice. "But I didn't want it to be like this."

"I ... I don't know what to believe," Louie muttered and shook his head. "It's all a big mess. I thought I already knew my dad. But he wasn't real. And now ... now I meet you, and I don't even know you ..."

"You know me better than you think," the man said. "Even though it wasn't me you talked to, it actually was in a way. The siren copied me down to the smallest detail, and it stole my memories. The only thing it lied about was when it tried to turn you against your mother and Phil. I would never do that."

They looked at each other for a long time.

"Dad," Louie said, as though he tried out the name.

Dad reached out his arms. Louie stepped forward into the embrace. Dad's body was boney and weak and cold, but he squeezed Louie firmly, and Louie started to cry quietly, cried from exhaustion and fear and confusion. Dad just stroked his back. They stood like that, at the top of the staircase, for a long time.

The next morning, Ellen found Louie's door still locked. When her knocking wasn't answered, she started banging and yelling.

"Louie! That's enough now! You come out here, right now!"

A loud clicking noise from the other side, as something made of metal hit the wooden floor. She bent down and looked through the keyhole. The key was gone, and she could make out part of the desk and the window. The curtain moved. The window was open.

Ellen was suddenly gripped by fear. She got the key from the bathroom, prayed it would fit—and it did. She burst into Louie's room and found exactly what she was afraid of: an empty room.

The next minutes disappeared in blind panic. She ran to find her phone, almost called the police, then tried Louie's number instead. She heard his phone ringing from his room.

"Calm down, calm down," she whispered to herself and shut her eyes for a moment and fought to collect her thoughts. "All right. He left because he was angry with me. He must have been on foot. He couldn't have gone very far. Where is he?"

The answer was so obvious it took her a few seconds to see it. She almost forgot to get dressed before leaving the apartment.

The morning traffic was sparse, yet the drive through town felt like it lasted forever. All the way she prayed to the higher powers, promising all the things she would do differently from now on, if only they let her find Louie safe.

When she finally parked on Park Road and jump out of the car, she was stricken for a moment at how much the house had changed. It had once been a lovely home, *her* home, full of life and color and hope. Now, underneath the grey October sky, the building, empty and ramshackle, was a poor sight.

She found the front door locked, tried the terrace door, and finally got in through the garage. She almost stumbled over her sleeping son.

"Oh, Louie!" She kneeled down and grabbed his shoulders. He was alarmingly cold. "My God, have you spent the whole night here?"

She shook him. Gently at first, then harder. She called his name, but got no reaction. The fear started to creep back in. No matter how loudly she spoke, he didn't come to. She checked his breath and his pulse. Both were faint but there.

Ellen was on the verge of tears now. "Why won't you wake up?" she whispered.

A noise made her turn her head. The door to the house opened slowly with a creak. Ellen held her breath, expecting someone to step forth.

But the doorway was empty.

Louie straightened when someone called his name.

Dad must have heard it too, because he opened his eyes. They had been sitting leaned against the wall in silence. Earlier they had played rock-paper-scissors. Then they had exchanged memories. Finally, they had both become tired, so they sat down shoulder to shoulder to rest a bit.

"Who was that?" Louie asked.

The voice called again. He thought it came from the hallway.

"Mom," he gasped and jumped to his feet.

"Louie, wait," his dad began.

But Louie ran out of the living room. He looked both ways in the hallway, listened, heard the voice once more, now as a whisper, barely audible: "Why won't you wake up?"

Louie turned towards the door to the garage. It was ajar. He suddenly remembered he had completely forgotten about the garage door when he was looking for a way out. Now he went and pushed the door open. The sight made him freeze.

On the floor lay Louie sleeping, exactly where he had dropped down when he came. Above him was his mom kneeling. She turned her head towards the door and stared right at him. Her face was full of panic.

"Mom," Louie breathed.

She didn't answer. Instead, she looked down and shook the sleeping Louie once more, before she started rummaging through her bag.

"Mom, I'm right here," Louie said, wanting to go to her, but a hand on his shoulder stopped him. He looked up at his dad.

"Don't, Louie. She can't hear or see you."

"But she can wake me up!"

Dad shook his head. "No one can."

Mom found her phone and dialed a number.

"Of course she can, she just needs to shout and ... and shake me." He was again about to step forward, but his dad stopped him once more.

"Listen to me, Louie. You're not just sleeping. You're ..."

"Yes, I need an ambulance," his mom said. "My son is ... I'm not sure what happened, but I can't wake him up ... no, he's not unconscious, it's like a very deep sleep ... no, I *can't* wake him up, I just said that! He's completely gone, almost like ... like he's in a coma or something ..." She gave her name and the address. After she had ended the call, she started stroking Louie's hair and whispering to him.

Louie felt a lump in his throat. He fought a wild urge to throw himself into her arms. Seeing her caress his sleeping body was almost too much to bear.

"She's just as pretty as I remember," his dad muttered.

Louie noticed tears in his dad's eyes. Then, it hit him. "You can show yourself to her, Dad. You can tell her we're here."

"Sssh," his dad hushed, furrowing his brow. "Don't say that out loud, Louie."

"Why not? It's a great idea. If she sees you, she might guess that I'm here too. Maybe she can ..."

"Louie."

"Maybe she can find a way to wake me up."

"Be quiet."

Louie couldn't stop talking before his dad put a hand across his mouth. He tried to get free, when he realized his dad was staring towards the garage door. It was open.

Louie almost ran for it. But then he remembered they probably couldn't leave the house even though the door was open. Afterall, it had been unlocked for several years. It must be the evil powers of the sirens keeping them imprisoned here.

And then he saw the figure out in the darkness. It moved across the lawn in a weird rocking gate, and when it got closer and its features started becoming clear, Louie gasped into his dad's palm.

The siren stopped in the doorway and looked inside with its big, white nightmare eyes. The wide mouth smiled. "You have a visitor, we see," it screeched with its whiney voice.

It turned its face towards his mom. Louie felt like screaming to warn her, but his mom didn't notice anything, she just kept whispering to her sleeping son.

"We won't try anything," his dad said. Louie could here the fear in his voice, yet he kept it firm. "We just wanted to see her one last time."

"And now you've seen," the creature said. "Go inside and close the door."

Dad took his hand away from Louie's mouth and put it on his shoulder. "Come on, Louie. She's not in any danger."

Louie, who was glued to the floor, couldn't move an inch. He stared at the nightmare creature.

The creature stared back, tilting its head sideways. "Is there something you would like to tell us, Louie? How hurt you feel, maybe? Or perhaps you want to ask us how we could do something so terrible to you? Using the memory of your poor dead father. You see, we never get tired of hearing things like that."

Louie clenched his fists.

"Don't answer, Louie," his dad said.

"Why are you doing this to us?" Louie asked.

It looked as though the creature smiled, but it was hard to tell the feelings in the awful face. "We are the ones who create nightmares, Louie. But we can't do it without you. Your fear is kind of like our ... inspiration."

"But why *us*?"

"Because you are dreamers. The livelier one's dreams, the easier it is to get lost in them."

"So we're not the only ones?"

"Oh, no. There are many others. Once we get one, we usually get the whole family." The creature glanced at Louie's mom. "We think your mom will be easy to lure, once you start showing up in her dreams."

If his dad hadn't caught Louie's arm, he would have jumped on the siren. "Don't touch my mom, you monster!"

The creature closed its huge eyes for a moment and whispered, as though to itself: "So much fresh fear. We will surely enjoy your stay, Louie."

Louie looked at his mom, and felt a pain in his heart. He had to force himself to look away and let his dad take him into the hallway. Dad closed the door behind them, but right at that moment Louie was seized by a sudden impulse. He grabbed the door, tore it open, pointed at the siren and said: "You haven't won yet."

He just had time to see the furious look in the creature's empty eyes, before his dad pulled him back and shut the door again.

"That was a stupid thing to do," he said, pulling Louie into the living. "Nothing good ever comes from taunting them."

"But I have an idea, Dad."

Dad stopped and turned towards him. "Please listen, Louie. You have to accept it. There is nothing we can do."

"Yes, there is! I got the idea when I looked at Mom. I think it will work, but even it doesn't, isn't it at least worth a shot?"

Dad took a deep breath. Then, he kneeled down and whispered: "All right. Tell me then. What's your plan?"

Louie told him.

Meanwhile, Ellen was sitting on the cold garage floor, her son's head in her lap, waiting for the ambulance. She was consumed by worried thoughts and hadn't even noticed the door into the house closing itself.

When the ambulance arrived, the paramedics asked her questions while examining Louie. They lifted him onto a gurney and carried him out of the garage. Ellen followed them to the ambulance.

"Do you want to drive with us, or will you follow in your own car?" one of them asked when Louie was in the ambulance.

Ellen tore loose her gaze and mumbled: "I'll drive myself."

"Are you o.k. to drive?"

"Sure."

She went to her own car and unlocked it. Just as she opened the door, her eye caught a movement in the kitchen window. It appeared someone was in there, waving out at her.

Ellen squinted her eyes. Yes, there really was someone in the window.

She blinked, confused, and looked around to make sure it wasn't just a reflection of someone standing behind her. But the street was empty except her and the ambulance. When she once more looked at the kitchen window, the person had gone.

My imagination, she told herself. She got into the car and followed the ambulance.

In the kitchen, Louie and his dad were looking after the car as it drove out of sight.

"Did it work?" Louie whispered. "Did she see you?"

Dad swallowed and nodded. "Yes, she saw me. I just hope *they* didn't."

Louie followed his eyes and saw the sirens, who were making the darkness alive with their silent dance. He shivered. "They can't do anything about it now. If she really saw you, she'll come back. I know she will."

Ellen spent the next three days in the hospital. She didn't leave Louie's side for a moment. The staff brought her meals she barely touched. Doctors came to speak with her, but she had a hard time understanding the words.

Louie was in a coma, and no one could explain why. He had no traces of trauma or internal damage, no illness or fever. The only thing wrong with him was that he couldn't be awakened.

At first, Ellen tried to explain to the doctors how the same thing had happened to her late husband. She did her best to convince them, she even pleaded with them, to find John's old records, but they no longer existed, and the doctors were not convinced. When Ellen started shouting at them, they referred her to the crisis counselor.

After that, she gave up and surrendered to the silence of Louie's room. She wanted to believe the doctors would find a cure and make Louie wake up. But they had failed her trust once before, eleven years earlier, and when she was told on the third day that Louie's condition had become slightly worse, she realized they wouldn't be able to help this time around either.

Ellen was back in the hell she had went through once already. And this time it was even more unbearable. When John had died, at least she had had Louie, and with him a reason to go on in spite of the pain. This time she would lose all she had left.

Days and nights crept by in a stream of changing light. She didn't sleep, but she wasn't really awake either. At some point she must have drifted off, for she dreamt of the figure she had seen in the kitchen window.

When she awoke, Louie had lost a little bit more of the color in his cheeks and looked ever so slightly more shrunken.

Ellen knew she had to do something. She couldn't just sit here anymore watching her son dwindle and die. So she left the hospital.

She drove through town without really realizing where she was going before she parked in the driveway. It was evening, and the house looked even more like a ghost house than last time.

She went in through the garage, stared for a long time at the concrete floor where she had found Louie, and asked herself why she had come. The answer, of course, was that she didn't have anywhere else to go. Louie had spent many hours in this house, so maybe she would find an answer. It was a frail hope. But it was all she had left.

She opened the door to the hallway and stepped into the darkness of the house.

Louie and his dad were in the attic, where they took turns looking at the moon through the telescope, when they heard a floorboard creaking somewhere below.

"She's here," Louie whispered wide-eyed.

Dad nodded. "Stay here, Louie. There's nothing you can do anyway." He crawled down the ladder.

Louie waited for a minute. Then he couldn't hold it any longer. He crawled down as well and went to the stairs. By crouching down at the top step, he could see downstairs to the living room.

At that moment, his mom entered from the other end. She looked terrible. Her hair was messy and her eyes red. She walked like a sleepwalker, glancing drowsily around, as though looking for something.

Dad was in the middle of the room. He darted a glance out into the yard, where the sirens were dancing. They didn't seem to have noticed the visitor. Not yet, anyway.

Louie saw his dad close his eyes, and suddenly his reflection appeared in the dark glass of the terrace windows.

Mom didn't see him at first. She sighed—it was an awfully tired, exhausted sound—and rubbed her eyes. Then, she turned towards the terrace and froze. "J ... John?" Her voice was trembling with disbelief.

Dad nodded.

"Are you ...? Is it ...? How can ...?" Mom gazed around the living room, but couldn't find Dad anywhere. She looked back at the reflection. "I don't understand anything."

Dad made a word with his lips, which was unmistakable: *Louie.*

Mom gasped. "Is he here with you?"

Dad nodded.

Mom covered her mouth. From between her fingers, she whispered: "It's the same thing that happened to you. He's going to die."

Dad shook his head.

Mom slowly took her hand away. "Can he ... can he be saved? How? How, John?" She stepped closer to the window. "Tell me what to do. Please, John, help me save our boy!"

At that moment Louie noticed the figure entering from the hallway. The siren glided across the room headed for his dad. Its mouth was contorted into a wry sneer.

Louie's heart leaped to his throat. "*Dad!*"

Dad turned and saw the siren coming at him. He gave a startle and backed away. "No, wait! I didn't ... I just wanted to ..."

"John?" Mom exclaimed, putting her hands on the cold glass, fumbling, pushing. "John? Where did you go? Can you still hear me? Come back, please. *John!*"

The siren swept right passed Mom, who didn't even sense it.

"You ought to know better, John," the creature hissed. "Have you forgotten what happens if you try to cross us?"

"Leave my dad alone!" Louie yelled and jumped down the stairs. He ran over and tried to push the siren in the back, but his hands went straight into something which felt like cold fog.

Dad stepped forward and caught him, pushing him behind his back.

The siren stared at them, furiously, and it looked as though it grew until it almost reached the ceiling. Behind it, Louie could see his mom still searching in the window.

"Don't hurt him," his dad said. "It was my idea."

"You're lying!" the creature screeched. "You know you can't fool us, John. Give us the kid."

"No!"

"*Give him to us!*"

"Get lost!" Louie shouted. "You have no right keeping us here!"

The nightmare creature screamed, grabbed his dad and flung him aside, making him go sliding across the floor. Then, it caught Louie by his arms and lifted him high up into the air. He screamed and writhed to get free, but the grip of the soft, scaly claws was immensely powerful.

"Look at me, Louie!" the siren demanded.

Louie stared down into the terrible face. The eyes grew bigger, filled his entire field of vision, swallowed up the world in their milk-white emptiness.

Louie experienced a hundred nightmares at once. They all tore through his mind. Horrible pictures. Crippling terror. Evil dreams worse than he had ever imagined. And these he couldn't awaken from. The fear strained his mind to its breaking point.

In the hospital bed eight miles away, something happened to Louie's body. The pulse spiked, the muscles in his arms and legs contorted, and the eyes flickered underneath the eyelids.

If it had gone on for more than a few seconds, Louie would probably never have been the same.

But then it stopped.

The nightmares left him, like a storm passing.

"Never cross us again, Louie," resounded the shrill voice.

Louie blinked and slowly got his vision back. Dad was bent over him with an anxious look on his face. Louie trembled all over. He glared around and saw they were alone in the living room. The siren was gone, and so was his mom.

"It's over," his dad assured him. "That was very stupid of me. I should never have gone along. I'm sorry, Louie."

Louie fought hard to collect his thoughts. They felt scattered and sore. He wanted to asked his dad if the plan had worked, if his mom had caught the message, but he couldn't speak.

Dad picked him up and held him while whispering soothingly in his ear. Several minutes passed before Louie regained his voice.

In the car in the driveway, Ellen was sitting, silently brooding. She no longer felt like crying. Instead, she felt an illogical hope. It was stupid, almost insane, but still a hope. Either she had lost her mind, or everything suddenly made sense.

John hadn't died from the cancer, but had suffered some unknown fate. A fate which had made part of him live on in this house. Louie had come into contact with John and had somehow become contaminated with whatever it was that had taken John, and now it was taking Louie.

It must have something to do with the dreams. It didn't really matter, though. What mattered was that it wasn't too late for Louie. John had assured her of that.

But John couldn't help Louie. He had shown himself to her because it was up to her.

So what was she supposed to do? If she could only reach Louie somehow, if she was able to talk to him for just a few seconds, he might be able to tell her—

Ellen sat up straight in the seat when an idea hit her. She grabbed her bag and fumbled out the phone. She made a quick search online, found a number, and called it.

"Yes, hello, my name is Ellen Taylor. I know this might be a somewhat unusual request, but I hope you can help me …"

Louie wandered restlessly about the house.

It had taken him most of the night recovering from what the siren had done to him. He had felt weak and anxious, not able to calm down. Now, he was all right again.

"Louie?" Dad called from the living room.

Louie went there.

Dad was sitting against the wall. "Come sit down, buddy. Try to think about something else. Listen, did you ever find the answer for the riddle?"

Louie went and sat down next to his dad. "The riddle about Venus? Yes, I did. Men ... how do you know about it?"

"I came up with it."

"You did?"

Dad nodded. "The siren stole it from me. Tell me, then. Why can Venus only be seen during mornings and evenings?"

"Because it's closer to the sun than Earth is. It can never go to the nightside."

Dad smiled tiredly. "Great work, Louie. You know, in a way the riddle worked as a metaphor for how I tried getting in contact with you."

"How's that?"

"Well, I could only reach you when you were right between sleeping and being awake. That is, when you were waking up or falling asleep. Just like Venus. You see?"

Louie thought it over. He was just about to say something, when a distant, dreamlike voice said: *"Louie Taylor?"*

Louie froze. He looked around and listened. "Did you hear that?"

"What?"

"Louie Taylor, do you hear me?"

The words were faint and weirdly distorted, as though someone was speaking through a funnel. Louie jumped to his feet.

Dad looked at him, alarmed. "What is it, Louie?"

"I've come to talk with you, Louie."

He stared eagerly at his dad. "Don't you hear it? Someone is talking to me!"

Dad frowned. "I don't hear anything. Are you sure you heard something?"

"Yes, I—"

"I'm sitting here with your mom, Louie. She is very worried for you. If you can hear me, please answer."

Louie finally realized the obvious: the voice was in his head. "It's Mom," he breathed. "She has found someone who can talk to me."

Dad got up and grabbed his shoulders. "Answer them, Louie. Quickly!"

Louie closed his eyes and concentrated hard on one word.

In the hospital bed, Louie whispered: "Mom."

The word crept over his lips, no more than the subtlest breath. Both the clairvoyant and Ellen stared at the comatose boy.

"Yes, Louie, I'm right here," Ellen exclaimed, grabbing his hand.

In the house on Park Road, Louie heard his mom's voice. He was just about to answer, when someone screamed behind him. He spun around to find the siren come rushing across the room, eyes wild with fury and arms reaching for him.

"*You cursed brat! We warned you!*"

Louie let out a scream of fear, but the moment before the siren could grab him, he was shoved aside by his dad.

"Make her ask you, Louie!" he yelled and blocked the way for the siren. "*Hurry!*"

"You will both regret this," the nightmare creature promised, opening and closing the long, clawlike fingers. "We will make sure you get nightmares that never end!"

The siren pounced upon Louie's dad.

Louie clasped his ears and closed his eyes hard. *Ask me again!* he yelled in his head.

"Ask me again," Louie whispered from the bed.

Ellen stared from the clairvoyant to her son. "What did he say?"

"Ask me again, Mom," the sleeping Louie whispered, a little louder.

A moment of intense silence in the hospital room. Ellen couldn't utter a word.

"What do you want your mom to ask you, Louie?" the clairvoyant helped.

Ellen leaned over her son, clutching his hand and holding her breath. She stared at the lips, which were slightly parted, but not moving.

Louie couldn't answer, because his concentration had been broken when the siren had grabbed his arm. The creature had turned his dad into a limp figure lying on the floorboards, and now it glowered lividly at Louie.

"Louie?" the clairvoyant repeated in his head. "Do you still hear me?"

"Look us in the eyes, Louie," the siren cried.

"No!" Louie shouted.

Ellen saw a twitch in the corner of Louie's mouth. She suddenly got the feeling her son was close to waking up, that he was somewhere right beneath the surface. She fought a strong urge to grab him and shake him.

Instead, she whispered: "Louie? I'm right here. Tell me what I should ask you."

In the dim living room, Louie heard his mom, but he wasn't able to answer, since he was being shaken violently by powerful hands, making his head rip back and forth, and straining his neck to the point of breaking.

"*Look at us, you little coward! Open your eyes, or we will tear your eyelids off!*"

Louie opened his eyes. The face of the siren was right in front of him. Its eyes grew big as two sick moons. Louie felt the creature penetrate his mind. The terror of a thousand nightmares seeped into his body, way worse than before. This time, Louie knew, he wouldn't survive.

Then, his mom's voice sounded in the midst of it all: "Please talk to me, Louie."

The siren heard it. For a brief moment, sheer amazement made it loosen its grip on Louie.

Ellen leaned over her son.

Suddenly, the lips curled back in a sneer, and Louie spoke with a voice far too hoarse and shrill: "Back off, you damn bitch. He's ours, finally ours."

Ellen pulled back with a startle.

The clairvoyant jumped in his chair. He blinked and fumbled at his glasses. "My goodness, I've never heard anything like that. What do you mean, Louie? Why are you suddenly talking like that?"

"It wasn't him," Ellen heard herself say. And she knew it was too late. Whatever had gotten her son had won.

And still she leaned forward again, squeezing his cheeks with her palms, putting her nose against his and whispered: "I know you can hear me, Louie. I want you to come back to me. Tell me what you were about to say. Tell me, sweetheart."

Louie heard her.

The nightmare pictures were rushing through his mind, rapidly growing, shredding and tearing everything on their way. But for a few seconds, as the siren turned its attention towards his mom, Louie felt a sudden relief. He instantly seized the opportunity, tore himself lose and turned his back on the creature.

An indeterminable twitch slipped across the face of Louie. For a moment Ellen feared the horrible voice would speak again.

Then he whispered softly: "Ask me where I want to be."

Ellen was for an instant too shocked to say anything at all. Then, she cried out: "Where do you want to be? Where do you want to be, Louie? *Where do you want to be*?"

The question rang out in the house, in the world, in Louie's head.

The siren gave a startle. It had once again grabbed Louie, turned him around and forced him to look it in its eyes, and was just on the verge of releasing all the world's nightmares into the head of the boy.

And now it froze in terror. Just for a moment. But that was enough for Louie to shout: *"With you, Mom! I want to be with you!"*

The words were like a roaring thunder making the house tremble.

The siren glared at him, and now the white eyes were full of dread. It laid back its head and uttered a long, howling scream, piercing Louie's head. He clapped his hands over his ears, trying to keep out the noise. The scream seemed to go on forever.

When it was finally over, Louie blinked and looked around.

Dad was lying on the floor. They were alone in the living room. The siren was gone. The house was completely silent.

"Are you all right, Dad?" Louie asked.

Dad came slowly to his feet. His eyes sought the terrace windows and widened. Louie followed his gaze and saw them.

The sirens were standing right on the other side of the glass. There were many, too many too even count. They stared into the house, their eyes glowing with malice, their mouths contorted into silent screams.

"I think you kicked her out," his dad said and coughed.

"So ... it worked?" Louie asked.

Dad shrugged and looked around. "I don't see anything different. Do you?"

A loud snap somewhere in the house.

"What was that?" Louie asked.

Dad stared towards the hall. "I think that was ... the lock on the front door."

They went out there together.

Dad looked from the door to Louie. "It's open. It's been locked ever since I came."

"Does that mean we can go out?"

"I think it means we are free."

Louie gleamed. "We did it, Dad! Come on, let's try ..." He took his dad's hand, but his dad didn't follow.

He smiled, but his smile was tired. "I can't go with you, Louie."

Louie felt his heart wrench. "If you leave, you'll die."

Dad kneeled down. "I'm already dead, Louie. This place has just been keeping me artificially alive." He poked Louie's stomach. "But you're going back to your life. Back to your mom. You guys have a lot of good years in front of you."

Louie felt the tears coming. "I was hoping those years could be with you."

"Don't look at it like that, Louie. The way I see it, my death should have been the end. But against all odds, you and I got to meet one final time, eleven years later. Can't you see how lucky we've been?"

Louie sniffed. "So, in a way ... in a way, the sirens did us a favor."

"Exactly! They thought they'd won, but we were too clever—no, *you* were too clever. I'm so proud of you."

Louie smiled, but the smile broke into crying. He hugged his dad tightly.

"All the time I've waited here doesn't feel like a waste anymore," his dad said in his ear. "I would gladly do it all over."

Louie held on for a little longer.

Then, his dad said: "We'd better go, buddy."

Against his will, Louie let go, wiped his eyes, and reached for the handle. The door opened out to the grey world. He halfway expected the sirens to come rushing, but they were nowhere to be seen; only the dim front yard and the driveway.

He looked back at his dad. "Are you going with me?"

"I'll wait to make sure you get off safe."

Louie bit his lip as an idea entered his head. "Maybe you could stay a little longer?"

"What do you mean, Louie?"

"It's just ... you don't have to leave right away. I could come back and visit. That way, we could have a little more time together."

Dad seemed to consider. Then he smiled and nodded. "I'll stay a little longer. Go on now. And say hi to your mother from me."

Louie smiled. "I will. See you, Dad."

He left the house and heard the front door close behind him. He was halfway down the driveway when the man in blue came running out of the darkness. Louie's first impulse was to run back to the house, but the man in blue stopped at a safe distance and held out his hands.

"Louie," he panted. "I finally found you. You have to listen to me. It was all a trick. They want to trap you in here forever."

Louie hesitated for a moment. "You're lying."

"No! I'm telling the truth. They've kept me trapped. The man you met in the house is not your real father. *I* am." He poked his chest with a finger for emphasis.

For a moment Louie almost believed him. The desperate plea in the eyes was very convincing. But then the man smiled, and the smile was a bit *too* desperate.

"You have to believe me, Louie," he went on. "I don't want you to end up as their slave. We have to get you back to your mom. But you need to hurry back inside and lock the door."

Louie looked up at the house, pretending to consider going back. In the kitchen window he saw dad. His face removed the last shred of doubt in Louie's mind. He raised his hand and his dad waved back at him.

"Look at him," the man in blue sneered. "He's a fraud. Can't you see it, Louie?"

"You're the fraud," Louie said, walking on towards the road. "Leave me alone."

The man in blue jumped in front of him. "No, Louie, wait!" He reached out his hand, as though he wanted to grab Louie. But something prevented him from doing so, and he pulled back his hands.

"You can't touch me," Louie said. "I don't belong in here anymore. Get out of my way."

The man in blue stayed where he was for a moment and looked at him, expressionless. Then the face contorted into an angry sneer. "You little rat," the siren said, using its real voice. "Don't feel safe just because you got away this time. We'll get you."

"Move," Louie said.

The man in blue stepped unwillingly to the side.

Louie walked out of the driveway. Behind him, he could hear the siren breathing in furious, rasping heaves. But he didn't look back.

Louie opened his eyes and immediately closed them again when he felt a sting of pain. It felt as though he hadn't used them for days.

Just a moment ago he was walking along the driveway. Now, it felt as though he was lying flat on his back. And the darkness had gone. Instead, he saw this bright light which hurt his eyes.

When he finally managed to open them, he looked around and realized he was in a hospital bed. Mom was by his side, sniveling into a paper napkin. Louie opened his mouth and tried to speak, but no sound came. His whole body was heavy and immovable like marble.

Some time passed before his mom lifted her head and met his eyes. At first her expression was the same. Then, the eyes started growing bigger until Louie felt sure they would fall out of her head.

"Louie," she whispered. "Are you awake?"

He managed to blink.

Mom was over him in a second, covering his face with wet kisses and tears, burying him in her hair. Then, she shouted for a doctor.

The noise was grindingly loud in Louie's ears, but he didn't care.

He was alive. And he was awake.

Louie and his mom moved into the house on Park Road in early December.

Since the property was apparently unsaleable, they got it at auction price. It was Louie's idea, and even though his mom was hesitant at first, she finally agreed.

The transformation of the vacant ghost house into a bright and living home went incredibly fast. It was almost as though the place had just been waiting for new owners. Both Louie and his mom felt at home right away.

Louie started school again a few days after he was discharged from the hospital. His classmates had a lot of curious questions.

"How did it feel to be in a coma?"

"Do you remember anything?"

"Did you dream?"

Louie lied and said he hadn't dreamed anything.

Marc was mostly interested in knowing if it was true they had moved into the haunted house, and if they had seen any more of the ghost.

Louie smiled and said he thought the ghost must have moved out.

That wasn't true either. Dad was still around. Louie would often speak with him. That is to say, his dad never spoke, but Louie knew he listened, because once in a while he made an answer.

When Louie got stuck on his math homework, his dad helped him by typing in the result on the calculator. A plate which Louie dropped didn't go to the floor, but was caught midair. Sometimes his dad would tease him. If Louie had just made his bed, as soon as he turned his back, the blankets would be on the floor. Or the left shoelace would be untied as he was tying the right. Louie would laugh and push the air. Dad showed himself now and then in mirrors or windows, but only to Louie.

Ellen also sensed John.

Not all the time, but when she was sitting alone in the living room with a book, or at night, when she lay in the wide bed waiting to fall asleep. In wasn't a feeling of intrusion, like being watched by a stranger, but rather a comforting feeling of not being alone. Sometimes she would even wake up in the middle of the night and be surprised that the other side of the bed was empty.

Louie told her that John could easily hear everything they said, but Ellen never spoke to John. She didn't know what to say. And it didn't really feel necessary.

They spent Christmas in the house, and Phil came to visit on Christmas Eve.

The mood over the dinner was a lot better than Louie had anticipated. Mom had explained to Phil as much as she could, and Louie had apologized to Phil.

It was as though all three of them had made an agreement to go back to how things were before they started going wrong.

Louie and Phil went to the cinema and watched a movie about space. Mom started once again to sound in love when she spoke to Phil over the phone.

Winter came, bringing its cold weather. The snow melted away and made room for spring. At Easter, Phil cancelled his apartment and moved into the house with them.

Already the first night something happened which told Ellen it was time for a change.

"That's odd," Phil said, picking up his toothbrush from the floor. "I was sure I put in the cup next to your guys' toothbrushes."

And after they finished brushing their teeth, that was exactly where he put it. But the next morning Ellen found it once again on the floor under the sink.

"Hold up, Louie," his mom said and stopped the car in the garage after she picked him up from school the next day. "I want to talk with you."

He had already grabbed his bag and opened the door, eager to get in and say hello to his dad. Now, he closed the door again. "All right, Mom. What is it?"

"It's about your father."

"What about him?"

"You told me he stayed behind when you left the house. He stayed even though he was going to leave. Right?"

"Yeah, so?"

Mom took a deep breath. "I don't know how to say this without upsetting you ..."

"You think it's time Dad leaves."

Mom looked very surprised. "I ... I just think it might be for the best. Now that Phil is here. Imagine how your father must feel about that."

Louie nodded. "I know. I think it's what Dad wants, too. I can feel he's very tired." Louie looked down. "I just don't want him to go away. If he leaves the house, he dies for real."

Mom reached over and stroked his cheek. "I understand it's hard losing him again. But this time you have the memories. They'll never go away."

Louie nodded bravely. He promised to talk to his dad. Then, he left the car and went into the house.

Ellen stayed in the car and stared at the wheel for a minute or two. Then, just as she was about to get out, she caught a reflection in the rearview mirror.

John's blue eyes watched her from the backseat.

Ellen glanced over her shoulder, but saw nothing. She met his eyes in the mirror again. He smiled and looked awfully tired.

"Did you hear everything?" Ellen asked.

John nodded.

"You understand why I said it, right?"

John nodded again. He raised his left arm and pretended to look at his watch.

Ellen got the message. It was time. She felt her heart beat heavily. "We never got a chance to properly say goodbye. You were sleeping all the time, and you were so ... different ..."

John held her gaze. His eyes were shiny.

"I've never really let go," Ellen whispered. "I couldn't." She sniffed and dabbed her eyes with her sleeve.

When she looked in the mirror once more, John held up a hand and waved.

Ellen smiled. "Goodbye, John."

She opened the door and left the car.

Later that evening, as Louie was lying in his bed and staring at the ceiling, he realized it was time. He had spent the whole afternoon with his dad. Had pushed the inevitable. He couldn't push it any longer.

"Dad," he whispered and sat up.

The desk chair turned slightly, and Louie knew his dad was listening.

"There's something we need to talk about. Do you remember how you promised to stay a little longer?"

No answer came. The room was silent.

Then the door suddenly opened gently, and light from the hallway came streaming in.

Wondering, Louie pushed the duvet aside and went to the door. He looked down the hallway and heard the floorboards creak. He followed his dad and stopped by the ladder to the attic. The hatch was pushed open. Louie climbed up into the chamber. The telescope was standing under the skylight. It turned slowly, carefully adjusting its coordinates.

"What do you want me to see?" Louie asked and went over to take a look.

At first, he saw only darkness. But then a fireball suddenly shot past.

Louie gasped and pulled back. "What was *that*?"

He stared at the calendar nailed to the beam next to the window. The date was marked with a big, red circle. The meteor showers. He had completely forgotten.

Louie sat spellbound watching the incredible show on the night sky with his dad. He let out an excited sound whenever he caught a fireball in the telescope. The hours slipped past.

Sometime during the show, his dad must have left the attic. Louie didn't notice him going. But suddenly he realized he couldn't feel his dad's presence any longer. He glanced around and knew he was alone.

John left the house through the front door. He felt the cool night air through the old hospital gown. He was tired, so tired, and he was looking forward to what was to come. In the driveway, he stopped briefly to look back up at the skylight. He smiled. Then, he turned his back to the house and started walking.

Louie kept on having lively dreams, but he never visited Dreamland again, and he saw no more of the man in blue. Instead, he often dreamt about his father.

***

I wrote *Dreamland* during a difficult time in my life. I was stressed out of my mind, to the point where I could barely remember my own name. Writing this story was a very welcome relief. While I visited this world, I felt stress-free. To this day, I'm still amazed at how I did it. I guess sometimes, bad energy finds a positive way of expressing itself.

Only a few years after writing this story, my own father passed away from cancer. My relationship to him was much like the one between Louie and his father, so as you can imagine, losing him broke my heart. It also made *Dreamland* one of the most personal stories I have written.

HUMAN FLESH

The following is a presentation of all written material so far legally available for publication in what is publicly known as the Freyston case. The material has been corrected for spelling and punctuation errors, but is otherwise unedited.

1

Email sent from Michael James Cochran to the travel agency Ski Top, Saturday, February 11, 2017, 11:41 PM.

Hello Ski Top,

I've tried calling your local office, but I just missed your calling hours. I have made a reservation for a family cabin for seven days in Pittsfield. Unfortunately, I'll need to cancel, due to an unforeseen accident. I've read the cancellation policy on your website, but I'm not quite sure how much of the advance payment I'll get back, if any.

I know it's a late call, but I really hope we can still cancel and let some other lucky people enjoy the cabin. (The kids were really looking forward to the trip. What a shame!)

I've attached to this email the necessary information. I'll also call you first thing Monday morning.

Thank you and sorry for the hassle.

Best wishes,

Michael Cochran

2
Text message conversation between Caroline Cochran Wilson and Otha Cochran, Sunday, February 12, 2017, 9:11 AM – 9:42 PM.

Hi sweetie <3<3 Dad just told me you guys aren't coming for the trip??? Something about your dad breaking his leg? :S

Hi Caroline <3 Yeah, he fell in the driveway yesterday while shoveling snow. It was only the ankle, though, and they said it's just sprained. But he won't be able to drive—what awful timing! :-(

OMG, bummer! :'(But can't you just come with us then? And maybe Hugh too? I think we can all fit in our car …

Hugh already suggested that, but Dad said your cabin is only big enough for 4 people.

I know, I just asked him, and he says we won't be able to fit in the car, eight, what with all the luggage :-(OMG, I feel so sad … It just won't be the same without my favorite cousin :'(

I know :-(

:'(Who will help me learn to ski then?

You'll just have to remember what I told you last year. Put your weight from side to side and make sure to do nice, wide turns. I'm sure you'll be fine!

:-) I hope so …

If you like, you can always hire a teacher. Maybe that guy with the brown eyes is there again this year—that wouldn't be too bad now would it? ;-)

Haha :P <3

Just send me a thought while you're sitting in the snow drinking hot cocoa :-)

I definitely will! <3<3<3

3
Transcription of voice mail message from Michael James Cochran to Frederick James Cochran,
Sunday, February 12, 2017, 3:02 PM.

[...] Hi Dad, it's me. I was hoping to catch you, but ... well, I guess you're probably busy shoveling snow, right? [brief laughter] ... Boy, it's really coming down, huh? We're almost up to our waists around here, and I just heard it was even worse for you guys up there ... Anyway, uhm ... I was actually calling to ask if you, uhm, I know it's been a while and all, but, uhm ... how would you feel about having the kids come visit you for a week or so? We were going to Pittsfield ... you know we usually go there in the winter holidays, right? ... Well, you see, I managed to fall down and sprain my ankle out in the driveway. Nice going, huh? [grunting laughter] So, uhm ... no skiing for us this year. But then I thought ... [clears throat] ... the kids might go and visit you instead. They'll bore themselves silly spending the week in the house with me, so I, uhm ... if it's fine with you, of course ... I could put them on the train tomorrow morning ... But, you know, I understand if you have other things to do, that's perfectly fine, we'll just figure out something else then ... Anyways, uhm ... I'll let you go. Give me a call when you get the message, all right? Thanks, Dad [...]

4

Text message conversation between Hugh Cochran and Otha Cochran, Monday, February 13, 2017, 08:11 AM – 08:48 PM.

Check out the guy next to me :D
   Hello???
   Why aren't you answering?

   Because you're being really rude. What if the guy sees what you're writing about him?

   Come on, he's not seeing anything ... he's snoring like a bear xD
   Seriously, did you hear that?? That noise he just made :D

   Hehe :-) Yeah, I heard it. You're not being very nice, Hugh.

   I'm just bored 0:)
   Hahaha! Hear that? I think he's dreaming xD

   He's tired, poor guy :-) He's probably on his way to work.

   I'm glad it's not me xo When will we be there?

   Two more hours.

   Fuuuuck! :-| Seriously, I had no idea Maine was such a long state :S

   I think the train is going slower than usual due to the snow. Could you please stop texting? I'm trying to watch a video.

   Do you have data? :o

   Yes.

   I don't, mine ran out yesterday >:(I'm bored ...
   Otha?
   Hello?
   I'm boooooored x'(

   That's not my problem. Look out the window.

   There's nothing but snow and fields to look at :-| God, Maine is a boring place ...

I know.

I wanted so badly to go to Pittsfield :-(

Me too.

What was that she said on the speaker?! :o Was it our stop next?

No. I just told you it'll be another couple of hours.

Damnit >:(
The snoring guy just got off :D
What are you doing now?

Well, my eyes are closed, so what do you think I'm doing? Why do you keep texting me? I'm sitting right across the aisle. You can just speak to me.

Because the other passengers can't know what we're saying. It's top secret B)

You really are bored.

Yes! :X
Are you excited to see Grandpa?

Sure.

Do you remember him?

Of course. Don't you?

Not really ... I was only five the last time we saw him.
Helloooo?

Cut it out, Hugh. I'm trying to sleep. I'll turn off my phone if you keep texting.

Nooooo! Entertain me!
Please don't turn off your phone! :'(
Otha?
I know you haven't turned it off. I can still hear it vibrating :P Or is that a dildo in your pocket?

You really are a pain in the ass :-| I'm turning it off now.

Are you going to write on your blog while we stay at Grandpa's?

There probably won't be anything to blog about.

You don't know that. It might be an awesome holiday! :D

Yeah, right. On an old farm in the middle of nowhere? No one wants to read about that. I'm turning it off now. Don't wake me up until they say Freyston.

Noooo! Waaaait!
Otha?
Hellooooo?
x'(

5
Entry from the blog *My Otha Life* by Otha Cochran,
Monday, February 13, 2017, 11:08 PM.

This was supposed to be a short entry. I just wanted to tell you guys how the planned vacation I have been looking forward to for months was cancelled at the last minute, thanks to my clumsy dad who tripped over a pile of snow in the driveway and sprained his ankle.

Instead he arranged for me and my brother to go visit my Grandpa who lives all the way up in Maine. Sounds awesome, right? #sarcasm

At first, I thought it would be too lame to write an entry telling you about what's going on up here, but I've actually changed my mind. A few things happened today which made me think the vacation won't be as dull as I feared. In any case, writing a few entries will give me something to do. I apologize in advance if these aren't going to be the most thrilling entries I've done.

(By the way, I wanted to once again thank all you guys following my blog. I still can't believe the everyday life of a nineteen-year-old hopefully-someday-writer is that interesting, but I'm very flattered.)

All right, here goes.

The train ride was, as expected, dreadful. It lasted 8 hours! We were delayed several times due to snow on the tracks, and apparently about a million people were going home on winter holidays, because the train was stuffed to the rafters.

When we finally got off, it had (surprise, surprise) started snowing. Like, really snowing. It was drifting so much you could barely open your eyes—which of course didn't bother Hugh in the slightest; he immediately threw himself down and started making snow angels. (Sometimes I seriously consider if he has some sort of undiagnosed mental disorder.)

I couldn't see Grandpa's car anywhere; in fact, there were no cars at all in the parking lot next to the station. I had to bite off my glove in order to get to my phone and call him up, but he didn't answer. I tried a few times, but no luck. I thought he was probably just running late.

So, we started waiting.

Twenty minutes later, still no sign of Grandpa. I was halfway dead from the cold, and I was just on the verge of crying, when our savior showed up.

A large pickup truck came plowing through the snow and stopped right in front of us. At first, I actually thought it was Grandpa, as he too drives a pickup (I guess pretty much everyone drives a pickup up here), but it wasn't him.

As the window rolled down, a young guy with a beard said in a thick accent: "Hello there. You guys don't look like a regular pair of maniacs."

"Well, we're not," I said, feeling very confused.

He laughed aloud, like it was some kind of joke.

I explained to him that we were visiting and our grandpa was supposed to pick us up. He asked me for Grandpa's name, and I was puzzled at this at first, but then I realized that of course everyone knows each other up here. And sure enough, the guy lit up when I told him Grandpa's name.

"Well, what do you know?" he laughed. "I had no idea Old Fred had any grandchildren, that darn old-timer."

Then he offered to take us to Grandpa's house. Now, normally, I would have turned down an offer like that in a heartbeat—although the guy seemed friendly, you just never know. But I was about half a minute away from pneumonia, so I decided to take the chance.

Inside the car, the air heater was blowing at full force, and there was a pleasant smell, not cow dung or armpit sweat like I'd expected. The cabin was pretty clean too, except for a few candy wrappers on the floor.

The guy drove responsibly, the conditions considered. He kept saying how "greasy" the road was—I'm not fluent in Maine-lingo, but I think he meant "slippery"—and we didn't meet any other drivers who had dared venture outside. He was pretty talkative, and according to all my prejudices, he was dressed in a thick work jacket with a big woolen collar, worn-out jeans and heavy boots.

"You know, I could tell right away you guys were flatlanders," he said at one point. "Where are you from? Boston?"

I told him yes, we had come from Boston, and we were going to spend the week at Grandpa's due to the cancelled skiing trip. He told us his name was Martin, but everyone called him Mowgli.

Hugh asked him where he got the nickname from.

"I loved climbing trees when I was your age," Martin said with a shrug, and I could tell right away Hugh got himself a new idol.

The two of them started talking about skiing, and Martin offered to take Hugh out on a beach one of the days. His plan was to tie a rope to the car and drag Hugh behind it, skiing—or "car-skiing" as he called it. "I've done it a million times with my friends," he boasted, blinking at me in the rearview mirror. "That way, you get to do a little skiing after all. How about you? You want to try?"

"No, thank you," I said, trying to sound firm, but I think I accidentally smiled a little.

Yeah, I know what you're thinking. And yes, Martin is quite charming, if you can get past the accent, and if you're into the farmer-type. I don't know, there was just something very open about him, the way he just talked to us like he'd known us forever.

But before you guys go apesh*t in the comments, let me make it clear nothing will happen, all right? First off, I don't even know if Martin has a girlfriend or wife. He didn't wear a ring (yes, I checked, okay?) but you never know. And secondly, he's like ten years older than me.

Good. Glad we got that out of the way. Back to the story.

Grandpa lives about ten minutes outside Freyston, a tiny dump of a town. As we drove up the icy driveway and saw Grandpa's house up ahead, Hugh noticed all the lights were out.

Now, I just need to explain real quick about Grandpa's property. It's an old farm consisting of four buildings: the machine house, the barn, the cow barn and the main house. I won't bore you with the architectural details, my point is simply how large a place it is for one old guy. And all the four buildings were black as night in the already dim evening.

Martin parked in the courtyard, and as I looked up at the dark windows, I got a really odd feeling that we might find Grandpa dead from a heart attack. I can't explain it, it was just a thought.

I thanked Martin for the ride and offered to pay him, to which he simply laughed. But he said he would stay in the car until we were sure everything was all right, which made me feel a little better. So, we left the car with our bags and rushed through the snowy wind into the house.

Seeing and smelling the old scullery brought back memories from my childhood, and my Grandpa's old dog, Skip, a small terrier mix, came running out to greet us. He has gotten a few more gray hairs around his muzzle, and he honestly didn't seem that excited to see us, in fact he was more whimpering than anything. I just tell you this because it struck me as very odd, and because it enhanced my sense of something being wrong.

Hugh, on the other hand, clearly had no worries. He kicked off his boots and ran up the stairs, calling for Grandpa. I figured Grandpa was probably taking a nap in his upstairs bedroom, and Hugh would be sure to wake him up.

I had started freezing again after we left the car, so I kept my jacket on and went out to the kitchen. It was pretty obvious Grandpa lives alone, judging from the piles of dirty dishes. I couldn't find the light switch, so I went on to the TV lounge, which was also cold, dark and empty; the ancient leather furniture looked even more worn than I remembered.

I suddenly realized just how cold the house was, and I noticed the window being ajar, the curtain swaying in the draft. I quickly closed it and felt the radiator: completely cold. I had no idea why Grandpa would have shut off the heat and opened the window.

Upstairs I could hear Hugh still calling and opening and closing doors, obviously looking for Grandpa. My sense of dread increased still further, and I was just about to turn around and go upstairs when my eye caught something through the French door into the dining room. It was dark in there, too, but the windows were visible as bright rectangles, and in front of one of them stood a tall, gangly figure. It kind of looked like Grandpa, except I didn't remember him being that thin.

I went and opened the door, but the man by the window didn't move as I entered the room. I could tell he had his back to me, as though he had gone to look out the window and then fallen into a trance.

"Grandpa?" I asked low, not wanting to scare him.

No reaction.

Suddenly, I got a very strange feeling that the man *wasn't* my Grandpa. I know it's totally silly—I mean, who else could it be?

I squinted my eyes in an effort to see his features more clearly, and I realized to my astonishment he was naked except for a pair of white undies.

I'm not kidding. I know I should have felt embarrassed, but for some reason it just made me even more uneasy. Something was definitely not right.

"Grandpa?" I said, louder.

Still, the man didn't stir. I noticed the faint whisper of the wind blowing through the room, and I noticed the windows in here were also standing ajar.

Finally, it dawned on me to turn on the lights. I can't believe I didn't think of it earlier, but the situation was just so unreal and I was really confused and scared. I found the switch and flicked it.

At long last, the man by the window reacted and started turning slowly around. I gaped at him. It was my Grandpa all right, but I almost didn't recognize him. His cheeks were hollow, his lips thin and dry, the skin around his eyes was very dark, the eyes themselves were really haunting, being way too dark, like almost black, as though the pupils had grown to blot out the white.

There was something strange above his head, too, although it must have been the shadows playing a trick on me—but for a brief second, I could have sworn Grandpa had a couple of branches sticking out of the top of his skull. Yeah, I know. It sounds completely bonkers.

It was all over in a blink of an eye, then Grandpa looked exactly like I remembered him—the only odd thing about him being the missing clothes.

"Well, if it isn't Otha," he said, his face lighting up. "I was just wondering when you guys would show up."

The situation was still pretty weird, but I think I managed to ask him why he wasn't wearing anything.

He looked down himself. "Oh, right. I was just about to grab a quick shower before you came. I guess I fell into a brown study."

He welcomed me with a hug, and once I smelled him and felt the warmth from him, my nervousness finally went away. It really *was* my Grandpa. Of course. Whatever I had just seen had to be some sort of trick of my imagination, probably caused by my fear. Just shows how much a scaredy-cat I am and how vivid my imagination is.

I asked him about the open windows, and he just shrugged and said he was letting in some fresh air.

At that moment, Hugh came bursting into the dining room and greeted Grandpa with a hug.

I suddenly remembered Martin still waiting in the car. I went out and opened the front door, sending him a thumbs-up. He returned the gesture, honked once and drove out of the courtyard.

When I returned to the house, Grandpa had gone to take his shower, and Hugh was unpacking, complaining about the cold. I went around closing the windows and turning on the heat. Grandpa had been really serious about airing out the place, because I found the windows opened in *the entire house*.

When Grandpa came out of the shower, the radiators were booming out heat, and we were finally able to take off our jackets.

"Did you forget to come get us?" I asked him.

Grandpa looked at me with surprise. "Come get you? From where?"

"Well, from the train."

"Did you guys come in with the train?"

"Yes. Dad said you would pick us up by the station."

Grandpa frowned. "I don't recall him saying that. But how did you get out here from the station?"

I told him about Martin, and Grandpa simply nodded and said he would have to thank him the next time he saw him. Then he went on to tell Hugh how big he had grown.

I remember looking at him while he chatted with Hugh, feeling pretty weirded-out. I'm pretty sure my dad had told Grandpa about the train, but he must have forgotten. I mean, he is more than seventy years old, after all, so I guess it happens. I just couldn't shake the feeling it had something to do with the way I found him ...

The rest of the evening went very well, Grandpa was completely himself. We ate roasted goose and had ice-cream for dessert. Afterwards, we played cards.

I think it just might turn out to be a nice stay up here, in spite of the weird start. If anything interesting happens, I might do a few more entries.

Till next time.

Love, Otha.

6
Text message conversation between Hugh Cochran and Otha Cochran, Tuesday, February 14, 2017, 02:18 – 02:27 AM.

Are you asleep?
   Hey, are you asleep? Please answer if you're awake … :-(
   Please, Otha :'(

   Why are you texting me in the middle of the night?

   Because I'm scared :'o

   Come in here then.

   I'm afraid to get out of bed :'o

   Why? My room is right next door.

   But I think someone is in my room :'o

   It's probably just Skip.

   No, he sleeps in Grandpa's room. I think it's a person.

   You must have been dreaming. Go back to sleep, Hugh.

   I can't. The wind is keeping me awake.

   The wind?

   Yeah, don't you hear it? It sounds like it's whispering :o

   It's just the wind, Hugh. You've had a bad dream. Think about something else, and you'll fall asleep again in no time. I'm really tired. I'm going back to sleep.

   I tried thinking about something else, it doesn't work … It's the wind, Otha … That's what I can feel in the room …

   What do you mean? Is there a draft? Did you open the window?

   No, but it's like the wind is trying to get in here … I'm really scared :'o Can't you please come?

Otha?
Hello?

Stop texting. I thought I heard something.

Do you hear it too? :o

I don't know. Let me listen for a minute.
All right, I see what you mean. The wind does sound a little like a voice whispering.

I told you! I wasn't just dreaming! Can you hear what it's saying?

It's not saying anything.

Yes, it is ... it's telling us something over and over again. Can't you hear it?

I can hear the same noise repeating, yes, but that's just something to do with how the wind is hitting the roof of the house or whatever.

I guess you're right ...

Get it together, will you? You're not a baby anymore ;) Let's go back to sleep, okay? Sleep tight.

You too.

Otha? Are you asleep?

Yes.

I can hear what the wind is saying now ...

Honestly, Hugh ...

It's saying 'indigo' ... Don't you hear it?
Don't you hear it??

Yes, all right, I hear it. Can we please go back to sleep now?

What does it mean? What does 'indigo' mean?

It's a color or something. You'll have to Google it.

Now it stopped ...

I think I can fall asleep now :-)

Great. See you in the morning.

See you :-)

7

Entry from the blog *My Otha Life* by Otha Cochran, Tuesday, February 14, 2017, 8:43 PM.

Right, I think I better start by clarifying something from yesterday's entry. Several of you guys have asked me to go into more detail about what I saw when Grandpa turned around at me right after we got here. I would like to do so, but the thing is, I can't really explain it better than I already did. Reading now what I wrote yesterday, I honestly think it was nothing. I was scared due to the cold and the darkness and the weird situation. And it was really fast, like a fraction of a millisecond, so I'm not really sure I even *did* see anything. I think we need to chalk it up to an unexplained delusion and let it rest, okay?

I also want to thank the reader who brought to my attention what Martin found so funny about what he said when he saw us, the thing about us being maniacs. Evidently, he didn't say "maniacs" as in "crazy people," but "Maineiacs," a term used to describe the people up here. Today I learned …

All right, with that out of the way, I have something new to report from up here in the cold and merciless climate of northern Maine.

It has been snowing all night, so we woke up to even taller drifts outside the windows. Grandpa was already busy in the kitchen when I came downstairs, frying eggs and making toast.

During breakfast he told us he had to run a few errands today, as one of the neighbors, an old widow, had called him to come help her remove a tree which had been downed by the snowstorm. Hugh wanted to join him, so they left as soon as they were done eating.

I watched them go from the kitchen window, Grandpa's truck plowing through the heavy snow of the driveway. I cleared off the table, then went upstairs to get a book from my bag. As I passed by Grandpa's bedroom, I noticed an odd smell. I opened the door and almost gagged. Something smelled seriously rotten. (And I know that smell, because my dad once forgot about a packet of raw meat in the fridge.) I opened the roof light all the way and checked the room for anything nasty, but I didn't find anything. Once the smell had cleared out, I went to close the window, when I noticed something very strange.

Outside, on the roof, were imprints in the snow. It almost looked like something had been hurled out the window, but I couldn't see anything but the imprints. I also noticed a small puddle on the floor from melted snow. Grandpa must have opened the window sometime during the night.

I decided to go outside. When I visited Grandpa as a kid, I loved to feed the chickens and collect eggs, and call me a nostalgic fool, but the thought still excites me. So, I went out the front door—Skip joining me and immediately zooming off to somewhere important.

The barn is where the cattle once was, but now the empty booths are all that's left—it's quite an eerie sight, to be honest. Anyway, in one of them Grandpa has made a chicken coop. The birds were eyeing me curiously through the wire—they are such funny little animals! If you ever get to see them, you'll know what I mean.

There were a dozen fine eggs in the nest, so I filled my jacket pockets and carefully went back outside.

To my surprise I found a blue car in the courtyard, a set of footprints leading up to the front door. Someone had come without me hearing it and simply entered the house. I guess it's not unusual out here in the country, and I wasn't really scared. Probably just a neighbor, I thought.

I went inside and heard the noise from a vacuum. In the living room I met a small, Mexican-looking woman humming loudly to herself while cleaning the floor. When she saw me, she didn't really seem surprised, she just turned off the vacuum and smiled beamingly at me, revealing a row of tiny grey teeth.

"Uhm, hi," I said. "Who are you?"

"My name is Esme," she said in a slight accent. "You must be Fred's grandchild? He didn't tell me you would be here, but I noticed your shoes and jackets."

We chatted politely for a few minutes. Esme told me she lives three miles up the road, and that she cleans for Grandpa a couple of times a week. Of course he hadn't mentioned this to me either.

I told Esme I didn't want to disturb her, so I placed the eggs in the fridge and went upstairs to read one of the books I had brought along—it's *Alone in the Moonlight* by A. C. Reeler, and God, it's good! Just the right amount of sappy.

About an hour later I heard the sound of a car and got up to see Esme's car making its way out the driveway.

I went downstairs to find everything neat and tidy. She had left a short note on the kitchen counter with her hours and a few things Grandpa needed to know, something about him needing to buy more food for Skip, as the bag was almost empty, and that his clothes were in the dryer.

I was surprised to find out how Esme seems to be more than a cleaning lady, almost a domestic helper. But maybe Grandpa needs someone like that now that Grandma isn't around anymore.

I remembered Skip and went to let him in. But when I opened the front door, I let out a scream of surprise as a tall person stood right in front of me.

"Christ, you gave me a heart attack," Martin said and laughed.

"*You* had a heart attack?" I asked, clutching my chest. "What are you doing here? I didn't hear your car."

He held up a paper bag. "I brought cake."

"Well ... I'm home alone right now," I told him.

"More cake for the two of us, then," he simply smiled. "Do you know how to make coffee?"

I do, although I don't drink it, so I made him coffee and a cup of tea for myself. I'll be honest, it was quite weird being alone with a strange guy in Grandpa's house, but Martin didn't seem to mind; he just sat down, cut the cake and chatted along, and Skip even came and jumped onto his lap, as though the dog was used to seeing him. I was glad I had done my hair and put on a bit of makeup that morning.

"So, how's the old-timer doing?" Martin said as I sat down across from him. "Hasn't been up to anything funny, has he?"

"What do you mean?" I asked, sipping my tea.

Martin shrugged. "Well, he can get a little spooky once in a while, like he suddenly forgets what he's doing."

I felt kind of relieved that Martin had also seen Grandpa fall into a stupor like that, and I told him briefly about how I had found him yesterday.

Martin listened intently. Then he smiled once more and said: "Yeah, that sounds like Old Fred, all right. Well, let's have a taste. It's my mom's home baking."

"Your mom?" I asked surprised. "Do you still live at home?"

"Hell no. I moved out a long time ago. I just didn't move that far. We like to keep it local up here, you know. We don't want any of the good genes going to waste."

I raised one eyebrow. "Isn't that what you call inbreeding?"

Martin laughed aloud.

"So people around here only marry other locals?" I pursued.

"You're right," he joked. "Imagine if any big city blood got mixed into the population—that would be a catastrophe."

Seizing the opportunity, I asked him: "How about you? Would you date anyone from not around here?"

All right, all right, I know. It wasn't the most elegant or subtle way of asking, but it felt okay in the moment, and Martin didn't seem to find it awkward.

"Nah," he just shrugged. "I would be glad to find anyone willing to put up with me for a longer period of time."

He smiled at me, and I found myself smiling back, then hastily averted my eyes.

The conversation drifted onto other things. Martin asked me about school, and he told me about himself. He works in his dad's company, a building firm of some kind. Right now his dad is in Japan to negotiate a deal, and Martin is in charge while his dad is away.

I have to admit; I was quite impressed. The first impression Martin gives off is more like that of an overgrown teenager, but if he can take care of a business with more than twenty employees, he has to be pretty responsible, don't you think? I discretely lured him into telling me his age: twenty-six. Not as old as I had guessed.

A few minutes later I saw Grandpa's truck coming up the driveway. One minute later, Hugh came bursting in, babbling about how they had cut up the fallen tree and showed off a twenty-dollar-bill the old lady had paid him for his help.

Grandpa came in and greeted Martin like he wasn't at all surprised to see him.

I told him about Esme and gave him the note she had left.

"Oh, thank you, sweetheart," he said. "I thought she might come. She's not really on a schedule, she just comes a couple of times a week, and—" At this point, he cut himself off, reached for the radio and turned up the volume. It was the weather forecast, and they said something about a mild thaw coming tomorrow. "They're wrong," Grandpa muttered to no one in particular. He looked out the window, as though he saw something out there, but I couldn't see anything but the open, snowy fields. "It'll get colder," he prophesied. "A lot colder. It's only just begun."

For some reason I got the chills when he said that. Honestly, he reminded me of Ned Stark, the way his voice got all hoarse, like he was foreboding something awful. I glanced at Martin and saw him noticing it too. Hugh, however, was busy stuffing himself with cake.

I've been wondering about it later on, and I really just think Grandpa is a little weird, if you know what I mean, like old people will sometime become. Not like mental or anything, just from living alone out here.

He came to after a few seconds and smiled at Martin. "So, Mowgli, I understand you already met my grandchildren?"

"Yeah, I found them lost and abandoned in the snow and figured I better drive them home."

"That was nice of you," Grandpa said. "I had completely forgotten they would be coming with the train, although their father reportedly told me so."

"That's what I keep telling ya', old-timer, you need to get yourself a hearing aid," Martin teased him.

Grandpa pointed at Martin. "Just so you know, you're not too old to get hit by a snowball when you're not looking."

Martin laughed, and I couldn't help but smile. He really has a way of taking the tension out of the situation, probably because he is so authentic. You automatically relax around him.

"So, are you going out with the shovel tomorrow?" Martin asked. "The shovel," I found out later, is a snowplow Grandpa has which he uses to clear the driveways of most people in the area, so they can get out during periods of heavy snow.

"If it's going to snow tonight, which I'm sure it will, then yes," Grandpa said.

"Well, I was thinking I could come by and take your grandchildren for a ride out to the beach, you know, entertain them while you're out."

Hugh looked up. "Are we going car-skiing?"

"I'm afraid your sister says it's too dangerous, and she's probably right," he said, winking at me. "But I had another idea: We can use the tube from a tractor tire as a sled. You know, like a big donut. You'll be both safe and comfortable sitting in that."

Hugh almost couldn't deal with the excitement. He begged Grandpa for permission to go, and of course Grandpa gave in, but at least not before making Martin promise not to go too fast.

And that's how I got invited on a date tomorrow. I know my brother will be there too, but still. I'm actually looking forward to talking with Martin again.

All right, commence the chatter, you gossipy girls you!

8

Email from Martin Edwin White to Edwin Harold White, sent Tuesday, February 14, 2017, 9:43 PM.

Hey Dad

Tried calling you earlier, but the connection is really spotty. Heard someone say a lot of phones can't make calls from up here due to the snow tipping over an antenna or something.

How are things going in the East? The Japs treating you all right? :-) We're holding up fine around here, I've got things covered, and Paul and Sue have been great helpers, managing the New York contractors.

Wanted to talk to you about something else. I don't know, it's probably nothing. It's about Fred. His grandkids are visiting—did you know he had grandkids? I talked with one of them today, Otha is her name, and she told me Fred had one of his episodes. You know, one of those where he just all of a sudden spaces out. Like that time at New Years. You told me to come tell you if I ever noticed anything like that again.

I'm not sure if you can reach me on the phone, but try Skype.

See you.

—Martin

9

Entry from the blog *My Otha Life* by Otha Cochran,
Wednesday, February 15, 2017, 7:43 AM.

I know it's kind of weird posting an entry this early in the day (I'm still in my pj's and haven't even had breakfast yet), but I just have to share with you guys a story my Grandpa told us late last night. It was so intense, it literally gave me nightmares.

I woke up a few minutes ago by the sound of a car engine outside the window. It was Esme, she's cleaning downstairs right now, I can hear her bustling about. I think it's really early for her to come by—it's only five past six right now—but it's also nice not being the only one awake, as I'm sure Hugh and Grandpa are still snoring.

Let me just start by saying thank you for your concern, guys. Many of you have pointed out that Grandpa's tendency to lose touch with the world for brief periods might be the beginning signs of dementia. That would also explain why he forgot to pick us up from the train.

I read a little about dementia online, and I see your point. I don't think I'll talk to Grandpa about it, though. He's a stubborn old farmer, and he's always been proud of taking care of himself, so he probably won't listen anyway. But if I notice any other strange signs, I'll call my dad and talk with him about it.

That being said, once you guys read the story I'm about to tell, I think you might see why I don't think it's dementia causing Grandpa's episodes, but rather something else. Please feel free to give your feedback in the comments.

Okay, here goes.

When I had finished yesterday's entry and posted it, I went downstairs and joined the others in the TV lounge. Hugh was playing on his laptop, Grandpa was watching the late news and sipping from a cup of coffee, and I got my book and started reading.

"Grandpa?" Hugh suddenly asked, taking off his headphones. "Why didn't you ever marry again?"

I think Grandpa had drifted off slightly, because he straightened up and cleared his throat. "Marry again? I'm afraid it's too late for me."

"You could get a girlfriend," I butted in. "Don't you get lonely up here, all by yourself?"

"Nah, I'm not lonely," he said, looking up at the black-and-white wedding photo on the wall. "And besides, your grandmother was the love of my life."

There was something very sad but also very beautiful in Grandpa's expression. Call me a hopeless romantic, but I hope I someday will find someone to love me as much as Grandpa loved my grandma.

"How did she die?" Hugh asked bluntly, causing my heart to skip a beat. Grandma's death really isn't something we talk about in the family. I remember asking Dad once, when I was little, and he got very quiet. I finally managed to squeeze out of him something about a plane crash, but that was all he ever told me.

I looked tensely at Grandpa, forgetting all about my book. I thought I saw his demeanor charge somewhat. Then he muttered: "It was a terrible accident. A plane we were on went down."

Hugh's eye grew big. "Holy s**t, are you serious?"

I told him to watch his language. "And do you really think it's something Grandpa wants to speak about?"

Hugh actually looked embarrassed for once, but Grandpa simply said: "It's all right, sweetheart. It's no secret, really. I can tell you the story if you'd like."

I didn't know what to say.

Grandpa muted the television and started telling the story. He didn't look at us as he spoke; he just stared out the window, where the snow was once again falling in big, fat flakes. I'll try my best to tell it the way he did.

"We rented a cabin up in Canada," he began. "Every year in January we would go there for a week or so. We would drive to Quebec and go by plane even farther north, to a small town called Wabush, and from there we still had a four-hour drive to the cabin. The nature up there is simply amazing. The woods are mostly uninhabited, and in some areas no man has ever been.

We'd made the trip many times before, but that year was particularly snowy. Most of the flights from Quebec were cancelled, but not ours. It was already close to midnight, and we were glad we didn't have to spend the night in a hotel.

I fell asleep as soon as we took off. Your grandmother didn't sleep; she never could sleep on a plane. She had a mild fear of flying, you see. Me, on the other hand, I wasn't the least bit worried. Of course, I knew smaller planes aren't quite as safe as larger ones, but I also knew the pilots up there have a lot of experience with flying in harsh weather.

And, actually, I don't think the weather was the cause of the crash, although I never really found out; it was probably some sort of engine failure. All I know is, suddenly we were going down. Everything was shaking, the lights were blinking, everyone woke up and started shouting or crying or praying. I remember your grandmother squeezing my hand, and the next moment I was lying in the snow.

Something numbed me; I'm guessing the cold, or maybe the shock. Either way I couldn't feel a thing, even though I would later find out my shoulder had been dislocated and I had a deep cut in my hand."

At this point, he held out his hand so Hugh and I could see a long, ragged scar across the palm.

"But all I could think of at the time was finding your grandmother. Now, as to describing the scene, if you guys ever saw a movie with a plane crash, that pretty much sums it up: wreckage, tipped over trees and a few flames. It was fairly easy to see, due to the moonlight, but it was also freezing cold, and the howling wind just made it worse. I'd guess we were well below minus twenty, and in weather like that you get frostbite within minutes if you're not dressed properly.

"I managed to find your grandmother, who was still buckled into her seat, unconscious. I managed to shake her gently awake. Except for a blow to the head which made her dizzy, she was miraculously unharmed.

"There were only two other survivors: the copilot, a Canadian named Cliff, and a German tourist at around my own age named Jürgen. I checked as many of the other passengers as I could find, but they were all dead, all thirty-two of them, counting the pilot.

Cliff, the copilot, was badly injured. I think his hip was broken, because his legs faced the wrong way, and the blood was pumping from a gash in his thigh. The German had gotten off with a dislocated elbow and maybe a few cracked ribs—at least he kept grunting and clutching his side. Now, as I think back, I would guess he was bleeding internally.

I suppose I was the lucky one of the bunch; my hand was so frozen it was barely bleeding, so I had no trouble bandaging it with a piece of cloth, and although my shoulder felt a little stiff—and still does so to this day—it had popped itself back into place, making me able to use my arm.

First thing I focused on was finding clothes. I took jackets from the bodies and found gloves and scarves and hats in the suitcases. Cliff, however, didn't want me to put any of the clothes on him."

"Why not?" Hugh exclaimed. I don't think he intended to interrupt Grandpa; he was just so wrapped up in the story he couldn't help himself.

"Because he knew he wouldn't make it," Grandpa said calmly. "He could neither walk nor crawl, and the wound in his leg was too big to do anything about. He was doomed, and he preferred the cold to take him sooner than later, instead of prolonging the pain."

Hugh looked terrified at this, but didn't say anything.

"Cliff was a brave man," Grandpa went on. "He spent his last minutes helping the rest of us. He told me where to find the radio, and I actually found it, but it was smashed to pieces. Then he told me how to read our coordinates. I found a map and followed his instructions. We couldn't pinpoint our exact location, but we had at least 250 miles to the nearest town. There might have been a few lonely cabins around, but they didn't show on the map, and finding them was like finding a needle in a haystack. With his dying breath, Cliff told us to walk south, and then he said something about taking a short rest. He closed his eyes and died."

Grandpa made a brief pause, still not looking at us. We both waited for him to go on.

"The German guy was an engineer of some kind, and he was confident he could fix the radio with his pocketknife. He might have been able to do it too, if it hadn't been for the cold. The shock had almost left me by now, and I found my body rigid and shaking with cold. Our breath literally froze to ice, and even with many layers of clothes on, we still had to keep moving not to freeze to death.

"Jürgen took off his gloves to work on the radio, but within seconds his fingers were stiff and purple. He only spoke a little English, but I think I made him understand he needed to give it up and come with us. That even if he got the damn thing working and got hold of someone, it would still be hours before anyone could reach us.

"But he just shook his head and kept saying 'nein, nein' while he worked desperately on the radio. I grabbed his shoulder, but he tore himself loose, shouting: 'Nein!'

"And so I left him. I helped your grandmother to her feet and told her which way we had to go. She looked back at the crash site with all the dead people strewn about, and I could tell she was happy to leave.

"If Jürgen ever got the radio working, I don't know, but he was never found. He—" Grandpa's voice faltered suddenly at this point, and for the first time, I detected a slight hesitation. "He had left the crash site and probably died somewhere in the woods.

"Well, your grandmother and I started south, tramping through the snow. As long as we kept going, we could barely hold off the cold, but if we stopped to rest for just a few minutes, it would seep right through our clothes and start gnawing at our skin.

"The woods just went on forever. Now and then we would pass a clearing or cross a frozen stream, and those were the only signs that we weren't just moving in circles.

"The night became day, and the sunlight provided a modest warmth, giving us the opportunity to slow down a bit. The wind settled down too, and I think the temperature even crept above zero. But the days aren't very long that far north in the winter, and soon the darkness came back, giving the cold renewed strength. The night lasted forever, or so it felt, and we walked without pause until the next morning finally came.

I don't know how many miles we put behind us, probably close to a hundred. We didn't talk much; we didn't need to. We both knew we were fighting for our lives and against pretty bad odds. When we got too tired, we slept for ten minutes. When we got thirsty, we drank the snow. Had one of us slipped and broken an ankle, that would have been the end, and the other would have had to go on alone.

In the beginning the hunger was there all the time. But by the third day, something happened to it. It left our bodies, and—I know it sounds strange, but—somehow the hunger joined forces with the cold, which by now had become a living thing. We felt it all around us, skulking, like a predator waiting patiently for its prey to tire out so it can move in for the kill. It was only a trick of the mind, of course, and probably not uncommon when people are fighting for their lives. That would also explain why the wind started whispering."

Grandpa stopped talking at this point, though his lips kept moving a little while. Both Hugh and I waited breathlessly for him to continue. When he didn't, Hugh finally lost his patience.

"What did the wind whisper, Grandpa?"

Grandpa didn't answer. He was still staring out the window, out into the snow and the darkness, as though he could see back through time. (All right, that might be a slight exaggeration, but I'm just trying to give you guys a feel of the mood in the room.)

"Grandpa?" Hugh asked.

Grandpa blinked and came to. "Yes?"

"What did the wind whisper?"

"The wind?"

"Yes. You said it whispered."

"Did I?" Grandpa shook his head smiling. "I must have been lost in thought. Well, I think we'd better call it a day; it's getting late." He was about to get up.

"No!" Hugh exclaimed. "You have to tell us how it ended."

I would have told him off for yelling at Grandpa like that, but honestly, I too was very eager to hear the rest of the story.

Grandpa hesitated for a moment, looking from Hugh to me. Then he said bluntly: "Your grandmother froze to death. I had to leave her behind. I kept on walking for two days, until I reached a town and was saved."

Silence descended over the room, as I felt the excitement drain from the air. The story had been ended way too abruptly.

"So, if Grandma could have gone on for just two more days," Hugh began.

"Hugh!" I hissed at him.

"She couldn't have taken another step," Grandpa said soberly. "She had spent her last strength and then some. I was just lucky I ..." He got up suddenly, clapping his hands together. "Well, I'm off to bed. It's been a long day."

He gave me the usual kiss on the forehead and ruffled Hugh's hair briefly before he went upstairs.

Hugh and I just sat there for a minute or so, staring at each other. I could tell Hugh felt the same frustration at the way Grandpa obviously had cut the story short.

"You heard what he said, right?" Hugh finally breathed. "About the wind?"

I just nodded. (I need to explain something real quick: Last night, Hugh thought he heard the wind whisper outside the house. It was of course just his imagination, but I understand why he was a little scared.)

When I lay in bed a few minutes later, I couldn't help but listen to the wind howling outside. I thought I would never fall asleep, but somehow I did, and I had terrible dreams about plane crashes and endless, snowy woods and a predator lurking in the darkness ...

Phew!

I have to say, it feels good getting the story out of my head. I'm a lot more calm now. Oh, and I think Esme has gone by now; I thought I heard her car leave a little while ago. Grandpa is up; I can hear him whistling downstairs. He's probably making breakfast. I'm starving.

I'm still looking forward to seeing Martin today.

Maybe I'll post another entry tonight, to let you guys know how it went.

10
Handwritten message from Esme Beatriz Durrant to Frederick James Cochran, Wednesday, February 15, 2017, approx. 07:30 AM.

1.5 hours

Came a little early, have to take Mr. Furry to the vet, Jud couldn't bring him, working today. Let Skip out to pee. Didn't vacuum, didn't want to wake you or the kids, it can wait till Saturday. Taking the empty bottles. Brought a squash cake, it's in the fridge.

Esme

PS. Come to dinner next Sunday. It's Jud's birthday. Bring a bottle of [ends abruptly]

11
Transcription of voice mail message from Freyston Animal Hospital to Esme Beatriz Durrant,
Wednesday, February 15, 2017, 09:14 AM.

[...] Morning, Ms. Durrant, this is Beth Devareaux calling from Freyston Animal Hospital. I'm reaching out because you had an appointment this morning at nine o'clock. It was a, uhm, desexing of a male cat. So I just wanted to make sure you didn't by chance forget about the appointment ... Of course, you might have been unable to come due to the weather, we get that a lot lately ... So, uhm, yeah, if we don't hear from you soon, we'll assume your appointment is cancelled, and we'll need to reschedule. In any case we'd appreciate you getting back to us when you get this message. Thank you, and have a nice day [...]

12
Entry from the blog *My Otha Life* by Otha Cochran,
Wednesday, February 15, 2017, 11:13 PM.

I heard some pretty awful rumors about Grandpa today. Up here, nasty gossip seems to flourish really well. Perhaps it's because everybody knows everybody, or maybe it's just because they don't have anything else to talk about.

Sorry if I come off as hostile, but I'm actually pretty pissed right now, and I need to get this off my chest.

The day started off fine, although I wasn't exactly well rested after that restless night of continuous nightmares, and I could tell Hugh hadn't slept well, either. Grandpa, on the other hand, seemed completely normal.

(By the way, he was right about the weather: It has been snowing all night, and the thermostat in the kitchen window read 6 degrees—I think that's the lowest temperature I have ever experienced.)

Martin came right after breakfast, and Hugh and I left with him half an hour later.

Hugh had a million questions for his new best friend slash hero, so I barely got a word in all the way to the beach. I didn't mind, though. I was sitting in the backseat looking out at the white landscape, once in a while sneaking a peek at Martin in the rearview mirror.

The beach was covered in a flat blanket of snow, the waves came rolling in, leaving rims of grey foam, which were lifted up by the breeze and strewn about in large chunks.

Hugh almost couldn't take the excitement as he and Martin went out to fasten the giant donut to a rope behind the car. I used the opportunity to slip into the front seat and give the heater another nudge upwards.

When Martin came back into the car, his cheeks were pink and his eyes had watered.

"Damn, that's wicked cold," he said, blowing into his hands. (He uses that word constantly, "wicked." I found it annoying to begin with, but it's actually pretty sweet.) Then he rolled down the window slightly, and called out: "Ready, Hugh?"

"Ready!" Hugh called back.

Martin started the truck, driving slowly across the beach, dragging Hugh behind it, who was sitting in the big black donut, laughing his head off, signaling Martin to go faster.

"It looks like fun," I said, looking at Hugh in the sideview mirror.

"You want to go next?"

"Think I'll pass."

"Suit yourself. So, you guys never been to the beach in wintertime, eh?"

"Nope."

"You never tried winter bathing, then?"

"No! Do I look like a crazy person to you?"

Martin laughed. "It's actually wicked fun."

"It sounds awful. I don't get why anyone would do that to themselves."

"Well, you feel very much alive afterwards, for one thing."

"I feel plenty alive already, thank you."

We drove a little in silence, while Hugh whooped and laughed from behind the car.

"Listen, what we talked about yesterday," Martin said, and I could tell from his voice what he was going to address. "Has your grandpa done anything else, you know ... out of the ordinary?"

"No," I said, trying to sound casual.

Martin just nodded.

When I realized he wasn't going to pursue it, I decided to ask: "Do you think it might be dementia?"

He looked at me, then quickly looked away again. "No. I mean, I'm not a doctor or anything, but my own grandpa suffered from dementia before he died, and he never acted like Old Fred does. No, I think it's something else ..."

"Like what?"

He didn't answer right away, because he had to turn around and go back, following our own newly made trail.

"You didn't answer," I urged him.

Martin turned off the radio. "Right, listen. I have a buddy who served in Iraq, and he got into a shootout one time, where he lost two of his friends. So now he has that thing ... what's-it-called? Post something ..."

"PTSD?"

"Exactly. He gets these episodes, where the memories just come barging in, and he has a panic attack or faints or something. I don't know, the way he describes it ... something about it reminded me of your grandpa."

I realized my heart was pounding away for no apparent reason. Somehow, I knew exactly what Martin meant, although I couldn't put it into words. But I got the same feeling when Grandpa told us about the plane crash and Grandma's death, that it's somehow connected to Grandpa's episodes.

"You know, I found him once, like you did the day you came here," Martin went on. "Except worse." Martin threw a glance into the rearview mirror, as though to make sure Hugh couldn't hear us. Then he started speaking in a low voice: "It was New Year's Eve some years back. I remember I just got my license a month or so before that, so I guess I was only seventeen. We were having guests over, and Fred was invited. But he didn't show up, and he didn't answer his phone either, so my mom sent me to go check on him. It was a wicked cold winter that year, but not as bad as this one. I found the house exactly like you did, dark and empty and freezing cold due to the open windows. But Fred wasn't in the house. I saw him through the living room window, down by the stream. I ran down there."

Martin paused and shook his head.

"He was standing not *by* the stream, but *in* the stream, and he was butt naked. He had stepped right through the ice, and the water reached his knees. I'm telling you; his legs were *blue* ... He must have been standing there for quite a while, because I remember his prints were gone, snowed over, you know. I was sure he was dead on his feet, frozen like a damn popsicle. But when I grabbed his shoulder, he came to, and so I quickly dragged him back inside and helped him get some clothes on."

Martin made a grin, which wasn't at all pretty.

"The weirdest thing about it was how he talked to me like everything was normal. Apparently, he couldn't remember what he had done, and he didn't believe me when I told him. But he could tell I wasn't joking around, so he told me not to tell anyone. I wanted to call an ambulance and everything, but he said it wasn't necessary, that he was fine." Martin shrugged. "So, he combed his hair and we drove to my parents' place. We told my mom Fred had just forgotten the time, and no one suspected anything. I told my dad about it a couple of days later, but no one else knows about it."

Some moments of silence followed inside the car as Martin stopped talking. I was kind of relieved I wasn't the only one who had experienced Grandpa like that, but I also felt worried for what it might mean.

"Has he had any other episodes since then?" I asked.

"A bunch," Martin said. "But never as bad. Most of the time he's just gone for a couple of seconds or so. My dad has been keeping an eye on him ever since that New Year's Eve."

"Then why do you think it's PTSD?"

"Because it always happens in the winter. I think the cold reminds him of your grandma and ..." Martin broke off at this point and threw a look at me. "You know how she died, right?"

I nodded.

"He never told anyone around here about it," Martin went on. "We only know the story through rumors. How did he say she died exactly?"

I was kind of surprised Martin would ask me that directly. I told him she died from cold in a cabin they had come by to seek shelter.

"From cold," he repeated thoughtfully.

"Yes, from cold," I said. "What else would she have died from?"

Martin bit his lip. "Maybe we shouldn't talk anymore about it."

"It's kind of too late now," I said.

Martin turned the truck around once more, then said: "All right, listen. You might as well hear it from me. There are certain rumors going about. Some people think your grandpa killed your grandma."

It honestly made me laugh. "That's ridiculous. He loved her more than anything." When Martin didn't reply, I crossed my arms and asked him: "Why on earth would he have killed her?"

"To survive, of course. There was this whole case concerning the plane crash. Fred was detained by the Canadian police for like three months before he was allowed to return home. He was the sole survivor, so no one could really confirm what he said had happened."

"Why would that need to be confirmed? He had nothing to lie about!"

"The police apparently thought your grandma was murdered by someone. They never found her body, you know. I guess that's kind of weird."

"Yeah, well, it doesn't mean he killed her," I told him—I probably sounded pretty angry by now, because I was.

"Listen, I'm on your side," he said. "I'm just telling you what people are saying. I've known your grandpa my whole life, and I don't think for a second he could hurt anyone. All right?"

I realized I was completely tense all over, and I tried to relax. "Sorry," I muttered.

"It's okay," he said. "Fred was charged with murder—or so the rumors say, anyway—but he was also acquitted. The story is that he and your grandma came to the cabin and found something edible there, but seeing as they still had a long way to go, it wasn't enough for the both of them, so if they shared it, they would both die. That's why your grandpa ... allegedly, anyway. But like I said, the police couldn't prove anything."

I scuffed. "That's just ludicrous. They didn't find anything to eat, and Grandpa would never in a million years kill the love of his life just to save his own life."

"I don't think so either. But I can't imagine what it's like knowing you're going to starve to death."

"Sounds like you still think he might have done it?"

"No, I'm just saying, hunger makes people desperate. The rumors were fueled even more by how different Fred seemed after he came home. The first year or so he practically didn't leave the house. He looked like a caveman when he finally showed his face in town. And some people said they saw not only grief but also remorse in his eyes. But it wasn't until I spoke with my buddy—that guy with PTSD—that it finally hit me."

"What hit you?"

"That thing about remorse. My friend felt very guilty about himself surviving when his buddies died. I think it has a name ..."

(Martin couldn't think of the name, but I just Googled it. It's called "survivor guilt." From Wikipedia: *a mental condition that occurs when a person believes they have done something wrong by surviving a traumatic event when others did not, often feeling self-guilt.*)

Martin stopped the car at this point, and Hugh got up from the donut and came into the car, his face red, his eyes streaming with tears and his teeth chattering, but still he was grinning. "That was fun," he stammered, wrapping himself in one of the blankets Martin had brought along.

"All right, who's next?" Martin asked, looking at me.

"I'll pass."

"Sure?"

"Positive."

"Well, I guess I'm up, then."

"Wait, I can't drive the car," I told him, as he unbuckled and pulled off his shoes.

"That's all right, you don't need to. I'm going for a swim instead."

Hugh let out a gasp. "Are you ... are you going swimming ... in the *water*?"

"Hard to swim in anything else," he grinned. "I'll probably regret it, so keep that blanket ready for me, all right?"

"Are you sure it's not dangerous?" I asked. "I mean, couldn't you go into shock and drown?"

He looked at me very gravely. "If I don't come back, tell my mom I died fighting."

Before either of us could say anything else, he had jumped out of the car, pulled off his shirt and pants and was running across the snow towards the water. He threw himself into the waves, was gone for a split-second, then emerged again with a roar and came sprinting back to the car. As he threw himself into the car and slammed the door behind him, I could still feel the coldness emanating from his skin. Hugh gave him the blanket, and Martin dried off his face and hair.

"Christ, you're insane," I told him, but couldn't help smiling.

"That was awesome!" Hugh said, jumping in his seat with excitement.

On the way home we talked about all kinds of stuff, and I almost forgot about what Martin had told me about the rumors. But as soon as we saw the farm up ahead, the thoughts returned. I could tell Martin was also brooding as he parked in the yard. He was gazing out of the window and almost didn't hear me when I said goodbye.

I've spent most of the day wondering about it, asking myself whether the nasty rumors could have any truth to them. But I don't think so. I think people just love to talk. Of course, Martin might have had a point when he said that thing about hunger making people desperate, but I'm still convinced Grandpa would have died before hurting Grandma.

Oh, by the way, I got Martin's number. He told me to call if I felt like talking.

I just wanted to comment on one last thing. Several of you guys mentioned the fact that Hugo heard the wind whisper last night, the same way Grandpa said it had whispered to him and Grandma when they were fighting for their lives deep in the Canadian woods. I know it's kind of creepy, but of course it's just a freaky coincidence.

Well, that grew into a long entry. Hope I didn't bore you guys too much. Thank you for reading. Sleep tight everyone.

13
Email from Edwin Harold White to Martin Edwin White, sent Thursday, February 16, 2017, 11:02 PM.

Martin,

Tried calling you, but you're right, no connection in your area. Wi-Fi here in the hotel is also pretty spotty, so couldn't Skype you. Hope this mail comes through.

Negotiations going fine, the Japanese are easy to talk to. Not sure if I can get the 40%, but they're definitely interested.

Not good, the thing with Fred. Was worried it would happen again. What exactly did that Otha girl see him doing? Keep me updated if anything new.

Love you,
Dad
Kind regards,
Edwin Harold White
CEO, Northern Whitewares™

14
　Transcription of telephone conversation between Jud Durrant Jr. and Ellsworth Police,
　Thursday, February 16, 2017, 7:11 PM.

OPERATOR:
Ellsworth Police, Deputy Abigail Davis speaking.

CALLER:
Yes, uhm, hello. My name is Jud Durrant.

OPERATOR:
Evening, Mr. Durrant. How can I help you?

CALLER:
Yes, eh, I'm calling 'cause my wife hasn't come home. And, uhm, I can't reach her on her cell. Nobody around here knows where she is, and, eh, I've been driving round looking for her all afternoon, but I can't find her anywhere …

OPERATOR:
All right, hang on now for one moment, Mr. Durrant. Let's take it from the top, please. What's your wife's name, sir?

CALLER:
Esme. Esme Durrant.

OPERATOR:
Esme … how do you spell that?

CALLER:
E-S-M-E … yeah, she's from South America. Been living here for almost twenty years, though.

OPERATOR:
I see. And when was the last time you saw your wife?

CALLER:
Yeah, well, uhm, that would be yesterday morning, I guess. Right before I left for work.

OPERATOR:

That makes it almost two whole days ... Right, Mr. Durrant, can you think of anything your wife might have had to attend to yesterday after you left for work? Any errands, appointments or visits?

CALLER:
Well, she was going to clean at the neighbor's, that's all.

OPERATOR:
Did you talk to your neighbor since the last time you saw your wife?

CALLER:
Yeah, uhm, he said she'd been there all right. But from there I can't for the life of me figure out where she might have gone. I mean, she always tells me if she goes to visit someone, but, you know, with all this goddamn snow I'm afraid she might have driven off the road somewhere ...

OPERATOR:
Right, I understand your concern, Mr. Durrant. Normally two days isn't enough for us to put out a missing person report, at least when it's an adult, but—

CALLER:
But you need to go look for her. I mean, if she's trapped in her car somewhere, you have to find her and help her before it's too late!

OPERATOR:
You didn't let me finish, Mr. Durrant. I would like to contact Highway Safety Patrol. If you give me your address, they will probably be able to tell me if they've had any reported accidents in your area. If not, we can rule out that scenario. Would that be okay with you, sir?

CALLER:
Sure.

OPERATOR:
Right, and if your wife doesn't come home or if you haven't heard from her come Saturday morning, you call me back, and we'll put out an APB. All right?

CALLER:
Yeah ... thank you.

OPERATOR:
You're welcome, Mr. Durrant. Now, if you could just give me your address ...

15
Excerpt of transcription from hearing of Frederick James Cochran by Canadian State Police,
Sunday, February 22, 1998.

POLICE:
How did your wife die, Mr. Cochran?

COCHRAN:
I told you a hundred times.

POLICE:
We need to go over it again.

COCHRAN:
She died from hunger or cold, I'm not sure which one got her first.

POLICE:
Were you present at the time of her death?

COCHRAN:
No, I was outside the cabin.

POLICE:
You were chasing this predator you mentioned?

COCHRAN:
I wasn't chasing it. I tried to scare it off.

POLICE:
Can you elaborate on what kind of animal you believed you saw? A bear, a cougar, a wolf?

COCHRAN:
It was none of those.

POLICE:
Did you see it?

COCHRAN:
Never up close.

POLICE:

And yet you are certain it was a predatory animal?

COCHRAN:
Yes.

POLICE:
Earlier you stated the animal had antlers. Only moose and a variety of different deer have antlers, and those aren't predators. Can you explain that, please?

COCHRAN:
No, I can't. All I know is, it had antlers on its head.

POLICE:
What makes matters even more confusing is the fact that you claim this animal was walking upright. The only predatory animal in this area able to walk for an extended period of time would be a bear.

COCHRAN:
It was way too skinny to be a bear. And it didn't have any fur.

POLICE:
Could it have been a human? Perhaps one of the other survivors?

COCHRAN:
It wasn't human.

POLICE:
You stated earlier you heard Jürgen Strauss calling for you.

COCHRAN:
That was only my imagination.

POLICE:
But you heard *something*?

COCHRAN:
Yes. But it wasn't the German.

POLICE:
Then what was it?

COCHRAN:
Don't know. The wind, I reckon.

POLICE:
In an earlier statement you said you suspected this predator might have impersonated the voice of Jürgen Strauss in an attempt to lure you out of the cabin.

COCHRAN:

I thought so at the time.

POLICE:
I'm only trying to figure out whether this predator was real or a figment of your imagination, Mr. Cochran.

COCHRAN:
I guess that's your problem. I only know what I heard and saw.

POLICE:
I hope you understand that without your cooperation—

COCHRAN:
I am cooperating. I'm answering your questions, aren't I?

POLICE:
Let's move on. The word 'wendigo'—does that mean anything to you, sir?

COCHRAN:
That was the word the wind whispered to me. I told you already.

POLICE:
When you say "the wind," do you refer to the predator again? It's difficult to get a clear picture on this point; it almost seems like you regard the wind and the predator to be one and the same—would that be correct?

COCHRAN:
I don't know. The wind ... the wind was the voice of the predator. I can't explain it any better than that.

POLICE:
And the predator would repeatedly whisper this word, wendigo?

COCHRAN:
Yes.

POLICE:
What does that word mean to you?

COCHRAN:
Not a damn thing.

POLICE:
Do you know the story of Swift Runner?

COCHRAN:
Of who now?

POLICE:

Swift Runner was a Crew Indian who lived in this country more than a century ago. He was sentenced for the murder of his entire family.

COCHRAN:
I never heard of him. What does that have to do with anything?

POLICE:
We just needed to know whether you knew of the story.

COCHRAN:
I didn't.

POLICE:
Very well. Returning to the time of death of your wife, sir: how much time would you say you spent outside the cabin?

COCHRAN:
A few minutes.

POLICE:
And when you reentered the cabin, your wife had died?

COCHRAN:
Yes.

POLICE:
Did you feel for a pulse?

COCHRAN:
Let me ask you this: Have you ever seen a dead person?

POLICE:
Actually, I have.

COCHRAN:
Then you know there's no doubt.

POLICE:
If one is in shock—

COCHRAN:
She was dead!

POLICE:
There is no need to yell. After you felt sure she was dead, you decided to eat off of her?

COCHRAN:

I didn't decide to do it. I was forced to. And I waited for more than two days. By that time I couldn't stand the hunger anymore.

POLICE:
You stated earlier how the predator was lurking around the cabin at this time, whispering to you, trying to convince you to eat your wife's body. Is that correct?

COCHRAN:
Yes.

POLICE:
So the predator could speak?

COCHRAN:
Yes.

POLICE:
Are you aware of the absurdity of this statement, Mr. Cochran?

COCHRAN:
I don't care how absurd it sounds. I just want to go home. I haven't broken any laws.

POLICE:
The psychiatric evaluation suggests you might have suffered from delusions brought on by shock and hunger. Do you acknowledge this assessment?

COCHRAN:
That's probably about right.

POLICE:
You don't seem convinced.

COCHRAN:
How should I know whether I was temporarily crazy or not? I'm not a shrink.

POLICE:
Our reports are consistent with your explanation that your wife was dead when you ate off of her, as the remains of her found in your stool show that the meat was frozen at the time of ingestion.

COCHRAN:
Of course it was. She turned to ice as soon as her heart stopped beating.

POLICE:
How much would you say you ate of her?

COCHRAN:

Christ Almighty ... what do you want me to say? You want me to give an estimate in ounces? I didn't happen to carry around a goddamn scale! Do you really think I cared to notice how much I ate? What kind of a question is that?

POLICE:
I understand the question is very sensitive, but I need you to answer. Please take a moment to think.

COCHRAN:
I ate part of her thigh.

POLICE:
And did you eat from anywhere else on her body?

COCHRAN:
No.

POLICE:
Are you sure?

COCHRAN:
Yeah, I'm sure, damnit!

POLICE:
How did you remove the flesh from the body?

COCHRAN:
Jesus Christ ...

POLICE:
I'm sorry, but we need the details. Did you use your teeth?

COCHRAN:
Yes.

POLICE:
You didn't have a knife or any other sharp utensils?

COCHRAN:
No.

POLICE:
What did you do with the rest of the body once you had eaten off of it?

COCHRAN:
I left it in the cabin.

POLICE:
Did the door have a lock?

COCHRAN:
What? How should I know? You tell me, you guys searched the place.

POLICE:
We need to know how much you remember.

COCHRAN:
Well, I think it had a lock. Yeah, I guess it must have, because I locked it so the predator couldn't come in.

POLICE:
And did you lock the cabin when you left it?

COCHRAN:
How could I? The lock was on the inside.

POLICE:
So you left the cabin door unlocked?

COCHRAN:
I guess so, yeah.

POLICE:
Could a predator have gotten the door open once you had left? I'm not referring to the unspecified predator you claim to have meet, but a regular predator, like a cougar, for instance.

COCHRAN:
I guess it could.

POLICE:
Could that be an explanation for the missing body?

COCHRAN:
I don't know. Isn't that your job? Finding out what happened to my wife?

POLICE:
There were no traces found anywhere near the cabin except for yours, Mr. Cochran. No blood stains outside or in, either.

COCHRAN:
Of course you wouldn't find any blood. She wasn't bleeding, she was frozen stiff.

POLICE:
Then how do you explain the absence of any traces of any predator?

COCHRAN:

Well, the predator I'm talking about didn't leave any traces. Somehow it was able to walk atop the snow without making any imprint.

POLICE:
I see. Do you understand why the missing body concerns us, Mr. Cochran?

COCHRAN:
Sure I do. It concerns me too. And honestly, I think it's lousy police work that you haven't found her, and that you would even dare to suspect me to have hidden it. Why in the name of God would I do that?

POLICE:
Perhaps you were ashamed of having eaten off of your wife's body?

COCHRAN:
I am ashamed. But I didn't try to hide her.

POLICE:
So what do you believe happened to the body?

COCHRAN:
I prefer not to answer that.

POLICE:
How come?

COCHRAN:
Because none of you will believe me. You already think I'm nuts.

POLICE:
Nothing in the psychiatric evaluation suggests any mental problems, Mr. Cochran. Please understand that we're on your side in this. We wish to find your wife's body, so we can put an end to the case and let you return home.

COCHRAN:
You'd better go looking, then.

POLICE:
We searched more than a thousand square miles of the forest, both at the crash site and by the cabin. Our investigation clearly shows that your wife walked to the cabin on her own accord. But from there, we have nothing to go on, no traces at all. You, Mr. Cochran, are the last person to see your wife both alive and deceased. That's why we're so keen on hearing what you think happened to the body.

COCHRAN:
(...)

POLICE:
Would you repeat that?

COCHRAN:
I said: the predator took her.

POLICE:
Are you referring to this unspeci—

COCHRAN:
Yes, that's the one I'm referring to. It obviously came back and took her after I had left. It's a scavenger, and it only eats frozen flesh. That's why it waits so patiently for its prey to freeze to death.

POLICE:
How would you know that?

COCHRAN:
I just know.

POLICE:
But surely you must have some kind of explanation as to this insight into—

COCHRAN:
I know because ... because I also ...

POLICE:
Because you also what, Mr. Cochran?

COCHRAN:
I have nothing more to say.

POLICE:
The interview isn't over, Mr. Cochran. We may take a break if you like, but I have more questions for you.

COCHRAN:
I'm not answering anymore of your questions. And that's final.

POLICE:
You do understand that without your cooperation, your chances of being acquitted of any suspicion diminishes.

COCHRAN:
I don't care anymore. Do whatever the hell you want with me.

16
Excerpt of website visited from computer belonging to Martin Edwin White, Friday, February 17, 2017, 01:43 AM.

THE TERRIBLE TALE OF SWIFT RUNNER

In the spring of 1879 a man named Swift Runner arrived at the Catholic mission in Alberta, Canada, stating that he was the only one in his family to survive the harsh winter. Yet the priests grew suspicious at the sight of the man, who seemed well-fed and healthy, and local police were notified.

When they visited Swift Runner's home in the woods, the remains of a woman and six children were uncovered. All had been methodically killed, dismembered and eaten. The man confessed to the terrible crime of butchering and consuming his family, although he claimed an evil spirit had possessed him and made him do it. He kept to this explanation until his execution that following winter.

The hanging was carried out one freezing cold morning in December. Some minor problems with the noose caused a short delay, which allegedly caused Swift Runner to say: "I could kill myself with a tomahawk. Save the hangman further trouble."

Moments later, as he was standing with the rope tight around his neck, he was asked if he had any last words, and he stated calmly: "I am human no longer."

Swift Runner was hanged till death, cut down an hour later and buried in the snow.

The tale of Swift Runner is not a singularity. During the nineteenth century, Northern Alberta saw a wave of cannibalistic murders. Some say cold and hunger drove people to desperate acts to survive, but amongst the natives the phenomenon has been known for a long time, and was named after the wendigo—a demonic spirit believed to reside deep in the endless forests, capable of possessing human beings with an irresistible craving for human flesh [...]

17
Email from Martin Edwin White to Edwin Harold White,
sent Friday, February 17, 2017, 01:58 AM.

I think something's really wrong, Dad. I'm not sure exactly what you think Fred might be up to, but he's not being himself, that's for sure. I can tell from looking in his eyes ... It's hard to explain, but I think you know what I mean.

I went over there yesterday, and I noticed car tracks in the snow leading to the machine house, but no tracks going the other way ... I don't know, I just thought it was odd, you know ... I could tell they weren't from Fred's truck, so what was another car doing in there?

I didn't want to ask him, what with his grandchildren being around, so I just went home. But I couldn't shake it, I just kept thinking about it all day. It was like my gut was trying to tell me something, and you always tell me to listen to my gut, so I decided to go back over there when I was sure Fred had gone to bed.

I turned off the lights a mile up the road and parked at the end of Fred's driveway, so the sound of the car wouldn't wake him. I ran up to the house. I damn near never got there ... it's snowing around the clock, and I couldn't see anything ... but I made it and went straight to the machine house.

You'll never guess what I found.

Esme's car. That little blue Nissan.

Isn't that weird? I know what you're thinking, Dad, that he might have offered to fix something for her, but get this: it was hidden under a tarp. Why the hell would he do that? Like he didn't want anybody to see it ...

But that wasn't even the weirdest thing I saw, 'cause once I got outside again, I heard something. At first, I just took it for the wind, but the more I listened, the more it sounded like someone was saying something, like the same word over and over again ... And then I looked up and saw someone standing on the roof of the goddamn house! I know it sounds crazy, but I'm almost certain it was a person ... a tall, skinny guy ... I don't know if it was Fred, the snow was getting in my eyes, so I couldn't see clearly. It was only a brief moment, then the person was gone. Guess I should have gone around the house to see if I could find the guy, but honestly, I was about shitting myself at this point, so I just ran up to the car and drove home.

I can still recall the word I heard in the wind. It was "wendigo." I have no idea what it means, if it's a name or whatever ... but I just Googled it, and I found a pretty sick story about an Indian guy who killed his entire family and ate them ...

I don't know, Dad. I'm pretty worried. What do think I should do?

Martin

18
Excerpt from diary of Frederick James Cochran,
Saturday, January 4, 2003.

The nightmares are driving me insane.

Every night I'm back in Canada, wandering around in that damn forest. Sometimes Jane is there with me, other times she is already dead. But I can always feel it. The predator.

I think it's the cold. It's bad this year. That's why the dreams are back. I don't feel like myself. It's worse at night when the temperature drops. I've had periods where I can't remember anything. I'm sleepwalking. More than once I've woken up somewhere in the house, missing the last few hours.

Last night I almost got myself in a real gaum. I suddenly came to and found myself in the middle of the courtyard, only wearing pajamas. I must have been standing there for quite some time, because I was ankle deep in newly fallen snow, and my skin was all blue.

Perhaps I ought to talk to someone. But who the hell would believe me? Anyone would laugh if I told them what I saw up in that forest. Or they might think I'm crazy and get me locked up.

I've decided to write it down instead. Maybe this way I can get it out of my head. I'll tell everything exactly as I remember it. Allow myself to live through it all. For five years I've been trying to forget. Maybe I need to face it instead. Maybe that will help me sleep.

I'll begin from where I first noticed the predator. That was about the time we started hearing the wind whisper. Actually, Jane heard it first. She would stop every few minutes to listen. When I asked her what she had heard, she just shook her head. A little later I heard it too. The same word, repeated endlessly. Very faintly at first, but growing ever stronger. It was trying to brainwash us, to make us give up hope, break our spirits. Somehow, the wind and the predator were one and the same.

I knew I was probably losing my marbles, but the feeling of the predator was very real, and I also knew we had to keep going, because if we stopped, something far worse than cold death would come for us.

I think it happened on the third day. I don't blame her. No one can. We hadn't eaten or slept for days, and nothing drains you like fighting off a constant, gnawing cold.

She simply collapsed in the snow. Said she couldn't go on. It was morning, and the sun was rising.

I begged her to go on. Just a little farther. She tried, but couldn't. She told me to leave her. To go on without her. I wouldn't. I couldn't. If she was going to die, I would die with her. I was about to sit down next to her, and I knew that as soon as I did, I would never get up again, so, I looked around one last time. That was when I saw the cabin.

I carried her over there. It was abandoned. No furniture, tools or anything. But at least shelter. Perhaps there had once been a road leading from the cabin to the nearest town, but it had long since disappeared, so we were none the wiser as to which way to go from here. For now, we were just thankful to get out of the wind.

I tried to light a fire in the fireplace by rubbing two branches together, but they were too frozen, and I was too weak. Instead, we lay down close together. I fell asleep immediately and dreamed about the predator lurking around the cabin, whispering and trying to get in.

When I woke up, it was nighttime and pitch darkness. The wind was howling down through the chimney and shook the woodwork. It was an effort just to sit up. My legs were numb, my head was spinning, my stomach aching.

Jane was alive at this point. I know, because I checked her breath. But she was sleeping deeply. That's why she didn't hear the German's voice.

He called for me. From somewhere outside. Sounded desperate. Like he knew I was nearby. His voice carried with the wind. Still recall the words.

— Hilfe! ... Ich sterbe! ... Hilfe!

I thought it was my imagination. But the more I listened, the more real it sounded. He could have followed us. If we had made it this far, maybe he had too.

I got to my feet and staggered to the door. As soon as I turned the knob, the door was ripped open by the wind. Snow whipped into my face. The trees were swaying, threatening to break.

I called his name. Got no answer. He had stopped shouting. I went outside, still calling for him. I moved still farther away from the cabin, making sure not to lose it from sight. But Jürgen was nowhere to be seen. I turned to walk back inside.

And then I saw him. Standing in front of the open cabin door. He was taller and thinner than I remembered. Something was perched on the top of his head, it looked like branches. But the most disturbing part was that he was naked.

I called out his name.

He turned slowly to look at me. Finally I realized it wasn't him. It looked like him, but it wasn't. It was the predator. It had tricked me. The branches were its antlers, protruding from the skull. The eyes were tiny and black.

I was paralyzed for a moment. But the fear of losing Jane was greater than the fear for my own life, and I found myself charging at the creature. But I didn't reach it in time. It stepped inside, bending down far to get through the doorway, and closed the door.

I burst into the cabin a second later, but a second too late.

Jane was still lying where I had left her. The predator was gone. I shut the door and kept watch for a while, ready to fight if the predator should return. But it didn't. And when I finally lay back down beside Jane, I realized she was dead.

It looked like she had gone quietly in her sleep. But I knew the truth. The predator had killed her. It was my fault. I had let it trick me.

My heart broke, and rage overtook me. I ran out into the snow, screaming at the dark forest, telling the beast to come and get me.

I fell down, and the shock of the cold snow was what brought me back to my senses. Some survival instinct took over and brought me back inside the cabin. I sank to the floor and wept.

I understood the predator wasn't going to take me. Not now, at least. It had just eaten. It wasn't hungry anymore. It could wait for days, maybe weeks. It wasn't exactly in a hurry. I was too weak to leave the cabin. I was trapped and could only wait to starve to death.

A few days passed by. Thinking back, I can't tell you what kept me from taking my own life. I could have gotten it over with quickly and painlessly. All I had to do was lay down in the snow and close my eyes.

But I stayed inside the cabin, kept warm, drank melted snow and waited. I wondered how long a man can live with no food. I tried to figure out how long we had traveled. How long I would have to go on to reach a town. But it didn't matter. I couldn't go anywhere. I was too weak. I had nothing to eat.

Nothing.

Nothing—except ...

It was the wind that planted the idea. It whispered to me all through the night. Told me I still had a chance. Told me she was already dead, that she wouldn't mind, that she would have wanted me to do it.

At first the thought revolted me. But as time passed, I became more and more desperate.

So I did it.

May God forgive me.

Afterwards, I fell into a deep sleep.

When I awoke, I felt well rested. Stronger. I kissed her goodbye and thanked her. Then I left the cabin. The storm had passed, and it was a quiet afternoon. I began walking.

I walked all day. I walked as darkness fell. I walked on through the night. The voice in the wind came back as I had known it would. That cursed word, over and over. The predator was hungry again. I was going to be its next prey. It just waited for a sign of weakness, a moment to strike.

I sensed how it followed me. I felt its stare, smelled the rotten stank from its skin. I heard its wheezing breath and its creeping steps in the snow behind me. But when I looked back, I saw only my own tracks. I glimpsed it several times out of the corner of my eye, but it disappeared between the trees whenever I looked closer.

I tried not to look, though. Tried not to listen. Not to stop walking.

The whisper of the wind increased to a shrill falsetto. It hissed, whined, roared and shrieked. It breathed down my neck, tucked at my sleeves, whispered in my ear, told me I was going to die, that I might as well give up.

But I didn't believe it. Something gave me hope. I could tell it was desperate. It knew I was going to make it.

And suddenly, I saw it. It was just before dawn. The light appeared between the trees ahead, a faint glow. And then I was out of the forest. I stopped and stared down at the town before me. My legs gave way, and I sank to my knees.

I heard something behind me and turned my head.

It was standing just inside the tree line. In the dim light from the city I saw it—really saw it—for the first time. I might have been halfway insane from exhaustion at this point. And yet I'm sure of what I saw.

It looked like Jürgen. But it also looked like a hundred other people. At the same time, there was nothing human about it. It was too tall, too skinny, its arms and fingers too long. And of course there were the antlers, rugged and pointy.

It sneered at me one last time, then it disappeared back into the forest.

Later I would start wondering whether that final sneer looked more like a smile. And as time has passed, I'm beginning to understand why.

It isn't Jane haunting me in my dreams. Nor what I did to survive.

It's the face of the predator, smiling at me. Something in that smile scares me more than anything. Something ... familiar. The more I think about it, the more that smile reminds of what I see when I look in the mirror.

Even though he was never found, I know what happened to Jürgen. I know what he did to survive. I know it was the wind that persuaded him in the end. I also know why he left the crash site: he tried to get out of the forest before the predator could get him. But it was too late. It had won. He had sealed his fate.

And so had I.

The predator can go into hibernation. It will sleep for months on end. It doesn't need to feed all summer. In fact, it can sleep for several years if it has to. It will only wake up when the winter is cold enough, when the temperature gets extremely low. Then it smells prey. It doesn't feed on human flesh alone, but also on fear and desperation and guilt.

I feel it when the winter comes. Feel how it stirs. Luckily, the temperature doesn't get low enough around here. I pray it never will.

And I pray the nightmares might end now that I finally admitted it to myself. The terrible truth I have never been able to face.

I didn't escape the predator who killed Jane and Jürgen.

I brought it home with me.

19
Email from Edwin Harold White to Martin Edwin White, sent Friday, February 17, 2017, 11:11 PM.

Martin,

Go straight to the police. Tell them Fred is psychotic and very dangerous. Tell them you saw Esme's car at his place. But <u>keep away</u> from him. You got it? It's <u>very important</u> that you don't go over there, no matter what. I'll try to get in contact with the local police myself.

Dad

Kind regards,
Edwin Harold White
CEO, Northern Whitewares™

20
Entry from the blog *My Otha Life* by Otha Cochran, Saturday, February 18, 2017, 02:03 AM.

I'm writing this in the middle of the night. I'm scared out of my mind right now.

I tried calling my dad and all of my friends, but I have no signal. I even tried calling Martin. I don't want to wake up Hugh, so I'm writing to you guys instead. I might not even post this, but I just need to feel like I have someone to talk to.

I woke up about an hour ago. I needed to pee really bad, but as soon as I got out of bed, I felt something really unpleasant. It's hard to put into words. It was like the whole house was possessed or something. The wind was roaring outside and the air in my room was way too cold. Like, I could see my breath. I had to put on my clothes before I could leave the room.

As I passed by Grandpa's room, I could smell that awful smell again—the one from the other day, I think I mentioned it in a previous entry. I had to find out what caused it, so I opened the door. Grandpa's bedroom was even colder. Honestly, I've never felt cold like that. I could literally feel it hurting my lungs and stinging my face. The window was open, the curtains blowing like crazy, and snow was drifting in and covering the floor. The bed was empty.

I called out for Grandpa in a low voice, still not wanting to wake up Hugh, but I got no answer, so I hurried to close the window, trying not to breathe in that horrid smell, and through the snowstorm I thought I glimpsed the lights from a car up by the road. But it was probably just my imagination—who the hell would be out driving in the middle of the night in a blizzard?

I left Grandpa's room and slipped downstairs. I had expected to find him in the kitchen, thinking he had probably gone down to get a glass of water, but I found it dark and empty. He wasn't in the bathroom, either.

Instead I found someone else: Skip was sitting in the corner, shivering all over. It was obvious the poor dog was frightened out of his mind. I tried soothing him, but he hardly noticed me. When I had peed, I lifted him up and brought him to my bedroom. As soon as I sat him down, he slipped under the bed.

I decided to check the rest of the upstairs. So I started with Hugh's room. He was snoring deeply. The other rooms were empty. The only logical explanation was of course that Grandpa had gone down to pee, and that we somehow missed each other as he had gone back upstairs. That's why I figured he had to be in his bedroom.

Oh, God, just thinking about it ... Why did I open the door?

I just had to know, I guess.

I don't even know if it was Grandpa. I'm not sure exactly what I saw.

A thin, boney figure was crouching on the roof outside the window, staring directly at me through the glass with small, black eyes. I screamed, shut the door, ran to my bedroom and locked the door. For maybe five minutes I just paced around the room, unable to sit down or relax, debating what to do, trying not to panic. Skip was whimpering under the bed; the wind was howling louder than ever.

I started trying to call someone, anyone, but couldn't get a signal, and then suddenly I realized the wind was completely quiet. The mood had shifted once more. Everything seemed somehow calmer. Skip had even come out from under the bed, and was now lying curled up on the floor, sleeping.

I honestly don't know if I'm going mad. If I just sleepwalked and dreamed the whole thing. I would actually sleepwalk quite a lot as a kid.

I decided to write the whole thing down, in case I forget about it in the morning. I think I'll upload this post. Sorry if it's a complete mess, I haven't proofread it. Let me hear what you guys think.

I'm really tired. I think I can sleep now.

21
Excerpt from article in *Portland Press Herald*,
Monday, May 15, 2017.

- The guilt is the worst part.

That's how Edwin H. White begins the story of how he lost his son. As I meet the CEO in his beautiful home this sunny afternoon, I can instantly feel the burden of grief weighing heavily on the large man's shoulders.

Of course, no one can blame him. It's been less than three months since his son, Martin E. White, known lovingly as "Mowgli," died. The case has been all over the news, but this is the first time Mr. White has agreed to an interview.

- I knew the winter would be a bad one, he goes on. - So I knew there was a chance that Old Fred would start acting weird again. But I had no idea any of this could have happened.

Old Fred is of course Frederick J. Cochran, the lead suspect in the Freyston case.

In my research, I've noticed how several others of the survivors and their relatives have mentioned this thing about the winter being very cold, so I ask Mr. White what he thinks that means.

- It was the cold that did it, he retorts with no hesitation. - Don't ask me how I know it, and don't ask me to explain it, because I can't. All I know is, he would always become strange whenever the winters were particularly cold. That's why I should have stayed home. It was my responsibility, as I was one of the only people who knew how serious it was.

Mr. White draws a deep sigh before continuing.

- But work demanded I go. And I thought, even if Old Fred would become a little weird, he had so far not shown any tendency towards violent behavior ...

I ask him what he means when he says that Frederick Cochran—or "Old Fred"—would become strange. He tells me briefly about a few episodes in the past, where Old Fred had been found somewhere on his property in the snow, wearing no clothes at all, and appearing to be in a trancelike state. One time, Mr. White even found him on the roof, staring out into empty space, even though it was snowing heavily and the temperature was well below zero.

- Martin was the one who found him the very first time. He came to me and told about it later, because he knew he could confide in me. We always had a close bond ...

The large man squeezes his lips together at this point. I let the silence pass through the room as I wait for him to start talking again.

- If I had come home a little earlier, or if I hadn't gone away in the first place ... would my son be alive today? I've asked myself that question a million times. The truth is, I don't know. I don't know if I could have stopped it. But at least I could have tried. That's what's killing me. Instead, I was halfway around the world, unable to do anything ...

I round off the interview by asking Mr. White how he feels about Frederick Cochran still being at large.

Before answering, he looks towards the window facing the garden, where everything is in bloom and the birds are singing. It's easy to forget how everything was covered in several feet of snow just a few months ago.

– I'm not afraid, Mr. White says finally, shaking his head firmly. – He can't do anything worse to me than he has already done. Martin was my son, my heir.

The words die out. Mr. White keeps looking out into the garden. I have to ask him what he thinks will become of Frederick Cochran, if he still hopes the guilty will be put to justice.

Mr. White breathes deeply before meeting my eyes. He says simply: – Wherever he is, I hope he stays there. As far as I'm concerned, he can rot in hell.

22
Text message conversation between Otha Cochran and Martin Edwin White, Saturday, February 18, 2017, 10:12 – 10:21 AM.

Hi Martin. Tried calling you, but no signal. Please write me back if you get this ...

Hey, just got your message :-)

Thank God. Would you please come get us?

Well, sure ... Are you guys ok?

I don't feel safe being here. Grandpa is acting really weird this morning.

Be right over.

Thank you! <3

Did he do anything to you or Hugh?

No, but ... he's not himself.

Should I call the police?

They've already been here.

They have!?

Yeah, two officers came by to ask about Esme. Her husband has reported her missing.

Shit

I know :-(Grandpa told them he didn't know anything about it. He was acting all normal when they were here, but once they left, he just went back to staring out the window. I'm really scared to be here right now, Martin :'(

On my way.

I'm really thankful.

Sure. You guys can stay with me.

Thank you, but I think we'll just get on the next train home.

The trains aren't going. Because of the snow.

Oh, fuck :-(

Don't worry. You can stay at my place for now.

That's sweet of you :-) I already packed our stuff. When will you be here?

5 min.

Great, I'll just find Hugh.

Does Fred know you're leaving?

No, I'm afraid to talk to him :'(

Where is he?

Downstairs.

Maybe it's better if he doesn't see you leaving ...

I think so too. Jesus, this is just awful :'(What do I do?

Try to get him out of the house. Tell him one of the hens is dead.

All right, I'll tell him.

I'll wait for you at the end of the driveway. As soon as he leaves the house, you take Hugh and run to me.

I don't know if we can run with the suitcases.

Then leave them. As long as you guys get out of there.

Okay ...

I'm here now.

I just told him. He's leaving. We're coming.

23
Transcription of voice mail message from Otha Cochran to Michael James Cochran,
Saturday, February 18, 2017, 9:02 PM.

[…] Dad? … Hello? … Oh, crap, I think it's gone to voice mail again … Hi, Dad, it's me again … I tried calling you like a hundred times, but the connection is still bad, so … I don't know if you're getting these messages, but if you do, please come pick us up … I know your foot is messed up, but we really need to get away from here and the trains aren't operating … (sigh) … I-I don't know how to explain it, but … it's Grandpa, Dad … something's seriously wrong with him. Something, like, mentally wrong. We're at Martin's place—he's one of the neighbors and a close friend of Grandpa's. We'll be spending the night here. He promised to drive us home first thing in the morning if I still haven't heard from you by then … (pause) … I'm really scared, Dad. I'm trying not to frighten Hugh … I don't think he really gets what's going on, but … it's something about the cold … it's making Grandpa weird, and … and tonight they say it'll be a new low record or whatever … like an all-time lowest temperature or something. I know it sounds crazy, I know, but … Jesus, it's blowing like mad outside … (muffled sounds) … We're two miles down the road from Grandpa, but I'm still scared that he might … I don't know … I just don't feel safe, you know … I mean, what if he comes? We left earlier without a word, and … and I don't know, Dad … Jesus … And Esme … that's Grandpa's cleaning lady … she's disappeared, and the police are looking for her … they came by this morning, they wanted to speak to Grandpa, because Martin told them he saw her car at Grandpa's place, and … but I don't know if they found it or if they're even suspecting Grandpa … I don't know … I wanted to tell them something was wrong, but … what was I going to say? He hasn't done anything … Maybe this is all just … I don't know … I just feel like Grandpa is hiding something, you know? … (inaudible voice in background) … that was Hugh … he's afraid the wind is going to tear off the roof … (pause) … Listen, Dad … Grandpa told us about Grandma. He-he told us how she died, and … and I think … I think it might have something to do with her, but … I have no idea what … I just keep thinking Grandpa might have hurt Esme … (sniffles) … Jesus, I'm a mess … (muffled sounds) … sorry, Dad … please call me back if you get this, all right? … Love you […]

24
   Transcription of telephone conversation between Martin Edwin White and Ellsworth Police,
   Sunday, February 19, 2017, 03:11 AM.

OPERATOR:
Ellsworth Police, Officer Stevens speaking. How may I help you?

CALLER:
Yes, hello, my name is Martin White, I'm calling from Four Old Deer Drive just outside Freyston. You need to get out here right away. Someone is lurking around outside the house, and I think he's trying to get in here ...

OPERATOR:
All right, just stay calm, sir. Is this person doing anything? Like, knocking on the door maybe?

CALLER:
No, he's just walking around out there. We saw him by the window just a minute ago.

OPERATOR:
How do you know he's trying to get inside?

CALLER:
I just know, okay? Just come and help us, please ...

OPERATOR:
Take it easy, sir. You need to explain to me what's going on. Do you know the person outside your house?

CALLER:
Yeah, it's my neighbor, Fred. Something is really wrong with him, he's fucked up somehow, like ... mentally. He wants to ... what's that, Hugh?

OPERATOR:
Are there others in the house with you?

CALLER:
Yeah, two others ... Hold on a minute ... What? ... Are you sure?

OPERATOR:
Hello? Sir?

CALLER:
We can hear something from above. I think he's climbed onto the fucking roof. He's looking for a way in ... Right, listen, you really need to send someone ... If he gets in here, he's going to hurt us. Do you understand?

OPERATOR:
I'm sure he can't get in through the roof. Are all the windows closed?

CALLER:
Well, what do you think? It's minus a hundred goddamn degrees outside, of course the windows are closed! But he can easily smash one of them, or maybe he'll—

OPERATOR:
Please try and remain calm, sir. Does your neighbor have a weapon?

CALLER:
I don't know ...

OPERATOR:
Then why do you think he wants to hurt you? Has there been some sort of dispute between you and him?

CALLER:
He's fucking crazy, I just told you! He's not thinking clearly. He's—

OPERATOR:
Hello?

CALLER:
Shut up a second ... Do you hear that, Otha? ... The wind just stopped ... It's totally quiet now ...

OPERATOR:
Can you still hear your neighbor on the roof?

CALLER:
(...)

OPERATOR:
Hello? Sir?

CALLER:
I think ... I think I hear something ... It sounds like it's coming from inside the wall ... Oh, fuck me, I think ... no, that can't be ...

OPERATOR:
What's going on, sir?

CALLER:
I-I can hear him inside the chimney ... (fast breathing) ... He's coming down the fucking chimney!

OPERATOR:
Now listen, it's not possible for a fully grown man to squeeze through a chimney. He would never be able to—

CALLER:
Lock the door to the living room, Otha! Hurry up! I can hear him in there!

OPERATOR:
Has the person entered your house, sir?

CALLER:
Yes, goddamnit! He's in the living room! Come out here, damn you! Four Old Deer Drive! Hugh, come over here! Get away from the door, Otha! ... (loud crash, followed by screaming) ... *Shit, he's trying to break down the door!*

OPERATOR:
Right, we'll send someone right away. Please remain on the—

CALLER:
About fucking time! Hurry!

OPERATOR:
Remain calm, sir, and try to—

CALLER:
(repeated crashes, breaking of wood) ... *Fuck, fuck, fuck! He's punched a hole in the door! I think he can come through!* ... (loud, female scream) ... Oh, fuck, oh my fucking God! Who the hell is that? Who *are* you? ... (more screaming) ... He's naked ... Is-is that you, Fred? (crying voices) ... Fuck, stay away! *No, stay away, goddamnit! Don't touch him, Otha!* ... (loud crack, as the phone apparently is dropped to the floor, audible commotion, furniture being tipped over, more screaming) ... *Let her go, goddamnit!* ... (continued screaming, commotion, breaking of glass) ...

OPERATOR:
Hello? ... What's going on? ... Sir? ... You still with me?

CALLER:
(silence)

OPERATOR:
Hello?

CALLER:
(sound of footsteps, scrambling noises, as the phone is apparently is picked up from the floor) ... He-hello?

OPERATOR:
Hello, who is this?

CALLER:
(hectic breathing) It's ... it's Hugh ...

OPERATOR:
Tell me what just happened, Hugh.

CALLER:
I think ... I-I think it was Grandpa ... (hard sobbing) ... b-but I almost couldn't re-recognize h-him ... He-he was all naked, and ... very skinny, and ... his skin w-was all grey ... and he h-had something on h-his h-head ... it looked like antlers ... I don't know, I don't know ... It happened very f-fast ... (hiccups, sobs) ... I'm af-fraid ... I don't know ... (panting) ...

OPERATOR:
All right, all right, listen to me, Hugh. Take a few deep breaths through your nose. Can you do that for me?

CALLER:
(deep, trembling breaths)

OPERATOR:
Good. Now, help is on its way, so don't be afraid. It sounds like it's very quiet on your end. Are you alone?

CALLER:
I ... I think so ...

OPERATOR:
Where did the others go?

CALLER:
Grandpa took Otha ... he jumped out the w-window ... and Martin ... I think, I think he went to follow them in his c-car ...

OPERATOR:
Do you know where your Grandpa might have taken Otha?

CALLER:
I don't know ... Home, maybe ...

OPERATOR:
Do you know the address of your Grandpa?

CALLER:
Uhm ... Old Deer Drive ... Seven, I think ...

OPERATOR:
Good. Just keep talking to me, Hugh. A couple of officers will be with you shortly
...

25
Entry from the blog *My Otha Life* by Otha Cochran,
Friday, August 4, 2017, 01:02 PM.

Well, I'm finally back. Sorry it took me so long.

I want to begin by thanking you guys for all your support. Since the time from my last entry, sweet, warming messages have been pouring in every single day. It's totally overwhelming to know so many people care for me. You have definitely helped me get my life back.

I'm still struggling most days, but my therapist is helping a lot, and I'm finally beginning to experience days that don't feel like a nightmare.

I know the case has been everywhere, and some of you may have already heard me tell the story on TV (by the way, I know I've always wanted to become famous, but this wasn't exactly the way I pictured it) but I still want to tell everything here on the blog as detailed as I can. I think I owe you guys. And I think I'm finally ready.

So, here goes.

We went to Martin's place just before noon that day. I was simply too scared to stay in the house with Grandpa at that point. Once there, we played cards and tried to make the time pass, Hugh, Martin and me. I tried calling home many times, but I couldn't reach my dad.

At bedtime, Hugh and I got the guestroom, and I lay awake for a long time, listening to the howling wind outside. Finally, I must have drifted off, because I awoke abruptly when Hugh whispered my name and told me the wind was speaking again.

He was right. The wind really was speaking to us. It was repeating that single word over and over again: wendigo. I had no idea what it meant at the time; it wasn't until much later I found out. But I'll get to that.

Even though I didn't know the word that night, I knew exactly what it meant. Grandpa had come.

I grabbed Hugh and ran to Martin's bedroom. We woke him up, and the three of us went to the kitchen. Martin called the police, and he actually got through, but of course they didn't really take him seriously. I was mad at them for a long time, but I honestly don't think it would have made any difference. They would never have gotten there in time anyway.

Martin had made sure to lock the doors and shut all the windows. But Grandpa came in through somewhere completely unexpected; he climbed down through the chimney. I have no idea how he did it, but he did. And before we had time to do anything, he had forced his way into the kitchen.

Everything happened really fast from this point on, and I only saw him briefly, as he came through the kitchen door, but I just had time to register how much he looked like that creature I had seen when we first arrived, and this time I could tell the things on his head hadn't been my imagination. He really did have a huge set of antlers. Yes, antlers. Like on a stag. Oh God, just thinking about it ...

The following minutes are kind of hazy in my memory. I've talked with Hugh about it, and he can't remember that much either. I think I tried to fight back as Grandpa grabbed me. But it was no use; he was inhumanly strong. He picked me up and threw himself out through the window.

I remember faintly I was screaming as I hung over his shoulder and he ran through the icy night. Even out in the open I could smell the stink coming off of him—that's one of the details I remember most clearly. He reeked of rotting flesh. I also remember his skin. It was cold and leathery.

I have no idea how long he ran with me—it must have been at least a few minutes. I was halfway unconscious from shock at this point—but suddenly we were back at Grandpa's place. He carried me down to the cellar, and I started struggling to get free. He didn't turn on the lights, so I couldn't see anything.

As he opened the freezer, a sharp, yellow light hurt my eyes just before he threw me down there. I landed on top of something hard and frozen. Looking up, I saw him glaring down at me in a split second before he rammed the lid shut. That was probably the clearest view I ever got of his face, and that's the picture that's been haunting my dreams.

The eyes were small and black—the same eyes I had seen staring at me through the window in Grandpa's bedroom, that night he had crawled out onto the roof. Nothing human was in those eyes, only hunger. The skin on his face was thin and clung to the skull, and the lips were broken and peeled back. The nose was nothing but two tiny holes.

Then he shut the lid, and everything went dark. I reached up and pushed hard against the lid, but I couldn't move it an inch. I started to feel the cold—I was already freezing from the night air, but now my skin began to hurt.

I tried turning over, tried to get to my knees in order to push my back against the lid, but there wasn't much room in the freezer.

Instead I remembered the phone in my pocket. I managed to get it out. My hands were shaking at this point, I couldn't feel my fingers, and the air hurt my lungs with every breath. When I got the screen activated, the light from it gave me a brief feeling of comfort. I was just about to call someone—I'm not sure who, actually, maybe the police, maybe Martin—when I saw her face. The brown eyes were staring at me.

It was Esme.

I couldn't see that both her arms and most of her lower body was missing—if I had, I would probably have passed out, and I might never have gotten out of that freezer. The forensic scientists found out that Grandpa had gradually been cutting pieces off of Esme's body for several days after her death. They checked both mine and Hugh's stool, but—thank God—didn't find any traces of human flesh. Grandpa didn't cook or serve anything of Esme to us.

What he did do with the flesh, the police can't tell, since they still haven't found Grandpa. But I'm pretty sure what happened: Grandpa would sneak down into the basement every night to eat from Esme. They say at least 50 pounds of her was missing, and that Grandpa couldn't possibly have eaten that much in a few days. But I still think he did so.

Well, back to the story.

I obviously panicked when I saw Esme's dead body and I dropped the phone. I just screamed and screamed and banged on the lid, twisting and turning and trying everything to get out.

Those minutes I spent in the freezer were definitely the worst. I was sure I was going to die. It really felt like hours, although now I know it wasn't more than two, maybe three minutes, because they told me afterwards that the oxygen would have run out within four or five minutes tops.

Then, suddenly, I heard Martin's voice. It was very distant, but he was calling my name. After Grandpa took me, Martin had run to his car and driven straight to Grandpa's place. I screamed for him, and I could hear him coming closer. He rummaged with the ropes Grandpa had used to tie down the lid of the freezer, and then he opened it.

He lifted me up, I was bawling like a baby, and my arms and legs were hardly functioning. The only light in the basement came from the open freezer, and I remember how pale Martin looked.

"We have to get out," he whispered. "Can you walk?"

I tried, but it was hard, and Martin had to support me as we staggered across the room to the stairs. But then, at the same time, we both noticed the smell, and we stopped abruptly.

Out from under the stairs stepped the creature who wasn't really my grandfather. In the dim light I could only make out its silhouette, tall, skinny, long swaying arms and with those awful antlers almost reaching the ceiling.

Martin shouted at it while pushing me behind him. But the creature was obviously not going to back off, and it didn't want to lose its prey either. It charged at Martin, and I was flung aside. Martin started wrestling with the creature, shouting: "*Get out of here, Otha! Run!*"

And I did.

I ran.

I've asked myself many times if I did the right thing. If I should have stayed instead, trying to help Martin. At the time I couldn't think of anything but my own survival. I wasn't brave like Martin. Honestly, I don't think I could have done anything to help. The creature was impossibly strong, and had I stayed to fight, I would have been killed too.

But still, the question haunts me. The survivor guilt.

I made it up the stairs as I could still hear Martin fighting against the creature, giving off moans and grunts. I ran through the scullery and out through the open door, bursting into a police officer. The headlights from the police car were blinding me, and another cop came running towards the house.

I explained sobbing about Martin who was still in the basement with my grandfather, and one of the officers pulled out his gun and ran inside, while the other took me to the car and helped me into the backseat, where Hugh was already sitting. He started crying when he saw me.

Through the window I saw the officer run into the house to join his partner. But a second later there came a loud scream from inside. Half a minute passed. Then one of the cops came back out, his face bloody and his arm obviously broken.

He stumbled to the car, tore open the door and grabbed the radio. As he called for backup, I didn't take my eyes off the front door. I was sure the creature would come bursting out at any moment. But it didn't.

"Jesus," the officer moaned, clutching his broken arm, as he put down the radio. "Jesus Christ."

I asked him what happened, and he turned halfway around to look at me. I'll never forget the terror in his face.

"They're dead," he simply said. "I think it escaped."

I remember his words very well. He said "it." He saw the creature. He knew it wasn't human.

I looked out and realized the wind had suddenly gone quiet. I understood the danger had passed. The creature had disappeared. I wanted badly to run back into the house. I wanted to find Martin. Perhaps he wasn't dead. Perhaps he was only wounded.

But I stayed in the car.

Ten minutes later, the lights from several police cars came rolling up the driveway. Six officers came pouring out, and four of them went into the house. An ambulance had arrived too. The medics helped me, Hugh and the wounded officer.

Martin came out on a stretcher a few moments later. Luckily, I didn't see any blood. But I knew instantly he really was dead.

Phew.

I did it. I told everything that happened that night.

The rest of my story is less dramatic. Back in Boston, I couldn't sleep for several days. I was convinced Grandpa would still come for me. I had terrible nightmares and would lie awake every night, listening to the wind.

Grandpa disappeared from his house without a trace—literally. The area was searched thoroughly the following days, and the conditions were really optimal, the police told me. I think it was because no new snow had fallen, or something like that. In any case, they would be able to find even the slightest marks in the snow. But they found none. It was like he had simply vanished into thin air.

As the days turned into weeks, I slowly began to relax. And when the temperature finally started rising, and the snow began to melt away during March, I knew it was over. I knew Grandpa had turned into himself again, wherever he was.

About my Grandpa ... I'm not sure he understood exactly what was happening. Or maybe he did. The police showed me a few notes from his diary, where he has written about the accident up in Canada. I think he somehow knew the creature was living inside of him, but he tried to live a normal life. But when the cold came around, he couldn't control it, and the creature took him over.

This past winter isn't the only time it has happened. As you probably already know from the media, the police found DNA traces from four other people in Grandpa's freezer—all people who have disappeared from the area the past 14 years.

So, what is it? This creature.

It's a wendigo. Try Googling it, if you want to see pictures, but I'll tell you right away: Even the most imaginative illustration doesn't even come close to the real thing.

It's a kind of demonic spirit, believed in by the old Native Americans residing in Canada. Put in modern terms, I guess you would say the wendigo is the personification of the desperation a human feels when freezing and starving to death. That's how the Indians thought the creature originally came into being: Some poor souls were forced to eat human flesh to survive, and that terrible experience turned them into wendigos.

From this point on, it gets very confusing. Some myths say the wendigo will steal human souls; others say it will kill and eat human beings; others again say it only possesses a person to get him or her to eat other people. Some believe it's a kind of insanity—some psychologists even use the term "wendigo psychosis"—while still others believe it to be a supernatural being.

I don't know what happened to Grandpa. But I do know there is no natural explanation for the things he did.

And I guess that leads me to the final question: Will Grandpa ever be found? Again, I don't know. And honestly, I don't care. Of course I hope there won't come another winter cold enough to wake the creature inside him. But something tells me that won't happen. I still believe Grandpa is a human being in his core. I think he did his best to keep down the wendigo for all these years, and even though he failed more than once, I believe he will win in the end. I have to believe so.

Well, that was all, really. For once I think I would like to ask you not to post any questions for me. I probably won't be able to answer them anyway, and I've said all I can. Now I just want to focus on getting my normal life back.

Thank you so much for reading.

Love, Otha.

26
   Letter found on the corpse of Frederick James Cochran in an abandoned cabin in Northern Alberta, Canada,
   Tuesday, November 14, 2017.

Should have done this a long time ago. Instead I've been hiding up here.

Guess I ought to go to the police. But what's the point in dragging things out? It would probably only make the pain worse for a lot of people if they had to see me alive. I can never undo the things I've done, and our society is too humane to give me what I deserve.

If anyone needs closure, let this letter be my confession. I did it. I regret it deeply. I couldn't help it.

And now, as winter is coming once more, I can feel it moving again. The predator is waking up. It's hungry.

Luckily, I can still stop it this time. I hope Jane will be waiting for me.

May God have mercy on my soul—or what's left of it.

***

When I set out to write *Human Flesh*, I was pretty anxious about the format. It was kind of daunting, only allowing myself to tell the story using written evidence. The only chapters I got to dive into the characters' thoughts just a tiny bit were Otha's blog posts. But surprisingly, it wasn't constricting at all. As soon as I got going, it turned out to work really well, and I enjoyed coming up with creative ways of painting the picture, if you like.

I had no idea how readers would feel about this way of telling a story, but the feedback I've gotten has been almost entirely positive. If you like this format, then you should check out another story I wrote in a similar way. It's called *Blind Gods*, and it revolves around a police interview that goes horribly wrong when it turns out supernatural forces are at play. You can download it for free at **nick-clausen.com/blind-gods**

BONUS STORIES
Never before published

Contents

Introduction		#
1.	A Taste for Blood	#
2.	The Whisper of the Dolls	#
3.	A Life for an Idea	#
4.	House of Echoes	#
5.	Creepy Crawlies	#
6.	Nightmare	#
7.	Eternal Snow	#
8.	Beast	#

Introduction

These eight stories you're about to read have never been published before. As you may have guessed, they were meant to become *Chills & Creeps vol. 3*, but they never got that far. So, for years, they've been lurking in the darkness of some obscure folder in my Google Drive. I honestly never thought they would get to see the light of day.

When I decided to put together *Monsters at Midnight*, and I went back to pull out these dusty old stories, I was elated to find that among them were some of my personal favorites. I really think these eight stories would have become the strongest in the *Chills & Creeps* series. Needless to say, I'm thrilled that you get to read them after all.

Without further ado, let's dive in!

A Taste for Blood

Elliot opens his eyes.

At first, he doesn't remember anything. Slowly, he looks around.

He's lying in a strange bed in a strange room. The walls are white. Next to the bed is a small table, and from a tall tripod hangs a clear bag of liquid. A tube runs down to his hand and disappears under a patch.

Elliot turns his head. The room has no windows, only two doors, one of which has the text TOILET written on it.

So, he's in the hospital. But why? Is he sick?

"Hello?" His voice is barely working, his throat is so dry. "Hello? Is anybody here?"

He listens. No answer comes. In fact, he can't hear any sounds at all. Perhaps it's nighttime? There is no clock, so he has no way of telling the time.

He needs to pee really bad. He tries to get up, but it's difficult. His body is very heavy.

Why is he here? And why can't he remember anything?

He pulls aside the blanket and looks down at himself. He's dressed in a white hospital gown. He scratches his hair—and feels the gauze. It's tightly wrapped around his head. Did he hurt his head? Is that why he's here?

"Hello?" This time he calls louder. "Somebody? Please come!"

Elliot is starting to feel nervous. Something is wrong.

His strength has returned a bit, so he's able to get his legs off the side of the bed and put his feet on the floor. For a moment he feels dizzy. Then, it passes. He stands up, but after a few steps he feels a tug from his hand. He remembers the tube. He has to bring the tripod, which, luckily, has wheels. He rolls to the bathroom.

It's not Elliot looking back at him from the mirror. He looks terribly pale and weak, with dark circles under his eyes and tufts of greasy hair sticking out from under the bandage.

Elliot pees and washes his hands.

When he opens the door to leave the bathroom, a woman is standing there.

Elliot jerks with surprise. "Fuck, you scared me!"

"I apologize," says the woman with a smile. She has black hair and wears a white nurse shirt. "It's best if you stay in bed. Come on, let me help you back." She gently takes hold of his arm.

"What happened to me?" Elliot lets her take him back to the bed and sits down. "Why am I here?"

"You were in an accident. You hit your head. Lift your legs, please."

"Oh no," Elliot mumbles. He lies back down and stares at the ceiling. "Is it bad? The injury, I mean."

"A little, but you'll survive. In a couple of days, you'll feel better. Then, you can go home."

Elliot feels relieved. "Where's my mom?"

"Your mother was here earlier today." The nurse pulls the blanket over him. "She will be back tomorrow."

"Is it nighttime right now? Why aren't there any windows?"

"Yes, it's nighttime," the nurse says with a smile. "I have to take a blood sample." She goes to the closet, where she finds a big syringe.

Elliot isn't afraid of needles, but he isn't particularly happy about them, either, and this one is really big. Of course, he can't be a baby, especially not in front of the nice nurse. So, he smiles as she rolls up his sleeve.

"You'd better look away," she says. "It can be a little bit unpleasant."

Elliot looks at the ceiling. He feels the sting and does his best not to wince.

"Great, that's it." She pulls the needle out. The syringe is completely filled up. The nurse puts a small ball of cotton on the wound and fastens it with a piece of tape. "Does your head hurt?"

"No."

"Good. Then the pill you got earlier is still working. But I think you'd better get another. We wouldn't want the pain to come back now, would we?"

Elliot swallows and shakes his head no.

The nurse finds a small bottle in her pocket, opens it and fishes out a pill. It's pink.

Elliot takes it, but hesitates. "Uhm ... can I get something to drink? I'm actually really thirsty."

"Of course. One moment."

The nurse opens the closet again and finds a cup. She goes to the bathroom and returns a moment later with the cup, now full of water.

Elliot swallows the pill and empties the cup. The water feels wonderful in his throat.

"Thank you," he sighs and puts the cup on the table.

For a moment they look at each other. The nurse is very young. In fact, she looks more like a big girl than a grown woman. She is also very pretty. Her hair is smooth and shiny, her eyes are big and green, her lips are red, her teeth perfectly white when she smiles. Elliot feels a little shy.

But there is also something strange about her. He just can't put his finger on it.

"Try to get some rest," she says. "I'll be back to check on you later."

"Okay."

She leaves the room and sends him one last smile from the door.

Elliot is left to the silence. He can still taste the pill in his mouth. He looks at the ceiling and sees a big cobweb. A spider is hanging right in the middle of it. It's weird. Hospitals are usually very clean. Maybe they just forgot to clean his room. They probably didn't want to disturb him while he was sleeping.

Elliot yawns.

He tries to remember something.

He remembers plenty. His name is Elliot Hartford White. He's eleven years old. He is in the fifth grade. His mom's name is Linda. His dad's name is Arnold. They are divorced. Elliot lives with his mom. As does his little sister, Sophie.

Elliot yawns again. He is starting to feel sleepy.

What else does he remember?

His best friend's name is Tom. His favorite food is chicken with fries. He's good at computer games. Every Monday and Wednesday he goes to soccer practice.

Elliot tries to remember anything about the accident. Nothing comes up.

What is the last thing he remembers, then?

He racks his brain. It's hard to remember. His memory feels heavy and dull. His eyes are starting to close. He's falling asleep.

Then something pops up. A memory.

He's on his way home from soccer practice. He's riding his bike. The sports bag is hanging from his shoulder. The sun has almost set, the streetlights are on. He goes for a shortcut through the park. The path winds itself among the big trees. He's going fast. He's a little scared because of the darkness. He looks back. All of a sudden, a figure steps out in front of him. Elliot shouts out. He doesn't have time to turn. He closes his eyes.

That's the last thing he remembers.

Elliot drifts into sleep.

***

Elliot opens his eyes.

At first, he doesn't remember anything. Slowly, he looks around.

"I see you're awake."

The voice makes him jump.

A young nurse is standing at the side of the bed, smiling. "I didn't want to wake you. I've brought you some food. You must be hungry."

"Where ... where am I?" croaks Elliot.

"You're at the hospital."

"Why?"

"You've been in an accident. You hit your head."

Elliot raises his hand and feels his forehead. His fingers find a bandage.

"Don't worry," the nurse says. "It's not that serious. You just have a slight concussion. In a couple of days, you'll be ready to go home. Are you hungry?" She points to the table where there is a tray of food. It's a burger from McDonald's with fries and a large Coke.

"I'm really more thirsty," Elliot mumbles. He tries to sit up, but it's difficult. He feels very weak.

The nurse helps him and gives him the cup. Elliot guzzles down most of the Coke, then lets out a loud burp.

"Does your head hurt?" the nurse asks.

"No."

"Good. But as soon as you have eaten, we'd better give you a pill. We wouldn't want the pain to come back now, would we?"

Elliot definitely does not want to feel pain. Then, he asks: "Why can't I remember anything?"

"That's completely normal. It's because of the accident. Your memory will return soon. You'd better eat."

Weirdly enough, Elliot doesn't really want the burger. He usually loves McDonald's, but it feels like he's had it a lot lately. Still, he picks up the burger—mostly to please the nurse. She is very pretty, and she is smiling at him. Elliot begins to eat.

"Your mom was here earlier, but you were asleep. She told me to say hi."

"Thanks. When will she come back?"

"Tomorrow morning."

Elliot notices the room doesn't have any windows. He has no idea what time it is. "Is it nighttime now?"

"Yes."

Why does she bring him food in the middle of the night? Perhaps she's been busy with her other patients.

"What's your name?" Elliot asks.

"My name is Sevi."

"That's a pretty name."

She smiles. Her teeth are very white. The smile makes Elliot shy.

Elliot finishes the burger. The fries are kind of soggy.

"I just need to take a blood sample," Sevi says. She gets out a syringe from the closet and rolls up his sleeve. "You'd better look away. It can be a little ..."

But Elliot has already seen the red dots on his arm. There are four of them. "What's that?"

"Eh ... it's from the other samples."

"Did you already take *four?*"

"I've taken one a day."

"What? Have I been here for *four days?*"

"Yes."

"But ... I can't remember that at all!"

"Calm down. It's because of the accident. Your memory will return soon."

She sticks the needle in his arm. Elliot clenches his teeth. The red blood slowly starts to fill the syringe.

"What happened?" Elliot asks. "In the accident, I mean."

Sevi is staring at the syringe. "You got hit by a car."

Elliot tries to remember, but nothing comes to mind. Strange.

"That's it." Sevi pulls the needle out and fastens a piece of cotton to the wound. "Do you need to go to the bathroom? I can help you get there."

Actually, Elliot does have to go. Sevi helps him. It's a little awkward to walk, because his legs are kind of numb, and he needs to bring the tripod.

Sevi smiles at him as he closes the door.

Elliot sits down on the toilet. His gaze falls on the toilet paper roll. It looks like something is written on the back of it. Elliot rolls out the first piece.

don't trust Sevi!

she's lying!!!

Elliot stares at the note. It's written with a pen.

Sevi knocks on the door. "Are you all right in there?"

"Eh ... yes, sure! I'm almost done."

Elliot's heart is pounding. He can't remember having written the note, but it's unmistakably his own writing. Why did he write it? What is Sevi lying about? The accident?

Elliot finishes up. He throws the note in the toilet and flushes. When he opens the door, Sevi is standing right outside.

She smiles. "It took you a long time. Are you ready to take your pill?" She shows him a tiny pink pill.

"Uhm ... actually ... I would like to see a doctor."

Sevi's smile disappears. "Why?"

"Because I ... I would like to hear what ... uh ... happened ... and ... when I can go home."

"But I already told you."

"Yes, well ... I would still like to hear it from a doctor."

She looks at him. Then, she puts the pill in her pocket. "All right. I'll get him."

"Thank you."

Elliot shuffles back to the bed and sits down. Sevi leaves the room.

While he waits, Elliot checks out his other arm. There he finds six dots.

Ten blood samples, he thinks and shivers. If Sevi has taken one a day, he must have been here for ten days.

Some minutes pass. Finally, the door opens.

Sevi enters. "All right, here's the doctor."

A tall, skinny man in a white coat strolls in. His hair is black and grey on the sides. He shuts the door and gives Elliot a hard look. "My name is Pram. I'm a doctor. What's the problem? My time is short."

"I'm sorry, I just wanted to ask—"

"About when you can go home? In a couple of days."

"Okay. What happened to me?"

"You have a concussion. I thought Sevi already explained these things ..." He glances at the nurse.

"I *did*," Sevi says. "He *insisted* on talking with you."

"Why can't I remember anything?" asks Elliot.

"Because of the concussion, obviously," the doctor says. "It's completely normal. Your memory will return soon."

This isn't getting me anywhere, Elliot thinks. The doctor is just saying the same phrases as Sevi. If he can't trust her, he probably can't trust the doctor, either.

"I would like to call my mom."

"It's the middle of the night," the doctor says.

"I would like to call her anyway. Where is my phone?"

"Phones aren't allowed in the hospital."

"Then please show me where to find a phone." Elliot gets up.

But Sevi gently takes hold of his shoulders. "You're not at all well enough to go outside the room. You risk fainting."

"Does your head hurt?" Pram asks. "I think you need a pill."

"I think so, too," Sevi nods. "We wouldn't want the pain to come back."

Elliot looks at them. Something about the situation is off. Why don't they want him to call Mom?

"Could you give a pill, Sevi? I really don't have time for this. There are many other patients to tend to."

"How many days have I been here?" Elliot asks.

Sevi and the doctor answers simultaneously.

"Four."

"Eight."

They look at each other.

"Oh, right," Pram mumbles. "Four. I must be thinking about another patient. Well, speedy recovery." He turns around, coat flapping, marches out of the room and slams the door.

Sevi smiles and offers him the pill. "Here you go. It's for the pain."

Suddenly, Elliot knows that she's lying. The pill isn't meant for the pain. But what then? Could it be a sleeping pill?

He smiles nervously. "I think I would like to skip it."

She looks surprised. "Would you want the pain to come back?"

"No, but ..."

"When you came in here you were screaming constantly. It was an awful noise. I really think we should show consideration for the rest of the patients. They're trying to sleep and get better."

Elliot hesitates. What if it's true? He doesn't want to feel that much pain. He takes the pill. Sevi hands him a cup of water from the table. She stares at him. He has no other choice than to put the pill in his mouth. He tries to hide it under his tongue. Then, he drinks.

The smile on Sevi's face returns. "Now, try to get some rest. Your mom will be here tomorrow morning."

Elliot lies down. Sevi leaves the room.

Elliot realizes that the pill is gone. He accidentally swallowed it. He briskly sits up. If it really was a sleeping pill like he suspects, he'll soon fall asleep, and when he wakes up, he might not be able to remember anything. He has to write a new note for himself.

Desperately he looks around for something to write with. In the corner he sees his sports bag. He gets up and crosses the room, but he forgets about the tripod, and with a yank the tube is ripped out. Elliot stares at the patch on his hand. Slowly, he pulls it off. There are no marks on his skin. The tube was just there to fool him.

Elliot is really frightened now. He rummages through the bag. The training suit smells sour, like it really needs a washing. There's also a milk carton and a couple of other things. In a flash he suddenly remembers: His mom gave him some money and asked him to go by the grocery store on his way home from soccer practice, so he did. The last thing he remembers is riding through the park. Someone jumps out in front of him, and after that ...

Elliot yawns. His eyelids are getting heavy.

In the side pocket he finds a pen. But he doesn't have anything to write *on*. He looks at the table, nothing. He's starting to feel dizzy. The pill is already having an effect. Soon, he'll faint.

Elliot turns to the bed, grabs the pillow and writes on the cover. Then, he turns it around and hides the pen underneath. He lies down on the bed and immediately falls asleep.

Just before his eyes closes, he looks at the tripod and thinks: *Oh, shit, I forgot the tube!*

Then, he's gone.

***

Elliot opens his eyes.

At first, he doesn't remember anything. Slowly, he looks around.

He's in a strange bed in a place that looks like a hospital room. Why is he here? Is he sick?

"Hello? Is anybody here?"

No answer.

There are no windows. He has no idea what time it is. It could be nighttime. Maybe that's why it's so quiet.

Elliot feels very tired, but he also needs to pee, so he gets up. A tube is attached to his hand, and the other end goes to a bag of clear liquid hanging from a tripod. He brings the tripod and goes to the bathroom.

The boy in the mirror doesn't look like Elliot. He looks older, weaker and completely exhausted. It looks like he's withering away. A big bandage is rolled around his skull, which means he must have hurt his head. It's strange how he can't seem to remember anything.

Elliot pees and washes his hands.

He leaves the bathroom and tries to open the other door, but it's locked. Elliot is puzzled. How weird. Why would he be locked in? It's got to be a mistake.

He shuffles back to the bed. As he sits down, he accidentally knocks the pillow to the floor. He bends down to pick it up—and notices the writing. He reads it with deeper and deeper wrinkles in his forehead.

you can't trust Sevi or the doctor!

they say you've been here for 4 days, but it's much longer!

the tube isn't even attached!

they won't let you call Mom!

and the pill makes you go to sleep—whatever you do, don't take it!!

Elliot recognizes his own handwriting.

The message scares him. What does it all mean? Who is Sevi? What pill is the message talking about?

At that moment, he hears steps from the hallway. Quickly, he turns the pillow around and lies down.

The door opens and a young nurse comes in. Smiles at him. "I see you're awake. I've come to take a blood sample."

"Are you ... are you Sevi?"

She looks at him with surprise. "How do you remember that?"

Elliot shrugs.

Sevi smiles. "I only ask because your memory has been a little hazy. It's completely normal. It's because of the accident."

"What accident?"

"You were hit by a car. But it seems your memory is returning. That's a good sign." She comes closer. "Do you remember anything other than my name?"

Elliot tries to think. Then, he shakes his head.

"Do you remember leaving the bed?"

"No."

"I was in here earlier to check on you. You had pulled out the tube." She points to his hand.

"It ... it was probably something I did in my sleep."

"All right, but you have to be more careful."

"I will."

"I also found a pen on the floor. Did you write something?"

"No."

Sevi goes to the closet and finds a large syringe.

Elliot stares at her as she comes to the bed and starts rolling up his sleeve.

"You'd better look away," she says. "It can be a little bit unpleasant."

Elliot turns his head. But he sneaks a peak and sees five dots on his arm.

"That's it." She puts on a piece of cotton with tape. "Do you need to go to the bathroom?"

"No."

"Are you hungry or thirsty? I can bring you something."

"No, thank you."

"All right. You'd better take your pill, then ..." She sticks her hand in her pocket.

"I would like to call my mom," Elliot exclaims.

Sevi looks apologetic. "That's probably not a good idea. You see, it's the middle of the night. But your mom will be here tomorrow morning. You can talk with her then."

Elliot feels that Sevi is lying. He can tell.

She finds a tiny pink pill and hands it to him. "It's for the pain."

Elliot remembers the message: *the pill makes you go to sleep—whatever you do, don't take it!!*

"No, thank you," he smiles. "I'm not in any pain at all."

"But you will be if you don't take the pill. A lot of pain."

"Can't you just leave it here? I'll take it later, if the pain comes back."

Sevi smiles. She has nice white teeth. But for some reason Elliot doesn't like her smile.

"The pill must be taken at a certain time."

Elliot is desperate, but he tries to hide it, as his brain scrambles for a way out. "Uh ... actually, I do need to pee after all."

"All right. I'll help you." She puts the pill on the table and helps him to the bathroom.

As soon as the door is locked, Elliot rips off the patch. The tube is not attached—exactly as the message said. Elliot is beginning to understand. Sevi is not really a nurse, she's just acting.

But why? What on Earth is going on here?

He stares at himself in the mirror for a moment. Then, he has a thought. He loosens the bandage and removes it. He checks his head for wounds or anything else, but he finds nothing at all.

Was there even an accident? Does his mom know where he is? Does *anyone* know?

A knocking on the door. "Are you all right in there?"

"I'm fine! I'll be done in a minute."

Elliot wraps the gauze around his head again and opens the door.

Sevi is standing with her back to the door, but she quickly turns around. "Oh! I didn't hear you ..." She has the syringe in her hand. Elliot notices that half the blood is missing. He could swear that he remembers her filling it up all the way when she took the sample from him. So, what happened to the rest of the blood?

Sevi smiles. "Well, are you ready for your pill?"

Elliot just gapes. He stares at her teeth, which were shining white just a couple of minutes ago, but now they're bright pink.

Sevi has blood on her teeth.

His blood!

"Eh ... yes ... I ..." Elliot can't find the words.

"Do you know what? You'd better get two." She finds another pill and puts it on the table next to the other one. "That way we'll make sure the pain doesn't return."

There is no more doubt in Elliot's mind. Something is terribly wrong here.

What can he do? Attempt to wrestle Sevi to the ground? Run? He's not sure he has the strength to any of that. Besides, if the doctor is in on whatever is going on, there might be others, too. For all he knows, they could be waiting right outside the door.

He decides the smartest thing to do is to keep pretending. So, he smiles and goes to the table. Picks up both pills, turns his back to Sevi and puts them both in his mouth. Or rather, he makes it look that way. In fact, he keeps the pills in his hand, while swiftly grabbing the cup and drinking a large gulp, seemingly swallowing the pills.

"There," he says and turns around. "Now I think I'll try to sleep."

Sevi smiles again, her teeth are still red. "That sounds like a great idea. When you wake up, your mom will be here." She leaves the room, and Elliot notices the sound of the lock turning.

He waits a minute before going to check, just to be sure. But the door really is locked. He grabs the pillow and rereads the message.

Elliot is starting to get a picture of what is going on. But it's almost too crazy to be true. Yet, he can't see any other logical explanation. Because he saw Sevi drinking the blood, he really did. And now that he thinks about it, she fits the description perfectly. Beautiful, black hair, white skin, red lips.

Sevi is a vampire!

And the same probably goes for the doctor. They are keeping him trapped here, while they systematically drain him for blood, so they can drink it.

The last thing he remembers is a figure jumping out in front of him. That also makes sense now. They knocked him out and kidnapped him.

Elliot starts to shake all over. What can he do to escape? There is only one way out, and it's locked.

Should he try shouting? Banging on the walls? Perhaps he can get in contact with the other patients.

But—is this place even a real hospital? Elliot listens. It's absolutely quiet. He looks around. In the corner there's a flap of wallpaper sticking out. He pulls the tube off his hands and walks over there. When he gently pulls the wallpaper, he finds a brick wall underneath it.

Elliot sees the sports bag, grabs it and rummages through it. He finds his training suit, his towel, a milk carton and other grocery stuff, but no phone. They took it when they took his clothes.

He has to be clever now. He knows their secret, and *they* don't know that *he* knows. That gives him an advantage. He might be able to fool them.

Perhaps he can use something from the bag? He checks the milk. The date says March 22. He has no idea what day it is today, but the carton is bulging. The bag also contains a can of tomato soup, and—

Elliot gasps.

Garlic! A whole pack!

He can use it as a weapon. But how? What's the best way to use it? Should he just take a clove of garlic and stick it in the face of Sevi the next time she comes in here?

No, because he has no idea how she will react. Perhaps she gets furious and attacks him. He has got to be more sneaky about it. Maybe even sneaky enough that she won't even know about it.

How do you use garlic against a vampire without the vampire knowing?

Elliot has an idea. He can eat it. The garlic will go into his bloodstream. Sevi drinks the blood, and …. And what? Will she die? Perhaps. It's worth a shot.

He rips open the pack and peels off a clove. It's too big to swallow, so he chews it. The taste is really strong, it burns his mouth. But it feels good, makes him feel protected. Elliot eats two more cloves.

Then, he goes back to bed and remembers to attach the tube to his hand again, so Sevi won't know that he has been out of bed.

He waits. He's way too excited to sleep. But after a while, sleep comes creeping.

***

Elliot opens his eyes.

This time, he remembers it all.

It's the sound of footsteps waking him up. They stop outside the door, the lock turns, and the door opens.

Sevi enters the room, smiling. "I see you're awake."

"Where am I?" Elliot asks. He has to play confused. "What happened?"

"You were in an accident," Sevi explains. "I just need to take a blood sample."

"An accident? Is it serious?"

"Oh, no." She goes to the closet. "You just had a minor concussion, that's all. In a couple of days, you'll be ready to go home." She brings the syringe and rolls up his sleeve. "You'd better look away …"

"I know, it can be a little bit unpleasant."

Sevi looks surprised at him. Then, the smile returns. "Exactly. Have you tried this before?"

"I can't remember," Elliot lies. He looks away, he plays it cool. But on the inside his thoughts are going a hundred miles an hour. He prays for the plan to work.

Sevi sniffs. "What's that smell?"

Elliot freezes. "What do you mean?"

"There's a terrible smell." Sevi looks around. "Where does it come from? It's burning in my nose."

"I can't smell anything." Elliot holds his breath. Perhaps she can smell the garlic on his breath.

Sevi looks very uncomfortable. She finishes the blood sample, but the whole time she keeps looking around the room, as though she's trying to figure out where the smell of garlic is coming from.

"I'm actually pretty hungry." Elliot is trying to distract her. "Can I get something to eat?"

Sevi manages to look at him briefly. "Of course. I'll bring you something." She hurries out of the room.

This time, Elliot doesn't hear the sound of the lock turning. She forgot! The smell of garlic confused her so much so that she forgot to lock it!

Elliot pulls off the tube and goes to the door. He opens it just a little and peeks out. The hallway has no windows. At one end there's a door, at the other there's a staircase leading up. This definitely is not a hospital. It looks more like a basement.

He runs to the stairs and looks up the steps. There's a door with the word EXIT. Elliot jumps up the steps. But the door is locked. He pulls hard, but to no use.

There is still another possibility. He walks down the steps again and goes to the other end of the hallway. He stops by the door and listens. Someone is talking in there. A man and a girl. The voices are familiar.

"Are you sure it was garlic?"

"Yes. No. Not completely sure."

"Where could it have come from? He can't all of sudden make garlic appear, Sevi."

"I know, Dad."

"I think you must've mistaken the smell for something else."

"Fine, you go and check, then."

"I will."

Elliot gasps. He turns around and sprints back to the room, closes the door and jumps up in bed. He fumbles with the tube, attaches it, and just as he pulls the blanket over himself, the door opens.

A tall, skinny man in a white coat comes in. Elliot vaguely remembers having seen him before.

The man doesn't look happy. "My name is Pram. I'm a doctor. How are you feeling today?"

"I'm a little tired, but other than that—"

"That's completely normal. You've been in an accident." Pram doesn't seem at all interested in talking. He paces around the room and looks around, as though he's searching.

"Is ... is something wrong?" Elliot asks.

"One of our nurses noticed a funny smell in here. I just wanted to make sure that everything is in order."

"I don't smell anything."

"It was probably just a misunderstanding." Pram goes to the door, but stops halfway there. He sniffs the air. Turns towards the corner where the sports bag is.

Elliot holds his breath.

The doctor goes to the bag, kneels down and opens it carefully. Then, with a hiss, he jumps up. "By all the devils in hell!" He glances quickly at Elliot. "Uhm ... I mean ... the smell seems to be coming from this bag. We can't have things like this in a hospital." He goes to the closet and rummages through the shelves before he pulls out a couple of rubber gloves. He puts them on and picks up the bag. He's very careful, as though there's a bomb in the bag. On his way out, he remarks: "You look tired. Try to get some sleep."

The he slams the door and turns the lock.

Elliot is left to the silence. He just lost all his garlic. Now, he can only hope that his plan will work.

An hour or so passes.

Elliot tries to count the minutes. It's difficult without a watch.

Finally, he hears footsteps. The door opens and Sevi comes in.

Immediately, Elliot notices that she is not well. She looks sick. Her cheeks are red with fever, her hair is greasy, her eyes are bloodshot and she's sweating.

"I just ... need to ... take a ... blood sample ..." She almost can't speak. "Very important ... need blood ..." She stumbles to the closet.

Elliot looks to the open door.

Sevi is looking for the syringe.

Elliot slips quietly on to the floor.

At that moment, Sevi turns around. Her eyes grow big. "Hey! You can't get out of bed ... Stop! Come back!"

Elliot goes for the door. Sevi grabs at him. Her nails scrape his arm, but he gets past her. He runs to the hallway, slams the door and turns the key. She screams through the door and bangs it violently.

Elliot looks towards the staircase. He knows that the exit door is locked. He has to try to find another way. The only option is the room where he heard Pram and Sevi talking.

He sneaks down the hallway. Listens by the door. No noise is coming from the other side. He tries the handle. The door opens, and very cold air meets him. The room is pitch black. He feels for a switch, finds it, pulls it down. A single naked lightbulb turns on. In the center of the room is a table with two chairs. On the table is two tall glasses. They are empty, but have traces of something red and sticky on the sides.

The room is too big for the lightbulb to illuminate it all. But he can make out two large coffins against the far wall.

He can't see Pram anywhere, though.

Elliot steps into the room. On the table is a key. He reaches for it.

"Sevi?" croaks a voice.

Elliot jumps.

"Is that you?" the voice continues. "Did you get the blood?"

It's coming from under the table. Elliot bends down. Pram is laying on the floor. His eyes are closed, and his arms are wrapped around his belly.

"Oh, I need it so bad ... fresh blood ... I don't know how ... he tricked us ... that little piece of ..." While he speaks, Pram opens his eyes. He stares at Elliot. "You! Come here, you! I'm going to kill you!"

Elliot steps aside as Pram reaches for his leg. He grabs the key and runs for the door.

"You come back here! You little devil! I'll drain every last drop of blood from your—"

A loud bang sounds as Pram tries to stand up and hits his head on the table. Elliot doesn't see any of it. He just sprints out the room and down the hallway and up the stairs.

Behind him, the vampire roars with fury.

Elliot fumbles with the key. Sticks it in the lock. Turns it. A click.

Heavy steps below him. "Don't you open that door! You hear me? *Nooooo!*"

Elliot opens the door and stumbles out into the bright daylight.

***

I honestly can't remember where I got the idea for this one from. I just thought it was really creepy to have this poor guy kept hostage without him knowing what was going on. It was tricky writing it from his point of view because I couldn't reveal anything until he (re)discovered it.

Anyway, hope reading this story hasn't scared you out of ever going to the hospital. After all, not all doctors are vampires—probably just a few of them.

Oh, and by the way, I left a clue in the story as to what Pram and Sevi really are. Did you get it? Try combining their names and rearrange the letters ...

The Whisper of the Dolls

It's nighttime. Beatriz is in her bed, very close to sleeping, when suddenly she hears someone whispering.

"You think they're asleep?"

"No, not yet."

The voices are very low. The words are hard to hear. Beatriz isn't completely sure they are even there. She lifts her head slightly from the pillow, listening as best she can.

Nothing.

She turns over with a sigh, deciding it was probably just her imagination. Mom always says Beatriz is very good at making stuff up in her mind. She yawns and closes her eyes.

She's drifting off when the voices come again.

"What now? You think they're asleep now?"

"Be patient, dear. It's only half past nine. The only one sleeping at this hour is probably the kid."

Beatriz sits bolt upright.

This time, she definitely heard something. It came from under the bed. Her pulse is beating away, so much so that she can hear it inside her ears. Dad once told her a scary story about trolls living under some boy's bed. What if the trolls from that story have become real and moved in here?

No, that's silly. Beatriz is eight. She's too old to believe in trolls.

So, even though she's scared, she gathers her courage and sticks her head out over the edge.

There's nothing scary under the bed—just a sock and some dust bunnies.

"Can't we just settle for her then?"

"No. It has to be all three of them."

Beatriz hears them better this time. It's coming from under the floor. From the basement. She keeps absolutely still and quiet as she listens. The voices keep whispering to each other. It sounds like a man and a woman.

"I don't know if I can wait any longer."

"You have to."

"Why?"

"Because I said so."

"You're not the boss of me, Tom."

"Listen, dear. Don't you want to be free?"

"Yes, of course."

"Good. Then I'm telling you, we have to get rid of all three of them. Otherwise, they'll just continue."

"All right." Tom sighs. "I guess you're right, dear."

Beatriz feels fear rise as she eavesdrops on what is clearly a private conversation. She knows who those voices belong to. It's the dolls. Tom and Tina. That's what Mom named them. Just as a joke.

Beatriz uses the trick Dad taught her for when she's having a nightmare: She pinches her arm. It hurts. But she doesn't wake up. So it's not a dream.

She sits up and shouts, "Mom! Dad!"

Shortly after, she hears footsteps. The door opens. Dad peeks in and turns on the light. "What's wrong, Bea?" Dad is big and strong. Beatriz always feels safe when he's around.

"I heard something," she tells him.

"What did you hear?"

"Voices. It came from the basement."

"It was just the TV you heard. Mom and I are watching a movie."

"No. I think it's the dolls, Dad."

"The dolls?"

"Yes. Tom and Tina."

Dad smiles. "You must have had a dream. The dolls can't talk. They're not alive. You know that, sweetheart."

"But I pinched myself, just like you showed me, and it didn't make me wake up. I really heard it, Dad."

Dad comes over and kisses her. "Go back to sleep, Bea. It's late. You have school tomorrow."

Beatriz suddenly isn't too sure of herself. Now that Dad is here and the room is bright, it all seems kind of silly.

"Sleep well, sweetheart. Goodnight."

"Goodnight, Dad."

Dad turns off the light and leaves. Beatriz turns toward the wall. She lies there for a while and listens. The voices don't return. She starts once again to drift off. She finds that she's very tired now.

Just before she falls asleep, she hears, "That was close. The kid heard us. We need to be more careful."

At this point, Beatriz is too sleepy to react, and she falls asleep.

And when she wakes up the next morning, she's forgotten all about the voices.

***

"Bea? Have you seen the lighter?"

Beatriz looks up. She is sitting on the floor with Anne. They are in the middle of a game of Jenga. Mom is standing at the door, hands on her hips.

"No, Mom."

"So you haven't borrowed it?"

"No, why would I? It's your turn, Anne."

"Well, maybe you needed to light a candle or something."

Anne carefully removes a red block. The tower remains standing.

Beatriz rolls the dice. "Yellow! This one's going to be difficult ..."

"It's just strange," Mom says, biting her lip. "I used it yesterday, and I'm sure I put it back in the drawer. This is the second time it disappeared."

Beatriz taps a yellow block. The tower wobbles but doesn't fall.

"Bea?" Mom asks. "Have you seen Dad smoking cigarettes?"

"Nuh-uh. He quit, remember?"

"Yes, that's what he says."

Beatriz nudges the block again. It drops out, but the tower keeps standing.

Anne grins. "Phew! That was close. You got lucky."

"Well, if you happen to see the lighter, let me know, okay?"

"Sure, Mom."

Mom closes the door behind her.

The girls continue playing for a while.

Beatriz rolls another yellow. This time, it's impossible.

"Hey, do we want to continue?" she asks. "Shouldn't we just call it a draw?"

"No. If we stop, I win."

Beatriz looks at the tower. She decides to give it a try. She sticks out her tongue, concentrating. Just before she touches the tower, there's a bump on the floor. The tower topples over.

"I won!" Anne shouts.

"No, that's not fair! I didn't even get to do anything."

"But it was your turn."

"Yes, but I didn't knock it over. Didn't you feel the bump?"

"Yeah, I did," Anne admits. "Where did it come from?"

"I think it came from the basement."

"Isn't that where your parents have their business?"

"Yeah, it is."

"How many sunglasses do they have?"

"Many. I think a million."

"Wow! Can I see them?"

Beatriz suddenly remembers what she heard last night. She doesn't feel like going down to the basement. "They're not that exciting. They're just stored in boxes."

"I really want to see them. I've never seen so many sunglasses all at once."

Beatriz can't really come up with a good excuse, so the girls go to the basement stairs. Beatriz reaches in and turns on the light before descending the steps. The basement is divided into five rooms. Two of them are for storage. One is the packaging room. Then there's the laundry room. And the last one is the photo room. That's where the dolls are kept. The photo room is right below Beatriz's bedroom.

The girls enter the storage room.

"Wow, there are so many!" Anne stares at the shelves. They cover every wall, from floor to ceiling. Boxes, boxes, boxes. All filled with sunglasses.

Beatriz has seen it plenty of times, so she isn't really impressed.

"Do customers come down here to buy them?"

"No. It's not a real store. People order them online, and Mom sends them with FedEx."

"Can I try some of them on?"

"Yes, sure. Just don't break 'em."

Anne picks a box.

Beatriz glances towards the photo room. The door is slightly ajar. Did Mom or Dad forget to close it? They come down here every day to pack and ship orders. But they only really use the photo room whenever new models arrive. They need to take pictures for the website. That's what they use the dolls for; they're models.

"How do I look?" Anne asks. She's put on a pair of sunglasses.

Beatriz giggles. "They're way too big."

Anne takes them off. She points. "What's in there?"

"Not much," mumbles Beatriz. "They just take pictures of the glasses in there."

"Can I see?"

"It's probably not a good idea. The camera is very expensive. If anything happens to it, Dad will get very angry."

"I won't touch anything." Anne has already walked over there. She pushes the door open and turns on the light. Then she lets out a little scream.

Beatriz startles. "What's wrong?"

Anne turns around with a nervous smile. "I got scared! I thought there was someone in here."

Beatriz approaches the door.

Tina is standing on the photo table. The doll only has a head, neck, and shoulders. But it's made very realistically. Every little detail is there. Real hair, color in the cheeks, even a gleam in the eyes. Beatriz always gets goosebumps when she sees the dolls. It feels like they're looking at her. Like, really looking. As if they can see her and know who she is.

A white canvas hangs on the wall behind the photo table. Large lamps are set up, and in the front, there's a stand with a camera and a laptop connected to it.

When Beatriz was little, Dad brought her down here. They took silly pictures of each other. That was before the dolls arrived.

Anne takes a closer look at Tina. "Do they use her as a model?"

"Yes. They put sunglasses on her and take a picture. That way, customers can see how the glasses look when worn."

"Smart." Anne smiles eagerly. "Shouldn't we try putting some on her?"

"We're not allowed to," says Beatriz. "We're not supposed to be in here at all. The dolls are very expensive, and ..." Suddenly, it hits her. "Hey, where's Tom?"

"Who's Tom?"

"The male doll."

The girls look around. They can only see Tina.

Then Beatriz spots him. He's lying on the floor, halfway under the canvas. She picks him up. "He must have fallen down. Maybe that's what we heard."

Fortunately, nothing has happened to the doll. Tom looks just as lifelike as Tina. He appears a bit more serious. Beatriz has always felt more uneasy around him. She quickly places him on the photo table and discreetly wipes her palms on her pants.

"Come on," she says. "We better go. Before Mom hears us."

***

"Have you started smoking again?"

Mom looks across the table at Dad. They're having dinner.

Dad swallows and looks surprised. "No, why do you ask? Do I smell like smoke?"

"No. I just can't find the lighter."

"I haven't taken it."

"I haven't either. And Bea says it's not her."
Mom and Dad look at her. Beatriz shakes her head.
Dad grabs a potato from the pot. "It must have gone missing."
"It doesn't just disappear on its own," Mom says. "It happened last week too. I found it in the laundry room."
Dad shrugs. "I really don't know how it ended up there."
"Someone must have had it in their pocket," Mom says. "And then forgot to take it out before the pants went in the washer."
Dad puts down his knife and fork to look at Mom. "So, you think I'm lying?"
"No, no. I'm just saying. It seems strange. And now it's gone again. I couldn't light the fireplace today."
"Then we'll have to buy a new one." Dad resumes eating.
Mom doesn't say anything more.
"By the way," Dad says. "When you change the batteries in the smoke alarm, remember to put new ones in."
Mom looks at him, confused. "What do you mean?"
"Well, the smoke alarm in the kitchen." Dad points with his fork. "It was open when I got home. The batteries were removed."
Now Mom looks outright bewildered. "I haven't changed the batteries."
"No, you haven't. You only removed the old ones."
"I haven't touched the smoke alarm, John."
"Then who did? Bea can't reach it."
"Well, I really don't know."
"Hmm," Dad grumbles. "Apparently, mysterious things are happening."
Mom and Dad continue eating in silence.
Beatriz has lost her appetite. A grim suspicion dawns on her. She remembers something one of the voices said the previous night.
"We need to get rid of all three of them."

***

Every evening, Beatriz listens for the voices. But she doesn't hear them.
During the next week, more mysterious things happen in the house. Mom still can't find her lighter, so she buys three new ones. Dad puts new batteries in the smoke alarm, but they disappear again that same night. The next day, Mom's lighters are also gone.
Mom and Dad argue a little. They both suspect each other of playing a joke.
Beatriz knows what is really going on. It's the dolls. They're alive. Not only can they talk, but they're also able to move on their own. And what's worse, they're clearly planning something. But *what?* Why would they need lighters and batteries?
She has to do something. She can't tell Mom and Dad about it; they wouldn't believe her anyway. And she's afraid to go to the basement by herself.
One day, when Mom is working, Beatriz goes down to join her. Mom is in the storage room, whistling along to the radio. The basement doesn't seem nearly as spooky now.
"Hey, sweetie," Mom says when she sees her. "What do you want?"
"Nothing," Beatriz says innocently. "I'm just a little bored."

"Did you do your homework?"

"Yes."

"That's good." Mom continues packing.

Beatriz saunters into the warehouse. She strolls along the shelves, approaching the door to the photo room. She casually opens it and steps inside. Tom and Tina are both at the table. Beatriz keeps a close eye on the dolls while she carefully searches the room.

Under the table, she finds them. Four lighters and six batteries.

"Mom! Could you come in here, please?"

Mom enters the room. "What is it, Bea? I really should be working."

"Look!" Beatriz says, pointing.

Mom bends down, sees the stuff under the table, then looks at Beatriz. "Is it you, Bea?"

"No! I swear, Mom. I just found them."

Mom looks at her doubtfully. Then she kneels down. "Bea, listen to me. I'm not angry. But it's dangerous to remove the batteries from the smoke alarm. If there's a fire, we might not notice it. And lighters are not for playing with, either."

"It wasn't me, Mom!" Beatriz lowers her voice, glancing sideways. "It was *them* ... the dolls."

Mom looks confused. Then she smiles. "All right. Thanks for showing me. I'm glad we solved the mystery." She stands up, strokes Beatriz's hair, and goes back to the packing room.

Beatriz feels like crying. Why won't Mom believe her? Maybe she should tell them what she heard the dolls whispering about? No, that would probably just make the matter worse.

Beatriz is about to exit the photo room when something makes her freeze in place. What did Mom just say?

"If there's a fire, we might not notice."

Suddenly, it all falls into place. The dolls' plan. They want to set the house on fire! That's what they needed the lighters for. They would probably do it late at night. Without batteries in the smoke alarm, the whole house would go up in flames before any of them could wake up, killing them all in their sleep.

Beatriz stares at the dolls. Tom seems to be smiling.

Beatriz rushes out, slamming the door behind her.

***

Beatriz wakes up in the middle of the night. She needs to pee, so she quietly slips through the house to the bathroom. Back in bed, she waits for sleep to come again.

And that's when she hears them.

"Are they asleep now?"

"Yes, definitely. I can hear the fat one snoring."

Beatriz holds her breath and listens intently.

"Darling? I'm not comfortable with this. I think we should drop it."

"Drop it? Why would we do that?"

"Because we were almost found out!"

"No, we weren't. The bitch thinks it's the kid who took the batteries and lighters. You heard her yourself."

"Yes, but it's the kid I'm worried about. The way she looked at us. I think she's on to us."

"And so what? Nobody believes her. She won't be able to stop us. Not before it's too late, anyway."

Beatriz lies stiff as a board.

"But now they're keeping an eye on us. With the batteries, I mean."

"I know that. We need to change the plan. Something they don't expect."

"Do you have an idea?"

"Of course I do, darling. Listen up ..."

Beatriz holds her breath. Her heart pounds in her ears. She tries very hard to listen, but Tom lowers his voice even more, to the point where she almost can't make out the words.

"Are you going to do it now?"

"Sure, why not? They're all asleep."

"Okay, but be careful, darling."

"I will. You keep watch."

Fear shoots through Beatriz. She sits up in bed. The dolls are going to do it right now! She has to wake up Mom and Dad.

"Just give me a hand," Tom says. "I can't reach the window."

The window?

Beatriz hears rustling and then a squeaking sound. Did they just open the basement window?

"Wait for me here," Tom says. "I'll knock when I need to come back in."

"All right. Please hurry, darling."

Beatriz rolls out of bed. She slips over to the window and pulls the curtain slightly to the side. In the garden, she sees something small and bright darting across the grass. She covers her mouth in shock. It's Tom! The doll has no legs, yet it moves effortlessly somehow, using its shoulders.

He heads straight for the shed.

What is he up to?

Tom hesitates in front of the shed door for a moment. Then he jumps up and latches onto the knob. Beatriz can't see it clearly, but it seems like Tom is using his mouth to open the door. He jumps down and disappears inside.

Beatriz waits behind the curtain, her bladder feeling full again even though she just went to the bathroom. She shifts her weight back and forth. Should she wake up Mom and Dad? Perhaps it will be too late. Maybe Tom will already be back in the basement by the time her parents come. And Beatriz needs to see what he's up to.

After a few minutes, the doll emerges again. It's carrying something in its mouth. It looks like a small bucket. Tom places it in the grass, pushes the shed door shut, and picks up the bucket by biting the handle. Then it rushes back toward the house. Beatriz pulls aside the curtain a little more. She mustn't be seen.

Tom disappears from view.

A moment later, she hears a tapping sound.

The basement window opens, then closes again.

"Oh, you did it, darling!"

"Of course I did. It was a piece of cake."

"You're so brave. And you brought the bucket."

"Yes. Now we just need to make sure they don't find it. This time, we must hide it well."

"It doesn't look very big. Is it really enough? For all three of them?"

"Trust me, it's more than enough. I read about it on the internet. We can kill ten people if need be."

Tina giggles. "And we only have to kill three."

"Two and a half, actually," Tom corrects.

The dolls laugh quietly together.

Beatriz feels like screaming. She runs into her parents' bedroom.

"Dad! Mom! You have to wake up!"

Mother lifts her head with a grunt. "What? What's happening?"

"It's the dolls. They're out to kill us! I heard them again!"

"What are you on about?"

"Bea?" Dad mumbles. "What's going on?"

"She had a nightmare," Mom sighs.

"No!" Bea stomps the floor for emphasis. "No, it wasn't a nightmare. I'm completely sure. I saw him myself!"

"Who did you see?"

"The doll! Tom! He ran into the shed. He took a bucket down to the basement. They're going to use it to kill us! You have to believe me!" Bea starts to cry.

Mom elbows Dad. "You and your stories about trolls."

Dad sits up, rubbing his eyes. "Come here, sweetheart." He embraces Bea. "Some dreams can be very lifelike."

Bea sniffles. "It wasn't a dream, Dad!"

"Okay, okay." Dad sighs. "If we go down to the basement and check that there's no bucket, will you feel better?"

"That ... that won't work," Bea says. "Because they've probably hidden it."

"All right, then we'll check the shed. If nothing is missing out there, then it was a dream. Deal?"

Bea hesitates for a moment. Then she nods.

Dad starts getting dressed.

***

Five minutes later, Dad and Bea stand in front of the shed. Dad has a flashlight in hand. He opens the door and steps inside.

"Well," he says, looking around. "Let's see then. A bucket, you say? How big was it?"

"Not very big. Maybe like this," Bea shows with her hands. "And it was black."

Dad scans the shelves with the flashlight. "Hmm. Black, black. A black bucket. Well, I don't see—" Suddenly, Dad falls silent as the light stops at an empty spot. "What the heck? Where's my paint thinner?"

"What's paint thinner?" Bea asks.

"Something you mix in paint," Dad mutters, striding to the shelf to take a closer look. "Hmm, that's odd. It's gone. I just bought it last week, because your mom keeps pestering me about painting the fence."

An uneasy thought crosses Bea's mind. "Is ... is paint thinner toxic?"

"Very toxic," Dad says. "Definitely not something you should—" He suddenly turns and shines the flashlight on Bea. "Did you take the bucket, Bea?"

"No, Dad! I keep telling you, it was the doll! Why don't you believe me?"

"Because dolls aren't alive, Bea. And paint thinner is not a toy."

"I *didn't* take it!"

"Fine, let's say you didn't. So you're telling me the doll brought the bucket into the house?"

"Yes, through the basement window."

Dad nods. "Let's check the basement, then."

As they step back out of the shed, Bea notices the doorknob.

She gasps. "Look, Dad!"

Dad shines the flashlight on it. "What's this now? Why is the doorknob all scratched up?"

"Those ... those are bite marks," Bea whispers.

Dad glances at her but doesn't say anything. She hopes very much that he's starting to believe her. They go back into the house and down to the basement. Dad turns on the lights in every room.

"So, where could they have hidden it?" he asks.

"I don't know," Bea whispers. "Maybe in the photo room."

They enter the photo room. Tom and Tina are standing at the table, their lifeless gazes welcoming them. Bea feels like the dolls know she heard their plans.

"You check in here," Dad says. "I'll take the storage."

"No, Dad, don't leave ..."

But Dad has already gone into the adjacent room. Bea is left alone in front of the dolls. She starts searching. Nothing under the table. Not behind the door, either. There aren't many hiding places. She can feel the dolls watching her, but every time she turns towards them, they stare straight ahead.

She can hear Dad in the storage. If he wasn't with her, she wouldn't dare be down here.

She's about to leave when she spots the grate in the floor. Over in the corner. She walks to it. The grill is all rusty. She kneels down, trying to pry it open.

A sound behind her.

Beatriz turns her head and gasps.

Hasn't Tom moved? She feels like the doll has come closer. And he has turned slightly towards her.

He can't move as long as I'm watching.

Beatriz doesn't take her eyes off him. She fumbles with the grate. Somehow, she gets her finger stuck. "Ouch!" she exclaims.

She takes her gaze off Tom. It's only for a second. Then she turns her head again.

Beatriz is on the verge of screaming.

Now, Tom is right at the edge. Directly facing Bea. As if he's about to pounce on her.

"Dad!" she shouts.

Dad comes running. "What's wrong?"

"I think I found something. Under the grate here. I just can't get it open."

Dad approaches. Bea keeps a sharp eye on Tom.

Dad picks up the grate. He reaches down into the hole.

And up comes the bucket with paint thinner.

***

Mom and Dad are convinced that Beatriz did it.

They don't scold her, but they don't believe her either. She can hear them talking after she's been put to bed.

Dad: "I don't think she lied. I can tell when she's lying."

Mom: "So it *was* the dolls then?"

Dad: "Of course not."

Mom: "Someone has taken the bucket from the shed, though."

Dad: "She probably had a bad dream. Maybe she sleepwalked."

Mom: "No wonder she has nightmares when you tell troll stories."

Dad: "It was a fairytale! And it was your idea to read bedtime stories."

And so on. None of them take the threat seriously. Only Beatriz knows how close they came to things going very wrong.

Or was it just a nightmare? Did she really just sleepwalk? Was it all something she dreamed? She considers the thought. No. She really saw Tom take the bucket. She was awake. As awake as one can be.

The dolls wanted to poison them. Pour thinner into the milk while no one was home. Or maybe directly into their mouths while they slept.

Beatriz starts to tremble under the covers.

The dolls are silent in the basement. Or maybe they whisper so softly that she can't hear them. Making new plans.

***

"Bea! Come here!" Mom calls from the living room. "We have someone you should meet!"

Beatriz gets up from her homework and walks into the living room.

As she opens the door, she is greeted by joyful barking.

A small, light-haired dog comes running towards her. It jumps up and licks her face.

Beatriz is speechless. "What ... what is this?"

"That's a dog," Mom smiles. "His name is Bonito."

"You like him?" Dad asks.

Beatriz tries to pet the dog, but it's going crazy, yelping and licking her hands. She starts giggling. "Yes! I do."

"Good, because he's yours."

"He is?"

"Yes," Mom says. "We thought you could use a sleeping companion. So you won't have any more nightmares."

Beatriz crouches down. Bonito licks her chin, nips at her hair, and nearly knocks her over. She laughs and gives him a hug.

Maybe it's not such a bad idea, Beatriz thinks.

Maybe Bonito can keep watch. Let her know if the dolls try anything.

***

A week goes by.

Bonito sleeps in bed with Beatriz. Down at the foot of the bed. The first few nights, he's a little restless. But then he starts sleeping heavily. He even snores a little.

Beatriz doesn't hear anything from the dolls. She checks on them occasionally. When Mom is downstairs packing. They're just standing on the table in the photo room. Bonito always follows her closely, no matter where she goes.

The first time he sees the dolls, he sniffs them. Then he whimpers a little and backs away.

He doesn't like them, Beatriz thinks. *He can sense they're evil.*

Beatriz begins to feel safe. Finally, someone believes her. And the dolls probably won't do anything when the dog is around.

***

Suddenly, one night, she wakes up.

The dog growls. He's sitting upright; his ears and shackles are raised.

Beatriz sits up. "What's wrong, Bonito?"

Bonito stares at the floor as if he heard something.

Beatriz listens carefully. Her first thought is the dolls. Have they started planning again?

But she can't hear anything. After a while, Bonito falls quiet. He whimpers a little and lies back down. Beatriz reaches down and scratches him behind the ears. He sighs and settles down.

It was probably nothing, Beatriz thinks. She lies back down to sleep.

But now she needs to pee. She throws off the covers. Bonito jumps up and wags his tail.

"We're not going to play," Beatriz whispers. "I just need to pee, but you can come with me if you want."

Bonito doesn't need an invitation. He's already jumped to the floor, shaking his fur.

They walk together through the house. Beatriz doesn't turn on the lights. It's not necessary when the dog is with her.

Suddenly, Bonito slips into the kitchen.

"Hey! What are you doing? That's not the way," she says, following him. He runs around and sniffs the floor. Then he stops by the counter and lets out a low bark.

"Be quiet," Beatriz hushes. "You'll wake Mom and Dad."

Bonito barks again. He stretches his neck and scratches with his front paws as if to show her something.

"What are you doing?" Beatriz walks over there. "What can you smell?"

She looks at the counter. There's a package of sandwich bread. Next to it is the knife block. One of the knives is missing. It's strange. Mom is very protective of her knives. No one else is allowed to use them, not even Dad. They were very expensive. She sharpens them all the time, and she always puts them back in place after she's—

Bonito growls again.

Beatriz looks at him. He has turned around. Now he's staring into the living room.

Beatriz gets goosebumps. "What is it, Bonito? What do you see?"

At that moment, her question is answered. A small figure darts past the doorway. Beatriz doesn't see if it's Tom or Tina, but she does catch a glint from the knife.

"Jeez!" she cries out.

Bonito barks and charges forward.

"No, Bonito!"

But it's too late. The dog has disappeared into the living room. Beatriz follows him quickly. In the shadows, she sees Bonito and Tom wrestling. They roll around on the floor, halfway under the coffee table. The dog snarls and snaps. The doll writhes, trying to break free. It has dropped the knife.

"Let me go, you vile beast!"

Bonito sinks his teeth into Tom's throat.

The doll gasps and tries to scream, but it sounds muffled. Bonito shakes him, and Tom starts to gurgle.

Beatriz stands there, stunned, and watches.

Tom's eyes roll back. Bonito shakes him again. This time, Tom doesn't resist, and he looks to have gone limp.

Out of the corner of her eye, Beatriz sees something. Tina emerges from the shadows. She picks up the knife. It looks strange because she has no hands, but she manages anyway.

"Hold on, Tom!" she squeals. "Hold on, my beloved!"

She leaps forward and stabs Bonito with the knife. The dog lets out a loud howl. Tom falls to the floor.

"*Noo!*" Beatriz screams.

Bonito flops onto his side. He whimpers meekly. Beatriz can see blood in his fur and on the knife.

Tina turns toward her. "You!" she hisses. "It's all your fault!"

Her eyes are full of rage. The doll screams and lunges forward.

Beatriz spins around. She flees through the kitchen. She nearly slips. She can hear Tina. The doll is right on her heels.

Beatriz runs into the hallway. As she rounds the corner, she sees the basement door is ajar. Beatriz gets a sudden idea. She jumps behind the door and stomps on the floor six times. She hopes it sounds like she's running downstairs.

She hears the doll catch up. It stops right on the other side of the door. "You can't hide down there!" it screams.

Beatriz peeks out. Tina is standing right at the top of the stairs, peering down into the darkness. The bloody knife trembles in her grip. If she turns her head, she'll spot Beatriz.

"I've got you now," she whispers. "There's no way out."

Beatriz pushes hard against the door. She feels a thud as it hits Tina. Then a scream, followed by a series of crashes. She hears the doll tumble down the stairs.

Beatriz opens the door. Reaches in and turns on the light. Tina lies at the bottom. Her eyes are closed. Her mouth is open. There's a large gash on her forehead.

"Beatriz?" Mom's voice. She comes out of the bedroom, staring at Beatriz in astonishment. "What the hell is going on? Was that you screaming?"

"It was the dolls," Beatriz whispers. She starts to cry. "They attacked us. Bonito is dead, Mom."

***

Bonito isn't dead. He's just injured. Dad takes him to the emergency vet. He only needs a few stitches.

Mom and Dad think it was all a dream. That Beatriz was sleepwalking. They're not mad at her, but they send her to a psychologist.

The dolls are useless. Tom is covered in bite marks. Tina's head is cracked open. Dad throws both of them away.

Beatriz stands at the kitchen window and watches the garbage collector empty the bin one morning. She feels very relieved.

Bonito recovers quickly. Before long, he's running around the yard and playing again.

Beatriz sees the psychologist twice a week for a month. She has given up trying to convince Mom and Dad. So she just plays along. Pretends it was all a nightmare.

Soon, everything goes back to normal.

Until one day, when Dad comes home with a big cardboard box.

"Oh, hi, Bea," he says. "I thought you were at school."

"I got out early. What do you have there, Dad?"

"Oh, just some new glasses."

"Okay."

There's something in Dad's voice. Beatriz can sense he's lying. He takes the box down to the basement. She sneaks after him.

Dad puts the box on the floor. Cuts it open with a box cutter knife, then lifts something out of it.

Beatriz gasps.

It's a male doll. Not quite like Tom. This one has blonde hair. But it's just as lifelike.

Dad spots her. "Damnit. You weren't supposed to see this, honey." He lifts up another doll. A woman. She has red hair.

"Why, Dad?" Beatriz whispers. "Why did you buy new dolls?"

"We need them, Bea. We have to take pictures of the sunglasses."

Dad places the dolls on the photo table.

Footsteps are coming down the stairs. Mom appears. "So, they've arrived? Well ... Bea! What are you doing here?"

"I got home early."

Mom sighs. "Now don't get scared, all right? They're just dolls."

Beatriz doesn't say anything. The three of them stand there, looking at the dolls.

"What do you think they should be called?" Dad asks with a smile. He's obviously trying to lighten the mood.

"Well ... I don't know," Mom says. "Is it a good idea?"

Dad thinks for a moment. Then he says, "How about ... Paul and Piper?"

***

Days go by. Beatriz is a bit nervous. She listens for voices every night, but she doesn't hear anything. Bonito doesn't growl either.

She starts to relax again. The new dolls are apparently not alive, like Tom and Tina were. They have no plans to harm them.

One morning, Beatriz sits on the couch. She watches TV and eats cereal. Mom comes up from the basement. She goes into the kitchen, where Dad is drinking coffee.

"Take a look at this," she says.

"Oh, are these the new photos?"

"Yes, I just took them."

Mom and Dad are talking in low voices. Apparently, it's something Beatriz isn't supposed to hear. She leans in to listen.

"Isn't it strange?" Mom whispers.

"What? I can't see anything strange about it."

"Look at the mouth."

"What's wrong with the mouth?"

A brief pause. Beatriz holds her breath.

Then Mom whispers, "Doesn't it look like it's smiling?"

***

Before I could do this writing gig full-time, I worked a lot of odd jobs on the side. One time, I worked for a family that ran a home business like the one in the story. The basement was full of sunglasses. They also had a photo room with two mannequins. Sometimes I had to take pictures of them. I'm not particularly scared of dolls, but those two were pretty creepy, maybe because they were made to look very realistic. I constantly felt like they were staring at me. Did one of them just raise an eyebrow? Was the other one standing there a moment ago? I could become quite paranoid if I was alone with them for too long. It was obviously a very potent inspiration for this creepy story.

A Life for an Idea

"Goodness, Lau! Where *do* you get your ideas from?"

The whole class looks at Lau.

He smiles, shrugs his shoulders modestly, and says simply, "That's a secret."

Bitten laughs out loud. "Well, of course. I suppose a true writer never reveals where he gets his ideas from."

She called me a true writer!

Lau feels warm inside. He has always dreamed of becoming a writer, ever since he was little. He has written and deleted, written and deleted. Year after year, the right ideas just never came.

Not until now. Finally, he's getting good ideas.

"You should try submitting your stories to a publisher," Bitten suggests. "Reach out to an agent. I think you have a great chance to get these stories published."

Lau feels a surge in his stomach. The thought is almost enough to make him dizzy. A real publication. A real writer. Him—Lau Jessen. At the tender age of only 13!

Someone whispers behind him. Lau hears something about "... getting a life ..."

He turns in his chair. Two girls at the back are giggling. One of them is, of course, Sofia. Who else?

Lau pretends not to notice. He turns back toward the teacher.

"Now I'm going to read the story," Bitten says. "The rest of you can learn something from Lau. His imagination is truly incredible!"

"Truly incredibly boring," Sofia whispers.

Lau feels the heat rise in his cheeks. Why is she always on his case? What did he ever do to her?

She better watch out. If she doesn't, she'll become my next idea.

Lau is startled by the thought. He looks around guiltily. But, of course, no one heard him. It was just a thought.

Bitten starts reading aloud, "It's really pouring down. Peter is soaking wet. He runs down the street, trying to use his collar as a guard against the water, but it seeps in anyway and trickles down his neck ..."

Lau closes his eyes. He listens to the words. He knows them by heart. He wrote them himself. He wrote them last night. As the dark man whispered them in his ear.

It all began a month ago.

***

Lau is very close to throwing in the towel.

He sits for hours every day, staring at the screen. The blank page mocks him. The cursor blinks teasingly.

No words come. No matter how hard he tries. And if any do come, they sound stupid, and he deletes them right away.

He even prays to God. Every evening before going to sleep, he recites the Lord's Prayer and ends with, "Dear God. Won't you please give me an idea for a story? I'll do anything."

But God never listens; Lau receives no answer. No ideas.

Finally, one day, he's had enough. Lau is furious. He slams his laptop shut so hard that the screen cracks. He punches his pillow and screams into it. The anger turns into tears. He lies on the bed and sobs until he falls asleep.

He has a strange dream. Something about the Devil.

When he wakes up, he has an idea. Not for a story. But for something new to try. That same evening, he will pray to the Devil instead of God. Maybe *he* will help him when God won't.

So, at bedtime, Lau doesn't recite the Lord's Prayer. Instead, he prays, "Dear Devil. If you give me an idea, I'll do anything in return."

Then he lies down to sleep.

***

At midnight, he is awakened by a sound.

Lau sits up. The door to his room slowly swings open. A tall figure appears in the doorway. It looks like a man wearing a black coat.

"Dad?" Lau mutters, rubbing his eyes. "Is that you?"

"No," says a deep voice.

Lau gasps. He reaches for the bedside lamp.

"Leave it be, please," the stranger says. He only raises his voice slightly, but it's enough for Lau to jump and quickly pull back his hand.

As the guest enters the room, the floorboards creak and groan under him, as though he weighs ten times that of a normal person. "We don't want the light on," the stranger goes on. "It's easier to talk when it's dark. Don't you think, Lau?"

"W... who are you?" Lau asks weakly.

"You know very well. You summoned me yourself."

Lau becomes even more frightened.

"I've come to negotiate," says the stranger. He reaches out for Lau's office chair, drags it across the floor, and sits down on it. The chair sounds like it's about to break.

A strong smell of something burnt fills the air.

Lau discreetly covers his nose with his sleeve. "Negotiate about what?" he asks.

The stranger throws out his arms. "About an idea, of course. I gathered that's what you're after, am I right?"

"Uhm, well, yes. But ... I don't have much money, you see."

The stranger scoffs. "I'm not after money, Lau."

"What then?" Lau feels his fear diminish slightly. The Devil apparently hasn't come to harm him. In fact, he's acting very friendly, almost like the two of them know each other intimately.

"Oh, nothing big," the Devil says casually. "Just a little life."

"A *life*?"

"Yeah. A life for an idea. Seems only fair, doesn't it?"

Lau frowns. "So, you'll give me an idea for a story, if in return, I give you ... a life?"

"Exactly."

"How would I do that?"

"It's very easy. You find an animal and you give it poison. That's all."

Lau shakes his head. "No, I won't do that. I can't."

The Devil falls silent for a moment. "Very well," he says. "I was under the impression you'd be willing to do anything. In fact, I seem to recall you using those exact words. But I must have misheard you. My mistake." He gets up from the chair and straightens his coat. "Well, it was nice meeting you, Lau. Sorry we couldn't do business together."

"Wait a second," says Lau.

The Devil has turned to leave. Now, he stops in the middle of the room to look back over his shoulder. "Yes?"

"What kind of animal are we talking about? I mean, if I agreed to it."

The Devil shrugs. "Just a tiny one."

"Like a ... snail?"

The Devil smacks his lips. "Noo, a little bigger than that. Let's say ... oh, I don't know ... a cat, perhaps."

"A cat ..." Lau feels his throat close up. "I'm not sure if I can do that. I mean, even if I wanted to, I don't have any poison either."

The Devil turns back around to face Lau. "I can provide you with the poison; you don't need to worry about that. The rest you'll have to handle yourself."

Lau bites his lip. It's insane. But he's actually considering it. His mind runs through potential victims. The first one that comes to mind—and the obvious choice, really—is Møller's old cat. Mom is sick of it. It always brings dead birds onto the terrace. And it pees on the doormat. She's told Møller a thousand times to keep it indoors, but the old guy doesn't give a damn. The cat is very old, too. So maybe it wouldn't be so bad if it—

"What do you say, Lau?"

Lau looks up at the Devil. He can't see his face. It blends with the rest of the darkness.

"Will it hurt the cat? The poison, I mean. Will it be painful?"

"Not at all. The poison acts very quickly and completely without pain."

"And you promise I'll get a good idea in return? Like, a *really* good one?"

He can hear the Devil is smiling. "You'll get the best one I have."

Lau takes a deep breath. "Okay," he whispers.

"Do we have a deal?"

"Yes."

The guest extends a hand. The skin is black. Not like a Black person, but black as ink. Lau cautiously takes the hand. It's burning hot. And it holds great strength. They shake hands, then Lau quickly lets go again.

"Now I'll explain to you how you make the poison," the Devil goes on. "Come with me over to the window."

Lau slips out of bed. Barefoot, he goes to the window. The Devil parts the blinds with two black fingers, allowing Lau to peer outside. The backyard is bathed in pale moonlight.

"Do you see the plants down there? At the bottom of the garden?"

"The ones with the white stems?"

"Exactly. They're called Cicuta virosa, or water hemlocks. You'll need to wear gloves when you touch them. Pick two. That should be plenty. Then you take ..."

Lau listens, holding his breath. The stench from the guest is really bad up close.

"That's it," the Devil says after relaying the instructions. "That's all you need to do. Will you remember everything?"

"I think so."

"If not, you can just summon me again. I'm always ready to help. Thank you for the deal, Lau."

"What about the idea?" Lau asks as the Devil goes for the door again.

"You'll get it as soon as the cat is dead," he says, not stopping.

"You promise?"

"Oh, Lau," chuckles the Devil, turning in the doorway to look back at him. "If there's one thing I'm known for, it's that I *always* keep my promises."

***

The very next day, Lau prepares the poison. He follows the recipe given to him by the Devil. He ends up with half a cup of a greenish liquid, which he pours into a jar and screws the lid on tightly.

Lau goes to the kitchen and pours full fat milk onto a plate. He opens the jar of poison again, very carefully. The Devil instructed him that ten drops should be enough, but Lau wants to be on the safe side, so he adds a good slosh. He then goes out to the terrace and places the plate in the corner closest to the hedge separating the garden from Møller's. He closes the door, sits down on the couch, and begins waiting.

Minutes go by, but Møller's cat doesn't show up. It's unusual because the cat is always around, just not today.

Lau eventually grows tired of waiting and moves on to do other things.

Later, his mother comes home from work, and Lau forgets all about the poison until bedtime. As it suddenly comes to mind, he runs out to the terrace. It's dark, but in the moonlight he can make out the plate. It doesn't appear the milk has been touched—except for a dead fly floating around the surface.

Lau sighs. "Well, I might as well leave it overnight," he mutters to himself.

He sets his alarm to ring an hour earlier than usual, goes to bed, and sleeps restlessly.

***

The next morning, the poison is the first thing on Lau's mind.

He rushes downstairs, heads for the terrace door, and freezes in place. Next to the plate lies Møller's cat, lifeless.

And there's something else there too—a hedgehog. Also dead.

***

All day in school, Lau can't think of anything else. He just wants to go home to his computer.

He also feels guilty about the cat. He buried it in the garden along with the hedgehog.

Finally, when school ends, Lau pedals home as fast as he can.

His fingers tremble as he unlocks the door. He rushes to his room, not even taking off his jacket. He boots up the computer and sits down by the keyboard, opening a new blank document.

Then he waits.

And waits.

Why isn't anything happening?

He stares at the cracked screen, then down at his fingers. They're not moving. "Come on," he urges them.

But his fingers don't obey. No idea comes to him.

Lau slumps back in his chair with a sigh. "He tricked me …"

***

That same night, Lau wakes up again at midnight.

The dark man is there once more. "So, Lau, are you ready?" he asks.

"Ready for what?" Lau sits up. "I already killed the cat, you know."

"Yes, I know."

"But I didn't get any idea like you promised. You cheated me! You didn't—"

The Devil holds up his hand in a stop-motion, and Lau abruptly ceases talking. "I came as quickly as I could, Lau," the Devil says calmly. "I'm not very fond of daylight, you see."

Lau's heart is racing. "So, you … you have the idea for me now?"

"Of course."

Lau slaps his hands together with excitement—then he remembers not to make too much noise, and he lowers his voice. "Where is it?"

The Devil taps his temple with a long, pointy finger. "In my head. Come on, get ready now, Lau. I don't have all night." He gestures towards the computer.

Lau jumps out of bed, slips across the floor, and sits at the computer.

The Devil comes to stand beside him. Just as Lau opens up a new blank document, the dark man leans in, places a heavy hand on his shoulder, and in a soft whisper, he begins to tell the story into Lau's ear.

Lau quickly writes it all down.

It's the fastest he's ever written anything. His fingers move with incredible speed, dancing like crazy ballerinas, tapping away like a machine gun, and yet they find the right keys without a single misstep.

It takes twenty minutes.

The story fills almost forty full pages. Afterward, Lau is completely exhausted. He's trembling and sweating. His fingers ache and his eyes sting.

"Thank you," he murmurs hoarsely. "That was a really good story. I—"

Lau falls silent as he notices he can't smell the smoke any longer. He looks around to find that he's alone in the room.

Dazed, he crawls back into bed and immediately falls asleep.

***

Bitten is very surprised by the story. It's the best thing Lau has ever written, she says. One of the best she has ever read, in fact. She reads it to the class.

Lau is over the moon.

His joy lasts the rest of the day and all of the next day. He reads the story again and again. It's truly good.

Then the high starts to fade.

Life becomes dull again.

Lau wants to write a new story. He tries on his own, but it's like before—nothing happens. No ideas come to him.

He begins to wonder: Should he summon the Devil again? He doesn't want to kill more animals. Yet he still has the poison. The jar is hidden behind the freezer in the garage.

Then it hits him: the hedgehog!

He already killed two animals. The Devil owes him an idea.

***

That evening, Lau prays to the Devil. And at midnight, he appears.

"Hello again, Lau. You summoned me?"

"You owe me an idea."

The Devil tilts his head. "Do I?"

"Yes, for the hedgehog."

A brief pause. "It wasn't part of the deal."

"No, it wasn't intended. But it died anyway. So you got two lives, and I only got one idea."

The dark man is silent for a long moment this time. "You're brave, Lau. Not many dare blackmail me."

"I'm not blackmailing you. But we had a deal. One life for one idea. Right? That's what you said."

"Yes, I did. And you'll get another idea."

Lau throws off the covers and jumps out of bed.

"But," the dark man says, raising a thin finger, "a hedgehog is smaller than a cat. So the idea won't be as good."

"As long as it's still somewhat good."

"It is. All my ideas are good."

"Great. Come on, then."

Lau has already started the computer.

The Devil comes over and whispers in his ear.

***

The story is good. Not as good as the first one, but still somewhat good.

Bitten isn't as impressed. She doesn't read the story out loud.

Lau isn't as happy, either. The joy only lasts for a few hours. After that, he actually feels kind of disappointed.

So he decides that he must try again. With a really good story this time.

The problem is that it would require a bigger sacrifice. Lau deduces that if a cat is better than a hedgehog, then a dog must be better than a cat. And preferably a big dog.

But where does he find such a dog? Lau doesn't know anyone who has a dog. He never liked dogs. In fact, he's a little afraid of them. He doesn't know if he dares to get close to one of them.

On his way home from school, he rides his bike slowly through the city, pondering the problem.

At a traffic light, he stops for red. Something catches his eye. Someone has drawn with a marker on the lamppost right next to him. It's a lightbulb with an arrow pointing to the right.

Lau looks in that direction. He sees a narrow path between two hedges.

Lau furrows his brow. *It's almost as if ... No, that can't be.*

Still, he gets off his bike and drags it along. He just wants to check it out. So, he veers towards the path. It leads between two gardens. He walks a bit farther in, not really knowing why. He passes several gardens.

Suddenly, he hears a loud bark.

Lau topples with his bike. Behind a picket fence, a big black dog runs back and forth. Lau catches glimpses of it between the boards.

Lau gets back on his feet, jumps into the saddle, and hurries back to the road. He stops by the lamppost and catches his breath.

Then he notices that the drawing is gone. He walks around the lamppost, checking all sides, but it's completely clean. Lau is no longer in doubt.

The Devil just gave him a helping hand.

***

Lau spends all day planning.

He has to be very thorough and cautious if he wants to pull this off without getting caught by his mom.

So, while she prepares dinner, he goes to the garage. He takes a bag of pork chops from the freezer and smuggles it into the bathroom. He thaws it under the hot tap, then takes it back out to the garage. He retrieves the poison, pours it all into the bag along with the pork chops, then ties a firm knot, and hides the bag behind the freezer.

In the evening, he stays awake.

His mom goes to bed at eleven.

Lau sneaks out of the house, bringing the bag along. He rides through the town, encountering only a few cars and a late dog walker. He discreetly hides his face, just in case.

At the intersection, he looks around, making sure no one sees him. Then he slips onto the path. As he approaches the picket fence, he parks his bike. His legs begin to shake. He stops in front of the fence, expecting the dog to bark at any moment.

But it doesn't happen. He steps closer, peering into the empty garden. There is still light in the house.

"Darn it," Lau whispers. He hadn't thought about the fact that the dog would obviously be inside for the night. Now he can't execute his plan. If he throws the meat into the garden, it will probably just be eaten by various other critters during the night.

Just then, the terrace door opens. A chubby woman with a lit cigarette appears in a cloud of smoke. "Come on, Hector," she snaps. "Out you go. Do your business."

The black dog slinks out, and the woman slams the door shut. The dog starts sniffing around.

Lau can hardly believe his luck. He purses his lips and whistles softly. The dog raises its head. Lau whistles again. The dog starts moving in his direction, looking both suspicious and curious.

"Come, Hector," he calls. "I have a treat for you."

The dog growls at his voice. Lau quickly puts on the gardening gloves, opens the bag, and takes out a marinated pork chop. He sticks it through the picket fence.

Hector barks loudly. Lau is startled and drops the meat. The terrace door swings open. Lau is about to flee.

"Hector! Shut the hell up!" scolds the woman. "You're waking up the entire neighborhood."

Hector stops barking. The woman huffs and closes the door again.

Lau stands frozen in place for a moment. His pulse pounds in his throat. He can hear Hector breathing and sniffing on the other side. He picks up the pork chop and tosses it over the fence.

He looks through the gaps in the fence. Hector approaches and sniffs the meat. Then he snags it and swallows the entire thing!

Lau doesn't want to see what comes next. He quickly jumps back on his bike and pedals away.

***

Half an hour later, Lau sneaks back into his room. He closes the door and is about to turn on the light, when—

"Good evening, Lau," says a deep voice.

He spins around.

The dark man is sitting in the office chair, revolving slowly. "You've been hard at work, I see."

"I ... I just wanted a new idea."

The Devil nods. "And you shall have one. You deserve it."

"So, the dog," Lau whispers. "It's really dead?"

"Stone-cold, rest his soul." The Devil makes the sign of the cross and bows his head in mock grief.

Lau feels both relieved and terrified at what he's done. He decides then and there that the dog will be the last one. He won't do it anymore. If he gets caught, they'll throw him in jail. And what's even worse, no one will ever buy his books once he becomes a real writer.

"Come now, Lau." The guest gets up and gestures towards the chair. "Let's get to it."

Lau sits down at the computer.

***

Hector isn't going to be the last one.

The story Lau got for him is really good. Better than the one for the cat. Bitten reads it out loud in class. She asks if she can take it to the teachers' lounge and show it to the others.

Lau feels extremely proud.

This time, he goes for a full month. He tries to write something every day. But he's back to square one. No inspiration. No words. No ideas. No matter how hard he tries.

One day, Bitten hands out a written assignment in class. She winks at Lau. "I'm very excited to see what you come up with."

Lau tries even harder, but he just can't get any words down. And the assignment is due tomorrow.

Reluctantly, Lau starts considering the idea. Should he make another deal with the Devil?

He has no more poison, but he knows the recipe. And the hemlocks are still there, at the bottom of the garden. So, that same afternoon, he starts making a new batch.

This time, he has no plan. There's no time. He just takes the glass with him in his jacket pocket. He rides out in the middle of the night. It's Wednesday, so most people are sleeping.

Lau goes through the pedestrian street. It's deserted. The row of lampposts stands like silent soldiers, passing by one after another. Lau pedals, and scans, and ponders. Where will he find a suitable victim?

Suddenly, one of the lampposts flickers. He stops under it. Now it's lit normally again.

Could that be a sign?

Lau barely has time to look around before a door opens and a man stumbles out. It's a tavern. Muffled music can be heard from inside. The man has a beer in his hand, his clothes are dirty, and his beard is greasy. He's very drunk. He struggles to walk.

Lau plays with the idea. A human? No, he just can't.

But on the other hand ... who would miss a drunkard? He probably doesn't even have a family, let alone a job. Maybe it'd be kind of a service to society. And to the poor guy himself! He can't possibly be happy living such a life, getting drunk on a Wednesday, smelling like dirt ...

The man seems cheerful enough, though. He's singing softly to himself as he reaches the corner of the building. He tries to unzip his pants. It's difficult with the beer in his hand. So he bends down and puts it on the ground, almost keeling over as he does so. Then, with both hands free, he turns his back and resumes the battle with his zipper.

Lau stares at the beer bottle.

It's his chance.

And he acts before he can think. He parks his bike. He takes out the jar, opens it, and creeps toward the man. Lau can smell him as he gets closer. Kneeling down, he takes the bottle and pours out half of the beer.

The man starts urinating. "Aaaaah," he sighs contentedly, as piss splashes all over the ground and his boots.

Lau pours the poison into the bottle, filling it all the way up. It should be more than enough. He spills a little but doesn't get any on his fingers.

He hurries back to his bike, puts the lid on the jar, and slips it inside his pocket. As he pulls back into the shadows, he checks to make sure no one has seen him.

The drunkard finishes up. He walks back toward the door without his beer.

"Hey!" Lau shouts, startling himself as much as the drunkard.

The man turns his head. It takes a few seconds before he spots Lau. "Wha'?" he grunts.

"You forgot your beer," Lau says, pointing.

The man looks back. "Goodness, me! You're right, I did. Thanks, kid!" The man sends him an exaggerated bow, nearly losing his balance again. "The world needs more people like you, son," he drawls.

Then he waddles back and picks up the bottle. Puts it to his lips and drinks greedily.

Lau hurries home.

***

The idea he gets for the drunkard is really good. The best so far.

This is the story that Bitten suggests he send to a publisher.

That same evening, Lau prays to the Devil again. As usual, the Devil shows up at midnight.

"Nice to see you again, Lau," he says, sitting down on the chair. "You want a new idea?"

"I'm thinking about it," Lau admits. "I would like to try to send a story to a publisher. But it would need to be longer. Like a novel."

"I see," says the dark man. "That would be much more pricey."

"I have already given you a human life," Lau says, frowning. "What could be worth more than that?"

"Well, you see, a life isn't just a life. The value of a particular person's life varies greatly. The drunkard was, to be honest, not worth very much. Even for a human. He was old, ugly, disgusting. No one loved him anymore." The dark man leans forward on the chair, causing it to creak loudly. "If you want a great idea, I need a child. A healthy child. From a loving family. Lots of good years ahead."

Lau feels sick to his stomach. "I can't," he whispers. "I could never do that. I'm not *that* evil."

The dark man gets up and goes to the bookshelf. He casually runs a thin finger across the books. "A real book. A real book with your name on it."

Lau feels a warmth spreading on the inside. It's his innermost desire. His one ambition in life. To write a great book and have it published, for thousands of people to read it. He could become famous. Rich. By touching so many readers' lives, he would influence them in ways he can't even imagine. He would become immortal, in a sense.

"And you're only 13 years old," the Devil goes on, as though having read Lau's mind. "It would be very impressive. The newspapers would definitely want to interview you. Maybe they'll even put you on TV." The dark man picks a seemingly random book and pulls it out. He brings it over and hands it to Lau. "Everyone would be talking about you. The young, promising writer."

Lau forgets to breathe as he sees the cover of the book.

A Life for an Idea, it says. By Lau Jessen. The front page is beautiful and captivating. Lau takes the book from the Devil with trembling hands. He opens it up and leafs through the pages. They are full of words. *His* words.

He closes the book again. The front page has changed. Now it's just a random book from the shelf.

"It can become reality," whispers the Devil. "Right now. If you want it to."

"Right now?" Lau repeats, feeling dizzy.

The guest nods. "I am willing to make an exception. You have been diligent and easy to work with. This one time only, I'll give you the idea in advance. The payment can wait."

Lau bites his lip. Part of him knows he shouldn't do this. Even just considering it is madness.

But another, larger part of him wants it so badly that it physically hurts.

"Okay," he whispers finally.

***

The next day, Lau is completely wasted.

He was up all night. Writing, writing, writing. His fingertips are red and swollen. The story is close to two hundred pages. A proper novel.

It was worth the effort. The story is more than good; it's fantastic. Soon, he can call himself a published writer. He only needs to print out the story and send it to a publishing house. They can't not accept it—there's just no way.

And of course, there's also the payment.

The Devil gave him three days.

Lau prefers not to think about it. He doesn't want to decide who it will be. He simply trusts that a fitting victim will appear on their own once the time is right. Like the dog did. And the drunkard.

He drags himself through the school day. At recess, he's slumped over his table, almost nodding off, when someone slams their hand down his desk hard.

Lau sits bolt upright. "I'm awake! I wasn't sleeping!"

Loud laughter. He blinks and looks around. Everyone is howling and pointing at him. Sofia smiles. "I got you good!"

Lau feels anger rising. "Go away," he snarls.

"You look like a zombie," Sofia says, ignoring him. "Didn't you sleep at all last night?"

"Actually, I didn't."

"Why not? You peed your bed?"

New laughter, even louder this time. Lau feels a stab in his heart. A long time ago, he was secretly in love with Sofia. That's why it hurts even more whenever she bullies him or makes fun of him behind his back.

Lau stares at Sofia. "Why do you always act so mean to me? Can't you just leave me alone?"

"Come on, can't you take a joke?" Sofia says. "Are you that sensitive?"

"You better be careful, or I'll make you my next story." Lau gasps. He didn't realize what he said until the words slipped out.

"Uuuuh," Sofia says, grinning. "That sounds cool. I'd love to be a character in one of your stories. I would make a great hero. Super Sofia, who saves the world!"

The others laugh again. Luckily, none of them understood that Lau was actually threatening Sofia. He gets up, grabs his bag, and leaves the classroom.

"Hey, where are you going?" Zena calls after him.

Lau doesn't look back.

He's got something else to think about now.

The victim just revealed herself.

***

That same afternoon, he gets a text from Lea.

Hey Lau. I'm throwing a party on Saturday night. The whole class is coming. If you want something to drink, you have to bring your own booze. We start at ten. Hope to see you there!

Sofia will be there too. Lau is sure of it. She loves to party, and her and Lea are close friends.

Lau spends the night making a new portion of poison.

***

Saturday comes around, and Lau parks his bike in front of Lea's house at 10:05. He can hear music from the inside.

He has the poison in his pocket. Instead of the jam jar, he put it in a small shampoo bottle. It'll be a lot faster and easier to use. Just a small squeeze, and—

The door opens.

"Hey, Lau!" Sofia grins at him. "Did you bring any booze?"

"Uhm, no," he mutters.

"You're not gonna get drunk?"

"I don't think so, no."

Sofia sighs. "Why are you also so boring? Can't you just relax for once?"

Lau is instantly annoyed. "I am not boring. I'm just—"

"Yes, you are. You are always just sitting alone at your house, writing those weird stories."

Lau throws out his arm. "I want to be a writer! I'm practicing my craft."

"A writer?" She wrinkles her nose. "To be honest, Lau. That's the dumbest thing I've ever heard."

She sends him a wide smile, daring him to rise to the insult.

But Lau just smiles back. As they stare at each other, Lau thinks to himself, *Good. Keep being mean to me. That'll only make it easy.*

"Anyway, you can have some of mine," Sofia says.

"Some of your *what?*"

"Booze, you moron. You're not gonna be the only sober person at the party. Come on, come with me." Sofia grabs him by the arm and drags him inside. "Don't you want to take off your jacket?"

Lau shakes his head. "No. I'm good."

She sends him another look. "You really are strange."

She pulls him through the living room. The others greet him. Sofia takes him to Lea's room. Lea and Tobias are on the bed, making out. Lau feels instantly embarrassed and looks away. He tries to go back outside, but Sofia holds on to his arm firmly.

"Whoa," she grins. "We didn't know someone was already in here."

Lea looks up at them and smiles. "Oh, hey, Lau!"

"Hello."

"I'm going to fix Lau a drink," Sofia says, going to the table, on which there are a lot of colorful bottles. "Dumbass didn't bring any of his own. He thought it was a mocktail party. Anyway, sorry for disturbing you guys."

"It's fine," Tobias says, getting up from the bed. He's obviously drunk and almost loses his balance. "I was gonna go take a piss anyway."

Lea gets up too. "You guys can have the room," she says, blinking at Lau as she passes him.

She closes the door after her, leaving Lau and Sofia alone. Lau's pulse is picking up speed. He can feel his heart pound against the shampoo bottle in his inner pocket.

Sofia is busy mixing the drink. She sends him a look over her shoulder. "Seriously, take off that jacket, will you? You look stupid."

"No, I'm still a little cold."

She grunts and shakes her head. "You're hopeless, Lau." She turns around with a tall glass. "Here! My special recipe. It'll warm you right up."

Lau takes the glass and sniffs it carefully. It smells sweet.

"Thank you," he mumbles.

He's surprised at how Sofia is acting, and he can't really figure out what her motives are. Is she trying to get him drunk so that he'll embarrass himself, and she can make fun of him? That's not unlikely.

She places her hands on her hips. "Well, are you going to taste it or just stand there? You think I poisoned it?"

Lau feels the blood drain from his face. He tries to act normal, and he quickly takes a sip of the drink. "It tastes fine," he mutters.

"Good. Now it's your turn."

"My turn?"

"Yeah!" Sofia gestures toward the table. "Make me a drink."

"Oh ... Okay."

Lau goes to the table and puts down his own drink. He picks up an empty glass and starts pouring from different bottles.

This is almost too easy. As if someone is helping me.

He darts a look over his shoulder. Sofia is lying on the bed, stretching. "I hope you make it a good one," she says. "Have you ever mixed a drink before?"

"Yes, sure I have," Lau mutters. He discreetly zips down his jacket and slips out the shampoo bottle. If anyone comes through the door in the next few seconds, they'll catch him red-handed.

He carefully pops open the cap with his thumb, making sure to cover the noise by clearing his throat. But Sofia doesn't seem to notice anything. She's busy looking at her phone now. He pours a healthy swig of poison into the glass. His hands are shaking so badly, he almost spills. Then he takes a stirring stick and stirs it vigorously.

"I was afraid you wouldn't come tonight," Sofia says suddenly. "I wasn't sure nerds like you even went to parties."

Lau slips the shampoo bottle back into his pocket and turns around. Suddenly, his nervousness is replaced by anger. He turns around and glares at her. "Why do you always have to be like that?"

Sofia looks at him. "Be like what?"

"You always call me names. Nerd, geek, moron, dumbass. You're constantly making fun of me. You laugh at my stories. You mock me. But you're always nice to everyone else. So why are you riding me? What have I ever done to you, Sofia?"

Sofia gets up and comes over to him. She takes the drink from his hand and looks him right in the eyes. "You don't understand girls, Lau."

Then, before Lau can say anything else, she leans in and kisses him. Lau never kissed a girl before. It's warm, wet, and surprisingly soft. Their lips part with a smack.

Lau is dumbstruck. He just stands there, mouth open and eyes wide, as Sofia goes back and sits down on the bed.

"Does ... does that mean ...?" Lau swallows. "Do you ...? Are you ...? I mean ..."

"Yes, your fool," Sofia says, grinning. "I've been crazy about you since fourth grade. Are you seriously telling me you never got the hint?"

A lot of things happen inside Lau at the same time. Different emotions tumble around, bumping into each other. He suddenly sees everything in a completely new light.

"I wanted you to take the first step," Sofia says, shrugging. "You just never did. I got tired of waiting."

She puts the glass to her lips.

Lau leaps across the floor and slaps the drink from her hand. The glass hits the floor and shatters.

Sofia blinks with surprise. "Why did you do that?"

"Did you drink any of it?" Lau grips her face, staring at her lips. "Did you drink any of it!?"

"No," she says, frowning. "Jesus! I didn't even get to taste it."

"Good," Lau sighs, feeling immense relief.

"Lau, what the fuck is going on with you?"

"I have to ... I have to ... I'm going home ..."

"Home? But you just got here!"

Lau leaves the room, marches through the house, rips open the front door, and jumps on his bike.

***

Lau strides around his room restlessly. Constantly checking the clock on his phone. It's close to midnight.

There are eight unread messages and four missed calls. All from Sofia.

Suddenly, the light goes out. Lau turns around. The Devil is standing by the door.

"Good evening, Lau."

"I didn't get you a life," Lau blurts out.

"No, I noticed. I'm very disappointed."

"There was a problem. I had chosen a victim, but ... something completely unexpected happened, and ... and I just couldn't do it ..."

"I know what happened, Lau," the Devil says in an overbearing tone. "I know why you didn't kill Sofia. But the thing is, I still need a life. That was our agreement."

"Yeah, I know. I'll get you one. I promise. I just need a few more days. I'm making more poison."

The Devil seems to be thinking for a moment. "Well, you have kept your promises until now."

"Yes! That's right, I have. And I will keep this one, too. Just please give me—"

"You have twenty-four hours."

"Okay. Okay, that's fine. Thank you so much." He sighs with relief.

The dark man turns to leave. But then he stops. He sniffs. "What's that I smell? Is it ... *a lie?*"

Lau's insides turn to ice.

The Devil turns around slowly to face him. "Are you lying to me, Lau?"

"No," Lau croaks, shaking his head stiffly.

"Yes, you are. You are not going to kill anyone else. You can't do it anymore. Your mind is all filled with Sofia. You're ... *in love.*" He pronounces those last two words as though they're disgusting to him.

"No," Lau says. "No, I ... I'm just a little confused right now ..."

"You are planning to run away. To try and hide from me."

The Devil comes very close, and the burnt smell fills Lau's nose.

He tries to pull back, but the dark man reaches out a hand and grabs him around the neck. The grip is crushingly hard. Lau can't breathe.

"You got your idea, Lau," the Devil whispers. "Now I want my life."

Lau lets out a hoarse wheeze as he's lifted off the floor.

The face of the Devil hovers in front of him, but Lau doesn't want to look at it. Instead, as darkness closes in on him, he squeezes his eyes shut and thinks of the moment Sofia kissed him.

***

You know how Stephen King often has (struggling) writers as his main characters? I never really did that before. It just didn't appeal to me. For one thing, I can't help but wonder how many people can really relate to such a job? Of course, King is great at making it relatable and all, but it just didn't feel right to me. Until the idea for the story you just read came along. It was obvious I had to finally tell a story from the viewpoint of a young, struggling author. And I do think his struggles are pretty easy to see yourself in, if you're being honest. I mean, when we really want something, we're sometimes willing to do some pretty messed-up stuff. It might start with something small. A minor compromise. Then something a little bigger. And step by step, before we know it, we're making deals with the Devil. To me, that's what's really scary about this story.

By the way, did you notice anything familiar about the opening of the very first story? The one the teacher read aloud for the class? They were taken from another one of my short stories, the one called *Under the Skin*. It's featured in *Chills & Creeps vol. 1*, which is also in this collection.

House of Echoes

"How long has it been vacant?"

Tim is sitting on the windowsill. Outside, the rain is pouring down. It's late, and the street lamps are lit. On the other side of the residential street is the empty house.

Julius shrugs. "As long as I can remember."

"So, no one wants to live there?" Tim asks.

"Guess not. The last person was an old man. I think Mom said he died. That was before I was born."

Julius looks over at the house. The rain makes it look distorted. The black windows almost resemble eyes, and the picket fence looks like crooked teeth. Julius gets the feeling the house is looking back at them, and he can't help but shiver.

Tim grins. "Maybe he's still hanging around over there."

"Who? The old man?"

"Yeah. Maybe that's why nobody wants to live there. Because it's haunted."

Julius snorts. "I don't believe in ghosts."

"So you'd be willing to go over there?"

"I've already been over there. Last summer. Helen and I were playing frisbee. She threw it over the fence, and I went in to get it."

"So you were only in the garden?"

"Yeah. But I looked through the windows."

"Did you see anything in there?"

"Nah. It's completely empty. No furniture or anything. Not even curtains."

Tim doesn't answer right away. Julius can tell his friend is getting fired up by the thought of the old, creepy house, so he decides to try and distract him.

"Should we watch that movie? It's getting late."

"It's strange that it's just sitting there," Tim says, not even hearing what Julius said. "Why doesn't the council tear it down or something?"

"I believe they wanted to. Mom said so a few years ago. They even brought machines and a big container, but ..." He trails off.

"But what?" Tim demands. "What happened?"

Julius shrugs. "Nothing. The machines were just there. After a few weeks, they left again. They hadn't touched the house."

"No, because they couldn't." Tim is whispering now. "You can't demolish a haunted house. The ghosts won't allow it."

Suddenly, a thunderclap rumbles in the distance.

"Yeah, right," Julius snickers nervously. "They probably just changed their plans. It was most likely—"

"Let's go over there." Tim's expression has turned excited. "I want to see the inside."

"I told you, there's nothing to see. Just dust and cobwebs."

"Then there's nothing to be afraid of," Tim teases.

"I'm not scared. I just don't want to get wet."

"It's the perfect weather for a ghost hunt. The rain and thunder set the right mood." Tim smiles wryly. "This is when the spirits come out to play, you know. You didn't see anything last summer because it was bright daylight when you looked in there."

Julius sighs. He knows Tim won't give up. Once he gets an idea, he can't let it go. "Okay, just a quick look. But Mom mustn't see us. She'll get mad."

***

The boys sneak out through the back door. Tim doesn't have any rainwear, so Julius grabs his mother's umbrella. The wind is picking up now, almost to the point of storming. Julius nearly loses the umbrella.

As they cross the road, a car passes by, spraying water to the sides. The empty house is sitting there, waiting for them with its gaping, black eye holes. The roof sags a little, the walls are cracked, and the picket fence is missing some boards.

Tim looks at the mailbox. "There's no name on it."

"It's probably worn off. I think his name was Mortensen or something."

"Is the front door locked?"

"How should I know?"

Tim goes up the stairs, tries the door, and it opens. He smiles at Julius. "After you."

"No, after *you*. This was your idea."

Tim makes chicken noises and laughs, then turns and disappears into the darkness.

They should have brought a flashlight. Julius realizes this now, as they stand in the dark hallway. Fortunately, Tim has his phone. He activates the light and shines it around. With Tim leading the way, Julius folds up the umbrella and follows. The light reveals the bare walls; everything is gone, not as much as a nail left. The air is heavy and stale, obviously having been standing still for years.

"Damn," Tim whispers. "This atmosphere is really creepy ..."

Julius doesn't reply, hoping that Tim will soon want to leave.

They wander around the house. All the rooms look the same, stripped down and left empty.

The only things left are the echoes. Every step they take produces a resounding noise. Julius can almost hear his own breathing bouncing off the walls and returning to him.

Tim notices it too. "It's quite echoey in here, huh?"

"Yeah," Julius whispers. "Hey, what's that?"

"What's what?"

"Over there. In the corner." He points.

Tim shines his phone light.

There are three empty beer bottles, some candy wrappers, and an old garden cushion.

"Somebody has been here." Tim moves closer. "Probably a homeless person."

A new thunderclap, this time closer.

Tim looks around. Then he calls out loudly, "Hello?"

"... hello? ..."

"Stupid echo says what?"

"... what? ..."

Tim laughs, and his laughter echoes throughout the house, multiplying, rising in volume, until it gradually dies out and leaves the place completely quiet.

Julius gets goosebumps. "Okay, we've seen it now. Let's go home now."

"Why? Are you afraid of an echo?"

"No, but Mom will soon notice we're gone, and she'll rip me a new one. We're trespassing, you realize that, right?"

Tim doesn't care; he just looks up at the ceiling, and muses, "What if the echoes are voices of the ghosts?"

"What are you talking about?"

"Maybe that's how they communicate? Through echoes? We just think it's our own voices coming back, but it could be the ghosts responding."

"You've lost your marbles." Julius is actually scared now but tries not to show it. "Come on, Tim. Let's go. I mean it."

"Julius," Tim whispers.

"Yeah?"

"Julius," he says again, a bit louder.

"... *Julius* ..." the echo replies.

Julius frowns. "Stop that."

"Juuulius!" Tim shouts.

"... *Juuulius!* ..." the echo repeats.

"Come on, man ..."

Tim takes a deep breath and shouts as loud as he can, "*Julius!*"

A deafening thunderclap shakes the house, drowning out the echo.

"All right, I'm outta here." Julius turns and heads towards the door. "You stay here and play around, but I'm going."

Behind him, Tim laughs. "Wait, man. I'm just teasing. There's one last thing."

Julius reluctantly stops and turns around. "What now?"

"Should we christen it?"

"Christen the house?"

"Yeah!" Tim walks to the beer bottles. "When you christen a ship, you smash a bottle of champagne against it." He picks up one of the beers. "This one should do. What should we call it?"

"I don't know."

"I've got it!" Tim raises the bottle. "I christen thee ... Echo House!" He hurls the bottle against the wall, and it shatters with a loud bang. Glass rains down onto the floor.

This time, there's no echo. In fact, the house suddenly falls very quiet. The storm can't be heard anymore; it's as if the house is holding its breath.

The boys stare at each other in the silence.

Then the sounds slowly return. It's like someone is gradually dialing up hidden speakers until the volume is back to normal.

"What the hell just happened?" Tim whispers.

Julius swallows dryly. "I don't know. But I'm leaving now."

"Yeah, me too."

They rush out to the hallway.

Tim opens the door, and the wind and the rain greet them. As soon as they step outside, Julius breathes a sigh of relief. He's never been so glad to be in the rain.

They're halfway down the garden path when it hits him. "Damnit! I forgot Mom's umbrella ..."

He goes back and opens the door again. As he slips inside, the wind slams it shut behind him. "Just the wind," he whispers. His heart is pounding in his throat. "It was just the wind."

The umbrella is lying on the floor, only three feet away. He reaches for it, and as he does, he senses someone behind him. He turns around, but there's no one there, just darkness. But it *feels* very much like someone is close by.

"Wh... who's that?" Julius croaks.

"... *that*? ..." whispers the echo.

"Hello?" he says a bit louder.

"... *hello*? ..."

Only silence.

He shakes his head and turns towards the door. "Just my imagination."

"... *see you, Julius* ..."

Julius rips open the door and rushes out of the Echo House.

***

That night, Julius has nightmares.

He dreams he's back in the Echo House, running through the rooms, trying to find the door. But it's much, much bigger now, like a labyrinth, and someone keeps whispering his name over and over.

"... *Julius ... Julius ... Julius* ..."

It's the echoes. The voices of the ghosts. He can feel their cold breath.

Then, he wakes up screaming.

Outside, the thunderstorm is still rumbling. Tim is snoring on the mattress on the floor.

"We shouldn't have christened it," Julius whispers to himself. He's not exactly sure what it means; his brain is still groggy, and he's pretty much talking in his sleep. "Now they have come alive. We shouldn't have christened it. Should've never gone over there in the first place."

He slumps back down, falling into restless sleep again.

***

Days pass, and Julius manages to almost forget about the incident.

Then something strange happens.

Julius is on his way home from school when he abruptly stops when he sees the Echo House. The picket fence has been repaired, the missing boards have been replaced, and the rest of them have been painted. They used to be gray and greenish, but now they shine white in the sun.

"How did this happen?" Julius mutters. "Who's fixing the place up?"

He asks his mother as soon as she comes home.

"Apparently, someone has bought the property," she says. "They are probably renovating the house before moving in. Finally! That's very good news. Frankly, it was depressing, having that old dump just sitting there. Don't you think?"

***

Mother seems to be right. The Echo House is being renovated rapidly. Every day when Julius comes home from school, something new has changed. The mysterious thing is that Julius never sees anyone there. Not even a car.

He tells his mother about it.

"They're probably busy," she says. "They might work during the day and do renovations late at night."

Julius wants to see it for himself, so he stays up one evening, keeping an eye on the house. Nothing happens. He stubbornly stays awake, but by 1 AM, he still hasn't seen anything. Eventually, he falls asleep.

***

The next morning, the Echo House has undergone further renovations. The speed of the transformation is truly impressive. First the walls, then the roof, the windows and the front door. Soon, the whole house is repaired and looks almost like new.

Something is bothering Julius every time he looks at the Echo House. He can't put his finger on it, but for some reason, he has a feeling something is off.

One afternoon, he's sitting on the front steps, staring at the Echo House—when suddenly, it strikes him: The Echo House looks exactly like their own house, down to the smallest detail.

Getting to his feet, Julius stares back and forth between the two houses. They are not only similar; they look like identical copies.

No, he thinks, feeling goosebumps climb up his back. *Only one of them is a copy. Or rather ... an **echo**!*

***

After three months, the Echo House is finished. Now there's light in the windows in the evenings. A vehicle has appeared in the carport—a metallic red CitiCar, identical to Julius' mom's.

"Mom," Julius says one day, finally mustering the courage to talk with her about it. "Something is wrong with the house across the street."

"What do you mean?"

"It's exactly like ours. Can't you see it?"

Mother looks out of the kitchen window. "Yes, now that you mention it, it does look quite similar. But that's probably just a coincidence, don't you think?"

"No, I don't think so. I think ... I think they're imitating us."

Mother laughs. "Imitating us? Well, if they like our house that much, I take it as a compliment."

"But everything is just like ours," Julius goes on. "The mailbox, the curtains in the windows, the doorbell, the flowers in the garden, even the car's license plate!"

"Noo," Mom says in an overbearing tone. "That can't be true. Two cars can't have the same license plate, that's not how the system works."

"I'm telling you, they're the same! And I've also noticed—"

"Please calm down, Julius," Mom says, frowning. "There's no need to get so worked up. And frankly, I don't like you spying on them. They're our new neighbors. In fact, I meant to go and say hello to them. I think I'll do so one of these days."

Julius considers it. Perhaps Mom is right. Maybe there's no reason to freak out. After all, they don't know who lives there. They could be perfectly ordinary people.

***

That same evening, Julius lies in bed, unable to sleep. He tosses and turns. Finally, he sits up and reaches for the window. He pulls the curtain slightly aside. The Echo House is dark. The people over there must have gone to bed.

"Who are you?" he whispers.

An idea occurs to him. He gets up and pulls the curtain all the way aside. Then he goes to the light switch, and turns on the light. As he does so, he looks through the window, keeping an eye on the Echo House.

A few seconds later, one of the windows over there lights up.

Julius gasps. He quickly turns off the light.

Shortly after, the light in the Echo House goes out too.

Julius turns on the light again. The Echo House does the same.

He leaves the light on, goes back to the window, and gasps.

There's a silhouetted figure in the window over there, staring right back at him.

Julius squints, trying to see the face, but the person has the light behind them. As far as he can tell, it's a boy. He looks like ...

Julius raises his arm. The person in the window does the same. Julius raises the other arm. The person mimics him.

Julius' heart is hammering away in his chest. Suddenly, his fear turns to anger. Someone is playing tricks on him, and he wants to know who it is. He opens the window. The figure across the street does the same. The night is calm and silent.

"Hey?" Julius calls out. "Who are you?"

"Hey?" the person calls back. "Who are you?"

"This isn't funny," says Julius. "Tell me who you are!"

"This isn't funny," the person repeats. "Tell me who you are!"

Furious, Julius slams the window shut again. If this is a prank, it has gone too far. He's going to trick the guy over there to reveal himself. He goes and turns off the light. The Echo House does the same. Then he returns to the window. He takes out his phone, activates the flashlight, and holds it under his chin. His face is illuminated from below.

He stares at the Echo House. Two seconds later, in the middle of the dark window, a face appears. Julius feels his blood freeze.

*It ... it's **me**!*

Julius staggers backwards and turns off the flashlight. A moment later, the face in the Echo House disappears.

He crawls back into bed. His head is spinning. His thoughts are running in circles, trying desperately to find a logical explanation for what he just saw. But there seems to be none.

He doesn't get much sleep that night.

***

The next day, Julius stays home from school. He tells his mother that he's sick—and he really is. Sick with worry.

His mother leaves for work at nine. Julius keeps watch from the window. He sees her walk to the car, get in, and start the engine. She drives out of the driveway and disappears down the road.

Julius waits with bated breath. "Please," he whispers. "Don't let it happen. Don't let it happen."

But a few seconds later, it does happen.

The front door of the Echo House opens, and a woman comes out. She looks exactly like Julius's mother. Same hair. Same coat. Same handbag. She even stops to adjust her hair in the reflection of the car window, just like Mom did a moment ago. Then she gets into the car and drives away.

Julius feels dizzy. He can't believe it. But apparently, what he feared is true: It's not just the house that is imitating—it's also the family living there.

In that moment, he spots the boy. He's sitting over there in the window, looking back at him, his expression worried.

Julius gets up. He decides it's time to confront their new neighbors.

***

On legs shaky with fear, he crosses the street. He has to. He can't live with the fear of the unknown any longer. So he walks up to the front door of the Echo House and rings the bell.

The doorbell plays the same melody as theirs—of course.

A few seconds pass, and then the door opens.

Julius stares at himself.

At first, it feels like looking into a mirror. But then he realizes there *is* a difference. The boy does indeed look just like him, down to the smallest detail—but his skin is slightly paler, and there are dark circles under his eyes. He looks like a sick version of Julius.

Julius clears his throat. "My name is Julius," he says. "What's yours?"

Also clearing his throat, the boy says, "My name is Julius, too." The voice is just like Julius', only a bit weaker and slightly hoarse.

Julius blinks. "So you *can* talk? I mean, talk properly, not just repeat what I say."

The boy raises his eyebrows. "Why would I repeat what you say?"

"Because you're just an—" Julius stops himself. "Because you did so last night. When I shouted to you from the window."

The boy shrugs. "I don't remember. What do you want?"

"I just ... uhm ..." Julius doesn't know what to say. He doesn't know what he expected. Certainly not this. He gets an idea. "I just wanted to welcome you to the neighborhood."

"All right. Thanks." The boy shows no emotions. He just stands there, completely still, staring at Julius.

There's something strange about him. Julius feels like he's putting on an act. He decides to play along.

"So, where are you from?" Julius asks conversationally, as though he doesn't even notice the weirdness of the situation. "I mean, where did you live before?"

Another shrug. "Not really anywhere."

"What does that mean?"

"I don't know."

"Are you going to start school here?"

"Maybe."

Julius looks at the house. "You've made the place very nice. Did you and your family do it yourselves?"

"Yes."

"How many of you are living here?"

"Three."

"Your father, your mother, and you?" Julius already knows the answer, of course, but he hopes to trick the guy.

"No. My mother, my little sister, and me."

"Okay. So what's your sister's name?"

"Helen."

"That's my sister's name, too."

"Oh." The boy couldn't care less. He's like a zombie. The words have to be dragged out of him.

"Is your sister at home?" Julius asks.

"She's at school."

Julius knows it's a lie. Helen hasn't mentioned a new girl in her class. But if Echo-Helen isn't at school, where is she? And if Echo-Mom isn't at work, where is *she*?

"Well, it was nice meeting you." Julius makes as though to turn around. "I guess we'll see each other around."

"I guess we will."

Julius goes back. But as he reaches the sidewalk, something makes him turn around.

The boy is still there, looking after Julius. And now, he's smiling. Then he steps back and closes the door.

***

"Come on, Julius. That sounds like something you're making up."

"I'm not making it up! Everything I've told you is true."

The boys are in the schoolyard.

Tim looks skeptical. "Are you sure they're not real people?"

"I'm absolutely sure! They're echoes, Tim. We brought them to life when we smashed that stupid bottle."

"Awesome," Tim grins. "This could be front-page news! You'll become world-famous, dude."

"I don't want to be famous. I want them to disappear!"

"Why?"

Julius slaps his forehead. "Why? Well, why do you think? Because they're not real, you idiot! They're supernatural! They're evil!"

Tim shrugs. "How do you know they're evil?"

"I just know. I can *feel* it. That smile he sent me ..." Julius shudders at the thought. "It was an evil smile, Tim. I'm telling you."

Tim still doesn't seem convinced. "Have they done anything?"

"Not yet. But they're planning something."

"Planning what?"

"I don't know! But we have to stop them."

Tim throws out his arms. "How are we going to stop them when we don't know what they're up to? Maybe they're not up to anything. Maybe they're just a little weird."

Julius groans. "You don't get it."

Of course Tim doesn't get it. He hasn't seen a living echo of himself. He hasn't had the eerie experience of looking at someone who looks so much like yourself that they could be your twin.

"Okay, so call the police," Tim suggests. "Report them."

"What good would that do? The police can't do anything. And then the echoes will figure someone is suspicious of them." Julius shakes his head. "No," he mutters. "I'll just have to wait. Keep my eyes and ears open."

***

Mom is home early that day. She's in the kitchen, slicing a cake, when Julius comes home.

"Hey, Julius!" she says with a smile. "Just in time. Our new neighbor is visiting."

Julius freezes.

"She baked a cake. Isn't that sweet? Come on in and say hello," Mom says, leading the way to the living room.

Julius hesitates for a moment, then follows her. He sees the woman sitting on the sofa, an unsettling resemblance to his mom. She looks weaker, with paler skin, bleached hair, and empty eyes. She briefly glances at Julius without smiling.

"This is my son," Mom introduces, placing the cake platter on the table. "Julius, don't be rude now. Say hello!"

"Hello," Julius mumbles, extending his hand.

The woman takes his hand and shakes it. Her touch is cold. "Hello," she responds.

"Guess what this nice lady's name is," Mom says, smiling widely.

"Pernille," Julius mutters.

"Yes!" Mom exclaims. "Just like me. Isn't that funny? And you know what? Pernille has two children too—a boy and a girl, and you'll never guess what? They're named Julius and Helen. What a coincidence, huh?"

Julius doesn't say anything.

"Help yourself to some cake," Mom goes on. "We have plenty of it, because both Pernille and I baked one. I took mine over just as she was taking hers out of the oven. We apparently had the same idea."

They all have a piece of the cake, and there's a moment of silence in the room as they eat.

Julius can't take his eyes off Echo-Mom. She chews slowly and looks around the room. Her eyes are kind of dreamy. She's pale, just like her son, and dark under the eyes.

"It's a nice home," she remarks.

Mom smiles. "Oh, come on. It's nothing compared to yours. Julius, you should see it. They've decorated it so beautifully."

"You've been inside?" Julius is shocked.

"Of course. I got a tour. It's really cozy. I'm actually a bit jealous. They have the sun on their terrace in the afternoons. We don't have that here."

"Why don't we just swap houses then?"

The woman puts it out there casually, like it's a serious suggestion. Julius stares at her in horror.

Mom just chuckles. "You don't mean that. Yours is much newer and prettier than ours."

"No, I really do mean it," the woman says. For the first time, she seems to come alive a little. "We'd love to live here. Your house has more ... soul."

"That's sweet of you, but we can't afford it. Your house is much more expensive, and besides—"

"We'll just swap," the woman interrupts. "No money involved."

"Really?"

"Yes, really."

Mom takes a bite of the cake, contemplating the idea. Julius can't believe what he's witnessing.

Mom smiles at him. "What do you think, Julius? Would you like to move?"

"No!" He vehemently shakes his head. "I won't live there. Not in a million years."

"Julius, mind your manners," Mom says, frowning. "That's not a nice thing to say."

"But there's something wrong, Mom. With the house. And with them. I've told you," Julius insists.

"Julius! That's enough." Mom raises her voice.

Julius looks at Echo-Mom. His heart rate is rising, but he decides to confront her. "How can your house be number 6? Our house is number 6. It makes no sense."

The woman slowly puts her plate down on the table. "It was supposed to be a number 9. The workers hung it upside down by mistake."

"See?" Mom says. "There's nothing wrong."

"Yes, there is," Julius mutters. "I don't want to move, Mom."

"Okay, okay," Mom smiles at Pernille. "We're just playing with the idea anyway."

Julius glances at Echo-Mom, who stares back at him with a dark gaze.

The coffee machine gurgles in the kitchen.

"I'll get the coffee," Mom says, getting up.

She's barely left the room before Echo-Mom leans forward and grabs Julius' arm, almost making him scream.

"Listen here, kid," she snarls. "Do you think it's fun being a copy of others? To be destined to mimic them? We appreciate the chance you've given us, but we have the right to a life. A *real* life. And you won't stand in our way. You understand?"

"Y-yes," he whispers.

She releases her grip and leans back.

Mom returns with the coffee. "Do you take sugar or milk, Pernille?"

***

Days go by, and Julius keeps an eye on the Echo House. There's not much else he can do.

Mom becomes good friends with Pernille. They often meet on the street or invite each other over for coffee.

Helen meets her echo, and they get along well. They have the same dolls.

Julius can't understand how Mom and Helen can't sense that something is wrong. But, in a way, it makes sense. They do have a lot in common with their echoes. And they have no idea that they aren't real people.

Julius hates it when Mom or Helen visits the Echo House. He sits by his window, watching and waiting for them to come back home.

Mom discusses the idea of swapping houses with Pernille. Initially, it's just talk, but Mom becomes more serious. She mentions it often during dinner. Helen is excited about it, but Julius always says a firm no.

He doesn't know what will happen if they swap houses. But he remembers all too vividly what Echo-Mom told him.

"... we have the right to a life. A **real** life."

***

One day, Mom calls for him. She's sitting in the living room with Helen.

"There's something I want to tell you," she says, looking eager. "I've made an arrangement with Pernille. Can you guess what it is? We're swapping houses!"

"Yay!" Helen shouts, clapping her hands. "I'll get a new room!"

"Mom, we can't do that," Julius says, horrified.

"Of course we can. Please don't start with all that nonsense again. We've already contacted the realtor. We're signing the papers tonight. We'll move this weekend." Mom is obviously very excited about the idea. "You can both start packing your stuff."

***

Julius calls Tim, demanding that he come over immediately.

Tim arrives ten minutes later, panting from biking fast.
"What's up, man? You sounded serious."
"It is serious," Julius says. "We're moving."
"Moving? Where to?"
"To the Echo House."
"*What?*"
Julius explains the situation.
Tim looks worried. "Jesus. This is not good, Julius. It really sounds like they're up to something."
"Yes, I know! That's what I've been saying all along."
"What do you think they want?"
"They want to be real people. That's what she told me."
"So, what do you think will happen when you swap houses?"
"I think they'll get their wish. They'll become real people."
"Well ... maybe that's not such a bad thing?" Tim suggests. "Maybe they'll become more ... normal."
Julius leans closer. "But what do you think will happen to *us*?"
Tim looks stunned. "Oh, right. Damn."
Julius nods. "That's what worries me."
The boys talk all afternoon, discussing the situation, turning it over again and again, searching for a possible solution. They come up with an idea that just might work.
"This is how it works in movies," Tim says. "You have to break the curse, fix the damage."
"I know," Julius says. "I'll give it a try. But if it doesn't work ..."
"We'll call the police."

***

In the evening, a storm is brewing. Darkness arrives early. Distant thunder rumbles.
Julius waits in his room, looking over at the Echo House. The door to his room is opened, and his mother sticks her head in. "Are you ready?"
Julius goes out to meet them. Mother and Helen are dressed in their shoes and jackets. They leave the house and cross the street as the rain begins to drizzle. Julius is hiding something under his jacket.
Echo-Mother opens the door. "Oh, it's you." He turns and shouts: "Mother, they've arrived!"
"Show them in, dear!"
They step inside, take off their shoes, and Julius keeps his jacket on.
"Aren't you going to take off your jacket?" his mother asks.
"I'm cold," he mumbles.
They enter the living room.
"Wow, how cozy!" Mother looks around enthusiastically.
Julius doesn't find it cozy at all. In fact, he feels sick.
The living room is dimly lit with lots of flickering candles. The table is covered with a black cloth, and there's a bottle of blood-red wine, six glasses, and, of course, the papers.

The Echo family stands shoulder to shoulder, neatly dressed.

"Welcome," says Echo-Mother. "We wanted to make it look nice here, especially since it's our last evening. We're so excited."

"We are too," Mother smiles. "Are those the papers? We might as well get it over with."

"Yes, let's do that, and then we can toast afterwards," Echo-Mother says.

Mother walks over to the table. Julius' heart pounds wildly. It's now or never. He moves away from the others.

Echo-Julius spots him. "Wait a moment," he says. "Julius still has his jacket on."

Everyone turns to look at him.

"Aren't you going to take off your jacket, Julius?" Echo-Mother asks. Her tone is friendly, but he can sense something darker underneath. Something which says, 'Don't you cause any trouble now.'

"Um ... yeah," Julius mumbles. He unzips his jacket, puts his hand inside, and fumbles for the item. "I just need to ... let me just ..."

"He's a bit strange," Mom says, smiling apologetically. She takes the pen. "He's probably just excited about this, like the rest of us."

The echoes don't take their eyes off Julius.

He gets hold of the empty bottle and pulls it out.

The echoes all gasp.

"Stop him!" Echo-Mother screams.

Julius raises the bottle. "I take back the name!" he shouts. "This is no longer the Echo House!"

"*No!*" Echo-Mother squeals, as both her and Echo-Julius rush towards him.

Julius throws the bottle as hard as he can, but ... it's no longer in his hand. He turns around; Echo-Helen has snatched it. "No, gimme that!" he shouts, grabbing for it.

That's when Echo-Julius jumps on him. They tumble to the floor, wrestling fiercely.

"What in the world are you doing?" Mom yells. "Stop it, boys!"

"Sign it!" Echo-Mother demands, handing Mom the pen. "Right now!"

Echo-Julius ends up on top of Julius and wraps his hands around his neck. He can't break free, and he can't breathe. He squirms, looking up. Echo-Mother has a knife. She points it at Mom.

"What ... what is going on here? Why are you doing this, Pernille?"

"Sign it now," Echo-Mother hisses. "Get it over with, and no one needs to get hurt."

"Don't ... do it ... Mom," Julius croaks.

Echo-Julius tightens his grip. He's unnaturally strong, and Julius feels like he's about to faint.

Mother leans over the table, starting to sign her name.

No! Julius screams in his mind. His vision goes blurry.

Helen starts crying, and Echo-Helen goes to comfort her.

Just as he's about to lose consciousness, Julius sees his chance. He kicks out with his leg, hitting Echo-Helen's ankle as she passes by. She's still holding the bottle. As she falls, she drops it. It flies through the air, hitting the wall, and shatters.

The echoes all jump in surprise.

For a moment, there's complete silence.

Then lightning strikes. Everything is illuminated in a flash. In that instant, they all look the same. White skin, big eyes. No one knows what has happened.

Then comes the thunderclap.

"Nice try," Julius' echo hisses in his ear, tightening the grip even more. "But it was too late."

Julius faints.

***

He wakes up with a start. His heart is pounding. He gasps for breath. He's in his bed. It's early morning. Birds are singing outside the window.

Was it all a dream?

He sits up, looking around. The room looks the same. He's back in his own house. Julius breathes a sigh of relief. He did it! He broke the curse.

But what about ...?

He rushes to the window.

The Echo House is still there. It looks just like he remembers: An exact copy of the house where Julius is. But it must be empty. The Echo family must be gone. Julius sent them back to where they came from—wherever that is.

The door to his room opens.

Helen peeks in. "Hi, Julius. Are you awake?"

"Yes, come in."

Helen comes to the window. "What are you looking at?"

"At the house over there."

"Why?"

"Don't you remember? Something happened last night, which—"

Julius stops abruptly. He stares at his little sister. She looks pale, and there are dark circles under her eyes. Her face is expressionless.

"But you ... you are ..."

Julius looks back at the Echo House. It looks incredibly alive, more than usual. The front door opens over there. Julius himself steps out, followed by Helen. They have a frisbee and start tossing it to each other. They laugh together. Their skin has color. Their eyes are alive.

"What's wrong, Julius?" Helen looks up at him with a questioning expression.

Julius stares at his hands. His skin is completely white. Almost transparent. The truth hits him like a hammer.

I didn't make it ... I didn't make it in time ...

***

Over the next few days, Julius becomes weaker and weaker. He feels tired all the time. The same goes for his mother and Helen.

Julius tries to seek help. He calls Tim, but his friend can barely hear him. He runs out onto the street, stopping cyclists, but they can't really see him.

Soon, Julius can't leave the house. It requires too much effort. So he stays indoors, skulking around the house. Even the interior fades away. The furniture disappears one by one. The wallpaper crumbles. Dust settles in layers. Spiders move in. Soon, everything is bare.

Across the street, the new family seems happy. The mother goes to work, the children go to school, and they have friends over. Tim visits and plays with Julius—the real Julius. In the evenings, there's light in their windows.

Only rarely do they glance at the house across the street.

The house that is now empty and abandoned.

The only thing left is the echoes.

***

Back when we lived in our first apartment, I was standing in the kitchen one day, and I could hear sounds coming from the neighbor's house. Every time I moved, there was a sound. It fit perfectly, as if someone next door was echoing me. It gave me goosebumps. Of course, it was just a coincidence. But it gave me the idea for this story.

Creepy Crawlies

"This is totally awesome!" Nikolaj swings a branch, hitting it against a tree trunk. The sound echoes through the forest. "I can't believe we're all by ourselves. It's like real survival!"

"Yeah," says Frederik, grabbing his backpack. "Only the strongest will make it. Just like in nature."

"That's actually a misunderstanding of what Darwin proposed."

The boys turn to their group's third member. Stefan is the smallest of the bunch. Both Nikolaj and Frederik are disappointed that the scout leader put him in their group.

"What's a misunderstanding?" Frederik asks.

Stefan pushes his glasses up his nose. "That it's the strongest who survives."

Nikolaj throws out his arms. "What are you talking about? That's like a law of nature."

"Yeah," Frederik agrees. "It's called evolution, everyone knows that."

"It's called natural selection," Stefan corrects him. He's slightly out of breath from carrying the backpack. It's almost heavier than himself. "And it's not the strongest but the one who is best adapted that survives."

Nikolaj and Frederik exchange a glance.

"Oh, that's right," Nikolaj says. "I forgot for a moment we got a nerd with us. Isn't there something about you having a nude poster of that guy Edwin?"

Stefan furrows his brow. "I think you mean Darwin. And he's not nude."

"Yeah, whatever!"

"I also have his book, *On the Origin of Species*," Stefan goes on. "It explains everything. How nature selects the best-suited to survive and pass on their offspring."

Frederik scoffs. "Jesus, man. You'll never get close to a girl if you talk like such a huge geek all the time."

Nikolaj laughs.

Stefan looks down.

The boys continue walking. The trees cast long shadows. Dusk is falling. Flies and mosquitos buzz around their ears. It's May, so the weather is warm but not too humid.

Frederik groans. "Doesn't this forest ever end? We've been walking for like an hour."

"How much longer do we have to go?" Nikolaj asks. "What does the map say?"

Frederik takes it out. "Almost there."

"How far are we from the cabin?"

"Three miles."

Nikolaj grins excitedly. "That means no running home in the middle of the night if one of us gets scared." He nods his head toward Stefan.

Frederik chuckles.

"I don't get scared," Stefan says defiantly.

"Oh, right," Frederik scoff. "We forgot you're the best-suited to survive. You'll get to pass on your offspring."

"I never said that. I just said –"

"If it's not the strongest who survive," Nikolaj interrupts, "then how do you think we three would manage on our own out here? Instead of just one night, let's say it was a whole year. Who do you think would come back alive?"

Stefan wipes a lock of hair away from his forehead, and says simply, "It depends on who will be best at adapting."

"You mean, like, finding food? Building camp? Keeping predators away?"

"Yes, among other things."

"I still think the strongest would have the best chances," Frederik says.

"Maybe," Stefan says with a shrug. "Maybe not. Strong people also require more food to survive." He gestures with his hands as he talks. "Nature is constantly changing. Take the seasons, for example. What happens when winter comes? Can we still find meat? Or can we survive on plants? How do we know which ones are poisonous? Can we learn to cultivate vegetables? And what about water? If the streams freeze, then what? Can we break through the ice? Or melt it with fire?"

Nikolaj strikes another tree with his stick. A piece of bark comes off. "Damn, that's gross! Look at this!"

Stefan and Frederik look closer. The tree is teeming with woodlice.

"Nasty," Frederik says, wrinkling his nose. "It's a whole colony."

"Did you know they're edible?" Stefan asks.

"Seriously?" Nikolaj exclaims. "Then try one of them!"

Stefan shakes his head. "They need to be boiled first, but it's a good example of something you might have to do to survive."

"Fuck that, I'm not eating insects." Frederik shudders. "Just the thought makes me nauseous."

"If there's no other food …" Stefan shrugs. "Then you'll die of hunger."

"Okay," Nikolaj says, swinging the branch over his shoulder like a golf club. "I'm starting to get it. Muscles aren't always enough." He glances at Stefan. "Maybe it's not that bad we have you around."

Stefan smiles.

Suddenly, Frederik stops. He stares into a thicket.

"Frederik?" Nikolaj asks. "What's wrong?"

"I think I saw something in there …" He steps closer, then gasps. "Shit!"

Nikolaj and Stefan come over.

On the forest floor lies a deer. It's clearly wounded. Its breathing is labored. Its tongue hangs from its mouth.

"Damn, man," Nikolaj whispers. "What happened to it? Was it hit by a car?"

"Not likely; the nearest road is like five miles away."

"I don't think it was a car," Stefan says, kneeling by the animal. "None of its legs are broken. But look here. There's blood in its fur." He points at the animal's back, and the others notice several wounds along the spine.

"Something bit it," Nikolaj says. "It must have been a predator of some kind."

"There are no large predators around here," Frederik says. "I think the biggest is like badgers or something."

Stefan shakes his head. "I don't think those are bite marks anyway."

"What the fuck do we do?" Nikolaj asks. "I mean, we can't just leave it here. The poor guy is suffering!"

"Not anymore," Stefan mumbles, as he gets back up.

Frederik takes out his flashlight and shines it on the deer's face. It's no longer breathing. Its gaze is empty.

"What do you think happened to it?" Frederik mutters, glancing at Stefan.

"It's quite strange," Stefan says. "The wounds could be from a knife. But they're not bleeding that much. So I'm not really sure what did it."

Nikolaj throws his arms up. "What do we do with it? Should we bury it?"

"That would take all night," Frederik says. "We only have the small foldable shovel to dig shit holes. I say we press on."

Stefan nods. "I agree. It's getting dark soon. We need to set up camp before that happens."

***

"Here it is!" Frederik exclaims. It's ten minutes later. He has pulled the map out again. "This clearing here is where we're supposed to set up our campsite."

"Finally," Nikolaj says, stretching his back. "Let's get the tent up, so I can lie down."

The boys pitch the tent and light a fire like they've been taught to do. They unpack the food they brought and begin eating. The darkness has grown thick all around them. Anything outside the range of the fire's light is no longer visible.

"That was creepy," Nikolaj says, taking a bite of the jerky. "I mean, with the deer."

Frederik looks up from a can of corn. "What was creepy about it? That's just how nature is—right, Stefan?"

Stefan doesn't respond. He's sitting completely still, staring into the flames.

"Hey, Stefan?"

"Hmm?"

"I asked you—"

Frederik is interrupted by a sound from the darkness.

"You guys heard that?" Nikolaj whispers.

"It was just the wind," Frederik says, trying to sound confident.

The boys listen for a moment. They can only hear the crackling of the fire. The forest is completely silent, as if the trees are holding their breath.

"We're not in any kind of danger," Frederik says. "All animals are afraid of fire."

"Not all of them," Stefan corrects him grimly. "Some are actually drawn to it." He gets up and retrieves the flashlight.

"You're not planning to go out there and look, are you?" Nikolaj asks. "You have no idea what made the noise."

"Are you scared?" Frederik teases him.

"Of course not. I'm just saying, this is how every horror movie begins. Something goes bump, and some asshole has to go check it out, and then everyone is eaten alive."

"Come on, man. This isn't a movie. There's nothing—"

Suddenly, there's a buzzing sound. It resembles an electric motor. Something comes floating out of the darkness. It's some kind of nightmare creature. It has transparent wings and thin legs and is the size of a large bird, only there are no feathers or beak. It's heading right for the boys.

Nikolaj jumps to his feet. "Fuck! What is that?"

The creature comes for Frederik who's closest to it. He tries to stand up but trips over his bag. The creature buzzes eagerly, hovering over him, apparently about to land on him. Frederik crawls backwards, attempting to get back on his feet. "*Get it away! Get it away from me!*"

Nikolaj grabs his stick and swings at the creature. It dodges the blow, emitting an angry buzz, and instead comes for him. Nikolaj swings again and again, backing away. "Now it's after me! *Do something!*"

Stefan snaps out of his stupor. He thinks quickly, grabs a stick from the fire, and rushes behind the creature. Thrusting the burning end of the stick up at the creature, he sets one of its wings on fire. The creature whines shrilly, then falls to the ground, buzzing and writhing.

Nikolaj seizes the chance and begins pummeling it with his stick.

"Okay, it's dead," Frederik says finally, pushing Nikolaj away from what is now a messy pile of broken legs and wings. "Jesus, what the hell kind of alien thing is that?"

Stefan kneels down, examining the long, thin legs. "It almost looks like an insect."

"Last time I checked, insects aren't that big. Just look at that thing sticking out of its face!"

"Yeah, I know. It seems to be its proboscis."

"Pro-*whatnow*?"

Stefan retrieves his pocketbook. He flips to the section about flies. "It's a forest mosquito," he confirms, turning the book over for the others to see. The image is identical to the beaten-up creature on the ground.

"It says they're only seven millimeters long," Nikolaj notices. He glances at the dead insect. "That thing is more like thirty inches."

Frederik does the math. "That's a thousand times too big! How did it become so large?"

"I have no idea," Stefan mutters. "But I'm pretty sure it's the one that killed the deer. Or, rather: It's one of them."

"You think there are more?" Nikolaj asks, his voice shrill as he darts a look out into the darkness. "What makes you say so?"

"Because mosquitoes only bite once. The deer had obviously been bitten many times. And judging by how this one came for us, it was apparently hungry, which means it hasn't had any blood recently."

The boys look in all directions. Suddenly, the darkness feels suffocating.

"We need to get away from here," Nikolaj concludes. "It's not safe. If there are more of those monsters out there, then—"

"Where will we go?" Frederik asks, throwing out his arms. "We can't find our way back to the cabin in the dark. We risk getting lost."

"Maybe we can find one of the other groups," Nikolaj suggests.

"We don't know where the others are! That's the whole point of this trip: We have to fend for ourselves."

"Then we'll use the phone."

"It's only for emergencies."

"Are you kidding me? This *is* a fucking emergency!"

Stefan steps closer to the fire. He grabs the water bottle and pours it over the flames. The fire goes out with a hiss.

"What are you doing?" Nikolaj exclaims. "Now we have nothing to defend ourselves with!"

"They're attracted to the light. Turn off the flashlight, Frederik."

"Yeah, okay. Good idea." Frederik turns it off.

The boys stand in the darkness. After a while, starlight begins to filter down. They can see again. They observe the dead giant mosquito.

Nikolaj pokes it with his shoe. "It must be a mutant. From a nuclear disaster or something."

"I'm pretty sure we would have heard of it if there'd been a meltdown," Frederik says. "Besides, shit like that only happens in the movies. There's gotta be a natural explanation." He looks at Stefan. "What would Darwin say about something like this?"

Stefan doesn't answer. Instead, he bends down and reaches out his hand.

"Ew! Don't touch it," Nikolaj says. "Just leave it alone, man."

Stefan pulls something out of the messy pile. "Turn on the flashlight again, Frederik. Just for a moment."

Frederik turns it on.

They stare at the object in Stefan's hand.

"Is it ... a *collar*?"

"Looks like it. And there's something written here." Stefan adjusts his glasses. "Molly—Gen. 53,661."

"Molly?" Nikolaj repeats. "Is that its name? Molly the mosquito?" He bursts out laughing.

"What does the last part mean?" Frederik asks.

Stefan ponders. "I think I have a guess. But it can't be true. I—" He gazes into the darkness. "What was that?"

"What was what?"

"I heard something rustle. It came from the trees over there!"

Frederik shines the light in that direction. "I can't see anything."

"Yes, right there! Higher up!"

Frederik lifts the beam, and suddenly it hits something. Something big, round, and shiny with a spiral pattern. It takes a moment before the boys recognize the object.

"Oh, shit," Nikolaj whispers. "That's a fucking snail!"

"A giant fucking snail," Frederik corrects him, swallowing audibly.

The snail is attached to the trunk, hanging upside down. Its tentacles move slowly. The snail's shell is the size of a beach ball.

"Fuck, that's nasty!" Nikolaj says. "Look at that trail. It's all gooey and sticky."

"It has a collar, too," Frederik notices. "Can you see it? Right there on the shell?"

Stefan walks toward the tree. "Give me the flashlight."

He gets it from Frederik and climbs up. As he approaches the snail, it doesn't react much to him, as if it doesn't care.

Stefan reads from the collar. "Speedy—Gen. 56,912."

"Cool name for a snail," Nikolaj grunts.

"That's really far-out," Frederik says. "Is this forest teeming with these creatures?"

"Yeah, there's no way we're going to sleep," Nikolaj says. "But what do we do?"

"I see light," Stefan says, pointing in a certain direction. "Looks like a house. About half a mile away."

"You sure?" Frederik goes to the bag, takes out the map, and shakes his head. "There shouldn't be a house anywhere near these parts."

"Maybe it's abandoned?" Nikolaj suggests.

"Then there probably wouldn't be any lights on."

"Oh, right. Should we go there? I know we'll fail the task if we come into contact with anyone, but honestly, I don't give a damn about the diploma. I just want—"

A branch snaps somewhere. The boys spin around. Something big dashes away through the forest.

"I think that settles it," Frederik mutters. "I don't know about you guys, but I'm staying here."

The others agree. So, the boys quickly pack up and leave camp.

***

They walk for twenty minutes or so. The forest is treacherous in the dark. They only have the light from their one flashlight. More than once, one of them trips over something or almost walks into a branch.

Nikolaj is noticeably nervous. He walks in front, constantly looking back. "Damn, I really hate insects. Where's that house? I can't deal with being out here—"

"Stop!" It's Stefan shouting.

Nikolaj spins around. "What's wrong?"

Frederik raises the flashlight beam and gasps. "Fuck, man! You almost walked right into it."

Nikolaj spins back around. His stomach turns to ice.

Right in front of him, between two trees, a gigantic spider web is stretched out. It's nearly invisible in the dark, only the light from the flashlight makes it shimmer.

"Holy crap," Nikolaj breathes. "Thanks for the heads up, man ..."

"What's that up there?" Frederik whispers. He shines the light beam up at the corner of the web. A small lump is hanging from the threads. It's the size of a football with black feathers sticking out at the bottom.

"It's a bird," Stefan hears himself say. His mouth feels dry. "I think it's a crow."

"You guys see the spider anywhere?" Nikolaj asks.

"It's hiding," Stefan says. "Maybe up in the trees, ready to pounce if someone touches the web. Come on, let's go around it."

"Wait," Frederik says. He picks up a branch. "Should we try?"

"Try what?" Nikolaj asks.

"To throw something into the web, of course."

"Are you crazy? You wanna end up like that bird up there?"

"I don't think it's a good idea either," Stefan agrees.

Frederik tosses the branch aside, muttering, "Scaredy-cats."

The boys go in a wide circle around the web.

***

Finally, they arrive at the house.

It's more like a small farm, really, and it's located in a modest clearing. The main building has white walls and an old-fashioned, thatched roof. The buildings are old, but someone obviously lives here and takes care of the place. The courtyard is illuminated by two lamps, and a pickup truck is parked in the middle.

"What a creepy place to live," Nikolaj mutters. "It looks like something straight out of a ghost story. Now I just hope they have—" Nikolaj cuts himself off. "Stefan? What's wrong, man?"

Stefan is looking towards the stable, his forehead all wrinkled. "Look at the doors," he mumbles.

The boys go over to take a look. The stable has four doors, all locked with padlocks. Each one has a picture painted in black.

"It looks like a butterfly," Frederik says.

"And that one is a centipede."

"What about this one? A grasshopper, or what do you guys think?"

Stefan nods. "Yeah, and this last one ..." He points to the farthest door. "It just has a crown."

Nikolaj walks up to a window. The panes are small and dark, covered in moisture, but from the inside. "It's pitch dark in there. You can't see a thing. But the glass feels warm."

Frederik puts his ear to the door and shakes his head. "I can't hear anything, and the door is locked." He turns to the others. "What the hell is going on here? Is this an insect farm or something?"

"Yeah, I think so," Stefan says. "Some kind of mega-terrarium. They probably hatch them here. That was actually my guess. Darwin studied animal breeds, and stuff like that. That's how he got the idea for his theory. If you want to make a tiny dog, you take the smallest from each litter. Over several generations, the breed becomes smaller. It's called artificial selection. It's not nature that chooses; it's humans."

"And does it work the other way around too?" Frederik asks. "If you take the biggest insect?"

"Yes, then it gradually gets bigger."

Nikolaj looks sick. "They must be insane. What the hell do they get out of breeding these monsters? I mean, that's seriously—"

Suddenly, the door to the house opens. An older man steps out. He's dressed in a dirty jacket, a cap, and wooden clogs. He carries a shotgun over his shoulder.

"Oh, will you stop being so dramatic?" he calls to someone inside the house. "I told you, it's probably just the transmitter acting up again. You know it's caused trouble before."

The boys retreat into the shadows. They huddle close together, watching the man descend the stairs. One of his knees seems very stiff, and he's limping.

A woman appears in the doorway. She's quite heavy. "I sure hope it's that transmitter again. Because if something has happened to her ..."

"She's fine. I'll find her."

"Just be careful, Paul."

The man stops in the gravel to glance back and wag a dismissive hand at his wife. "Don't you worry about Molly. Just keep an eye on the girl, will you? If she tries anything while I'm gone, give her a good smack on the head. Got it?"

The woman nods hesitantly. "Okay, Paul. Hurry back home."

"I will." The man limps across the courtyard, unlocks the pickup truck, opens the door, and gets in. The engine starts with a dry cough. The truck rolls out of the courtyard.

The woman waves, then closes the front door. The lock snaps.

"Shit!" Nikolaj whispers. "Did you guys hear that? Molly! He's going to check on the mosquito we killed!"

Stefan nods. "It must have had a transmitter, probably in its collar. He must be able to track it."

"What happens when he finds it?" Frederik furrows his brow. "I don't think he'll be happy. And he had a freaking shotgun."

"We need to get the hell out of Dodge," Nikolaj says, looking like he's about to make a run for it. "Before he comes back."

"Wait a minute," Stefan says, grabbing his arm. "Didn't you hear what he said? Something about a girl."

"Yeah, so what? It's probably just their daughter."

"They're at least 70 years old. They're too old to have young children."

"Then it's their granddaughter! Whatever, man! Let's just get away ..."

"No," Frederik says thoughtfully. "Stefan is right. Something strange is going on here. I think we should find out what it is before we run away."

Nikolaj doesn't look thrilled, but he follows along as Stefan and Frederik go towards the house. They peek through the nearest window, only to see an empty utility room. They sneak around to the back garden, checking the windows along the way. They see a bedroom, a bathroom, a kitchen, and finally a living room, in which a fireplace crackles warmly. Faint music is playing. In an armchair sits the woman, knitting away at what looks like a beanie.

Frederik—who's the tallest of the boys—stretches his neck, then gasps. "Oh, fuck! Look over there!"

The others stand on tiptoes. They can just make out the girl. She's sitting on the floor, knees pulled up to her chin. One arm is tied to the leg of the heavy dining table with a rope. Her eyes are big and frightened.

"Holy shit, that's ... Agnes!" Nikolaj gasps. "They've taken her captive! But why? And where is the rest of her group?"

Frederik looks at the others. "See? I knew something was fucked up here. These people must be psychos. We need to call the police."

Stefan has already taken off his backpack. He finds the emergency phone. Dials 1-1-2, but then hesitates. "We can't tell them where we are. We have no address to give them."

"Just tell them the name of the forest."

"But it's huge! It would take them all night to find us. I think it's better to call Torben."

"Then do it. But hurry!"

Stefan calls their leader. The others listen in. The call is answered.

"Hello?"

"Torben? It's Stefan. From group 3."

"Oh, hey, Stefan. So, are you guys having trouble?"

Stefan quickly explains the situation.

Torben sounds very serious. *"Oh, Geez. This is really bad. Where are you?"*

"We're not sure. About half a mile from where we were supposed to set up camp."

"Give me the coordinates. There's GPS on the phone."

Stefan checks and reads out the numbers.

"Damn it," Torben says. *"You've gone way too far. You've entered a private part of the forest."*

Nikolaj shoves Frederik and hisses at him: "You idiot! You misread the map ..."

"Stay where you are," Torben tells them. *"I'll call the police."*

"Okay. Thanks, Torben." Stefan ends the call.

The boys exchange glances.

"Now what?" Nikolaj asks nervously. "We can't just sit around while Agnes is trapped in there. She's in danger. That old hag could hurt her. We have to get her out of there."

"But the woman locked the door," Frederik says. "We can't get into the house."

"Maybe we can find a window that's slightly open," Stefan suggests.

The boys follow the wall and find a small window. It's sitting high up, but it's ajar. Nikolaj reaches in and unlocks the latch, opening the window.

"It's the bathroom," he whispers. "But I can't squeeze through."

"I think I can if you guys lift me," Stefan says.

"Wait a second," Frederik says. "What's the plan here?"

Stefan points at Frederik. "You go around and knock on the door. That will lure her away from Agnes. Nikolaj, you keep an eye on the living room through the window. As soon as she gets up, you whistle. Then I'll know the coast is clear, and I'll run in there and free Agnes."

Frederik nods. "Okay. Do you have your knife? To cut the rope."

Stefan checks. The knife is in his pocket.

Nikolaj folds his hands. Stefan steps up and squeezes through the window. His jacket gets caught, but he manages to free himself. He finds himself in a small, dark bathroom.

"Ready?" Frederik whispers.

"Ready!"

Stefan waits in the darkness. He can hear the music playing. Then a distant knock. The music stops. Someone says something. Then, a moment later, Nikolaj whistles.

Stefan opens the door. The hallway is dark, with many doors. He slips in the direction of the living room and peeks inside. The armchair is empty.

He steps inside, and there's Agnes. She's fumbling with the rope, and then she looks up in surprise. "Ste... Stefan? What are *you* doing here?"

Stefan places a finger to his lips and quickly goes to her. He kneels and takes out the knife, starting to cut the rope. It's wrapped around the table leg multiple times, but luckily, the knife is very sharp.

"They're insane, Stefan," Agnes whispers, almost crying. "I think they were going to kill me. They were debating what to do with me. They couldn't let me go, because I'd seen too much. They mentioned something about ... 'feeding me to the queen.'"

Stefan shudders. He remembers the door with the crown—that's got to be where "the queen" lives ... whoever she is.

"Don't worry," he whispers. "We'll get you out of here. Nikolaj and Frederik are waiting outside." He's almost through the rope now.

"I got separated from my group," Agnes sniffles. "I went behind a tree to pee, and I couldn't find my way back. I must have been wandering around for an hour or so, when I found this place." She looks at him. "Stefan, I think they are breeding—"

They hear shuffling footsteps approaching.

"It's her!" Agnes whispers. "She's coming back, Stefan!"

Stefan cuts the last rope just as the woman—Bente—enters the living room. Agnes frees herself from the rope and gets to her feet.

"There was no one out there," the woman mutters, not looking in their direction. "If it's some of your friends out there, they'll regret it. As soon as Paul gets home, he'll make sure—" Bente stops abruptly as she finally sees them.

Stefan hesitates, shifting his weight from side to side. The woman is blocking the door, which is the only way out of the room.

The woman's expression is a mix of shock, confusion, and anger. She takes a step forward, as though she wants to grab them.

Stefan instinctively holds up the knife. "Stay back!"

The woman stops. She's heavy and much taller than when she was sitting in the armchair.

"Move aside," Stefan orders her. His voice trembles a bit, as does the hand holding the knife. "Let us pass!"

The woman hesitates, then steps aside. For a moment, Stefan thinks they'll be allowed to leave. But the woman goes to the fireplace and grabs the iron poker.

"If you ... if you try to hurt us in any way, you'll go to jail," Stefan warns her, backing away. Agnes stays behind him. "We've called the police. They're on their way."

Bente seems not to hear him. She comes closer, brandishing her weapon like a baseball bat. "Damn kids. Coming here, poking around, trying to ruin our work."

Stefan and Agnes edge around the table.

"Just let us go!" Agnes pleads. "We won't tell anyone, we promise!"

Bente stops, then goes the other way around, staring at them across the table. Her eyes gleam with madness. "You won't be leaving. You know about the animals. We're not going to let anyone take them away. All those generations. All that work. Our family has bred them for centuries."

Stefan catches a glimpse in the window. It's Frederik's face. He's trying to signal something. Stefan doesn't catch what it is. He needs to buy time.

"What about the mosquito?" he asks. "Was that yours too?"

The woman stops again, going the other way, not letting them get close to the door. "What have you done to Molly?" she whispers. "If you've harmed her even the slightest, you'll pay for it. Just wait till Paul gets home. He'll—"

Stefan barely sees the stone coming. It smashes through the window with a loud bang. The woman screams and spins around. Broken glass rains down onto the floor.

Stefan reacts quickly. He grabs Agnes by the arm and pulls her along as he darts for the door.

Bente stares at the shattered window in shock.

"Run, Stefan!" Nikolaj shouts from outside. "Get out of there!"

The woman spins again. Stefan and Agnes are already gone. They run through the kitchen, into the utility room. Stefan grabs the door, yanks it. It's locked. He twists the lock. He can hear Bente. She's coming this way fast.

"Hurry!" Agnes squeals.

Stefan yanks the door open. They tumble out of the house, right into Paul's arms.

"Hey, hey! What's the hurry!" He grabs Stefan by the arm. In his other hand, he's holding the rifle. "Who are you now?"

"Let me go!" Stefan tries to pull free, but Paul's grip is too strong.

Agnes flees across the courtyard.

Bente appears in the doorway. "Paul! Thank goodness you're here! They're trying to escape!"

"Yeah, I can see that." Paul turns around and aims the rifle at Agnes. "I'll stop her ..."

"*No!*" Stefan grabs the barrel, forcing it down.

"Let go, you little shit!" Paul sends him a stinging backhand.

Suddenly, Stefan finds himself on the ground, staring up at the sky, dazed. His face throbs from the blow. He manages to focus on Paul, who's standing over him, grinning. He points the rifle at Stefan, then says: "Cover your ears, Bente."

Stefan closes his eyes.

Then he hears voices yelling and someone screaming.

He opens his eyes again and manages to sit up. He sees Nikolaj and Frederik. They've come to his rescue and are fighting Paul. Bente screams and joins in. She swings the poker and clocks Nikolaj hard over the head, causing him to collapse. He stays down, not moving. Frederik tries to wrestle the rifle away from Paul, but the old man wins the tug of war, and Frederik turns and runs. Paul takes aim. There's a deafening bang. Frederik falls with a scream.

Stefan's ears are ringing. He's barely aware that he's moving. It's like his body is acting on its own accord. He gets to his feet and picks up a handful of gravel.

"You damn little brats," Paul snarls, rounding on Stefan. "One good thing about this, the queen is going to eat well tonight."

Just as he raises the gun again, Stefan hurls the gravel at him. Most of it hits him right in the face. Paul curses, and staggers backward.

Stefan spins around and flees. He runs around to the back of the stable. As he rounds the corner, he almost bursts into Agnes.

Her eyes are huge, her face pale in the darkness, and she's breathing fast. "He shot Frederik. Did you see that? He shot Frederik, Stefan!"

"Yes, I saw it."

"And Nikolaj is unconscious. We have to help them, Stefan!"

"We can't do anything. He has a shotgun, Agnes."

"Wait a second." Agnes fumbles in her pockets. "Where is it? Where is it?"

"You'd better show yourself!" Paul shouts from the courtyard. "If you don't, I'll shoot your friend here!"

Stefan's head is still spinning from the blow. He tries to think clearly. If they run, Nikolaj dies. But if they don't, Paul will most likely kill them all anyway.

"Here it is!" Agnes pulls out a lighter. She looks at Stefan. "We'll burn down the stable, and all those creepy monsters! It will give us a chance to save Nikolaj."

"And the police will see the fire," Stefan mutters. "Good idea. Hurry!"

Agnes has already lit the lighter. She holds it up to the thatched roof, which is very dry and immediately catches fire. The flames rapidly climb up the roof.

"Come on," Stefan says. They run around to the other side of the stable, and from the corner, they peek into the courtyard.

From this angle, they can see Frederik. He's still lying in the gravel, moaning. He seems to have been shot in the leg. Paul stands over him with the rifle. A little farther away lies Nikolaj, with Bente keeping watch over him. She still has the fireplace poker.

Then Paul shouts, "I'll count down from ten! If you don't come out by the time I reach one, I'll shoot your friend! Ten! ... Nine! ... Eight!"

Agnes grabs Stefan's arm. "We have to do it, Stefan. We can't let him shoot them."

Stefan is about to step forward.

Suddenly, Frederik yells, "Run, Stefan! They'll just shoot you the moment they see you! I heard them say it!"

"Shut up!" Paul roars.

"Shut up yourself, you psychopath!"

Paul aims the rifle at Frederik and pulls the trigger.

The shot echoes across the courtyard, reverberating through the surrounding forest.

The ensuing silence is deep. A crow caws somewhere.

Stefan is on the verge of vomiting. He closes his eyes, taking deep breaths through his nose. Beside him, Agnes sobs, trying to stifle the sound with her hands.

Stefan's thoughts are spiraling. Frederik is dead. And Paul still has Nikolaj.

"Did you find Molly?" Bente's voice.

Paul sighs. "She's dead, Bente."

"Oh, no! I knew it! This is your fault, Paul."

"My fault?"

"Yes! You wanted to set them free!"

"I thought they deserved to experience freedom. Besides, they always come back."

"But look at poor Molly now!"

Paul doesn't respond.

Then Bente asks, "What do we do with this one?"

"Throw him in with the queen."

"And what about the other two?"

There's the sound of the gun being cocked. "I'll go find them. They won't get far. I know this forest inside out."

Stefan peeks around the corner. Bente lifts Nikolaj's leg and drags him toward the stable. Paul hobbles in their direction, heading straight for them.

Then Bente screams, "Paul! The stable is on fire! The stable is on fire!"

"For heaven's sake!"

Stefan hears Paul's running footsteps. They disappear around the other side.

"Wait here," Stefan whispers to Agnes. He sneaks along the wall and peers out.

Bente has moved away from Nikolaj. She just stands there, panicking and screaming. The flames have taken hold now, and the roof is ablaze in several places. Paul limb runs toward the house. "I'll get the fire extinguisher! Find the ladder, Bente!"

Bente runs to a shed.

Stefan runs over to Nikolaj. He's still unconscious. Stefan grabs his leg and is about to drag him along, when—

"It was you!"

Stefan whirls around. Paul is suddenly there, no longer holding the rifle. Now he has a fire extinguisher. His eyes gleam in the glow of the flames.

"You little monster. You set our animals on fire!"

Paul raises the fire extinguisher to strike.

At that moment, a screech is heard. It's not human. It comes from the stable.

Paul gasps. "Oh no! The queen!" He limps toward the stable door, fumbling in his pocket, finding a key, and fidgeting with the padlock. "Hold on, my love!"

Meanwhile, more screeches are heard.

Stefan can only watch in horror. The thatched roof is now engulfed in flames. Parts of it have collapsed. Paul finally manages to open the door. Smoke billows out, and he coughs, waving his hands.

Then something large bursts out, knocking him over.

Stefan feels his knees go weak. The scene is simply too grotesque, like something out of a horror movie.

A brown wolf spider, the size of a large Rottweiler, is attacking Paul. It's burnt in several places, but that doesn't stop it from grabbing him with all eight legs.

The old man lets out a cry. "*Stop! It's me, my love!*"

But the spider doesn't care. Holding him firmly in place, its jaws snap audibly, biting Paul in the chest, then the shoulder, then the neck. He tries to defend himself, but the spider is too fast. Soon, Paul stops screaming. He goes limp.

The spider releases him and turns toward Stefan. It has eight black eyes, all fixed directly on him. He's completely exposed and defenseless. As the spider sprints toward him, he prepares himself for the pain.

Then a hiss, and a thick, white mist appears from behind him.

Agnes has come running. She's picked up the fire extinguisher and is now using it against the spider. The large insect screeches, backing away as the foam sticks to its body.

Then the entire roof of the barn collapses. A large chunk of burning thatch falls onto the spider. It goes completely crazy, twists, screeches, all eight legs thrashing desperately.

"*No!* What have you done?"

Stefan and Agnes turn around. Bente stands there with the ladder. She drops it and rushes to Paul and the spider. She falls to her knees. The arachnid is already dead, its legs giving off some last twitches.

Agnes points the fire extinguisher at Bente, and Stefan picks up the poker, ready to strike her if she comes for them. But Bente stays down, sobbing weakly.

Something catches Stefan's eye. He looks up and sees a huge, burning butterfly flutter up toward the black night sky.

***

Half an hour later, the farm is swarming with police officers. There's an ambulance too. Frederik and Nikolaj are being taken away. Nikolaj survives with a concussion. Frederik is not so lucky. The second shot killed him instantly.

Stefan and Agnes are taken away in a police car.

Bente is arrested, and Paul's body is examined.

The stable has burned down, and all the insects are dead. Cleanup is about to begin.

Two young police officers observe the devastation.

"It's almost a shame," Janus says. "I mean the insects. I would have liked to see them."

"You still can," Dennis says.

"What do you mean?"

"Haven't you seen the silo? Behind there?"

"No."

"Come with me."

The two officers walk behind the stable. There's a tall silo camouflaged by common ivy. The door is securely locked, but there's a large window.

"They think it's a colony," Dennis says. "It even goes underground. There could be hundreds inside."

"Hundreds of what?"

Dennis points. "Take a look."

Janus steps closer and peers through the glass. On the other side is sand. It seems the silo is filled with it. There's a tunnel dug through it. Just then, a giant ant comes crawling by right on the other side of the glass. It stops briefly to peer out at them before it crawls on.

    Janus gasps. "Oh, Jesus ... That's the biggest ant I've ever seen!"

    "Yeah," Dennis says, chuckling. "You might even say it's giant."

    Janus looks at him. "What's so funny?"

    Dennis throws out his arms. "Get it? Gi*ant*."

    Janus sighs. "You have a sick sense of humor, Dennis."

***

I'm not particularly afraid of insects. I'm not exactly thrilled about them either. But I don't run screaming when I come across one. My wife, on the other hand, does. She tries her best not to panic when she spots a spider in the house. This story is for her and everyone else who can't stand creepy crawlies (big or small).

Nightmare

"Hey, Markus. So, you're back again. I was hoping not to see you anymore." The doctor smiles at him.

Markus stares at the table. The light in the ceiling is very bright. The room's walls feel suffocating. The silence is deafening. The only sound is his mother's sniffling. Somewhere in the building, someone is laughing loudly. Or maybe the person is screaming.

The doctor leans forward. "I understand the nightmares have returned?"

Markus becomes very aware that the mark on his arm is visible. He discreetly tries to cover it with his sleeve, but the T-shirt is not long enough.

The doctor notices it, of course. "Have you been scratching yourself?"

Markus shakes his head.

"Looks like scratch marks to me."

"It was a jellyfish," Markus mutters.

"A jellyfish? You got stung?"

Markus nods.

"Were you dreaming about swimming?"

"Not exactly," he says, talking slowly. "I was in the sea, but far from land. I think I fell off a ship or something."

The doctor makes a note on his laptop. "And what happened while you're in the sea? Were you attacked by jellyfish?"

"No, it was just one. And it just kinda swam by. I don't think it did it on purpose. That's not what's unsettling about the nightmare."

"What is unsettling, then?"

Markus hesitates.

"Were you drowning?" the doctor guesses.

Markus shakes his head. "I don't know yet. I just had this feeling that ... something terrible was gonna happen."

"Were you alone in the dream?"

"Yes. I was completely alone out in the middle of the sea."

The doctor looks at his screen. "Your previous nightmares were about being trapped in a burning house. Or being bitten by rats. Chased by a werewolf. Strangled by—"

"Do we really need to go through all that again?" Mom interrupts. She stares at the doctor with teary eyes. "We thought it was over! Why has it come back now? Why does he suffer from new nightmares?"

"That's what we're trying to figure out," the doctor says calmly. "That's why we'll keep Markus here for a few days. We have a new drug that I would highly recommend. It has a very good effect on ..."

Markus isn't listening. He knows the routine. Hospitalization. Pills. Talks. The nightmares will go away. He'll come home again. After a few weeks, it starts all over.

"Markus?"

The doctor's voice brings him back.

Markus blinks. "Yes?"

"Do you have any other injuries? Besides the mark on your arm?"

Markus shakes his head.

"Not yet," Mom says grimly. "But they will come. They always do. At first, it's just small things."

"Anne," the doctor begins, using a very parent-like voice. "I think you're scaring Markus. Maybe it's better—"

But Mom doesn't listen. "Suddenly, one morning, I find him covered in wounds. His hair is pulled out in tufts. He has bruises and bite marks. *Bite marks*, for God's sake! How can someone bite themselves in their sleep?"

The doctor takes a deep breath. "It's not uncommon at all. There are worse cases than Markus's."

"But how do we make it stop?"

"We have to figure out what the dreams mean. Why they started. What's causing them."

"It began ... it began after his brother died."

"Exactly. And *he* suffered from nightmares too, correct?"

Mom nods and sniffles. "They ... they killed him."

"It says here that Thomas died of cardiac arrest while he was asleep. It wasn't technically the nightmares that—"

"But it was!" Mom exclaims. "He was going through a really bad period. He would wake me up every night. Screaming and kicking. He rambled about Nazis chasing him. They wanted to kill him with a poisonous injection. I didn't listen. I was so tired of his episodes. And Markus was so young. So I had to take care of him." Mom starts sobbing again. "I should have woken him up. But I was so tired. I couldn't take it anymore. So, I put in earplugs. And the next morning ... the next morning, I found him ... completely cold ... his eyes—"

"I think we'll stop here," the doctor says, clearing his throat. "Like I said, we'll keep Markus under observation for the first few nights. Just until the medication starts working. There's no reason to worry."

Mom picks up her bag and wipes her eyes as she leaves the room.

At the door, the doctor stops and turns. He looks at Markus with a serious expression. "Your mother is just worried about you. I promise you, you don't need to be afraid. You're in good hands here. What your brother died from was a heart condition. It had nothing to do with the nightmares. Nightmares are not dangerous—just unpleasant. Okay?"

Markus forces a smile and nods.

He knows better, of course.

**

Mom kisses him goodbye, completely distraught. Markus watches her leave the building.

Then a nurse shows him to his room.

"This is where you'll stay. You can unpack if you like."

The room is furnished with a bed, a table, and a small bathroom without a lock. The windows can only be opened a few inches. He has a view of the garden. It's nice. He sits for a while and watches the birds.

At 5 pm, it's medication time. Markus goes to the common room, and stands in line. There are children of all ages. Some look like zombies. Others smile nervously. Some seem very sad.

"Hi, Markus," Lone says. "Nice to see you again. Well, you know what I mean."

Markus smiles. He likes Lone. She is a small, kind lady with gray hair.

She finds him on the list. "Okay, I see you're getting a new medication today. We've had good results with this one. I think it will help you."

Markus tries to look optimistic. He takes the small cup, swallows the pill and washes it down with water.

He goes to the sofa area and sits down, watches TV until dinnertime. Some of the other residents play Scrabble. Someone is humming as they walk around the room.

At 9:45 pm, it's bedtime. The TV is turned off. The lights are dimmed. Some have already gone to bed. The rest are helped along by the staff.

Markus goes to his room. He brushes his teeth in the bathroom. Takes off his clothes and puts on his sleeping shirt. He sits on the bed and waits. A minute later, Lone comes in.

"Well, I see you're ready," she says, taking a seat in a chair. She has a book with her. "How are you feeling?"

"Okay."

"Are you scared?"

"Only a little."

"That's good. I'll just sit here if you need anything."

Markus crawls under the covers. "Goodnight, Lone."

"Goodnight, Markus."

Markus closes his eyes. Takes a deep breath through his nose.

This is the worst time of the day. Just before he falls asleep. Because he knows what awaits. He always lies awake for a long time, trembling. Thankfully, the medication helps, and he falls asleep fairly quickly.

***

The first hours of the night pass peacefully.

Lone manages to read ten chapters of her book. It's a good one, keeping her engrossed and preventing her from getting tired. By the time it's 3 am, she has only yawned once.

Now and then, she glances at Markus. The boy is sleeping peacefully.

***

Around 4 am, he starts mumbling in his sleep.

Lone listens but can't understand the words. It doesn't sound like a nightmare, so she waits a bit. Reaches over and touches him on the forehead. He's quite warm. In fact, he's sweating. Maybe she should crack open a window.

Lone gets up.

At that moment, Markus lets out a hoarse scream.

Lone spins around. Now he's tossing his head from side to side. Whispering in his sleep. Trying to scream. His eyes are squeezed shut. He flails his arms.

"Markus! Wake up!" Lone hurries to the bed. She grabs him by the shoulders, shaking him. "Wake up, Markus! You're dreaming."

Markus opens his eyes. He looks around wildly. Gasping for breath.

"You're not in danger, Markus. It was just a nightmare." She steps back a bit, giving him space to breathe. "How are you feeling?"

"My ... foot ..." he croaks. "I cut myself ... I'm bleeding ..."

"Your foot is fine. You just had a dream."

Markus sits up. He wipes the sweat off his forehead with his sleeve. "My foot," he mumbles again. "It hurts ..."

"You just need to wake up properly. Something to drink might help. You want a glass of water?"

Markus doesn't answer; he pulls back the covers.

Lone stares at his foot. Stares at the blood that has stained the sheets red. "How ... how on earth ...?"

"I stepped on a sharp stone," Markus whispers. "It cut me."

Lone regains her composure. She checks the foot. There's a gash on the heel. It doesn't seem too serious. She also senses a distinct smell of salt. It must be his sweat. There are actually white patches on the boy's skin. She's never seen anyone with such salty sweat before.

"Wait here, Markus. I'll go get a wash cloth and a Band-Aid."

***

The next day, the doctor is called in.

A nurse helps Markus into the meeting room. He struggles to put weight on his left foot. The heel is bandaged. It throbs a bit from the wound. Thankfully, it didn't require stitches.

"Hi, Markus," greets the doctor. "Looks like you had a restless night."

Markus doesn't respond. He just plops down on the chair. The nurse leaves the room.

"Your mother hasn't arrived yet," the doctor says. "I thought we'd have our conversation here first." He smiles encouragingly. "Waking up to that must have been quite a shock, huh?"

"Yeah," Markus mutters.

"I'm actually a bit confused. Lone didn't see how it happened. She thinks you might have cut yourself with your toenail. But the on-call doctor said the wounds were too deep to be caused by a toenail. So, I'm hoping you can tell me how the wound came about?"

Markus stares at the doctor for a while. Then he says, "I cut myself on a stone. It was on the seabed."

"Now we're talking about the dream, right?"
"Yes."
"So, you were back in the sea?"
"Yes. But this time, I could touch the bottom. I must have been closer to land."
"And you stepped on a stone?"
"Yes."
"Did anything else happen?"
Markus hesitates. "I ... I felt someone."
"Who?"
"I don't know."
"But there was someone in the water with you?"
"I think so. It was very foggy. I couldn't see well."
"What happened then?"
"Nothing else. Then I woke up."

The doctor types on his computer. "I have to ask you something, Markus. You know that knives and other sharp objects are forbidden here in the ward, right?"

Markus nods.

"Did you have anything sharp with you when you arrived? Scissors? A nail file? Anything that could cut?"

Markus shakes his head. He doesn't break eye contact with the doctor.

Then the doctor smiles. "The brain can do incredible things, Markus. It can actually turn imagination into reality. Did you know that? If you imagine something and truly believe in it, it can manifest in the body. I once saw a woman who believed she was pregnant. So, her belly started to grow. But there was no baby inside. Isn't that amazing?"

"I guess."

"That's why it's important not to believe in the dreams. You understand?"

"I do."

The doctor closes the laptop and folds his hands. "Tonight, I think we'll try something different. You'll have someone on guard, of course. But in addition to that, I suggest we restrain you. It might sound a bit extreme, but it's not dangerous. It's just to prevent you from scratching yourself in your sleep. What do you say?"

***

Mother comes by an hour later.

She is horrified by what happened. She scolds the nurses, saying that Markus might as well be at home if they can't take better care of him here.

But she doesn't suggest taking Markus with her when she leaves.

***

At bedtime, Markus enters the room and stops in the middle of the floor. The bed looks like something from a torture chamber. The belts are thick and brown. He can't help but wonder how many insane people have been strapped down before.

There's a gentle knock on the door, and Lone enters, smiling at him. "So, Markus, are you ready?"

"I guess."

Lone nods toward the bed. "Have you tried the belts before?"

"No."

"They're not nearly as bad as they look. If you lie down, I'll help you."

Markus lies down, and Lone gently fastens the belts. One around each ankle, one on each wrist, and one around his waist.

"Is it okay? Not too tight?"

"It's fine."

"Good. If you start feeling uncomfortable, just let me know." Lone takes a seat in the chair with her book and a big cup of coffee. She smiles at Markus. "I'll make sure to wake you up if you have nightmares."

Markus tries to smile back, but he's already afraid. The medication makes him groggy as well. Nonetheless, it takes a while before he falls asleep.

***

Lone drinks all the coffee, not wanting to risk falling asleep this time. The caffeine keeps her awake, but unfortunately, it also gives her a strong urge to use the bathroom.

At two o'clock, she can't hold it any longer. She puts her book down, glances at Markus, who is finally asleep, and sneaks out to the toilet, leaving the door to the room slightly ajar. She listens carefully while she pees, but there's no sound from Markus.

Afterward, she washes her hands, dries them with a towel, and steps back into the room.

She immediately freezes in place.

Markus is sitting upright in bed, as much as the belts allow him. He stares directly at Lone.

"Markus?" she asks, swallowing. "Are you okay?"

The boy's eyes are big and white in the dim room. His lips move, and he whispers something.

"Markus?" Lone suddenly isn't sure whether he's awake or not. She approaches the bed. "Markus, can you hear me?"

Markus responds in a whisper.

"What are you saying?" she asks, leaning closer.

"Baikokudo," he whispers.

"Markus, you must be dreaming," she says, placing her hand on his shoulder, but she pulls it back abruptly as Markus snaps his teeth at it.

"Baikokudo!" he shouts, staring accusingly at her. His face contorts in anger. "*Baikokudo! Baikokudo!*"

"Markus! Wake up!" Lone grabs his arm and shakes him hard.

The boy blinks, gasping, and comes back. The rage dissipates, and he starts crying. "I heard them ... they're after me ... they're after me, Lone!"

"There, there," she says, quickly loosening the belts and embracing Markus. "There's nothing to be afraid of. You're awake now."

The door opens, and a nurse peeks in. "Is everything okay in here? I heard someone yelling."

"He had a nightmare," Lone explains. "Get the on-call doctor. We might need something to calm him down."

The nurse nods and disappears again. Lone rocks Markus and comforts him.

"I heard them," he whispers. "They want to hurt me."

"Who did you hear?" Lone asks.

Markus sniffs and whispers, "The men on the beach."

***

"Well, Markus, it seems like the belts worked well. You don't have any new injuries," the doctor observes. "But you seem a bit unwell. I understand you had another nightmare?"

"Yes."

"Were you back in the sea?"

"Yes, but I'm close to the shore now. I can see a beach."

The doctor makes notes on his computer. "What's happening on the beach?"

"It's very foggy. There are men riding horses. Some kind of warriors. They're searching for me."

"How do you know that?"

"Because they're shouting at me."

"Do they call your name?"

"No. They speak a language I don't understand."

"What do you think they want?"

Markus's breathing becomes quicker. "They want to hurt me."

"How do you know?"

"I can feel it. I can hear it in their voices. They're just waiting for me to reach the shore."

The doctor falls silent for a moment. "We'll increase your medication. It should start to work and reduce the nightmares. For now, I think we should keep the belts on, just to prevent you from hurting yourself."

Markus doesn't respond.

"I also think we should try a sleeping pill."

Markus looks up abruptly. "No, I don't want that."

"It's just to ensure you have a peaceful night."

Markus shakes his head vehemently. "It doesn't work. It just keeps me from waking up. We tried it last time. It was terrible. I don't want it!"

"Okay, calm down, Markus." The doctor holds out a hand. "Then we won't do it."

Markus calms down again.

"I do remember you had a bad experience with it last time. But you also need sleep. And you look like someone who could use it."

"I'll manage," Markus mutters. "Just, please, no sleeping pills."

***

Before dinner, Markus walks around the garden. It's springtime, and the trees are budding, the birds are singing, and the sky is blue. By the other end of the lawn, a couple of boys are playing soccer.

"Hey, Markus," Lone says, smiling at him as she comes towards him. She must have just arrived for work. "How are you doing?"

"Fine," Markus replies.

"I wanted to talk to you about something that happened last night," Lone says.

Markus kneels down and plucks a dandelion. "Okay."

"You were sleep-talking. You repeated a word several times, and I wrote it down." She takes out her phone. "It was … 'baikokudo.'"

Markus feels a hint of déjà vu and starts pulling the small yellow petals from the flower. "I remember that. It's what the men were shouting."

"Do you know what it means?"

"No."

"Well, I looked it up. It's Japanese and means 'traitor.'"

Markus feels a surge of goosebumps under his jacket. It makes sense. The men in the dream were angry with him. They apparently believed he had betrayed them in some way.

"I just find it strange," Lone says, looking up at the sky for a moment. "That you spoke a word in perfect Japanese. But I figured, it's probably something you've heard, like from a movie or something."

"Yeah, probably," Markus mutters, dropping the dandelion.

Lone smiles. "I don't know why I asked. Forget about it, okay, Markus?" She gives his shoulder a gentle squeeze. "The nightmares will soon pass. I'm sure of it."

***

After dinner, Markus goes to his room and takes out his phone. He searches for the word from the dream, not knowing how it's spelled, so he tries different variations. He finds information about Japan, its ancient traditions from the Middle Ages. Suddenly, he finds a relevant result.

It's about betrayal, considered the worst crime, punishable by the harshest sentence: death by beheading with a samurai sword.

"They're samurais," Markus whispers. "The men on the beach are samurais."

He continues reading, shaking so much that it's hard to keep the phone steady. After the beheading of the traitor, the body is cut into seven parts—head, arms, legs, chest, and stomach. That's what the men want to do to him. Markus feels nausea rising in his throat. He puts the phone down and holds his head in his hands, sweating.

Tonight, he'll probably reach the beach in the dream. He mustn't let the men see him. If they catch him, they'll kill him. Markus doesn't want to die. He needs help.

***

There's a knock on the door.

"Come in," Markus says.

Lone enters the room. "Hi, Markus. It's time again."

"Yes," Markus says.

Lone comes to his bed, smiling at him. "If you lie down ..."

"Not yet."

"Is there something you want to talk about?"

Markus bites his lip. "You have to help me."

"Of course, Markus. That's why I'm here." Lone pulls over the chair and sits down.

"You need to wake me up every half hour, so I don't dream anything."

Lone tilts her head. "I don't think that's a good idea, Markus. You need to sleep, and if I keep—"

"It's just for a few days until the medication starts working. Until the nightmares go away."

"I promise you, I'll wake you up if I see you having a nightmare. I'll keep a close watch."

Markus swallows dryly. "I just hope you're faster than the samurais then," he whispers.

"Samurais?"

"Yes. The men on the beach. They're samurais. They think I betrayed them. They want to behead me and cut me into seven pieces."

"My goodness, Markus! What gave you that idea?"

"I just know," Markus mutters. He feels like crying. "But it doesn't matter. You don't believe me anyway. No one does."

***

It takes Markus two hours to fall asleep. He's more frightened than usual.

Lone feels sorry for him and hums while stroking his hair. Eventually, he's completely exhausted and finally drifts off. He starts snoring softly.

Lone takes her book and opens it to the bookmark.

She can't really concentrate. She keeps thinking about what Markus said about the samurais. Was it a mistake to tell him about the word he said in his sleep? But where did he even hear that word in the first place? Is it just from a movie? Or could the nightmare possibly be ...?

Be what? Real? Now she's being silly.

Lone shakes her head and continues reading her book.

Markus is very quiet.

The first thing she notices is the sweat. It beads on his forehead. She pulls the blanket aside and observes him for a while. His sleep still seems calm. She can't be sure if he's dreaming, but it doesn't seem that way.

Ten minutes later, his breathing changes. It becomes slightly faster. Lone puts the book down, leans over him, and asks, "Markus? Are you dreaming?"

He doesn't respond.

She reaches out, taking him by the shoulders, just about to shake him when he suddenly opens his mouth and screams, "*Leave me alone! Go away!*"

Lone almost falls off the chair. She instinctively pulls her arms back.

Markus jerks his head from side to side. "*Nooo! My legs!*"

His arms and legs begin twitching wildly. They're kept in place by the belts. Lone stands frozen for a second, and in that moment, she sees something incredible. Red streaks appear on Markus's legs. They are scratches, and some of them start to bleed.

"What on earth ...?"

"*No!*" Markus shrieks. "*Let me go! Let me go!*"

Lone lunges forward and slaps him on the cheeks. "Wake up, Markus! Wake up!"

His eyes open wide. They are the wildest eyes Lone has ever seen.

"It's me, Markus! You're awake now ..."

Finally, she sees recognition in his eyes.

The boy starts sobbing. "They almost got me ... they almost got me ... one of them grabbed my shoulder ..."

Lone doesn't know what to do. She looks at Markus's torn legs and notices something else. His feet are suddenly covered in sand.

At that moment, the door swings open. "What's going on?"

"Doctor!" Lone shouts. "Right now!"

The nurse disappears again.

Lone looks at Markus. "I'm going to loosen the belts, Markus, so you can sit up."

"My shoulder," Markus sobs. "He grabbed my shoulder ..."

Lone notices something. The skin around Markus's collar is dark. She pulls down his T-shirt and gasps.

There are clear bruises from four large fingers.

***

Lone is sitting in the meeting room when Markus enters. She looks very tired.

"Good morning, Markus," says the doctor. For once, he isn't smiling. "Please have a seat."

Markus sits down. He glances at Lone, who sends him a faint smile.

"Lone's shift actually ended an hour ago," says the doctor. "But she offered to stay a little longer. We have already discussed what happened last night. Maybe you can help us, Markus."

Markus doesn't say anything.

"May I see the injuries?" asks the doctor.

Markus pulls up his T-shirt.

"Yes, it does indeed look like a handprint," the doctor mutters. "What about your legs?"

Markus stands up and pulls up his pant legs. The scratches aren't very deep. Most of them don't even need bandages.

"Thank you, Markus. Have a seat again." The doctor looks at the monitor. "You were restrained. No one else touched you. And the injuries weren't there when you went to sleep, right?"

Markus shakes his head.

"So how in God's name did it happen?"

Markus remains quiet for a while. Almost a full minute. The doctor and Lone both wait for him to start talking.

"I reached the shore," he begins. His voice is weak and hoarse. "I fled along the beach. It was hard to see anything because of the fog. But I could hear them. I could hear their horses. I ran up into the dunes. There were thorn bushes. They were the ones that scratched me. I almost got away ... but one of them ... one of them was lying in wait." Markus starts rubbing his thighs under the table. His voice rises. "He grabbed me while he was grinning. Then he called the others. I tried to break free, but he was too strong. The others gathered around. They were just about to ... they were just about to ..." Markus breathes quickly now.

"It's okay, Markus," says the doctor. "We don't need to talk about it anymore—"

"They were just about to behead me!" Markus blurts out. "And afterwards, they were going to chop me into seven pieces. They're planning to try again tonight. I can't sleep anymore. It's too dangerous." He looks imploringly from the doctor to Lone. "You have to help me. You must give me something to keep me awake. You must—"

"Calm down, Markus. It was only a nightmare. A very scary nightmare, but it wasn't real."

"Yes, it was! Where else do you think I got these injuries from?"

"I think you caused them yourself," the doctor states bluntly. "Either you did it while Lone wasn't looking, or it's your psyche that has caused them because you still believe the dreams are real."

"So either I'm lying, or I'm crazy?"

"I didn't say that."

Lone clears her throat. "There was also sand."

"What?" the doctor asks, frowning. "Sand?"

"Yes, there was sand in Markus's bed. At his feet. Quite a lot, actually. I don't ... I don't understand where it came from."

The doctor shakes his head. "It must have been the cleaning staff who overlooked it. What's your point?"

"I'm just saying ..." Lone hesitates. She bites her lip and glances at Markus. "Maybe it's not just something Markus imagined. Maybe there's another explanation."

Markus feels a great relief. Lone believes him! Finally, someone believes him!

The doctor doesn't look pleased. "Let's not put more ideas into Markus's head. He's already scared. We risk making his condition worse."

Markus jumps up, the chair goes flying backward. "Why don't you believe me?"

"Markus, calm down. Otherwise, we'll have to—"

"I can't take it anymore. I want to go home!"

"You can, of course. But I still think—"

Markus doesn't listen. He walks over and pulls open the door.

***

Markus has just finished packing his bag when Lone enters the room.

"Can we talk for a moment?" she asks.

"Okay." Markus plops down on the bed. Most of his anger has dissipated. Now, he just feels exhausted and anxious.

Lone comes over and sits down next to him. "I think it's better if you stay, Markus."

"Why is that? You're the only one who believes me."

"Exactly. And I have the night shift again tonight." Lone rubs her forehead. "I have no idea what you're going through. I've never seen anything like it. I don't think anyone has. That's probably why no one believes you."

Markus's heart starts racing. "Only my brother believed me," he whispers. "He went through the same thing."

Lone meets his gaze. "Maybe it's your mind that's making it real. Maybe it's a rare illness. Or maybe ... maybe you have a connection to something we don't understand." She shakes her head. "Whatever the explanation is, it's not just nightmares. I think you're in danger. And I want to help you."

Markus is close to breaking into tears of relief. "How?"

"We'll do what you suggested. I'll wake you up every half hour, so you don't have a chance to dream."

Markus embraces Lone. "Thank you. Thank you so much."

Someone clears their throat. In the doorway stands a young nurse. He didn't knock, so they didn't hear him.

"Yes?" Lone asks.

"Markus has a visitor. It's his mother."

Markus gets up. Wipes his eyes. "Okay, I'll come now. Tell the doctor I changed my mind. I want to stay here."

The nurse smiles briefly. "Sure thing."

Just before he closes the door, he glances at Lone.

***

Of course, Mom starts crying as soon as she sees Markus.

Markus sits and waits for her to finish. Suddenly, a thought strikes him.

"Mom," he says. "There's something I want to ask you. It's about Thomas."

Mom wipes her nose. "What about him?"

"You said he dreamt about Nazis. And that they wanted to poison him. Did he say anything else?"

Mom dabs her eyes and shakes her head. "I can't remember, Markus. He said so much. Most of it was nonsense."

"It's important," Markus insists. "Please try to remember."

Mom gives him a puzzled look. Then she shrugs. "There was something about the Nazis threatening him. They didn't want him to tell anyone about them. They called him a snitch and stuff like that. Sometimes he also spoke in German. In his sleep, I mean. It was really strange."

Mom says more, but Markus stops listening.

Suddenly, he understands it all. Why the samurais called him a traitor. Why they're after him. It's obvious, really: He has told Lone and the doctor about them. He has told them everything. That's why the nightmares have only gotten worse.

He can't help but shiver. Thank goodness Lone agreed to help him. Otherwise, he wouldn't survive the night. He's sure of it.

***

Lone is not the one handing out medication that day.

"Name?" asks the new nurse.

"Markus Grøndal. Where is Lone?"

"Lone is not here. Here you go." She hands Markus the cup.

Markus doesn't take it. "But ... she said she had the night shift."

"She got off. Take your medication, please."

Markus stares at the cup. Suddenly, the connection dawns on him. The male nurse overheard what Lone said to him. He must have snitched to the doctor. And the doctor has suspended Lone. Or maybe even fired her.

"No," he mutters, shaking his head. Fear overwhelms him. The thought of a night without Lone to wake him up is too much for Markus. He knocks the cup out of the nurse's hand.

"Hey! Why did you do that?"

Markus spins around and sprints towards the door. He doesn't think about his belongings. He just wants to get away from here.

Someone calls after him. Markus dashes down the corridor. Just before he reaches the main entrance, a nurse steps in front of him and grabs him.

"No, I want to go home! Let me go!"

Markus squirms and wriggles.

Another nurse joins in. Markus keeps fighting. The nurses talk to him, asking him to calm down. But Markus can't. He's too scared.

Other patients gather around. Markus sees a row of pale faces through a blur of tears.

A tall figure appears. It's the doctor. He says something Markus doesn't understand.

Then he feels a prick in his butt.

Shortly after, everything goes black.

***

Markus opens his eyes slightly. He's in his room. It's dark outside the windows. He's restrained. He's very, very tired.

He manages to turn his head. The young nurse is in the chair. He's wearing headphones. He notices Markus and takes off the headset.

"Hey, Markus. My name is Michael. I'll be with you tonight."

Markus tries to speak. His lips feel strange.

"Don't worry, buddy," Michael smiles. "You've been given a sleeping pill. So you'll get a good night's sleep. Just close your eyes."

Markus panics. He tries to fight against the sleep. But it comes over him like a black wave. His eyes close. And Markus drifts away.

One last, coherent thought flies through his mind: *I should never have told them ...*

***

Michael keeps it up until 3 am. He listens to the music, humming along, drumming the rhythm on his knees. He tries his best to stay awake.

The patient just sleeps peacefully. There are no problems.

At some point during the night, Michael dozes off.

With a start, he wakes up again. The room is bright. It's morning. He immediately looks to the bed, and sighs with relief.

The patient is still there. He's lying under the blanket, his head turned away.

Phew, that was lucky, Michael thinks. No one has noticed that he slept. He takes off the headset. Stretches. "Well, Markus. Time to wake up. Breakfast will be served in a few minutes."

He reaches over and nudges the boy. He doesn't react. The sleeping pill really knocked him out good.

"Good morning, sleepyhead!" Michael says loudly.

He pulls the blanket aside.

And starts screaming.

***

For years to come, the incident is still talked about.

The screaming nurse who needed crisis counseling. The doctor who moved to another department. The month-long police investigation which came up without any reasonable explanation.

And, of course, the patient who was chopped into seven pieces during the night.

***

Nightmare is based on an urban legend a friend once told me. I can't recall the details, but it was something about an ancient punishment where a person would be chopped into seven pieces in their sleep. Pretty gruesome, huh? Of course it immediately gave me the idea for the story you've just read.

As I wrote it, I was aware that it was also drawing inspiration from *A Nightmare on Elm Street*. Those movies certainly gave me nightmares as a child. That's why I purposefully didn't go into the dreams to describe what happened there; I didn't want it to be too much like the Elm Street movies, and I also wanted to keep it kind of a mystery what exactly Markus was dreaming about. That's why I switched viewpoints whenever he was dreaming.

Hope the story won't mess with your sleep tonight. And if you dream of someone calling you a traitor, you might want to do everything you can to wake up …

Eternal Snow

"*Good afternoon, it's 5 o'clock and time for a weather update. It's still snowing all over the country, and it looks like we're heading for a record-breaking white Christmas. However, there are also reports of traffic accidents. Several drivers have been caught off guard by the slippery roads. It is therefore advised not to venture out unless absolutely—*"

The voice on the radio is cut off as Mom reaches over and changes the channel. "Shouldn't we listen to something with a bit more Christmas spirit?"

She finds a Christmas song. It's some cover version of *I'll Be Home For Christmas*.

"Have you tried calling again?" Dad asks, gripping the steering wheel tightly. He's trying to follow the road, but it's difficult even seeing it with all the snow.

"There's still no coverage," Mom replies. "Never mind. I'm sure Mom will understand that we're a bit delayed due to the weather."

Leo sits in the backseat, looking out at the white, wave-like landscape. Heavy snowflakes fall from the dark sky. Some of them land on the window and then melt and slide off.

Beside him, Emmy plays on her tablet, some kind of Christmas game. Now and then, she cries out when she falls through the ice or gets crushed by a giant snowball.

"How much longer until we get there?" Leo asks, stretching his neck. He tries to see the clock on the dashboard. It's 4:58. They should be at Grandma's by now.

"We're one mile closer than a mile ago," Dad answers.

Leo sighs. "Very funny. Mom, when will we be there?"

"Not much longer now, Leo. We're almost there."

"Sure hope they cleared the road to her house," Dad says. "Or we might have to walk."

Emmy shifts in her seat. "I want to play in the snow! I'm going to make a snow angel."

"It's dangerous to lie down in the snow," Leo says. "You might get buried."

"Mom, Leo is going to bury me!"

"I didn't say anything about that. I just said you might get buried."

"But you mean you'll bury me."

"Only because you need a bath." He leans over and sniffs. "Phew, you smell like farts."

"No, I don't!" Emmy looks back at the tablet and lets out a shriek. "Ow, now I'm dead!"

"Will you two please be quiet?" Dad glances in the rearview mirror. "It's difficult enough to concentrate without all the screaming."

"Emmy," Mom says, "we agreed that you would only play three levels. Put the tablet away now, okay?"

Emmy obeys, sending Leo a dark look. "I've lost my last elf hat because of you."

"Oh, wait a second!" Dad suddenly slows down. "I think this is it."

The sign sticks out from the snowdrifts, easy to overlook. Dad makes the turn. The engine works hard to plow through the snow.

"Who's going to push if we get stuck?" Dad asks.

"Not me!" Emmy exclaims.

"Not me!" Mom says.

Emmy nudges Leo. "Leo! You forgot to say, 'not me.'"

Leo doesn't respond. His gaze has caught something in the darkness. For a moment, there was a light. It blinked yellow and then disappeared in the snowfall.

It was probably just the light from a nearby farm. Or, perhaps, from another car that had dared to venture out.

Leo doesn't know why, but he feels a slight unease in his stomach.

Emmy shifts again. "Mom, I really need to pee."

"I know, dear. I have to go too. We're almost there. We can use Grandma's toilet. Look! The house will be visible as soon as we turn here."

The road makes a slight bend. The car's headlights follow the curve. The house comes into view in the darkness. There's light in the windows. Leo is looking forward to the crackling fire in the fireplace and the smell of Grandma's Christmas food.

"Does Grandma have a Christmas tree?" Emmy asks.

"I'm sure she does." Mom turns in her seat. "Start putting on your jackets now."

"Can we unbuckle?"

"Yes, go ahead. Dad will be careful during the last hundred yards."

Dad looks straight ahead and mumbles, "Looks like she hasn't cleared the yard."

"Of course not. She's 79, Henrik. She's had enough to do with the food."

"I'm just saying."

They pull into the courtyard. Leo and Emmy put on their jackets, hats, and gloves.

"It looks quite dark," Dad remarks, stopping the car. "Are you sure she's home? Maybe she changed her mind and went to your sister's for Christmas."

Leo looks outside and realizes Dad is right. There's no light in any of the windows. It was just the reflection from the car's headlights he saw.

"Oh, cut it out," Mom snaps. "She's probably just taking a nap. Come on, kids. Remember to wipe your boots before going inside."

Leo opens his door. He steps out into snow up to his knees. The snowflakes hit him in the face, and he pulls his beanie further down. He kicks the snow as he makes his way around the car. He stops when he sees the tree. Grandma has put up string lights on the branches, but the small bulbs are off. Leo's unease returns.

Maybe she's waiting to turn them on until we arrive. Yes, that must be it.

He runs after Mom and Emmy. They've already reached the front door. Mom opens it and steps inside. Leo follows and takes off his beanie. He expects to be greeted by a warm blast of air, but the temperature in the hallway is not much higher than outside. And it's as dark as night.

"Remember the snow, like I said," Mom reminds them.

Leo and Emmy stomp their boots.

"Where's the switch?" Mom asks.

"I really have to pee!"

"Yes, yes. Come with me. Leo, go in and let Grandma know we're here. If she's sleeping, don't wake her. Just help Dad with the gifts, okay?"

Leo nods and takes off his boots. Mom and Emmy disappear down the hallway to the bathroom. Leo walks toward the kitchen door. Just as he's about to unzip his jacket, something makes him keep it on.

When he opens the door to the kitchen, he's met with the same darkness and cold. He stands still for a moment and listens. No music. No humming. No crackling of flames. Not even a creaking floorboard.

"Grandma?"

He steps onto the wooden floor, fumbling along the wall. He finds the light switch. It clicks, but there's no light.

Power outage, Leo thinks. *That's why the lights on the tree aren't on.*

His eyes have already adjusted to the dark. He senses the table, the sink, and the stove. He walks through the kitchen and looks into the living room. The furniture is sitting there like dark shapes—armchairs, sofa, TV. The fireplace isn't lit. In the middle of the room is a large, decorated Christmas tree. Presents of different sizes are on the rug beneath it. The star on top nearly touches the ceiling, but it seems dull and lifeless, just like the rest of the decorations.

"Grandma?"

A small, white cloud forms in front of his mouth as he speaks. The living room is just as freezing cold as the kitchen and hallway.

Leo is no longer uneasy; he's genuinely afraid now. He runs back to the front door. Dad is about to enter, carrying a lot of gifts.

"Hey, watch out, Leo. There are a few more still in the car. Would you mind—"

"Something's wrong, Dad."

"What? Help me with these, please."

Leo takes some of the gifts. "I can't find Grandma, and there's no light. The whole house is freezing cold."

Dad finally catches on. He looks toward the kitchen door. "What do you mean? Hasn't she turned on the heating?"

"No. And I think the power is out."

Dad furrows his brow. He puts the last gifts down and takes off his shoes, then goes into the kitchen. "Margaret?"

His voice trails off in the darkness.

"That's really odd ..."

Dad continues into the living room, and Leo follows closely behind.

"Did you check upstairs, Leo? Maybe she overslept."

"No, I haven't been upstairs."

The toilet flushes.

A moment later, Emmy rushes into the kitchen. "Grandma? Oh, who turned off the lights?"

Mom comes in with a puzzled expression. "The lights aren't working in the bathroom, so we had to ... wait, what's going on in here?"

"The power is out," Dad says. "And your mom didn't light the fireplace. I don't think she's home, Bitten."

"Of course she's home. I spoke to her half an hour ago. She was preparing the duck. Mom? Hello?" Mom goes out into the hallway, calling up the stairs. Leo can hear a touch of worry in her voice now.

"Where's Grandma?" Emmy asks anxiously.

"We're trying to find her, sweetheart."

Leo goes out and follows Mom upstairs. He catches up with her at the light switch, which clicks futilely.

"No light up here either," she mumbles. "Mom? Are you in the bath?"

She opens the door to the bathroom. Empty, dark, and cold. Now, Mom starts opening doors quickly.

The sewing room. The bedroom. The guest room. No Grandma anywhere.

"What's going on?" Dad calls from the kitchen. "Have you found her?"

"No!" Mom yells. Leo can hear her hurrying down the stairs.

He runs after her.

When they are all gathered in the kitchen, Mom suggests, "Try calling her, Henrik."

"I just did. I have no signal out here."

"What about the garage?" Leo asks. "Maybe she went out to get a flashlight or something when the power went out."

"Good idea, Leo," Mom says. She runs to the entrance hall. A moment later, the front door opens.

"Dad, I'm scared," Emmy says, close to tears. "Why can't we turn on the lights?"

"There's no need to be scared, dear. The power just went out. It's probably because of all this darn snow."

"But where is Grandma?"

"We'll find Grandma in a moment. When we do, we'll take her to Aunt Heidi's. How about celebrating Christmas there instead?"

Leo notices the oven. "There's something inside," he mutters.

He goes over and opens the door. A faint smell of roast duck comes out. In a baking dish lies a duck, half-cooked. But when he touches it, the skin is cold and soft.

"She had started on the food when the power went out," Dad murmurs. "You can tell she was in the middle of it."

Leo looks over the table. It's filled with utensils, a bowl of red cabbage, a cutting board, and much more. The whole house reminds Leo of a video game on pause.

Emmy spots a glass bowl with Christmas sweets. She goes over and reaches for a piece of marzipan. She puts it in her mouth but quickly spits it out. "Yuck! It tastes like dust."

"Emmy, for goodness' sake. Be polite."

"But it really tastes like dust, Dad."

Leo takes a piece and bites into it. Emmy is right. The marzipan tastes old and dry, as if it's been out since last Christmas. Leo shivers. It's not just because of the cold.

The front door opens. Mom comes in with snow in her hair. She shakes her head. "She wasn't there."

"Now I know what happened," Dad says. They all look at him. "Grandma was in the middle of preparing Christmas dinner when the power went out. She couldn't get it back on, so she eventually called Aunt Heidi. She asked them to come and get her. Maybe she couldn't reach us, possibly because our phones don't have coverage out here. So instead, she didn't lock the house when she left. Of course, she turned off the fireplace to avoid accidents while the house was empty. I'm sure she's waiting for us at Aunt Heidi's. It's only a half-hour drive from here. I say we leave right away. That way, we can still make it in time for the meal."

"Why didn't she leave a note?" Leo asks.

"Maybe she did," Dad says. "We just haven't noticed it in the dark. Or maybe she forgot it in the confusion."

"You're right, dear," Mom says. "That must be how it happened."

Leo doesn't believe Dad's explanation. He feels like it has something to do with the light. The little blinking light he saw way out in the darkness. He just can't explain why.

"Put your boots back on, kids," Dad says. "We're going to Aunt Heidi's."

***

Soon, they are in the car again, steadily making their way through the snow. The wipers battle the constant stream of snowflakes, and the headlights can only pierce a short distance into the darkness.

"Have you tried calling again?" Dad asks. "Maybe we have a signal now."

"No, still no connection," Mom mutters. "Do you think a phone mast fell in the area?"

"I'm pretty sure they put the cables underground these days."

Emmy makes a sound. She has taken out her tablet and is busy saving elves.

Leo looks out the window, and his breath fogs up the glass. He thinks about the light. The little blinking light.

Leo's restlessness gnaws at him. He can feel it in his chest, like a rat trapped and trying to get out. But it's not just inside him. The atmosphere in the car is heavy. Even the music doesn't help much.

Something terrible has happened. We just don't know it yet.

The radio plays a familiar tune, and then a voice says, "*Welcome to the news, it's 5 o'clock. The snow continues to fall across the country. Everything seems to indicate that ...*"

Leo straightens up. "Did he say it's 5 o'clock?"

"Hmmm?" Mom says. "I didn't pay attention."

"He definitely did."

"Maybe it was a mistake." Mom reaches over and changes the channel. "I could use some Christmas music now."

A melancholic song fills the cabin.

Leo furrows his brow. "It's the same song."

"They play the same things over and over again during Christmas," Dad says. "There aren't many songs to choose from."

Leo looks out the window again. There's something almost magical about the snow-filled darkness. There are no landmarks. Nothing to reveal where they are. If he stares too long, he can almost make it seem like they're standing still. As if it's only the snowfall moving around them. As if the car is stuck on an invisible treadmill.

"What the heck?" Dad exclaims, slowing down. He looks at the sign they just passed. "I didn't know there are two roads named Beacon Lane out here ..."

"Guess there must be," Mom says.

"It did look like Grandma's road," Emmy says, looking up from her elf game.

"I thought so too," Dad murmurs. "But it can't be. We haven't turned around."

"Are you sure we didn't make a wrong turn somewhere?"

"Yes, I'm sure. We haven't turned at all. I haven't seen a single side road. But you can't see a thing in this weather, so we probably just passed it, or maybe—"

"Okay, okay," Mom interrupts. "Let's just drive back to Grandma's house."

"Why? She's not home."

"No, but maybe we have to wait. Just until the snow stops. You said yourself that you can hardly see where you're driving."

Dad grumbles something, as he sharply turns the steering wheel and enters Beacon Lane.

"Is Grandma home now?" Emmy asks.

"Maybe," Mom mumbles, without conviction.

The half-baked lie doesn't deceive Emmy. In the light from the tablet, Leo can see her chin trembling. He reaches over and takes her hand. It's freezing.

"Don't cry, Emmy."

"But Grandma is gone."

Leo forces a smile. He wants to reassure Emmy. "Grandma is probably just—"

Emmy points out of Leo's window. "Look, Leo! There's a light."

He stares in that direction. His heart picks up speed. "Where?"

"It was out there in the darkness. Now it's gone." She looks thoughtfully at Leo. "Do you think it could be Grandma? Maybe she went out into the snow with her flashlight and got lost?"

Leo chews on his lip. "I don't know."

But the light is the answer. The answer to whatever has happened.

He's sure of it.

Just then, they see the house again. Leo is once again fooled into thinking there are lights in the windows. But as soon as they turn into the courtyard, he can see that it was the car's headlights.

"Okay, listen," Mom says, looking at them. "We'll go into Grandma's house. We'll light the fireplace. We'll wait here until we get in touch with Grandma. Or until the snow stops."

They zip up their jackets and leave the car. The snowstorm rages with the same force. Leo walks with Emmy holding his hand. They are almost at the front door when something dawns on Leo. He stops and looks back.

"Come on, Leo!" Emmy pulls on him. "I'm getting snow in my eyes!"

"There are no footprints," Leo mumbles. He grabs Dad's sleeve. "Dad, look. Our footprints from before ... they're completely gone."

Dad glances over the courtyard. "Of course they are; it's snowing like hell. Come on, let's go inside before we get buried alive."

Emmy lets go of Leo's hand and goes with Dad. Leo lingers for a moment. It's not just their footprints. The car's tracks are also gone. The snow is perfectly smooth. Completely untouched. As if they were never here.

"Leo!"

Mom pulls him out of his trance. He hurries after the family into the house. The cold and darkness welcome them back.

"I'll light the fire," Mom says. "Try to find some blankets. We can stay warm until the fire starts."

Leo goes up the stairs to the second floor. He's not entirely sure why. It's as if something is drawing him. He enters the sewing room and stands before the blackness of the window. The icicles make the window look like an open, square mouth. Or an opening to another dimension.

At first, there's nothing but darkness and snow. But then he spots the light. It blinks away bravely. A gust of wind shakes the roof. Leo shivers all the way down his back.

"The answer," he whispers.

He stands there for a long time, staring at the light in the snowstorm. He loses track of time. Everything else fades around him. It's just him and the light. Blinking. Blinking. Blinking.

Dong! ... Dong! ... Dong!

Leo becomes aware of a sound. It's very far away, almost too faint to hear. He snaps back. Now the sound is gone. Maybe it was just his imagination. Maybe it was his own heartbeat. But it sounded like ...

He looks around. A grandfather clock is standing by the wall. When Leo was little, he loved sitting in front of it, waiting for the clock to strike the hour. The chimes sounded like something from a fairy tale.

He walks up to the clock, listening. It's not running. Leo knows it doesn't run on electricity; it needs to be wound up. Maybe Grandma forgot to do it. The hands are frozen at 4:58, just two minutes away from the hour.

But I just heard it ... Or did I?

In the living room, Mom exclaims, "It's unbelievable. None of the matches work. I can't even get a spark."

Leo goes out into the hallway. He's about to go down the stairs when he catches a movement out of the corner of his eye. He turns.

The door at the end of the hallway. It has just opened ajar. A faint light seeps through the crack. It's Grandma's bedroom.

Leo's heart races. He's not sure if it's relief or fear that's making it pound.

Leo walks toward the door. Just before he reaches it, a voice comes from inside.

"Yes, of course I've tried calling them. Six times now!"

Leo recognizes his grandmother's voice. She's talking to someone on the phone.

He pushes the door open, and in that moment, the light disappears. As if someone switched it off.

The bedroom is empty, cold, and dark. Just like the rest of the house. The bed is neatly made and untouched. The snowstorm presses against the window, trying to get into the room.

Was it just his imagination? Some sort of daydream?

He walks over to the bed and notices a slight indentation in the duvet. He places his hand there and feels a faint warmth.

Grandma was sitting here, just a moment ago. But where did she go?

Leo spins around, feeling like he's not alone. He senses that someone else is in the room with him.

"Is that you, Grandma?" he whispers. "Where are you? What happened?"

"Leo?"

Leo lets out a yelp and spins around.

Emmy is standing in the doorway, looking startled.

"Jesus, you scared me!" Leo breathes.

"Who were you talking to?"

"No one. Just myself."

"Dad says we're leaving again."

Leo follows Emmy down the hallway. As they pass the sewing room, he says, "Wait a second, Emmy." He enters the room and opens the window, which is a bit stuck due to frost. But he manages to get it up. The wind hits him.

"What are you doing?" Emmy asks from behind.

Leo reaches up and breaks off an icicle. He throws it out into the darkness and closes the window.

Emmy looks at him skeptically. "Why did you do that?"

"It's just an experiment. Come on now."

They go downstairs and find their mother in the living room.

"I can't get the fireplace started," she says, rubbing her arms. "It's as cold as the grave in here. But your father thinks the snow has eased up a bit. He's gone out to start the car. We're trying to make our way over to Aunt Heidi's."

Leo just nods. He goes with them outside and puts his boots on again.

**

They drive through the endless darkness and the endless snow, which is pouring down as if it wants to bury the whole world.

Leo doesn't take his eyes off the window. He's looking for the light. He knows it will appear soon.

Emmy has started playing her elf game again. Mom and dad are talking about calling Grandma.

The radio is playing its tune. The feeling of déjà vu washes over Leo.

"Good afternoon, it's 5 o'clock and time for a weather update. It's still snowing all over the country, and it looks like we're heading for a record-breaking white Christmas. However, there are also reports of traffic accidents. Several drivers have been caught off guard by the slippery roads. It is therefore advised not to venture out unless absolutely—"

Mom reaches over and changes the channel. "It's Christmas Eve. Why aren't they playing music instead?"

"Didn't you hear that?" asks Leo. "They said it's 5 PM. They said the same thing last time."

"That must be a mistake," Mom mutters, seeming absent-minded. She finds a Christmas song instead, "I'll Be Home For Christmas."

"What time is it really?" Leo asks.

Dad looks at the dashboard clock. "It's 4:58. We still have plenty of time."

"But ... that can't be right. The clock has already been 5, twice."

"Leo, look!" Emmy says. She grabs his arm and points. "There's the light again!"

Leo almost throws himself against the window, shielding his eyes with his hands. He catches sight of the light. It's still blinking. It almost seems teasing, as if it's deliberately keeping its secret.

"We're getting close to Grandma's house now."

"Did you see it, honey?" Mom exclaims. "That sign back there?"

"Yes," says Dad. "It looked like it said Beacon Lane. But that doesn't make any sense. We just drove away from Beacon Lane."

Mom and Dad discuss for a bit and agree to drive back to Grandma's house.

Leo keeps his eyes fixed on the window, seeing the reflections of the car's headlights. They pull into the courtyard. There are no tracks in the snow.

"All right, kids," Mom begins.

Leo has already unfastened his seatbelt. He opens the car door and jumps out. He runs to the house and lets himself in. Everything is still dark and cold. He takes the stairs two steps at a time, enters the sewing room, and stops in the middle of the floor.

The icicles are still hanging there. All of them. None are missing.

Leo feels his stomach drop. *What happened at two minutes to five?*

He catches sight of the light. It blinks at him from the darkness.

"They were supposed to be here by now," a voice says. "I'm really worried, Heidi ..."

The voice makes Leo turn. Grandma comes walking past the door, but it's not really her, just an indistinct figure. She holds a cellphone to her ear. Then she's gone again.

"Grandma!" he exclaims, rushing out into the hallway.

It's empty. Grandma has vanished.

Okay, that's it. I want to know what happened.

Leo remembers something. He scans the room with his eyes. On the top shelf of the bookcase is what he's looking for: Grandpa's old binoculars. Leo borrowed them when he visited Grandma last summer. He steps up on the lower shelf, stretches, and manages to tip the binoculars down and catch them.

He goes to the window. Pauses for a moment.

From downstairs, he hears his family.

Emmy: "Is Grandma home now?"

Mom: "I don't think so, dear."

Dad: "Try to find some blankets. I'll light the fireplace."

Leo lifts the binoculars and searches in the darkness. And then he finds the light.

He feels his heart stop. Or rather, he realizes it has already stopped.

Leo stares at the back of a car. Only one corner is visible. The rest is buried under the ice of a frozen lake. One of the taillights is blinking. In the orange glow, he can barely make out the license plate. But he doesn't need to read it. He knows the car.

Leo drops the binoculars on the floor. He goes downstairs. Finds the rest of his family in the living room.

"I don't get it," Dad grumbles. "It just won't light. I've used up all the matches."

"It's almost warmer in the car," Mom says. "Maybe we should leave again?"

"It won't do any good," Leo says evenly. "We can't get away."

All three of them look at him.

"What do you mean, Leo?" Dad asks.

"We're trapped in a loop. Can't you see it?"

Mom and Dad exchange a glance. Emmy looks frightened. She comes over and takes his hand. Her fingers are icy.

"Leo," she says, looking up at him with pleading eyes. "Why are you saying such scary things?"

Leo swallows hard. His throat hurts. "Listen, everyone. What I'm trying to say is ..."

He looks at their faces. They are expectant. Pale. Scared.

What will happen if I tell them?

He has no idea. He just knows he can't say it. So instead, he forces a smile. "Nevermind. Forget it."

Their faces relax a bit.

Dad blows into his hands. "Phew, I'm freezing. What do you say, guys? Should we try to make it to Aunt Heidi's?"

"Yes, let's do that," Mom says. "Put your coats on again, kids."

Leo goes with them to the hallway. He feels empty inside. He doesn't know how long this will continue. Maybe forever. But he does know when it started.

At 4:58.

When time stopped.

When their lives stopped.

Emmy takes his hand again. She stares up at him, anxiously. "I'm still scared, Leo."

"You don't need to be," Leo reassures her. "There's nothing more to be scared of, Emmy. I promise you."

She bites her lip, considering. "I don't know what's going on," she says thoughtfully, and she sends him a tentative smile. "But I'm glad we're at least together."

Leo feels tears form in his eyes. "Yeah," he whispers. "Me too."

***

When I started this story, I didn't know how it would end. I just saw Grandma's empty house in my mind. I could feel the strange atmosphere in the car. And I imagined how the radio kept repeating the same news. Like Leo, I became more and more uneasy. I knew it was about the little light in the darkness, but I didn't understand what it meant. It was only when Leo stood with the binoculars that it struck me. And suddenly, it all made sense.

Beast

Connor is awakened by a wet snout nudging his knee.

He sits up in bed and rubs his forehead.

Hunter is sitting by his side, her blue eyes shining eagerly, her tail wagging. Connor scratches the wolfdog behind the ear, making her give off a pleased sigh.

"Morning, girl." He yawns and is about to get up when he notices something hanging from the dog's whiskers: a tiny, red pearl. He rubs it off with his finger and examines it closely. It can only be blood. He looks at the dog. "What did you poke your nose into this time?"

Hunter gives him an innocent look. She's a big dog, even for her breed, and immensely strong, yet she would never harm anyone. The blood has probably come from a tiny cut in the dog's mouth. That wouldn't surprise him, as she loves to chew on sticks when lying around in the yard.

Connor gets up and gets dressed and trudges downstairs. In the living room he finds his mom smoking like a chimney.

On television a news reporter is talking with a very serious voice: "... making it the third in a row. All the murders have happened within a month, and police are now asking the citizens of Muttville to come forward with any information regarding ..."

"Did he say Muttville?" Connor asks.

Mom gives a startle. "Christ, Connor! Why are you sneaking up on me like that?"

"I'm not. Is he talking about our town?"

Mom inhales a long drag on the cigarette. "Yeah, isn't it crazy? This is the third one they've found. A woman my age. They haven't given a name yet—I just hope it's not someone we know." She snatches her phone from the table.

Connor stays and watches the news for a while. They show scenes from a street he's familiar with. An area is closed off by plastic bands, and three police cars and an ambulance are present. They cut back to the reporter.

"Hi, Penn!" his mom exclaims. "Have you heard? ... Yeah, you know who it is?"

Connor goes to the kitchen and grabs an aspirin from the bottle in the cupboard. He's used to getting a headache whenever he spends too much time around his mom and her deathly fog. He glares at the packet of Corn Flakes for a moment, but he has zero appetite.

He turns to see Hunter standing behind him. "How about you? You hungry?"

The dog licks her mouth.

Connor opens the cupboard, but finds the bag with dog food empty.

"Goddamnit," he mutters and opens the fridge instead. On a plate he finds a couple of dried-up pork chops from last night's dinner. He shows them to Hunter. "How about these?"

Hunter whines impatiently.

"All right, all right, remember to chew them."

Connor drops the meat in her bowl, and Hunter immediately wolfs them down.

"I know, it's awful!" Mom comes into the kitchen, phone to her ear, cigarette in the other hand, nodding eagerly. "Completely mauled, they said—just like the first two. As if a wild animal had—" Mom breaks off as she sees Hunter. "Oh, come on, Connor. You're not feeding the dog our dinner."

Connor shrugs. "There's no more dog food."

Mom sighs. "No, Penn, it's just the boy—he's feeding pork chops to the dog. Yes, the dog!" Mom sends Connor a triumphant smile. "Penn says you should feel ashamed."

"Show this to Penn," Connor sneers, holding up his middle finger.

"Don't you get an attitude!"

"Come on, Hunter. Let's get out of here."

Hunter swallows the last bite of the meat and eyes his mom for a brief moment before following Connor out of the kitchen.

Connor goes to the mall and buys dog food with a crumpled-up bill he found in his mom's jacket. When he comes back out of the store, Hunter is sitting patiently waiting.

"Good girl," Connor says. "Come on, now."

The dog follows him across the parking lot.

"You ought to keep that cur on a leash," a cantankerous voice hisses.

Connor turns and sees a fat lady rolling by with a shopping cart who has gotten the ungrateful job of carrying most of her weight, as she is slumping over the handlebar.

"It's illegal, you know," she goes on. "It also has to wear a muzzle."

"What business is it of yours?" Connor asks calmly. "She's not bothering you."

The lady stops the cart and shows her yellow teeth in a sneer. "No, but it sure could. Or maybe it will attack a child."

"Hunter never did anybody any harm."

The lady doesn't hear him, she's staring at Hunter with obvious disgust. "A beast that big isn't a pet. They should be banned!"

"Fuck you," Connor says and walks on.

"Next time, I'll call the police!" the lady shouts after him.

"Call a personal trainer instead," Connor mutters under his breath.

Unfortunately, he's no stranger to that sort of comment. He doesn't care, though; he has no intention of keeping Hunter on a leash. Why would he? He trusts her one hundred percent. She would never do anything without him telling her to. She stays on the sidewalk, she ignores other dogs, doesn't care about cats, and she always comes when he calls. The worst she has ever done is dig up a couple of his mom's flowers.

Connor stops abruptly. Without realizing it, he has come to the street from the news report. Two of the police cars are still here, and a small crowd of onlookers are buzzing around. One of them turns and sees Connor, waves and comes over.

It's Steve from his class.

"Hey, have you heard?"

"Yeah, it's another murder."

"Isn't it fucked up? I mean, in our little town. And I think it was someone I knew."

"Who?"

"I don't know her name, but she's the mother of that kid Donald from fourth grade. You know, that annoying redhead?"

Connor knows Donald very well. A sad little pudgy guy who hasn't any friends and seeks attention from anyone. A couple of days ago he shoved Connor in the schoolyard, making Connor drop his phone. As payback, Connor kicked him hard. Donald started crying and ran away.

After school, a red-haired lady was waiting outside for Connor. She was furious and started berating him as soon as she saw him. She threatened to tell the teachers about his "violent attack" on her son. She promised she could get him expelled.

"Connor?"

Steve's voice pulled him back. "Yeah, I know Donald."

"They said she was all torn to pieces. Like she had been through a harvester. It took the police three hours to find all of her. Fucking hell, it's like something out of a horror movie."

Hunter gives off an impatient whimper. She's looking towards the crime scene.

"Easy, girl. We'll go in a minute."

"Hi, Hunter," Steve says, patting her head. "Oh, right, that reminds me ... they said the police thinks it might be a dog that did it. A big dog."

Connor stares blankly at Steve. "So?"

Steve throws out his arms. "I'm just saying ..."

"You're saying what, exactly?"

"Come on, man. I'm not accusing you or anything. I know Hunter, I know she's a good dog. I'm just saying, maybe you should—I don't know—keep her indoors until they catch the guy."

Connor breathes heavily through his nose. He suddenly realizes a lot of the onlookers have turned and are now staring at him and Hunter. He nods. "You're right, Steve. Maybe I should."

That evening, Connor is playing on his computer. It's eleven thirty; he better get to sleep. But he still needs to let Hunter out for her bedtime pee.

He gets up. "Come on, girl."

The dog gets up from her place by the window and trudges after him. As soon as Connor gets near the living room, his temples start pulsing. He peeks his head in and sees his mom lying on the couch. The TV is on, but she's snoring loudly. On the table is an empty wine bottle, and a cigarette is burning in the ashtray.

Connor sighs. "One day she'll burn the fucking house down." He goes and puts out the cigarette, opens a window, and pulls a blanket over his mom.

She grunts in her sleep. "... let out the dog ..."

"I'm doing it now. Good night, Mom."

"Mmmm ... love you."

Connor goes to the back door and opens it so Hunter can slip out into the yard. She knows the drill.

Connor leans against the wall, finds his phone and forgets the time. Suddenly, ten minutes has passed, and Hunter hasn't returned.

He steps out on the stairs and looks around. "Hunter? What's the holdup?"

The dog doesn't come. Connor slips on a pair of his mom's flip-flops and goes out to the yard where the grass is wet with dew and glitters in the light from the street. He can't see Hunter anywhere.

He whistles. "Hunter? Where are you?"

From the bottom of the yard comes a noise, and a moment later, Hunter comes out of the darkness.

"What were you doing?" Connor asks.

Hunter sits by his side and licks his hand, leaving a dark stripe. She has dirt in her mouth.

"Have you been digging in the flowers? You know Mom will get angry."

Hunters whines.

Connor goes down to check. His eyes are getting used to the darkness, and he sees a spot in his mom's flower bed where the dirt has been dug up, but to his surprise there's no hole, which must mean Hunter has covered it again. But why would she do that?

Maybe she buried something.

Connor kneels down and sticks his fingers in the ground. He digs around for a moment before he feels something and pulls it out. It's some sort of fabric, perhaps an old rag. Connor gets out his phone and activates the light.

It's not an old rag—it's a part of someone's pants, all torn-up and smeared with blood and dirt.

"Fucking hell ..." Connor stares from the piece of cloth to Hunter. "What have you done, girl?"

The wolfdog stares back at him, her black eyes shining in the light from the phone.

"Okay, it's not what I think it is," Connor tells himself. "She just found it and brought it home. It doesn't mean anything."

Connor turns off the light and quickly buries the piece of fabric again before going back inside. On his way across the yard, something attracts his gaze from the other side of the fence. There's light in a window in the house next door, and a figure steps out of sight.

Alfred, that nosey old prick. Oh, well, he was probably just taking a piss. He couldn't see anything anyway, it's too dark out here.

"Come on, Hunter."

He brings the dog inside and locks the door. As he washes his hands thoroughly, he feels the dog eyeing him.

He glances down at her. "We're not telling anybody about this. All right, girl?"

Hunter seems to agree.

As soon as Connor wakes up, he immediately looks for Hunter. He finds her lying by the window as usual.

Connor gets dressed and goes to the bathroom. But as he crosses the hallway, he notices small traces of dirt on the floor. He follows the trail to the back door and finds it ajar. He shuts it and turns the lock.

Mom must have been out for a smoke during the night. She was drunk and probably didn't notice the dirt coming off her feet.

Connor goes to the living room and finds his mom still snoring on the couch. In the kitchen he pours himself a bowl of cereal, although his appetite is zero. Just as he's about to begin, the doorbell rings.

Mom stirs in the living room. "Huh? Was that the door?"

"Yeah."

"What time is it?"

"Half past seven."

"You mind getting it, sweetheart? It's probably the delivery guy—I ordered something online."

Connor gets up with a sigh and goes to open the door. It's not the delivery guy. It's a young man in a shirt and tie.

"Morning. My name is Roger Johnson, I'm an investigator with the police." He briefly flashes a badge before putting it back in his pocket. "Are you Connor?"

Connor's mouth opens, then shuts again.

"I just want to talk to you," the officer says, smiling. "Don't look so worried, you haven't broken any laws. Actually, it's not you I want to talk about. May I come in?"

A torrent of thoughts rushes through Connor's mind. If it's not him the officer has come for, then it has to be his mom. What will the officer say when he sees her lying on the couch, hungover? A lot of people know Connor's mom drinks a lot. Has someone called Child Services? Maybe a teacher from school? Will he be taken away and put in a foster home?

"I see you're getting ready for school," the officer says. "It'll only be ten minutes, I promise."

"Uhm ... all right." Connor doesn't know what else to do, so he lets in the officer. "My mom's ... uhm ... not up yet."

"That's fine." The officer hangs his jacket on the rack. "I just need to speak with you for now."

"Connor?" Mom appears in the doorway wearing a robe, hair messy and eyes squinty—although they grow a lot bigger at the sight of the officer. "Oh, no ... what have you done, Connor?"

"Morning, ma'am," the officer smiles, reaching out his hand. "I'm Roger Johnson, I'm from the criminal police. Your son is absolutely fine, ma'am. This is just an informal talk."

Mom shakes his hand, but doesn't seem convinced. "About what?"

For the first time, the officer hesitates. "Well, it's about the recent murders. I'm sure you've heard about them."

Mom turns even paler.

"But, like I said," the officer hurriedly adds, "this isn't really about Connor. I just have a few questions I'd like to ask him. We're still investigating different leads."

"Right then." Mom nods slowly. "Should I ... put on some coffee?"

"No, thank you. I'll be off again shortly."

"Let's talk in my room," Connor says, regaining a small amount of control.

"That'd be fine."

Connor leads the officer down through the hallway. The situation is completely surreal. He opens the door and steps in, making room for the officer. But Johnson stops in the doorway, his gaze suddenly stiff.

"What's wrong?" Connor asks—but then he sees Hunter. She's sitting by the window, back straight, ears perched, eyes fixed on the officer. "That's just Hunter. She's harmless."

The officer comes to, clears his throat and forces a smile, then closes the door behind him.

Connor sits down on the bed, gesturing towards the desk chair.

Johnson sits down and takes out a pen and paper. "So, Connor. You're probably wondering why I'm here."

Connor rubs his thighs.

"We got a call earlier this morning. A person saw you out in the yard late last night."

Connor freezes. Alfred! So he did see me. And he called the fucking cops on me! What the hell was he thinking? That old piece of—

"Connor?"

He blinks. "Yeah?"

"Is that true? Did you bury something in the yard last night?"

Connor considers telling the truth for a moment, but then he looks at Hunter. The dog is sitting still as a statue, like she's following the conversation.

Connor shakes his head. "Nah. I was just letting Hunter out for her evening pee."

The officer glances at the dog. "And how about Hunter? Did she find anything in the yard?"

"Like what?"

"Well, the person who called said it looked like a piece of clothing."

Connor swallows dryly. "I didn't see her finding anything," he managed to croak.

How the hell could Alfred have seen that? Does he have a fucking night scope?

Johnson looks at the wolfdog. "She seems like a very obedient dog. What breed is it?"

"A Czechoslovakian wolfdog."

He makes a note. "Has she ever strayed from the property?"

"No."

Another note. "Does she sleep in here with you?"

"Yes."

"Every night?"

"Yes."

A third note. "And she's never outside at night?"

Finally, it dawns on Connor: this "informal talk" is about Hunter. She's the suspect. His voice hardens. "Hunter never did anybody any harm. She's very good-natured."

The officer nods, but doesn't meet Connor's eyes. "Would you mind if we had a quick look in the yard?"

"Why?"

"Maybe we'll find the piece of clothing, it's probably easier to see in daylight."

"I ... uhm ... I need to get going, actually."

But the officer already got up. "Me too. We'll check the yard on our way out." He leaves the room.

Connor stays behind for a moment, glancing at Hunter. The dog stares at the doorway, a deep, low growl escaping her throat.

"Quiet," Connor whispers. "I'll take care of this, girl. You stay here." He rushes out to catch up with the officer, showing him the way to the back door.

As they come out to the yard, Johnson looks around, sees the farthest corner and goes there to kneel down. It's obvious the ground has been dug up recently, and there are many dog prints.

Connor's heart is beating right under his chin.

"Do you have a shovel?" the officer asks.

Connor feels a faint hope. "No, we don't."

"Oh, well." Johnson rolls up his sleeves, then sticks his hands down in the ground and starts digging it aside. Connor watches the officer as he burrows through the dirt very meticulously. He tries furiously to come up with an excuse for how the piece of clothing could have ended up here without incriminating Hunter. If there is any evidence linking a big and powerful dog like her to the crimes, she will definitely be taken away—probably even put down. But Connor can't think of anything.

Johnson grunts and stands up, brushing his hands; they are dirty but empty. "There doesn't seem to be anything buried."

Connor can hardly believe it. "That's ... that's what I told you."

The officer eyes him for a moment, but quickly turns the stare into a smile. "Thank you for the talk, Connor." He leaves the yard without looking back.

Connor breathes a sigh of relief. He's shaking all over as he stares at the ground. Where did the piece of clothing go?

Something makes him turn and look across the fence. Alfred is standing in the window, but quickly slips out of sight.

Connor bites down hard. "Hope you enjoyed the show, you old fool."

That evening, as he's going for a walk with Hunter, Connor notices something is different. Everyone he meets is staring at him. He tries to chalk it up to him being paranoid, but he can't quite convince himself.

The next day, he speaks to Steve about it in school.

"Of course people are staring," Steve says. "They think Hunter did it."

Connor frowns. "They think she killed three people? Come on, people can't be that stupid. They're just pissed because I don't use a leash on her."

Steve raises his eyebrows. "Are you serious? Haven't you heard the rumors?"

"What rumors?"

Steve darts a glance around, then lowers his voice. "Everyone knows the police were at your house, man. They are saying on the news the victims all had bitemarks from an animal, a big dog, probably. And Hunter is the biggest dog in town."

Connor feels a white-hot rage rise up in his chest. Alfred, that fucking tattletale. This is all his fault ...

That night, Connor sleeps badly. He twists and turns, sweats and moans. A terrible nightmare keeps haunting him, and suddenly, he wakes up with a start.

He pants and looks around. It's still dark outside the window, but something breaks through the darkness: a blueish light flickering across the ceiling. There's also a noise coming from outside. Is it ...?

Sirens, Connor realizes.

At that moment, he feels something wet on his hand, and he looks down to see Hunter, sitting next to his bed, licking him between the fingers.

"Stop it, girl," he mumbles, removing his hand, which feels sticky with drool. But he's too preoccupied by the light and the sounds of sirens outside to worry about it—now he can hear several engines getting closer, cars stopping outside, doors opening and slamming.

He gets up and goes to the window, but can't really see anything from this angle. Instead, he trudges out to the kitchen, where he finds his mom leaning over the sink, sucking eagerly at a cigarette and peering out the window.

"Have you seen it, Connor?" she whispers as she sees him. "There are police and paramedics right outside."

Connor looks out. Two men in colored vests come out of Alfred's driveway, carrying a stretcher between them. A figure is lying on it under a blanket.

"Poor Alfred," his mom mutters. "I hope it's not another murder."

Connor hears his own voice speaking. "It's probably just a heart attack."

"The police don't show up for a heart attack," his mom sneers, blowing smoke into his face. "Look, they're blocking off the area now. I have to tell Penn—where's my phone?" She goes looking for it.

Connor watches for a minute as the police put up the tape around Alfred's driveway. His head has started to throb. He staggers back up to his room, but freezes right before the door, looking down. A trail of wet blotches runs from his room and down the hallway. Apprehensively, he follows the trail. It leads to the back door, which is standing ajar. Connor peeks out into the yard. The grass is wet with dew.

He closes the door and hurries back to his room, his heart racing, only to find Hunter perched by the window, watching the blue lights and listening intently. As she hears him coming, she turns her head and looks straight at him.

"Have you ... have you been outside, girl?" he whispers.

The wolfdog doesn't move a muscle, the blue eyes gleaming in the dark.

The back door is never locked—the key broke in the lock a few years back, and his mom never got it fixed. So Hunter could easily open the door on her own if she wanted to; she's certainly tall enough—and clever enough.

Connor approaches her cautiously, kneels down and examines her around the mouth. Her muzzle is caked with something dark and sticky. It could be mud, but it could also be ...

No, it can't be!

Connor rubs his forehead, but stops again immediately as he feels his fingers are sticky. He stares at his hand; it was the hand Hunter was licking when he woke up. It's not drool, and it's not mud. His fingers are red and shiny with blood.

"Oh, fuck me ... Jesus Christ, Hunter, what have you done?"

The eyes of the dog remain alert.

"Come on. Quickly!"

He pulls her to the bathroom and into the shower, where he washes her muzzle. He also rinses off his own hands thoroughly. Afterwards, he shuts Hunter in his room and uses a towel to wipe off the wet prints down the hallway, ending by the back door.

Just as he finishes, there's a loud knocking.

Connor almost screams.

"Police!" a gruff voice shouts. "Open up!"

Connor just stands there, unable to move, until his mom comes rushing by a few moments later.

"Why haven't you opened it?" she asks him, just as the knocking repeats. She opens the door.

An officer in full uniform shines a flashlight in their eyes. "Police. Is everything all right in here?"

"Y... yes," Connor's mom says, squinting against the light. "We're fine. We just woke up."

"Have you heard or seen anything from the house next door?" The officer turns the flashlight to Connor's face.

He shakes his head, discretely hiding his hand behind his back.

"No," his mom says. "Like I said, we just—"

"Stay in the house," the officer demands. "And lock the doors." Then, he's gone.

Mom closes the door. "My God, I need another cigarette," she mutters and scuffles off.

Connor goes back to his room. Hunter sends him a greeting look from her place at the window. He sits down on the bed and buries his hands in his hair. He's scared, but oddly enough it's not Hunter scaring him. He simply sees no reason to; she might be a killer, but Hunter is still his friend, and she would never hurt him. In fact, as he goes over the recent events in his head, he begins to see how Hunter has actually been helping him.

The blood he noticed in her whiskers the other day; that came from Donald's mom, as did the piece of clothing. Hunter knew Connor was cross with her. So, she sought vengeance on his behalf.

And now Alfred. Hunter must have realized he was the one telling the police about Connor. She probably saw him from the window, she knew he had seen Connor burying the piece of clothing, so she went out later that night to get properly rid of the evidence. That would explain the dirt on the floor by the back door. And then she gave Alfred what he deserved.

What about the other two murders then? Connor didn't know them by name, but he felt certain they had somehow done him wrong at some point. Plenty of people had.

But how could Hunter know about all these people who had bothered him?

Well, the answer was pretty obvious. He had told her about the episodes himself, as he has a habit of speaking to the dog as though she was a person. He remembered being angry and muttering about Donald's mom that day, just like he had been cursing Alfred earlier this evening. Hunter had heard it all. And she understood.

Connor stares at Hunter and suddenly sees her in a new light. She isn't just a dog, she's his undying friend and protector. She has been getting rid of his tormentors and covered it up as best she could.

Connor reaches out his hand. Hunter comes to him, and he caresses her gently.

"Good girl," he whispers.

Connor lies back down, feeling a lot more at ease, and surprisingly, he drifts off almost immediately.

Early the next morning, Connor takes Hunter for a walk.

Alfred's driveway and frontward are blocked off by yellow tape. One police car is still remaining, and a couple of officers are standing next to it, talking. One of them is Johnson. Connor hurries down the street before he is seen.

They go for a walk through town. Connor's mood is very gloomy. He has a strange feeling it might be the last walk they'll ever share. It's almost a sense of foreboding, as though he knows something bad is going to happen.

As they come back home, his fears are confirmed. The police car is still there, but the officers are gone. As soon as he opens the front door, he can hear sobbing from the living room. He goes in to find his mom sitting next to Johnson on the couch. She's crying and blowing her nose.

The officer gets up when he sees Connor. "There he is now."

"Connor, oh my God," his mom cries, her mascara is all runny. "They say ... they say that Hunter is the one who ..." The rest drowns in more sobs.

Connor turns to stone on the inside.

The wolfdog growls ominously at his side.

Connor doesn't take his eyes off Johnson. "And why do they think that?"

"We've found a trace leading from your backyard to Alfred's bedroom window. That's where the murderer entered the house. The traces are from a large animal."

"Hunter spent the night in my room. She hasn't been outside."

Johnson breathes deeply. "Listen, Connor, here is what is going to happen. I'm taking Hunter with me. She will be placed in a shelter; it's only temporary. I would like for you to come with me as well, so we can have a proper talk."

Mom sniffles. "Oh, Connor ... how could she?"

Connor clenches his teeth. "And what if I don't want to?" he asks the officer. "What if I don't allow you to take Hunter?"

Hunter growls once more, deeper this time.

Johnson glances at her before looking back at Connor. "If you resist, you will be placed under arrest. That would be a very stupid thing to do, though. So far, I have absolutely no reason to suspect you had anything to do with the murders. You will get through this with a clean record, if you cooperate."

Connor looks down at Hunter, and she looks back up. She's ready. Ready for whatever he decides. He can see it in her eyes. She's just waiting for him to say the words.

Mom's sobbing is starting to get on his nerves. A vicious headache is pounding on the inside of his skull. Out of the corner of his eye, Connor notices the officer's hand reaching discretely inside his jacket. He probably has a weapon.

Connor realizes there is nothing he can do, unless he wants to risk Hunter getting shot. So, he sighs deeply. "I'm sorry, girl. We need to part for a short while."

The next days pass by in a daze.

He's been interviewed twice. The same questions, over and over. He answers as truthfully as he can. Makes sure not to incriminate Hunter.

He visits Hunter several times a day. She's locked in a cage, her sad eyes stabbing Connor like a knife in the heart.

All over town, people are talking about the killer dog who finally got caught. There's a vicious mob-like mood in the air. Everyone wants Hunter put down.

Finally, the verdict falls. Johnson comes by one afternoon to tell Connor what he already knows. The officer's face looks sympathetic, but Connor can hear the hidden triumph in his voice.

It will happen in a few hours. Connor will be allowed to be there, giving him the opportunity to say goodbye.

Mom drives Connor to the shelter. It's a big, ugly building at the outskirts of town, right next to a big forest.

"Do you want me to come?" his mom asks quietly as she parks the car outside the shelter.

Connor shakes his aching head and gets out. A brisk wind hits his face as he walks to the front entrance, making his eyes water. Weirdly enough, he doesn't feel like crying, he just feels empty inside.

Johnson greets him right inside. "Hi, Connor. I'm glad you came. She will feel better with you around." He sends him a reassuring smile.

Connor just stares back.

Johnson leads him down a long corridor. Somewhere, a dog is howling. There are a lot of unpleasant odors in the air: detergents, misery, fear, death.

"It's right in here," Johnson says, stopping and opening a door.

Hunter is strapped to a table with strong leather bands. She is breathing rapidly. A man, whom Connor takes to be a vet, is standing by a desk, preparing something.

Connor goes to Hunter. The sight of her face makes his stomach churn. He tries his best to sound cheery. "Hi there, girl. Did you miss me?"

Hunter whimpers. She lifts her head as high as she can, and he strokes her muzzle. She licks his hand in return.

"I'll give you a few minutes," Johnson says

Connor leans over Hunter, inhales the smell of her fur, feels the beating of her heart. Already she seems a lot calmer, now that he's here.

She thinks I can protect her, like she protected me. She's convinced that somehow, I'll be able to get her out of here.

The thought almost makes him tear up.

Johnson puts a hand on Connor's shoulder. "All right, Connor. We'd better get it over with."

Connor stands up straight, takes Hunter's paw and holds it tightly.

The vet comes over to the table, bringing a large syringe. "It'll be absolutely pain-free," he promises. "She'll simply go to sleep."

The lump in Connor's stomach grows larger, harder, hotter. He realizes he's shaking all over, and he suddenly feels dazed. Something starts firing in his brain. Brief images. Bloody images.

"Wait ... wait a moment," he mumbles.

The vet hesitates.

Johnson's voice is firm. "You had your chance to say goodbye, Connor. Now we need to do it."

The vet proceeds, bringing the needle closer to Hunter's neck.

"I said WAIT!"

Connor's roar echoes between the walls like a thunderclap, making both the officer and the vet jump.

Connor breathes fast as he starts speaking. "It's ... it's not right ... Hunter didn't kill anybody ..." A scene appears in his mind. Hunter, licking his fingers. The blood didn't come from her mouth, though. It was already on his fingers; she was just trying to clean them off.

Johnson shakes his head. "We've been over this, Connor. It has already been decided—"

"Hunter is innocent," Connor interrupts, his voice suddenly turning hoarse and deeper. It's difficult for him to speak now, and his whole body is burning from within, like something is pushing to get out. "I know ... who the real ... killer ... is ..."

Johnson crosses his arms, trying to look skeptical, but the way he stares suspiciously at Connor tells him the officer is nervous. "Really? And you just remember so now? Who is it then, Connor?"

Connor gives off a grunt as his muscles contract and start to swell. His whole body is growing, his clothes start to rip. He manages to force out one last word, more of a growl than anything: "Me."

Johnson gasps with horror and the vet backs away into the desk.

Then, Connor's vision turns black and his brain shuts down. The last thing he perceives is the distant sound of the men's terrified screams.

Connor is awakened by Hunter licking his face.

Feeling dazed he sits up and realizes he's naked—and covered in blood—like the rest of the room. It's everywhere, screaming red at him; the floor is soaking, the walls are splashed over, even the ceiling has stains. It's like someone emptied several buckets of the stuff.

The table is tipped over, and beneath it he can make out part of what he assumes is Johnson's body—it's hard to tell, since only a few inches of the skin is intact. In the farthest corner the vet is lying splayed out, like a big doll some kid got tired of playing with.

Only Hunter is completely unharmed, and she's also free—the leather bands have been ripped open.

Connor notices a metallic taste in his mouth. He feels something between his teeth, reaches in with a couple of fingers and pulls out a dollar-sized piece of skin. He groans in disgust and wipes his mouth; his lips are sticky with blood.

Connor slowly gets to his feet, stumbles and reaches for the wall. He grabs a coat from a hook next to the door and swings it over his shoulders. Luckily, it's just long enough to cover his groin.

He opens the door and checks the hallway. It's empty. He shuts the door again and goes instead to the window and pushes it open.

"Come on, girl," he says and climbs out.

Hunter follows him, easily making the jump.

They walk around the building. From the corner, Connor sees the car. Mom is sitting behind the wheel, smoking and talking on her phone. Connor sees the silver ring on her finger and instantly feels his head start to throb.

He sneers and turns away, instead looking down at Hunter. "I think we can manage on our own from now on. Don't you?"

Hunter gives his hand a quick lick.

Connor starts walking into the forest.

Hunter is right at his heels.

***

I hope you enjoyed the story as much as I enjoyed writing it. I usually don't plan out my stories beforehand, but with *Beast*, I knew the twist all along. It was still tough writing that scene leading up to the climax, though, where Connor takes Hunter to be put down. My heart was thumping like mad! I just love dogs so much, even the thought of a fictional one almost being euthanized made me want to kill that police officer. Does that make me a psycho? I'll let you decide.

Anyway, that's it! We've reached the end.

I really hope you enjoyed this mixed bag of tales. If they kept you up even five minutes past your usual bedtime, I consider my job done.

If this was the first time you came across my work, and if you liked what you read, I have great news: There's much more where that came from!

One monster that didn't get too much screen time in this here collection were zombies. I rectified that by writing a full series called *Dead Meat*, which follows the end of the world one day at a time as the undead take over. You can binge the whole thing for just 99 cents/pence at **nickclausen.com/dead-meat**

I also have another complete series called *Under the Breaking Sky*. That one is also about monsters, but not zombies. I consider it my best work yet, and I hear from a lot of readers who tell me I raised my game with that one. So, if you want some epic, high-quality thrills, check it out at **nick-clausen.com/breaking-sky**

Or, if you feel like taking our relationship to the next level, I'd be thrilled to welcome you into my reader club. It's basically a free newsletter, and it's the best way to keep in touch with me since I don't really do social media. You also get three free books when you sign up at **nick-clausen.com/free**

Here's to many more cool stories!

—Nick

Printed in Great Britain
by Amazon